PETER NEVSKY

and the True Story of
the Russian Moon Landing

BOOKS BY JOHN CALVIN BATCHELOR

The Further Adventures of Halley's Comet (1981)
The Birth of the People's Republic of Antarctica (1983)
American Falls (1985)
Thunder in the Dust: Images of Western Movies,
by John R. Hamilton; text by John Calvin Batchelor (1987)
Gordon Liddy Is My Muse, by Tommy "Tip" Paine (1990)
Walking the Cat, by Tommy "Tip" Paine:
Gordon Liddy Is My Muse II (1991)
Peter Nevsky and the True Story of
the Russian Moon Landing (1993)

PETER NEVSKY

and the True Story of the Russian Moon Landing

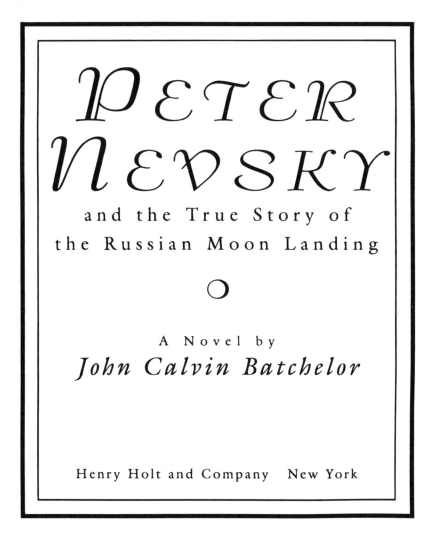

A Novel by

John Calvin Batchelor

Henry Holt and Company   New York

Henry Holt and Company, Inc.
Publishers since 1866
115 West 18th Street
New York, New York 10011

Henry Holt® is a registered
trademark of Henry Holt and Company, Inc.

Published in Canada by Fitzhenry & Whiteside Ltd.,
91 Granton Drive, Richmond Hill, Ontario L4B 2N5.

Library of Congress Cataloging-in-Publication Data
Batchelor, John Calvin.
Peter Nevsky and the true story of the Russian moon landing:
a novel / by John Calvin Batchelor.—1st ed.
p.   cm.
I. Title.
PS3552.A8268P48   1993
813′.54—dc20   92-29075
                                                CIP

ISBN 0-8050-2141-8

First Edition—1993

Designed by Paula R. Szafranski

Printed in the United States of America
All first editions are printed
on acid-free paper.∞

3   5   7   9   10   8   6   4   2

For my Sam

One word of truth outweighs the whole world.

—PROVERB

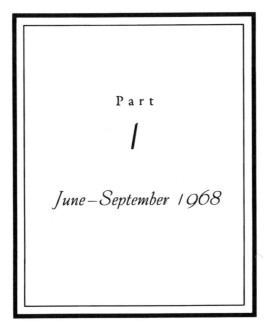

Part

1

June–September 1968

Moon-gazing

I was very, very young on the starry night it all began. It was a white night, June of 1968, so the stars above me were blurred by a flush of midnight sunlight that lit up the talcum veil of the last quarter moon low to the west. In those days I didn't gaze at the moon idly, however, as if it were just another astronomical body; rather I gazed with the power of a boy-man's eyes to see the quarter moon so sickle-shaped and gilt-edged that it was like an icon blazing above the citadel of the Russian empire. I could roll my head up and look upon the moon not just as a cold satellite but also as a whole new planet beckoning me to come and conquer for Russia and for myself. I remember that particular moon-gazing moment with the stars fading and the sun flashing and the quarter moon whitening as if it were just last night, and I also remember how I announced, "You're for me, moon, I'm going to land on you, here I come."

I think I laughed, for I was just twenty-two years old and confess that I gazed at the moon a lot and talked to myself about the moon even more and, when I caught myself, laughed about it all. I had been a junior lieutenant in the Air Force for two weeks and was so full of my prowess that I never felt the ground. I was hugely happy; I soared more than walked; wherever I was I could blink and I was in the sky. To look at I wasn't much more than the next dreamer, but then I was a little more, for I'd won my wings, first cadet in my class from the legendary Orenburg Academy, and I could drive all the high-performance aircraft in the arsenal as well as read, count, and obey as true as any falcon in the Air Force. I had studied and worked for what seemed all my life to get what I wanted, and what I wanted was the peerless victory of the moon. I had been sure for as long as I could remember that I was going there; and perhaps I can't explain it better than to say that I felt so moonbound that all the wondrous mystery of the world around me, my childhood and education, the Air Force and the might of Russia and the triumph of the space program and even the crisp brown uniform I wore, the good leather boots I'd bought so dearly with my first monthly paycheck as a commissioned officer, the glimmer of my hammer-and-sickle brass buttons, all of these details had come my way in order to keep me on my surefooted march toward my appointment on the moon.

I understand that what I'm saying might sound strange to you now. The moon, you say, why would any sensible boy want to quit the fruitful Russian plain for the lifeless, airless, colorless seas of the moon? My answer is impossible unless you've lived—as I have—a lifetime in pursuit of interplanetary flight. I wanted the moon not only for myself but also because I believed that it was the first hard step toward the planets and the stars, because to get way out there you have to start just there, at Tranquillity Base, where I have been and where I have sent boys such as I once was. My answer, too, is that the moon once looked to be a profound part of mankind's destiny. In those days Russia and America, the two most powerful empires in history, were caught up in a race for the moon that was as outspoken and pell-mell as my own. However their moon race wasn't for some utopian vision of the future in interplanetary space like mine, but instead because it was believed that the first men on the moon would win for their nation an unshakable superiority over all others for eternity. This might seem an extreme exaggeration to you, but I guarantee you that the Cold War of those days had made all competition between the superpowers no less than a fight to the death on the field of Armageddon. The race to the moon was a fact, not a legend, and it was an all-consuming fact that dominated the passions of the two most aggressive military forces ever assembled for twenty-five years. And it took as much folly and luck as common sense before the moon race was done and the Americans had won and we had lost. This is what I want to tell you now. This is what I'm sure you've not heard in all these years of talk about the secrets of those days. For the truth is I know the complete story of the moon race, I know in detail about the preparations for and execution of the *two* landings that took place on the moon on July 20–21, 1969; and though what I have to say is often dark and heartbreaking to me, I can still smile to know that I was there. I did my duty. I knew the men who won and the men who lost. They were my comrades and friends. I loved them.

On the white night I've chosen to begin my story, the moon race was more than a year from the finish. On that particular white night, my moon-gazing made me feel grandiose because as a reward for my graduating first cadet from Orenburg I had been assigned to the Cosmonaut Corps; and it was my certainty that the Corps was going to win the race, beat the Americans, finish what it had started with *Sputnik* and Gagarin. The orders in my pocket told my tale more matter-of-factly: My name was plainly Peter Nevsky then; and my rank and serial number and candidate Party number were routine; and my birthplace was commonplace but very special to me for I'm a Petersburger, born and raised, though we called it Leningrad then and I proudly called myself a Leningrader; and at the bottom of my orders came the wonderful part of my assignment, where it read, "Special Duty. Chkalvo Air Force Base. Moscow Military District." In Air Force talk, this meant that I was headed to Starry Town, the home of the Cosmonaut Corps outside Moscow, in order to begin the year-long training course for cosmonaut candidates. In my imagination, my orders also meant that I was actually, finally, genuinely on my way to the moon, for Russia and for me.

The date was June 17, 1968, however, so my imminent moon landing was still farfetched, and at the moment I first remember acutely I was doing my moon-gazing while propped on my motorcycle on the aft deck of a flat-bottomed military barge churning up the Volkhov River. Among diesel-oil fumes and the thumping of a screw propeller, I was enjoying a gentle passage upriver between dark green shores rich with waterbird life—the red-throated and black-throated loons, cackling "gag-ga-gagara," were the prizes of the region—and lined by the towering Siberian spruces and firs and larches mixed with the poetical white birches of the everlasting Russian forest. I had found the military barge on the Neva and had left Leningrad the day before, first to Lake Ladoga, where we'd been pounded by a sudden wind, and then to the shelter of the narrow Volkhov River. My goal was Moscow, via the inland waterways. But for my motorcycle, I suppose I could have hopped a military train and been there in a day instead of the two weeks it eventually took me. But that wasn't for me, since I wasn't due to report to Starry Town until July and since I couldn't afford to ship my motorcycle. It was my treasure. True, it hadn't worked for two decades, and I'd had to patch the tires and center the wheels just so that I could push it along like a cart, and otherwise it was rusted junk with a goatskin seat I'd fashioned into a perch; and yet my hope was that, once I got to Starry Town, I could store it somehow and find the parts to repair it. It was another of my boyish ambitions, I admit, but worth the risk for such a priceless trophy—a wartime BMW.

It was also a son's ambition. The motorcycle was my inheritance from my father, Colonel-General Apollon A. Nevsky, the bravest man who ever flew for Russia. The story was that my father got it for me the day I was born, in the spring of 1946, and though he was dead some twenty years, the motorcycle had come to me as a present for graduating my father's alma mater, Orenburg. Two weeks before, in Leningrad, my Great-Uncle Lev had handed me the motorcycle key. For two decades he'd secretly stored it in a river warehouse, he told me, planning for just such a day. "Your patrimony, Petya," Great-Uncle Lev had announced in his portentous, playful way, making it sound as if I'd satisfied all creation, "and I'm supposed to say, 'Keep going.'"

I must explain that this was my father's motto, "Keep going." It had once been displayed beneath the cockpit of his fighter planes. In the heroes' archives at Orenburg, I'd seen the photographs of my father that had been taken after he had come back from yet another murderous sortie against the Germans—his squadron and regiment mauled again by the Luftwaffe and ground fire, the duty roster reduced by another five names, the war going badly and the flying weather worse—and there in his cockpit would sit my beautiful, cock-of-the-walk father, Apollon Nevsky, the canopy thrown back, his goggles up, his wind-scarred face intense and yet cheery, vibrant, aggressive, those black eyes fixed faraway on the next mission already; and on the fuselage just below his face, among all the red stars that meant kills, was the hand-painted motto KEEP GOING. The truth was that Colonel-General Apollon A. Nevsky was my gallant father, the number-one air ace of the Great Patriotic War, truly Russia's Apollo at war's end, and I worshipped my father more than space travel. Though I didn't have any time with him—he died when I was three, and I have no clear memory of his face or voice—nevertheless to receive the BMW from him when I was twenty-two made me feel that I had grown up as momentously as he would have wanted, that I'd pleased him all these years of missing him and my mother and my two sisters, and that I was right to believe that my ambition for the moon only required me to follow his motto and "keep going."

My obedient progress to the moon wasn't so demanding that night that it could keep me awake. Soon after I'd told the moon I was coming aboard as a conqueror, I must have napped a little. It wasn't a deep sleep, more snoozing at midnight, yet just enough to keep me unaware, so that I startled when an Army captain came up behind me and shouted, "Ho, little falcon! Help me settle a fight!"

I stood and saluted courteously. I'd chatted with him at boarding when I'd bragged about my posting to Starry Town. He had coveted my motorcycle and had tried to get me to say it was for sale, and I had too timidly communicated that it was an heirloom. The captain was a tanker, about forty, and I never got his name, though from his look he was one like tens of thousands of others in the Army, a red-faced, steel-toothed lout with a bad boil rubbed raw on his neck. That night he was so drunk he was bobbing even faster than the vodka in the bottle he was waving at me, but I didn't snub him. As a new lieutenant I gave all superior officers my respect, and even his calling me "little falcon" was tolerable, since I wasn't fat like him and I was a falcon, which is Air Force slang for pilot.

"An ignorant mudcrusher," he said, pointing belowdecks to the crew quarters, "says Yuri Gagarin, yes, famous Yurka—" He wobbled against me like a man out of control trying to recover his cunning, then he continued, "—says Gagarin was fried in some secret spaceship. You know about it, eh, spaceman? He was your brother!"

I replied, "Sir, Colonel Gagarin died in a training exercise."

"No, no," the captain breathed on me, "you can tell me. I know he ain't dead, just scrambled eggs, so they can't show him on television. Say it's right, and I win a bet from the boys."

"Sir," I tried too earnestly to assure him with facts, "Colonel

Gagarin died in a training flight in March, at Starry Town, a plane crash. It was a tragedy. He was buried at the Kremlin. You must remember, it was on television."

The captain pinched my right shoulder and pulled at the falcon insignia on my gorget patch. "Have a nip." I declined, stepping back to get his hands off my new jacket and his breath off my lieutenant's star. The captain gulped a drink and stepped close again in order to come to his true motive, my motorcycle. "You selling it?" he asked.

I spoke firmly. "No, sir."

"What's it worth to you?" he bargained. "I can make us a profit. Partners, what about it? Be my brother, little falcon."

When I didn't reply, he became my enemy, calling me, "Shithead, Air Force shithead, think you can shit on me from the sky." He kicked at a tire and ranted, "Frig you and your frigging scrap heap!" and then wandered away through the two tanks lashed down on the aft deck, but not so far that he didn't turn and fling the bottle at me and curse me once more, "You shitheads are all alike."

I realize this must seem a foolish episode; and yet I have outlined it carefully because it was a profound part of my fate that night, for that drunken tank captain was the first of many twists that were ahead of me on my pathway to the moon.

Within two hours, the sun up rosy white to port and the curtain of mist off the river and the local plover and sandpiper population awake for breakfast, the bridges and quays of Novgorod were just ahead. The barge crew came on deck in order to prepare for a landfall at the wooden wharf to starboard. The bargemen were as drunk as the tankers belowdecks, and there was soon predictable woe. We were off line for the wharf, so the quaymen flapped at us to go about, but the barge pilot plowed blindly onward and then, much too late, reversed his engines to avoid an unavoidable collision. I was ready for the impact but not the recoil. The wharf tore like cardboard, the barge lurched backward, the propeller shuddered and jammed, and the heavy machinery crates on the foredeck broke loose and dipped the barge like a bar of soap, aground and wrecked. By then I was on my backside, holding on to my motorcycle half atop me and trying to figure how to get my bike off before we sank.

The emergency didn't upset many others. The quaymen laughed and shouted at the barge pilot, "Bravo, Comrade Blockhead!" and "Welcome to Novgorod!" while the Army tankers poured on deck

to celebrate, since now there'd be days free for drinking until someone else cleaned up the mess.

It was all familiar folly to me, the corruption of the ranks, the
derogation of hooligans, and I didn't fret about it. I was Air Force
and believed that, outside my duty, nothing else signified. Russia was
too big, too old, too magnificently impenetrable for me to explain or
to solve. What is more, my Great-Uncle Lev had taught me the
simplest of lessons: "If you can't love strangers, leave them alone."

What I could do about the wreck was to stay clear. The quaymen
flung a ramp to the barge deck to off-load the crates and, after waiting my turn, I walked my motorcycle over the gap. I wasn't quick
enough for the tankers, however, who were sitting on their machines
and mocking everyone's labor, particularly mine. "He's going to fly
that shit to the stars!" they cried. "Stand back, boys, here goes the
takeoff!" they called. "Hey, little falcon, show us how to fly!" I
lowered my head and got off the wharf quickly. The Air Force training in me said to fight, but not with my motorcycle that close to the
river.

A kindly quayman pointed me to the shack of the river agent.
"You can find another barge by nightfall," he told me. "Good luck
to you." He eyed the motorcycle and asked, "Not for sale, is it?" I
said it wasn't and wished him "soft landing," too. The quayman
glanced at the wrecked barge and joked, "Soft? Shit." I smiled in
return, for it was unlikely that he knew that the Air Force talk for
good luck is "soft landing."

The river agent turned out to be a half-naked man who cracked
the door of his shack and growled at me, "Don't know nothing, go
away." None of this bothered me. I felt peaceful, with more money
than I'd ever had at once, one hundred and fifty rubles in my boot,
another fourteen in my pocket. Wasting a day wandering around
Novgorod looking for transportation south to Moscow wasn't a
challenge, though hunger was, for at supper on the river the night
before all I'd managed to buy from the bargemen was bread, a sizable slab of butter, a decent onion, and tea. I needed to find a bakery
before I went looking for another barge ride. I am certain that my
sightseeing was an afterthought. I wouldn't have stopped at
Novgorod more than to stretch my legs except for the accident, but
once there I became curious. I'd spent the last eleven years in school
barracks and seen almost nothing of Russia outside of Leningrad and

the steppes of Orenburg. I'd flown the southern Urals and northern Kazakhstan, but that didn't count, and now here I found myself in the father of Russian towns, Lord Novgorod the Great, city of the legendary Prince Alexander Nevsky (who is no forebear of mine). I told myself to risk the curfew and poke around. If a policeman stopped me, I'd tell him the truth.

After an hour of pushing my motorcycle, I was still hungry, and I hadn't seen much worthwhile beside several magnificent red-throated loons dipping toward the lake and a cautious goshawk patrolling the tree line. Novgorod had been leveled in the war, and after twenty years it was only half rebuilt on opposite shores of the river. There were stained Khrushchev houses, a fenced-in dye factory, wooden quays, and concrete single-span bridges and almost nothing of the thousand-year-old imperial city. I drifted deeper into the citadel quarter on the western riverbank, where the structures were better built, some Romanov blue and yellow. The streets remained grim and deserted. Secondary cities in those days were on short rations and mean finances. The bosses spent most everything on themselves and their servants, such as the military and State Security, and that left little for paint or window glass and nothing for new buildings. The exception to the general gloom was Novgorod's magisterial five-hundred-year-old citadel, sitting on the riverbank in the flush of the white night, as if a Romanov emperor had just gone out, to return by noon.

It was right then that fate started its work on me. Up broad Dmitryyevska Street I spied the tankers from the wrecked barge, nine of them, looking rowdy, nasty, and drunk. I guessed that they hadn't come looking for me, but that now that they'd found me, I'd do as a target of opportunity and my motorcycle as plunder. I had no plan. I hurried across the birch park for the biggest refuge in sight and the citadel was that, with its massive crenellated brick walls, awe-inspiring bell towers, and peaked gun towers. I veered toward the high main gate. It should have been shut but wasn't. I didn't look back. Head down I shoved my bike into the broad flat courtyard. I needed cover but there wasn't any to be seen—a gray stone armory and whitewashed Byzantine cathedral to the left, a decayed, green Romanov palace and ramshackle barracks to the right. I didn't think about my trespassing, nor that I had just trapped myself inside. I let my alarm carry me across the drive and to the center of the courtyard, where there was a monument of a famous bell once dedicated by a Romanov tsar. By then the tankers had appeared at the main gate and were pointing and waving to me to come back to them: they wouldn't hurt me, they shouted, they just wanted to talk. I needed a cubbyhole, but every doorway was sealed. I remember that I first thought about trying for the Romanov palace to the right, but because there were several long black limousines there I shied away toward the river. I reached the river gate and realized that now I was trapped up against the beach—the old bridge over the Volkhov was just two pylons and trash. I figured that if I tried down the beach they'd catch me in the sand, so I backed up. The weight of the BMW pulled me off balance. Once I'd righted myself and looked up, there was the gold dome of the Saint Sophia, beckoning me.

You can see how I hesitated, how my thinking kept rejecting routes, how I did everything I could, but still I kept turning back toward Saint Sophia. It was as if the ancient allure of the place was reaching out to pull me inside, or as if the invisible hand of fate was shoving me like a child toward my destiny. Do I believe this now? Yes, I do. I believe my fate delivered me into Saint Sophia and that all my struggle and panic was incidental. Perhaps you don't believe in such things as fate and the inexorable, so I won't argue harder here. But there was something overpowering that made me turn back toward the tankers and then, just when they thought I'd given up, there was something irresistible that made me slide around the yard and spot the open door within a door on the north face of the cathedral and enter eight-hundred-year-old Saint Sophia.

I wrenched the BMW through and shut the small door. There was no dead bolt, just a loose latch. The cathedral was damp, shadowy, smelling of wet earth and long-forgotten death. The enormous iconostasis on the east side was ripped and blackened by candle smoke. The floor had large gaps where the Nazis had buried gold and artifacts. Saint Sophia wasn't a consecrated church any longer, just an abandoned shell left to the care of babushkas and the curiosity of the young, but being inside such a hushed stone cave did make me feel uneasy. I didn't believe in God then; I'd been raised to be a soldier who believed in the Air Force and his duty to the Air Force. Yet part of a falcon's education was to remain superstitious at all times, so I treated the inside of the cathedral as if it were a bad weather system that deserved caution. I rolled the BMW down the north aisle and found a shallow hole like a grave at the base of a pillar, where the motorcycle fit exactly. I listened for the tankers but there was nothing, for the brick and stone walls sealed out the world so well I could hear my pulse. I knew I had to do something useful to stop my panic, such as cover up the hole, but with what? When I turned to the right, I spotted the imperial pew in the choir, a two-meter-tall hollow box made of hard dark wood. It was the only movable object in the vast choir so I had to try to move it. I reached out to test its weight and, with half a shove, realized there was a magnificently beautiful woman inside.

It was right then that evil came into my life, so I'm reporting the moment to you carefully; and if I'm too painstaking of the events, it's because after all this time it still amazes and terrifies and confounds me to know that I was there, that her unrelenting ruthlessness came at me. Was she evil? She was certainly an evildoer, for she hated without mercy and was as cruel, depraved, and demonic as anyone I've ever met. That magnificent woman in that pew was the primary mystery of my life, and it will take me some time to explain to you the whole truth of her.

"Who are you?" she demanded from her seat in the pew.

She was more than magnificent, she was magisterial—seated there potently and serenely as if she'd been born to the ceremony of this church and everything performed here in the last eight centuries—and she was watching me with burning black eyes and the most beautiful face I'd ever seen.

"Tell me your name," she said.

I obeyed. "Junior Lieutenant P. A. Nevsky."

"Give me your hand," she said. "Help me down."

I obeyed.

"You were looking for me?" she asked. This was more an accusation than a question.

I said I was sorry to disturb her and tried, "I didn't know you were here." I repeated myself, "I'm sorry to disturb you."

She stared at me for too long to be polite with big burning black eyes that were almond shaped and wide set and as aggressive as knowledge. "Your name is Nevsky?" she said, asking tentatively, "What's your patronymic?"

"Apollonovich," I answered. I spoke my full name clearly. "Peter Apollonovich Nevsky."

She startled and said, "You're his son! I knew it. I knew something like this would happen if I came here. I knew they wouldn't let me come home without trying something at me. But who could have thought, and how did they know—you! You! His son! Peter, you're Peter Nevsky!" As she exclaimed, her features changed as if she'd aged thirty years—her radiant beauty fading to a pasty brittleness—and then she recovered herself a little, so that her complexion ripened again, and as she breathed in she started to laugh with a most despairing tone. She extended her right hand to give a shove at my chest, and when I didn't give way, she grasped my tunic coat and pushed harder and harder against me until her face was so close I could smell her strong scent of perfume and tobacco. Her performance went on too long for sense, punctuated with small asides to herself in French that I didn't understand, and all the while she wouldn't stop shoving me, as if either she wanted me to go away or she didn't believe that I was real. I didn't know how to react and just stood still like a dumb doll and let her do what she wanted.

I wouldn't learn her full identity for several months. I can tell you now that she called herself Madame Eudaemonia Romodanovsky and was called Daemonia. At first I thought she was foreign, for her French expressions, extravagant elegance, and very educated Russian, but no, she was a most Russian beauty, and her accent, style, and airs were high Muscovite, those of a woman born to the highest privilege in a classless land. She was also cultured, wealthy and well-paid, divorced and childless; and as for her French language, she'd spent the last fifteen years living in Paris in a sort of self-elected exile. When I met her she was fifty-one years old and yet still as beautiful as she was when she was half that age—darkly complected and regal, with her dyed black hair, her fashionable wardrobe. She stood about my shoulder height in her foreign shoes and smelled of a kind of sweet carnal splendor that was part a powerful French perfume and part her natural scent. There was nothing natural or nurturing about her high-handed manner, and her voice was authoritative, vivid, forceful, at times melodic and yet never not spiteful and threatening. These were all simple facts, however, and none of them would have told me then that Madame Romodanovsky's life had been lived in parallel with the history of tyranny, brutality, and stupidity since the Revolution and especially since the war, that Madame Romodanovsky's life was filled with what Great-Uncle Lev would have called "evildoing." I know now that it wouldn't have mattered if I'd had any of the details. I wouldn't have understood what she was even with her name, and I wouldn't have believed any of her crimes regardless of the truth. Great-Uncle Lev once told me that evil has to be suffered before you can open your eyes and turn and see that it exists in the world. Madame Romodanovsky was a woman who knew evil intimately, who had suffered it and suffered it upon others. She was also a woman who knew how to protect herself and get what she wanted with her seductive fury, and I have to believe that I glimpsed the truth of her that first meeting, though I didn't understand it, when she tried to push me away and I looked into her black eyes burning with decades of anger, lust, betrayal, and viciousness. My old eyes are entirely open now, and I promise you the truth of her was so black that no one but an angel could have seen it at once and endured it.

Madame Romodanovsky's odd fit finished, and she ordered me in her scolding way, "Tell me, now, do what I say. They sent you, didn't they? You're going to tell me, and don't think you're not. Sasha did this, didn't he? Just him, it's like him, to send *you* like this. Is it some sort of insult, or is it meant to be a warning, are you here to warn me?" She hesitated in thought and then demanded, "But how did Sasha know that I was coming back? Why did he send you? How did you know I was here? How did you find me? I've just been back a week! Tell me!"

I couldn't think what she meant. I figured she'd confused me with someone else, so I shook my head and apologized again. She still hadn't let go of my jacket, and she banged her whole body against me. We were like enemies locked in a dance or like lovers who'd decided to hate each other for no reason, raging at our predicament to be joined together in a desecrated cathedral in a destitute city in a doomed empire.

Then we were no longer alone. The small north-face door flew open and the drunken tankers came in fast. "Here you are, baby," the tanker captain mocked. "He's here!" he called to his mates. "You shithead! Now we've got some settling up." The tanker saw the woman and hesitated, calling out, "So, boys, here, here! Look what a piece he's got!"

I saw the threat and, instead of my brain, I used my temper and my head, charging into them with the Air Force training of ram at them, just ram, fight and fight and ram. The tankers used their boots. What I'd learned from ten years of barracks brawling was useless, since they meant to cripple me. Still, my training said to ram, to forget retreat or escape, to go faster and ram. Before I couldn't see for pain, I dragged the tanker captain down and bent his arm like a twig, using my forehead to bash him senseless, kicking out at the others to keep them away from the woman.

Madame Romodanovsky just watched and waited, and I remember her smoking. Soon the groaning and screaming wasn't me, it was the tankers, who were attacked from behind by a team of State Security men. A half dozen stout bodyguards in the distinctive black leather jackets of State Security's goons used blackjacks, brass knuckles, belts, and pistol-whipping to rip at the tankers. The tankers didn't resist; they knew they were dead men. The bodyguards beat them anyway, and then the slaughter was done, and the tankers' pleading had ceased, and the last of them was dragged out like a sack. A bodyguard rolled me over and asked, "Can you sit, boy?"

"Yes, sir," I said and obeyed him. My belt was loose, my coat open, my tunic ripped, my boots half off, and my wristwatch was gone. I didn't feel any holes in me, and all my fingers worked. The bodyguard shoved my cap at me. I knew what he was. No Air Force officer could mistake State Security's black leather jackets, close-cropped haircuts, black little grins. I straightened my jacket coat and felt for my ripped shoulder board. My breeches were slashed open at the knee, and again I checked, but there was no blood. I sounded weak when I told him, "I'm ready, sir."

"Yeah." He wiped his hands on my sleeve. "Listen, boy, General Iagoda wants to talk to you. Are you going to vomit?"

I replied, "No, sir."

"Get up," he ordered.

I say I knew what the bodyguard was, but I didn't know much else. I didn't know why State Security was present, nor who General Iagoda was. Then I recalled the black limousines I'd spotted in front of the Romanov palace and realized I was in a good deal of trouble. I heaved erect and checked myself once more to find that my rib cage hurt, my face was puffy, my knees were on fire, and yet none of this was as unsettling as what I faced.

Across the choir in the shadows beside the pew stood Madame Romodanovsky, and next to her, like a chaperon, was a tall, slim, gray-headed and most handsome man, looking like a scholar in owl-like steel-rimmed eyeglasses. He was Gen. R. G. Iagoda of State Security. Both of them were smoking with meerschaum holders and watching me as if I were a foundling who might live after all. There was a long, discordant pause, a State Security trick to drain you, and then: "Thank you for what you did," General Iagoda began. "Nine to one. Or was it less? And you didn't lose, did you? How are you now?"

"Sir!" I reported. My salute stung me everywhere. There were simple Air Force rules when up against State Security: don't talk, obey, wait, obey, shut up.

"Yes, yes, fine officer," Iagoda said, "I'm sure, at ease, come closer, no displays necessary, just stand here, we'll talk."

I obeyed to within a few meters. Two bodyguards kept to my right and left, working their hands like bullies. There was no more weeping and begging from outside; there was just the cool tomb of Saint Sophia and the crackle of Iagoda's shoes on the stone floor.

Iagoda examined my face and suggested, "You could use a doctor."

"Yes, sir," I said. "Thank you, sir. Just fine, sir."

"Your nose could," Iagoda offered.

My nose is so beakish, and I was then so self-conscious about it, that I heard this as a criticism. I resisted checking to see if it was broken.

Iagoda waved me to calm myself. He was about fifty, and he talked with education, discretion, sincerity. He was a commanding figure in an offhanded way—a man who was used to being listened to—and he was attractive like a foreigner, well groomed, well dressed in a light suit, well shod in gleaming brown shoes. His manner was paternal, as if he knew what you wanted and tolerated you for being little and weak. Undoubtedly he was also, I believed as the Air Force had taught me, as rotten as his branch of service, the Committee for State Security. Iagoda had my papers in his hand and showed them to Madame Romodanovsky.

"I told you," she said to Iagoda.

Iagoda blew smoke from his nose. "Your father was Colonel-General A. A. Nevsky, yes? And you're posted to Starry Town, yes? Cosmonaut candidate, yes? . . ."

He continued to interrogate me, and I answered each question succinctly. You already know what I said, so I'll add here that, while I stood there, I was terrified and I was right to be. General R. G. Iagoda was one of the highest lords of the Lubyanka, the chief of the Fifth Directorate, the rot of the rot, the State Security boss responsible for crushing all dissent in the empire—political, national, religious. Add this to the library of things I didn't know at the time but could feel, and you can understand why I stood helpless before him. Even the Air Force general staff in those days backed off from confrontation with State Security. The Lubyanka lords were thieves, extortionists, every kind of lawbreaker; worse, they were torturers, sadists, mass murderers. If you're young, you don't know—you can't know unless you felt them. I won't forgive them and don't ask me to. They tortured and murdered everyone I held dear, and they did it for no reason other than that they were rotten souls.

"Very well, good report," Iagoda finished, his eyes raised as if he were addressing the iconostasis behind me. "You came off a barge. You were chased by thieves. You fled here. You hid your machine there. You meant to drag the pew over it. That lot came in. You defended yourself. That's all of it, yes?"

I returned, "Yes, sir."

Iagoda addressed Madame Romodanovsky, "Anything else, Daemonia? It seems direct enough."

Now that I've recalled this exchange, I see that Iagoda did use her name: Daemonia; her true name: Daemonia Romodanovsky.

Madame Romodanovsky turned on me and softened her voice. "Why are you here, Lieutenant? I asked you before. Tell me."

I knew not to speak and anyway couldn't think to.

She tried softer still, almost maternally, "You can tell me the truth. You haven't done any harm."

I stood obedient and silent. I could do no other.

She dropped pretense and assailed her strange point. "It's Oryolin isn't it?" Her beauty changed again, twisting this time, her mouth spraying spittle as she demanded, "It's Sasha Oryolin, it's him, he sent you? Why? How did he know I'd be here? Why are you here!"

Iagoda objected, "It makes no sense."

"Tell me the truth!" Madame Romodanovsky said. She approached me, closer and closer, until I could smell her again, and she could use that ploy of hers of putting her hand on my breast. "You have a strong heart." Her power of seduction was violent, and she squeezed her hand on my chest, pushed harder and harder at me. "I can feel your heart," she continued. "I can feel you want to tell me. But you can't. Perhaps you don't know yourself. But I know it's true, Oryolin sent you. Tell me the truth and then tell me why."

Her trickery made me break the rules and talk. "I've never met Colonel Oryolin," I stated. "I know him, though, I mean, I know him through my family, well, through my father. He's one of my uncles, well, not really. He was one of my father's fliers, one of the Martian Troika."

"You heard him!" Madame Romodanovsky shouted at Iagoda.

I didn't know what I'd done wrong and tried again, "The Martian Troika—they were my father's men, in the war, but I was young. I wasn't born until after the war. I was told they were like my uncles. I might have met them, when I was little. I don't think I remember meeting them. Colonels Oryolin, Strogolshikov, and Zhukovsky. I just call them my uncles. They're not really my uncles, more like my godfathers." Madame Romodanovsky stared blackly at me, and I tried again to correct myself. "I might have imagined that I met them once. But they really are my godfathers, and so I call them Uncle Alexander, Uncle Konstantine, and Uncle Dmitry. I've always thought of them as my uncles. But I was a child when I met them, or think I did, or imagine I did. After my father died, I never heard from them again. But I'll see them now at Starry Town. They're going to be my senior commanders there." I tried once more to qualify my tale. "I call them my uncles, but really, I only know them by their reputations. They're famous, you know, every Air Force officer knows them. Every schoolboy has a postage stamp of Colonels Oryolin and Strogolshikov in *Voskhod 2,* but—"

"Your uncles!" Madame Romodanovsky shouted me down. "You're lying! They sent you here! Stop lying to me!"

I said, "They're not really my uncles. It's just what I've always called them since I was little. But I've not heard from them ever. They don't know I'm here—they don't know I'm anywhere. I'm going to them now, and they probably won't remember me."

Iagoda waved me to back off, and I obeyed. Madame Romodanovsky and Iagoda then quarreled entirely in French. Most of it was absolutely beyond me. I heard names, pronouns, half sentences, crumpled thoughts, much harsh whispering and hissing ejaculations, but no recognizable phrases. She was cold, cross, impatient, he was conciliatory and frustrated, and I'd never heard so much of a foreign language at once.

Several times as they talked I was able to pick out the three critical names, Oryolin, Strogolshikov, Zhukovsky—the three men I called my uncles, the Martian Troika. The Martian Troika was a war name that had shaped their legend. During the war they had served in my father's air regiment, and they had come to be called the Martian Troika because, it was said, the god of war flew as their wingman, from Stalingrad to Berlin. It was a nickname more about their luck to survive than it was about their skill at war, though it was that, too, since they became aces by outlasting all odds, and since Uncle Alexander, as my father's wingman, surpassed even luck to become the fifth air ace of the war after my father and three dead men. You might know of them as cosmonauts from the moon race days, Alexander Oryolin, Konstantine Strogolshikov, and Dmitry Zhukovsky. You should know the whole truth of them. They were my father's favorites, they were three of the most decorated falcons in the war, they were winged victory itself, they were heroes of heroes, and that was just when they were my age. Two generations later, they were senior cosmonaut-pilots at Starry Town. Alexander Oryolin and Konstantine Strogolshikov had flown the first spacewalk mission in *Voskhod 2*. Dmitry Zhukovsky, at that time, was said to be the leading candidate for *Soyuz 2*. You will meet them soon, my uncles, the Martian Troika, and judge for yourself. I still think of them as my family, as my uncles, but the more complete truth is that they are the heroes of my story. And though several more generations have come and gone since then, my uncles Alexander, Konstantine, and Dmitry might be the only heroes I ever knew after my father. I don't mean heroic for wisdom, virtue, dignity, which they missed, being too often no more than hotheads in uniform and at times very dangerous men who were capable of limitless violence; nor do I mean heroic for victory, since in the end they risked everything they had and failed and fell and died; instead I mean heroic because they were my heroes and I loved them.

In Saint Sophia I wasn't thinking of heroism. I was ashamed for having spoken of senior brother officers in front of State Security. I'd violated the Air Force's rules that you must never, never give State Security a personal fact, a reason to remember you, a detail from your life; you must stand fast as Air Force. And what had I done but brag, apologize, equivocate, and humiliate myself. Worse, I'd spoken of my uncles as if they were my intimates, which was untrue. Great-Uncle Lev had told me that they had visited Leningrad when I was two years old and had patted me on the head, though even this was a questionable anecdote that Great-Uncle Lev might have made up to please me. In any event this tale of head patting was our entire kinship. Otherwise I'd seen them only at the Orenburg archives in group photographs of my father's squadron, their grinning boyish faces staring into the sky like restless birds of prey, their Yaks and MiGs and even Spitfires parked behind them like winged coffins, the three of them shoulder to shoulder and kneeling beside my bold father. I'd come to imagine them as part of the family I'd always wanted, and I'd boasted at Orenburg how they were my uncles. I'd also come to believe they knew who I was. Now I'd turned a boy's make-believe into grown-up trouble. I asked myself if I'd compromised them, and the answer was yes. I knew this intuitively, but I couldn't be certain of it, and I wouldn't admit it to myself for some time. There was nothing to be done except to wait on more of the same strange fate that had pulled me into the cathedral.

I think Iagoda lost the quarrel, or at least he looked pained when Madame Romodanovsky threw his hand off her arm and cursed him in violent Russian, "Do what I say, damn you, and do it now! Find out the truth!" With that she tossed her cigarette holder in a tantrum, scraped her heels across the stone floor, and left us, a bodyguard in lead, another behind her.

Iagoda smoked while watching her depart. The truth was that he was in love with her, and if I hadn't been so naïve of love, I could have seen this as nakedly as his authority. Iagoda loved Madame Romodanovsky as many strong men had loved her before him, for her amazing beauty, her unyielding pride, her boundless, seductive, enslaving power, and for no explicable reason at all, just because he loved her, just because there might be some decency in rotten hearts that makes them love as needfully as the rest of us. Madame Romodanovsky was a woman whom men want to possess and, failing at it, come to crave as something as unattainable as bliss and as perilous as defiance. Iagoda exhaled smoke like vapor in the shadows and told me, "I want you to do something for me, Lieutenant Nev-sky. I want you to do me a favor."

I was most confused and tried, "Sir? I didn't lie to you, sir. I didn't know anyone was in here, sir. It was all an accident, me coming in here."

"Don't bother explaining again. I understand. I believe you." He digressed, "I was wrong to let her come in here alone. What might've happened is awful to think." He coughed and addressed me again, "I thanked you, and I'll do it again. Now, I need your help, I'm asking for your help. Don't think of it as an order."

I was feeling better because he said he believed me. "Yes, sir."

Iagoda looked at me as if asking himself how stupid I could be to listen to a Lubyanka lord. "When you get to Starry Town, I want you to tell Colonel Oryolin that I want a truce between us, between him and me. He doesn't know me, but he'll understand when you tell him about me. Will you do this for me?"

I had no notion at all what he was talking about but still I snapped, "Sir!" Iagoda could have told me to cut off my hand and I would have said, "Sir!" just as obediently, and I would have done nothing about it just as determinedly.

"It's not necessary for you to understand why I ask. Tell him what I've said. Tell him what happened here. Tell him it was just a chance meeting. It's shocking to think, but there it is—it was chance, an accident." Iagoda sighed and added, "And tell him there's a truce between us, just that, a truce, and leave it there."

Iagoda fixed and lit a new cigarette as he circled the pew to come toward me. I laugh at myself now for not knowing what that pew was: Five centuries before, Ivan the Terrible had prayed there each morning before he went across the river to torture Novgorod's thousands to death. How sentimental of her, Madame Romodanovsky, I see now, how vain and operatic of her, to stop at Saint Sophia on her way back from Paris to Moscow just in order to sit in Tsar Ivan's pew. It was her only weakness, her vanity to see herself as some sort of an empress of all the Russias, but then it was a monumental weakness and a pathetic delusion, and her yearning to be more powerful than she was had cost her the few happy times she would ever know and the true love and heartfelt understanding she might have had despite her crimes.

Iagoda moved closer to examine me, the same trick Madame

Romodanovsky had used, and as he neared I could feel his vitality and also the strain of his decisions. "Your father was a brave man," he started.

I realized what he'd said and added, "Yes, sir."

Iagoda meant to charm me and made a speech, "I admired him, your father, everyone did, I suppose, every living Leningrader. I'm one, you know. Your father was just six years older than me. His flying in Spain, we all read about it. He was famous years before the war. And then that day he downed five Messerschmidts in two different planes—was shot down in one and went back in another. Didn't they give him one of his gold stars for that? Legendary stuff, everyone knew about it. I remember, I was in the Kuban, and we were mad for the stories of the great Nevsky, and they often mentioned him on the news dispatches on the radio. He was an all-union celebrity, of course, they decorated him more than once, I remember seeing it in the newsreels. You weren't born yet, but you should know. I admired your father as much as I've ever admired anyone, and when I was young I wanted to fly like him, though my eyes, I never could have made the grade. But you're obviously the great Nevsky's son. And now you're off to Starry Town. Good for you."

I didn't know why Iagoda was talking about my father, but I was sure this was a trick; and as warm as Iagoda's remarks seemed to me, I knew not to respond.

"After you've settled in," he continued, "when you get into Moscow, call this number. We can visit. I'll send a car for you. We can visit." He returned my orders and with them his card; and then he moved to the door, hanging his head but not turning when he asked, "You don't want a ride to Moscow, do you? You'll want to go along on your own, won't you?"

I was relieved to be free of him. "Yes, sir, I'd like to go on my own."

"Yes, it's best, I suppose," he said. "We'll leave this as a chance meeting ended by chance." Iagoda ducked out and was gone.

I waited to a count of five and then chewed the card he'd given me until it was spit and then put the spit on the floor. I told myself that I was right to destroy his card, though I do wonder, now, if I'd kept that card, and done what he'd said, would it have changed our fate? If I'd passed on his message immediately to Uncle Alexander, or if I'd called Iagoda's Lubyanka telephone number and told him I wouldn't do his favor, or if I'd done the least he'd asked and gone to Uncle Alexander with the news that I'd met a beautiful and incomprehensible woman in Saint Sophia *by chance*—would any of this have stopped our fate? I know I shouldn't debate such things, and yet it still pains me to think over those days and see how helpless I was before the momentum of events. I want to reach out from my ancient roost and give a hand to my youth, or perhaps I just want to touch what it was to be so young, naïve, full of hope, so fate filled. I can only watch it happen the same as you do, and though I know more than you do now, and though I know the course of the tragedy, it profits me nothing. My fate was as fixed as the pole star, and it was only mine to find it and follow it.

I keep mentioning fate. "All Russia is fate," as Great-Uncle Lev taught me, so what was so special about the fate I met that morning? There was nothing special, except that it came at me, I was there, and I survived it to remember it like a lost world that's now a relentless and too often pitiless dream. It was my life. There is much I can't explain until I dig into my memory, however I can say now that my fate at Saint Sophia was to cross the path of the only two people I've ever met who meant to destroy me and everything I ever loved and believed in. I can also say that it was their fate, General Iagoda's and Madame Romodanovsky's fate, to conspire and fight and fail, murderously and without meaning. And I can say that it was the fate of my uncles—the legendary Martian Troika, my undying heroes, my Three Musketeers—to conspire and fight and fail, too, with not a little of the murder that cursed those days, though they failed stubbornly like the true falcons they were, though their failure was no disgrace but came from the theme of their lives to attack, to ram, to fight, to keep going as my father had taught them, to go faster, farther, to go too far and then to go again.

What was my fate? I'm not all grim turns about myself. I can joke about what a bumbler I was enough to say that after the black-and-blue prologue of Saint Sophia, it was mine to keep my beak out of other men's reach until it healed. It was also mine to do my duty, since that was all a junior lieutenant could rely upon, duty and duty again, and if they asked you what you were doing, say "Duty, sir." I can smile now at the games I played in order to cover up that I was a boy: I was so arrogant and know-it-all; I was always posturing as one of Pushkin's "priests of the momentary and successes of the earth," sure that no one and nothing would get me to admit I found the world, the flesh, and the devil overwhelming. I pulled my BMW out of the hole and, backing it up, looked up to thank Saint Andrew, patron saint of Holy Mother Russia, for watching over me right there above me in the grimy iconostasis. I was godless then, a swell-headed little socialist ignoramus who couldn't have imagined there was a deal of high talk beyond the rote Leninisms I'd memorized to pander to my teachers, yet the part of me that was a son of a son of a son of a God-fearing serf knew the luck of heaven when it showed itself. I suppose, too, that I knew I needed a saintly hand, since I was a pauper again. The bodyguards had searched me thoroughly, and gone with my watch was my money. No, I remember, they'd left the coins. I had about ten rubles for the five hundred kilometers to Moscow. I should add that my fate at Saint Sophia was also to start walking.

"Welcome to Starry Town!"

Two weeks later I quit my last barge ride in the waterway north of Moscow and pushed inland from the riverbank. At first light I heard shrieking engines ahead of me, and they guided me to the airfield as if I were marching to the sound of guns. It was a moonless Monday morning, July 1, coolish and damp, with light fog off the streams and in the dells, so the Tumansky turbojets I'd heard were my guiding beacons, two of them, a flight of MiG-21s, descending from the northeast. It was already sunup where they were coming from, and they were feeling their way down through the last hundred meters of muck. Smelling high octane made me hurry, and it took me only a half hour to get my motorcycle over the rise, another half hour to clear the lorry road that bordered the outposts of the gigantic Chkalvo Air Force Base, and then, there it was, as I'd been told, the unmarked turnoff into the forest and the country lane to Starry Town. It was just a gravel cut in the pine groves, wide enough for a single vehicle, no signs, no special fences or redoubts, as plain as any country hamlet. But to my happy eyes it was the runway to paradise. On my first day, at my first view, every detail seemed larger than life and more perfect. I saw colossal Siberian fir, Scotch pine, Daurian larch, stone pine, and the omnipresent silver birch; I saw gorgeous blue veronica, rouge cranberries, dark bilberries, the sweet-smelling lichens and mosses and humble horsetail plants; I saw bounteous goldfinches, darting gray shrikes and white wagtails; and to my eyes the toadstools were as grand as thrones.

A kilometer down I glided to the sentry post and propped my BMW against the white barrier. There was no guard in sight so I busied myself with my appearance, brushing my tunic coat, wiping down my boots, debating if I should wear my breeches cuff loose in the Orenburg custom or tucked trim in Moscow's custom. I stayed with the familiar. My beard was scraped smooth; my hair was acceptable; my fingernails were clean; my buttons were fresh polished; my nose was entirely healed. I looked hungry but acceptable to any quick inspection.

The sentry ambushed me, demanding, "What do you want?"

I returned the salute he hadn't given me. He was an Air Police corporal, puffy faced with drink; he'd been urinating in the woods.

"Say it, Lieutenant," he said. "Don't expect me to guess."

I presented myself and emphasized that I was a cosmonaut candidate. "Reporting for duty as ordered," I closed.

He wasn't impressed and pointed at my bike. "Christ, what's that?"

I was so tired of the trouble my BMW had caused me since Leningrad that I tried to cut off the bargaining. "It's not for sale," I said.

"Pity." He kicked the tires and patted the handlebars. "I could get you a fair price. Goods like that are gold."

I kept shut. He sniffed at me and went to telephone his duty officer. I waited while wondering what sort of slipshod discipline they had around here. Any sentry caught absent at Orenburg would have been flogged, and I mean in the timeworn way, with a knout on his bare back. I'd been flogged more than my share in my time and admit my attitude then was that you didn't forget your mistake. But

I didn't care that much about this laggard, since the Air Police were notorious thieves. There was grumbling from the sentry post, a slammed phone, and he returned annoyed, telling me, "You're not expected until Saturday."

"I'm here now," I said as politely as I could.

"You'd think I wanted you here," he complained to no one. "What should I do? It's too early for Corps commander's office." He scratched under his tunic in order to make a show of his disrespect. "Go to Major Tronko, he'll see you," he said. "The Party clerk, Major Tronko. You should be his problem if you're anyone's. You know the way?"

I looked up the lane and waited for help.

"It's the administration building, new one on the circle." He nodded at the BMW. "They won't like that. Park it with me?"

"Thank you," I said, "no."

He snorted and at the time I thought his parting advice was silly, "Careful, Lieutenant, you're virgin to them," though he was actually warning me that Starry Town had its share of snares and traps, and he was one of them.

I only had big eyes for wonders, such as several teals in a pond by the lane or the ancient lemon tree at the foot of the circle or the new-built residential apartment towers behind the spruce line. Down to the right, in the glen, were the low-slung training and medical center and the bulky indoor and outdoor sports complex. Starry Town was exactly as I'd been told, brick-built and buffed, snug up against one of the airbase's heavy-duty runways, completely self-contained with food and goods shops, grammar schools, even its own cultural center. Starry Town, the headquarters of the Cosmonaut Corps since Gagarin's *Vostok 1,* was the most elite and envied Air Force bivouac in all Russia; and now I was arrived, it was happening to me, a dream of joy come to life. I remember now that, as I cleared the circle drive, at just that moment, an old prop bomber lifted heavily above the trees, banking east, and I saw it as if it were a great gyrfalcon welcoming me to the nest. Do you know the gyrfalcon? I suppose you've noticed that I care a deal about birds; it's a lifelong passion, and I can't not remember those days without recalling my bird sightings, even my make-believe sightings. The gyrfalcon is the largest and hungriest of our birds of prey, and its chilling "kyak-

kyak!" means supreme threat is on the wing. Sighting a gyrfalcon, even in winter, is very rare, and I was pretending I'd spied one in a boyish way to mark the moment of my life when I knew I was home forever.

The squat administration building was a cold welcome. None of the clerks would talk to me, keeping their noses in their tea glasses and scurrying frantically. It was because of the discipline trouble that morning, and, though I wasn't at fault, I was headed for the mess. I was lost within steps down the two-toned corridors because the signs were undecipherable acronyms. I roamed the first story and became even more confused until I twice passed the two captains at the T-corner and stopped to ask for help.

They were beautiful pilots, both very fair, blue-gem-eyed, sensational young men. Later I'd learn they were the two best MiG drivers in the Air Force, by reputation and design, and the two most mercurial Don Juans at Starry Town by same: Captains Valya Glavtop and Kolya Grin, both then twenty-nine and at the brink of their fame. Perhaps you know them only as the grand old air marshals weighted down by ribbons and medals, longtime co-chiefs of the Russian Air Force. You should also know that when they were young they were universally admired rogues. Right then they were proudest of being cosmonaut-pilots and members of my uncles' squadron, and they were least happy with being the source of the trouble that morning. As I went by them the second time, Glavtop said to Grin, "Not a navigator, is he?" It wasn't possible to distinguish between their beauty; they were two celestial white-blond darlings who had their own intimate language, like twinned gods enjoying their mortal days. "One of ours, you think?" Grin said to Glavtop.

I saluted them. "Excuse me, sirs, I'm to report to Major Tronko."

"Distinctly one of ours," Glavtop said to Grin.

I didn't mind the teasing. They were not only falcons but also, by their class rings, they were Orenburg graduates. They also looked banged about: Glavtop's left thumb was bandaged, Grin's cheek was cut, and both showed bruises. I could guess that there'd been a fistfight, not long ago, leaving ripped knuckles, a red ear, and that they were sitting out here like truants waiting on the switch.

Glavtop gave me directions, six doors down to the Party clerk's office, and then told me to go straight in. "Dear Tronko's a lonely fellow, he'll see anyone anytime." Grin added, "Beware, dear Lieutenant, he's got unmarried daughters."

I thanked them eagerly, for their playfulness was electric, and I was already having more fun than during all my years at the academy. I felt special in a new way, for first I'd found two cinematic falcons in the hall and now there were unmarried daughters up ahead. I couldn't decide if the daughters were good things or bad things to find, and so I opened the door onto their father, Major Igor Tronko, the worrywart of Starry Town.

Major Tronko's opening was characteristic of his nature. "Yes, yes, our early bird, God help us, what're we to do with you? We'll need your signature about two dozen times. Stop bouncing about, rest your feet, Lieutenant!" Tronko was stocky and squint-eyed behind bottle-thick lenses, and he was badly suited to Starry Town, a dull concessionaire lost among gate-crashers. He's gone forty years now, and I should be more generous toward someone who, in his retirement, atoned for his pettiness and became a man of many good works around Starry Town. Back then, everyone mocked and ignored him except candidates like me. He was petty in the extreme, for he worked for the Air Force political directorate, as Party clerk, which meant that he maintained something like an attendance sheet in bound leather books, and it was his job to report you if you didn't fill out all his forms and keep them up to date. Tronko was chiefly a creature of the Party. There were tens of thousands of Tronkos across Russia, in and out of uniform, from airbases to fertilizer factories to fisheries. The Party was an overgrown and overage schoolteacher always threatening to punish if you didn't attend to mandates. Perhaps I should say an overgrown and undying headmaster, since wasn't that all Ulyanov was in the end, the son of a headmaster who gave to Russia the same sort of dusty, brutal didacticism to be found in his father's back-country schoolhouses? Mind your ABCs and multiplication tables and we'll make revolution with honors, so don't miss a day or else you'll miss your head! I'm not going to waste words in this tale on Lenin's Bolsheviks and the fat, petty Communist Party of the Soviet Union that it became. Look at Tronko and you see the supreme example of the new socialist man, the longed-for genius of the dialectic, a pen-pushing clerk with an attendance sheet. Otherwise little had changed from the Petersburg pen-pushers Dostoyevsky liked to lampoon. Above the Tronkos of the land there were the same old bosses who'd always ruled Russia. Stalin, a boss of bosses who lived up to his reputation, started out a schoolyard bully who fooled his teachers until the moment he blew their brains out with nine grams. Lenin's revolution turned the classrooms into the slave camps and the books into files of denunciations in the Lubyanka archives. Stalin's revolution just took the next step of murdering everyone who complained that school wasn't what it used to be and then went on to kill anyone who might have ever gone to school. What a revelation: Russia isn't a schoolroom. By the time I arrived at Tronko's door, in 1968, it was evident to everyone that Russia had tossed off Lenin's headmastership and Stalin's gunmanship and settled back to the familiar ways of a dictatorship of bosses. The CPSU had become the same old heaps of big bosses and bigger bosses—crude, greedy, aimless figures who came from nowhere with nothing to say and went to nowhere with nothing to show—and that's all there was to the Party after fifty years of power: a pointless, meaningless crush of bosses across all Russia. If I sound fatalistic to you, you're half right. Yet I was once young enough to believe I could get what I wanted regardless of who was in charge, and I'm old enough now to realize that it never mattered who the bosses were, it only mattered who obeyed them. All Russia is fate, recall, and back then this meant that we got the fate we believed we deserved. We expected nothing and got nothing. I can't tell you what the bosses ever did for the Air Force besides shortchanging us our pay and counting our heads with dupes like Tronko; and yet still we accepted this as our due, and that means we wronged ourselves. I see now that a large part of what my uncles did for me was that they showed me how to demand a better world.

After an hour of his questions that had nothing to do with my duty, Tronko worked to an important detail. Where was I going to sleep and eat? "Candidate barracks can't receive you," he worried. "Not until next week. And the mess is closed for repairs, and we wouldn't know how to record your expense anyway, and we can't have you wandering around base without proper identification, how would it look?"

What followed was typical clerkship: I said that I could sleep anywhere. "I could bunk at the airbase, sir. I'm sure I can make friends with the flight crews." I didn't want to make it sound too easy, because I'd found charity on my journey but not plenty and was ravenous and broke. "Maybe I could use their mess, too," I tried.

"No, no," he said, "once you're here, you can't leave until you're officially here."

"I could go away and come back," I tried. "No one would know, sir."

"You've signed in!" he exclaimed as if I were mad. He checked the forms I'd signed, since they were the proof that I was now his problem to solve. "Let me think on it; maybe my wife would help. We'll see. I'll look into it. With the children away, you see, we have the room." The family portrait on his desk displayed a chunky wife and two dark, bony teenage girls. "So we'll see. Now, take this, and this, and go on to Corps commander's office to present yourself, and then come back to me, and we'll get on to the check-in at medical center." Tronko stacked folios in my hands and tsk-tsked me to the door. "Base commander's office is down the corridor, eight doors. Ask for Lieutenant-Colonel Maximov, and please," he indicated my trousers, "tuck those in before you do. And Lieutenant, watch your step. It's not a good morning to make difficulties."

The commander of the Cosmonaut Corps was Lt.-Gen. N. P. Kamenin, sixty-five, an orthodox falcon and once upon a time a daring arctic flier, one of my father's heroes and early commanders. I'd seen Kamenin speak several times at Orenburg and liked him for his devotion to the Air Force. I expected a benevolent interview, since seniors like Kamenin always mentioned my father to me and this made me feel happy, as if, though he was dead, he were still looking out for me. As it turned out my father's reputation was looking out for me that morning, but not until I'd found the trouble that had been building all morning.

My preliminary contest was with the Corps' deputy commander, the urbane, degenerate Lieutenant-Colonel Maximov. I recognized what Maximov was as soon as I made my way through the outer office of buzzing clerks and into his small office with portraits of Brezhnev, Lenin, and Dzerzhinsky on the wall and with an antiseptic desk that had pencils lined up like bullets on the ink blotter. Maximov was very carefully groomed, like a barber expecting customers, and though he was over forty, there were no wings on his jacket. Can you guess what he was? Maximov was State Security's spy on the Corps, a rat, trained to wear our uniform, to share our quarters, to take the pay scale of a falcon and then to denounce a few of us each month. Everyone knew who he was, since the Air Force taught you to know who the rats were and to give them nothing.

Maximov didn't look up when he put his hand out for my folios. I stayed at attention, and I recall that I spotted a pair of muddy officer's boots on the chair by the window and wondered why. Maximov couldn't find an error on Tronko's paperwork. He picked up a new sheet from his desk and placed it neatly on top of the folio of papers. "You've important friends in Moscow," he said.

I resisted answering. I wanted to deny everything, but all I could do was sense what was coming and outlast it.

Maximov still wouldn't look at me. "I've been telephoned recently," he said. "It seems you're a favorite of a prominent general in a most important Moscow post." He said all this dryly, as if he were not overly impressed, except that he was. "You're a special favorite of a very important man in Moscow."

I knew he meant General Iagoda. My shame came back at me as if it had only been moments since Iagoda had tried to compromise me; no, since Iagoda *had* compromised me. It was the way of the world back then: you couldn't refuse State Security. You said yes or nothing at all, and denying it only made more trouble for yourself or, worse, made your friends doubt you. It was like black magic—if they touched you, you were unclean. I knew that sheet of paper Maximov had added to my folio was Iagoda's tattletale report on the incident at Saint Sophia, and it would follow me forever.

"Yes or no?" Maximov asked.

The only way out of the trap was to counterattack, and I risked it. "I don't think that my friends, sir, that who they are, that it isn't my duty to report who they are, sir."

Maximov looked up and flicked his shiny fingers. He was a simple sadist, and he liked that I'd just cut my own throat. "So, you're a little shit, well—"

I won't quote the details of his threats against me, since I was rescued by my uncles, the legendary Martian Troika, that is, two-thirds of them. With a bang of the door, two stunning cosmonauts showing the three stars of colonels on their shoulder boards pushed into Maximov's office.

"You skinny ass, Maximov!" announced the brawny, bald colonel, who I knew instantly was my Uncle Konstantine. He was twenty-five years older than the photos I'd seen at school but he was still the same bald bear of a Cossack's son rumbling through life with a sunburned copper melon head and a large nose that had been battered too many times to call it simply broken and giant brown eyes hooded by furry brows. Here was K. K. Strogolshikov, at forty-seven, called Kostya, the uncontested clown of the three of them, the bad punster, the worse husband (married and divorced many times), who'd been born on the Don with a horseman's blood on both sides of his huge, rapacious family at Rostov-on-Don. I knew him like I knew heroism, for his walking-out coat flapped open to flash a rainbow of ribbons and his *two* gold stars—twice a Hero of the Soviet Union, in 1944 for combat and in 1965 for *Voskhod 2*. But then Uncle Konstantine didn't know me, and so he rumbled at me, "Give way, darling," while clearing me aside with an elbow. "You've engineered this frame-up," he told Maximov, "just to get me up too early. You've brought charges against innocence itself. And now you've done it, you've got me up from my morning dreams."

Maximov stood up and cursed, "Bugger off, Strogolshikov."

Uncle Konstantine grinned and replied, "I like you when you show your teeth, such pretty teeth. Doesn't he have first-rate teeth, Mitya? All of them like that, no steel or gold, just God's best bridgework ear to ear?"

"I see I'll need more tea," said the other cosmonaut-colonel at the door, Col. D. M. Zhukovsky, called Mitya, who was my Uncle Dmitry and who hadn't changed a tick since the photos of him at twenty-two. Tiny, trim, gauntly bony-faced, his small head covered by little brownish-gray curls, he looked like an aesthete, which was his fantasy, and he carried himself like a diplomat, which was his talent. He was the peacemaker and compromiser of the three of them, and he was also the good husband and loving father. Out of uniform he might have been a Muscovite dilettante, much at the concert hall or poetry reading. In uniform, those combat ribbons and *two* gold stars dominated, since he was also twice Hero of the Soviet Union, 1942 and 1945, who was credited with killing four German aces at Kirsk. Perhaps Uncle Dmitry was a little older around his sky-blue eyes, and he looked careworn as he took a tea glass from a clerk in the foyer, tucked his cap under his arm, smiled sardonically, and pretended to arbitrate the argument. "Right then, please, comrades, without the pleasantries, just speak your thoughts as you have them; we'll sort this out for the best."

Uncle Konstantine and Maximov obliged, accusing, cursing, and lashing each other. "Your putatively innocent friends have disgraced themselves!" Maximov would cry. "Prove it, ha-ha, prove anything!" Uncle Konstantine would boom back. Uncle Konstantine kept going at Maximov as if to smash his teeth, but each time Uncle Dmitry checked him and advised, "Sort this out for the best, Kostya."

Throughout the argument I was blocked from the exit by Uncle Konstantine's bulk and ignored like a coatrack by Uncle Dmitry. I understood this much of the yelling. The night before had been the year-end Cosmonaut Corps banquet at a Moscow hotel. Afterward the married men had gone home, and the bachelor officers had gone out on the town. Later there was a brawl at the Bolshoi Theater between several uniformed State Security officers and three unidentified cosmonauts. It was said to have been over a young woman who'd been roughed up by the Chekhists, something to do with her polio braces. Note this, as I did, that the cosmonauts came to the rescue of a young woman wearing a polio brace. The result was that the Chekhists required many splints. The question this morning was, who were the three cosmonauts? Maximov, Starry Town's chief disciplinarian as well as rat, had determined, on the basis of their rakish reputations, that two of the brawlers had to be the beautiful blond captains I'd met in the corridor, Glavtop and Grin. Their bruises and cuts had supported Maximov's theory. The third brawler was in question, for the only clue Maximov had was a pair of muddy officer's boots. It seemed that later last night, three drunken officers returning to Starry Town had run a car into the pond by the lane and fled the sentries, leaving the boots behind. It was Maximov's theory that the boots belonged to one of the guilty three, and when Glavtop and Grin had refused to try on the boots, Maximov had determined they belonged to the third brawler.

Yes, it was as ridiculous as it sounds, and yet it was also typical of how rats like Maximov went at you in those days, not because of what you'd done, but because he could catch you at it. The worst of the incident was that it had happened at all. Cosmonauts scrapping with Chekhists was reckless for the Corps and for the individuals involved, since State Security never forgot a slight and never forswore revenge. That three cosmonauts should break bones at the Bolshoi was disgraceful, no matter the cause. Yet it had happened, and it was a telltale example of how scandalous the Corps had become by the time I joined it. That's the truth of it, I know now, that the Corps felt drained, powerless, dragged down by the bad luck of false promises, failures, crashes, deaths, accidents, stupidity. There had been no manned spaceflight for fifteen months; the premier spacecraft was still an unproved prototype suited for robot guidance; and the premier boosters were unavailable or unbuilt, as you will see at the Cosmodrome. What I had come to, in July 1968, was a hang-dog Corps—with poor morale, bad discipline, aimless high jinks, drunken and wanton conduct, and palpable defeatism. But this is the high-handed opinion of an old soldier, and that morning I knew none of this and wouldn't have thought to condemn the very heroes I wanted to join. I let myself become swept up by their inspired vanity to bamboozle a rat like Maximov. All I cared for was how amazing Uncle Konstantine and Uncle Dmitry were when they toyed with a foe. Whatever they said, did, wanted, I was for it. They were the Martian Troika. You must understand that *my uncles were gods to me*. They were living proof to me that my father had been a hero of heroes. They were as close to my father as I could ever come. Their medals, ribbons, and gold stars, their splendid cosmonaut badges, everything they had earned, was what I aimed for myself. I didn't see two middle-aged troublemakers—comical, fleshy, provoking Uncle Konstantine; lofty, condescending, provoking Uncle Dmitry—no, what I saw was two legends with whom I could go to the moon. I could look at them and know my life was going to be a success worthy of my dead parents and family. I could look at them and believe that I was right to be here, that I must take any pain to stay here, including, as it happened, going along with their nincompoopery.

The argument came to its ludicrous finish. "You have a pair of boots," Uncle Konstantine taunted Maximov, "some sniffy Chekhists who fell down steps at the Bolshoi, a car stuck in the bushes, and the testimony of an innocent girl, no doubt terrified by your inquiries, that three Air Force officers defended her honor from several pigs. That's your case? If it is, perhaps it's best to bring charges against these clumsy Chekhists before we bother two of our brothers who, if it's true, deserve congratulations for their victory."

"Get out!" Maximov cried.

Uncle Dmitry hoisted the muddy officer's boots at arm's length and then dropped them on Maximov's nine pencils. "Let me help," he tried. "Justice requires more than hasty decision making. Why don't we try to use the physical evidence provided?" He ordered one of the eavesdropping clerks to fetch Glavtop and Grin. Presently Glavtop and Grin, more innocent looking than spring lambs, eased into the office. I still hadn't been able to slip free and was now jostled into the corner behind Uncle Dmitry. It became clear why Uncle Dmitry had kept me here, for he was planning a burlesque gesture. "How does the fairy tale go?" he said. "Cinderella wears the slippers, no one else. If we find the feet, we find the man." Uncle Dmitry measured Glavtop's foot, then Grin's. "Fruitless," he declared. He swung the boots at me. "On with them, Lieutenant."

I thought he was joking except that no one laughed, so I obeyed, exchanging my boots for a stranger's. They were excellent officer's boots, but they fit badly, much too big and deep.

Uncle Konstantine pointed at me. "Here's our culprit. You've already captured him, Maximov, and you were going to surprise us. Congratulations, case solved." More cursing followed. What was odd about the scene was that none of them laughed genuinely, only mockingly, as if they'd lost heart even for their pranks. The duel with Maximov was a tired charade and, if I'd admitted it to myself, a sad display for their uniform and rank.

The boots did belong to the third Bolshoi brawler, my Uncle Alexander—my father's wingman and the capstone of the Martian Troika—who was too sick with drink and too indifferent to State Security's machinations to come in to face his accuser Maximov. Uncles Konstantine and Dmitry had come in less to defend Uncle Alexander than to rescue Glavtop and Grin from serious discipline. Everyone present knew the truth of the debacle; so did most in Starry Town, except me. I wobbled in Uncle Alexander's boots and hoped I pleased Uncle Konstantine and Uncle Dmitry. My uncles didn't notice me beyond my use as a straw man. And when Corps commander General Kamenin arrived, I was kicked out.

General Kamenin looked like a pinched, white-headed rooster, burdened by too many disappointments for the Corps, too many frustrated, delinquent cosmonauts, and certainly by the bad luck of Gagarin's death—who had died in a 21 trainer, drunk as a lord—which was still a dark stain on Kamenin's command. He tossed his cigarette out the window and warned everyone, "Don't do this, don't, don't. Am I a grandmother? I'm going to break the whole of you! I'll try it, you know I will. I don't care how long we've known one another. I'll defend myself and break you! The year's over, it's over. We had a terrible year, and we drank to future success and went home to our beds and then this scandal. Fistfighting at the theater! One man's jaw is wired shut and the others, I'm told, can't walk for their broken bones. What am I to tell the marshal if he calls? What's to say?" General Kamenin shook the distress from his limbs. "Get out, all of you!" he ordered. "Except you two." He meant my uncles, and they followed General Kamenin through the connecting door to his office. My uncles were obliging, as if they were relieved not to have to misbehave any longer; for now they could begin the adult work of negotiating Glavtop's and Grin's penalty and determining whether Uncle Alexander would be humbled publicly or privately.

It was my turn to be humbled immediately. I still had on Uncle Alexander's boots and didn't have a way of getting back my own without dropping down and changing in front of Maximov, and this was clearly impractical. Maximov waited until my uncles had gone and then ordered Glavtop and Grin at attention before his desk and then casually whacked at me with an officer's baton he got from his desk. He pursued me through the duty room and to the entrance, where he made a specific threat for all the clerks to hear, "Report to me tomorrow, o-six-hundred," and then turned back to punish Glavtop and Grin.

I fled into Major Tronko, who already knew, via a grapevine faster than a telephone, what I'd been caught up in. "What did Maximov say to you?" he asked. I avoided the question and just mentioned the 0600 appointment. "That's bad, Lieutenant, but we'll see, and you'll have tonight to rest. I've arranged everything. My wife has agreed to let you use our daughters' room for the week." I didn't want this but kept quiet in the hope that the Tronkos' generosity might mean I could find a breakfast. "Come with me now," Tronko continued, taking my arm as if I were a child. "Medical center wants you to check in this morning, and I told them you're available for the balance of the week."

We started down the stairs, and it was then that I revealed my affection for my uncles to a man sure to spread the word throughout Starry Town that a long-lost nephew had come calling. Tronko asked, "What must I say to help boys like you? Stay away from that pitiable lot. Understood?"

I was confused. "You mean the Martian Troika, sir?"

"Who?" he asked.

I corrected, "You mean Colonels Oryolin, Strogolshikov, and Zhukovsky, sir?"

"All of them!" Major Tronko insisted. "Especially them! Drunkards! Headed for a hole they've dug. Your record is blameless. Your father, heavens, he was the very best! Please, just stay away from them. The candidacy's plenty rugged without the Maximovs and the Strogolshikovs. You've only been here an hour, and you're already playing along with drunkards!"

"They're not drunkards, sir," I replied immediately. "The colonels were my father's best men, and it was an accident I met them this morning. I didn't play along, sir. I did what I was told. They don't know who I am, I'm sure of it. They haven't known about me ever, and I don't know if they'll care to know now. I'm here on my own. They're not my family, sir. And if I've said they were my godfathers, it's just how I think of them."

Major Tronko's manner softened. He said something inarticulate such as "So? So?" and looked at me closely.

What I'd done, I know now, was alert my uncles that I'd come to Starry Town as loudly as if I'd fired a flare. At the time I felt stupid for having again explained too much about my uncles and myself. My stupidity widened when we reached the walkway. I'd parked my motorcycle against a retaining wall, and, with a glance, I knew it was gone, stolen, just gone. My duffel bag was there on the grass, my kit bag was there, if rifled, but the bike had vanished, and I felt cold and ruined. Tronko didn't care, nor did he entirely believe me when I explained about the BMW, how I'd walked it from Leningrad, how it was a present from my father. He wouldn't let me search. The most he'd concede was that if the bike was gone, it was probably impounded by the Air Police and I was better off without it, since I couldn't hope to keep it at Starry Town. Tronko stayed on my heels the rest of the day. He'd adopted me, I could see that, like the uncle you never wanted to have. We spent the day at the medical center, where there was food at last, though meanly for the tests to come. In the afternoon, there was more medical center for exams that were designed to waste time and deposit me naked in anterooms waiting for another probe of my eye, ear, nose, throat, and rudder. It was as if I'd arrived suspect of being an alien. I found the doctors typical vivisectionists, but their machinery was new-fashioned and sinister. My dreams of cosmonaut training had always been the centrifuge, the pressure chamber, and the orientation tester (dubbed the Devil's Windmill, the Tank, and the Iron Maiden) to prove how fit I was to fly anything on earth or off, but I was told bluntly that those were for cosmonauts, not candidates. The doctors didn't care about me as a pilot. I was a lab animal to prick and wear down. And I suppose that all this medical time-wasting was yet more evidence, if I'd been able to look past my disappointment with how I was being treated, that the Corps had lost its purpose and was adrift in the hands of clerks and rats and laboratory technicians.

My first evening at Starry Town ended in Tronko's care. He took me home to his plush apartment in one of the residential towers and to his abundant wife, who was his twin in a print dress and who insisted I call her Nadia, not Mrs. Tronko. My relief was that supper was choice and plentiful—roast chicken, mushrooms, turnips, straw-berries—and that I didn't have to talk too much while I ate. I was relieved that the two daughters, who were university snobs, were away on vacation. Major Tronko fixed the conversation on my stories of my uncles: he wanted to know whatever I could tell him about my father; he wanted to know how it was that my uncles had never contacted me, though I was at Orenburg for eleven years; he also wanted to know why I'd never reached out to them. I replied, "It wasn't something I would've done, sir," but didn't explain that I'd worshipped them from afar all my life and hadn't intended to present myself to them until I was a falcon and cosmonaut candidate who deserved their respect.

To avoid more of Major Tronko's questions, I went to bed early and was up at 0300 the next morning. I knew my day was going to be trouble, since Colonel Maximov wanted me in his office to bully me in three hours, and Major Tronko wanted me in his office to coach and interrogate me the more in five hours, and the medical center wanted me for more torture tests of coordination and pain tolerance in six hours. This left me a quick chance to find my motorcycle before it was sold off in pieces, since not even the naïf I was then could believe the Air Police had impounded the BMW: they'd stolen it, that sentry had taken it. I dressed silently and slipped out to begin a hectic search under last starlight for the culprit and the bike.

My fretting did come to a novel success. My uncles were waiting for me after all. They had indeed forgotten that I existed for almost two decades, but now in twenty-four hours they'd used me as a prop, then abandoned me to Maximov's ire, and then, finding out who I was thanks to a late call from Major Tronko to Uncle Dmitry, my uncles had decided to surprise me. I was headed their way, and they knew it, and they were waiting. During the night, members of their squadron had been approached by a certain Air Police corporal who had offered them a BMW. They had determined the fellow was a thief and, due to Major Tronko's tidbit about my bike, had then reclaimed my motorcycle, though they hadn't taken it simply for me, more as a lure and collective entertainment. It was like my uncles in that dull summer before the battle began, and it also illustrated how the wasted years had worn them down, for my uncles were come to being pranksters, wastrels, and show-offs.

I asked enough questions at the lane sentry post to guide me to the Air Police barracks. I couldn't find the thief there, but other enlisted men told me my motorcycle had been sold to cosmonauts, and they directed me to what they called the "Black House," located in the woods east of the lake. They said the Black House was where the cosmonauts kept their treasures, and if I wanted my bike, I would have to pay them dearly. I followed a forest path, overhung with heavy pine and spruce and littered with broken bottles, to an opening at a fallen stone wall. There on a low rise was my uncles' infamous Black House. Once it had been an old-fashioned farmhouse, two stories, stockpen below and living quarters above, without a chimney so soot-coated and therefore "black." Now, thirty years since it had been abandoned, it was a sagging, mossy, spider-rich wreck, fit for bats, rodents, and, as it happened, cosmonaut-pilots.

Stranger than even the Black House at first sight was that, seventy meters across a scrub field behind a cyclone fence, were eight beautiful MiG-21s parked at the lip of one of Chkalvo's short runways, and they each stood at the ready with a two-man flight crew, fuel, and auxiliary trucks and starting carts. I circled closer to see they weren't standard 21s; rather, from their features, they were prototypes with the new R-13 turbojets that made them the quickest air interceptors in the arsenal. I turned back to Black House dumbfounded that out here in the woods there should be a flight line of 21s prepped for a scramble and launch adjacent to a peasant roost. The truth of it was that the Black House was my uncles' hermitage, saloon, hideout, clubhouse, and those 21s were their toys.

A dog's yap announced the shenanigans; then I heard an urgent voice from the house, "Go away!" I'd rehearsed what I was going to say and addressed the four shutter-hung windows above the porch overhang. "I'm looking for my motorcycle! I was told it might be here!"

There was pounding and more yapping from the house, and then a small mustard-yellow mongrel dog popped out of the center window and scooted across the porch roof. There were suddenly four men in flight suits who came out of the windows and stomped across the overhang to where they could descend by a series of makeshift steps, using the stock door, a rain barrel, and a wheelbarrow. The leader of the four splashed himself out of the rain barrel and kept on across the scrub field toward the flight line of 21s. The others turned back and beckoned me to come to them to a spot just between the porch and a massive stand of Siberian firs.

It was Capt. Vitya Artzybashev, twenty-seven, who started their game with me. Artzybashev was a darkly handsome fellow, a glib talker and flagrant gambler, who already regarded my motorcycle as his own possession, part of a bad debt the Air Police had owed him. He challenged me, "You're the one."

I saluted him. "Sir, I've been told my motorcycle was here."

"Your motorcycle," Artzybashev chided. "Ours now! A bargain at two thousand."

I fell for their game as if I were a hireling. "Yours, sir?" I asked. "You couldn't have bought it, sir. It's mine."

"A transfer of goods," Artzybashev said.

His wingman, Capt. Kopa Kandidim, twenty-six, a spry, extroverted, penny-pinching gambler, contributed the facts of the deal, "Water-cooled, twin exhausts, before 'forty-two, a modest bargain.

If we were to rebuild it, the cost would appreciate several hundred percent."

As they continued their game, I realized I was dickering with Orenburg men. Artzybashev and Kandidim had once been famous upperclassmen to me, both with scandalous reputations as card-sharps. I knew the third falcon too, the one listening in—he was the kind and serious Genka Stumpelkin, twenty-four, a dark-skinned Siberian, who had been two years ahead of me as first cadet of the Orenburg cadet corps.

I did try to defend my position. "But he stole it from me, sir, yesterday, while I was inside the administration building with Major Tronko."

"You have proof of this?" Kandidim asked. "A bill of sale? Something from Tronko?"

I said, "It's my bike, sir, you know it is."

Artzybashev hooted, "Oh, we know, do we!"

What bothered me was that the more we argued the more I was disgusted with myself for accusing Orenburg brothers as thieves. I was divided between demanding my property and backing off and accepting the hard lesson that this Starry Town wasn't as friendly as I'd hoped. I couldn't accept that Orenburg brothers would do this to me, yet every time I began to tell them I was one of them, I shut up. I didn't want to start at the Corps as a pleader or favor-seeker. It turned out that all eleven of my uncles' men were Orenburg graduates. Like me they'd volunteered for the Corps and were rewarded with Starry Town, either by their credits at Orenburg or by their family connections (three of them had Kremlin relatives). At the same time they were brats. They called themselves a squadron, though it was more a gang, and they wasted their training and pay with nonsense, while the spacecraft they'd been promised hung wasting at the Cosmodrome.

As the argument continued, more falcons came out of the Black House, some in flight suits, some in the orange jumpsuits of the Corps with the cosmonaut patch I coveted. They all looked fun-loving if stiff and slow-footed, hung over as they were after a night-long carouse celebrating Glavtop's and Grin's luck not to be court-martialed for crippling State Security officers.

"What's the bother here?" asked the chubby little Miserbiev, a chatty busybody who would become one of my lifelong comrades.

Artzybashev said, "He's accused us."

"What of it?" asked Miserbiev's pal, Yurka Adama-Bibliov, a long-legged Olympic skier and one of the seven of them who'd give his life before the end. I miss him the more for introducing him like this, a cautious man who did his duty and should have had a long, happy life.

I remember it was Zhora Fedyuninsky, the always smartly turned-out Maj. Zhora Fedyuninsky, thirty-two—he preferred cravats, combed his wavy hair like a crown, and had the left-eye squint of a monocle wearer, and at Orenburg he'd had the reputation of being snobbier than Romanovs—who eased into the gathering and tried to intimidate me. "You're Nevsky, we've heard. Something about another son of the Revolution. Who needs more attention to his kit." Fedyuninsky flipped at my dusty brass buttons. "Not very tidy, are you? Haven't you a date with dear Maximov? Now, shoo!"

I resisted. "I'll go with my motorcycle, sir."

Fedyuninsky called, "Bring out this prize." Artzybashev rolled it from the stockpen. They'd dismantled its junk engine and stripped off my goatskin seat and electrical tape, so the bike was just a frame on patched wheels.

Fedyuninsky tried more intimidation. "How does the fairy tale go? Half for you, and half for us?" There was a call, "Get the torch!" and suddenly two of them were wheeling out a cart bearing an acetylene torch and large cutting shears.

I decided to stand my ground, though I might have been firmer, because I think I said, "Please, sir, it's my graduation present, sir. You know it's mine."

By then nine of the eleven of the squadron (absent the miscreants Glavtop and Grin) were lined up on the stoop and around me, chewing oranges, sipping tea, smoking hand-rolled cigarettes, stretching and groaning. They were a very good-looking lot, and they knew it, and they were the best fliers in the Corps. I can see them now as vividly as I did that day, like a tableau that hangs forever in my mind's eye: the two majors, dashing Fedyuninsky and the squadron's stumpy mother hen Cherryntevsky; the larcenous duo Artzybashev and Kandidim; my good friends Miserbiev and Adama-Bibliov; the two colorless chess masters Tevyelook and Schtange, who were also our most qualified aeronautical engineers. They were a gifted, well-loved, most-rewarded lot, who were also as mature as runaway schoolboys. And since Uncle Dmitry wasn't here to supervise them, nor Uncle Konstantine to divert them, they couldn't stop the sport they were making of bewildering me.

We were interrupted by the whim of the one man I wouldn't have believed would have tolerated these antics—my Uncle Alexander, Colonel A. A. Oryolin. He'd been the one who'd been first off the Black House and up to the 21s. Uncle Alexander signaled from the flight line that he wanted me brought to him, and this ended the game over the bike. Genka Stumpelkin took my arm and said, "The colonel wants you now," and I was swept along and ushered up the rise to the flight line and to my worst disappointment so far. Uncle Alexander stood before me like pride gone to dross. No one could have been more changed from the photos I had seen of him at twenty-three and still have resembled himself. Forty-eight years old, a Herculean leader of men, Roman-headed and Tartar-dark, square-shouldered and long-fingered, with short, thick, straight, silver hair, a jaw chopped out of an engine block, deep set and angry black eyes, everything was the same yet undeniably sadder and grimmer. It was as if he'd been beaten and starved and broken and killed yet none of it had changed the outside, rather the inside, so the façade was generally in shape but the soul was in trouble. I didn't know what a soul was then to argue this all to myself, but now I do, and I know that the soul I met that morning was as pitiable as imaginable. What I witnessed over the next year was a try for his soul to heal itself, and if he failed, I still believe he died trying.

Uncle Alexander's body also looked poorly that morning. His grimace was splotchy, swollen-eyed and reddened by drink, and he couldn't stand erect, bending to flex his bad knees. While the others came up to listen in, he turned from us, unzipped his flight suit, and in the custom of old fighter pilots, relieved himself on the front wheel of his 21. The man who turned back to examine me was a sleepless, moody drunkard, a square-shouldered hulk, a grim-jawed fool, who was also the chief surviving air ace of the war, my father's wingman, test pilot of the MiGs, Sukhois, and Yaks, the pilot of *Voskhod 2,* the senior cosmonaut-pilot of the Corps, a king of a falcon, and three times Hero of the Soviet Union.

"You've got my boots on," he mumbled. Uncle Alexander was a

mumbler, it was his way, unless he wanted something done, and then he barked like a stentorian madman. He repeated himself, "My boots, there, are on your feet, Lieutenant."

I saluted. "Sir!" I did have his boots on, stuffed with two extra pairs of socks.

"We've been waiting for you," he mumbled.

"I didn't know, sir."

"Where've you been?" he asked.

"Major Tronko's, sir, I've just arrived."

"No, no," he said, pushing sleep from his eyes. "Where've you been since I last saw you?"

The squadron laughed. I didn't know if I was supposed to remain quiet or tell him my life story, so I compromised, "I've just been assigned to the Corps, sir."

"Orenburg?" he asked.

"Yes, sir."

Genka Stumpelkin spoke on my behalf, "He was first cadet this year, Colonel, I knew about him. First cadet with honors, sir. A respectable driver."

Uncle Alexander half listened to Stumpelkin and then mumbled at me, "You're here anyway, aren't you?" while scratching his Adam's apple; he was days past shaving. "Why'd you come?" he asked.

Confused and defensive, all I could think to reply was, "It was my duty, sir." Uncle Alexander seemed to ponder this, and there was a long pause. I hoped that I'd said the right thing. Uncle Alexander's unreadable face did appear to lighten as he stared at me. Still I didn't have confidence in myself enough to keep quiet, and I added, "I wanted to, sir. I've wanted to come to Starry Town as long as I can remember. It's the only thing I've ever wanted, besides going to the moon and planets, sir."

Other men might have guffawed at my naïve confession, other men might have cut me off with a remark about my pretentiousness and ignorance, but then other men weren't at the edge of space in 1968. I was finally in the right company for my boyhood fantasy. None of them reacted in any way but soberly to my remark. Uncle Alexander pronounced, "Good, it's done, good, you're here. Welcome to Starry Town."

I'm certain I blushed and can only hope the poor light concealed my coloring. I think I said, "Thank you, sir," and I know I felt cosmic.

Uncle Alexander asked, "Interested in a job?"

"Yes, sir!"

"I can't offer interplanetary flight just yet," he said. "Are you still interested?"

"Sir!" I cried.

"Close as you'll get to the moon for now is," he said, jerking a thumb to the 21s.

"Yes, sir, they're beauties," I tried.

"Let's see what we've got here," Uncle Alexander said of me to the others. "We'll see if old Nevsky left us something special after all."

I asked, "You mean now, sir?"

If I'd known the man better, if I'd been less a bright-faced puppy and stumbling boob, I would have known he always meant *now*. Uncle Alexander looked away from me and up, grunting at the fresh sky, brilliant with broken clouds to the west. He didn't give an order, he just moved his head and everything around him was in military motion. The flight crews pounced to finish preparations on the lead four 21s while I was handed a flight suit, helmet, gloves, and flying boots. I can't remember thinking much about the challenge at the time. Uncle Alexander wanted me to fly, and I was happy to obey. I was too dazzled to look at motives, and I'm certain my mind wouldn't have been much beyond wanting to please Uncle Alexander, wanting to prove myself to him and the others; yet now I see how characteristic it was of Uncle Alexander to test me right away, as if what happened in the air were more profound than anything to be said on the ground. If I felt right in the air to him, it didn't signify what I wanted or what I had to say about my life; and if I couldn't drive up to his standards, then all he or anyone could do wouldn't overcome my inadequacy. It was truly Uncle Alexander's way—to fly, not to talk, to throw a thing up and see where it comes down, no maneuvers beforehand, just attack and attack and attack and ram ahead, just as he'd attacked his life and exactly as he was about to attack the moon landing.

That morning began my education from Uncle Alexander about how to carry myself. I watched the easy way he climbed up and folded himself into his cockpit and the calm way he let the flight engineer tuck him up. I imitated him, settling into my cockpit, pulling on the helmet, glancing at my panels, turning on my radio to ask ground control permission to start engines. The puzzle was that there was no ground control for the cosmonauts. They did what they wanted when they wanted. Not understanding this then, I looked to Uncle Alexander. He gave thumbs-up to his flight engineer. The crews pulled off the engine cowls and did the last preflight on hydraulics, signaling all ready and then starting power to our cockpits. Uncle Alexander fired his engine, and I imitated him. The R-13 gave a deep whine and then a hurling roar. It was clearly bigger than anything I'd ever sat on, since that's what the MiG felt like then, a man astride a sleek turbojet. We continued as irregularly as we'd begun: taxi to takeoff, no clearance, canopy down, no clearance, launch position, no clearance, and then Uncle Alexander's mumbling order on the radio: "Launch on burners, at my count, three—two— one—execute." I obeyed and followed. The point of no return was meaningless; fuel consumption was meaningless; g-load was meaningless. My 21 rolled and bumped and then I was airborne, wheels up with that raw throb through my ribs and the electrical joy that came to me whenever I was fresh airborne. I didn't have to think about what I was doing anymore, I could just follow Uncle Alexander tip to tail, and we powered up and banked until he called, "Burners off," and I shut down afterburners and the roar eased to a steady growl. We climbed without talk. The sky was blue cloth and endlessly new above and below, and I felt more like a bird than ever before, swimming free in the ocean I owned as long as I stayed fast and at Uncle Alexander's eight o'clock. Artzybashev and Kandidim had launched behind us and took up positions to the east. I listened to their chatter on our band as they explained to Uncle Alexander why they should be allowed to keep my motorcycle. "It's scrap to him," they argued. "We won't charge him for storage," they schemed. "We'll share it with the whole squadron, and if he stays on, he can have his share." I didn't respond, but what they were trying flabbergasted me, and rather than relaxing with the hot feel of my aircraft after five weeks on the ground, I was arranging counterarguments in my mind, so that when the break came, I was decoyed and out of position for the test. It happened at eight thousand meters. Uncle Alexander had throttled to cruising speed and headed us northeast for the empty taiga zones. I assumed we'd exercise somewhere away from settlements, and I wasn't paying attention to his actions when Uncle Alexander began his supersonic stunts.

"Now, Lieutenant," Uncle Alexander mumbled, and that was the only alert I got before he went vertical. He was reckless, and the simplest way I can describe the test was that we power climbed to pure vertical, went over the top at eleven thousand to an Immelmann, throttled forward past Mach 1, zoomed into another power climb, and this time went over the top into lunacy—Uncle Alexander kicking the rudder and dropping into a power dive from thirteen thousand meters. This summary can't include what my aircraft was doing while I abused it, the shudders and creaks, the heat vapors I felt at my feet, the shaking in the controls and scream of the burners. It was an exercise that the 21 either endured or it didn't matter what its parts had suffered. All the while I followed Uncle Alexander tip to tail and suffered for it more completely than my aircraft. What happens is spots, then black and white instead of color, then red-out and you lose time. It's a momentary unconsciousness, but when you're zooming like that, bearing up to seven negative g's, it's crazy-making, with the earth's coming up like a gravestone. You do it by not thinking about it, and since this is impossible to do—not to think about dying—you do it best when you're twenty-two with reaction time well ahead of fear and no sense of mortality. My altimeter twirled and then it didn't, since I wasn't there for a few seconds, and then I was back and had to do something. At my one o'clock was Uncle Alexander still going down. No g-load limit, no deck limit, he was flying like he fought, and it was as if he were attacking the earth, as if we were going to ram the planet unless it got out of our path. I stayed with him, and the red-out happened again, and then I recall that we were coming down on a railway line, then a village, then a black lake, like two needles falling out of the blue and into the pit.

I think we bottomed out at five hundred meters, but I didn't have an eye for the lowest point, I was working hard to get my nose up. If I'd had any humor in those days, I might also have been watching for Uncle Alexander to get out and walk on his wings just to see if I could match him. I didn't, I was a pious first cadet, and when we finally did unload and start the climb back up, I kept my silence and acted as if what I'd just witnessed were routine duty.

At cruising altitude Artzybashev and Kandidim joined up with us, and they didn't treat the incident casually. "Did you puke?" they asked me. "I would have lost my last five meals," Artzybashev said. I shook my head and couldn't figure if they were teasing me or not. I marvel now at how much of my time then was concerned with not looking as foolishly young as I was. Even when Artzybashev told me, "The colonel did," meaning Uncle Alexander had gotten airsick when we achieved altitude again, and even when Kandidim prodded me with, "The colonel's sleeping it off, you wore him out," I said nothing.

We floated while Uncle Alexander recovered himself. I watched my fuel gauges and wondered how long we were going to wait before turning back. Eventually Uncle Alexander waggled his wings and rolled a gentle turn, aiming home. My fuel gauges said I was red line, but I wasn't going to speak up and spoil what I believed was a test to drive at the limit of the envelope. When the automatic warning flashed at six minutes, I turned it off; when the alarm sounded at two minutes, I canceled it. I figured that we were going to pop and eject, and that this, too, must be part of the test, and that perhaps cosmonauts could waste 21s just to exercise—in brief, I figured that these men, especially Uncle Alexander, had no limits. Finally the field was ahead, with an Antonov crossing on final approach to a heavy runway; and again we didn't make a request, we didn't ask tower clearance, we just went in tip to tail. The best I could suppose at the time was that it was as if the cosmonauts had carte blanche, as if they could come and go without rules and reason, which was true, and which, I see now, was more evidence that the Corps had cut loose its tether and that Uncle Alexander was out of control.

We went in by twos, with Uncle Alexander and I last down. I guessed I had less than a minute of fuel before flame-out when I taxied back to the flight line and shut down, popped the canopy, raised my helmet, and waited for the next test. The boy in me did hope for some reward, at least for an acknowledgment that I could follow orders regardless of the danger, yet there was nothing. Uncle Alexander tossed his helmet to his flight engineer and, vaulting down from his aircraft, headed to the Black House for a nap, or his pipe, or more of his "juice" and his brooding. The other four 21s were still airborne. The flight crews rushed to ready our four for more of the squadron.

I felt forgotten and was slow to give over my flight gear to the aircrew. There was only one cosmonaut who paid mind to me, Lieut. Genka Stumpelkin, who'd spoken up for me before and was ready to show the brotherliness that characterized our lifelong friendship. Stumpelkin handed me my coat and hat; he also had my own boots. I didn't understand that he was being generous with me, and I asked what was going to happen next.

"We'll carry on, and you'll have boots that fit." When I didn't smile, Stumpelkin urged me, "Get on, now, Lieutenant. He'll see you later. It's fine now."

I glanced at the 21s behind us. "What was that for? Why'd we have to do that?" I asked.

"I suppose it was an interview," Stumpelkin told me. "You've had your interview, you could say. He does things like that. Who knows what it means?"

I still didn't understand. "The colonel flies like that with every new candidate?"

"He just flies like that," Stumpelkin said, "and some mornings are better than others." Stumpelkin took my questions as soberly as I asked them. He had the worst case of Alexander-worship in the squadron, beside me. "It's a good one, so far," he added. "The colonel doesn't usually go so long. He's happier in the mornings. Sometimes, he's not. It depends on how it goes. He's going to the Cosmodrome soon, you know. He'll get more flight time then."

"That's his?" I asked about the 21.

"Those're ours," Stumpelkin said of the whole flight line. I must have opened my mouth in awe that anyone could possess a squadron of the fastest air interceptors on the planet. "Don't worry about it, Nevsky," Stumpelkin added gently, as was his way. He had a sweet face as a young man; in his great age, with white hair and round cheeks, he could appear beatific, and that morning he showed me his most benevolent smile. "You'll do fine here. I remember you. You were the big-nosed little cadet who was always first in line at morning mess, right? Wasn't that you, first every morning? Two years behind me and always in front of us for eats. The hungriest first cadet, correct? It's easy to like a man who drives on his stomach. Orenburg doesn't make mistakes about that sort of thing, and neither do our colonels."

I felt much better and was surprised it didn't embarrass me to be thought of as hunger itself, since indeed I was hungry a lot and was always ready for my favorite meal of breakfast. I covered up my lip-licking by making a mistake. "The Martian Troika, you mean?" I asked.

Stumpelkin stared at me as I tidied up my trousers. "Who?"

Once again I'd embarrassed myself with my childhood fancy, for no one in the Corps called them the Martian Troika. I tried to recover myself. "What should I do?"

Stumpelkin smiled. "Relax, if you can."

I heard this as sound advice and thanked him as I retreated to the woods. I still didn't understand, you see, that the morning's swash-buckling had been orchestrated for virginal me. I headed onto the path in a mixed mood. I'd lost my motorcycle and a deal of useless pride, but at the same time I'd gained a fantasy world of rocket-driving, and it made me feel woozy. A shout of cheer and a lot of yapping from the Black House porch made me look back to see Uncle Konstantine, bigger than life in his orange Corps jumpsuit and waving his huge hand like a three-meter brown bear, and at his huge feet was his dog Little Laika, who was actually the daughter of the first dog in space and the squadron's mascot. While I'd been barn-storming, Uncle Konstantine and Uncle Dmitry had arrived at the Black House to take their turn on the flight line and in the playpen. "Darling!" Uncle Konstantine called to me. "Welcome to Starry Town!" Little Laika yapped harder and leaped up like a performer. "Welcome, baby!" Uncle Konstantine called.

I wasn't certain how to respond, so I called back, "Sir! Thank you, sir! Do you want me there, sir?" Uncle Konstantine was distracted by Little Laika's tricks. He flipped her a hard-boiled egg, and she picked it out of the air and back-flipped. As I waited for a response, Uncle Dmitry came out on the porch. At a distance, he was child-sized next to Uncle Konstantine's bulk, a tiny curly-haired brain next to the giant bald buffoon. Uncle Dmitry puffed hard on his cigarette and looked at me as if studying a child off to the first day of school.

Uncle Konstantine called out again, "Petya, you're a darling!" He flapped and pointed toward the airbase. "Keep going! You know! Keep awake, darling, and keep going!"

I waved goodbye and obeyed. He'd used my father's motto and it made me feel special, it made me believe that my uncles approved of me after twenty years of silence. I felt important to them, or, as

Uncle Alexander had put it, my father had left "something special" after all, or, as Uncle Konstantine said, I was a "darling." I glowed with the moment because my life so far, in my quick opinion, was going well.

I wasn't so confident of my position that I didn't doubt myself, for now that I'd found my uncles and gained their notice, I'd also discovered that they'd surrounded themselves with the pick of the crop from almighty Orenburg, eleven prodigies with a born talent for MiG-driving—not to leave out their notorious discipline problems, excepting Adama-Bibliov and Stumpelkin, who'd been first cadets like me. In all, the eleven falcons around my uncles were so peerless that my self-doubt was redoubled that I could go farther than just being noticed as my father's son. It was all so much boyish longing, I know now, but it colored every decision for me. I longed to be liked, longed to be noticed, longed to join them, longed to be like them, longed for love. I'd survived Orenburg longing to become the best. I'd come to Starry Town longing to become the elite. And now, in two days, I'd found something even more daunting to long for, to become one of my uncles' otherworldly squadron. It's funny to me now to think how quickly I looked past what I'd seen of my uncles' and their squadron's wheedling and very stupid flying. What I'd learned from their example instead was that if they puffed and swaggered, I would, if they drove 21s past the envelope and showed no fear at stupid risk, I would. I'd be a superb candidate, I'd be a fearless cosmonaut, then I'd be just like them—my mornings idling in the Black House, my own blood-brown 21, my nighttimes misbehaving like the rest of them.

Surely you can see that the fantasies of a twenty-two-year-old idiot are too vain to debate. No one but the young could endure being so young. Still my innocence did help me get through my appointment with Deputy Commander Lieutenant-Colonel Maximov later that morning, for it was Maximov's notion to demonstrate that I wasn't welcome at Starry Town until I'd bent my head some. He shouted at me, then he threatened me with various punishments that sounded feeble. He did use his officer's baton on my ears now and again. I took the knocking about in righteous silence, since already in my imagination I was emulating Uncle Alexander's heroic posture, and I'd only watched him preen, mumble, perform, puke, and wander off once.

No, I won't end my presentation here with Uncle Alexander laid open as if he were only a drunkard and Uncles Dmitry and Konstantine were only accomplices to nonsense. It's wrong only to say that my young eyes were blind to them in their pranks and stupors. I saw heroes because they were heroes. I knew the facts of their youth even if I didn't know the events that had ravaged their lives over the past twenty-five years. I knew that once upon a time those three had thrown themselves into the sky along with their generation of falcons, and that they had seen more beastliness by my age than I would ever see. I knew details that still amaze me, such as the fall and winter of 1941–42 at Stalingrad, how my father's air regiment of fighters, attached to the Second Air Army, was thrown into battle in order to buy time for the Army and Air Force to reorganize; how my father's air regiment flew nearly three hundred sorties and scored eighty-five kills; how on that wretched Christmas eve my father had led one of his squadrons of Yak-1s to support a big airstrike of Il-2s that didn't appear in time, leaving my father's fifteen fighters to cover the advance of our naked armor column; how Father and my uncles strafed and strafed until their ammo and fuel were gone and then one at a time the remnant dived into the German positions; and how all of them should have been killed but weren't because half had already been shot down, including my father and Uncles Alexander and Dmitry. Do you believe that they rammed antitank batteries with Yaks? My father ordered it. Uncle Konstantine rammed a tank and survived without a broken bone; he later claimed that he just bounced off and flopped over like a decapitated chicken, and that landing upside down and backwards was easy as long as you kept your head in the mud and feet in the sky.

The war stories are nightmares, and I have one for every photograph of them roughhousing beside their aircraft back from another sortie; and though I won't tell another now, I'll make the case that men who have boyhoods in such murder and evil don't ever see life and death as the rest of us do. For them, truly, war was war and blood was blood and peace of mind was incredible, and if they said they were going to do something, they meant it and didn't mind what or who was in their way or how savage they'd have to be to keep going. My uncles were some of the very few survivors of a generation—only seven out of a hundred males of their age lived to see their fortieth birthdays—and I'm not yet speaking to what happened to them after the war. How can I know now, how could I know then, what they considered responsible? To this day, I ask myself how I can comprehend the sacrifice they were about to make on the way to the moon because they wanted to, for no other reason, because they wanted to, because they said it and meant it and could move heaven and earth and the stars in the sky to get it done. What I do understand now is that the moon awaited three men who couldn't be stopped.

③

My Katya

The next Monday my cosmonaut candidacy began in earnest. It was plenty rugged from the start, as Major Tronko had warned, and, despite all the troubles ahead, my candidacy was my major worry for some months afterward. The way they'd designed the course in those days was to assume we were favor-seekers and loafers and that the Corps must be protected from our careerism. They aimed to wash us all out and said as much to my class of nineteen. "We don't need you brains," Lieutenant-Colonel Khitrovo, chief of candidates, told us in our first assembly at the candidate barracks. "There're too many brains around here already and what good are they. Doctor this and doctor that, who needs to know the biology of an asteroid?"

My thought was that Khitrovo was one of those old-style falcons who believed that if a bear could drive an aircraft he'd be in uniform immediately and at the top of the duty roster. I was wrong, because Khitrovo patted his belly and looked at me. "Same for you fancy lot, we don't need you fancy boys either." By fancy he meant falcons. Of the nineteen candidates to report, only two of us were pilots. The others were scientists, engineers, and medical doctors. With the class of 1968–69, the Corps had started transforming itself into a school for passengers for the orbital spacecraft—supercargo such as geologists, meteorologists, internists, even a diplomat whose qualifications

for spaceflight didn't exist. I thought this was a wrongheaded decision, but I accepted it as the way of the bosses. I know now that it
was calculated policy. The falcons of Starry Town were randy, un-
ruly, arrogant fighter pilots who believed in staying fast. My uncles
and their squadron were the worst offenders, yet they were also fairly
representative of a Corps of nearly four dozen cosmonaut-pilots.
Since the first cosmonaut class of 1959–60, falcons had been recruited and trained to launch into orbit and then to get home again.
They'd been chosen just because they were the hottest, boldest test
pilots and therefore the most unbridled personalities. All had gone
well until the manned space program had slowed in 1966 and then
halted with the failure of *Soyuz 1* in 1967. The last year before I
arrived had been idle and futile, and the falcons, sitting on their
hands without even a spacecraft to count on, had become defiant.
The incident at the Bolshoi was outlandish but predictable mayhem.
The expedient solution for the bosses in Moscow was to order that
there were to be no more falcon recruits, rather a whole new Corps
of subservient passengers.

Despite Khitrovo's intimidation, I shrugged off the threat and
told myself that I knew how to play up to him. I wasn't without
guile, just without much wisdom. I recognized that Khitrovo and his
staff of instructors were all stiff-necks from the political directorate
and that I could easily hoodwink them with schoolboy tricks. Over
the next weeks of orientation, I set myself to obey all their trite
regulations, to memorize all their repetitious lectures, to mention
Lenin whenever I could during oral reports, to volunteer for the
medical center's tortures, to act like a team player at football, gym-
nastics, and swimming, and altogether to act the perfect first cadet
and boot-kissing drudge, certainly at no time to indicate that I was
their worst foe, a supersonic falcon.

My charade did cause me some difficulty with the other class
falcon, Arkady Volgamints, a bomber pilot with a harsh temperament. Volgamints thought I was a dupe to bow to Khitrovo, and he
belittled me at the barracks until one day early on we came to blows.
He was a large, quick fellow, redheaded and hotheaded, and he
boxed my nose bloody before I sent him down with a kick to the
stomach. It was stupid schoolboy stuff, but it worked between us,
because after that we addressed each other with respect and soon
came to joking about our fellow candidates, "the brains." Arkady

and I spent a lifetime in service together arguing about the great and small intents, and I suppose we never had anything in common but that fistfight; yet it worked, it sealed us like brothers. Also, our mockery of the brains did result in just the opposite, when Volgamints and I befriended the two smartest members of the class, Professor Lev Lympyet, the meteorologist from Moscow University, and Doctor Marcus Gogol, the internist from Sevastopol. You can find Lympyet's and Gogol's names in the history of the orbital missions in the 1980s before they both moved on to senior instructor posts in the Air Force. Along with Volgamints they served the Air Force all their lives, and I think of them dearly and miss them more so; and I can see that just by telling this tale I can find the peace of being with them again in memory.

I didn't see my uncles again until late August. My first six weeks at Starry Town were so demanding and exhausting—I fretted myself blue that I might flunk out—that I hardly left the barracks, and then only for walks around the lake beside the residential apartment towers. By my second week of training my uncles and most of their squadron had gone on summer leave. I learned from Major Tronko, whom I saw occasionally at the back of the lecture hall and who openly disapproved of my attachment to them, that this probably meant Uncle Alexander was at the Cosmodrome, Uncle Konstantine was in a bordello, and Uncle Dmitry was on vacation with his family at the Black Sea. The Don Juans, Glavtop and Grin, were about, confined to base as punishment for the Bolshoi brawl, and I often saw them on their way to the sports complex or to sneak off for romance. They were cheery to me, and whenever I came within earshot they would shout over, "Your boots are too big for you!" or other teasing remarks about our first morning together, all of which made me feel special.

And then there was the most special moment I ever knew, the one special person each of us may find in a lifetime if luck and kindness lead the way. Her name was Mrs. Ekaterina Prishkin—my Katya. I fell in love that summer with a woman who taught me honor and justice and devotion as well as the heartache that can't be described. Katya changed me profoundly, and I still love her as devoutly as I did that summer. I know now this is the way of first love, to hold on to it as tightly as a hand, but for me my first love was my truest. I don't want to labor my love for Katya, since it makes me miss her a little more than usual. She's a major part of my story, and perhaps what happened will make more sense to me for having described it to you. Yet what happened was so cruel that there might not be consolation even in revelation. The best I know to say for now is that it was our fate, and there's nothing I can do now but tell the truth.

The first time I ever saw her I didn't notice much more than that she was kind. We weren't even introduced, it was just serendipity. It was while I was still staying at the Tronkos' the week before my candidacy began. It was a Saturday evening, and I was just coming in from having been used as a human lab specimen at the medical center. I was feeling sore to my soul from an experiment in which they had run me on a treadmill for an hour then dunked me in seawater to measure my heartbeat. I was clumsy up the stairs and came through the door and into the vestibule without much care. I ran into the back of a tall, slender, fair-haired woman talking with Mrs. Tronko. It was Katya; with her was her four-year-old son, Daniel. I recoiled from the collision so quickly that I didn't see Daniel at my knees until I'd knocked him off balance. I caught him up and apologized, but Daniel was startled and began to cry. I did what I could to divert him and tried, "Wait, wait, what's this?" I used Great-Uncle Lev's sleight-of-hand and pulled a fragile olive eggshell from my ear—a hatched nightingale's eggshell that I'd found in the woods. The ploy worked. Daniel was fascinated and took the eggshell from me as a great treasure, asking, "For me?" Katya told him, "It's to look at, not to keep, isn't it beautiful?" Then she addressed me as easily as if we were old friends: "It's sweet of you to show him." I made a fuss about being an oaf, and she told me not to mind. I recall her saying this so gently. "Not to mind, Lieutenant." I suppose Mrs. Tronko must have introduced us at this point, though I have no memory of it and didn't know Katya's name for another month. I do seem to recall watching her smooth down Daniel's thick golden hair with her right hand. I think now I was envious of Daniel having such a pretty mother, with long fingers and a beautiful round wrist, who protected him and explained things to him in that melodic, loving voice of hers. Perhaps part of my first attachment to Katya was my longing for her provident maternalism, what I'd never had and didn't even know I missed. Who can say now? The episode was very brief, for Katya thanked me again and told Daniel to give the eggshell back. Feeling generous, just by her presence, I told Daniel I wanted him to keep it. When Katya started to protest, I added Great-Uncle Lev's tale that a nightingale's egg is good luck because nightingales were delivered by the hand of God. Katya stared at me, smiled warily, as if I'd said something extraordinary, and then she said goodbye to Nadia Tronko, took Daniel's free hand, and departed. Daniel waved goodbye to me and said, "Thank you, sir," and I felt most satisfied that I'd done something right.

You see that at our first meeting hardly a word passed, and it can seem to me now like a dream. It wasn't until early August that I'm certain I learned who she was, not only her name and status but also the nature of her unhappy heart. It was about August 6 or 7, and my candidate class was just back from three days in the Urals, where we'd had a fun time of it practicing fundamental crash-landing survival skills, though nothing serious, just routine abuse by the instructors to shake out the loafers among us. Serious training would have hung us on parachute shrouds from fir trees or thrown us into the steep taiga hills in snow season to simulate the crash-landing of uncles Alexander and Konstantine in *Voskhod 2*. No, this was child's play, mostly sleep deprivation and bad food. My friends Gogol and Lympyet were exhausted by it all and, when we arrived back at the barracks, leaned on me and Volgamints for support. Later at mess, Volgamints and I competed as to who could act more awake on no sleep. I ate two portions of everything and bragged I was going for a walk around the lake in the soft late sunlight. It was in this dopey, boyish mood, while tracking some yellow wagtails along the shore, that I came across Major and Mrs. Tronko. "Candidate Nevsky!" Major Tronko called loudly. "We've been calling for you. You're just back, good!" "Just the young man we need," Nadia Tronko insisted. They beckoned me to them and explained that they wanted me to come to a party they were giving that Saturday to celebrate the return of their daughters from Vienna or something like that. Mrs. Tronko said, "We've wanted you to meet our Nina and Maria. Such a fine young officer as yourself, and they have so many Moscow University friends your age. You'll enjoy yourself."

I must have showed my reluctance when I said, "Yes, ma'am."

Mrs. Tronko said, "There'll be so many young people for you to meet, so many sophisticated Moscow people, it will be good for you, a boy from away. And Colonel and Mrs. Prishkin are coming too. You've met Katya. Remember? The eggshell you gave little Daniel? Katya is coming along. You do remember."

I conceded, "Yes, ma'am, I do."

Mrs. Tronko negotiated with me the more, "Katya's asked after you, she has. And so has her husband, you know, Colonel Prishkin, at the medical center." What I knew was that Colonel Prishkin was the deputy director of the medical center and, by reputation, a transparent menace when experimenting on cosmonauts. Mrs. Tronko appealed harder, "Colonel Prishkin was a cosmonaut in the early days, you know, and he'll have stories for you—and Katya was once a cosmonaut too, did you know that?"

"She's a falcon?" I asked.

"No, no," Major Tronko corrected his wife, "just one of the four girls they recruited for the Vostoks, for Tereshkova's flight. She wasn't ever a falcon, she can't really fly. Just a recruit, you understand." He told his wife, "She's not a former cosmonaut like her husband. It was a political affair. You've confused the matter, dear."

"Oh, the difference wasn't ever clear to me," Mrs. Tronko said, and then countered, "She trained to go up in a Vostok, didn't she? And she was ready to go, wasn't she? And then because she didn't, and they canceled more Vostoks for women, how does that make her any different from any other cosmonaut? And, anyway, Katya is famous in her own right because of her family. She's Academician Univer's granddaughter." Mrs. Tronko was now speaking to impress me. "The famous Academician Nikhon Univer, you know, the Grand Constructor. I imagine you didn't know that she was his granddaughter, did you, Lieutenant?"

"No, ma'am, I didn't." I was by then much taken with Katya— the woman whom I remembered as kind and pretty but hadn't thought anything of until now turned out to be both a former cosmonaut candidate for the seat that became Tereshkova's 1963 *Vostok 6* flight as well as the granddaughter of Academician Nikhon Univer, the most legendary Russian rocket scientist. I still sounded unconvinced about the welcome-home party.

Major Tronko wagged a finger and closed the debate. "Cosmonauts have social obligations, Lieutenant. You need friends with positive connections and good influences, if you understand me. We'll expect you at eighteen hundred and don't be tardy."

I said I'd be privileged to accept their invitation if my duty permitted. Because they didn't believe me, I added a flourish. "I'll try to bring eggshells for the little boy again, for Daniel, for Colonel and Mrs. Prishkin's son, Daniel."

"Good," Mrs. Tronko decided, "you are a thoughtful young man."

What I thought was that I'd sooner hang in shrouds from a tree in the Urals than go to a party of stuck-up university students. My plan to get out of the affair was simple and practical; all that had to happen was that my class be delayed at a training exercise, so I'd have an excuse to miss the party. The next Saturday we were obliged to return early from the week's so-called challenge, zero-g simulation in a looping TU-4, because several of the brains grew so airsick they collapsed. I tried to draw out my shower and dressing, but even still I was only a little late leaving the barracks. Worse, two other of the candidates, both political appointments, had been invited to the party, and they saw me trying to drift past the apartment towers and called out to hurry or the champagne would be gone. My crankiness was complete, and I argued to the wagtails and buntings, my favorite audience in those days, that this was unfair, I was tired and wanted to be quiet, and what were a couple of college girls to me? Katya Prishkin was intriguing, I was willing to admit. If I'd been more honest, I would also have recognized that I wanted to talk to her again because she'd made me feel good about the eggshell, and because she was the prettiest cosmonaut I'd ever seen, and just because she was a Univer of Leningrad, one of the city's first families from the early days because of Nikhon Univer. I suppose the truth was somewhere in between having a fledgling crush on the mysterious Mrs. Prishkin—who'd asked about me, Mrs. Tronko had said—and wanting to meet the granddaughter of a Bolshevik genius. I knew what there was to know from magazines and books about the very old, very mysterious rocket pioneer Academician Nikhon Univer: I knew he'd founded the prewar Leningrad rocket club; I knew he'd been the mentor of the rocketeers who'd launched *Sputnik* and Gagarin in *Vostok 1;* I knew he was called, in respect for his great age and supreme socialist achievements, the Grand Constructor.

I see now that what I was up to was weighing social-climbing against antisocial humbughood. Perhaps I can see more: how fate kept at work; how I was again pushed or dragged onto the path that led to the moon. Through the Tronkos I met Katya, who was the granddaughter of Nikhon Univer, the one man whom my uncles needed if they were to get to the moon. You can't see any of this yet, it's just that I can see it. I wonder now if, that Saturday night I wandered around the towers debating to go in or not, there was nothing to be done but give in to my fate and say hello once more to the love of my life, my Katya.

It was a clear twilight, August 10, the moon not up yet and the forest rich with bird calls. Believing I could have been happy anywhere but at the Tronkos', I climbed the stairs to the fourth floor like the condemned. There was a servant to let me in, and the vestibule and rooms were a din of laughter and lust. I eased down the hall to the main room and felt instantly that I was out of place, since there wasn't a uniform to be seen, there were only tall, rosy university girls in expensive frocks and wealthy Party sons in foreign sports clothes and blue jeans and those coats they wore then called windbreakers. The drinking was excessive, and it wasn't cheap vodka, rather whiskey and much champagne. There were musicians, too, and servants circulating treats I didn't recognize as well as dishing out plates of smoked fish, cheeses, whole portions of lamb and other meats at the dining table. Everyone was scatterbrained, loud, attractive, artistic, fashionable, many speaking in French or German and not a rare English phrase. I was astonished, since this was the sort of Muscovite party I'd only read about in magazines or heard referred to in passing in television interviews with famous poets. I tried to tuck myself near the coatrack and eat as much as possible of the fish before I left. So it was gluttony that trapped me, for Mrs. Tronko spotted me soon enough. She cooed, "We've been watching for you," and then swept me over to introduce me to her two daughters Nina, twenty-two, and Maria, twenty, who were most different from their teenage photos. Maria was white-blond, vivaciously made-up, and she was draped on the arm of a university sports hero whose name I forget, though he was popular at the time, and I remember her later marrying him. Nina was the more troublesome of the two, for she was blond-streaked, buxom in a low-cut frock, and very drunk. Mrs. Tronko told them I was "the famous air ace's son, you all know, Colonel-General Apollon Nevsky." Maria giggled and said, "Mama, we don't know anything of the kind." However Nina studied me and said, "So you're the one, so you're the one, so, so," which was mysterious talk to me until I figured out she meant that I was the one who'd slept in her bed while she was on vacation.

After this difficult exchange, I backed away from the crowd and stood slumped like an alder, appetite gone and pride bruised, resigned to be unhappy for a while longer and then to flee regardless of Major Tronko's watchful eye. It was in this self-pitying estate that Katya found me.

She arrived like a rescuer. "You're the nightingale man, Lieutenant Nevsky," she started to me before I was aware she was beside me. "It's what my son calls you. Daniel, my little boy, you do remember. He marvels at the eggshell you gave him and wants to know what happened to the baby bird."

I felt better as if by magic and answered, "Yes, ma'am, thank you. I wanted to bring another one, but there were none to be found, though I wish I'd had more chance to look." I tried to present myself more courtly. "I can go out tomorrow morning, if you'd like."

"He's happy with the one you've given him already," she replied, "though it's sweet of you to offer."

This was the second time she'd said I was sweet, and I decided I liked it. I tried to begin formally all over again, hoping I'd think of something to talk about beside the eggshell. "Mrs. Prishkin, I'm Peter Nevsky . . ."

She smiled as if I were a child. "I know, Lieutenant, we've been introduced."

I think it must have been then that I was taken by her looks and my crush became passionate. She was very clean, very fair, with clear brown eyes, with a nose to match mine, with fine limbs and those lovely round wrists and her fair hair tied back in a bun, all told a very handsome, slender, tall, mature woman, much my superior, by far the most attractive and intelligent woman who'd ever talked to me alone and for myself. I particularly liked her voice, a smart, soft sound, drawing out her words playfully with the educated Leningrad tone and yet capable of the singsong gentleness I'd heard her use with Daniel.

She got the conversation moving again, back to the eggshell. "So what happened to the baby nightingale, what can I tell Daniel?"

I was flummoxed by her question. The truth was that I was in love with her from the first and didn't know it for some time. I wanted to talk about my name and rank and who knows what other pomposity, and she wanted me to talk poetry about nightingales. What I could think to offer was ornithology and told her, "The eggshell I gave him, it means that the chick was born in June and would be mature by now. Nightingales have a good survival rate around here, the newborns I mean. If he can, tell Daniel he can hear the nightingales best at dusk. Tell him to listen for the bird from his eggshell at dusk, and he'll hear it singing something like this." I did a low-volume version of the call of the thrush nightingale, "fee-you-eeee-trr," and added, "The real thing is much higher than I can reach. You could probably imitate it better for him. The song is impossible for me, it's more musical than anything I know."

Katya shook her head, I suppose in tribute to what a character I was. "I will tell him, and I'll practice my nightingale call for him, he'll like it. I do. Now help me, is there any particular direction to listen for our nightingale?"

I was feeling much more in control of myself and led the way through the room to the terrace. I pointed down on the lake. "I've found several nests on the other shore. Nightingales are ground nesters when it's safe, and the thrush nightingale hatched out in May or June, so there might be a few left like the one I found in July, though it will be difficult. I can show Daniel where to look, if he'd like."

"You can?" she said, sounding ever more impressed. "You do know about these things?"

I wanted to be modest, yet what came out sounded know-it-all. "My mother was an ornithologist and so was her father. I didn't know my mother much, since she went away when I was very young and didn't come back, but I've been told about her work, and I have her books from before the war. Ornithology is a family tradition from her side of my family that I've tried to keep up. Nightingales are easy, since they're famous. There are much rarer birds around here, you know, because a big airbase like this one is almost as good as a bird sanctuary."

"It is, is it?" she asked. "The aircraft don't bother them?"

"Not much," I assured. "It's people that do, settlements, and the base is a huge amount of territory with very few people. I've found a lot of new ones to me."

Katya spoke to me so warmly I was aglow, "Tell me how many, Lieutenant."

"My lifetime list is near two hundred," I bragged. "It sounds like a lot, but it's not much compared to my mother's when she was my age. I've got her notebooks, my great-uncle does, Uncle Lev, since it's his side of the family. He was my mother's uncle. My mother had sighted and recorded over four hundred by the time she was just eighteen."

The party noise roared over us in such a way that Katya had missed much of what I'd said, and so she ducked closer to me, took my hand for emphasis, and said, "I'm sorry, you were saying—your mother was what?"

Her soft hand burned me to my heart; it felt like nothing I'd ever been touched by, and it made me blush and grind my teeth. I swallowed my surprise and tried to keep to the facts as I knew them about my mother Marya. "Before the war, and even during it as best she could, my mother was a research assistant at the Zoology Museum in Leningrad."

"I knew you were a Leningrader," she said. "I am too."

"Yes, ma'am, I knew that too."

"You've heard about me?" She spoke in her loving tone, "I suppose we've both asked Nadia about each other; we have something in common after all. What else do you know about me?"

I said, "I know about your candidacy for the Corps."

"Yes, ancient history; I washed out, you must have heard."

"Mrs. Tronko said they put you out after Tereshkova's flight." I tried, "Did you learn to fly; can you fly?"

Katya might have shown her temper about what had happened to her, how she'd been drafted to the Corps and promised equality in space and then pushed aside once the Corps had achieved maximum propaganda with the first woman in space; she might even have given me a first lesson in her dangerous politics. Instead she smiled at my question and said, "Of course I can fly. You think only boys can drive MiGs?"

"You're a MiG driver?"

She laughed. "Only a two-seat Seventeen trainer, and I hope you don't hold against me that they never let me solo in a Twenty-one. I don't fly anything more than a little Ilyushin now, at Moscow University, at the flying club. I sometimes teach flying now, I suppose you could say, to young women like I was once. And sometimes I fill in with lectures at the astronomy department."

Mrs. Tronko hadn't mentioned about Katya's flying, nor had she told me that Katya was a part-time instructor in astronomy at the university, a doctoral candidate who had no ambition to pursue her research or get her degree. Before I swooned with amazement—a magnificent MiG-driving moon-gazer—I said, "And I also know about your grandfather, Academician Univer, though I knew about him from before I met you. I've known about him since I was a child, because of the rocket club he founded. Everybody knows about him."

Her response was significant: "Oh, my grandfather," she said and waved away the thought. The truth was that Katya disliked her grandfather, who was a loveless fanatic and who she hadn't seen or heard from him since she was a child. Katya's relationship with her grandfather was much more complex than like or dislike, however, so it's best to say now that she didn't like talking about him. She turned the conversation back to me, "Tell me, where did you grow up?"

"On the Fontanka, with my great-uncle and great-aunt," I said. "I grew up with Uncle Lev and Aunt Elizaveta, and now there's just Uncle Lev and me."

"I see." I thought she was going to give the standard condolence when someone guessed that your family was gone. My family was profoundly gone: my parents dead of accidents after the war, my two older sisters dead in the famine at the end of the war, and of my larger family of tens of uncles, aunts, nephews and nieces, and grandparents, only Great-Uncle Lev and a few cousins living in the Urals were left beside me. It sounds like a catastrophe, and I suppose it was, but it was not untypical for Leningrad in those days. Katya's reaction comforted me. She cupped her ear and, grinning and leaning closer still, both her hands on my wrist, she said, "Talk to me more about nightingales!"

I've gone on at length about our first exchange, and my excuse is that recalling it makes me feel closer to her than I have for more than sixty years. The sum of our conversation was that we liked each other. I knew I liked her, and the boldest part of me was willing to claim that she liked me, and what a joy the possibility of her liking me as much as I did her was to have in my imagination. Love is a flame that you can dream into an afterburner. Katya told me later that what struck her about me was how earnest I was when I was talking about birds or anything at all; she also said she liked that I didn't mock or deride anything or anyone. She said I was the most straightforward and serious young man she'd ever met in a uniform and that I reminded her of a character out of a book. I never did get her to tell me the name of the character, but once she did say that of all the heroes she knew in novels she liked the innocent ones the best. I puzzled about this for many years, and just recently I decided she was telling me I reminded her of Dostoyevsky's Prince Myshkin, the Idiot.

What I thought about Katya, beside that she was a MiG-driving goddess, was also colored that night by her husband Colonel Prishkin; and I must mention our meeting before I move on. Sometime well into our talk, Katya paused to introduce me to Colonel Prishkin when he came out on the terrace. He was tall, fair, successful, very neatly cut and kept, and he was strangely antagonistic to me right away. "So you're the one, so, so!" he roared.

It was Nina Tronko who was behind the private joke, for Prishkin and she were having an affair. It had been going on since the days Nina had started babysitting for Daniel, when Katya was teaching at Moscow University. Katya knew about it and did nothing for her own troubled reasons, not the least being that she was having her own affairs at the university. It was all a mess, and what I could see were clues that made no sense to me.

Prishkin expanded upon his teasing, "You're the one who's slept in Nina's bed, lucky fellow!"

Nina, who was even more drunk than before, was instantly at Prishkin's side, wrapping her arm around his and teasing. "Boris, he's somebody famous's son or something."

"Famous luck! Not many've had his luck," Prishkin said.

Nina bumped Prishkin. "No one has!"

Katya spoke up for me, "Lieutenant Nevsky's a candidate, Boris. You know, we've talked about him. He gave Daniel the nightingale eggshell."

"A lucky egg thief!" Prishkin said.

Nina told Prishkin, "They're always new ones and Daddy's always bringing one of them home for snacks."

Prishkin made a remark to Katya that I missed, no doubt vulgar.

Katya flushed at what he'd said and then excused herself from us. I wanted to follow her but understood enough of what I'd just seen to stay back. I was embarrassed for myself and for Katya and let the party drift around us. I hoped she might go so I could catch up with her outside, yet she occupied herself talking with several older women. Soon it was curfew for me, and I stopped by Katya to thank her and say good-night.

She took me aside. "You didn't have a good time, did you?" she asked.

"It was good to meet you, Mrs. Prishkin."

She made a face, squeezing her eyes shut and twisting her delicate mouth, a gesture of shared prejudice. "I hated it, too. It's just that there's things we have to do, and if I hadn't come, I would've missed out on the nightingale lesson."

I felt worried at this remark, not knowing why.

"I loved the bird talk, Lieutenant Nevsky," she assured me. "I've never thought about Starry Town being a happy place for anything, and now I can think of it as a bird sanctuary. It sounds utopian and a little fabulous. Perhaps you can tell Daniel and me about it again someday. He'd like that."

We said good-night. I was almost sure I was in love by the time I reached the barracks. How could I tell? If you're a boy like I was, what it feels like is that you can leap twenty meters and that everything you think is brilliant. If you're now suspicious of my unprecedented opinion, consider that she was thirty-five years old, another generation from me, and her family was one of Leningrad's most accomplished and prominent—not only for her grandfather, but also for her deceased father, a mathematician, and her mother, a senior instructor at the Kirov Theater, and that Katya herself was an intellectual, a lecturer in astronomy at Moscow University; she was also musical and played cello in Starry Town's quartet and had many friends and, though I knew nothing of this at the time, several loyal ex-lovers and one devoted current lover. She was way over my station, and we had nothing in common but Starry Town, and to fall in love with her made as much sense for me as to want to go to the moon. Naturally I was so lovestruck I didn't feel hungry for several days. It was our supreme incompatibility that overwhelmed me, and I daydreamed about her obsessively. My schoolboy crush on a new teacher had quickly become passionate longing for the forbidden.

There was no controlling my imagination, and I spent each evening after mess watching for her and Daniel down by the lake. On the third night, they arrived at sundown, and it was fate that my passion was about to be returned.

I saw that Katya was unhappy. Her very fair skin was bluish, as if she'd been ill for a long time, and her fine hair was unwashed and pinned up carelessly. She watched me approach as if asking herself if she wanted to see me, then she made a decision, tightened her face, and asked, "Out spotting more songbirds, Lieutenant?"

I apologized, "I hope I'm not disturbing you; I don't mean to."

"Please do," she said, "disturb, disturb!" I think she'd been brooding and that I had disturbed her bad mood. Something about my approach, probably that I was so fearful of rejection, made her soften toward me. She flipped her cigarette away and sounded gentler. "We've been listening for those nightingales, haven't we, Daniel?"

"Yes, Mama," was all he'd say; he was a fine-boned, yellow-haired doll, who stood between me and his mother.

What I then felt of my passion was a blushing modesty and a mighty desire to please. I thought to ask Daniel what birds he could hear just now, and he picked out an orphean warbler's "chek-chek-chek." I told him what it was, pointed out where to look, and began a discourse on the variety of warblers in the Moscow area, each identifiable by its song. I talked much too long, but it made me less anxious about being near Katya. Later, as we strolled together by the boat house, Katya said they'd be out for another walk Friday night, and she asked if I could show them the nightingale's nest. My "Yes!" embarrassed me and made her smile.

Was she flirting with me? I see now that she was troubled, trapped, lonely, and I was someone who could flatter her without asking much back. I don't believe there was more meaning to it for her than that, at first. Katya had been disappointed by her life for so long that she favored me as that rare find, a young man in love with his life and luck and place in the world. She was unhappy, and I was happy. I do believe it was that simple a pairing. Katya had grown up in a privileged Leningrad family that had suffered its reversals—including the imprisonment of her father for antisocialist behavior—but through them all Katya had been expected to succeed. She had triumphed all the way to Starry Town and the promise of being the first woman in space. She was a star of stars, and then one day the bosses changed their minds about her—perhaps because she was a genuine heroine—and chose a faceless factory worker named Valentina Tereshkova to be the first socialist workingwoman in space. Katya was shoved aside as no longer useful to the state. Her marriage to philandering Prishkin came in the aftermath of her rejection—and I later learned it was because she'd become pregnant—and all the poor choices she'd made since about herself had followed like bad weather. I think Daniel was the only thing she believed she'd done right for the five years before I met her. Now Daniel was the reason she couldn't save herself and get away from Prishkin and Starry Town. It was as common a tale then as now, and Katya's marriage to Prishkin wasn't even passionate enough for there to be fireworks at its finish. More than a lover Katya needed a friend, and this made it easy for me to be precious to her, the best friend she could want.

In those early days of our friendship, we didn't have much time or urge to say anything compromising to each other. I was satisfied just to see her and chat; and Friday night, at our first rendezvous, I again got an opportunity to show off on our long walk with Daniel as I lectured about song thrushes, buntings, larks, and willow tits. That night Katya and I tried a new topic, our shared love for Leningrad. Katya told me, "Daniel's not had a chance to get to know the city as we do. I don't like the idea of him growing up thinking of himself as a Muscovite, since we're not even in Moscow here. We're not really anywhere but on an airbase. I want Daniel to have Leningrad the way you and I do. We're going for a long visit at the end of the month, to my mother's, aren't we, Daniel?"

"Peter!" Daniel exclaimed, making Katya and me laugh, a fine moment for us. You must remember that in those days to call Leningrad by its tsarist nickname, "Peter," was thought peasantlike and backward. I think we laughed not just for Daniel's remark but also because we enjoyed being together, a make-believe threesome, mother and son and would-be father.

I saw Katya and Daniel several times over the weekend, once to build a paper boat fleet for Daniel; yet the next meeting of consequence was a chance event the following Monday evening. This time it was without Daniel. There was much critical to our fate that night, so I'll include the detail.

I didn't expect anyone to be out, for it was a most wet evening with passing rain showers, very dark for the cloud cover. I was taken aback when I spotted Katya alone on a bench that was well away from the apartment towers, and though I was certain it was her I approached warily. I was conscious of her black moods by then and knew that when she was smoking with her head down, she was likely miserable. I almost darted off before she saw me, but then my affection took hold and I called out of the dark, "Mrs. Prishkin, where's Daniel tonight?"

"He's home with a sitter," she said angrily. Her head was uncovered, her hair was matted with the damp, her overcoat hung open. "Where else would a little boy be on such a lousy night?" She didn't look at me when she added, "Boris and I were going to the theater, but it didn't work out. He made other plans."

I knew I shouldn't bother her and tried to get away by saying that I hoped she was all right.

Katya snapped at me as if I was the enemy, "What a dull thing to say! Do I look all right? Is anything all right in this lousy place? What's all right?" I stood dumbfounded. She seemed to change her mood: "No, no, I'm sorry, sit down here and talk to me," and then she was back to ridicule, "You don't smoke, do you? No, and you don't drink or run around in Moscow or do anything, do you? What do you do beside walk around and around this lousy lake."

Her sarcasm bounced me every which way. She had a dagger tongue, as Great-Uncle Lev would say, and she wasn't slow to use it, and I think now one of the stranger parts of her that I liked was that she could be nasty. When I think of her, I don't recall anyone plain, such as a good citizen, good mother, or good anything. She wasn't bad, but she was never someone Uncle Lev would have called good. Katya was a temperamental genius who never said or did what I thought she would. The truth was that she was always exciting to me, and I loved her contrariness and sarcasm as deeply as the rest of her.

She surprised me when she brought up my uncles. "I've heard we have a mutual friend in Dmitry Mikhailovich, your godfather. Isn't that what you call him?"

I asked, "You mean Colonel Zhukovsky?"

"Yes, of course, though you call him Uncle Dmitry, I've heard. Uncle Dmitry, Uncle Konstantine, and Uncle Alexander, your godfathers, your father's best boys. I've heard the tale twice now, from

Nadia Tronko and from Angelicka, Dmitry Mikhailovich's wife, Angelicka. It's a small town around here, you realize, and I play my cello with Angelicka's quartet. Your Uncle Dmitry's wife, do you know her? She knows about you."

I said no, weakly, because I was flustered to learn that my uncles should discuss me. "They're not really my uncles," I tried. "I just call them that to myself, I always have." I didn't want to explain the confusion again, so I qualified, "I just met them briefly last month, the second day I was here. I wasn't introduced to the colonels' wives."

"Just one wife," Katya corrected. "Dmitry Mikhailovich has a *wife*. A man is supposed to have just *one wife*."

I knew she meant something about Prishkin, and I suppose I had guessed they were having marriage troubles, so I tried to stay on neutral ground. "I've never known about their wives. I mean it's hard for me to think of the Martian Troika with wives."

Katya asked, "You call them what?"

I admitted, "The Martian Troika. It's from the war, and no one calls them that except me. It's something I grew up with."

Katya wouldn't leave my uncles alone. Boris Prishkin had hurt her and made her spiteful. She taunted me, "They're called other things here, and no one calls them husband except Angelicka. Strogolshikov would marry anything female at night and divorce her in the morning. And Oryolin hasn't ever been fit for a wife. I admire Angelicka for putting up with the three of them, but then, Dmitry Mikhailovich's tolerable, apart from the other two. What a cockeyed idea that Strogolshikov and Oryolin should have wives. God help such a creature if she exists."

I accepted her opinion. "Yes, ma'am."

Katya flashed, "Oh, stop being so damned good around me." I lowered my eyes like a scolded child, and this pose ignited her for one more tirade. "It's true, it's all you are, good and good and good," she said. "It must be your talent, the best little big boy at Starry Town. I bet you fly as good as you listen. They might just as well send the Corps home and make you the only cosmonaut they'll ever need, the best cosmonaut. Really, your goodness is fatiguing, you've got to stop it somehow. Complain or be pompous or make a pass at me or something normal. You do like me, don't you? Isn't that why you've been following me around with your eyes like a cat for his prey? Oh, shit, forget it, you don't understand what I'm saying, just forget it."

I didn't want to be the idiot who sat there saying nothing, yet I didn't have in me the sophisticated man she needed. I could feel her bitterness, and even if I couldn't help her, I knew that I could hold fast beside her.

Katya smoked in silence for a while, and I thought she was going to tell me to go away. But no, she was never a predictable personality, and once more she softened. "Tell me about yourself. And I don't mean your family or your duty, tell me about Peter Apollonovich."

We talked at length about me, and I tried to emphasize my imperfect parts—how I struggled at the candidacy, how I'd give anything to be a cosmonaut, how much and how long I'd admired my uncles. Several times I said I wasn't good at various skills, such as I was a poor footballer, poor swimmer, poor aeronautical engineer, and I noted how badly I'd scored on the first astrophysics exam.

Katya asked a number of sympathetic questions and then suddenly taunted me again, "Your uncles, do you know you've mentioned them every two minutes? You talk about them more than yourself. I want to hear about you, and all you can tell me is that you worship three drunkards. What sort of idols are they for a good boy? Selfish bastards is what they are, who haven't been sober as long as I've been at Starry Town. Oryolin and Strogolshikov are ridiculous. Listen to me, ridiculous."

She'd gone too far, and I pushed back, "The colonels are the most decorated falcons in the Air Force. They're my superiors, and I don't question their off-duty conduct." I spoke sharply, "No one alive has done more for the Motherland than the colonels. They were my father's favorites because they were the best. They're the best, just the best. Colonel Oryolin was my father's wingman; he saved my father's life more times than I will save anyone's." I shut my mouth and looked away.

Katya lit another cigarette. She was acting perverse and said, "See, my good lieutenant does have a temper. And you're stubborn too. I'd like it better if you'd argue with me. We'll wait on that. Just tell me that I should back off about your revered ones. Particularly Oryolin. Angelicka tells me that all you young ones follow him around like he was the Pied Piper. Because why? Because he once, one thousand years ago, killed one million Germans in airplanes? Is that a reason to admire a man like that? Tell me, I want to know, don't worry about what I'll say, give me your reason."

Katya had gone to the heart of my idolatry—I think of it now as Alexander-worship—so I avoided her baiting and answered simply. "Colonel Oryolin is my superior officer."

Katya laughed. "I wish I were as loyal as you."

Our conversation wasn't all one-way however, for toward the end Katya spoke about herself. "I know you've been wondering why I'm out here alone and not at home. It's part of being all grown up with nowhere to go—do you understand that much? Oh, I don't mean to sound this way, it just comes out sometimes—" She caught her words then, as if she was also catching off a sob. In the dim lamplight, I watched the fine lines in her face deepen; I saw her hand tighten into a fist and then release; I watched a beautiful woman admit to herself that she was losing hope. I understood by then that she was heartsick about her failed marriage. I think now that she was angry at herself for being unhappy, though it might also be true that she was just angry at everything. She told me, "You know what I hate? That I've become a pest. What's worse than a woman who can only say what a gyp her life turned out to be?"

I wish that I'd had poetry for her to make her fears go away. Pushkin would have grabbed up her foot and told her that a whole world can turn for years on an ankle as exquisite as this one. Such gay talk wasn't in me; all I had was dumb devotion and the beginnings of a strong desire for everything from her toes to her ears.

Fate delivered a very noisy blow before we parted. Near 2200 hours and my curfew, we were battered by a massive airlift of heavy An-24s going out from two runways in tight intervals. The roars shook the pine trees and seemed to jell the lake, wave after wave going out as if the air itself had turned into a flood tide. Katya and I sat together as if huddling from a storm until the thunder eased, and then I discovered that Katya's mood had changed once again. She didn't care for more confessions; she wanted to argue in a new direction. "What was that?" she asked about the sky.

It was Monday, August 19, 1968, and if you've done your lessons, you'll remember the answer to her question. It was twenty-seven hours before Operation Danube, the invasion of Czechoslovakia by the Warsaw Pact nations directed by the Kremlin bosses. The books say now that, at the time, not even the bosses were certain what was going to happen. A day before the invasion, the bosses still hadn't voted to attack. My reading of the history books tells me that those fools weren't sure which hand was going to pick up the glass until they were drinking. What must have been true was that on invasion eve, someone, somewhere, had orders to prepare us to go to the brink of a world war. Knowing none of this then, what I did know was how to sound authoritative, "It was at least composites of five divisions worth of An-24s." I also registered my puzzlement. "It's strange. The transport boys don't like to work late, and this time of night, with such a tight launch, it's almost like a war exercise. A tight launch like that is war footing, you know."

Katya revealed her ruinous politics for the first time. "What's strange about it? Those jackasses live for it, them and their ass-kissing general staff live for playing war games. It's almost as fun for them as cocking up, and lying to us about it, and beating up anyone who talks back."

I felt cold in my soul at her words. I understood what she'd said, and I knew what she was saying was dangerous. I'd read how the Moscow intelligentsia were always making trouble for themselves and others. They were called dissidents back then, and they would be destroyed to a man and woman in the next years. In 1968, no less in '78 or '88, I wasn't savvy enough to respond to such fury. I sat silent, a coward before the woman I loved, frightened not only of Katya but also what might come out if I spoke one word.

Katya took mercy on my idiocy, flicked ash at our feet, and rescued me. "Whatever those planes are, now I've got a head like a drum they're beating on." The wind swept the tree line and made the forest seem deep and mysterious. "Let's walk," Katya suggested, as if all we'd disagreed was forgotten. I missed her gesture at first and said I only had ten minutes to curfew. "Forget the curfew, you can be late just once. Listen to me: being on report will suit you, make you fit in with your bad boys and your ridiculous, I can't help but repeat it, your ridiculous old war eagle Oryolin, one of the most anachronistic of Stalin's damned little heroes, and I guess one of yours, too."

Calling Uncle Alexander "anachronistic" was what intellectuals regarded funny—and Katya laughed and pulled me up. My reward for her derision was a stroll together that I thought wonderfully close and much too brief. She held my arm and paraded me down the empty pathways to my barracks, and when she said good-night she squeezed my arm and laughed again, this time kindly. I sneaked through the duty room while the watch officer was on a smoke break and undressed for bed feeling love like a newfound compatriot. I loved Katya more than I had reasons for—which I know now to be the only way to love, without conditions or explanations. She was moody, sharp-tongued, racy, patronizing, world-weary, and impatient; she spoke way over my head most of the time, and whenever she didn't she was probably mocking me for being naïve; yet none of this touched me a flick compared to the fire I felt whenever she turned her face to me and said something as simple as, "Listen to me, Peter."

My harder point about the evening is that those roaring Antonovs were all any of us at Starry Town knew ahead of time about the invasion of Czechoslovakia. I promise you, none of us were prepared, no one truly guessed beforehand that they'd do it. Yes, some of the smarter folk knew the bosses had been banging fists all year at Svoboda and Dubcek; and even I knew that there had been a series of Warsaw Pact war games over the spring and summer, with some of the reserves called up before the harvest began. None of this was a credible warning. War games were routine during the Cold War, more a sign of the status quo than a crisis. How do you hear a warning that you're about to bash your own face, forever exposed as a rotten thing called the Soviet empire? Czechoslovakia was such a stupid crime that, out of all the offenses of those days, it can still make me throw down my pen. Why didn't we ever jail the rot who ordered it? We jailed so many more of their successors for much smaller catastrophes, why didn't we pull those felons out of their old-age flats and charge them with war crimes? You, now, listen to me: Czechoslovakia was invaded and ransacked and a whole generation was smothered because of the decisions of a handful of men, less than three dozen. I can name them, and you could, too, after some simple research. Why weren't they punished? Because their crime was too big? Because their lies were even bigger? Does anyone know? Is justice only for the young?

No matter the answers, Czechoslovakia was a crime that shook all of Russia like nothing since Stalin's death. It also shook the flabby Cosmonaut Corps into action. Czechoslovakia was no passing crisis.

It was a turning point in Russia's history. Czechoslovakia was like a storm front that you couldn't climb over or run from, you could only trust yourself and drive through. Before Czechoslovakia, the state had been like an old bear that no longer roared and was too slow to worry about. After Czechoslovakia, the old bear again became a beast, and there wasn't anyone safe from chaos. Before Czechoslovakia, the Corps and my uncles in particular were as toothless and spiritless as pensioners. After Czechoslovakia, my uncles awoke as if from a drunk and went out to fight for what they wanted. Remember there was no justice in Russia in those days, not for the young or the old; there was only crime and the limitlessness of torturers and murderers like State Security and the very few men and women who could resist the darkness—men such as my uncles with their profound desire to do what I call heroism and what they would have called their jobs.

The day and the moment I learned of the invasion are as vivid as murals in my mind. It was two days after my argument with Katya, Wednesday, August 21, around noon. My candidate class was at the lecture hall in the medical center, and we were just finishing a lecture about g-forces. They'd promised us an exercise in the Devil's Windmill soon—the big centrifuge in the medical center—and it made my friend Lev Lympyet very nervous. I remember Volgamints was leaning forward from the back bench to tease Lympyet, "At fourteen g's, it'll put your balls in your brainpan." Volgamints tried to pull me into his sport, "Tell him, Peter, how the spots eat your eyes and you get your lunch up your nose."

I told Volgamints to shut up. It was then I glimpsed several officers entering the hall at the front, from the doorway behind the podium. The guest lecturer, a dullard of an aeronautical engineer, carried on; however, Colonel Khitrovo stepped over to the officers and they whispered together while Khitrovo looked back over his shoulder at the map on the wall.

Arkady Volgamints told me, "It's bad news." Doctor Gogol, at my left, leaned close and asked what Volgamints had said. "Bad news," I repeated, and as I said it I believed it. There's always something gloomy in the air when bad news arrives, and I've known you feel it before you learn it.

Colonel Khitrovo acted shaken. "Wait, wait!" he called out, stopping the lecturer. He crossed his arms over his big belly and faced us;

his words came out tongue-tied. "I've just learned that this morning, it seems, that Warsaw Pact members, this morning it seems, in defense of order . . ." What Khitrovo was trying to find a way to say was that the 103rd Guards Airborne had overrun Prague's airport at 0100 hours Moscow time. By the time we learned it, half a million Warsaw Pact troops were in motion across the Czech border. Prague's Wenceslaus Square was a bullet-ridden trash heap. Earlier that morning, Czech radio had played the national anthem up until it was cut off by our paratroopers at 1057 hours Moscow time. Svoboda and Dubcek were under arrest, and State Security was the new order in Czechoslovakia. The jeopardy of all this bad news was that Russia might be at war with NATO within hours. World war was a very likely, very imminent possibility that day, and that meant catastrophe on a planetary scale. We knew it, and Khitrovo showed it in his clumsy remarks. All summer the political directorate had been preaching international friendship with Prague, and now what we had was international thuggery. "Get to mess, I think it best," was Khitrovo's best oratory that day; he added that the reservists were to pack kit bags and prepare for call-up, the serving officers were to remain on base.

The class rose as one and then scattered. Our hubbub was not quite a panic, but that's how we felt. You who've grown up without the Cold War, you can't know what it's like to live with world war always a crisis away. In those days it was as if we were all grim together. Whenever there was another face-off between Russia and the West, you didn't think: Is this the real thing? You thought much more simply: Here's what I'm supposed to do next.

Volgamints, Lympyet, Gogol, and I headed for the barracks to wait on news. Volgamints was ghoulish about what his mates in bomber command would be doing at the moment: "On-loading the goods," was how he liked to talk about the nuclear weapons arsenal. Doctor Gogol thought this primitive claptrap and told Volgamints so. We were arguing about the prospects of a full-scale NATO counterattack in Germany when Glavtop and Grin called out for me while they were crossing the green catercorner to us. I told my friends I'd catch up later and rushed over to them. They were their usual handsome selves as well as looking like warriors headed to bar the gates. Glavtop teased me, "Our navigator! Here we've come to find you, and you find us!" Grin told me, "You're to come with us. We're rounding up you lads."

I explained that Colonel Khitrovo had ordered us candidates back to barracks.

"To hide under your beds!" Grin teased. "Listen here, Lieutenant," Glavtop said, "be on the flight line by thirteen thirty." Neither of them would be clear, and Grin kept up the doubletalk. "Our young navigator's easily lost," he teased. "You remember the way? Our pile of lumber in the woods?"

I guessed, "You want me at the Black House, you mean?"

Grin said, "You're volunteering."

I asked, "You want me to go with you?"

"We're ferrying to the Cosmodrome," Glavtop clarified at last, "and you're assigned. Orders from the colonels. They want our aircraft down there, understand, and we were one short on drivers until they included you. You're it. The colonels said you're it."

I felt blessed. "Sir!" I shouted, "you want me? They asked for me!"

Grin said, "We'll file the flight plan. You need to find your way to the flight line, the one with the aircraft on it." Glavtop added, "And grab a bite on the way. We're likely to be scrounging gas and food all night."

What all this dauntless talk meant—and I've illustrated it to show how romantic my uncles and their squadron were to me from the very first of my time with them—was that my uncles were caught down at the Cosmodrome without their private air fleet in what looked to be a world war by weekend, and so my uncles had ordered the squadron to assemble at their feet. Not everyone of the eleven cosmonauts could get back to Moscow in time, so I and several of the flight sergeants were drafted to help Glavtop and Grin and those falcons on hand to ferry the squadron's fourteen blood-brown 21s, clean on auxiliary tanks, the five thousand kilometers to the Cosmodrome in southwestern Kazakhstan. If you blink at this move— cosmonauts redeploying high-performance interceptors while the Air Force mobilized on war alert—then you don't understand how wide open Russia was in those days, especially at senior military levels. The lesson is that it was a totalitarian state where all commands came from the top, all permission waited on the whim of the bosses. For the Air Force, however, there was a deal of what could be called freedom. We had our orders and we were obedient, but then after a written-down point there was whatever you could get away with. As cosmonauts, as monumental falcon heroes, as very well paid members of a powerful elite, my uncles had a sort of unconditional authority that served as carte blanche, and they used it. If Oryolin, Strogolshikov, and Zhukovsky said drive, we drove; if they said drive the moon, we readied the launch.

Wednesday was a wild day everywhere, for not just the military but all Russia was on the run from the invasion news. I can guess there was more drunken despair than ever that night. Yes, it was fear of war and fear of catastrophe, yet I think now it was also a visceral fear of a fall back into the random cruelty of Stalin's time. We Russians knew that if the bosses could do this to Czechoslovakia—and lie about it brazenly, calling it an intervention to maintain order— then what they could do at home was unbounded. I didn't think this, I admit, but if I'd had a sharper mind I would have, and I would have been right. Most everyone believed that the bosses had gone too far, that we'd acted recklessly, that NATO and the Americans could only respond the same way. I remember the stunned, hopeless faces I saw at Starry Town: mothers hurrying to shop before there were shortages; babushkas weeping in the shadows and whispering that this was just like 1941; children called in from play as if they could be protected from the news. It was a criminal act to scare women and children like that, and I hold those bosses as liable for every tear I saw that day as I do for the murders they ordered in Prague. Let the whole of the misery they caused charge and condemn them. Yet what happened on August 21–22 was the least of the brutality that was to follow as all Russia again turned as black as a moonless night.

I'm ashamed to confess now that, at the time, I was anything but sorrowful. Educated to shun politics as if it were treason, I was indifferent to the suffering around me. Worse, I was joyous, and my joy was airborne, for my uncles had asked for me, they had chosen me specially, Glavtop and Grin had said so: "You're it." What my thick head could think was that they cared about me enough to make me part of their squadron just like that, no talk, no more tests, no conditions. I had a vision of us flying off to war within days. Surely I would rise to be Uncle Alexander's wingman. You see how far afield a boy can roam if you feed him gold stars and high octane. The more I manufactured my fantasies, the more I preened and pranced. I also pushed aside any doubts about flying to the Cosmodrome, such as whether Glavtop and Grin had cleared my departure with Colonel Khitrovo, which they hadn't. I was careful to avoid Volgamints when I got back to the barracks—I didn't want him to taunt my mood—and slipped into the mess to stuff my pockets with bread, onions, and fruit. I did wave goodbye to Doctor Gogol, who looked puzzled what I was about. No, I remember now, I told Doctor Gogol and he said, assuming this could be war, "Well, then, soft landing," and I felt as brave as a myth as I dashed into the woods to the Black House and the 21 flight line behind it.

I did register some of the fright I saw at Starry Town. I recall one mother in particular, who probably was my age though I thought of her as grown up, a dark-haired woman with a toddling red-haired child, and I saw them sitting on a bench watching for their husband and father to come running from the airbase. I don't know who they were, but I can picture the pain in their eyes as if they were thinking that he would never come running to them again. You see what war is, don't you? It's madness. Who but a madman could do that to those two helpless souls left waiting for love forever? I doubt if I put together any of this at the time, yet I'm sure it occurred to me, as I scrambled to get away, that I should call on Katya, to make sure she was safe. It was an impossible urge. I had no claim on her, and I certainly couldn't go calling on her apartment, so it was just a boy's notion. Yet I know the idea pleased me in a surprising way. Putting someone before my duty was new to me. Great-Uncle Lev had taught me that if I couldn't love a stranger, to leave the stranger be; but he hadn't told me what to do when you loved the stranger so much that you never wanted to leave her. For the first time in my life I was leaving love behind, and it hurt.

④

The Grand Constructor

Late Wednesday afternoon I took off for the Cosmodrome in formation with Captains Glavtop and Grin and the five junior members of the squadron, senior lieutenants Miserbiev, Adama-Bibliov, Tevyelook, Schtange, and my wingmate Genka Stumpelkin. I was AWOL from Starry Town, but none of them mentioned it, and I was most reluctant to ask. My uncles' falcons carried themselves with a relaxed iconoclasm that made me think it would insult them if I asked about regulations. I was stuck halfway between being the best little first cadet at Starry Town and the newest swaggerer in the heavens, a dilemma that was laughable to everyone but me. At the least I knew that fretting about Lieutenant-Colonel Khitrovo's permission was useless once I'd taken off. I can see now that I so wanted to be accepted as a member of the squadron that I would have done anything they asked. Fly sleepless all night five thousand kilometers from my station? Walk on my wings? Yes, sir! What a little mimic and show-off I was, how I longed to be more like them than they were. It's no excuse to say that all of what I said or did the next week was either to please the squadron or to demonstrate to my uncles that I deserved the trust they'd already given me. I think of the squadron now when I think of Pushkin asking about heroes in his "Poltava": "What remains of those proud men, so strong of license and of lust?" And I answer that what remains is my memory that once upon a time they were my guides to the Cosmodrome and the moon.

Our flight wasn't routine: there was a bad-weather system across the Urals that obliged us to divert to the east, so that our flight path resembled a blind man's; and then, due to the mobilization, we had to beg for fuel at the first stopover, and we were on the ground half the night at Orenburg awaiting tanker lorries from the stores. We raised Star City's beacon before dawn Thursday and, when the clouds scattered at first light, we descended over the skinny Syr-Darya River toward the town. It was my first glimpse of a spaceport

I'd dreamed of for a decade; I doubt if anything could have disappointed me. What I could see were the glaring white concrete patches of the city center up against the dark blue string of the river. Star City was actually a former river village on the caravan route that had been raised into a futuristic-looking miniature metropolis of geometric shapes and vast, empty boulevards right alongside the sod and canvas hovels of the desert peoples. The sharp lines of the new buildings cast long morning shadows out across the plain, making the settlement resemble an oasis of lost angles cast into the midst of the swirling yellow dust of the dry steppe.

Glavtop and Grin started the fun by breaking from formation and performing a shallow dive and then a textbook scissors, so that their contrails hung an X in the blue. I couldn't resist my spirits and signaled my wingmate Stumpelkin with a hand gesture that we should follow the game. Stumpelkin agreed, and we pushed into an imitation of their run at Star City, eventually easing up and performing a series of scissors—more a weave of diamond shapes—and then waggling our wings like shivering robins. I wasn't entirely sure I should have tried to show up my superiors, but then Glavtop called me, "Adequate, Cosmonaut," and Grin added, "Distinctly adequate, distinctly," and my pride flamed. I hadn't ever imagined a finer entry into Star City's airspace, and now I'd been congratulated for it by the two best 21 drivers in the world, who'd called me a cosmonaut. I felt that the rest of my life would envy this morning. Below me I didn't see the yellow steppe as a salt flat–pocked desert in southwest Kazakhstan, I saw it as yet another new planet for me to conquer; I didn't see the rocket range of the Cosmodrome—about ten kilometers to the east of Star City—as a vast wasteland, I saw it as a stepping-stone to history in the heavens. My pretensions were as boundless as my pride that morning, and I made the same sort of private speeches that had long swelled me up when there was something new to challenge. "I'm the one you've been waiting for," I told the yellow steppe; "I'm the man who's going to get us the moon," I told Star City; "I'm the first man on the moon," I told the Cosmodrome. I don't recall laughing at myself as I had when I was moon-gazing on the Volkhov. In two months I'd come to take myself as seriously as a bronze plaque, so that my youth, driving a 21 in the company of men I worshipped, was as humorless as it was vain.

The airfield was midway between Star City and the Cosmodrome and offered several heavy hangars, a large tank farm, a sizable operations shack, and two long, heavy runways that could take An-24s and -26s. The landscape was treeless, shadowless, wind-scorched, and most yellow. It all did have the feel that we'd voyaged to a whole new planet from the world of the deep green forests and pale brown taiga steppes to the north. I eased in on final approach tip to tail with Stumpelkin and came down like skating on a sea of yellow talc. The ground crews greeted us at the flight line and passed us "juice" and corrosive desert coffee, though we really needed water. I must emphasize that the direct experience of the yellow steppe was thirst. It's called a steppe out of custom, but it's really a dangerous desert that roasts by day and freezes by night, and always throws up a yellow dust that coats your skin, lips, lungs, and innards like paint.

Uncle Konstantine appeared soon after at the wheel of a bright green autobus to carry us to the Corps' elite billet. He was his usual happy self and crooned to us, "Hurry on, now, darlings!" He was bareheaded with a tan that was so brightly red that it made his head resemble a talking copper pot that glowed and laughed in booming roars, "Hah! Hah!" He broadcasted a menu that got my attention, "Roast pork for breakfast, darlings, and all the eggs you can eat!" and also made the others act gritty. We were sleepless, unwashed, and as determined as condemned prisoners at dawn, and so we heard the size of the meal as confirmation that we were going to the war front right after breakfast. The overnight news from Czechoslovakia and the West was so forbidding—Prague was sealed and blacked out, NATO was in emergency session, our reserves were mobilizing, our bombers were at their fail-safes in full feather—that we presumed the worst. I remind you that we weren't speculating, we had evidence, such as the redeployment of bomber command and several bellicose remarks by Western bosses quoted on the radio, to assume that world war was imminent. The jeopardy had the contrary effect of exciting us as if it were a great game and we were going to be the first on the field and likely some of the first to fall. I've seen men at war since then—I've been one—and know that when the shooting starts, few feel anything but a draining fear, and all you can think is to do what you're told. But that morning we held ourselves immortal. What foolishness it all was, what arrogance that young men should think that dying in combat was more worthy or sensible than dying of diphtheria or a car wreck, but that's how stupid war makes whole peoples and how feebleminded the invasion of Czechoslovakia made Russia, as if a lie like that were tolerable as long as we could exploit it for medals and glory.

There was glory enough for a century that day, but it wasn't to be found on earth. The reason my uncles had gathered us at the Cosmodrome was not to go to war but to the moon. I realize that even these many decades later those days can still look as if I dreamed them. I didn't dream any of it, I was there, I saw and heard and turned around and around in amazement at the march my uncles began on the yellow steppe. Yes, I believed in them too much, and I adored them beyond reason, and my faith in them then and now probably makes me a less than excellent witness. Yet if I'd been more mature, modest, and evenhanded, then what would I have achieved? If I'd longed less to follow them, then what would I have now to remember but doubts? If I'd missed out on my uncles, I would have missed out on the adventure of my life. Perhaps my fate wouldn't have been so remorseful, but then again I'm here, I remember, and that means to me there is a deal to be thankful for. I don't know about the darkest parts, the evil that was done and the timeless sorrow I feel; perhaps I would have missed out on that too. But can you answer for me how much of a life is willful choice and how much is unavoidable fate? I sometimes think now that from the moment I chose to go to Starry Town, from the instant I gazed at the moon on the Volkhov, then all that I've told you and have to say followed tip to tail on my drive to the moon.

The wonder of moon-driving started as soon as we reached the Corps' billet, a blockwork compound of three-story concrete barracks set off from the bare boulevards by an empty reflecting pool and a row of neatly planted saplings. I was assigned to bunk in with Stumpelkin, and after a gorging breakfast of pork chops, eggs, tomatoes, and a mountain of my turnips and onions in the first-floor mess, we hauled our kit bags to our room on the top story. The hallways gleamed, and whatever I touched seemed extravagant to me, the furniture, fixtures, carpets, even the washbasins and toilets. Since Star City had been built with the largess of the empire, a showplace for what the bosses called true communism, I was right to feel pampered. I knew I needed sleep but couldn't stop from inspecting everything in my room and then from roving out onto the cantilevered terrace at the hall's end. I wanted to see everything and never wanted it to end. I squinted east into the sunlight, letting my eyes prowl over the bee eaters and buntings flitting across the tree park, and then staring farther and farther into the desert in the direction of the Cosmodrome. I can still feel what it was like to loose my flight suit and let the desert air parch me. I was drinking water like ambrosia, and my mood moved from happy to drunken when I called out, "I love this!" I thought I heard Genka Stumpelkin come up behind me, and I turned to howl the more. Instead of Stumpelkin, it was Uncle Alexander in crisp tan tropicals. He was smoking his pipe and parading with his hands behind his back like a field marshal before the campaign, which was the truth of it, he was at the edge of the final battle of his life. He spoke formally, "Good morning, Lieutenant."

I saluted, redid my buttons, and saluted again, explaining, "Sir, we've just arrived, sir, and I was looking out to see if I could locate the launch towers from here."

Uncle Alexander glanced into the desert. "You can see the Rocketage," he told me. "Follow that road and find the profile in the heat. That's the big barn, the Rocketage. The primary launchpad's another kilometer on, two radio beacon towers like pencil lines. Maybe your eyes can pick them out, mine can't anymore."

He was speaking kindly, but because I usually felt inadequate before him I explained, "Yes, sir, I can spot the towers, sir. I saw the whole area when we came down, sir."

Uncle Alexander joked, "And a few windows came down with your lot." It wasn't much of a joke, yet it did make him smile, and this made him seem calm to me. If I'd only realized how exceptional it was that such a lonely man should show approval at a boy's exuberance. Uncle Alexander usually held his square shoulders and long arms as if he were either remote from life or possibly just uninterested in it, but that morning there was zest in him, his black eyes were warm, he smiled like a normal human being. All I could think was that somehow I'd pleased him by breaking windows when we'd buzzed Star City at the speed of sound. I stood by trying to think what I should say next. Stumpelkin saved my silence by stepping out on the terrace with us. "Sir!" Stumpelkin began, "thank you for calling us down here, sir! To be left out, it would've been unbearable to sit it out."

Uncle Alexander raised up to his imperial posture and asked, "How's that?"

What Stumpelkin replied was what we'd all believed—that we'd been ordered down here as a squadron in order to prepare for the war against NATO and the Americans. "It's because of Czechoslovakia, right, sir?" Stumpelkin asked. When Uncle Alexander didn't agree, Stumpelkin tried an alternative scenario. "Then we're here to defend the Cosmodrome from attack?"

Uncle Alexander shook his head and responded, "Nothing for us in Czechoslovakia, and nothing to defend yet." He spoke in his mumbly style, which was his way when he was thinking out loud. "We're for the moon, moon-driving's what we're about." He gestured toward the burning blue sky and the very faint silver sliver of the moon, one day short of new. "We're here for moon-driving, Lieutenants. Time for the moonship."

Stumpelkin and I couldn't resist our astonishment and glanced wide-eyed at each other like children who have just been granted a wish. It was too much for us, and both Stumpelkin and I started, "But, sir, the moon, but how?"

Uncle Alexander's dark gaze settled on us. I saw he was angry that we were questioning his word. It was an early lesson that he was burdened with a spontaneous temper. He waved off his mood and told us, "Briefing tonight, you can ask your questions." He sucked on his pipe and left us.

We waited only a moment longer than necessary before we hugged and hooted. "Did he say it?" Stumpelkin joked. I was more awestruck: "The moon, it's going to happen, Genka. We're going to see it, the moonship and the moon landing." Stumpelkin shouted down to the desert floor, "Yes! Yes! Yes!" like a man who is trying to get used to his good luck.

You might ask what did a couple of junior officers dancing on a balcony know about the prospect of a moonship and driving the moon? And if you've read some history of that period, you might also ask what chance did Russia have for the moon by August 1968? Wasn't the moon race settled by then? Hadn't all our mission disasters and booster failures and wasted opportunities lost us everything? Hadn't the Americans bought their way ahead of us? Wasn't what had started out as a fair match between mighty America and mighty Russia—step matching step, our Vostok with their Mercury, our Voskhod with their Gemini—now become so unequal a contest as to be a laughingstock? Wasn't our moon-landing program stalled per-

manently by the untested Soyuz spacecraft and an unbuilt
superbooster? Wasn't their moon-landing program headlong with
the sumptuous Apollo spacecraft and the flight-tested Saturn V
superbooster? Wasn't what was left for us just to hold their coats
while they made history? My answers now to all of these questions
and so many more detailed ones I could ask is my best old grin. If
you know history so well to follow my facts, then you also know that
nothing about the moon race was certain until it was finished and
Armstrong and Aldrin stood at Tranquillity Base in July 1969. Right
up until that moment, the moon race was to the luckier, and I mean
men, not machines. I'm telling you the truth: the moon race continued until Armstrong's luck to set down *Eagle* with no fuel left to
measure; the moon race continued until my uncles had lost luck and
were dead. I shall explain all of it eventually, but for now it's right to
say that there was a moon race as long as both sides aimed at the
moon and both sides boasted of a future of infinite possibilities. In
those days, it felt as if anything were possible at any moment, from
the sunburst of nuclear catastrophe to the phenomenon of extrater-
restrial life. We were all bound for the unknown together, and the
moon was the agreed-upon first leg in a collective leap for the planets
and the stars. On their side there was all the money and power
available and a lust for victory that colored the times. On our side
was the largest, cruelest, greediest empire ever constructed that had
at its center undeniable heroes such as Alexander Oryolin to declare,
"Time for the moonship." Then and now I think it was a well-
matched race, America versus Russia, Cape Kennedy versus the Cosmodrome, astronauts versus cosmonauts, for I will set wealth and
genius and pride against the fury of heroism anytime and wait for
luck to determine victory. Yes, there were critical mechanical problems on our side, while the Americans enjoyed a gifted technology;
and we cosmonauts were about to learn more about the obstacles to
us getting off the ground in time. Yet at the same time I remind you
that you don't think about probabilities when you begin a race, you
think about believing in winning. And we believed in Uncle
Alexander so completely that just to hear him say we were going to
drive the moon made it real and imminent to us. Haven't you ever
worshipped an idol? You don't doubt your hero. You believe that all
is larger than life and that no matter what, your hero will keep going
until the heavens take him in.

I floated to my uncles' briefing that evening at the billet's ground-floor lounge bar, a cool, pale room that smelled pleasantly of sweets, Turkish tobacco, and tangy desert breezes. The squadron wore its bright tropical off-dress uniforms that I couldn't yet afford, and it filed in two by two according to the pairings and spread out along the bartop. They were a very well-turned-out crew, bathed, combed, and fluffed for romance in Star City's native quarter later that night, and I can close my eyes and see them now like a rogues' gallery: Fedyuninsky puffing on a cigarette, Cherryntevsky munching peppers, Glavtop and Grin with their feet up, Kandidim reading an Italian smut magazine, Artzybashev humming a popular song, big-eared Tevyelook and his pal Schtange bent over their chessboard, my friends Miserbiev, Adama-Bibliov, and Stumpelkin eating more sweetcakes. And yet as exalted as the cosmonauts looked to me, they all seemed ordinary in comparison to the splendor of my uncles. Uncle Alexander stood alongside the shuttered window in the pose of a world conqueror, his hands clasped behind, his back as straight as a booster, his jaw set like an outcropping of granite. Beside him Uncle Dmitry sat patiently in an overlarge high-backed chair that made him seem even more dainty than usual. And Uncle Konstantine was in his favorite casual position on his backside on a bench, eating grapes and tossing the sour ones to Little Laika at his feet. She was a most hungry dog; I doubt I've seen any animal since eat fruit, nuts, eggs, and various trash as eagerly as meat, but then Little Laika, or Laikushka as she was called, probably seems as bizarre to you as most else about my uncles and their squadron. Yes, they were just three men in uniform with a raggedy yellow dog for a pet, but to us they were truly the center of all the heroic legends we'd ever wanted for ourselves. I speak for myself and for all of the squadron. Everything my uncles said that night was burned in our souls, and since I am the last of us, it falls to me now to tell you the truth of how it was at the very first of our campaign for the moon.

Uncle Alexander began the briefing with a domineering speech that was what I'd imagined my father must have sounded like twenty-five years before when he gave his famous speeches before another air battle—the shock commander at the front on the eve of the desperate battle. "Why are we here?" Uncle Alexander asked. He kicked open the floor-length window shutter so that the late sunlight emblazoned the floor. "The job we're here to do is to drive the moon. Who doubts it? Not any of us." He didn't point, he shrugged to the sky to the northwestern horizon, where the nearly invisible sliver of the moon was setting early. "We're here, and it's there. It's our job. It's what we were brought here to do, by Seryozha Korolev and them. They're gone now, and we're still here. No one's going to do it for us. We'll do it with what we've got. It's good enough and perhaps it's better than that." Uncle Alexander paced some, fogging his head in gray pipe smoke. He added what might have been a political comment—who could tell with him?—but was clearly an illustration that he thought of the moon race as a battle campaign: "Moon-driving's a job worth doing. It might be the only one that is. For me, it is. That's what I believe, it's for me. It's the center of the front; it's where the fight is; it's where we belong. Main force at the main chance is what we're here to do. Attack the center of the line and all the rest will follow. I don't care about what others have done or not done for us or against us, I care about my job. And my job is to get there any way I can, not next year, not next month—now, now." Uncle Alexander drew straight up in the posture I best remember him, a potent, silver-headed, square-shouldered, enigmatic fortress of a man with the bearing of a king who at the same time was able to sound like a mystic, and by this I mean that Uncle Alexander was a man who spoke to the future as well as to facts. "When they ask," he posed, "a hundred years on, who was there and what was done, the answer will come back that the Corps was there, and the Corps did the job at hand, that's what they'll say. What the Corps began eight years back, it's the Corps' to finish. We began it by taking orbital space. Now we're going to finish it by taking the moon. The moon's ours, the moon's for us. It's time to get our moonship and finish it."

The squadron was prepared to cheer in agreement, but Uncle Dmitry raised his hand for our attention. If Uncle Alexander was the king of the three of them, Uncle Dmitry was the prime minister who liked to make abstruse, diplomatic remarks and to find compromises between Uncle Alexander's willfulness and Uncle Konstantine's prankishness. "Now think about what we're about here," Uncle Dmitry began as if addressing schoolboys. "No place for your signing on in blood, this isn't piracy. You're to think for yourselves for the moment. None of you are ordered to this. We won't order you. The Corps has plenty of need for men who want the orbitals, and soon there'll be the space stations and the like." Uncle Dmitry's tone was cautionary, a mentor reminding us we were young. "A moon landing isn't a career," he continued. "If we get there—and there's no call to think we will, despite what Sasha says—it'll only be one or two of us. The others of us won't have much to speak of. If there were family men among you, if at least a few of you would conduct yourselves less ardently, then perhaps you could think more wisely about this decision. I know at your age it can seem that if you don't drive the fastest ship then you'll be left behind. I know the feeling. I was like you once, we all were. And it can be hard to know the difference between boldness and blockheadedness. So think, will you. If you sign on this, you could be signing off on your futures."

The squadron shifted about, and Artzybashev and Kandidim slumped over the lounge bar like impatient rascals. Uncle Dmitry saw his speech was lost on us and yet tried once more to slow the stampede to glory: "I'm telling you, I couldn't argue with one of you who says this isn't for him. I'd be proud of the man, at least he'd be showing he's thinking for himself. The moon's not a panacea, comrades. It isn't what your mothers were thinking when they gave you to the Motherland, and your children won't be able to eat it. Now, think, before I believe what you say back."

The squadron thought for a moment and then let Fedyuninsky reply for everyone, "Yes, Colonel, the moon isn't a ballroom. Let's get on with it, what's the question? It isn't as if we've got better offers these days." He addressed all of us, "Any of you lot too busy with some paradise not to get on to a bleak little estate like the moon?"

There were twelve of us, the squadron plus me, and we shouted out as if we were thousands. "Roll out the moonship!" "On to the moon!"

Uncle Konstantine tossed fatter grapes to Little Laika to make her yap like a Greek chorus and get our attention for another one of his fractured proverbs. "So," he chewed loudly, "so, you can't get drunk on another man's vodka—now pass the bottle!"

As unceremonious as all this seems, Uncle Alexander's fury followed by Uncle Dmitry's equivocation followed by Uncle Konstantine's buffoonery, it was how my uncles chose to announce their decision to drive the moon, and I suppose you could say that the squadron just as unceremoniously entered into the conspiracy of it.

From the very first, my uncles said they were going to do it just as simply as you might say you're going to go to Moscow. If you can spot trickery in all that I've shown, you've got a keener eye and ear than I did then and do now. My belief is that it was unironic heroism from the beginning, no greed or treason about it, as plain an ambition as that of a man crossing an ocean, climbing a mountain range, planting a foot and a flag at the top. What lesson I took from the moment was what I carried with me through my own ambitions: if you're after something grand, say so to yourself and all who will listen, and then keep going until you get it.

Afterward it was time to celebrate, and that evening was my introduction to many of the favors of Star City. The cosmonauts were indulged throughout the empire; however in Star City they were exalted. We toured the native quarter of the town along the river and were soon surrounded by a mob of hangers-on as we wandered through a maze of mud-built warrens, flimsy tin-backed buildings, and canvas-sided stables that the squadron knew like a child's sandbox. Half the night we raced from strange den to peculiar house, always welcomed by Russian and Kazakh hosts and toasted by sly drunks. There was singing, dancing, speechifying, and a heated swarming by the most beautiful of the women. I didn't drink, because I couldn't drink—vodka nauseates me—but I was soon woozy from just going along, and I couldn't ignore the women. Many of them were prostitutes, but not all, and I was struck by how different the Kazakh girls were from the Russian, with their dark complexions, small breasts, powerful hips, casual eroticism. I don't mean I went off with one of them, but I was kissed by several, and I did think about it when they made it appear so easy. I admit the women scared me a deal, and I clung to Genka Stumpelkin as if he were my chaperon. I've never been comfortable with voluptuaries such as Glavtop and Grin and Artzybashev, yet that night I was envious of how they enjoyed themselves. "Flesh," Artzybashev would cry when we arrived at another luxurious opium den, "can't you smell it!" I remember I could smell flesh that night, since there's something about the desert that makes even priggish men like me feel loose, tangy, and uncontrolled.

My uncles were well in control throughout the escapade. They joined in with the squadron, and Uncle Alexander and Uncle Konstantine could drink liters, but at no point did I see them act anything less than godlike. It was a profound transformation from the high jinks I'd seen the month before. Gone were the puffiness, sloppiness, recklessness I'd witnessed that first day, replaced instead by an authority that I can only describe as serene. It wasn't peace, I know now, it was the sort of calm that comes on to commanders when they've determined to attack and have given the order to go forward. At the time what I understood was that my uncles were now the towering figures of mastery that I'd always supposed. I don't recall thinking about fate, but now I do; and what I think is that night it was as if my uncles had finally settled on theirs.

It was Friday morning that I discovered that fate was not something that comes on suddenly, it's more a theme in the course of a man's life, and that for my uncles the fate of moon-driving was what they had been pursuing for many years. I was up as early as usual, after about an hour nap, in order to watch the sun color the desert and the larks complain while they fed. Genka Stumpelkin came out on the terrace and asked me how I was feeling. "Hungry," I said and laughed. "But more than that, I want to get out to the Cosmodrome and see this moonship. Do you think we can get out there today?"

Stumpelkin warned me right away that there was a problem about the moonship. "Who knows," he said of my uncles. "You can't be sure what they're going to do. Like yesterday. When Colonel Oryolin's in charge, anything's possible."

I heard a glum note from him and asked, "What's that mean?"

"Just that I hope something comes of the moonship talk this time. You shouldn't expect too much right away."

"What's wrong?"

Stumpelkin revealed his worry. "The moonship, Peter, it's not actually ready. It's not something you can look at, not something you can launch. You see, none of us has ever seen it."

I still didn't understand. "But Colonel Oryolin said it was time for the moonship."

"It's his way," Stumpelkin explained. "Colonel Oryolin has talked like this before. I didn't hear him myself, it's just what I've been told."

I demanded, "When?"

Stumpelkin's tale was insightful. "He's done it three times before that I know about. The first was three years back, after he and Colonel Strogolshikov got back from their crash landing in *Voskhod 2,* and the first thing Colonel Oryolin did was demand a moonship and a shot at the moon. He'd just survived the first crash landing from space, he'd landed his own capsule on a mountainside and walked away with Colonel Strogolshikov; and what'd he do but demand a moonshot. Then there was two years back, right after Chief Constructor Korolev died of a heart attack. It was the year before I got to Starry Town, and I've been told that Korolev was the brains and soul of the Cosmodrome—he chose Gagarin, you know, and he chose our colonels, too—and that when he died, everyone was paralyzed except for our colonels, who stood at the gravesite and again demanded a moonshot. Colonel Oryolin said that Korolev wouldn't rest in his grave until we got to the moon, and I hear Oryolin kicked stones into the grave and said that unless the Corps found its backbone and fought for its rights then we might as well get in there too."

I could picture Uncle Alexander's theatrics and nodded at Stumpelkin's story like a child at a puppet show.

"Last year I saw it for myself," Stumpelkin said. "It was right after *Soyuz 1,* even before Komarov's funeral, when we were hanging around the Rocketage waiting for them to fly back the capsule. Colonel Oryolin had gone up to see the crash site and what was left of Komarov. We were all upset—the whole Corps was there waiting for the heavy Mils—and then Colonel Oryolin starts singing this thing from the opera *Don Giovanni.* I thought it was very strange, and they told me later he was singing about when the statue comes to life and threatens the hero, or something like that. Colonel Oryolin, who can sing all right, he finished his song and then said just about what he said last night. 'It's time to get our moonship and finish it.' "

I stood still for some time after Stumpelkin finished, brooding about what this all meant. I don't take credit for what I said, it just came out, and even I wouldn't understand it for many years, perhaps not until I commanded men myself. "You mean he says there's a moonship whenever there's bad news? He's saying all this about a moonship now because of Czechoslovakia?"

Stumpelkin said, "I don't know. It did cheer everyone up."

Neither of us laughed. We were too young, and we were too full of ourselves, for us to have understood the genius in my uncles. Now I know that what Stumpelkin had described to me was a style of heroic leadership whereby all immediate setbacks and disasters were countered by fantastic ambitions. In 1965, *Voskhod 2* had crashed in the Urals due to systems failure, nearly killing Uncle Alexander and Uncle Konstantine; in 1966, Chief Constructor Korolev, builder of the rocket program and founder of the Cosmodrome, had died of a heart attack that left the Cosmodrome without leadership; in 1967, Colonel Komarov had crashed and died in *Soyuz 1*. In three years there had been three hard blows against the Corps, and at each instance my uncles had responded with swashbuckling bravado: parading their pride of place, calling for a moonship, speechifying that the Corps' job was to get on to the moon. It was as if the true power of heroism is that at the worst times, when defeat is imminent and the only reasonable choice is quitting, it's then that heroes stand up and start yelling attack, attack, ram. What I know now about such heroes is that they're pigheaded and wrongheaded at most every turning in history, and yet then there are those unexpected moments when they're right and brilliant and a gift from heaven. They arrive on the battlefield like Steppe Eagles and roar out "Keep going!" like madmen, and who's to say beforehand they aren't saviors?

All this was too simple for me to comprehend then, caught up in the power of my uncles' legend. What I could think was to ask Stumpelkin about facts. "Isn't there anything to what Colonel Oryolin said? There must be plans?"

Stumpelkin smiled. "Yes, yes, plans."

"But yesterday," I argued, "you were excited, too, when he told us. Right here, you believed him, I saw you did."

"I believe him, we all believe him. He can get us to the moon. I know he can. And someday they're going to give him what he needs to do it; someday the bosses will listen to him. And then they'll give him a moonship, and then what a day!"

I didn't challenge Stumpelkin as we dressed and started down to the mess hall for breakfast. I'd convinced myself, as young men who want to conquer worlds often do, that everything was as it should be and that fretting over details I didn't understand was so much foolishness. I tried to show Stumpelkin that I had put aside my doubts. "What you said, Genka," I told Stumpelkin, "maybe this is the day, maybe the moonship is ready today? It could be, couldn't it?"

"Oh, yes!" Stumpelkin said, and we laughed at last.

A good part of our joy was that it turned out we were right to believe in Uncle Alexander. Those were the days for the moon, and I was witness to my uncles throwing themselves forward as the men to win the moon race. The best part of all was that there really was a moonship, it did exist, and my uncles knew it did, just as they knew that the way to the moon was to walk on the heads of the rocketeers and bosses who had been holding the Corps back for years.

My uncles' campaign for the moon began Friday afternoon. Uncle Konstantine drove us out to the Cosmodrome in the autobus, again taking the wheel from our official driver, a rotund black-suited Kazakh woman named Zere Godzihkty, who was quickly appointed to teach us desert songs. Misha Cherryntevsky had brought along his guitar, and he accompanied our booming chorus with his frantic playing, making our ride out a dust cloud of broken notes and much laughter. I sat with Stumpelkin and felt privileged to be among such charmers, yet I also felt a great curiosity and yearning, and as we neared the huge rocket assembly barn—the Rocketage—I stopped singing and started staring. I think I was almost weepy before the Rocketage. That dry yellow salt flat was hallowed ground from my adolescent dreamlife, for out of such an indistinct landscape of saxual trees, salt bushes, broomrapes, and sand sedges had risen the man-made phenomena of *Sputnik, Vostok 1* and the Vostok series, the Luna series, the Venera series, *Voskhod 1* and *2*. I wasn't the only one in the autobus feeling the history of the Rocketage, for there'd been no manned launch for sixteen months, and my junior peers Miserbiev, Adama-Bibliov, Tevyelook, Schtange, and Stumpelkin hadn't ever toured the assembly line. We all hoped we'd come not only to flap around the boosters but also to see something of the building of the promised moonship. We exchanged knowing glances, but I was the only one not sophisticated enough to keep my mouth shut. I asked Stumpelkin, "Is this the day we get the moonship, you think?" He shook me off, so I asked Miserbiev, "Could this be it today?" and he passed me hard candy and shrugged.

It wasn't to be that day, nor the next, nor for a week yet. Our tour turned out to be a ruse, and we cosmonauts turned out to be unwitting foils as Uncle Alexander opened his final march on the moon with the guileful tantrum of a warlord. We roamed the Rocketage like hedgehogs. Outside it was molten in the desert wind, but inside it was vast, cool, and green-hued from the light through the translucent window banks. The Rocketage was like a railway terminal built by Zeus: the floor was crisscrossed with rail bed to roll the boosters, fixed horizontally on rail cars, along the line of assembly stations; overhead cranes swung fuel tanks, engines, and equipment about as if they were toys; and along the walls there were splattering sparks from welding torches and the rattling of what I took to be an entire tool-and-die factory. The whole arena was deafening with industry and smelled like a busy railroad—acrid, sulfurous, oily. Even the bird life was hard at work, for a phenomenon of the Rocketage that I always liked was that the desert birds had transformed its eaves and beams into a bountiful aviary.

The Rocketage's pace was misleading. None of this labor was for the Corps, none of it had to do with orbital flight or with the moonship. And we soon found out what had happened to our manned space program. Uncle Dmitry lectured as we weaved through the assembly stations, while Uncle Alexander stood off from the group, waiting his moment to start his tantrum. I don't remember Uncle Konstantine being with us; I think he stayed in the autobus to sleep off his breakfast. We juniors knew most of what we saw from our studies, but it was still exciting to see the R-7 laid out in thousands of pieces. The bulk of the assembly floor was for the R-7, the tough, powerful, faithful plowhorse of the Cosmodrome. The R-7 had carried every cosmonaut aloft, and the Corps so regarded it as its own property that in tribute it was nicknamed Old Number Seven, or just simply the Seven. The R-7 wasn't the moonship, of course, and hadn't been built to do more than orbital work and rehearsals for the rendezvous that would be critical to moon-driving. Any sort of lunar mission—fly-by or landing—required a booster with ten times the payload capacity of grand Old Number Seven.

Regardless, Uncle Alexander chose as his first target the trustworthy R-7 itself and as his first straw man the rocketeer most trusted by the Corps, Deputy Chief of the R-7 Doctor Mishuk. It was a very stylized attack, and I realized as we gathered around Mishuk that Uncle Alexander was acting contrived and sounding insincere. "Tell them, Mishuk," Uncle Alexander boomed out. "Explain to them why they haven't been given a Seven to fly for a year and a half."

Mishuk, at forty-one, was a porky, dainty man with eyeglasses like microscopes, and he cringed and stuttered in reply, "Ple-ease, Colonel, you know the answer." We were squeezed between two stripped-down RD-107 engines, the core stage of the R-7, and it was as if we were children at the bedside of two twenty-eight-meter-long patients and Mishuk was the surgeon trying to explain his work. Mishuk was frightened of Uncle Alexander's temper and appealed to Uncle Dmitry, "You understand, Colonel Zhukovsky, we're doing what we have to do, you know."

Uncle Dmitry soothed him, "You're ready to go when we go, isn't it true, Doctor? You're the master of our shock booster fleet, we know it. Tell the boys, you've earned it, brag a little."

"I can't," Mishuk told Uncle Dmitry.

Uncle Alexander spoke out loudly again so that as many rocketeers as possible could hear him over the din. "Who can't, Mishuk? You? Are you gun shy? Is it the Seven? Tell us!"

Mishuk was helpless. "Don't, Colonel Oryolin, please."

Uncle Alexander used half of the truth in order to humiliate a blameless man, "You can't give us a Seven, but you can cry about it! You can't give us the help we need, but you can beg me off! If your moaning was thrust, we'd've flown the link-up last year! What good is your work if it's not for us? What good are all these Sevens if we can't fly them? What good are you, Mishuk, if you can only sit on your hands and wait for orders that will never come?" and then Uncle Alexander walked away from us so ruefully that it occurs to me now that he must have been imitating some opera he'd once seen— the hero singing out his high-mindedness and then strutting his pride off stage.

The full truth that Alexander had left out and that Mishuk was frightened to speak out was that State Security had taken over the Cosmodrome's launch schedule. Since the winter before, all Mishuk's R-7s had been committed to launching recoverable photographic payloads, which was jargon for spy satellites. I've already shown you why: because of the Czechoslovakia crisis. The bosses had known for some time that they had to prepare for an invasion, and one of their schemes had been to keep track of NATO's warships and supply ships with spy satellites launched serially before the invasion and now during the critical weeks following. Mishuk had been launching R-7s every three to five days for three months, and the exhaustion we saw in him that day as he begged for understanding was the result of a superhuman effort to please all parties. Uncle Alexander knew this and knew he was unfair to Mishuk and the rocketeers, yet Uncle Alexander was never a fair-minded man, and he didn't care about State Security or Czechoslovakia or Mishuk's thin skin, he only cared to lay a preparatory barrage, warning the rocketeers that he was on the warpath again. Uncle Alexander's frenzy that day announced that the overbearing Oryolin was roused once more to try for the moon and that the rocketeers could only hope he was satisfied with some lesser victory before he damaged their careers and comforts at Star City.

None of this manipulation answered my question about the moonship, and so Saturday night, after a day roaming the warrens and cafés of Star City with the squadron, I took it upon myself to investigate. I was up on the billet roof with my friends because we'd heard that there was to be an R-7 launch of another spy satellite, though we didn't know when to expect the launch. We'd carried up our suppers and waited beneath a star-packed night sky. Stumpelkin traded his chicken for my beets; Miserbiev preached his mastery of astrology while finishing three extra pieces of honey cake; Adama-Bibliov, who was a very soft-spoken man, sat back and waited for Miserbiev to shut up so he could enjoy the black tea. The desert smelled of wormwood and seemed to surround us like a sea of cold dust lit whitish and smooth by the street lamps nearby. I don't think we were debating anything more significant than the talents of the local dancers we'd seen that day, when we were surprised by a pink-and-orange flash to the northeast, followed by a series of rolling cracks. Out of the smoky stew rose the orange flame of an Old Number Seven. We jumped up open-mouthed, tracking the red flame in the black sky. It was like watching an onion dome blast off. Near escape velocity, the four strap-on engines peeled away from the core like a spire shucking support arches, and four red dots fell away to the desert. The core pushed on until expended, then fell away as the third stage ignited. I had to imagine the last part, the insertion into orbit, as I lost the flame downrange in the stars. I felt like shouting. It was my first launch, and all I could think was how it might feel sitting atop it, like riding a cannonball.

Stumpelkin brought down my mood with a fair imitation of Alexander's temperament. "That should've been our Seven. What good is it unless it's ours. What's the use?" Miserbiev spoke with a mouth full of cake, "Whereth ourth?" Stumpelkin asked, "What?"

I repeated what Miserbiev had muttered, " 'Where is ours?' is what he said. And it's a good question."

"Not this again," Adama-Bibliov said.

"Why not again?" I asked, and then I did my best to take up Uncle Alexander's argument: "You joke about the moonship and all, but what about it? We haven't seen anything at the Rocketage nearly large enough to get to the moon, unless they mean the Proton, but that's only good for a fly-by, isn't it? So what's wrong with asking where's our moonship?" I was swell-headed with my remarks, and the others looked at me as if I'd been made commander of the Corps.

Adama-Bibliov had a subtle sense of humor, and he used it to catch me up in the wildest tale of all. He confided, "The moonship isn't anywhere we can look, Peter." He pointed into the desert. "It's out there."

I sensed I was being teased but didn't back off. "You mean it? Where out there?"

Miserbiev whispered the crucial nickname, "Tsar Cannon."

"What's that?" I asked.

The cosmonauts looked over their shoulders as if they were concerned with eavesdroppers. They were just playing along with a long-established game—to speak of Tsar Cannon as if it were a secret. "Have you ever heard of the Grand Constructor?" Adama-Bibliov asked.

He looked so sincere this time that I had to ask, "You mean Academician Univer?"

"That's him!" cried Miserbiev. "The Grand Constructor and his Tsar Cannon!"

My first thought was that they were teasing me about Katya: I guessed that somehow they'd learned about my crush on her and were sending me up with gossip about her grandfather. The twist of this was that I was wrong and that they were being forthright, up to a point: The moonship did exist, and its pet name was Tsar Cannon, and its inventor was the genius rocketeer Academician Nikhon Univer, who was both Katya's grandfather and the so-called Grand Constructor. Miserbiev didn't help my suspicions right away, however, for he recounted the story of the Grand Constructor and his superbooster Tsar Cannon as if it were all a fairy tale. Once upon a time, it went, Chief Constructor Korolev had painted a fantasy of a rocket that could launch an orbital nuclear bomber, and Stalin and the Kremlin bosses had ordered one immediately. Korolev, a camel-trading genius, had used the monies to build the modest R-7 and later the mightier Proton. Meanwhile, the superbooster had been left to the fantasies of Korolev's onetime mentor, Academician Nikhon Univer of Leningrad. Now Korolev was dead of overwork at sixty-five, the R-7 was in service and the Proton in trials, and the Grand Constructor was said to be undaunted in his eighties while his superbooster Tsar Cannon, after ten years of rumors but no facts, had become a fable like the Flying Dutchman—never believed and yet always thrilling.

"They say the Grand Constructor's out there," Miserbiev had whispered, pointing into the desert. "And on bright nights, they say you can hear him hammering and sawing the biggest launch vehicle on earth, he and fifty thousand elves."

I asked, "The moonship— Is it true? Does it exist?"

My friends rolled their shoulders and made passive faces. Stumpelkin said, "If it does, Colonel Oryolin's going to steal it for us, you'll see."

"Steal it how?" I asked.

Miserbiev teased, "Oh, he'll huff and puff until they beg him to take what he wants."

Genka Stumpelkin preached a bottomless creed that I would soon come to hold on to like love: "Colonel Oryolin's in charge. He can do anything."

Sunday afternoon, Uncle Alexander's huffing and puffing continued as he led us out to the Rocketage again, this time to inspect the Soyuz spacecraft. It was another roasting day, and we chugged water and opened our top buttons to get relief. We drove into the rear loading doors of the Rocketage, where the spacecraft assembly floor was sealed off from the dusty bustle of the booster assembly. Several Soyuz spacecraft hung on scaffolding, and Stumpelkin and I moved over to touch one as if it were a new 21. The Soyuz was said to resemble a bird of prey, but I thought this wrongheaded. I didn't see anything predatory about it, more fluttery, darting, benign. The first thought I had was that the Soyuz was an iron butterfly, perhaps because it had a reputation for being as fragile as clockworks, with its three discrete modules that resembled a head, torso, and tail, with solar battery panels for wings. Over the years the Soyuz would go through as many design changes as a butterfly metamorphosing, but the early prototype I saw that day was painted green, seven and a half meters long, six metric tons at lift-off—a sturdy iron butterfly. It wasn't the Soyuz's sturdiness that Uncle Alexander meant to attack that day. "Get me Sinebrykhov, now!" he ordered a rocketeer. The man cowered and said that Academician Sinebrykhov, who was chief of spacecraft design and assembly, didn't come out to the Rocketage on weekends. "Pass on a message," Uncle Alexander said. He scooped up a long screwdriver like a rapier and swung backhanded to whack one of the extended solar panels of a Soyuz. "Tell him that I'll take her clipped. She'll still fly."

This was such a heretical act that we grimaced along with every rocketeer in earshot. A senior rocketeer stood from his station and shouted at us incoherently. Another technician grabbed for a telephone as Uncle Alexander swung again and severed the panel from its bolts. It crashed to the floor and cracked. The squadron looked to see if Uncle Dmitry would stop the vandalism. Instead Uncle Dmitry crossed his arms and waited. Uncle Konstantine roared out, "Pluck her, too, Sasha, pluck her like a hen!" and then he made Little Laika bark in approval. Uncle Alexander had made his point and flung the screwdriver to the wall before he turned to us, his obedient foils, and began proclaiming dark prejudices: "Backwardness, that's why it's hanging there!" He pointed at the rocketeers staring down from the scaffolding ramp. "Backwardness, that's why they're hanging there! And there's new backwardness, listen to me, backwardness, backwardness like the old days!"

What followed was a detailed lecture on the failure of the top-secret Zond program, focusing on why five launches had been aborted in two years and why it would never get off the ground. The theme of his argument was blunt rhetoric: "Backwardness and backwardness," Uncle Alexander accused. "Backward, backward backwardness." I hadn't ever heard of the Zond program—a plan to send a lone cosmonaut in a truncated Soyuz craft to fly-by the moon and return to the earth in a great figure eight. It's long forgotten now, but back then the Zond program was a stepchild to the moon-landing program, a sort of cheat that would accomplish a propaganda triumph while at the same time practicing the logistics necessary for a landing. Importantly the Zond program called for the big, new, three-stage booster called the Proton that was meant to replace the R-7, when and if they ever got the Proton out of its troubled trials. Yet Uncle Alexander didn't care any more about the Zond program than he did about the Soyuz's status or the Proton's shakeout. The Zond wasn't for a moon landing and the Proton wasn't the moonship, and so they were no more than red herrings for Uncle Alexander's calculated public outrage: "The Zond is wasted work!" he bellowed. "The Proton is wasted half measure!" he growled. "The Zond program is all a waste!" he indicted. The rocketeers understood the message: Oryolin meant to carry on being hotheaded until he got his way; Oryolin was dangerous.

I remember watching Uncle Alexander perform—citing dates and specifications of the Cosmodrome's recent failures, bad-mouthing rocketeers who couldn't defend themselves—and thinking here was the one man who could push aside backwardness and bring us victory. If I'd been more mature, perhaps I might have recognized that Uncle Alexander was indeed a hothead, and his display of bluster was neither responsible nor worthy. I might even have guessed that just underneath the surface of his charade was a bloody tyrant who really did believe he could shout down the bosses and outshout the devil and shout up the heavens until the moon was his. I suppose it was my failure when I cheered Uncle Alexander as the boldest, fiercest falcon in heaven and earth, but then again I suppose, too, that if it were mine to do again, even with what I know, I would have cheered just as loudly.

Perhaps the best way I can show you what it was like to feel Uncle Alexander's power is just to report the stirring way he closed his bombast: "Backwardness must be defeated!" he cried, waving his arms as if they were golden swords. "The Corps must defeat backwardness! The moonship is ours! We've paid for it in blood! The moon is ours! We've bought in with the lives of tens of thousands of our comrades! We're the men for it, because we're the men here, now, to do our job!"

You might now ask what blood and what sacrifice he was talking about, and I can only answer that his exaggeration was calculated demagoguery. He was a great soldier, and within every great soldier might be the makings of yet another generalissimo dictator. Uncle Alexander was a courageous man, and who among us is strong enough alone to stand up to such a hero and say that once he was right to fight beyond reason, but now he is wrong to cut down sense for gain, and now he is going too far, and now he is becoming his own enemy? My response is: not me that day and not me today.

Uncle Alexander's performance felt exactly like the war stories of my father's speeches to his regiment before another battle, and I clapped as heartily for Uncle Alexander as I would have for my father, cheering, "Ours! Ours! Ours!"

I was so feverish after all this that, late Sunday night, I risked my own sense of limits and, with Stumpelkin's help, sneaked into the telephone switching board at the billet with my plan to call Katya at her apartment in Starry Town. I figured that if I could get past her husband, I could tell her what I'd seen and done and tell her more that her grandfather might be the Corps' deliverer. Actually my plan wasn't so careful, and my phone call was mostly a prank, a boy's fancy, and I have no good memory as to what I could have hoped to accomplish. I got directly through to a Moscow operator, and he, thinking it was a VIP call from Star City to Starry Town, connected me to Katya's line. There were four rings and then, "Hello?" she said.

"It's me." I stuttered some and knew right away that I didn't know why I was doing this. "I had to talk to you," I explained.

Katya asked, "Where are you?"

"At the Cosmodrome, close to it, at the Corps billet—with the squadron!"

"You're with them? Why?"

I tried my proud announcement: "We're going to the moon, Katya, soon we're going to do it! And it's your grandfather, he's building us a moonship! Academician Univer. The Grand Constructor! It's wonderful! I didn't know until two days ago! You should have told me. A moonship!"

Katya asked, "Peter, Peter, are you all right?" and then her tone changed from concern to discipline. "What have they been telling you? They're going to ruin your career. Don't listen to them. Who's going to the moon?"

Cautiously I answered, "Uncle Alexander mostly." I corrected my informality, "Colonel Oryolin says the moonship is nearly ready, and it's going to be ours."

Katya demanded, "What does Dmitry Mikhailovich say?"

I repeated what I'd already said about the moon, the moonship, and my uncles, leaving out mention of the extremes of Uncle Alexander's behavior. I didn't understand why Katya asked after Uncle Dmitry's thoughts, because I didn't know at the time that Katya was best friends with Uncle Dmitry's wife, Angelicka. Uncle Dmitry was the only one of my uncles whom Katya approved of, since, as I've told you, she thought Uncle Alexander a demagogue and Uncle Konstantine a knave not fit for his own dog. Perhaps I did sense all this while I talked, because I did go on too long and without a point, finally adding, "Colonel Oryolin says it can happen any day now, you'll see."

"You must listen to me," Katya countered, "I don't care what they've told you. There isn't any such a moonship and won't ever be. My grandfather's an old Bolshevik and a miserable bastard who's made slaves out of thousands and spent hundreds of millions on rubbish. My grandfather's a liar and a despot who thinks it's 1920 and this is some sort of a new world that justifies his fantasies of power. My grandfather—listen to me—is a madman who should have died decades ago in infamy, and it's only lies like they've told you that keep him out of his grave. They've lied to you, Peter, that's all it is."

I was confused and could only reply a soft no.

"Yes!" she said, and then came her politics again: "They've lied about Czechoslovakia, and they've lied about peace, and they're lying to you! It's all lies, Peter, everything you've ever been told, lies, lies. *Your life is built on lies.*"

I know now that what Katya said was more true than not; back then it was impossible to hear her say such a thing. My romantic telephone call was a humiliation. What was worse was that Katya had hit at the very heroic dreams that lifted me up the most. I tried, "Katya, please, I'm sorry, I can't," and then my conflict made me burst out, "I love you, I do, that's all I have to say. I love you, that's not a lie, I love you." It was Katya who cut the connection.

Stumpelkin, who'd overheard some of my distress, tapped me and asked, "What did she say?"

I couldn't explain and so I lied, "Oh, you know, 'Soft landing.'" I might have learned a lot more from Katya that night than just that she was willing to rock my soul if I didn't obey her. I might have learned that my brave Uncle Alexander was as ruthless as inspirational and that his quest for the moon was as wanton as daring. I might have also understood that what I was witness to that week wasn't the rising of the Corps against bloated cowards but rather a familiar Cosmodrome clash between longtime adversaries—the Cosmonaut Corps with its burst of glory versus the rocketeers with their firm hold on their budgets and their luxurious posts at Star City. At the least I might have guessed that my uncles' talk of a moon landing was based upon overreaching and not engineering.

The next Tuesday evening I had yet one more opportunity to see for myself that what I was caught up in was a tangled dance of jealous potentates. Late afternoon Uncle Dmitry and Uncle Konstantine led the squadron to a wedding reception in the big apartment compound at the center of town. Uncle Alexander had chosen to stay behind at the billet, I suppose because ranting wasn't appropriate to matrimony. One of several daughters of the Proton rocket chief Academician Faitelevitev was marrying a captain in the Rocket Forces. We falcons arrived in a cavalcade of high spirits at the compound off Sputnik Street. The wedding was a rich man's display under a gold-striped white tent that had been raised on candy-striped poles in the courtyard. There was music from two bands, roast pigs on spits in dug ovens, dancing on a platform, tables full of Russian treats and much Kazakh food I didn't recognize. The bride was in a long gown; the groom and most every Russian male were drunk on wine and dancing; and the weather was moderate for once with a cool desert breeze from the south.

Uncle Dmitry was an extraordinary courtier, a man whose manners would have raised him high regardless of the era, and he walked us directly to the bride as if we were approaching an empress. With bows and hand waves he introduced us to her one at a time and then signaled Artzybashev and Kandidim to place our gift on the table, a small heavy crate of some sort of French china obtained courtesy of Artzybashev's light fingers and limber tongue.

The bride was a plump, pretty girl, and she was thrilled by our generosity. She made so much noise that big-bellied Faitelevitev was quick to come over to attend his daughter's squeals and to confront Uncle Dmitry. From his look, I could tell that Faitelevitev wanted to hide, yet as the host, and as the father of a woman who was swooning over our gift, he made a start at welcoming my uncles.

Miserbiev and Stumpelkin made sure I spotted the other chief rocketeers, who were standing like dukes at the refreshment tables and watching closely for trouble. "There'll be a row, depend on it," Miserbiev whispered. I didn't know the bosses to see, so my friends identified Yangel, the acting chief constructor; Sinebrykhov, the spacecraft chief; Gendelmann-Grabovsky, the R-7 chief; and so many more whose names are lost in the records. What's important now is that they were all celebrated academicians of long-standing and weighty wealth, that they were by their postures all either dreary, dim-eyed, big-bellied, slack-shouldered, weak-kneed, or spineless humbugs and some all of the same. What was important then was that they'd had many reports of Uncle Alexander's antics at the Rocketage and our general mischief around town, and that they were both angry at us and intimidated by us or at least by the fact that we represented their failure to get back into space since Komarov's crash.

Uncle Dmitry knew better than they what they were afraid of— losing their jobs—and so he buried their suspicions with sudden camaraderie. He threw his arms wide to hug the much taller Faitelevitev and cried, "Father of the bride!" and "A good omen for all of us!" and other remarks meant not only to disarm the father but also to speak to Faitelevitev's powerful but dubious Proton booster. The ploy worked, and soon Uncle Dmitry and Uncle Konstantine had Faitelevitev happy and weepy enough to sing songs to love and luck. My uncles gathered us in a semicircle, facing the young couple, and led us in crooning some of the desert songs we'd learned, while the waiters poured and Uncle Konstantine fed wedding cake to Little Laika. The academicians stared at us as if we were the hired entertainment. No one should have been fooled by our blatant tactics, except that they were, and within a few rounds several of the chief rocketeers had drifted over to join in our songfest and to assure my uncles that we were great fellows, that this talk of a feud was just rumor-mongering, that they admired us and we'd make history together soon again. "To the moon!" my uncles toasted, and the rocketeers replied, "To the moon!"

I'm certain you can see now, as I couldn't see at all back then, that Star City's bosses and rocketeers were easily as puffed up as the Corps and were perhaps ahead of us a little in backstairs manipulation. Those academicians were as likely to double-cross the Corps as they were to lick our fingers, and what I should have learned at the wedding—which ended with ludicrous three-on-a-bottle drinking contests and Uncle Konstantine inviting several notorious courtesans in to dance for us and to please the old men—was that the men in charge of the Cosmodrome were a headless, fainthearted, rootbound clan of epicureans who would sooner risk their daughters than their jobs, and who would never get us to the moon unless the moon came down to Sputnik Street. And why were they such backsliders? At the time I couldn't fathom their inertia, but now I can try to make a case for them: Their master and mentor Sergei Korolev had built Star City, the Cosmodrome, Starry Town, and the Corps with a lifetime of toil (and not a few years in the camps as a slave), and what reward did he get for the R-7 and *Sputnik* and Gagarin but a heart attack while he was under anesthesia for hemorrhoid surgery, and what was his legacy but a grave in the Kremlin Wall and the drunken clattering of his beloved and pampered Corps, and why should the leaderless rocketeers he left behind throw away their lifetimes of career-climbing for an improbable climb into the heavens that could only bring more failure before it brought a single, fleeting success? My reply to this case for the rocketeers is the same as Uncle Alexander's—it was their duty to get us into space and to the moon, it was their job to finish the moon race they had helped start.

I hardly thought of the rocketeers or their duty at all back then. What I'd seen at the wedding were dusty old men who would either get out of my uncles' way or be removed by force, and I didn't care which. What I did care about was that my life as a cosmonaut candidate—as almost the top of the top—was a gift from God. I believe I even thought exactly this, a gift from God, though I was as uninformed about godliness as I was of the adultery I carried in my mind as well. Half my attention was for my pride of place, and the other half was for my longed-for possession of Katya. I aimed to conquer her just as if she were yet another new planet, and I told myself that the best way to confront her temper and doubts was to wait on the events that were certain to produce the moonship and the moon landing. I told myself that she would fall at my feet as the planets fell to my uncles' omnipotence.

That week was the most uninhibited I'd ever experienced as my friends and I raced all over the Cosmodrome in every available transport. We were boys in a great hurry to have fun at our duty, and we repeatedly took the autobus out to tour the Rocketage and the primary launchpad and to pester the rocketeers with trivial criticisms; we also rode around Star City in private cars and on motorbikes and one evening on camelback with several whores; we got flight time each morning in the squadron's 21s, roaming two hundred kilometers downrange to perform the usual cadet stunts. In the evenings, we called on many of the famous rocketeers we mocked by day and were introduced to the very handsome and well-to-do young women of the Russian quarter, who swooned over us as if we were cinema stars, though they weren't promiscuous like the Kazakh girls we saw later each evening. I did so many foolish things for the first time in my life that I felt as if I were dining on temptation as well as the best lamb dishes in Asia, but no, I was only carousing with falcons in their usual high jinks—the squadron falling back to its old wastrel ways—as we rubbed shoulders with gamblers, whoremongers, black marketeers, and camel traders, all of whom were happy to sell us anything on credit. Yes, it's true that I spent money on women, and on two different young women shamelessly. I suppose it's only right that I confess now that the Kazakh whores were unlike any women I'd known before, and I can't now say I've ever met such women again. They even smelled different from anyone I knew, and their notions of sexual intercourse were beastly, daunting, noisy, always muscular. What was left of my first swag after the women (my combined July and August salary was well over two thousand rubles, a fortune back then), I spent on keeping my friends in vodka, wine, koumiss, French cigarettes, and whatever else they wanted from the traders, while for myself I purchased, on credit, two tailored summer-weight uniforms, a richly lined greatcoat, and a perfect pair of handmade boots the equal of Uncle Alexander's. What it all came to was a week of joy, camaraderie, exhaustion, gorging, sex and more sex, and not a few long hours of the sort of weighty philosophizing boys like to do when they are fully attended and feeling higher than Steppe Eagles.

Our collective joy reached apogee Friday night with the rumor that the big bosses of the space program—the State Commission for Space Exploration—were flying down from Moscow the next morning for an open meeting with the rocketeers and the Corps. Suddenly everyone said that they'd known all along what my uncles were up to with their ranting and petting. My uncles, I was told, had known that the State Commission was under orders to get us back into space. My uncles had also known that the Czech crisis was easing, and so Doctor Mishuk's R-7 boosters would soon be released from State Security's tasks. The word was that the Corps was about to get its wings back and that my uncles had positioned themselves to be first in line for a mission. One rumor led to a dozen. The new talk my friends thought most likely was that the State Commission was coming down to give the new plum assignment to Uncle Dmitry, who would probably command a twinned Soyuz link-up mission to celebrate October Revolution Day. The rumor we laughed most over was that they were going to offer a Zond shot to Little Laika for a dog-around-the-moon spectacular.

Friday night the rumors became news as other senior members of the Corps started arriving at the Corps billet with news from Moscow. The Saturday meeting was definite, it was said, and Secretary Ustinov himself was coming down to oversee the debate and to deliver the decision of the Central Committee. Within hours the billet was ablaze with drink and talk, and it felt as if the Cosmonaut Corps had awakened from a long illness. All night, flight after flight of cosmonauts in their 21s roared out of all parts of Russia like a gathering of trailblazers come to claim their seats back into space. My friends and I watched Uncle Alexander break out of his pout long enough to greet the two other prominent cosmonaut leaders, Colonel Beregovoi and Lieutenant-Colonel Shatalov, and even to make some careful remarks about fraternity, which were not as honest as they might have been, since Uncle Alexander was not a man to share leadership. Uncle Dmitry made up for Uncle Alexander's moodiness by kissing Beregovoi and Shatalov welcome and speaking of all the tasks ahead requiring cooperation and teamwork. "All the darlings!" Uncle Konstantine kept shouting in the courtyard, "All the darlings!" and he would call out each of the fifty-two names of the Cosmonaut Corps so that no man, present or not, felt slighted by my uncles' apparent supremacy. The general spirit was that we were on the eve of a massive Russian invasion of space, and so it was the right time that the senior officers of the Corps agreed upon both their immediate and long-term ambitions.

The Corps' minimal demands, it was decided after an hour-long debate in the billet courtyard, were for a manned link-up of two Soyuzes in September and then for a Zond lunar fly-by in the October lunar window. The maximum demand was for my uncles' campaign for the moon landing. Amid back-pounding boasts and fist-pounding curses, the senior cosmonauts toasted the future, "The moonshot or hell!" and then Uncle Konstantine mangled a famous proverb, *"The bells toll often in Moscow, but not for supper, and not till you kick them yourself!"* We juniors were lightheaded, not only because we didn't sleep much that night, but also in anticipation of the next day's showdown: the Corps versus the bosses, with the stakes four hundred thousand kilometers overhead. I can remember dozing off in a chair on the terrace, not much before first light, with a fine view of the first quarter moon above me like a sickle-shaped talisman.

I'd like to report that Saturday was a success for my uncles and the Corps, and in truth it wasn't a defeat, more an augury of events ahead. It was another roasting day of intermittent dust storms hurtling across the yellow steppe, and in a filthy wind all fifty-two cosmonauts and a few supercargo like me marched in a body the kilometer from the billet on Sputnik Street to the Prelaunch and Launch Central Organization building on Korolev Square. Inside, the cosmonauts tossed their hats on a table and then strode into the lecture hall like paladins to join Corps commander General Kamenin and his personal staff. There were no rocketeers to be seen, so the Corps sat noisily in the hall for some time, trading remarks and smoking, as if we were an audience waiting on our lecturers. Eventually the bland little fellow Academician Yangel, the acting chief constructor of the Cosmodrome and the supposed boss of Star City, stepped out on the dais and, glancing at the Corps, he flapped his hands to usher in the other chief rocketeers from a side door. I was sitting on that side with my friends Stumpelkin, Miserbiev, and Adama-Bibliov, and we had a clear view not only of the sheepish rocketeers but also, back behind us, the calm faces of the senior cosmonauts, especially my uncles seated alongside of General Kamenin. It did look to be an unequal match: the Corps was about to condemn the rocketeers for all the delays and failures, and the rocketeers sat like the condemned.

After another few minutes, the side door opened again and the state commissioners and their staff strolled in as a pack. They did not look hesitant or intimidated, and the contest suddenly appeared to me more balanced. Along with assistants, lackeys, and runners, the Moscow delegation numbered over a dozen, but only three of them were critical to the debate that day. Sallow, miniature Blagonravov, sixty-eight, was chairman of the State Commission and therefore the government's spokesman and a laggardly toad whose task was to cheat and poor-mouth the Cosmodrome. Then there was silver-maned and elegant Keldysh, fifty-six, who was president of the Academy of Sciences and whose future depended upon more successes from the Cosmodrome. Finally there was the stern, bulbous Ustinov, then sixty-two, who was a secretary of the Central Committee and a candidate member of the Politburo and therefore the de facto boss of the entire space program, from Starry Town to Star City, the politician whose word settled all debates by fiat.

Air Force officers never wait. Once Ustinov had settled down, Corps commander General Kamenin raised his mighty rooster's head and offered a general challenge to the bosses on the dais. "We'd best begin this, and we'll not waste our breath on summaries. We'll be brief."

The gauntlet was thrown, and Chairman Blagonravov could only grab his chin and duck. President Keldysh tried his patrician charm, waving the cigarette holder in his hand and arguing, "General, it's not that bad. We're all on the same side."

Several of the cosmonauts cried, "Our backsides!" and then the Corps en masse laughed out like an ultimatum. I could see that the larger Corps could behave as arrogantly as my uncles and the squadron, and that there might not be anyone in the room concerned with peacemaking, not even Uncle Dmitry.

Chairman Blagonravov must have understood that even his authority was useless, and he started to whine, "Comrades, please, we're here to gather the facts necessary in order to make measured recommendations on the future of the workers of Star City."

General Kamenin didn't respond, instead nodding toward my uncles, "Get it said, Colonels."

My friends and I had to stand to see over the cosmonauts now on their feet between us and my uncles, who were grouped at the center of the room with both Beregovoi and Shatalov—the five senior cosmonauts surrounding General Kamenin like pillars. And yet I doubt if there was anyone who didn't know it would be Uncle Alexander who spoke for all of us.

"What we have is a job," Uncle Alexander began from his seat, his arms crossed and his head down. "It's our job," he mumbled, "to drive what you give us and to drive it as far and fast as we can." He mumbled so deeply into his collar that he sounded under water, but by then, the hall was his; he could have blinked his speech, and we would have understood him.

President Keldysh tried a sly appeal to interrupt Uncle Alexander's polemic. "You're the best we'll ever see, Colonel Oryolin. Your philosophy is irrefutable."

Uncle Alexander countered, "We don't think about it, we do it." The Corps snorted, and that was the last we'd hear that day of the so-called humanitarian benefits of space travel. Uncle Alexander added, "And we do it now."

Secretary Ustinov leaned forward and spoke back as bluntly as Uncle Alexander. "What is it you want, Colonel Oryolin? Say it, and let us decide when and if you can have it."

I believe now that here was the turning point. Everyone wanted Uncle Alexander to give them a goal they could reach. The rocketeers wanted a little flattery, just a hint of appreciation would have satisfied them, and then they would have eagerly rewarded the Corps with as many boosters and spacecraft as Uncle Alexander asked. For their part, Chairman Blagonravov and President Keldysh wanted to please the Corps too; they wanted to find a deal everyone could accept and applaud; they wanted the Corps happy and fat and no longer dangerous to their careers. All Uncle Alexander would have had to do was to ask for a Soyuz command for himself or Uncle Dmitry or Uncle Konstantine—just say that he wanted to assign the missions himself—and the state commissioners would have been relieved to reward everyone. It won't surprise you to learn that Uncle Alexander wouldn't have anything to do with flattery, deal-making, or happiness. I don't think there was mediation or negotiation in him, and I'm sure I never heard him mention concession. I could say that he had an extreme temperament, but that doesn't fully color his wrath. Uncle Alexander was a man who would not settle. What he showed me that day was that when a hero commits to a task, when a hero decides to drive, what he says is not rhetorical, it's truthful to him, he means it. And soon enough I would also see that when a hero starts to move, when the attack is launched, a hero doesn't know how to stop, he might not be able to stop, and he will very likely go too far.

"No more of this," Uncle Alexander answered Secretary Ustinov. "We want Tsar Cannon!"

Even though the Corps might have expected the demand, it was still stunned; and it was a moment before the cosmonauts started to join in a chant: "Tsar Cannon!" "The moon!" "The moon's ours!"

Yes, I'd heard this before, and yes, it wasn't a true surprise, but still to hear the fairy tale spoken aloud was a thrill. Uncle Alexander with one demand had swept aside the quibbling rocketeers, called the bluff of the state commissioners, and ignited the spirits of the Corps. I wanted more than thrills however: I wanted the facts of Tsar Cannon, and I leaned to Stumpelkin to ask, "Is this the day?" Stumpelkin shushed me, and Miserbiev held up his hand to silence me as Secretary Ustinov stood at his chair.

I thought something was going to happen—I mean something unambivalent and momentous—and I laugh now at what a child I was in the world of politics. Secretary Ustinov said nothing; he just turned and walked off the dais as casually as a man going to the W.C. What I saw was the end of the big showdown. In just four minutes the negotiation had turned into a stalemate—the irresistible Corps and the immovable State Space Commission—and in another few minutes the lesser bosses started to withdraw after their master Ustinov, off to another room to decide everything out of our earshot. The Corps behaved badly in response by standing, clapping, stomping, cheering, "Ooray for Tsar Cannon! Ooray for Oryolin!" and other hosannas, so that soon our celebration was transformed into an open taunt of the rocketeers still on the stage. They scattered through the several rear doors, leaving a brutally hot room in the possession of four dozen exuberant cosmonauts shouting, "Moonship! Moonship!"

I don't now think any one of us believed we could have the moon all at once—I can't believe even my uncles thought they could get it all in one leap—and so it wasn't a sharp setback to hear the State Commission's verdict after supper that night at the billet. The Corps was granted a dollop of its demands, with two R-7 boosters and two Soyuzes for an October link-up mission in earth orbit: *Soyuz 2* was scheduled as an unmanned orbital flight; *Soyuz 3* was scheduled for twenty-four hours later—a lone pilot to fly a rendezvous and docking mission with the *Soyuz 2* robot target. The insult was the pilot assignment. Uncle Dmitry, first in seniority on the list, was passed over, and instead Colonel Beregovoi was chosen as primary for *Soyuz 3* and Colonel Shatalov was chosen as backup. There was no mention of future missions, such as the Zond fly-by of the moon, so there was no way to mitigate the assumption that my uncles were being punished for their campaign for the moon landing.

My friends and I climbed on the billet roof that night to argue about the verdict. We were very disheartened by the news and at the same time bothered by the fact that the bulk of the Corps was celebrating the results. The general opinion was that the Corps had won something from the showdown with the State Commission; at the least the Corps was going back into orbit after a year and a half of idling. The billet courtyard was a gala reception for the lucky chosen cosmonauts, Beregovoi and Shatalov, and nearby Sputnik Street was lined by whores, black marketeers, gamblers, and other hangers-on happy to have the Corps back in town to spend money.

Yet we juniors hung back from the festivities as if they were a betrayal of my uncles. Our argument went in circles, each of us trying to outdo the other in cynicism. Stumpelkin complained, "Why'd Colonel Oryolin let them treat him like that? They're scared of him. Anyone can see it." Adama-Bibliov replied, "We're on the launchpad again, aren't we? It's more than we had last week. If anyone has been wronged, it's Colonel Zhukovsky." Miserbiev observed that, from what he'd seen the last week, the Cosmodrome was ready to go back into space but not onto the moon. "I haven't seen any evidence that they're serious about a moonshot," he said. "I think it might be smart to take what we can get for now. The low orbital missions now and maybe a high orbital station later."

The night wind flicked the cinders of their cigarettes around us like fireflies and made us look like four boys cut off from the fun below by a web of sparks. I felt so disappointed, especially by what Miserbiev said, since it was something I'd been thinking too, that I protested like a miniature Uncle Alexander: "We didn't come here for earth orbit. We came here for the moonship!" I controlled myself and tried, "You told me it's out there." I went on in the same whining manner for some time and then challenged them by pointing out into the desert. "Now either you've been teasing me, or we're on course for the moon, and Tsar Cannon's out there, and it's waiting for us."

Just then I heard that familiar mumbly voice from behind. "Exactly right, Lieutenant," Uncle Alexander began. He'd come up to smoke his pipe and brood. Since he'd removed his dress tunic coat and wrapped himself with a cotton shawl of some sort, he didn't carry himself with his usual severe military self, more like a parent or guardian.

Stumpelkin was the first to salute. "Good evening, sir!" I waited for the others to ask Uncle Alexander the obvious question about what he'd meant when he said I was exactly right; and when none of them did, instead bending their heads in respect, I swelled myself up and asked a direct question: "Excuse me, sir, is it out there? What you said today? About Tsar Cannon? Can't you tell us now? Does it exist?"

Uncle Alexander asked back, "Do you believe it?"

I answered, "I want to believe it, sir."

"Finish it," he said, a typical Uncle Alexanderism that sounded definite and final but usually confounded me and just confused the situation the more. I guessed that he wanted me to finish my thoughts. "I'll believe it when I see it, sir. When can we see it?"

Uncle Alexander lit his pipe with a big brass lighter and, just when I thought he was going to tell me something, he walked away. Within moments he was on the other side of the roof, lost in the blackness and, I thought, probably in his black thoughts. I was wrong about this: what I saw was a man on the eve of an advance. But then there was very little I understood about Uncle Alexander in those days.

My friends understood that I'd been impertinent, yet they were as eager as I to know the truth. "What did he say?" Adama-Bibliov asked. Miserbiev grinned and, standing straight-backed in imitation of Uncle Alexander, also imitated his mumbly style, " 'Finish it' is what he said."

Miserbiev's impression was funny, and we laughed in hushed guffaws. Stumpelkin wouldn't have it and, looking in the direction Uncle Alexander had walked, growled in defense of his idol, "Tsar Cannon is out there, sure it is, and he said he's going to finish it."

"But what does that mean?" Adama-Bibliov asked.

I was annoyed with my friends. They'd introduced me to the Tsar Cannon game, and now they wanted me to solve it for them. "If it's true about Tsar Cannon," I told them in a petulant whisper, "you wouldn't know it by what the colonel says. I guess you either have to believe it or not, and I believe it, and that's the finish for me." Not even I was satisfied with this, and I brooded alone that night, trying to penetrate Uncle Alexander's nature. What did "Finish it" mean? Was I to finish something, was the squadron, was the Corps? I'm still not sure.

What it might have meant was that the next day, Sunday, September 1, 1968, was the end of the waiting for the moonship. We spent the morning packing our kits for a return to Starry Town and engaging in more of our self-pitying confabs. And then after luncheon, about 1400 hours, Misha Cherryntevsky, the squadron's meaty little mother hen, called us juniors together in the billet's common room, where he announced, "No commotion, boys, just get onto the bus and keep your yaps shut." We assumed Cherryntevsky meant we were bound for the airfield and a long flight home, yet when challenged he explained, "It's Tsar Cannon. There's a test tonight. We've got invitations. The Grand Constructor himself's invited us." After having to repeat himself several times because we thought he was teasing us, Cherryntevsky admitted, "Yeah, it's a big show, a hurry-up. Colonel Zhukovsky said hush-hush. I say, move it!" And still we demanded to know more. Where were our colonels? What was going to happen? What sort of test—static, orbital?

Cherryntevsky couldn't control us, and so he called upstairs for help from Zhora Fedyuninsky, the squadron's executive officer when my uncles were absent. As usual Fedyuninsky was dressed in a uniform that never wrinkled, and as usual he treated us like tiresome schoolboys. "Is it a picture you want drawn?" he asked us. Since they were only nominally our seniors and had no actual authority unless we granted it, we resisted right up until Cherryntevsky bartered that he'd tell us what we wanted to know if we'd hurry onto the autobus and out to the field. Not even this could hold us, and we made certain every bystander we passed knew that we were being taken against our will to a secret test of a secret rocket at a secret site. Eventually Fedyuninsky and Cherryntevsky did have to answer our questions: Yes, we were flying out to the test site in a Il-14 prop that Artzybashev and Kandidim had secured for us with their gambling winnings. Yes, my uncles had gone on ahead in a Mil sent specially for them from the test site. Yes, we were to be on our best behavior tonight, put the bottles away, because the State Commission and the rocket chiefs were also attending. Yes, the test was scheduled after nightfall, because of State Security concerns about American spy satellites. And no, Cherryntevsky said, there was no truth to the rumor that Little Laika was launching tonight.

We were incorrigible while we settled into the Il-14 (a thirty-year-old prop that smelled of contraband whiskey and wine), tossing bottles and sausages back and forth across the cabin and reverting to our well-established patterns: Glavtop and Grin took over the flight deck with two of their Kazakh girlfriends, Schtange and Tevyelook restarted their eternal chess game, Artzybashev and Kandidim began calculating where they could obtain decent interior fittings for this new acquisition, and Cherryntevsky brought out his guitar and led with a new and smutty desert song that worked in mention of the fairy tale of Tsar Cannon. My friends and I sat back beneath the portals and laughed at everything as the Il-14 bumped and rolled and was then hard airborne. I recall my thoughts exactly because that night was the summit of my boyish fantasy. I believed everything I'd ever heard about my uncles. They were awesome, indomitable, the cleverest, smartest, luckiest falcons on earth, and this was true even before they got us to the moon. Katya was in my thoughts too, since she was the embodiment of Alexander-doubting, and I convinced myself that she'd misunderstood my uncles, and that she'd believe in them too as soon as I convinced her that her grandfather was the way to the moon and my uncles were the men to drive her grandfather's Tsar Cannon.

The Tsar Cannon test site was about a twenty-minute hop northeast from the Star City airfield. When we banked on the landing approach, what I saw below was most unimpressive: a single short runway, an operations shack, a fuel tank farm, and a handful of vehicles. There was a single-track rail spur that looped five kilometers across a cracked salt field to a patchy oasis. The oasis was actually a Kazakh village on a caravan trek, and it was now expanded greatly by a line of tents and tin huts. Beyond the tents were several ramshackle barns, and farther along were four giant man-made mounds arranged in a circle. My first thought was that we must have much farther to travel, since this couldn't be a rocket test site, an average desert wind might bury it. In fact, this was the whole of it, and the sod and skin-built Kazakh village of camel traders and goat herders not only was the housing and provisioning for the rocketeers, but also, as Katya had said of her grandfather, was the Grand Constructor's slave labor pool and the reason the fabled Tsar Cannon had survived for so long on so little state funding.

We glided to a perfect landing—Glavtop and Grin flew like mathematics—and deplaned in a rush, shouting, "Start the count!" and fanning out in the yellow dust to strike conquering poses just in case history had a camera. The treat of our arrival was that I met for the first time Research Assistant Isaacii Goldenberg, my dear friend Isaacii, and, though I knew him the rest of my life, whenever I would look at him over the decades we worked side by side, I often thought of that first night on the steppe and the childlike grandeur in his face. I think of Isaacii now, and it makes me feel blessed to have known him; he was a treasure of a man, a true pioneer, and if he'd been born American or European or even Asian he would very likely have risen to the stature of a Zeppelin or Goddard, and even if he'd been born in a Russia that didn't shame itself with anti-Semitism and the tragedy of the Communist Party he could have succeeded to a mark equal to Korolev's in the space program. I'm speaking as if Isaacii failed, and that's far from true; for that day he began the first of his many great deeds when he met us with a tiny autobus and a huge speech about what he called the most critical night in aerospace engineering. "Sirs! Sirs!" he called us. "Tonight we're cluster firing the RD-300s!" he pronounced. "He is the Grand Constructor, and we're cluster firing for a ninety-second test!" At twenty-five, Isaacii Goldenberg was an awkward, long-haired, near-sighted, excitable stick of a man. He was also the Grand Constructor's gifted protégé and major worshipper, and his opening remarks to us were colored by impassioned numbers: "Tsar Cannon has seven thousand metric tons of thrust! The core stage is sixty-two meters high and twenty-four meters across with the fins. It weighs . . ."

We were roaring at him by then. It was rude to laugh at him, but then, the notion of this high-pitched genius trying to teach us aerospace engineering or anything at all was hilarious. The squadron was about as studious as Little Laika. Artzybashev jumped to the front of the bus and immediately began an impression of Goldenberg's enthusiasm, solemnity, and gangliness, and we laughed so hard that even Goldenberg realized his lecture was useless. Soon enough I'd learn—we all would—that Goldenberg had a backbone the equal of any glamorous falcon's, and he showed a hint of his steadfastness by keeping on with his talk over our mockery.

"Sirs! Sirs!" Goldenberg announced as the bus cleared the rail spur and dashed into the oasis, and then he started again with his lecture as if we could follow him. It wasn't that we were stupid; it was that we thought of ourselves as drivers, not engineers and definitely not scientists, and so what we wanted to know about anything that flew was when and how, not why. Our bus passed through sheep and goat herds and about a thousand chickens, and then there was a drove of children waving for us to throw them treats from the windows, and still Goldenberg shouted, "Sirs! Sirs!" and kept up his technical discourse. We bounced across a rail spur where the Kazakh menfolk looked to be holding a camel auction, or perhaps they were just smoking after supper, and Goldenberg never stopped talking. We passed through the oasis and headed into the man-made mounds. "That's the rack, sirs," Goldenberg told us. "The count's at fifty-eight hours, and the Grand Constructor's holding it for our guests!"

At last we had arrived at a marvel that made us shut up and gaze in respect. The man-made mounds formed a broad shallow bowl that was misty with liquid oxygen and crowded with kerosene tanker cars and globe-shaped LOX tanks. At the center of the bowl were the concrete pillars and crossed girders of the static test stand that Goldenberg called the rack, and in the midst of the pillars, like a giant child in a swing, were the core and strap-on stages of Tsar Cannon— the superbooster from the waist down. The whole layout was all so big to see that Goldenberg's statistics didn't help me comprehend it. "Seven thousand metric tons of thrust," Goldenberg repeated himself, and there might have been some spite to the way he recited his numbers as we gawked and shook our heads, "and each of the twelve RD-300 engines weighs more than an R-7 with payload."

I could taste the LOX cloud like a topping on the kerosene stench. I counted and recounted Tsar Cannon's nine strap-on tail fins just to make sure I was seeing the same superbooster each time I looked. My thoughts were that nothing that big could fly. I asked Stumpelkin, "Did you really believe it was as big as this? I know you believed it was out here, but did you know it was so big?" Stumpelkin sighed in return, and I sighed back, and soon Miserbiev and Adama-Bibliov were sighing too, and we were all acting disoriented by the apparent contrasts of the galactic future and primitive past. The rocketeers climbing the rack were wrapped in rough dark cotton and looked like lumberjacks scrambling over the greatest tree in Asia; the Kazakh laborers were using camels to raise and lower the rack's lifts; and the village dogs were circling the LOX clouds and snapping at them as if they were ghosts.

The bus passed through to the other side of the mounds and stopped at the foot of a concrete command blockhouse erected at the crest of a mound. Behind the blockhouse, the rocketeers had prepared for the arrival of VIPs by raising a pavilion tent over a wooden deck and laying out tables of food and drink. Other than the village children we were the first guests to arrive, and Goldenberg ushered us off the bus like a cheery host. "Sirs! Help yourselves, sirs." For once the squadron moderated itself by choosing to drink just tea and that noxious desert coffee. The children came closer, and we started handing out fruit and sweets, while Cherryntevsky fetched his guitar to serenade the children. However it was another molten late afternoon in the middle of a wilderness, and soon the only relief from the sun was the tent and the pepper and lemon vodka bottles and pitchers of Armenian wine. Goldenberg pretended not to notice that so many cosmonauts were behaving so unprofessionally, and soon he excused himself gently, promising us, "The Grand Constructor welcomes you all, sirs. He'll be with you soon, sirs!"

We gave the tables of food over to the children and then out came the chessboards, cards, and usual paraphernalia, and the squadron settled down as if Tsar Cannon weren't just over the mounds. My friends Stumpelkin, Miserbiev, and Adama-Bibliov were more serious by half than all of the rest. We risked the heat and chugged up the mound to get a look down on the rack. We really needed Goldenberg to answer our fundamental questions, such as "What does seven thousand metric tons of thrust mean for a payload?" Miserbiev was the closest we had to a brain, and in his know-it-all way he calculated vaguely, "It can boost one hundred and fifty metric tons into low earth orbit, give or take, depending upon what they use for the upper stages, approximately—I guess."

Adama-Bibliov mocked his wingman, "Give or take nothing. That's impossible. Do you know how much that is?"

"It's one hundred and fifty tons," Miserbiev answered back, and then he tried to delight us the more with another crude calculation. "It's also about, give or take, seventy-five tons into lunar orbit, approximately."

None of us would accept this—it was just too much to believe all at once—so we waved to get the attention of Tima Schtange and Vasya Tevyelook, the only reliable engineers in the squadron. They broke off their chess game to climb up to us, and after we had outlined Miserbiev's claims they shrugged and nodded. "If they use high-energy fuels on the upper stage, it'll be more," Schtange said.

Miserbiev crowed, "I told you!"

Tevyelook pointed back southwest toward Star City. "If they use the Proton for the third stage, which is what they've always proposed, it'll be less, much less. Seventy-five is a high number."

Now we all were confused again, and even Miserbiev sought help, "Please, translate that for us."

"As you said," replied Schtange, "seventy-five tops for an LOR." Tevyelook finished, "And fifty-five at the very least for an LOR."

They were speaking in astronautical jargon, but what they said was critical. I watched a camel lumber up the side of the mound— they were clearing out the blast area—while I tried to calculate in my head what fifty-five to seventy-five metric tons represented. I knew the three-man Soyuz spacecraft weighed up to six metric tons at liftoff, and though I didn't know how much more a landing craft would weigh, I supposed at least half again and added three tons. My best guess was that the fuel supply would raise the combined weight of the whole payload to somewhere between forty and fifty metric tons. But these were all just numbers to me, and I didn't feel confident of anything just then; I wanted it said aloud. I asked, "But is it enough for the landing?" This was what we were all thinking, and my friends grinned in relief. "Easy," Schtange said. "By all means," Tevyelook said.

I tried once more, "Is it the moonship?"

Our laughter was the answer, and the answer was affirmative. Tsar Cannon was the largest launch vehicle ever conceived, almost twice the size and power required to thrust a lunar orbital rendezvous mission (LOR) with a three-man Soyuz and a moon lander. What we saw before us in a torrid veil of LOX and kerosene fumes was the fundamental platform for driving the moon.

Soon after, our excitement was drowned out by a heavy Mil that flew low over the rack and settled down the slope from the pavilion, where the pilot flopped near a stand of saxual trees, scattering sparrows and nightjars and dogs. It was the State Space Commission come to oversee the static test, and the bosses emerged from the Mil cabin looking hot and edgy. We noted right away that among the civilians were a number of general officers of the Rocket Forces led by Colonel-General Krylov and his chief of staff. This turned out to be a significant detail for the Grand Constructor's schemes that night, though at the time we were offended that our Air Force command, no less the Cosmonaut Corps command, had been left off the guest list. The VIPs moved in a herd up to the pavilion. The cosmonauts set aside their games, downed their drinks, put out their cigarettes, and even the desert children seemed to understand that the grownups had arrived and it was time to quiet down. Nearly simultaneously my uncles emerged from the command blockhouse in company with all the senior Tsar Cannoneers. The two groups closed on each other, suggesting another confrontation, so my friends and I slid around the side to try to eavesdrop. Uncle Konstantine and Uncle Dmitry were close beside Doctor Mstislav Lunin, the trim, hairless, goggle-eyed deputy chief of Tsar Cannon, and just behind them like a bride and groom were Uncle Alexander and Academician Nikhon Univer, whom everyone called the Grand Constructor, so I will too. My first reaction to him was disbelief, because at eighty-two, dressed severely in loose black breeches, an undyed sack tunic, a coarse wool duster, and a black forage cap, with a face dominated by a patchy white beard and steel-rimmed eyeglasses, the Grand Constructor looked like a caricature of a Bolshevik revolutionary, as if he'd been clipped out of a motion picture of the early days at the Smolny Institute or on Red Square. I know now that he looked exactly as he had since at least the 1905 Revolution—forbidding, inflexible, iron-handed—because, in addition to being an aeronautical pioneer and a rocket genius, he was also one of the last living fathers of the socialist state and therefore a tyrannical, slave-mongering, and not infrequently hate-filled fanatic.

I took my first lesson of his fanaticism at the pavilion. As the state commissioners neared my uncles and the Grand Constructor, one of the bosses said something insulting. It sounded to me no more rude than "Who invited them!" but it might have been rougher. Uncle Alexander pulled up and, just when it looked as if he would rant at the State Commission, the Grand Constructor overcalled him with his own cunning tantrum.

"This is my machine!" he shouted in that high-pitched voice of his, like a man in a permanent fit. "This is the finest machine ever built, and I'll do what I want with it, and if I want to shit on you with it, I'll do that too!" Some of the state commissioners tried to reassure the Grand Constructor that all was well. I couldn't hear enough of the fawning remarks to make sense of them, but I could see Blagonravov and Keldysh bowing beseechingly. The Grand Constructor kept up his fusillade of abuse. "Shit and fire!" he shouted back at one compliment offered him. "Devil mount your mother!" he shouted at another. And then he called out shrilly, "My machine is the greatest moment of your spineless lives, so squeeze your assholes tight and shut up!"

I suppose it would have been a farcical performance if the Grand Constructor had seemed more in control of his temper, but he was so vulgar, and everyone around him was so cowed, that the scene seemed very wrong. I mean by this that an eighty-two-year-old man in a sordid rage appears both mad and vicious, and from what I know now to be true about Nikhon Univer, both findings apply. Like the Revolution that had raised him up, the Grand Constructor had outlived justice. To be near him felt as if you were in the company of a bully; to trade on his undeniable genius felt as if you were dealing with a cold-blooded slave trader; to assist him felt as if you were somehow accommodating a man as soulless as Tsar Cannon.

The unexplained argument closed with a few squeaks from Blagonravov. The Grand Constructor took hold of Uncle Alexander's arm and ordered Doctor Lunin, "Make a little shit and fire with my machine!" and then he ejaculated a raw, piercing "ha-ha-ha!" All of us, the commissioners, Tsar Cannoneers, and lastly we cosmonauts, filed into the command blockhouse. My friends and I found a corner where we could be out of the way of so many sweating potentates and yet still see the rack. There was a moment inside to question Goldenberg about the argument, and while he didn't answer us directly or adequately, he did allow there had been some hard words because General Krylov had told the commissioners that he didn't think the blockhouse was secure. Goldenberg was apologetic and very grave. "We fell short of funds," he said. "We actually didn't fall short, we just ran out last year." He waved at the blockhouse, and it was a sorry structure—naked wiring and missing wallboards and the fetid smell of weary men and bad tobacco—and then he waved at the state commissioners. "We need whatever money they can give us," he said. "We don't need it for salaries or such as that, just for parts. We're out of everything."

Miserbiev solved the puzzle and laughed. "You're saying this bunker isn't safe, aren't you? That we're in a shack right next to a kerosene bomb?"

Goldenberg nodded and showed the first sign he had a sense of humor about his employer. "He is the Grand Constructor, but even the Grand Constructor can't do without insulated cables and good steel."

In those first days it could seem that Goldenberg was a blind adorer of a despot, yet in truth Goldenberg was not indifferent to the Grand Constructor's many faults; and in later times he would admit to me that it was often impossible to explain away the exploitation that he had to oversee as the master's apprentice. That night Goldenberg's halfhearted explanation about the blockhouse didn't reassure Adama-Bibliov, who argued with Goldenberg about the sloppy building materials while Miserbiev probed for details about the costs. I listened in, but the most I understood was that using the Kazakhs eliminated the largest costs. This was a dishonest way of admitting that the Tsar Cannon site was less a brave scientific outpost than a slave labor camp. Goldenberg understood that Adama-Bibliov was making a moral argument—I'd learn later that Adama-Bibliov was one of several cosmonauts with relatives who'd perished in Stalin's camps—and it wasn't long before Goldenberg argued back with some punch: "If we'd spent the way they do in Star City, we'd've been shut down three years ago. We've done what we had to. And if it wasn't for the Grand Constructor, all that you'd see would be dust. Would that make it better, that we were testing dust tonight?"

At the center of the blockhouse the Grand Constructor continued to harangue the state commissioners. I watched his posturing and thought about Katya's remarks that her grandfather was a liar and despot, and I acknowledged that what she'd said had some truth. I also acknowledged that it wasn't for me to judge such men—the Grand Constructor seemed more an archetype than a real man anyway—and that if one started to judge the space program on the basis of virtue then everyone was at fault. What was to be done with the facts that the command blockhouse was no better than a roost on a catastrophe, that the test site itself had been built next door to a helpless village of women and children? Weren't thousands of lives at risk in a gamble to win funds from Moscow so that the Tsar Cannoneers could take even more risks in future? I didn't even ask these questions, nor did any of the squadron care about them beyond a technical curiosity. It was as if we were all wordlessly agreed that driving the moon didn't need and probably couldn't stand up to common sense.

Soon enough a loudspeaker announcement from the firing house silenced the crowd: "This is Test Control. We are at eight minutes and resuming the count. Status board is clear. We are now at eight minutes and counting. Automatic sequencing. Our status board is clear."

The Grand Constructor turned from badgering the VIPs to berating his rocketeers at their console stations: "You bastards, get it right this time!" Doctor Lunin, who was running the test from the master console, signaled the rocketeers to continue, and indeed everyone carried on normally, either used to such abuse or just too weary to react. I positioned myself so that I could get up on my toes to peer through the slit in the wall above the command console. What I could see a kilometer below us, as the last desert light turned the LOX clouds a purplish gray, was that the rocketeers had already cleared the test site of lorries, tankers, and camels. The vapors had cleared the birds from their nests in the gantry. They sealed the blast doors at the firing house at the foot of the rack, and then a klaxon blared out rhythmically in order to empty the blast zone of every living thing above spiders. The loudspeaker noted, "Two minutes and counting. We are transferring to internal power. Status board is clear." Stumpelkin and I started laughing together. I might not have emphasized the fun of those days enough, so I want now to make sure you understand that there were moments when going to the moon was nothing but fun: despite all the lying and stupidity, regardless of the brutality and waste, there was never anything like those countdowns to make you laugh and tremble.

As they sealed the command blockhouse blast door, the Grand Constructor started to scold his men again in his high-pitched whine. Everything about him was irritating—I've called him a force, but he was also an obnoxious noise—and I suppose that if he hadn't been such a phenomenon he would have been a pest. He could build boosters, and he could hire first-rate rocketeers to help him, and those who worked for him were devoted; I suppose this and this alone was why the bosses coddled him and we needed him. As a weaponeer the Grand Constructor owned the secrets to the mightiest gun in the cosmos, and as a rocketeer he owned the moonship; yet as a human being he was a loveless and truly deplorable old man who, except for the firm faith of Isaacii Goldenberg, would die unloved and unmourned.

When the loudspeaker noted, "Test control at T minus fifty seconds. Clear. We are on internal power. Status is ready to fire," we all pulled down the goggles they'd given us and plugged our ears with beeswax. I divided my attention between watching the rack and watching Uncle Alexander, who stood there like a blazing bronze of himself.

The last seconds of the countdown were ominous, and I enjoyed each tick: "This is test control. We're counting down from twenty. T minus thirty seconds and clear. Clear. T minus twenty, nineteen, eighteen, seventeen, sixteen, fifteen, fourteen—all clear—ten, nine—ignition sequence starting—five, four—we have ignition, all engines running."

At ignition, red-and-yellow flames filled up and ran over the firing pit amid a cannonade of thunderclaps, and then almost instantly a man-made waterfall doused the rack's steel pinions so that a superheated torrent swirled up over the superstructure and hid the booster. Once the countdown reached lift-off, the dozen RD-300 engines were at full power to begin a fight against their imprisonment within the rack, and the contest was so equal that the thunder of the rocket thrust became a deep booming and shaking that made the blockhouse roll as if rippled by an earthquake. Tsar Cannon was trying to tear the desert out so that it could escape atop an upside-down volcano measuring seven-point-one thousand metric tons of thrust. The rocket quake flowed and flowed, and the heat waves lapped the blockhouse. It felt as if we were being tormented by fire and knout for thirty seconds, then a minute, then two and a half minutes, and then it ebbed as Doctor Lunin shouted, "Mark, ending mark!"

On command the flames folded, the steam cloud lifted like a tornado, the kerosene stench flooded the blockhouse, and the loudspeaker announced, "Shutdown at one-five-zero seconds." By then it was human cheers that were rocking the blockhouse as state commissioners, Rocket Force officers, and cosmonauts pounded their hands together, cheering and sweating. The Grand Constructor stood like a maestro come out for a curtain call, and he even managed to weep for us as he bowed and smiled and took credit for all behind him and all before him, a man who could rise from vulgarity to grandiosity without pause. Secretary Ustinov stepped forward to shake the Grand Constructor's hands and certify that the State Commission was now taking charge of funding a gigantic state success.

Stumpelkin and I moved over to be near my uncles. Uncle Konstantine was dancing with Little Laika, and Uncle Dmitry was hugging Doctor Lunin, yet Uncle Alexander was strangely still, the only one to stand off from the celebration. I was too happy to keep my distance and dared to put out my hand to him in congratulation. He responded formally. His gaze remained faraway in that detached manner of his.

Stumpelkin crowded in beside me and cried, "The moonship, sir, she drives!"

I tried to sound bolder, "Did you know Tsar Cannon was out here, sir? Did you know it was going to work?"

Uncle Alexander answered my questions in order, "It was always out here, and it was always going to work."

"But, sir," I pressed, "did you know all the time it was out here? All week, sir, did you know they were going to invite us here?"

Uncle Alexander ignored my foolish question—of course he'd known, of course he'd campaigned not for an R-7 or a Proton but for Tsar Cannon—and then he told me something much more important about the Grand Constructor and the future: "Without us, they've got no more than the steppe. With us, they've got the moon." He looked hard at me the way he did when he was candid. "The Grand Constructor needs us, Lieutenant, as much as we need him. Understand?"

"Yes, sir," I returned. I didn't understand yet that he'd just told me that he and the Grand Constructor were the same sort of unforgiving zealots, and that the both of them would forfeit any and all of us to get to the moon.

The celebration moved out to the pavilion, where Uncle Konstantine took charge like a royal fool to lead us in dancing, drinking, and howling at the moon, all of which made Laikushka yap and howl genuinely. I recall my three uncles standing together larger-than-life, like men who have just had their dreams come true. Stumpelkin bumped me in order to communicate that he spied their joy, too, and I think now it must have been then that we became bosom friends just because we both realized we shared the same vision of my uncles and yearned to be just like them, to be just like our godhead Alexander Oryolin. Stumpelkin told me, "We're lucky, Peter, aren't we, to be here?" I wanted to say, "Yes, we're lucky," but I held back and said nothing. What stopped me was that I also heard my Great-Uncle Lev's voice reminding me that "All Russia is fate." I knew this meant that it wasn't luck that had delivered us Tsar Cannon, it was fate, and I knew how fragile this made our luck and all our dreams.

It's time to get on to the rot of my story, and so I shouldn't linger at the one clean moment of triumph, the Tsar Cannon test, but still, recalling the flames and thunderclaps now makes some of the rot I have to tell sufferable. No, it doesn't. I'm wrong, no, nothing makes me tolerate the rot any more now than I did then. *Backwardness* was Uncle Alexander's word for the rot, and I think now that he was right, because backwardness fit what I saw exactly, the rot of Russian backwardness. It's not for me to forgive it or forget it or even to explain it. Nonetheless fate was busy at work that night. The fate of Tsar Cannon was that the State Commission for Space Exploration granted the Grand Constructor the funds he needed to build a vertical assembly barn, a first-rate launch facility, and several operational boosters, though how many boosters wasn't fixed, since the Grand Constructor knew how to use money meanly and conspiratorially. It was certain that the Kazakh labor camp was going to grow and that the oasis was going to blossom. The fate of my uncles was that the Grand Constructor granted them his machine. He wasn't generous about it; he didn't give Tsar Cannon away because my uncles were famous. The Grand Constructor was also the Grand Pinch-Penny and established scrupulous terms for the contract between the Corps and the Tsar Cannoneers. The central requirement was that the Corps had until spring—six to nine months—to demonstrate that it could man-rate the Soyuz and achieve the rendezvous and link-up necessary for a LOR and moon landing. If not, if the Corps wasted its time with lesser missions or failed to achieve the critical link-up, then the Grand Constructor said he would turn Tsar Cannon over to the Corps' chief competitors for such a superbooster, either to General Krylov and the Rocket Forces to launch an earth orbital bomber or to Academician Sinebrykhov to launch a space station.

There was humbug in the Grand Constructor's deal. Tsar Cannon was not only colossal, it was also colossally useless. The Rocket

Forces had no such orbital bomber to launch and never would have, and the rocketeers at the Cosmodrome were a decade from any orbital platform and would never design a payload that needed seven million metric tons of thrust. The Grand Constructor was making the only deal that could ever come to success: it was either the Corps and the moon landing or it was laughingstock on the yellow steppe. There was something disingenuous in my uncles' deal as well, for they were promising more than they could control to a despot who cared nothing for the Corps and little for the moon, who cared only for his own reputation and how he could expand it even beyond death. But this is to look back on those days with the prerogative of the future, and I don't want to erase the pleasure of the Tsar Cannon test just yet. I want to remember happily my view of my uncles huddling with the Grand Constructor. It was so much later it was more toward dawn, and my friends and I were standing around a bonfire we'd built for warmth. The State Commission had long since departed in a drunken haze of pomp, and the Tsar Cannoneers had either gone back to the oasis or were below at work on the rack under floodlights. The squadron's mood remained as radiant as the first quarter moon that was setting in Capricorn, and each of the long conversations was punctuated with the cry, "Moonship!" When the cosmonauts weren't bragging, they had Isaacii Goldenberg to question about his great machine. Goldenberg was delighted, for finally he had an appreciative audience for his tireless statistics, which he punctuated now and again with more of the biography of his idol, "Sirs! Sirs! We can do it again! Sirs! This is just a beginning! He is the Grand Constructor!"

Up on the mound above I could see the profiles of my straight-backed uncles and the bent-backed Grand Constructor. They were like shadow puppets in a victory dance, the Grand Constructor waving his hands over the new world his Tsar Cannon could bring down to earth, Uncle Konstantine throwing out his arms and making Little Laika yap, Uncle Dmitry holding his right hand at his mouth and musing, and Uncle Alexander standing slightly apart, not angrily for once, though at the time I couldn't interpret his posture. Now I think what I saw was a man at the precipice of a plunge into history. All that he'd done before, the war, the killing, the luck and catastrophe that I have yet to explain that took him from the top of the empire to the bottom and back up again, all that was inconsequential to him for those fine moments he stood above his moonship looking to find his fate somewhere between the steppe and the moon. I couldn't hear what they were saying—probably only the haranguing of the Grand Constructor and the laughing of Uncle Konstantine—but I could imagine it just as I could imagine their thoughts. My boy's sense of adventure told me that Uncle Alexander must be driving himself with my father's motto, "Keep going, keep going, keep going," though more likely he wouldn't have posed anything more imperative than "Finish it."

The truth is that they did finish it, my uncles finished it all the way to the moon. I promise you now, my uncles went from the steppe to the moon, and their course would have been true and their legend would have been topped by their footsteps on the moon if not for the rest of our fate to suffer the rot, the backwardness, the evildoing of those days. Though I have much to tell, you must understand that my uncles tried and failed and died not because of what was before them on their way to the moon, but because of their enemies at their backs, who were also my enemies, who were the same, General Robespierre Iagoda and Madame Daemonia Romodanovsky. I'm speaking of the rot ahead. Back then the Russian empire enclosed half the earth and the vast majority of mankind, and nowhere you went, north, east, south, west, were you far from the evil eyes of State Security. I started my story with my strange episode at Saint Sophia, and I have noted my run-in with Colonel Maximov at Starry Town, yet I'm sure you've missed, as I did, the eavesdroppers at the Corps' billet at Star City, the spies on the State Commission itself, the stealthy looks of goggle-eyed Doctor Lunin, deputy chief of Tsar Cannon. All of those rotten souls were working not only for State Security but also for General Iagoda's Fifth Directorate, and what was worse was that soon enough I was working for my enemies, too.

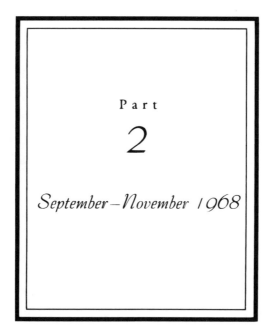

Part

2

September – November 1968

1

Evildoing at Starry Town

All September was punishment detail for me. I returned with the squadron to Starry Town on Monday evening, September 2, and the next morning, after mess and assembly and before the political directorate lecture, I was ordered to report to Chief of Candidates Lieutenant-Colonel Khitrovo. By then I suppose I knew I'd been AWOL for ten days, yet I was still so under the spell of my uncles that I assumed nothing would happen about it, or if it did I would be quickly pardoned. Instead Colonel Khitrovo cowed me right away by declaring, "Difficult times, Nevsky, and now you've done this. We are very disappointed in you, very disappointed, one of our good prospects, the best flier we have, aren't you? And why even discuss your patronage? And now what are we to do? What's worse is we have little choice here, little choice."

I knew he was talking about booting me out of the program, and I instantly lost the cockiness gained from a week with the squadron and started whining. I told a stupid pack of lies and half truths—"I was ordered!" "They needed me!" "They said you knew!"—and at one point tried to use the Czech crisis as an excuse, since Starry Town had been shut down for the week I was away. The words broke on my tongue, as Great-Uncle Lev would have said, and I knew I was only heaping more disgrace upon myself. I also knew Colonel Khitrovo was most serious about his duty, and he intimidated me when he folded his hands on his big belly, glanced at the shine on my brass buttons, and sniffed, "It's not up to me, Lieutenant, because if it was, you'd be on your way to the Chinese border. I'll pass on what you've said about your *dereliction of duty* and let you know the determination. Dismissed."

I recognized my defeat and spent the day in class feeling cold and useless. My pride told me to quit thinking about help from my uncles and prepare to face my fate with a backbone, and after a few hours of such dreary thinking I was sure Khitrovo would have to dismiss me from the Corps, if not break me from the service. There was no bottom to my gloom, and so it was a shock that afternoon to learn that I was spared the worst of the penalties. Khitrovo delivered the disciplinary board's verdict in the most humbling way, by posting it on the wall above my bunk. I was restricted to barracks indefinitely and demoted from the top of the class to the very last and assigned about a thousand housekeeping chores and fined one month's salary; yet I was not sent packing nor was I even sent to Maximov for another of his brutal conferences.

The single explanation I could think for my deliverance was that my uncles must have intervened for me. It turned out I was wrong about this. I learned later that Uncle Dmitry had spoken about me to Corps commander General Kamenin, yet that wasn't the primary reason Khitrovo was told to go easily. I didn't learn the truth of my pardon for two months, but I'm sure you can guess now, as I did not, that it was General Iagoda.

At mess that evening I boasted to my brother candidates Arkady Volgamints, Lev Lympyet, and Doctor Gogol that I was willing to accept my punishment because of what I'd gotten to see and do at Star City and the Cosmodrome. I knew I was being fatheaded, but I was so relieved not to be axed I couldn't hold back from trying to maintain I was too important a candidate to concern myself with Khitrovo's discipline.

My hard-won friend Volgamints was always a sour man, mostly because his father was an Archangel factory boss who'd taught his son that everything important was political, and he told me, "Shit, it's sweet shit when you got off a roasting because you have friends, ain't it?"

I knew that what Volgamints meant was that, as he was protected by his father and by an in-law on the Central Committee, I must be protected by some big boss. In other words I was a stooge. At the time I tossed off Volgamints's remark, yet as I've told you he was completely correct. (Colonel Maximov himself had passed the word to Khitrovo that I was to be pampered as a favor to a potent Lubyanka general.) My vanity was supreme and dazzled me from seeing anything but my conclusion that I was now on my way to becoming a member of the elite of elites, one of my uncles' chosen, and that my candidacy was no more than a tiresome formality. How choice I was for a fall, how fat I was for plucking, or as Great-Uncle Lev might have said, make yourself into a sheep and you'll meet a wolf nearby.

For the next few weeks I lived in daydreams of glory while I loitered like a lamb in the barracks. My major loss was that I wasn't free to get to the lake to see Katya, and gradually this deprivation wore me down as my heart pangs grew stronger and deeper. I was living almost all in imagination, so I was able, when I was marching around Starry Town with the class, to imagine her wherever I looked. The window of what I figured was her apartment's bedroom was my finest illusion, since it allowed me to dream of a day when she and I would live together in one of those elite addresses, and each morning she'd breakfast with me and see me off to my rocket ship. You must understand how dear remembering all this fantasy is to me now, especially the silly parts, for I know now that love like that comes only once to a boy and that as soon as you become a man one of the childish things you put away is that sort of devouringly sweet passion. In those September days my longing for Katya was such satisfaction that, as I went through my day studying, exercising, and waiting for them to recognize that I was the greatest candidate who ever walked into Starry Town, I moved more and more into a vision of myself either standing on the moon wearing Katya's scarf for good luck or lying with Katya while she wore a necklace of moon gems I'd brought her from the Sea of Cosmonauts.

Outside of my fantasy life there was trouble to be seen everywhere. If you recall, the Czechoslovakia crisis quickly turned into a black, black ruination. Each morning we candidates heard the political directorate's version of the invasion, a litany of distortions and lies that I won't bother to repeat. The truth was that Prague was sacked by our most famous airborne assault division, that the American leaders whom the Kremlin bosses were so fearful of—Johnson and Nixon were two of the names—so far from launching a counter-strike to rescue Prague, instead just washed their hands in public and ordered the NATO forces to hold position, that the Czech leaders Svoboda and Dubcek were dragged to Moscow to sign away their hearts, and that the Lubyanka lords were installed as the new order in Czechoslovakia. It's important to me to confess that I made nothing of all this tragedy, for I was just the sort of idiot who thinks politics doesn't matter. I was an idiot, you see, so whatever I didn't understand, such as politics, was idiotic to me. The most I might have thought—and I can't remember anything weighty whatsoever—was that since I wore the uniform of the Motherland, then whatever the Motherland did was mine to support. I didn't care about Czechoslovakia, I only cared about the medals and ribbons I would earn someday and how Katya would love me for being a hero.

I also cared about victory in space, and September 15 brought news that cheered Starry Town when the Cosmodrome launched *Zond 5* for history's first ever circumlunar flight. It was a robot test, and it should have been a manned shot, but still *Zond 5* flew. While we candidates followed the mission in bulletins, I flattered myself that, thanks to Uncle Alexander, I knew the complete story behind *Zond 5*. The Zond and the Proton were half measures, I told my friends, and the Zond program was half a loaf. If we could go this far, I said, then we could go to the moon now. And if the Zond flew so well, what had taken so long to get it up and why hadn't it been man-rated? My oratory was so adamant, and I was so much better informed than any other candidate, that it was a treat to follow the mission's progress like a sports contest that only I could interpret for the others. Two days later, we learned, ground control made a midcourse correction, and, on September 18, *Zond 5* looped the moon as close as 1,950 kilometers and then fired on a ballistic trajectory back to earth. I was such a know-it-all at the barracks that soon I had even the instructors asking me questions about the Zond, and what a special treat it was to learn that as the spacecraft emerged from the loss of signal on the dark side of the moon a prerecorded tape played a cosmonaut's voice making calculations as if the craft were actually manned. Rumor said that it was a recording of my uncles' voices, so I immediately claimed that I knew that spacecraft chief Sinebrykhov and Proton chief Faitelevitev had tried to make peace with Uncle Alexander by offering them the privilege. I even made up the detail that there was probably a yap at the end of the tape.

All such phony pridefulness launched me on a course for my own troubles, and I take no lesson from what happened except that I was a sheep in sheep's clothing. It started plainly enough: at evening mess, Sunday the twenty-second, when we learned they'd recovered the spacecraft from the Indian Ocean, I boasted, "We can do it! If it's man-rated, I say put a man on board! Let's get on!"

Volgamints blew smoke at me and baited, "If, shit. If, if, if, hog shit."

"You're wrong," I claimed, "and the next Zond should be ours. October's lunar window is out, because of Beregovoi's *Soyuz 2/3* mission. But November ninth to fourteenth, that's when we go. You'll see."

My friends had gotten used to my showing off the details I knew about the Cosmodrome, so Doctor Gogol disagreed with me shrewdly, "The reentry for *Zond 5* was ballistic, Peter, and that means it took a ten- to sixteen-g load coming down. If there'd been a man onboard he'd have suffered broken ribs, perhaps a burst lung and worse."

Lev Lympyet joined in against me. "And they used a water landing to absorb the impact, Peter. If there'd been a man onboard, and he'd been hurt, he couldn't have gotten out. And it probably took them a day to find the spacecraft beacon, so what you would have had is a dead man."

Doctor Gogol prodded me, "What would it prove if we brought back a cripple or a comatose case?"

I responded with a bombast equal to and informed by Uncle Alexander's. "It'd prove that the next falcon will get the job right. Driving's what we do. *Zond 6* will be ours! There's sure to be a manned fly-by in November! And then on to the landing!" To complete my mimicry of Uncle Alexander I threw down my fork, kicked back from the table, and made a show of walking out of the hall. My head was puffy with righteousness, and I recall feeling a frustration that I blamed on being trapped with so many doubters and backpedalers. My brilliant solution was to break even more rules and also get what I wanted, which at that moment was Katya. There must have been more cunning to my logic, since I'd learned before-

hand that Katya was in concert that night with Angelicka Zhukovsky's New Planet Quartet at the cultural center. In any event I told
myself that if real cosmonauts like Glavtop and Grin could chase
romance when under restrictions, I could, too.

I lied to the duty officer about a toothache and bounded out into
a chill fall rain, bypassing the medical center and stealthily doubling
back to the cultural center. I felt liberated and didn't hesitate to
sweep into the lobby and find a discreet but comfortable vantage at
the back of the hall. I remember the splendid vision of Katya on
stage in a plain skirt and white blouse with a simple black ribbon
holding back her fine hair. The quartet's leader, Mrs. Angelicka
Zhukovsky, was a much more striking beauty than Katya, her black
hair and sharp profile like a duchess in an oil painting, but at the time
I only had eyes for my strawberry-blond dream. I knew nothing
about the music they were playing, which I thought very sad and
complicated. There were few in attendance—I supposed because of
the rainstorm—and importantly Colonel Prishkin wasn't present,
nor, as I saw, were any other military men. Katya's son, Daniel, was
sitting with what I would soon learn were Uncle Dmitry's two
daughters, dear Anna, then twelve, and baby sister Marya at ten.
Mrs. Zhukovsky commanded the hall with passion and grace like the
virtuoso she was (once a third-place violin and twelfth piano at the
Tchaikovsky Prize), and she played one solo that awed my ignorance
and made the babushkas weep and the old men dab their eyes and
sigh. I could recognize that the music was moving, but what I didn't
understand was that the concert itself was intended as a high-toned
protest over Czechoslovakia, and Mrs. Zhukovsky soon hinted as
much. "Our final selection isn't on your program," she told the
audience. "We prepared it with this past summer in mind." A young
woman came on stage to take up Mrs. Zhukovsky's violin while Mrs.
Zhukovsky moved to the piano and announced, "Shostakovich. Piano Quintet. Nineteen forty." And then the five of them played as if
on turbojets, and this is my crude way of trying to say their music
was emblazoned, ominous, roaring, exact, implacable. I can still hear
it, and ever since, whenever I've heard any Shostakovich, I've been
transported back to that hall. At the close the musicians rose, bowed
as one, and walked off the stage in single file. There was no applause,
the audience just stood slowly and withdrew into the storm. Within
minutes the hall was empty and I was left standing and stymied, since

this wasn't following my fantasy of leaping on stage with the hot-house carnation I'd bought from the coatroom babushka.

What I could think to do was follow Daniel and the two girls, Anna and Marya, as they made their way through the front side door and up to the backstage level. Katya saw me before I saw her and she started scolding me immediately, as if it had only been a day or two since we'd talked on the telephone, "What do you want? Why are you here? I thought you were restricted to barracks."

Mrs. Zhukovsky stepped forward and, just like Uncle Dmitry, tried to soothe the tension. "Hello, Lieutenant Nevsky. We meet at last, Peter, after too long, much too long." She shook my hand and introduced me to Anna and Marya, whose eyes flashed when they heard my name because, as I learned many years later from Anna, they'd heard me much discussed at the dinner table as their father's godson and had decided on their own that I was their almost-cousin. I remember Anna's first words were as affectionate as her nature, "Pleased to meet you, Peter Apollonovich," and I believe she curt-sied. Even at twelve Anna was a pensive girl with wide, deep, wet eyes that made her seem very serious about life.

Introductions done and yet no change in Katya's scowl at me, Mrs. Zhukovsky tried, "You didn't tell me he had good taste in music, Katya. We might have sent him an invitation rather than let him wander in from the rain."

Katya closed her cello case. "Fine," she told Mrs. Zhukovsky, "I'll mind my manners." She turned to me and asked, "Are you all right? I heard they punished you—of course you're all right."

I was lost between wanting to say something romantic and want-ing to run away before I was rejected. Mrs. Zhukovsky must have spotted my lovesickness because she offered a compromise. "I'll take Daniel on with us," she told Katya. She told me, "We have sweets at my apartment after a performance, and we've asked several of my students to join us, and I hope you can too, can you? For an hour, no more."

Katya argued back, "No, he won't be. And don't make anything of this. I'll just walk him back a little way and then catch up, you go on." I think Mrs. Zhukovsky might have objected once more, some-thing about the rain, and Katya cried, "Please, Angelicka!"

What this mysterious exchange meant was that not only didn't Katya want me to visit with her, she also didn't want me near her ever again, and her prejudice wasn't because of husband Boris either. Her fear was much angrier and scarier than adultery, and it quickly led us to a profound upset. We ducked out of the overhang and got across to the bus shelter by the big spruces, where I tried to give her my cap and she refused and turned from me. Once we were away from all possible eavesdroppers she began loudly over the popping storm, "I'm going to explain myself, and I want you to listen. I don't know why I think I should explain to you, but I do, and you must understand. Things have changed, and we can't see each other anymore, not even a little." She continued painfully, saying she had been wrong to encourage me and that she wasn't going to pretend I wasn't "a little in love" with her and that she wouldn't deny she was "fond of" me.

I listened to what she said and kept trying to interrupt to make a suit I didn't have, but then she silenced me when she admitted that the reason we were finished was because of politics.

"I've signed a letter," she declared, and "I'm not going to say what was in it—it's not for you to know—but with some friends of mine at the university I've signed a letter. Last month we sent a letter to the Central Committee, and it's done and I don't regret it. I'll probably be leaving here soon."

I can still feel the heartache, it was like a blow in my chest, and I could only manage, "No," before spinning away and then turning back to grab her by the hand and wrench her out from the shelter and toward the trees. My overreaction wasn't baseless, since, idiot that I was, I knew that what she'd done was ruin. I screamed at her, "Can't you get it back or say it was a mistake?"

Katya yanked back her hand and pointed at me, and then she delivered some of her extraordinary ideology. "It was the most honest thing I've ever done. Get on! You're not a child. It's happening all over now. Those gangsters have gone too far. They can't lock us all up. We must make a stand for what we believe in before there's nothing left to believe." She swallowed the rest of her speech and told me, "You don't know anything about me, but you do know what will happen if you're implicated with me or any of my friends. I'm nobody to the Central Committee, just another treacherous Jew and dissident intellectual. But they'll break you, Peter, if you're found with me they'll shoot you, and you know they will, and I won't let that happen. Now, listen to me, this is serious. I want you to get on! If you care for me, if you care for Daniel, you'll not bother us again. Soon we'll be leaving, and you must get on with your duty you talk so much about."

I am pleased now to report that I resisted her: "What kind of friends would make you sign a letter to the Central Committee? Who are these friends? What kind of friends do you have? Do you mean Mrs. Zhukovsky?"

"My friends are my friends!" she countered. "Angelicka Zhukovsky has nothing to do with it, and you don't understand anything!"

I demanded, "When are you leaving?"

"Soon, when I can; now, get away from me!"

I begged, "Please, you can't go like this. We've got to talk. I've got so much to tell you." I tried all my news at once, "I saw your grandfather! He's amazing! Tsar Cannon works! We're going to the moon!"

She shouted, "Peter, leave me alone!" and then walked away.

I obeyed and didn't pursue her and returned to the barracks brokenhearted. I can't now reconstruct my twisted thoughts that night, but I can characterize them as black and hopeless. I think how many times folk like us must have had similar arguments in those days, how many fool intellectuals like Katya must have thought, They can't lock us all up, as if fate could be outfoxed, and also must have thought, We must make a stand for what we believe in before there's nothing left to believe, as if pretty words about faith are going to hold back monsters like Iagoda. You don't argue with murder; you don't debate, reconcile, compromise, speculate, plan, or hope in the face of guns; you don't do anything but survive if it's your fate. Katya, the truth was that you were doomed from the first you signed that letter, and though it enrages me all the more now to go over all the days we were together under the executioner's inevitable reach and know that there was nothing we could say or do to stop what was coming, yet still I tell myself that the love we gave each other must have come to something, it can't have been worthless. Perhaps what we achieved is that, after a lifetime of feeling that I failed you, I can still fall in love with you at the writing of your name.

Failure wasn't on my mind at twenty-two; love and conquest were, maybe just conquest. Within days I'd recovered enough to convince myself that Katya hadn't meant what she said and that we'd had a quarrel over matters that I didn't understand—politics, protests, petitions, anti-Semitism—and that it was mine to apologize and make up. I set myself to love-letter writing to win my girl back. I started my letters with safe themes such as Leningrad, the autumn bird migration, my candidacy, and my anxiety over slipping farther down the class ranking, but then because I hoped it might please her, I reported the highlights of my experiences at the Cosmodrome and carefully brought in mention of her grandfather the Grand Constructor. Eventually my shyness vanished, and I heaved raw heart into my postscripts, telling her that I hated sleeping because it was the only time I couldn't think about her, telling her that she was the most beautiful woman I'd ever met and that she could forbid me from meeting with her but she couldn't forbid me from desire.

My boldest ploy was to send the letter via Mrs. Zhukovsky's address, and when the first two didn't come back, I increased them to one every other day. I didn't expect Katya to reply; it was just enough to know that the letters might somehow be getting through and to imagine her reading them in her apartment tower. And yet then in October Katya did reply, but she didn't send me a letter, and at first I couldn't be sure it was Katya. On a Thursday I got an announcement of a recital by Mrs. Zhukovsky and one of her students that next Sunday at the cultural center, and after thinking about it for twelve hours I decided that this was Katya's way of arranging a rendezvous and that I was the luckiest man on earth.

My thoughts weren't all for love on earth, for that was the very same weekend the Americans launched a manned Apollo spacecraft for the first time, and I puzzle now at how tangled up Katya and I were from the first with the moon race, as if every lover's passion had to have wings that year. The race was on just as my race for Katya was on, and I can't say that I bothered to separate out my feelings between Katya and the moon. I do recall that waiting simultaneously for Katya and following the flight of *Apollo 7* on the radio and in the rumor mill made Friday and Saturday night pass sleeplessly quick.

How envious we candidates were of the Americans; how jealous I was that they were going to beat my uncles to the moon; and how much our collective competitiveness colored so many of the decisions made over the next year. It's important to report what I know of *Apollo 7*, because from the first its success established a pattern that would continue until the Americans won the race. The truth is that the Americans were luck itself—luck was their theme, their method, their reward. If this sounds sulky, then you aren't thinking like a cosmonaut, because I never drove a ship without luck at my side; and everyone knows that in all the universe the only thing that might be able to adjust fate is luck. The Americans found luck with *Apollo 7* as profoundly as they had lost luck twenty-one months before, in January 1967, when they had lost three astronauts in a fire in an Apollo while still on the launchpad. What had killed those three good men, Grissom, White, and Chaffee, wasn't poor planning or shoddy equipment but just bad luck, just as what had killed our Komarov in *Soyuz 1* in April 1967 wasn't a failed parachute but plain bad luck. The Americans had taken their casualties hard and had labored meticulously to launch five unmanned Apollo spacecraft in robot tests before girding their loins and trying their luck again. It is now my belief that from the moment *Apollo 7* flew, October 11, 1968, the Americans could feel they were on a winning streak just like a gambler's, and if they didn't feel it then I felt it for them, all Starry Town did. We candidates were so astonished by the extravagance of *Apollo 7*—a ten-day shakedown cruise with a three-man crew—that we pretended the Americans were buying their way up into orbit instead of driving there on beautiful machines. The mission's primary goal was to test the command and service modules, since there was no lunar module onboard, and a secondary goal was to practice close-rendezvous maneuvers with a drifting booster stage in the sort of maneuver that would be critical on an LOR mission.

I remember how, while waiting for the next bulletin on *Apollo 7* to be posted or just passed around by whispers, I tried to disguise my jealousy of the Americans from my friends with stupid remarks such as, "This is about getting to the moon, not looking good on television"—the Americans broadcasted television pictures back from orbit—or perhaps, "What the moon needs is a hungry falcon, you'll see."

Volgamints usually countered with cynicism such as Starry Town's most popular prejudice, "They're buying the moon, and who wants it anyway?"

I could counter this with more Alexander worship, such as, "The race goes to the winner, and Colonel Oryolin hasn't ever lost anything he's started."

But Volgamints could always overwhelm me with his cynicism when he would pose rhetorical questions such as, "What kind of frigging moon race is this? They do all the flying and we do all the watching? Let them have the frigging moon. What's it worth anyway?"

Doctor Gogol was usually able to philosophize around Volgamints's tongue and my worries, "The moon is worth the labor the workers provide to achieve it, comrade, read your Marx."

At the close of each of these arguments, however, Volgamints liked to remind us of his philosophy, something like, "Marx, shit, the moon, shit, as long as I get paid, shit."

Squabbling with knot-headed Volgamints didn't bother me, but being penned up with secondhand information did when instead I yearned to be at the Cosmodrome to follow *Apollo 7* in real time. I'd heard that my uncles had beckoned their squadron down to the Cosmodrome in order to monitor the *Apollo 7* intercepts, especially those of the passionate mission commander Schirra, who reported, "We're having a ball, she's like riding a dream." I told myself that my uncles had left me behind because I was on disciplinary report, and that as soon as I was a cosmonaut I'd be included in all their schemes. I only half believed this—mostly I figured they left me out because they'd forgotten about me—and I calmed myself by daydreaming and by showing off my knowledge of our upcoming *Soyuz 2/3* mission and finally just by waiting to see Katya.

By Sunday night I was so frustrated that I needed to take the risk to get out of the barracks as much as I needed to see Katya. I began my escapade by faking another toothache and asking to go to the medical center. I was sure the duty officer was going to reject my plea when he suddenly grinned in sympathy and said, "Get it yanked or learn to drink, boy." I got out before he changed his mind and raced direct to the cultural center. It was another damp night, threatening to storm later, and I took along a rain cape for Katya, since what I hoped was for a repeat of our last meeting, with a happier dialogue. I arrived at the hall just as intermission was over, and I carefully took position just outside the side exit, so that when I cracked the door I could see the stage and audience without being seen. I'd studied something about the program that night and the Mozart they played wasn't incomprehensible to me. When Katya came on stage to accompany one piece, I remember scanning the fairly large audience defensively for her husband or her son and not finding either. An hour later the program closed with a huge standing ovation, and then everyone started out past me and I was left adrift again until I was rescued by Uncle Dmitry's elder daughter, dear Anna. She walked straight up to me, as if she'd known where I was all along, and lowering her head spoke conspiratorially, "Aunt Katya asks if you can meet her at the lakeshore. She says you'll know where."

I kissed Anna's hand (Anna never let me forget how jealous I made her when I did this) and thanked her repeatedly and danced away in zero g's to rush to the lake and our famous bench. I wanted romance, not politics, certainly not debate, bossiness, intrigue, but then that was Katya, who at least did arrive soon after I did and ordered me, "Sit down and very carefully tell me what you know about my grandfather."

I balked at her temper and asked, "What about your grandfather? You mean the Grand Constructor?"

"You said in your letters you saw him in August, and now I want you to tell me what you saw and what happened."

I still resisted, "Yes, but why?" and stood there thinking that our meeting was already going badly, though I suppose now that I might have sensed that the reason she'd asked for this rendezvous wasn't because of love but rather because of trouble.

Katya looked sickly to me, and she was chain-smoking and her cough was worse than usual. When she yanked me down to the bench to sit beside her I could feel her dry, cold hands and something of her power. She wasn't in a panic, I'm sure, she was more angry than afraid that night, and I think now what most agitated and propelled her was her pride of place, her bottomless belief that she could control her life and master her fate with the same sort of vain and fervent genius that I'd seen in the Grand Constructor, so it was probably a family trait. Bluntly, Katya thought she was smarter than everyone else and that she could outsmart friend or foe whenever she wanted to. "I know I frightened you," she told me, "when I told you I was going away from Starry Town. I'm not going away, not now. I've decided I'm going to fight them. I was superficial to think before that they cared about what I do, or that they were going to persecute me because of a letter. Something else is going on here. It's not just the letter, and I don't know what's going on, but it has to do with Grandfather and perhaps with you, too. Or maybe something about Starry Town. I don't know yet, and that's why you must tell me what you saw in August when you saw Grandfather. Don't ask why, just tell me."

I tried to state the facts in chronological order just as if this were a debriefing. The wind blew hard over the lake and sent tiny rolling waves at us so that I had to raise my voice to finish my report.

Katya asked, "It was a complete success?"

"Amazing success," I reported. "Tsar Cannon is the moonship! It's the most amazing thing, and your grandfather is amazing." I caught my breath at this exaggeration and tried to conceal my doubts about her grandfather's character by exclaiming Goldenberg's praise, "He's the Grand Constructor!"

Katya was consternated, touching her lips and muttering, "It doesn't make sense," and then standing up abruptly and ordering me, "We'll walk now. I have to tell you something, and I don't want to sit here in the light anymore. I know I told you before that you should stay out of my business, but you're already involved, and you should know what's happened."

Katya held my arm close as she began to relate a riddle of events that at first seemed a story of anti-Semitic abuse but what I know now to be the first sign of State Security's evildoing at Starry Town. I've already mentioned Katya's politics, that the August week I was at the Cosmodrome Katya and her Moscow University friends—chief among them a literature professor named Ara Ovchennikov—had started to protest the invasion of Czechoslovakia with a series of defiant acts, such as sitting up all night in a lecture hall while reading poetry aloud or holding candlelight vigils out of doors while reading more poetry aloud. After a week of this sort of folly, the protesters sent a collective letter to the Central Committee in which they demanded an immediate withdrawal of our troops from Czechoslovakia, and I think they also declared the invasion illegal and immoral. The protesters all expected to be arrested by State Security. Yet, after a week more of poetry readings, they weren't even detained or obviously harassed, and they were left without an explanation. "It was as if they didn't care," Katya told me. It so happened that she was wrong about this and that State Security had a far more malevolent ambition than mass arrest.

It was about this time that Katya started receiving obscene telephone calls from an anonymous man who was undoubtedly a Chekhist agent. Katya said the calls were at first "dirty-old-man things," but that they soon became anti-Semitic and threatening. Importantly the caller only wanted to talk to Katya, since he rang off whenever Colonel Prishkin or the housemaid answered.

"I thought I knew what was going on," Katya told me. "I thought it was some perverted Chekhist who was having his fun with me before they arrested me. But then I found out that none of the others were being called and that I was the only one, and I was confused about it until the caller started mentioning my grandfather. He asked me if I'd ever 'had relations' with my grandfather. It was ridiculous, and I didn't know what to think until the letters started."

Katya received the first letter on October 2. She said it was terse and irrational. "It said I was a 'dirty traitor' and a 'Jew whore' and that Grandfather was a traitor, too. It was so obtuse I thought it was the work of a madman, maybe some old enemy of Grandfather's who'd found out who I was and was going crazy. But that didn't make any sense either, since I asked myself what does Grandfather have to do with me? And why should a Chekhist accuse me and Grandfather together of this nonsense? After all, I haven't seen Grandfather in more than fifteen years, and he's hardly a member of the family. He didn't even acknowledge my father's death, his own son's, and it's as if he's a stranger to my whole family, so why should anyone think I had anything to do with him unless he were crazy?"

The next letter threatened the Grand Constructor specifically, calling him a "Jew parasite," and a "Zionist wrecker." And then, the Monday before, Katya said she had received a letter that mentioned me, not by name but by implication, telling Katya to stop corrupting "innocent Soviet youth." Then there was a phone call that Katya said was all ugly, nonsensical stuff about "Jew corruption of Soviet youth."

I was dumbfounded to hear all this and am still ashamed to have to report it. What might have been harder to hear was that Katya told me that she'd heard much worse her whole life. At the time what truly worried Katya was not the race hatred but why her grandfather and I were being made part of the accusations against her.

"Peter, what have you and Grandfather to do with our letter to the Central Committee? I knew the Chekhists were ignorant bullies, but to this extent? And what they're doing not only doesn't make sense but they also don't seem to care much about me. I mean it's all impersonal, as if they've been ordered to scare me, but they don't know how to do it very well. They're so inept—the caller reads what he says, and he's such a poor reader, and the letters are badly typed and illiterate, and they can't spell. How scared can I be when my persecutors can't spell? I might have been scared at the start—it's frightening to think that they are doing this to you on purpose—but I've gotten so used to it now, I talk back. I correct his grammar, and tell him to speak up, and tell him how to spell *parasite.*"

Katya laughed at this point and her laugh startled me. What she'd said was so sickening to me that I couldn't think clearly. Perhaps I was wrong to take the world so seriously, but I did then and I do now, and I can still feel my fury at those Chekhists, and I can still admit that when Katya told me what they were doing I wanted to kill them. Do you understand? I felt the rage and murder in me as if it were my birthright.

By then we were walking along the lakeshore underneath bouncing pine boughs, and the storm was no more than minutes from breaking. Yet despite all this, the rain, the threats, the hatred and fear, Katya was able to rally herself and surprise me with an astonishing opinion. "I feel much better for telling you," she told me. "You see, I think I've figured out what they're doing. I think they're trying to scare me so much that I'll turn away from my family and friends. I think they're trying to isolate me so that I either go mad with fear or break down and confess to whatever they say just to make them stop. I think that's what they're doing, and I think I know how to fight them. I think I've got to fight back, yell back, and I think I've got to organize against them. They're ridiculous, they're dirty little gangsters, they can't even spell." To show how formidable she was feeling, she threw her cigarette into the lake and posed like a Joan of Arc in a wool coat.

I didn't feel so strong, and I clutched her, and I think I must have kissed her on the head like a brother. "Katya, please, don't worry," I started, but then I couldn't say what I felt and added, "It's terrible. What they're doing is terrible."

I believe it was right then that Katya made the critical decision that we were going to go on together intimately. I remember that, instead of pulling away from me as I'd expected, she moved up against me and touched my chin softly as if making sure my words of support were genuine. She asked me, "Peter, do you want this? Because if you do, you must listen to me. Otherwise, you must get away from me, and you must do it now and not come back. And no more letters, nothing."

I declared, "I'm not leaving you." I wanted her to kiss me so that I could kiss her, and as it happened I did eventually get kissed that night, but not before Katya had told me at length what to think and what to do. She charged me as scrupulously as any commander I'd ever had. I wasn't to write her any more letters. I wasn't to speak to anyone about her. I certainly wasn't ever to try to telephone her again. We were going to meet again but very carefully. Our first meeting was to be the next Sunday night after a piano recital, and we were to meet right where we stood, at the farthest-out lamppost on the lakeshore, and only then would we set another rendezvous date. In the meantime, Katya said, she was going to do what she could to warn her grandfather. She said she was going to write him about the abuse and tell him that she had admitted to nothing either about her own conduct or that of her family. Katya's remarks about her family were filled with a long-term regret. "He won't read it, probably," she said of the letter she would write to the Grand Constructor. "I don't know what he'll make of my writing him. Probably that I want something from him. He's been selfish like that as long as I've known him. My mother told me that he once accused my father of jeopardizing his reputation by being a second-rate mathematician. And this was after my father spent two years in detention rather than admit to some incredible conspiracy of academicians in Leningrad. And when my older brother was sick, and Mother wanted to get him into a special hospital only for families of the Academy, Grandfather refused to take her phone calls. Not that I was surprised, since Grandfather probably doesn't even acknowledge that he has grand-children. He's a bastard, I know that, and doesn't deserve anything from me, but he's still my only living grandparent, and he's still my father's father, and I'm doing this for me. It's important to me to try to protect him. I'll know I've done right even if he doesn't care."

Katya also said that she was going to start copying down what was said in the phone calls in order to help build a case against her persecutors. You might think it strange that she thought she could use law against State Security, since there wasn't any law in those days, there was just the Lubyanka; but then Katya was always an idealist even when she was feeling hopeless.

She was filled with hope that night and told me that she believed we could fight them together. Again she insisted that I tell no one, as she had not, because, she said, "It's not fair to them to get them involved in this. We can do it."

What she didn't say at the time was that, though she might have hidden the abuse from everyone but me, she hadn't been able to conceal her upset from her dear friend Angelicka Zhukovsky, and had had to lie to Mrs. Zhukovsky that it was all about her disintegrating marriage. I realize now that if not for that lie we might have survived everything; for Mrs. Zhukovsky would have told my uncles, and they would have intervened long before events became desperate. It was stupid to lie like that, more stupid than anything our enemies had done; and I blame myself more than Katya for not stopping the lie by breaking my promise to her and telling my uncles.

"You must promise me you'll tell no one," Katya repeated in her bossiest style. "Promise."

I promised, just as millions must have promised a wife or sister or friend before me as they tried to deny that they were doomed; and I even spoke aloud as if my promise was a contract between us, "I promise."

Katya's last gallant words that night were, "It's not illegal to write a letter to the Central Committee, and I'm not going to run from them. I'm a Party member, and Grandfather's a state treasure and untouchable. And you—here at Starry Town, you're out of their reach. I don't know what they're after. Maybe nothing, maybe they're just enjoying tormenting me. I can guess that if they already had what they wanted from me then I would have been arrested. Maybe not, I don't know. But I'm not going to cower from them like the old days. I'm going to defend myself and my friends, and I'm going to stand up for my family, and as long as I can I'm going to yell back at them that I'm right and they're wrong."

It was a fine speech, so fine that it moved her to kiss me on the cheek and then again lightly on the lips, and then she thanked me in her overthinking fashion. "If you change your mind, don't tell me about it, just don't come next week and I'll understand. This is a lot to ask of you, and for now, thank you. I feel better and cleaner and more sure of myself than I have my whole life, and this is very important to me. I think there's something sweet in you that makes me feel stronger. If that sounds muddled, then I suppose it's muddled, just like love is muddled."

I didn't get a chance to reply, because Katya broke away and hurried back toward the apartment towers in a way that told me not to follow. Still I felt rewarded. She hadn't spoken of my letters, she hadn't mentioned anything about her marriage, yet everything seemed in order between us. Katya commanded, and I obeyed, and I confess I liked it this way. Loving her was sometimes like being disciplined and sometimes like school-going, but it was always dear and made me feel loved in return, so that no matter how little we were actually together I always felt she was close to me.

The next Sunday, October 20, my toothache ploy to get out of the barracks failed, and I had to bribe the duty officer with a carton of cigarettes. The delay made me so late for the concert that I went on to the lakeshore to wait for Katya at the lamppost. Because I was early for the rendezvous, I came upon two strangers who were stumbling around the rocks down the walkway. They were not Air Force, and I guessed by their black leather jackets that they were State Security. I know it must sound crazy to you, but I wasn't frightened of them. This was Starry Town, and if they were State Security, then they were out of bounds and powerless. I went right at them and told them to get off the base as if I were shooing pests. "Now! Now!!" I ordered. "And if you're not gone in a minute I'm alerting the Air Police!"

What a bizarre incident, and I'm amazed now by what I did and how little I thought of it. Eventually Katya did arrive, and I let her kiss me greetings and tell me about her week—she said there hadn't been any more phone calls or letters—before I brought up the leather jackets. I meant to sound assured and conquering; but my attitude confused her, and her reaction was severe. "How did they know about us meeting here?" she demanded. I tried to calm her that perhaps it hadn't been State Security. "You mustn't ever do such a thing again!" she ordered. "Peter, promise me, you mustn't. What if they'd attacked you? You'd be arrested, and what's that do? Promise me!"

I tried to defend my performance, "This is Starry Town, Katya. They can't come in here, they know that."

She shouted me down, "You don't know what they can do! Starry Town is safe as long as they let it alone. You're to promise me! I won't have you fighting them. That's their way, they want you to do as they do, and you mustn't fight! If we become just like them, then we've lost, and what we're doing is wasted. Promise me you won't fight!"

She was being an intellectual, and I didn't understand her, but I promised anyway. I admit now that my promise was insincere and that I gave it because I wanted to please her, and also because I wanted to seduce her. She had kissed me greetings, and I wanted to kiss her passionately and soon did. It was in my mind to make love with her that night and no quarrel was going to get in the way. She had a firm white body, and I wanted to see it and touch it. I even had a plan, because I'd worn my new lined greatcoat and had looked into the boat house to find us a place out of the light rain. I know this all seems immature and selfish of me now—seducing a married woman, kissing her so hard that she couldn't argue, clasping her so tightly that we were like one—but then I was twenty-two, I remind myself, and I had never made love with a grown-up woman. She laughed when I told her I wanted to go into the boat house, though she didn't refuse and once inside she didn't stop me when I reached under her coat and felt her lovely small breasts and hard flat stomach, her smooth hips and buttocks. She was a beautiful woman, and once we were lying in my greatcoat she was the universe to me. Yes, we made love in the boat house just like students. And my memory is that we made love more than once that night, and that I felt that we could stay stuck together and just sail away. Of all the dear intimacies I learned that night, the one that still thrills me is that Katya liked to bite in her rapture; and she had a way of biting and saying "Don't stop" so that sex with her was like being bossed and consumed all at once. Later we huddled so that my legs were between hers and her legs were between mine—this seems impossible I suppose—and we spoke of how brave we felt together and how lucky we were to have just these moments, regardless what was to come. It was all so much big talk, yet it did feel brilliant at the time. "Love is a star," she told me. "A great red giant burning quick and wild. You go there with someone you love, and it's your private sun forever. You know you can't live on it. You know that it can't last and it will burn out and cool and empty someday. But it's yours, ours. Isn't it like that for you, Petrushka, my companion, my dear, dear lover."

Why was I so blind? Why did I go along with her foolish plan to stay on at Starry Town and defend herself? Why didn't I try to get her to go to her mother in Leningrad? And why didn't either of us tell our friends what was going on? Just one word to Mrs. Zhukovsky might have solved the deteriorating crisis—at least, it would have alerted my uncles there was jeopardy that was coming on against the most vulnerable and least defended of us. I suppose that our secret love explains all our folly, that because we loved each other covertly we had to guard everything from others. Our love was like a star, as Katya said, and to live there was as impossible as the sharing of it, yet we wanted to live there and struggled to keep our star to ourselves. I loved her because she was Katya. I loved her sight, heat, smell, fury; I loved just thinking about her. And Katya loved me because, I suppose, I was caught up in her pride of defiance, and so she felt less alone with me in love with her. I suppose I'm saying that Katya loved me because she needed me, and perhaps there was more to it, but this will do to explain her urgency. Her marriage was trash. Her Moscow friends were asinine. Her future was bleak. What she had was a four-year-old son she couldn't protect and a fleeting happiness with me, if only after dark by a lake.

October did pass like some sort of starry dream. I was so in love that I rocketed through my regime and stood loftily over the news from space until the news turned bad and our *Soyuz 2/3* was a failure. On Friday, October 25, a robotic *Soyuz 2* lifted from the Cosmodrome and achieved an excellent low orbit. Twenty-four hours later R-7 deputy chief Doctor Mishuk proved his claim to lift consecutive R-7s and launched *Soyuz 3* with Colonel Beregovoi onboard. The two spacecraft rendezvoused and closed to two hundred meters with all systems reported perfect for a docking. At this point ground control released *Soyuz 3* to Beregovoi, and he became captain of a swift ship in a calm sea. We candidates were listening in at the lecture hall, and we cheered, "Fly!" But within moments, when Beregovoi didn't report a successful lock on his target, it was clear that the mission was in trouble. Our instructors tried to cover up with nonsense that the first pass was just a test of the rendezvous radar, and that Beregovoi had backed off 565 kilometers to prepare for the docking the next day. But I knew, we all did, that it wouldn't work, that Beregovoi had aborted the docking and that *Soyuz 2/3* was a failure.

By the next Wednesday, Beregovoi had landed without docking, and it was impossible to avoid the feeling of defeat at Starry Town. I let the gloom spoil my own mood and that night acted childishly with Katya, and how my tantrum hurt us. We had taken to meeting at my uncles' Black House in the woods, because it was drier and warmer than the boat house and also because Katya hadn't gotten over the incident of those two mysterious leather jackets at the lake. Besides it was fun to use my uncles' refuge as our own. Katya had agreed to the Black House and even made a joke, "As long as we use sheets!" That night we were exuberantly alone in the musty, leaky living loft, the squadron either away at the Cosmodrome following Beregovoi's reentry and landing or, in the case of my uncles, out at the Tsar Cannon works. I'd started bribing my way out of barracks on weeknights, so it was the second or third time in a week that we'd been together. A roof and bed made me brazen, and the good sex made me want to show off, and as I've said the *Soyuz 2/3* failure made me cranky.

"It's a disgrace!" I declared of Beregovoi, who had landed that afternoon in a snowstorm in Kazakhstan. "His mission was to drive her to docking. We were years waiting for this. It would have worked!"

Katya lay beside me, and I remember how tender her voice sounded when she said, "Dear, it's not that meaningful, is it? You shouldn't let it bother you so; it's not good for your beautiful complexion; and look, you're fidgety again. Now lie back."

I remained petulant, declaring, "It does bother me! The Soyuz can fly, but they won't let us drive her. There should've been two crews up there. Rendezvous means nothing. We've got to dock. It's what we need for the moonshot. This was a test flight! Why didn't they test her?"

Katya teased me, "You do go on when your clothes are off."

If only I had turned to her wonderful scent and shut myself up with a kiss, but no, I rolled away from her and addressed the rafters above. "Colonel Zhukovsky would have done the docking or he wouldn't've come back. Glavtop and Grin would have roped the ships together. Colonel Oryolin would have launched another Soyuz if that's what it took. This was a battle in space, just like a battle anywhere, and we had to win!"

Katya murmured and then reached out once more to soothe me, even trying a joke, "What about this roping together. It sounds exciting. What do you have in mind?"

We must have made love again, as if all was forgiven, yet no sooner had we finished and slid apart than I started again with my fixation. "What did Beregovoi give us, tell me that?" I asked. "All he gave us was television!" I was shouting about the TV broadcast that they had beamed back in order to cover up the fact that Beregovoi had failed to rendezvous and dock with *Soyuz 2* on the second try. "What good is television? And television for what?" I mimicked Uncle Alexander, "I'll tell you for what! For backwardness! Backward, backward backwardness!"

Katya challenged my pigheadedness with her sharp mind. "It's all propaganda, Peter. What do you think Starry Town is? We're all just examples of socialist genius kept under glass, like a museum of lies. Don't sound off like such an innocent. You think you're paid so well because you're on some sort of frontier? You're a comfortable puppet, Peter. We all are. And the bosses pull the strings."

She had flabbergasted me again, and all I knew to say was more pretentiousness, "We're for the moon! Colonel Oryolin says that moon-driving is our job!"

I went on about the moon until Katya couldn't listen any longer and she had to flatten me, "Your Oryolin could just drink himself to the moon. Listen to me, your uncles-as-you-call-them are just cagey old drunkards. With all their hot air about the moon, I notice they keep on like the buffoons they are. And you're another dupe for them, another little boy to make them feel like big boys. I hope that someday decent young men like you will stop listening to bullies like Oryolin and his kind—*Stalin's damned little heroes!*—and then we might have a winter without famine and a child's shoe that lasts more than a month and a clinic that can save a man having a heart attack, not just watch him die! Do you hear me? I can't buy a pair of shoes for Daniel that last more than a month. And you walk around in handmade boots and have a coat that could keep a whole family warm!"

Katya's outburst had profound merit. She was so right about everything that I can say now that for want of a good shoe the empire eventually fell over its own bare feet. And yet none of what she said touched my master-of-the-sky polemic. I sat there naked as a crow and shouted that she should respect what I do, that the space program was built by men like my father and my uncles, that Starry

Town existed because of what I did. "I'm here to get to the moon!"
I bragged. "It's my duty. And if you can't love me because of it, I'm
not for you!"

In our frenzy I think she wept, though I couldn't be sure, since it
wasn't like Katya to act fragile when she was truly hurting. That
wasn't our first quarrel about my uncles and the moon landing, but
it was the first one in which I pushed back as hard as I could and
threatened her love. I confess that I meant to upset her and knew at
the time that I was being cruel and still kept on, as if I enjoyed it, and
perhaps I did enjoy it. Katya was no weakling, and she was always
eager for an argument. I think she crumpled that day not because of
what I'd said but because of her larger fears. She kept her back to me
as she pulled on her dress and coat and stuffed her knickers into her
pockets, and she had her boots just half on when she walked out the
loft door. I shouted more idiot remarks trying to provoke her, and
when that failed I let her go alone. I walked back to the barracks
arm-in-arm with righteousness, as Great-Uncle Lev would have said,
and swore to myself that I was done with her high-handed ways.

I capitulated within a day and wrote her a heart-filled apology. I
was so anxious that I couldn't wait the delay it would take to send it
via Mrs. Zhukovsky; so on Friday afternoon I cut away from the class
and, dashing over the gardens, delivered my note to Katya's building's concierge. I begged to see her at our lamppost at the lake. I
told her that I loved her more than boots or Starry Town or anyone,
and that I had to see her if just to apologize in person before she
rejected me. I felt so desperate that I did what I knew was rash, I set
a time for our rendezvous—after Daniel was asleep, at 2000 hours
the next night. Here was the mistake State Security was waiting on.
They were reading Katya's mail, listening in on her telephone calls,
watching my coming and going, yet they hadn't been able to plan a
way to ambush us together. Katya's precaution to set our rendezvous
only when we were together had worked so far, since State Security
wasn't supreme at Starry Town. The airbase was hostile territory to
the goons; they had to know when and where to wait. You had to tell
them beforehand, or at the least give a note to one of State Security's
snitches, such as a white-haired babushka who worked as a concierge.

As it happened, Saturday night began with Katya ambushing me.
It was a chill, starlessly black night, very still and silent, for even the

birds were muffled by the damp in the air that warned of snow coming. With *Soyuz 2/3* down, Starry Town was hectic again as the Corps returned from the ground tracking stations or the Cosmodrome; and there were many couples and groups of walkers out late around the lake. I was still on report and didn't want to run into Colonel Khitrovo, so I darted through the shrubbery and waited behind our lamppost like a sneak.

I suppose this meant that I knew the rendezvous was a mistake. When Katya arrived in what I could see was her darkest mood—smoking, coughing, slumping in her overcoat—I wished I could run away, but then I tried to show my best face and stepped out. She sputtered at me, "What are you doing in there; this isn't a game; come out here." Her mood deteriorated the more as she launched into a speech that was intended to strangle me. "I've done little but lie to you for months, and this is the end of it." She added that this had to be our last meeting and that she had only come out here to tell me goodbye. "I've told you lie upon lie, Peter, and I can't lie anymore. I won't go on. It's ruined for us. The lies are more hateful to me than anything." She admitted she had lied to me when she'd said that the obscene phone calls and letters had stopped, because they had continued daily. She also claimed that she had lied that she was brave. "My stealing around with you is cowardice," she said. "I'm a coward for this, and I deserve to pay a price. I should have taken Daniel and gone away in September. And now I might have waited too long, but I've got to try."

I think it was at this point that I attempted to stop the heartache I felt by asking something weak and off the point, such as was she cross with me because her husband had found out about us, or maybe I asked if she was annoyed at me for getting her out here.

"Stop it!" she yelled and then threw her cigarette at me and told me that her husband had known about us from the start and that he even knew she'd come out here to get rid of me. "He pushed me at you at the party; it was funny to him how we liked each other!" She said her marriage was another lie. She said Prishkin had not only urged her to take up with me but also, now that he knew she was in trouble, she suspected he was betraying her. "I think he's informed on us! He's too frightened to leave me. And he's actually afraid that you might leave me and I'd do something crazy like denouncing him as a pimp. And when I told him I was going to tell you to leave me alone, you know what he said? He said, 'Think again, he's just your kind, honey.' Boris the pimp! He's drunk every night waiting to be arrested for being married to a treacherous whore. You whimper to me about your duty. Do you know what your duty might be? Your duty these days is to screw me so that I won't go crazy and kill my husband. Didn't you know? They're playing with us!''

What she said was crazed, yet I couldn't curb her rage; and my inaction only made her wilder, for then she stabbed at my heart, "We can't fight them, Peter. They know everything we do. They're watching us all the time. I know what they can do! They've taken my friends! They've taken my friend Ara, and they'll take me when they want.''

Here was a lie that shocked me, for she told me in words I can't recall—or won't because it makes me crazy too to hear about him—about her friend Ara, that is the literature professor Ara Ovchennikov, whom she'd often mentioned as the chief letter signer but had never before identified as her lover. He was her lover when she met me, and she had continued to see him and me together for several weeks until he had been arrested. It was another of her lies that no one of the letter signers had been arrested, because Ovchennikov had been taken ten days before, in early October. "Ara's gone," she said. "And now they're going to take all of us."

Before I could react to the breadth of her lies, Katya lied one more time. "I know what they'll do, and I don't want to be brave!" she said, and this time there were tears. "It happened to my father. They took him and tortured him for two years. At least they murdered your father quickly with their nine grams; at least they let him die with his dignity and didn't torture him until he wasn't human before they shot him. They tortured my father for two years without charging him and then released an invalid who couldn't remember how to clean himself. We had to watch him die over seven years of a heart they'd starved to tissue paper."

Katya kept talking about her father's death, yet I'd stopped listening when she lied about my father's death. At the time I didn't know the truth of how my father had died, but then neither did she, and she lied when she said he was shot. What I'd known of my father's death was what Great-Uncle Lev had always told me, that Father had died in a MiG prototype test crash in the Far East in 1948. I know now that the truth was that no one ever knew how he died, nor did anyone know what happened to my mother, Marya, after she'd left me with my great-uncle and great-aunt and gone east to bury my father. My mother had buried my two older sisters, who had died during the famine in the siege of Leningrad; and she had buried her own family, who had died in the famine after the end of the war; and then she had gone to bury her husband, and the truth disappeared with her. In the winter of 1949 what was left of my once giant family was Great-Uncle Lev and Great-Aunt Elizaveta with me, a three-year-old orphan to raise in the rubble of Leningrad, and I had grown up with the story that my father had died a hero's death.

Twenty years later I couldn't accept that my father had been murdered; and even now I still struggle with the notion that they shot him, that State Security executed the greatest ace of the war just because he was the greatest ace of the war. I know that is probably what happened; I know that Stalin ordered tens of thousands of the best of our officers shot before, during, and after the war just because he was jealous of their talent and patriotism. And I don't mean starved to death or beaten to death or frozen to death or shoved in rivers or tossed in bonfires or all the other horrible ways State Security killed tens of millions in the slave camps, I mean executed by gunshot as an enemy of the state, taken out and shot in the back of the head by pistol shot, the infamous nine grams of a bullet. My father was likely shot in the head by Chekhist monsters who were themselves likely murdered by other Chekhist monsters; and they kept shooting and shooting for thirty years until there were more than three-quarters of a million murdered by nine grams; and there might be nothing more to do about such evil now but to declare that I refuse to hate those who murdered my father. A world of hate would mean that Lenin and Stalin and their kind had won out after all, so I refuse to hate those who murdered my father. I won't forgive them, and yet I won't hate them.

I still can't explain what it was like to hear for the first time that my father had been executed, and to hear it from the woman I loved. What I recall feeling was something like madness. No one had ever said such a thing to me before, not in school nor at the academy, and I'd never even thought it. Yet I knew as soon as she said it that I believed her. And then, my mind sealing up like a fortress, I didn't believe her, and I had to shut her up, and so I hit at her. I didn't use my strength, it was more a defensive blow as I recoiled; yet what I'd missed in force I made up for with words. I screamed hateful words at her. I called her vile names. I won't record them, though I confess what came out was misanthropic rubbish, the sort of thing you hear all your life and are ashamed to realize you can say aloud.

Katya withstood my wrath as if our souls had switched places, and she was come to comfort me. Rather than her yelling at me, and me standing there dumb, she grabbed me close and held on and waited out my fit. It was a profound transformation, and yet I think now it was possible because my terror had solved her terror. Seeing me afraid of the truth that my father had been murdered made her iess afraid of her fear of the truth that she was doomed. Do you understand how it is that only when you realize you are in fear of fear that you can recover yourself?

We remained knotted together like dancers. Katya wouldn't let me go and kept saying, "Petrushka, forgive me. I didn't mean it," while I wouldn't stop twisting to get away, though not very hard or I could have broken her hold instantly, so I must have wanted her close so I could denounce her, "You're lying, say you're lying!"

I know now that this was all so much soulful lovemaking between us, and it might have come to a deep reconciliation, it should have, for Katya seemed ready to love me not for the lies we'd told each other but for the little we had. She must have had something like this in mind, for she started me moving away from the lamppost and lake and toward the Black House. I will never know what might have grown between us that night, though I like to imagine that what we felt was the sort of bonding only childbearing can provide. But then what were we really fighting about? Not her lovers or lies or my stubborn idiocy, no, those were reactions to the facts we suffered along with everyone we knew: the fact of tyranny, the fact that we were trapped by fate, the fact that trapped animals turn on each other in despair.

Fate that night came at us in the guise of several State Security goons, who had been waiting for us to move away from the lamplight. Once we entered the woods we were helpless to the ambush. One struck me behind the right ear, and another kicked out my legs. Katya didn't scream, though she should have as I should have, for it was stupid to hold your tongue as if you were brave and make it easier for them to treat you like a victim. I think I saw them throw Katya's overcoat over her head, and I know I heard them stomp her.

Then they hit me again and put a gag and hood on me. I remember I could taste my teeth. My arrest was just like a robbery, except that the criminals didn't demand anything, because what they really wanted was my soul.

My Soul

The root of all the little evils baffling Katya and me was the Lubyanka lord General R. G. Iagoda. Yet at the time, even as we were arrested, we had convinced ourselves that what was happening to us was our own fault. I think that Katya believed she was being arrested because of her dissent, because she, her lover Ara Ovchennikov, and their comrades had sacrificed their families and lives for high-handed political principles and for nothing else. As for myself, even as they slugged us down I had the notion that we were being arrested because in some way we deserved to be punished for our adultery, because I believed that I'd dragged us both down by seducing Katya. We were both wrong—we were arrested because Iagoda gave the order to bring us in to advance a plot against my uncles—and yet now I puzzle if we were completely wrong. Hadn't we made ourselves into the sort of prey that wolves can take without running hard, two naked lambs refusing the help we needed because we were too proud to admit our weakness?

The Chekhists jammed me on the floorboard of a Volga sedan and drove me to the Lubyanka. It was over an hour drive into central Moscow, but, lying on my ear just above the drive wheel, I found I couldn't think clearly and eventually stopped trying to do more than keep my nose from rubbing raw every time we bounced. The reason I wasn't more frightened or enraged by the treatment was that I'd been trained to believe that the Air Force would protect me from State Security so long as I acquitted myself correctly and said nothing, obeyed orders, waited to be returned to my superiors. I might have just been in shock, since not only wasn't I worried for myself, but also I didn't feel any special concern for Katya. It must have been shock, perhaps those blows to my head, for my vagueness would soon lift and I would fret about everything to an extreme. Also, I might have passed out on the drive, and maybe I only came alert when the car turned several times and stopped in a stone-wall close. They hauled me out on my backside and removed the gag and hood. "Get up and shut up," was the order. The leather-jacketed Chekhists then gave me over to blue-tabbed regulars, four of them, who pushed me down several steps and through an iron gateway and then jammed me face first against a wet stone wall, where they took my belt, greatcoat, new wristwatch, money, and identity card. I had the sense that we had passed from the outside of a building to the inside. Though everywhere was equally shadowy, I felt that strange denseness you feel underneath a building. I was turned into a warren of doors and then pushed into a holding cell that was mostly a closet, without light or room either to stand up straight or to lie down flat.

They dropped the dead bolt, and I was left alone in silence. I remember slumping down like a dead thing, not because I was sick or scared, no, worse than that, because what dragged me down in my cell was a stupefying sense of shame. I had never experienced shame so totally, a cold, battering disgrace that left me feeling feeble, exposed, hopeless. I can still feel a piece of the shame; it can still make me feel cold. I think now that this same sense of shame weakened me from the moment they took me until now, these many decades later, when I'm able to write down what was done to my family, to my loved ones, to me. The telling of this story is the first thing I have found that can shove aside all that shame and let me see that it wasn't my fault, it wasn't the fault of the victims. It was done to us by men and women with rotten souls because they wanted to: not for some greater cause or because of a historical necessity or economic theory, but because they were rotten and because they wanted to do rotten things to us.

What was I ashamed of? At bottom I was ashamed of being so helpless, and since I know now that this was just my pride, then I suppose the real cause of my shame was my vanity. Regardless of the cause, however, the shame I felt twisted into a weapon that I used on myself. I was ashamed of being arrested; I was ashamed of Katya; I was ashamed of the truth; I was ashamed that what Katya had told me of my father might be the truth; I was ashamed of everything I'd done from birth to slumping there alone in a damp tomb. Shame so confused my mind that I couldn't tell the truth from the lie and blamed myself for everything that was happening. Soon enough the circle of self-shame and self-blame made me so disgusted with myself that I was certain that it would have been better that I had died when my mother left me rather than that I'd come to this, a stain on my father's name and on the Air Force.

I was left alone the remainder of the night in that cell that smelled fetid of earth, sweat, urine, rust, rifle grease, tobacco, cooking oil, concrete and coal, and long-dead things. I assumed I was at the Lubyanka, though as it happened it could easily have been Lefortovo Prison, which was then being expanded to accommodate the tyrannical crusades State Security planned for the decades ahead. You must have heard something of Lubyanka as a dungeon during the worst of the Red Terror, from 1934 to 1954. What you might not know is that, by the time I got there, it was more a museum of past horrors than a circle of current hell. The new State Security commandant, Andropov—who would eventually become the only Chekhist boss ever to rise to boss of bosses—had been granted thousands of millions to transform his command into a modern enterprise; and one of Andropov's first endeavors was to renovate the Lubyanka from a prison to a working palace. The sandstone façade was scrubbed and the roof replaced; the cells in the annex were emptied and remade into archives; the execution pits in the basement were torn out and replaced with a central heating system; the torture chambers on the upper floors were rebuilt for a battalion of clerks.

Not all the old personnel were so easily refurbished though, and one of the leftovers was the grotesque orderly who opened my door Sunday morning. At first I thought he was just diminutive, but he was in fact a dwarf in a shabby old-fashioned three-piece suit and rimless glasses that made him appear a miniature Lenin. He said that his name was Bukhtanovich, that I wasn't to talk—"Sssh!" was his favorite order—and that I wasn't a prisoner. He spoke in a purposeful whisper, as if we were in a nursery or church or somewhere requiring discretion. He returned my belt and greatcoat and said that I was to dress, and then repeated that I wasn't a prisoner. He said he was speaking on behalf of General Iagoda, and asked if I would like to have my wounds cleaned, and then, without waiting for an answer, told me to follow him. When I reacted to his mention of General Iagoda, Bukhtanovich again went, "Sssh!" and told me to follow silently.

It might amaze you to learn that I saw Bukhtanovich once more after that Sunday. Twenty years later, in the fall of 1988, I was walking with friends in Moscow off Gorky Prospect near the cinema. It might have been the day of old General Kamenin's funeral, though I'm not sure. In any event I was just ambling along watching the faces of the people, when I suddenly spied Bukhtanovich up ahead on a park bench, sitting by himself, wearing what seemed the same shabby old-fashioned suit of clothes underneath an equally shabby overcoat, so that he looked exactly the same to me, not a day older, though he must have been in his eighties. He was eating an orange while feeding crumbs to pigeons, just like every other pensioner waiting out the day in the autumn sunshine. I should have gone over and introduced myself and asked some sharp questions about whatever had happened to Iagoda—who had vanished from sight by then along with so many of the Lubyanka lords deposed in the general housecleaning of the mid 1980s—but I was too frightened to approach him. And I've told you why: I still felt the shame of what had happened to me; there was a part of my thinking that still held me accountable for all of it. I tried to hide in the crowd as I passed his bench, however I was fairly sure that he saw and recognized me. Maybe not, but I wasn't entirely anonymous by then, after several well-announced orbital missions, and I can suppose that Bukhtanovich was capable of spotting former prisoners as some schoolmasters can pick out their old students. The moment passed when he might have called out to me, and I left Bukhtanovich as if he didn't exist. I never saw him again.

I mention this not only to amaze you, but also to prove to myself that what I saw and felt at the Lubyanka that day was real and true, that such an obscene place did exist as I remember it. My Sunday stay there can get jumbled in my memory, as if it were a nightmare that I suffered after they beat me; but if I hold on to details such as Bukhtanovich, the events feel solid.

We climbed a staircase without a banister, and all the while Bukhtanovich was chatty like a tour guide. For example, on the second level he showed me where the library had been—I saw an empty chamber—and said that the Chekhov books had always been left untouched, explaining, "There's too much food in Chekhov. The prisoners never liked him because of the food." On the sixth level, we moved through ladders and over painter's tarps until we came to a small, empty anteroom, perhaps three meters by four, with a huge barred window. Everything was caked with plaster dust, and Bukhtanovich slipped up the window sash for fresh air. I could see it was raining and that it had snowed overnight, leaving the streets slushy. Bukhtanovich pointed to a large building down the hill and announced just like a guide, "The Metropole Hotel." I couldn't look: it felt as if the outside world was lost to me, as if the city I'd only seen once before, in August the weekend before the Tronkos' party, was only for the living. Bukhtanovich must have understood something of my fears, since he played on them the rest of the day as we waited for Iagoda. Bukhtanovich sat on a barrel of paint, now and again providing me tea and fruit from his own lunch pail, and told me serial stories of the terror at the Lubyanka. Each tale had petty but profane details that Bukhtanovich emphasized as if he were a curator of horror.

For up to twelve hours I held on to my discipline and didn't talk. There were occasional sounds and voices in the corridor, but if I turned my head to them Bukhtanovich would order, "Sssh!" As the hours passed, I came to believe that I was being tricked in some fashion—that this queer man and his sick tales, that the empty halls smelling of lead and turpentine, all were a way of intimidating me so that I would denounce Katya. I even came to think that the mention of Iagoda was a trick of a lie, and that Iagoda neither knew nor cared that I was under arrest because of my relations with a troublemaking intellectual. I know now that my thinking was the single-mindedness of a boy. I wanted Katya's safety; and since I had no way of winning it or even asking for it, I had convinced myself that I must shut up and wait my chance to defend her. It didn't come to me until much later that I was the one they meant to break and use.

I was feeling empty and frail when, at twilight, General Iagoda walked in. Bukhtanovich said, "Sir, good evening, Comrade General."

Iagoda began with his signature of command, "Yes, yes." He was in his overcoat and fur cap and looked confident and sophisticated but also distracted, as if just arrived from larger events. Iagoda waved his cigarette at me and said, "I asked you to give a message to Colonel Oryolin. Some months back. You didn't?"

My sudden fear surprised me so much that I shook in fear of my fear, and found I couldn't swallow.

Iagoda told me that, if I answered him candidly, I had nothing to worry about. "Help me here, Lieutenant Nevsky. I'm not against you. I need your help."

I got some control and reacted with my training by locking my knees, standing rigidly at attention, and remaining silent.

Iagoda knew what I was doing and cursed. He was the same master he'd been in June, though not as enthusiastic, for his motions were cheerless and slow. He told Bukhtanovich to bring me along, and we weaved through connecting rooms full of scaffolding, paint, and lacquer cans, sawhorses and tool benches, until Iagoda pushed a tarp from the last doorway and stepped into the shell of an office. The skylight had been removed and sealed up; the sills and windows were knocked out and framed by translucent sheets; and there were holes in the mosaic of the parquet floor. Iagoda uncovered two chairs and told me, "Please, sit." I obeyed. Iagoda addressed Bukhtanovich, "We need tea," and when Bukhtanovich delayed, Iagoda said, "Don't fuss, hurry, hurry." Then Iagoda, using the trick of delaying conversation, sat beside me, opened his coat, fixed and lit a new cigarette, exhaled heavily, and took papers from his letter case to flip through them cursorily. As the sunlight faded—and Iagoda wouldn't turn on a lamp—we sat there like travelers in a waiting room.

I couldn't then account for our strange setting, but now I understand that the reason Iagoda had arranged our interview in such a way, on a Sunday, in a half-renovated Lubyanka, was that there was little risk of listening devices or eavesdroppers. We were secure from all but Bukhtanovich, who was Iagoda's pet.

Bukhtanovich returned with a tea service and plates of snacks; and, despite Iagoda's complaints, he did fuss over us. Iagoda sipped his tea and began to interrogate me: "I wanted to see you today because I wanted to ask for your help to stop a disaster. You mustn't think of me as your adversary. We're together on this, in that a successful outcome will benefit the both of us. I know that neither of us wants to see our friends come to harm. Do we?" As skillfully as that, the chief of the Fifth Directorate began his pack of lies to me. And then he carefully introduced the threat if I didn't cooperate: "Your friend Mrs. Prishkin has caused herself harm already, hasn't she? And she needs your help too, doesn't she?"

I didn't react. The questions were too tricky for the fortified state of my mind.

Iagoda tried again, "Mrs. Prishkin is your special friend? Answer me."

This time I fell for the trick and nodded.

Iagoda exploited the opening. "And my friend, Madame Romodanovsky, I want you to know that she's also in danger today, and in much more danger than when you rescued her from those hooligans at Novgorod. You did rescue her, didn't you? And you would help me save her again, wouldn't you?"

This was the first time I had heard her surname, Madame Romodanovsky, and I remember thinking it was strangely magisterial, and that calling her the French *Madame* was mysterious and intimidating, as if she weren't human.

Iagoda knitted together the two strands of his argument: "Both of our special friends need our help, do you follow me? And it's my hope that by working together we can help them free themselves from all dangers, or at the least keep them from more harm."

The Air Force warning was that if you responded to State Security in any fashion then you were theirs to torment, so don't talk, don't answer back, don't argue. I knew this, yet I also knew that Iagoda was telling me that Katya was in danger. I wasn't strong enough to keep my mouth shut. "Sir, Mrs. Prishkin was attacked at Starry Town!" I was furious for what had been done and raised my voice, "She was beaten and taken, sir. Sir, Mrs. Prishkin is a Party member. Her husband is deputy director of the medical center, and her grandfather is Academician Univer. She was beaten by thugs, sir. At Starry Town. I saw it!"

Iagoda waved me to calm myself. "Yes, yes," he started, "I agree it was badly handled." He passed his cup and saucer to Bukhtanovich and continued, "But this is a crisis, Lieutenant. We're likely to have mistakes at lower levels, which is why you and I need to work together to prevent further deterioration."

I glanced at him as he talked and saw that behind his eyeglasses his magnified eyes looked zealous. Also, his voice was very relaxed, yet with a keen, intellectual manner. A man of equal rank and experience to Iagoda would have perceived that everything he said was deceitful, however the boy in me only heard masterful candor.

Iagoda began in a new direction, "Let me tell you a story about my friend Madame Romodanovsky and your so-called uncle, Colonel Oryolin. It will help you understand the crisis. It might also help you help me."

Iagoda told me a story that was so incredible it might at first seem fabricated to you. It was one vast lie, but then again the major revelations were true. More than twenty years ago, Iagoda said, Madame Romodanovsky had married Uncle Alexander, and they had had a child, a girl named Sophia. This was in Vienna, just after the war, and some time later Madame Romodanovsky, who was in the service of State Security, accepted an assignment elsewhere while Uncle Alexander stayed on in Eastern Europe. Some time after that the child, Sophia, contracted polio and died. Uncle Alexander blamed his wife and tried to murder her, and he was arrested and sentenced to twenty-five years plus internal exile. He was pardoned in 1955 and returned to duty. By then Madame Romodanovsky had gone abroad to a self-imposed exile in Paris, where she had remained until this past June, when I found her at Saint Sophia on her way to Moscow.

"They were married. They grew apart. They ended their marriage," Iagoda explained. "And then there was the tragedy of their child's death, and Colonel Oryolin had to pay the penalty of his crimes. It was a long time again, yet now it's like a feud between them. Neither of them knows how to stop hating each other for things neither of them can change. Do you understand what I'm telling you?"

Iagoda's lies were so violent that I felt as if I were being pummeled.

"I'm the one who is responsible for Madame Romodanovsky's security," Iagoda continued. "She has come to Moscow on state business. My duty is to make her visit comfortable and safe. Now you can understand why I asked you to speak to Colonel Oryolin for me. I wanted you to tell him that I wanted a truce between us, between him and me. My hope is that the feud can be stopped. If it can't be stopped, then at least we can try to maintain a truce. This is my hope, a truce."

Iagoda reached his subtle point, "Unfortunately, Madame

Romodanovsky isn't convinced of my hope. You see, Lieutenant Nevsky, for reasons I can't explain, she thinks that Colonel Oryolin sent you to intercept her at Novgorod. She thinks that you were sent there as a challenge of some sort, as a threat to her, like a gauntlet being thrown, something like that. I know this must sound queer to you, but you must accept what I say." He blew smoke in my direction and asked, "You weren't, were you? You weren't sent there by anyone to intercept us?"

I responded, "It was an accident, sir. You must believe me. I didn't know she was there, sir. I didn't know anyone was there. I was just hiding from the tankers. I told you the truth. It's the truth!"

Iagoda remarked, "I believe you," and then paused to let me enjoy his paternal confidence. "It was an accident, a coincidence, it was just fate that perhaps we can turn to good. You can see why I find you the best choice to carry my message to Colonel Oryolin. We must help Madame Romodanovsky and Colonel Oryolin through this crisis. You should think of yourself as a go-between chosen by fate to preserve the peace."

Iagoda did say this, "a go-between chosen by fate to preserve the peace," and now that I record it I lower my head in disgust at how easy I was to lie to, how readily I fell into the grasp of evildoing. What nonsense Iagoda told me, what lies upon lies, what a perverted version of Uncle Alexander's marriage. The truth was that Madame Romodanovsky had seduced and betrayed Uncle Alexander, and that she had wanted him dead ever since she'd abandoned him in Vienna in 1948, and that she had been responsible for Uncle Alexander's imprisonment in the camps—it was a lie that he had tried to murder her—and that through her years of self-exile she had watched for her chance to finish her desire, and that now that she had Iagoda's power at her hand she aimed to use it to destroy Alexander Oryolin. The truth was that Iagoda knew all this, and that he meant to give Madame Romodanovsky what she wanted.

I suppose the further truth was that Uncle Alexander and Madame Romodanovsky hated each other equally. Though Uncle Alexander had not tried to murder her, he represented a mortal threat to her as long as he lived. I see clearly now, as I did not then, that the dark truth of those two was that they were both murderous tyrants and an endless threat to everyone. What use is it to try to solve them now? I can't explain everything, but I can say that their marriage was cursed from the start. Their little girl, Sophia, fell sick with polio. Madame Romodanovsky abandoned her daughter to die alone. Since Uncle Alexander was already under arrest and on his way to the camps, he didn't learn of Sophia's death until years later, after his release. All of it was an appalling sadness that only a man who has lost a child can feel to its depths. Losing a child is the worst experience possible, and losing a helpless baby girl to malice would be enough to make a man insane; and I suppose that, yes, I can find an excuse for Uncle Alexander's rage, but no, I won't try to justify him more than telling the facts of his fury. He hated his wife. He held her responsible for Sophia's death. And the reason I am certain he didn't try to murder her is that if a man like that comes at you with a weapon he doesn't stop until you are dead.

It was all a tragedy told and retold millions of times back then. Perhaps the only part of it that surprises you to hear is that Uncle Alexander, one of the greatest of war heroes, spent five years in the slave camps along with Uncle Konstantine and Uncle Dmitry. Then again, little should surprise anyone about the insanity of those days. The simplest lesson for you to remember about tyranny is that if you think it can't get worse, it can get much worse. The truth was that my uncles, the Martian Troika, heroes of heroes, were once convicts, political prisoners, condemned to twenty-five years in doom. They were pardoned only because after Stalin's death and Beria's execution, the new Kremlin bosses discovered that the Air Force was short of qualified test pilots. My uncles volunteered out of doom to drive MiG, Sukhoi, and Yak prototypes. When they didn't die or get so torn up they couldn't walk while deliberately pushing aircraft until their wings and tails fell off, they volunteered into the Corps; and when they didn't die or go invalid riding the early centrifuge and then driving *Voskhod 2* into a mountainside, they volunteered themselves into the moonship.

I knew none of my uncles' postwar history then except what Iagoda told me, of course, nor did I know so many more of the critical details of Madame Romodanovsky's history. But then, I knew so little of what was happening to me that I was protected by my idiocy.

As Iagoda told me his lies, he kept asking the fundamental question: "Do we have an understanding?" He asked again and again in many ways, but he always came to the same bargain: "I need you to tell Colonel Oryolin that there is a truce. When you do tell him, we can help each other." Finally Iagoda slowed his story and asked me, "Tell me what you're going to do."

I knew I was being tricked, and yet I replied, "I'm to tell Colonel Oryolin there is a truce."

Though Iagoda said, "Yes, yes," he darkened at this point, and I think I know why. He didn't want to do what happened next; he wanted to hold just to manipulating me and to setting up his plot from long range. Yet he was as much under Madame Romodanovsky's power as I was under his, and he had her orders. He told me, "Please come along with me now, Lieutenant. Madame Romodanovsky has asked to meet with you. She wants to see you again. I ask you to please keep the arrangement between you and me in confidence. It won't do to upset her. So please, you must keep all we've said in confidence. Please, say you will."

It was a frank plea, and I wanted to agree; and yet even in my confusion I knew that this might be the best chance I would have to save Katya. I started, "But, sir, what about Mrs. Prishkin, sir? You said there was a mistake. You said we could help each other."

Iagoda's face was icy when he responded, "Yes, yes, I understand. She'll be released. Depend on it. I shall keep our arrangement."

I had enough cunning to try once more, "When, sir? When will she be released?"

Before he'd grant me my desire, Iagoda demanded I speak aloud my fate. "We do have an understanding, don't we?"

I ask myself now if I saw the bargain for what it was. Did I see that I was making a compact with the man who was behind Katya's torment and arrest, did I see that I was bargaining with a sadist, a ghoul, a man who meant to kill my uncles and anyone in his way to killing them? At least, did I see that I was being used? I want to be candid. I believe I did understand some of this. I hold now that in some way I did understand I was dealing with the devil. What I did about it was that I lied to myself even as Iagoda lied to me. I wanted Katya's release. It was the most important thing I believed I could take away with me. And so I lied to myself that, if I obeyed Iagoda, then whatever else happened I would have saved Katya. I confess that I knew what I was doing when I said it, when I did the worst possible, when I sealed our fate with the words, "Yes, sir."

From that moment, no matter what else can be said about my

conduct, I was a collaborator, a stooge, a toady; from that instant I was working for State Security and my enemy, Iagoda.

It was time to go, and Bukhtanovich held the door for us and then rushed ahead to call for Iagoda's car. Iagoda and I strolled the corridor to a private lift and then descended five floors. All the while Iagoda chatted about the renovation, about my candidacy, about the recent space missions. "Great excitement, isn't it?" he said of the Zond mission. When we reached the driveway between the main and annex buildings, we found that the slush had made the pavement slick, so that Iagoda had to take my arm to keep his step. Arm-in-arm he took the time to introduce me to other officials who were waiting for their cars, and he spoke of me generously. I was "General Apollon Nevsky's son," or "the air ace Nevsky's son," or "our brightest candidate at Starry Town." Iagoda's conduct was even stranger, because, as the others fawned over me and bantered with Iagoda, it was as if he were treating me like a son. I'm sure now that I wasn't misinterpreting him. It might be that what I experienced was an example of what the philosophers call a divided self—that half of Iagoda was proud of me as the son he might have had, and that the other half meant to break me. I don't know: a human heart is such a wilderness, you can meet anything there, from the horror of the Lubyanka to the nobility of love and faith. It's possible that a man such as Iagoda, who was a very ordinary creature, born in Leningrad to ordinary parents during the civil war, raised and educated ordinarily until he ordinarily joined State Security during the war and ordinarily worked and conspired his way to prominence, that such a man was as capable of love or hate as the next man, and that I am wrong to make him more complicated than an ordinary criminal who's kind to children during the day while he cuts the throats of mothers after dark. I didn't have any of these high thoughts at the time. I just felt Iagoda's contradictions in the same fatalistic way I felt the damp weather.

Iagoda's car arrived, and we roared at high speed out of the courtyard, around Lubyanka Place and the infamous statue of Dzerzhinsky and then down Karl Marx Prospect a half kilometer to the parking lot beside the Bolshoi Theater, where my shame deepened profoundly, because Madame Romodanovsky was waiting for us in her limousine. I'm certain that Madame Romodanovsky meant to humiliate me by making me come to her like a lackey in front of an audience. The opera was just let out; the crowds were charging across the green to the buses and Metro station; and Iagoda's Zil pulled up close beside Madame Romodanovsky's limousine. Bodyguards opened the doors, holding umbrellas for us, and Iagoda ushered me out to join him in Madame Romodanovsky's car, so that in front of hundreds of grim, huddled Muscovites, I was obliged to disgrace my uniform by walking and talking and sitting with Chekhist grandeur.

Once in the car my shame and humiliation ran together like streams of dirty thoughts, for Madame Romodanovsky was in a vulgar mood I can only describe as lustful. And I'm not going to claim I wasn't prey to her tricks, though it disgusts me to think of it, though I wish there was some moral defense for the fact that I fell prey to her powers. At Saint Sophia I'd seen a shocked and threatened woman; however in the car that Sunday, Madame Romodanovsky had regained all her authority, so that what I saw was what Great-Uncle Lev said of the prostitutes who trafficked in the cemeteries at Leningrad, "a whore of Babylon," "a bride of the devil."

"Young lieutenant," she called me. "You remember me," she cooed. She pulled me close, bathed me in her perfumed scent, brushed at my bruises and cuts, and I think she even kissed me on the cheek, though I can't be sure because I felt so embarrassed by her attention. Isn't that astonishing?—that I blushed for her attention and felt desire when she touched me? Madame Romodanovsky didn't keep her attention just to me, she also leaned over Iagoda (she was sitting between us wrapped in a fox coat) and kissed him both on the cheek and then on the mouth. I must emphasize that, though all this sounds overdone now, to me at the time it was most persuasive. She was a very, very beautiful woman, big-eyed and fine-boned and hot to the touch, and whatever she did seemed dignified and fluid. I couldn't see anything ordinary about her look or manner. She had enhanced herself by dressing in some sort of soft dark gown that showed much of her soft breasts; and she also wore an elaborate gem necklace that sparkled in the car light like stars, so that the overall effect was that you were being fondled by an opera star. And she didn't just talk, she sang and cooed and whispered with remarks that were both frivolous and charming, as if she wanted us to be as excited as she was and was trying to cheer us up. "Such handsome men to meet me after the theater!" she'd say, or "You've fallen in love,

Lieutenant. I can see it. Don't deny it. You're in love, aren't you? Oh, it's good to be in love in the rain!" or "Don't you love Moscow with the rain and snow? It makes me feel as if the centuries have dropped away and we're riding the streets in a troika, and I can pull my two handsome hussars close for warmth!" or "You must come to the theater with me, and soon! Do you know Rimsky-Korsakov's *Maid of Pskov*? Do you know any opera? Oh, you should. You're just like the young officers in the opera, so fine and straight and in love!"

I also recall that her laugh—which at Saint Sophia had sounded predatory to me—had become tingling, melodic, most inviting.

I wonder now what could have explained Madame Romodanovsky's behavior that night. It was as if she were drunk or demented or Parisian or what? She was wholly alien to me. I can guess now she was aroused by the opera—I suppose she'd just seen Rimsky-Korsakov—but would the extravagance of the Bolshoi be enough to make her so provocative that she did everything but paw under Iagoda's and my clothes, that she was pornographic? Then again, I think now that perhaps her bizarre conduct was just another part of her nature, that what I saw as erotic that night came from the same source that, on another day, would show itself as cruelty. If I'd been sharper, I might have seen that her uninhibited passion could easily become uninhibited evildoing. Over a lifetime I have learned too slowly that the evil in men is shrewd enough to mask itself at most instances, because evil is patient, remorseless, daring, and knows that there is no hurry to display the worst.

I have also learned something else about evil that I saw that night in the car with those two but didn't understand. Evil is stupid. It makes those who do it stupid. Yes, evildoers are clever and too often gain their way; but at the same time how smart can it be to spend your life with greedy, lustful, homicidal folk, how wise is it to win a fortune alongside men and women who believe in nothing at all and then to come to your end realizing you have lost your soul to rot?

Our limousine sped through the central city and twisted around famous buildings and down famous streets that I'd read about all my life in novels. I could only glimpse the city through the front window, since they kept the window shades drawn. My worst fear was they were going to drive me back to Starry Town, and I would be exposed to the barracks and eventually to my uncles as a stooge. Meanwhile Madame Romodanovsky rambled on, asking me questions she didn't let me answer, gossiping with Iagoda in French, reviewing the opera she'd just seen, patting my chest and arms and brushing my face. By then the limousine had crossed the Moscow River twice and doubled back on the boulevard to the Yaroslavl station, where we stopped at the intersection. It was then that Iagoda pushed up his shade, rolled down his window, threw out his cigarette, and waited for another car to pull right adjacent to us on his side. Iagoda asked me, "We do have an understanding, Lieutenant, don't we?"

I glanced over, as he knew I would, and just then the Chekhists in the adjacent car pushed Katya's face against the passenger window about two meters from Iagoda. I could see her through the opening in the window. Though I was fairly sure she couldn't see me, I wrenched back anyway. The headlights from the escort car behind us had made her look blue and lifeless. I was terrified, and I think now that up until then I had never known what terror was. If you don't know, I can't tell you, but I can say that it feels like frozen hell. My terror was all the worse because at the last, just when I had been lulled by Madame Romodanovsky's patter, just when I had convinced myself that Iagoda was a sufferable bully, I realized that everything they had done up to then was trickery, like a beast playing with its prey. Their coup de grace was that Katya's life was in their hands.

If I'd been ambivalent before about my collaboration, I was clear-eyed when I said, "Yes, sir. An understanding, sir."

At this, even as Iagoda raised the window and lowered the shade again, Madame Romodanovsky changed her mood from lustful to hateful. "Get out, both of you! I'm going home. Get out, now!" Her voice was guttural and spitting with anger. "You bastards get away from me. Both of you, get away!"

Iagoda tried reconciliation. "What is it, darling? What's happened? I thought we'd perhaps drive Lieutenant Nevsky back to Starry Town. Can you tell me what's happened?"

Madame Romodanovsky was fierce. "Damn you, get out!"

"Yes, yes," Iagoda conceded.

In return Madame Romodanovsky gave me the strangest clue of all about her true nature, one that should have burned in my mind until I solved it. She whispered hoarsely to Iagoda, and I only heard part of it because she changed to French in midsentence, but what I did register was, "Give him back his Jewess and get out and . . ." and the rest was in French and lost on me.

I knew I heard her refer to Katya as a "Jewess." I knew that she'd said this with contempt. I knew there was something about me being with Katya that enraged her. But I couldn't make any sense of it, and let it go as just another mystery. I'm not faulting myself for this, just noting it now as another way the evil in her came out like an old wineskin leaking at my feet.

Iagoda took the intercom and told the driver to radio for his Zil to come up for him. We three sat silently for a moment, and then there were car sounds behind us and Iagoda spoke to Madame Romodanovsky, "I'll join you later for supper, is that good for you? I have to stop off for a meeting at the ministry. And then I can join you after midnight? Is there anything I can bring?"

"I don't care what you do," she answered.

This was all that I ever witnessed of their love affair, if that's what it should be called, a harlot and her slave, a tyrant and her consort. Such a love felt uncomfortable to be close to, and didn't make sense to me; yet I think now that it isn't for others to make love that I can understand, it's enough that they give love to others. I know I've called Madame Romodanovsky and Iagoda evildoers, and they were, but they were also human beings with hearts and souls, too, who weren't born rotten, and whom I won't now deprive of the gift of love. The truth of them was never as simple as Madame Romodanovsky being a loveless demon, and Iagoda a hard-hearted monster, and the rest of us their innocent victims. It's my experience that folk who do evil are the same as folk who don't right up until they do the wickedness that divides the good from the bad like life from death. I confess that on quiet nights now, watching the swirling and reliable heavens, I can think of them and the love they showed to each other and can try to find pity for them, though no pardon: not even the fact that they could give love to each other can make me want to offer forgiveness to them.

Iagoda and I stepped out with umbrellas. I looked around at a dark intersection near the Yaroslavl station, the wind rippling the large puddles, several cars pulled at angles to each other. I saw Iagoda's Zil and several cars of bodyguards, but there was no sign of the Volga with Katya. Iagoda lit a cigarette while he watched Madame Romodanovsky's limousine roll away to the east. I knew he was going to make a final speech to me, and I prepared myself as best I could for more of his handling; yet when he eventually started to speak I was still surprised by how defeated he sounded, as if he were the victim and I were just a witness to his pain. "I'm counting on you, Lieutenant," he told me. "You can see the crisis. You can see how much she needs us," he told me of Madame Romodanovsky. "You must help me just as I must help you," he said of our bargain. "It's come to us to save them from worse and worse," he said of everyone.

Iagoda became very commanding and said, "Tell Colonel Oryolin that we have a truce, and that if he stays clear of her, then we'll all stay clear of each other, and all is well. Tell him I want a truce, simply that, a truce."

My Lubyanka ordeal was done. When Iagoda turned me over to the same goons who had arrested me, I felt my exhaustion like an illness coming on—my skin hurt, I felt chills and a scratchy throat, swollen glands and a sweaty fever. It was just like the flu. I wonder now if that's what was behind the breakdown I endured the next week. My suffering began in the car that took me back to Starry Town. I was nauseated immediately at the odors in the car: tobacco, dried vomit, garlic, gun oil. In the front seat the Chekhists talked about ice hockey, while I sat alone in the back and tried to fight off my wooziness by thinking of Katya. That didn't work for long, and soon my sickness weakened me the more, and my sense of shame returned like a blackness falling over me. I felt abandoned, cut off, lost, empty, and so guilty I couldn't think to defend myself. What have I done? I remember thinking. Why is this happening to me? What have they done to me? Why? Why?

I couldn't answer any of this, but I could accuse myself for falling into Iagoda's hands, and I could feel my shame for my bargain with him. "Never surrender!" said the Air Force and every word of every hero I worshipped, and what had I done in my test but quit.

My shame made me a stranger to myself and began a kind of torment that I can now describe as a crisis of my soul. Sunday evening at Starry Town, when I reported back to barracks, the duty officer waved me to go away and said he didn't want to hear my explanation for my violation of curfew. I was sure this meant I was to be punished, and I waited at my bunk for Colonel Khitrovo to arrive and interrogate me. He never came, and I collapsed and slept in my blouse and breeches. Then at Monday morning mess I first recognized what was to become a pattern of shunning. In the breakfast queue, no one addressed me at all, as if I weren't there, and later at the political lecture I sat in my usual chair and yet the chairs around me remained empty. When the lecturer called on me, the others hissed under their breaths, and though I didn't finish my answer to him, the lecturer said, "Excellent, Lieutenant." Later still at class, at noon mess, at the afternoon exercise in the medical center, the other candidates treated me as if I were invisible, the instructors treated me as if I were perfect.

I understood I was being shunned, and I knew why, since I'd seen it done to others at Orenburg. The word had gone round that I was a pet of State Security. The other candidates finally could explain to themselves why I hadn't been punished more for being AWOL in August, and how it was that though on restrictions I could vanish Saturday night and turn up the next day with no explanation for my absence or the marks on my face, and yet not get axed. I was a rat's rat to everyone, a stooge not worth the tarnish on my brass buttons. Gossip was so good that it turned out that they even knew I was the darling of a Lubyanka lord.

What I saw was that Volgamints had been right about the politics of stoogehood. Yet when I approached him for sympathy, even he spoke guardedly. "Well, now, Lieutenant Nevsky," he started, as if he'd never met me before. "Well, a rough night with the ladies, well?" The shunning was harder with my friends Lev Lympyet and Doctor Gogol, since they were compassionate men. When I saw the distrust in their eyes, I ran from them after only a few words.

My shame was worse than any virus. Over the course of the week it spread inside me and transformed into what I think now was a self-hatred that was killing me. I could look at my cut and bruised face in the mirror and see a mask that revolted me. At times I couldn't make my fingers use a pencil or button my clothes, and there was a definite loss of feeling in my fingertips. At other times I heard so poorly that it was as if I were deaf not only to those around me but also to the forest. I couldn't hear the birds! Gradually food came to taste like the fork and the spoon, so I stopped eating; yet I kept drinking larger and larger amounts of water that queerly didn't quench my thirst.

My darkest thoughts weren't for myself but rather for Katya. I was obsessed with Katya. I suffered these sick visions of how they'd beaten her to the ground, how they might have humiliated and vio-lated her, what surely would have come to her if I hadn't bargained with Iagoda. It was crazy-making—that I should think only of the tortures I had stopped. I can see now that I hated myself so severely that I could only manage hateful thoughts about the woman I loved. My mind wasn't rational, and I can't now reconstruct how my mind was working. I do remember imagining Katya being tortured the way Bukhtanovich had said they'd once done to the prisoners, with walking sticks, and such a sick vision doubled my shame and deep-ened my illness.

The strange fact was that I didn't know what had happened to Katya. I didn't know if she had been returned to Starry Town or was still a prisoner at Lubyanka. Yet for four days I neither tried to reach her at her apartment nor contact her through Mrs. Zhukovsky. In-stead I deceived myself that the best thing I could do for her was to pass on Iagoda's message to Uncle Alexander. I told myself that as soon as I kept my bargain, then Katya would surely be safe, whether I could see her again or not. You see what I was doing, using Iagoda's lie on myself, and you see how powerful a lie can be when you suffer it alone.

What I should have done was to break out of my solitude by finding one of the squadron and alerting my uncles. Just a single shout to Genka Stumpelkin—whom I saw Tuesday on the walk-way—would have done, and my uncles would have rescued me from myself. But no, I held back from Stumpelkin just as I held back from the truth of what was happening to me. I didn't want to be who I was. I didn't want to live anymore. I knew I was cursed. I knew I was a coward and dross. I knew I had to obey Iagoda and admit to Uncle Alexander that I was a stooge.

I recall the days as if I was in a fever, with Monday a silent tor-ment and Tuesday marred by sweats and cramps. I hardly felt the exercise that afternoon in the famous Devil's Windmill to nine g's, as if I were protected somehow from simple physical stress. By Wednes-day I was shivering in class and couldn't eat more than bites, though I was drinking water like a desert.

Thursday was the day I feared, because it was October Revolution Day, and the Corps was to march in the procession in Red Square. I assumed that at some point I'd see Uncle Alexander, and I would have to pass on Iagoda's message and disgrace myself forever in my uncles' eyes. The morning began grimly for me with a spontaneous nosebleed that woke me from a bad sleep. At sunrise we candidates rode an autobus into central Moscow to our assembly area off Karl Marx Prospect. It was a cold, gray, blowy dawn, and we candidates swam into a sea of thousands of soldiers in gray greatcoats and parade-dress uniforms. The Corps was to have its customary place of honor near the front of the procession, despite the fact that the parade that year was to be heavily military in support of the expeditionary force in Czechoslovakia. Marching in the October Revolution Day procession had long been a dream of mine, yet I felt like a fraud as I stood with my fellow candidates, who joked among themselves, enjoyed drinks and snacks, and shunned me. I suppose I was shunning myself, too, since I didn't want to be me, I wanted to vanish before Uncle Alexander arrived. Soon the senior cosmonauts arrived in a pack from the hotel across the plaza, where they'd been celebrating breakfast in their customary drunk. As they arrived I counted them off, dreading finding Uncle Alexander's face. He didn't appear, nor did Uncle Konstantine or Uncle Dmitry, nor did the *Soyuz 2/3* crew of colonels Beregovoi and Shatalov. I did see some of the younger members of the squadron—Artzybashev and Kandidim were prominent among the Corps—but again, I couldn't force myself to approach them. The way we were lined up, there was an open file between the candidates and the cosmonauts, and it was easy for me to tell myself that I shouldn't cross the chasm until I had to. I waited and waited, telling myself that momentarily my uncles would arrive and then I would do what I had to do. But then the parade marshals were around us, and it was time to go. The parade moved like a tide with band music scattered in the wind, and the Corps carried itself like a shining craft toward the shore. I was so caught up in my fears that I hardly noticed the hours of the parade itself. I can't now recall what should have been the apex of my experience, when the Corps saluted the Lenin Mausoleum, and though I know I crossed Red Square amid a division of tromping boots and growling diesel engines, I have only a flimsy memory of brass band music somewhere outside of me.

After the parade there was to be a reception for the Corps at the Great Kremlin Palace in honor of Colonel Beregovoi's so-called achievement in landing alive in *Soyuz 3*. Attendance at the reception was to end the Corps' obligations for the day and begin a ten-day general leave in reward for *Soyuz 2/3*. The other candidates were buzzing with their plans for their leave time, and I listened in on them as I walked behind with my head down. I must have looked sickly, because my friend Doctor Gogol couldn't ignore my bad pallor and listless behavior and came over to ask, "Peter, are you ill? Let me see your eyes." I didn't answer him and tried to veer away. My thoughts were as black as death. I had one lie to deliver, and I couldn't do it.

From what Doctor Gogol told me later, I collapsed sometime between when he first spoke to me and the Kremlin's Borovitskaya Gate, where we were to report for the reception. I have no memory of any of this period in here and have to rely on what my friends Gogol, Lympyet, and Volgamints told me. I broke down, or quit, or whatever you call it when you suffer a hysterical paralysis. I just sat down on a curbstone beside a flatbed tank carrier and waited dumbly for nothing, sweating, shaking, mouthing silent cries. Doctor Gogol guessed I'd picked up a sudden virus, because my clothes were soaked through by a fever and I couldn't balance on my feet. Volgamints wanted to leave me and get on to the reception, and said something typical of him such as, "Shit, let his frigging Chekhist pals baby him. It ain't our problem."

Doctor Gogol knew to ask the patient what he wanted, and according to him—since I'm blank on this—what I said astounded them. I begged them not to abandon me in the Lubyanka, not to leave me to the Organs, not to let them take my uniform and name and face away from me. I also wept and rolled on the ground. Doctor Gogol decided he must get me back to the medical center at Starry Town. He told Volgamints and Lympyet to go on without him. Volgamints was angry with me for being such a burden and cursed and whined as the three of them, like grumpy Good Samaritans, hired us a lorry ride back to Starry Town. After all their efforts, they discovered that the medical center's staff had already gone on leave. This meant that either I would have to be left to shake and sweat alone or they would have to stay with me; so they carried me to the candidate barracks, where Doctor Gogol worked to control my fever and dehydration.

Volgamints solved the dilemma in his crabby way when he decided that, if I was the wondrous little bastard I claimed to be, then my so-called heroes, my "frigging colonels," should take responsibility for me. He sneaked away to telephone Uncle Dmitry's apartment—the one of my uncles who was admired throughout the Corps—and Angelicka Zhukovsky picked up the call.

What I can next remember clearly is many hours later when Uncle Dmitry and Uncle Konstantine were standing beside my bunk, conferring with Doctor Gogol. It must have been the middle of the night, the early morning of November 9. Back over by the doorway Major Fedyuninsky was also there, carping about the general colorlessness of the candidate barracks, and over at the doorway were Volgamints and Lympyet alongside my friends from the squadron Stumpelkin, Miserbiev, and Adama-Bibliov, all of them talking with Lympyet about my collapse.

I remember Uncle Dmitry sitting at my side and rubbing my hand to get my attention. He was in his flight suit, and he looked worn down, a tiny, somber man trying to stay focused. He'd just flown seven hours against bad head winds from the Cosmodrome. It turned out that my uncles hadn't planned to be in Moscow for the parade at all—they'd stayed on at the Cosmodrome after the *Soyuz 2/3* mission—and that uncles Dmitry and Konstantine had come to Starry Town only after hearing of my distress. Uncle Dmitry started, "Petya, were you taken to the Lubyanka last Saturday night? You and Katya both? Petya, you can tell us? You're safe here."

I wanted his help but didn't know how to ask for it and tried, "Mrs. Prishkin, she was taken, too, sir."

Uncle Dmitry was consoling. "Katya's told us some of it now. She's with Angelicka, with my wife."

I asked the critical question, "Is she safe?"

Uncle Dmitry stated, "She is now."

I found some strength. "We were attacked!" I said. "Six of them, out near the Black House, Saturday after the recital. They jumped us and beat us and they took her away. I didn't see her again until Sunday night. I didn't know if she was back or not, but I couldn't see her. I didn't know what to do."

Uncle Dmitry looked grave. "You two kept this to yourselves. Why? And Katya's been hiding in her apartment. Why? And you, what've you done since Saturday? Why didn't you get word to us? Why did I have to learn all this by telephone?"

Arkady Volgamints stepped up to the bed and told Uncle Dmitry,

"He's been like this all week. They must have worked him over. We thought it peculiar, all those bruises and cuts, but we figured he was with them, you know, one of their best boys. Until he fell sick today, we didn't know he was bad off. I've seen this kind of thing before. Did they use the drugs on him? That's what I think. They used the drugs on him."

At the time I didn't know what Volgamints meant by "the drugs"—the torture drugs used by State Security—but Uncle Dmitry did, and he looked to Doctor Gogol for the answer. Doctor Gogol shook his head. "I've checked for that, Colonel. No needles that I can find, but I'd have to have laboratory work to be sure."

Uncle Dmitry addressed Gogol, Volgamints, and Lympyet. "You three have done well and thank you. My advice is that you should go on with your evening. You aren't in the same position we are here, and I don't want to have to tell you what to do." Uncle Dmitry was being diplomatic, though he was telling them that as candidates they couldn't withstand the sort of trouble that was ahead.

Doctor Gogol protested some because I was his patient. Gradually Uncle Dmitry persuaded him, and Gogol let Volgamints and Lympyet lead him away. In parting Volgamints leaned over to wink at me and to tell me, "Soft landing, Nevsky." He was a brave man, Arkady, and he fought as hard as any one of us for the Corps and for the moon mission, as you shall see, and lifelong he served Starry Town ably; and if I seem to knock him now and again for his tight-fistedness, I want also to emphasize that I always respected him, and for moments like this I loved him, too.

Once the barracks was secure of all but the squadron members, Uncle Dmitry started in earnest to me, "You must tell me what's been done to you and Katya. You must tell me everything."

I felt my shame like a wash of heat down my back and a spike in my throat. I turned my head to the wall.

Uncle Konstantine leaned over and smoothed my wet hair back, passing his hard, cool hand across my brow and speaking to me affectionately, "Easy, darling, the way to do it is easy. Listen now, just start talking by telling us how glad you are to see us. The rest will follow like a little brook stream. We'll tell you when we've fished here before."

Uncle Dmitry was not so patient. "I don't know what you've

been hiding, but you must tell me now. It's important. There's something gone very wrong at the Cosmodrome. We have to know if what's happened to you is part of it."

I knew the moment he told me there was "something gone wrong at the Cosmodrome" that my trouble was part of it, and that what I'd done was hurt my friends and aid my persecutors. This wasn't a logical assumption, more an intuition, and it overwhelmed me with a remorse that made me sob. I sobbed loudly like a mourner and yet also was able to react with my training to report properly by putting my feet to the floor, so that this hysterical, half-naked, bare-foot boy soaked in sweat was teetering before a wall of cosmonauts. Uncle Konstantine pulled me up into his huge embrace and kissed me on my cheeks, then laid me down like a wounded falcon. His voice was as warm as love when he said, "Who beat on you, darling? Was it Maximov? Just tell Uncle Kostya, and I'll see to it."

My soul broke free, and I was able to tell them the truth, point by point, from my first run-in with Iagoda at Saint Sophia to the last word he told me to tell Uncle Alexander at the Yaroslavl station, "Tell him I want a truce, simply that, a truce." I was surprised at how straightforwardly I spoke, leaving out my self-pity, keeping to the facts as I knew them and reporting word-for-word much of the dialogue between me and Iagoda. I also told of Madame Romoda-novsky, though in less detail because of my concern to record Iagoda's threats against Katya. You know all I had to say, indeed you know much more than I did at the time about Iagoda and Madame Romodanovsky, so there's no need to reproduce my debriefing by my uncles. They were exacting and, when I mentioned Ma-dame Romodanovsky, they were cold in the eyes, and you'll soon understand why. What is significant to say here is that my con-fession stopped the worst torment of my shame, my self-hatred, which I know now to be what it feels like to have your soul grabbed at by a wolf.

3

Abduction

I learned from my uncles that night that General Iagoda had grabbed at more than my soul, for he had also directed his agents to grab off the Grand Constructor, Academician Nikhon Univer, from Star City. Iagoda had abducted and imprisoned the Grand Constructor in order to bait a trap for my uncles, though the trap wasn't apparent to me for some days.

What should have been clear to me was that everything Iagoda had said was a pack of lies like a pack of wolves. Iagoda meant to destroy my uncles, yet because of their status and fame, and because of the might of the Air Force and the Corps, he couldn't move against them directly; he had to employ surrogates like me and he had to bait lures like the Grand Constructor. I emphasize that everything Iagoda had said was falsehood—when he said I was a go-between, he meant I was a dupe; when he said he aimed at a truce, he meant he aimed at assassination; when he said that if I did what he said then Katya would be safe, he meant that she was doomed.

If you don't see the lie yet just look at what had happened up to October Revolution Day. All those bizarre incidents were directed by Iagoda to a cunning point. The bizarre task Iagoda gave me at Saint Sophia's; the bizarrely easy time I had enjoyed at the barracks; my bizarre detention at the Lubyanka; Madame Romodanovsky's bizarre remarks about Uncle Alexander: all this was joined with the bizarre harassment of Katya and finally with the bizarre abduction of the Grand Constructor to Iagoda's point that this was the opening battle in a fight to the finish between himself and Alexander Oryolin. Much of what you've seen so far was all Iagoda's plan not to end a feud but to win one, and my part in his plan was to be the thrown gauntlet that started the feud all over again.

What was the feud about? I've thought long about it, more than seven decades now, and I do believe the feud was about love, at least some sort of love. Iagoda loved Madame Romodanovsky. Madame Romodanovsky hated Uncle Alexander. Uncle Alexander was caught between loving and hating her back and his disregard for Iagoda. You can judge for yourself, but after all the betrayal and murder I witnessed in that year of the drive for the moon and the fall from reason, my best opinion is that the feud I saw between Iagoda and Oryolin came to love and failed love and the terrible cruelty of that miserable woman who called herself Madame Romodanovsky. Yes, I know I'm sounding sentimental to say that all this violence turned on personal motives, but I've tried to find some larger meaning to the darkness and I can't see it. What I witnessed was a love triangle of two men and a woman who had limitless power available to them and who didn't hesitate to use it. Rather fault the political catastrophe that delivered up a Russia so prostrate before tyranny that three such cruel people could play out their passions without checks than to fault me for not solving this tragedy more than as a melodrama. Wasn't the truth of the Soviet empire that it was no more intelligible than slave quarters? Can there be anyone who doesn't see after all this time that when you make a great land like all the Russias into a slave empire that you make vicious slave-mongers like Iagoda into masters and whores of Babylon like Madame Romodanovsky into royalty and wronged heroes like Uncle Alexander into self-righteous avengers? The October Revolution was a fall from the anarchy of the Romanov puppets into pack wantonness and private vengeance and the wrath of a handful of nearsighted cranks called Bolsheviks. What Lenin's knotted, miserly, childless dreams rendered—he outlawed the twelve days of Christmas—was not a modern state but an ever more puerile one, where nothing mattered but the royal desires and the secret police's cravings and the Army's pride. And when Lenin was dead, when his bowels and desires and warped soul were gone, what remained was a mummified lie and criminals such as Stalin and Trotsky and Bukharin. All power to the supreme Soviet tantrum. From each according to his rage, to each according to his rampage. How surprising is it that, seven decades after the October Revolution, three potent Russians could make their base jealousies into a gang war; and how much less surprising is it to you that, nearly seven decades later, my memory of 1968 is that of a black melodrama of liars, killers, and despots, of whining, cheating, and back stabbing, of the most stupid of all sins, lust, and the crudest of all political programs, assassination.

At first light Friday, within hours of my confession to my uncles, I was put on the squadron's Il-14 transport and dispatched to Uncle Alexander at the Cosmodrome. By then I'd told my story to Uncle Dmitry and Uncle Konstantine at the barracks, and then again to Zhora Fedyuninsky on the way to the airfield and in the first hour of the flight as he took notes. My uncles didn't provide me with details about the crisis, just the fact that the Grand Constructor had vanished from Star City, and that they'd been looking for him for three days.

Until I'd told them of my ordeal, they hadn't understood why the Grand Constructor was missing. Once I'd mentioned Iagoda, they had a good notion that the trouble was the work of State Security. I think that Uncle Dmitry saw instantly that Iagoda was aiming at Uncle Alexander, that the abduction of the Grand Constructor was an opening move, not an endgame, and that Iagoda had moved skillfully because Uncle Alexander would not be able to keep back from a bold counter to protect the man who owned the moonship. I think, too, that Uncle Konstantine saw the challenge more plainly as a contest between two cocks who would fight to the death.

On the fourteen-hour flight I dozed, brooded, drank liters of water, and, after the refueling at Orenburg, slept more heavily than I had in some time. Genka Stumpelkin sat across from me, since he was my new guardian who, along with the other junior cosmonauts, Miserbiev, Adama-Bibliov, Schtange, and Tevyelook, had been sent south to work for Fedyuninsky. Major Cherryntevsky and captains Artzybashev and Kandidim had remained in Starry Town with Uncle Dmitry and Uncle Konstantine to press inquiries at the ministries in Moscow. No one confided in me. Fedyuninsky talked with me on the flight but only to review my report.

I did try to get information out of him. "But sir," I tried at an early point in the flight, "what's going to happen?"

My uncles had appointed Zhora Fedyuninsky chief of the investigation of the abduction, both because he was the squadron's executive officer and because he was a son of the procurator of Kazan—in sum because he loved playing detective—and he sat beside me in full-dress uniform and keen-eyed for his duty. "I'm to determine what *has happened*," he answered, snapping his fingers. "What's going to happen is that I'm going to answer all the questions that can be answered. One at a time I will have all the answers come to me like children."

I asked for sympathy. "Did I do this, sir?"

Fedyuninsky told me, "You didn't help it. It's my opinion that by withholding information you made everything worse."

"But why would they take the Grand Constructor?" I asked, and then I displayed the size of my naïveté about State Security. "I don't know why they took me. I don't know why they gave me back. I don't understand, sir, why General Iagoda told me there was a truce, and why if General Iagoda's trying to get a message to Colonel Oryolin, why he sends me with it, and what have I got to do with the Grand Constructor?"

My uncles had ignored my questions and Fedyuninsky gave me little more. "Lieutenant, it's not mine to answer your questions alone, it's mine to answer all the questions—who, when, where, and how—and why, too, I will get to why."

The other cosmonauts treated me like an invalid child, though at the time I took it as more shunning. What I recall vividly from the flight was my belief that I had ruined myself with the Corps and ended my chance to join my uncles' squadron. I believed that I'd shown myself weak, deceitful, and untrustworthy, and that they kept talking to me only because I was a source about Iagoda. How narrow an idiot's mind can be even when trouble is imminent: with all those wretched events spinning around me, what I worried about was my status.

I was also worried about Katya, though not as acutely as I might have been if I hadn't been a selfish little fool. I suppose what had happened was that I'd decided that my uncles could help her far better than I ever could. No, I see that why I didn't worry more about Katya was that I believed I'd failed her completely and realized I was a coward. For four days I'd done nothing to help her while I'd lied to myself that if I tried to contact her I'd make it worse for her. Uncle Dmitry had told me that she was safe with his wife, yet he'd not told me what she'd endured since being dumped back at Starry Town Sunday night—her hiding in her apartment with Daniel since her husband, Boris Prishkin, had deserted her and left Daniel in a neighbor's care, also her refusing the phone and the mail while she waited for worse and worse, and also how she'd lied to Angelicka the first time Mrs. Zhukovsky had called to see why Katya was not about. Only Volgamints's telephone call had alerted Mrs. Zhukovsky to the scale of the crisis, and she'd both telephoned her husband for help and gone to gather Katya to her arms. Katya had suffered a four-day terror, and I'd let it happen as if I'd had no responsibility, as if I didn't know her.

During my confession Uncle Dmitry had scolded me about my affair with Katya. "You could have been more honorable with her, a married woman, no?" he'd told me. I think now that Uncle Dmitry was more annoyed that his wife hadn't told him about Katya and me than he was with me. Uncle Konstantine had mocked him for his prudery. "What's honor to a hungry stomach? What's honor to a lonely soul? What's honor in the grave?"

Uncle Dmitry had flared back, "You know they've used them. You see what the Chekhists are doing."

Uncle Konstantine had rebutted, "I know that love isn't wrong—not for boys anytime and anywhere."

There was momentous mystery to their disagreement. I know now that they were arguing about Uncle Alexander's love for Madame Romodanovsky as much as they were debating how Katya and I were being used by Iagoda. Word of Madame Romodanovsky startled my uncles—in truth, Uncle Dmitry was stunned. I saw a darkness in him that I couldn't comprehend and was out of proportion to his paternal evenhandedness, so that his fine, bony face became waxy like death at her name. Even zany Uncle Konstantine reacted oddly at her name, laughing harshly when I reported what she'd said of them sending me to intercept her at Saint Sophia; and when I described her lurid behavior in the car after the Bolshoi, I saw Uncle Konstantine grimace for the first time ever—a man who grinned at hellfire blanched at my description of how she'd pawed at me.

At no point did they help me make sense of any of what I'd seen with Iagoda or Madame Romodanovsky. Several times they evaded me when I asked how was it that Madame Romodanovsky knew about me and my father. I was curious about it: "She talked about my father, sir, as if she knew him. Did she? How did she know about me? —She called me 'Little Peter.' Why didn't she believe me when I told her I didn't know you?" Perhaps I should have picked up on this clue that they wouldn't tell me what my father had to do with

Madame Romodanovsky and Uncle Alexander; but then, because of what Katya had said about my father's death in the camps, I was frightened of the truth of my father. I let Uncle Dmitry put me off with sympathetic silences and Uncle Konstantine with grunts.

I wasn't so reluctant to press Uncle Alexander. Friday afternoon, November 8, Uncle Alexander was waiting for our plane at the Tsar Cannon airstrip. We'd flown straight to the Tsar Cannon works in the desert, since my uncles were already anticipating their efforts would need a base of operations. I remember looking out to see the backwash of the props lift the hem of Uncle Alexander's greatcoat as he stood like a black statue on a yellow sea. He'd been camped at the Cosmodrome since August—both helping prepare Beregovoi's mission and visiting Tsar Cannon—and he looked trimmer and healthier, save for the new blackness in his eyes that I know now was vengeance.

While the others off-loaded the plane and helped with the refueling—Glavtop and Grin were flying Fedyuninsky and his investigation team on to Star City immediately—Uncle Alexander led me to the squadron's new-built bivouac. Kazakh laborers from Tsar Cannon had transformed the operations shack into an air station, including a long Quonset that was now a cozy hut barracks with tables, bunks, a new coal stove, a water tank, a diesel generator, and a radiotelephone station hooked to a naked radio mast that swayed in the gusts. It was most cold everywhere, the yellow dust flying like ice crystals against my neck and face. Even once we were inside, I kept my greatcoat on and my backside to the stove. Uncle Alexander sat on a camp stool across from me and lit his pipe with a taper. Except for that blackness in his eyes, he looked the poised commanding officer. "Tell me," he ordered.

I spoke for many minutes, repeating my confession as succinctly as possible, and all the while Uncle Alexander's face was a cipher to me. I listened to myself talk and, whenever I paused, I listened to the rattling tin walls and the crackling atmospherics of the radiotelephone. I'd had time to prepare my report so that it was chronological and, whenever appropriate, illustrated with quotes from Iagoda and Madame Romodanovsky. I didn't hesitate to report what Madame Romodanovsky had said of Uncle Alexander at Saint Sophia, nor what Iagoda had said to me of Uncle Alexander's marriage. I emphasized Iagoda's words. "General Iagoda said there's a feud, sir," I repeated. "With you and Madame Romodanovsky. He said he wants to stop the feud. He called it a crisis some times and a feud at others. He said I was his go-between. I said I would be." It didn't feel bad to admit my idiocy anymore, which I suppose is one way of saying that I was learning to handle myself.

At one point I tried, "General Iagoda said she was his responsibility," and Uncle Alexander set his huge jaw so that I thought he was going to respond, but he didn't. He didn't speak until I'd finished my chronology and, believing I'd done well and deserved some information in return, I tried to separate the truth from the lies. I asked, "General Iagoda said she was your wife, sir. Is that true, sir?"

Uncle Alexander, never not an obtuse man, snorted smoke around his silvery head and stared at my neck.

"He said you were married after the war," I said. "And that your baby girl, her name was Sophia, that she died later. Is that true?"

He exhaled smoke hard at this. I understood that I shouldn't ask more about his daughter, about Sophia. I believe now that it was cruel of him to hold back on me about Sophia, and he was wrong, very wrong. Yes, if our roles had been switched, I might have done the same; and I would have been wrong, too.

I tried in frustration, "Sir, can you tell me why General Iagoda is doing this?"

He replied, "No."

I knew at the time that he wasn't telling me the truth, yet it wasn't mine to challenge his declarations. I did try to get him to help me about what I now understand as our consuming subject, Madame Romodanovsky. "But how did she know about me, sir? At Saint Sophia, Madame Romodanovsky seemed to know everything about me. And, sir, why didn't she believe me that it was an accident I was there? Why does she think you sent me? Why should you do that?"

Uncle Alexander remained intractable. "It's done."

I whined some, "Did I cause this, sir? By going into Saint Sophia? Or by holding back about General Iagoda? Or by being with Mrs. Prishkin and all?"

Uncle Alexander said, "Get your rest. You'll need it."

In defeat I whined again, "But why did they take the Grand Constructor?"

Uncle Alexander barked, "Don't explain them!" And then he

pulled back, squared his big shoulders, and spoke evenly, "What is it you want to know, Lieutenant?"

What I wanted to know was about my father. I wanted the truth of his death. I wanted to know why Madame Romodanovsky knew about my father. I wanted to know why, if he and uncles Dmitry and Konstantine had spent five years in the slave camps, what their imprisonment had to do with my father. I wanted to know why all this was happening to me and around me and yet no one would tell me the truth. I wanted to know so much that what came out was self-pity: "I didn't mean to tell them anything, sir, about myself, or my father or you, sir. I tried not to. They tricked me."

Uncle Alexander flared again. "What of it! What use talking about what they've done. It's what we're to do that I care about. Your job is to get in line and stay there. Understood!"

I snapped to attention like a cadet. "Sir!"

Uncle Alexander lost interest in me, as if I were no more useful than the stove, and he bolted upright and strode out of the hut without a word, his boots like hammer blows on the planks. He continued on across the salt flat toward a construction crew that was making ready to pour concrete, and then, after he exchanged some words with the foreman, he was picked up by his command car and driven toward the Tsar Cannon oasis. I wouldn't see him again until Sunday. Indeed for two days and nights I would see only a few of the squadron in passing and was left alone at the barracks hut in company with the Kazakh women tending the mess and kitchens.

Friday and Saturday nights I had plenty of time to brood about Uncle Alexander but didn't make much progress. I've told you he was such a hero to me that it was difficult to begin to think of him as a man with troubles and faults like the rest of us. The larger truth might now be that Alexander Oryolin was a hard man in a hard world and he lived out his fate with as much nobility as perversity and that in the end he got what he deserved, which was no mercy and no peace on earth. I don't believe this all the time—that he deserved to die in failure—and even while I tell you what I saw of him, I also want to understand why he did what he did. Yes, he was a cruel man who didn't believe in justice, rather in himself and his comrades; and he got what he wanted with violence; and I never heard him speak of fairness. Some of this might be explained by his wild, troubled youth. I don't think I've mentioned that he was born a bastard during the civil war in 1921. I know a deal about bastardy. Do you think bastardy explains a man? Do you think if he'd known his own father—by one account a tsarist flying officer named Alexey Oryolin on the run from the Red Army who stopped off in Sevastopol long enough to fall in love, father a child, and then fall into the hands of bandits, who shot him when he couldn't pay a bounty—that then Uncle Alexander would have understood what I wanted from him about my own father? I can't rely too much on this account, since there was another version of Uncle Alexander's birth that says his father just seduced a young girl and then just fled when the Red Army arrived, and that Uncle Alexander grew up in a large successful family (which didn't survive the German occupation) after his mother married well to a ferry captain. Either way, I don't know if any one turn of bad luck in a man's life can explain all of it. It would be too easy to write off several generations of Russians as only bootless victims if you looked to the Revolution, the civil war, the purges and the war and the slave camps as explanation for their personal failure. I'll have more to say about Uncle Alexander's dark soul, so what I'll add now is that he was cruel because he wanted to be cruel, he was vengeful because he wanted vengeance, he wanted to win the moon because he wanted to win, and all the rest that can be said about his motives can sound to me as hollow as a lie.

I slept most of the weekend, forgotten like a stray cat, though at the time there was always the question for me as to whether or not I was a pariah. The Kazakh women fed me mutton stew and insisted I sleep near the stove for warmth. My solitude did allow me to regain my strength and the weight I'd lost since Sunday. I did spy Stumpelkin, Miserbiev, and Adama-Bibliov on Saturday morning when they landed in a Mil from Star City, but they were off again immediately, part of Fedyuninsky's investigation of the abduction. Otherwise, to fill my time at night, I watched the deep starry sky swirl around in a dome to a full one hundred and eighty degrees, and during the day I watched the Kazakh laborers work on the airstrip. They were just beginning the expansion of the airfield then— backhoeing, form-raising, asphalt and concrete pouring—and the heaviest work was months ahead. I note it now because it's a demonstration that even as early as October, my uncles had given orders not only to make the squadron's base camp at the Quonset hut, but also to make the desert patch into a shock airbase suitable for interceptors, heavy transports, Mil squadrons, and a stout Air Defense. Those laborers were preparing the way for work battalions to come, and I suppose this is proof that my uncles always knew the battle was coming to them.

I suppose this is also proof that my uncles knew what Iagoda and Madame Romodanovsky were about, and that they could have spared me much suffering if they'd told me the truth right away. Instead they treated me like a child to be kept in the kitchens with the Kazakh women. I don't now blame them and can even make excuses for them. They were hard pressed to face the trouble of the Grand Constructor at hand. Once that was resolved, I suppose they figured they could turn to me. What they did was leave me to my own hands. And I wasn't helpless, was I? I wasn't so stupid that I didn't realize there was more to the story of Madame Romodanovsky than what I'd heard. Look at it as plainly now as I could have then. Who was Madame Romodanovsky to me? Why did she hate Uncle Alexander? Because of their dead child? Then what did my father have to do with them? And why did she say I was a threat to her at Saint Sophia? The solution to the mystery of her and all of them was right in front of me, yet I couldn't see it because I was too concerned with my rank, my ambition, my empty vanity. *I wanted to be important more than I wanted to think importantly.* I agree with Great-Uncle Lev that you see and hear and turn and know the truth of yourself when fate permits, no sooner.

The next step in the crisis came Sunday evening when the Il-14 from Starry Town landed at moondown, bringing bad news for my uncles and trouble for me. I watched the landing from a hundred meters behind the barracks, where I had been poking at the charcoal remains of an ancient cooking oven from when the wadi had been a major crossroad of the caravan route to the north. I'd also been wandering around in self-pity and self-doubt since supper. Genka Stumpelkin came running right to me, since he'd not let me far from his sight since he'd arrived for supper. "We're to report in, Peter," he told me. "Word has it there's a big briefing within the hour— Zhora's going to solve the case, or something like that."

"Is that the colonels coming down from Starry Town?" I asked of the Il-14. But before he could answer I asked what I really wanted to know. "Are you sure they want me there?"

Stumpelkin was puzzled at my neediness. "I'm telling you the orders."

I wanted more from him and tried again. "Genka, I keep apologizing for what I did, and no one wants to listen. I don't know what you've heard, but I'd do anything to make up for what I've done. I didn't know what the Chekhists were after. I didn't understand it. Last June, up at Novgorod, I was on my way to Starry Town when some thugs jumped me. And then this General Iagoda of the Lubyanka made me promise to pass on a message to Colonel Oryolin. And I didn't do anything about it for months. I guess I forgot about it on purpose. I didn't want to have anything to do with the Chekhists. But last weekend they took me again, to the Lubyanka, and Iagoda made me promise again. I was trying to protect Mrs. Prishkin, so I said I would. I guess you've heard some about Mrs. Prishkin. I didn't want to do what Iagoda said. And I waited until it was too late anyway." What I'd said was incoherent, so I begged him, "Do you believe me?"

It meant much to me that Stumpelkin's dark eyes softened and he nodded in sympathy. "Yeah, I understand," he started, and then he philosophized in his own way. "When they come at you like that— I've only heard stories—but when they do, no man can stand up by himself—he needs friends." To cloak his affection he waved at the stars and changed the subject. "The sky's clear here three hundred days a year, did you know that? Go north or south three degrees, and you get lots of cloud cover. But here it's like a clear window on heaven. Maybe I'm exaggerating."

I so appreciated his kindness that I tried to disguise my gratitude. "I guess I'm tired or something. Maybe I have a cold. Maybe I'm not making much sense."

"Then eat," he said, producing a pastry from his tunic and handing it over. "Who knows when we'll see sweets again?"

I grabbed for the pastry and for the promise of being included in better days ahead. "Have they found the Grand Constructor?" I asked. "Are they going after him?"

Stumpelkin stared at the barracks and repeated his firm faith: "When Colonel Oryolin's in charge, anything's possible."

I felt much better as we started back to the bivouac friends again, and I had my head up as if I were part of the team. The Il-14 was taxiing into the floodlights at the tank farm, and most of the squadron had sauntered out to meet it. To the north I could see the headlights of the three cars that were bringing Uncle Alexander and senior Tsar Cannoneers to the briefing, and to the south I could see a weaving light at low altitude, which was Fedyuninsky in the Mil helicopter headed in for his grand performance. I knew all this meant there was a showdown imminent. I asked Stumpelkin, "It's bad, isn't it? The Grand Constructor's dead or something, and it's bad?"

The answer to my question was that it was very bad, and how bad I realized the moment I saw Katya swinging down from the Il-14 with Uncle Dmitry and Uncle Konstantine. I was surprised, yes, but stranger than that I felt very protective of her and wanted to take charge of her safety. It was pride that made me so pigheaded about Katya—I'd failed her and wasn't willing to accept my failure—and I know I made it worse for everyone when I raced ahead to speak to her. "Katya, please, wait," was how miserable I sounded. "I have to talk to you."

I deserved it when Katya turned on me and said, "Get away, now, Peter, get back." She looked vigorous in cosmonaut fatigues and a new greatcoat, though her face was gray and tense. She told me, "This isn't the time, Peter."

I was so upset I didn't care if my uncles were listening. "I wouldn't have done anything to hurt you. I love you. I'm sorry. I am!" I had to shout over the backroar as the Il-14 spun around to ready for a cargo off-load. "I thought I was helping you!" I cried. "I did it for you!"

"Peter, stop it!" she ordered and reached for Uncle Dmitry's arm. Uncle Dmitry advised me, "Not now, Petya."

I talked back, "But why's she here, sir? You said she was safe, and now you've brought her here, and that can't be safe."

Glavtop and Grin shut down the props; there was a pause while we all regained our bearings. Then Katya spoke so bitterly that I didn't at first recognize her words, "Who's safe? You haven't learned anything; you're a fool! Those bastards have done this, and I'm not hiding from them anymore, and I'm not running away! I'm going to fight back. I'm going to make them pay for hurting me and my family. It's my family that's been attacked. Mine! I'm going to get back my grandfather! He's mine!"

If I hadn't been so caught up in my own needs, I might have

noticed that Katya was far from the same prickly intellectual who'd told me in August that my uncles were "anachronistic" and that Uncle Alexander was a "ridiculous old war eagle." I might have seen that Katya was starkly changed from the pacifist who signed letters of protest to the Central Committee and who ordered me never to fight back. I might have noticed that she was talking not reason but revenge. Instead I tried more whining. "But Katya," I said, "but Katya, I was trying to help you."

She shouted, "Shut up!" but I couldn't let her alone. It made me feel crazy that she wouldn't hear out my apology and accept my protection. I was hysterical when I said, "Why are you doing this? What about Daniel? What about us? And you said your grandfather was a stranger to you! And you said not to tell anybody about what we were doing! I listened to you! You said we were together on our own star! I love you!"

Katya didn't pay mind, rather tucking herself on Uncle Dmitry's arm and marching away with him to the barracks. Only Uncle Konstantine took time to care for me, putting his arm on my shoulder and squeezing me. "It's good you say things like that, Petya. I like to listen to them. You say them well." Uncle Konstantine beckoned for Stumpelkin to close up so we both could hear his counsel, and we three bumped together with Little Laika whipping in and out of our steps. "It's good for the soul to say you love a girl," Uncle Konstantine philosophized. "Say it as often as possible. Love is the best, better than juice, better than flying, too. Keep saying it, my darlings, always say it, and all your troubles will vanish like the snows."

The truth, if I'd looked at it, was that Katya's troubles were vast, and that even if I'd been a mature man who could make love to her as wisely as she deserved, there might not have been release. Her life was a tragedy, with her husband an informer and deserter, her Party rights forfeited, her son left fatherless, one of her lovers in jail—Ara Ovchennikov had already been sentenced to twenty-five years—and the other a raw boy; and her prospects without money, status, a job, or credible security most reduced. I can see now that her decision to reach out to my uncles for help wasn't truly anger or revenge for her grandfather's abduction or her own abuse but rather the result of a desperate, hopeless fear. Katya was terrified in a world that didn't allow for her sort of genius, and I think her terror showed itself as fury. I can't be sure, but I do believe that when she said she wasn't hiding or running away anymore she actually meant that she wanted to but was too afraid to go off alone. Maybe not, maybe she was a vengeful person who had fooled herself into pacifism; and maybe she meant what she said when she claimed, "I'm going to fight back!" and took up with men with guns like my uncles.

There was something secret at the time that makes me believe Katya was not being honest about herself when she cried out for retaliation. She was pregnant some eight weeks with our child. I believe she knew this without knowing it, as sometimes happens with pregnancy, and that what I saw that day was a woman alone, cornered, as vulnerable as imaginable, and fighting mad for her baby and her life because she could think of no other refuge.

Would it have made a difference if I'd known? Probably not, though I wish I had, though now that I know what our love came to, I wish that I'd had just those few months of her pregnancy to enjoy for themselves, even if it wasn't our fate ever to have more.

After Katya's rejection I felt unwanted when I joined the full squadron assembled in the barracks room. It was a robust gathering, with the Kazakh women stoking the stove and serving plates of the excellent lamb stew and pots of tea and desert coffee to the cosmonauts, who in their rich fur caps and coats, good boots, militantly relaxed poses, looked to me overbearing, overwhelming, and, truth, wonderful. My uncles were seated like tribunes at the radiotelephone table. On either side of them were the civilians who had been flown in from Star City by Fedyuninsky for his report, including the town's chief religious man, Mullah Orzabai, two medical women from the hospital, and a Kazakh boy named Abdrahman Godzihkty, who was the nephew of the squadron's bus driver. On chairs by the stove were the guests from Tsar Cannon, such as Deputy Chief Doctor Lunin, Research Assistant Isaacii Goldenberg, and several deputy directors.

I folded myself in a chair and peered at Katya, who sat beside Uncle Dmitry, her head down, her hands folded for warmth. I wanted to flee but found my attention fixing on Zhora Fedyuninsky, who put on a very theatrical show in order to reveal the mystery of the abduction in a way that pointed to a solution. I remember fastidious and strutting Fedyuninsky so happily that it makes me smile to think of him swaggering before us, fluffing his scarf and brushing dust from his sleeves and bouncing on the balls of his feet whenever he made a specially keen point. "We have a crime!" he began, and the cosmonauts hooted at the anticlimax. But Fedyuninsky raised his right hand and gestured like an orator to carry on his tale.

He told us that between Monday evening and Tuesday evening last, November 4 and 5, the Grand Constructor had been abducted by persons unknown in Star City. Fedyuninsky waved his hand like a magician over the map he had unrolled on the plank floor. "There are many clues, and there is one solution."

The cosmonauts made more cigarette smoke and called for more stew and vodka. Uncle Dmitry leaned forward and ordered, "Get on with it, Zhora."

I wish she hadn't, but it was then that Katya panicked again and burst out with an attack of her own. "Get on with what!" she yelled, pointing at Fedyuninsky. "I've told you that I caused all this: I wrote my grandfather to warn him about the Jew-baiting, and they've got my letter and are going to use it to kill him. You know how they work! He's just an old Jew to them, and they're going to kill him, and he's probably already dead. You don't have anything to solve here. Just get back at them! What are you going to do about it?"

Fedyuninsky replied that he disagreed with Mrs. Prishkin, and that the letter she referred to was irrelevant as a provocation, and that this was a plain crime of abduction and nothing to do with the Grand Constructor's Jewish nationality.

It hurt me to see Katya's frenzy. "It's a pogrom!" she stood and cried. "And it's the Organs who are doing it again. And I want you to kill them for it! If you're the men you say you are, just shoot them and kill them. We have to fight back! When are you going to fight back? What are you waiting for? If you know who did it, shoot them first and then shoot those who ordered it and keep shooting until they're all dead!"

Uncle Dmitry reached to comfort her. She slapped his hand away and sat down. I felt her pain as well as my own and could only lower my head and fight off a rush of shame that came at me.

There was no hurrying Fedyuninsky. He tapped his boot toe on the map and resumed his presentation. The yellow steppe was like an ocean, he said, and Star City was like a desert island, and whoever traveled here was as exposed as a man in an open boat and had to be seen. He said he'd bribed officials at the airfield and the train depot and found no unusual activity over the last week, in or out, and that he'd also bribed the police in Star City and again found no unusual circumstances. Fedyuninsky summarized, "What we have is a Black Maria job—a small team, in and out quickly, standard Chekhist operation. A plain abduction. But we can do better than this."

I didn't know what he was talking about, yet at the same time I was paralyzed by my sense of shame and anxious of every word he said, because I believed he was eventually going to point his finger at me. It's my fault, I told myself, not Katya's, no one else's, mine for breaking Air Force rules and thinking I could bargain with State Security. I kept hammering at myself like this during the briefing, as if it mattered what an idiot boy had or hadn't done when thrown into the pit of the Lubyanka.

It was time for interrogations. I'm going to detail them because it will help you understand how the rot of State Security had spread throughout the empire—so that there was just a handful of men and women left to trust. Fedyuninsky introduced the two medical workers, Doctor Tatyana Mometov and her assistant, Illina Ivanov, both pharmacists at Star City's April 4th Workers' Hospital. Why they were significant, Fedyuninsky said, was because about 0200, Tuesday morning, the young woman Illina was called down to the admitting hall by a stranger who said he was Kuznetsov, a lorry driver, and who claimed to have a respiratory illness. And yet when Illina took him upstairs for treatment, Kuznetsov's coughing stopped and he offered her twenty rubles for a bottle of nitroglycerine tablets.

Stouthearted little Isaacii Goldenberg understood the clue and stood to announce, "His heart condition! He needs his pills. He can't sleep without them. They took him without his medicine!"

Fedyuninsky was prepared, holding up a pill case and explaining, "I found this in Academician Univer's quarters at the oasis. He'd flown into town without them, since he expected to return Monday night. When they took him, the Grand Constructor must have told them they had to fetch him more or he'd die, which was smart on the Grand Constructor's part. It not only established that they didn't mean to kill him—this is an abduction—but it also left us a trail to follow." Fedyuninsky addressed the pharmacist, "Please tell them, Doctor."

I recall Doctor Mometov dearly, a stout, handsome, gray-haired woman, very brave and loyal, who would stand by us to the end, as you shall see, and who would be the last love of Uncle Konstantine's life. That night was the first any of us had seen her, and she rose and spoke as confidently as a general. "When Illina brought Kuznetsov to me, I knew he was an old Chekhist reptile; I know them by their dung-colored eyes. I told him I didn't sell state supplies, and I'd give him enough until he saw a specialist. He folded his money and said it was for a relative."

Uncle Konstantine made a soft noise and just like that fell in love, though I didn't recognize it as did the others. He said to the room, *"This is a woman."*

Doctor Mometov looked at Uncle Konstantine and then continued, "I told Kuznetsov I made house calls. I knew what they were up to. They were torturing some citizen. And I don't leave any citizen to die alone. Kuznetsov said he needed three days' worth, and I told him to get out of my department and then thought better of it and sent Illina after him."

Goldenberg interrupted, "He's got to have them to wake up and to go to sleep."

The nurse Illina Ivanov stood again like a student. "The doctor sent me after him with a bottle of twenty-five pills. I caught up with him outside at his little lorry. He offered me money again, and I refused. Then he said he wanted to thank me and grabbed at me and kissed me. I got back and told him he was too old to chase me. He laughed and said if I was ever up at Old Dzhezkazgan to look him up at the sports club, and he'd show me how he'd catch me."

Fedyuninsky asked her to describe Kuznetsov, and Illina obliged, "Bad knees, sciatic hip. He leaned like this." Illina bent to her side and added, "He was awful, and his teeth were all steel." Fedyuninsky asked her to describe his lorry, and she said, "It was a little dirty one, with a canvas back, with big water cans, like the lorries you use, but older and dented."

With the abductor and vehicle established, Fedyuninsky next called on the boy, Abdrahman Godzihkty, who, he said, was the assistant to the chief mechanic at Star City's transportation ministry garage. At sixteen, Abdrahman was a small, desert-blackened boy with a huge heart and deeply felt patriotism for his steppe and his people; and I do believe that he began his rise to fame that day, for one day he would be elected the prime minister of the Kazakhstan Republic. Even in those days he was dignified when he rose and took off his forage cap and bowed to us in respect. "I'm Zere Godzihkty's brother's son—the son of Ali Godzihkty," he said in good if formal

Russian. "And I'm the firstborn of a firstborn. I am asked to tell you what I saw this week past, on the overnight shift at the first transport depot." Abdrahman bowed to Mullah Orzabai and added, "God is great, and I speak the truth, little father."

Fedyuninsky prompted Abdrahman, "Tuesday morning, o-five-hundred."

"Yes, khan," said Abdrahman, who told us that two men had come to the depot and paid him twenty rubles "under the table" to bring his tool chest outside and work on their lorry's engine. Abdrahman described the lorry and then described Kuznetsov as "an old monkey with an iron mouth." He added, "I told them I could patch the lorry but not fix it, because it needed a shop, the radiator was junk. They told me to do what I could so it would last three more days."

Fedyuninsky thanked Abdrahman and then crouched over his map with chalk and drew a circle that measured three days' drive from Star City.

Fedyuninsky's next interview was the hostile and defiant deputy district boss named Valoknok, who was dragged in from the outside door by two large Kazakhs. Valoknok was filthy in a baggy suit and ripped shirt and had clearly been beaten recently. When the guards slammed him into a chair, he groaned and cursed us in Russian. Fedyuninsky said Valoknok was in charge of the caravans in and out of Star City and was the man to bribe if you wanted to join a caravan with no questions asked. Valoknok cursed everyone again, this time so foully in Kazakh that Mullah Orzabai reacted by ordering Abdrahman to translate for us. "He called you dead pigs, khans," Abdrahman said. "He said your mothers copulated with blood sausages."

I didn't mention that Mullah Orzabai was a longtime friend of the Grand Constructor. Goldenberg told me later that the mullah had negotiated the original deal that had moved several Kazakh villages out into the desert to work for Tsar Cannon, and that what looked like slave labor to me was in fact the best work the Kazakhs could get on the yellow steppe. Also, the Grand Constructor was a favorite of the merchants in Star City, since his program was now very well funded and paid cash for supplies. The merchants had appointed the mullah the administrator of a huge reward they'd offered for the Grand Constructor's return. The local Kazakhs wanted their benefactor back. Valoknok was a dead man for what he'd done to help the abductors, and Valoknok must have known it when he crazily spat and cursed at the mullah in Kazakh.

The mullah, a meaty, bearded man in good boots and a maroon robe, spat back at Valoknok and then addressed us in Kazakh, which Abdrahman translated. "He apologizes for this dog of the desert who lives on for a few more empty hours." The cosmonauts laughed, though the mullah had just told them that Valoknok's throat would be cut as soon as we were done with him.

Fedyuninsky regained the logic of his interrogation and said that Valoknok dispatched two caravans every Tuesday and Thursday morning, and that by camel was cheap and by lorry was expensive, and that he had charged Kuznetsov five times the usual lorry rate because he'd known he was carrying more than electronics or pornography. At this point Valoknok cried out in desperation, "They said they were pensioners!" and then Fedyuninsky asked the crucial question, "Bound for where?" When Valoknok hesitated long enough to spit, the mullah flicked his hand, and one of the Kazakh guards leaned down to hold Valoknok by the hair and lay a knife blade on his lips. Valoknok gave up his life to fate and whimpered his answer, "Dzhezkazgan District."

Fedyuninsky pointed to the extreme northeast of the circle he'd drawn on the map and summarized, "Dzhezkazgan District, three hundred and fifty kilometers from Star City, a lorry caravan leaving here Tuesday morning the fifth and arriving there Friday morning the eighth. When we find a Chekhist pensioner named Kuznetsov, bad hip and steel teeth and desert lorry with a cracked radiator, we will find the Grand Constructor. I would start at the sports club in Old Dzhezkazgan." While the cosmonauts cheered and applauded, Zhora Fedyuninsky held his right hand in the air like an actor receiving adulation, then rotated slowly and bowed to my uncles. "The largest unanswered question," Fedyuninsky began again, "is how it was that Kuznetsov knew he could grab the Grand Constructor at Star City on Monday the fifth. This leads me to betrayal."

To my surprise my uncles didn't look pleased, and Uncle Dmitry cut off the spectacle by ordering the guards to get Valoknok out of the room and then telling Fedyuninsky to sit down. We were about to see Uncle Dmitry's own sort of skill at interrogation. He didn't mean to waste breath with trick questions and sharp deductions, rather he meant to let the guilty one confess. Uncle Dmitry looked closely around the room and said, "The Grand Constructor was betrayed by one of us." And then he repeated, "He was betrayed by one of us in this room."

I didn't even have time to think that he meant me, because, almost as if he'd been waiting for his moment to speak, Doctor Lunin remarked, "Yes, he was, Colonel Zhukovsky. He was betrayed by me."

Mstislav Lunin was the traitor, however he didn't sound contrite. In fact, with his baked baldness and thick glasses and small mouth, he looked harmless and dull, and yet when he spoke I could hear the ring of ambition. "They told me he was too old for the responsibility. They told me I should take over and if I wanted it to happen sooner rather than later I should send him into Star City and they'd make him understand it was for the good of the state. I can't tell you who approached me, because this was all done on the telephone over the last month. I thought about it and took them up on their offer last weekend. I asked him to take my place at the workers' council at the center, which was something he never did. And when he agreed I assumed he knew what I was up to. He's an old man but a very clever one, and probably thought he could talk them out of it and use their attempt to get us more money. My best guess is that he wanted to meet with whoever is after him. He knew he was going to be detained, and that's why he left his boy Goldenberg behind."

Goldenberg flushed scarlet at Lunin's insult but checked himself by rocking in his seat while the three other Tsar Cannon deputies shook their heads as if they'd expected this all the while.

Doctor Lunin sucked his cigarette and said that he hadn't realized they were going to abduct the Grand Constructor. "I thought they would retire him to Leningrad, if you care to know, and what I'd have to do was announce his retirement for health reasons. Queer how it worked out—I do hope he's not dead, I didn't want that." Lunin crossed his legs and added, "I hope you can get him back alive. He's a clever old fellow. He's taught me a lot through the years. I find now that I miss him."

I thought it peculiar that Uncle Dmitry then thanked Doctor Lunin for his candor and neither blamed nor threatened him for what he'd done, almost as if Lunin weren't responsible. I didn't understand why my uncles weren't angry at Lunin, but I've learned since enough about men to realize that Lunin wasn't a bad man, just another in those days who'd become so cynical about life that, when it was convenient and useful, he had betrayed his dignity and colleagues as mundanely as if he were applying for a promotion.

Uncle Alexander's response to Lunin's confession was the coldest of all. It was time for command and not for moralism. Uncle Alexander leaned forward, stared at the floor at Doctor Lunin's feet, and then shocked me with his ruthless logic when he mumbled, "What we need to know, Doctor, is if the Grand Constructor is retired for health reasons, can you go on with Tsar Cannon?"

Doctor Lunin answered, "Yes, Colonel."

Uncle Alexander asked, "Is he necessary to the success of the program?"

Doctor Lunin answered, "Not at this time, Colonel."

Uncle Konstantine guffawed at the cold-bloodedness of the exchange and taunted, "Well, Lunin, can you go on if we give him back?"

"Naturally, Colonel," Doctor Lunin answered.

Isaacii Goldenberg showed some of the backbone that made him such a trustworthy comrade. "The Grand Constructor is Tsar Cannon!" he shouted, pounding his fist into his palm like a pestle into a mortar and then screaming at Doctor Lunin's backside. "We can't do it without him! You know it! You haven't got any of us, Doctor, you know we don't work for you and have never worked for you. We work for the Grand Constructor." Goldenberg appealed to my uncles, "Sirs, without the Grand Constructor, it's useless, we'll never sort it out, we can't continue. A machine like Tsar Cannon is thousands of men working together all the time—I know, the Grand Constructor's told me many times, Tsar Cannon is a great machine because the men who've built it believe it's great and believe in what we're doing. A booster is tens of thousands of systems built by thousands of men, and we can't hold them together without him! It was in his mind before we built it. And if he's gone, there's no one to keep it up here and in here, in the heart, too. Sirs, sirs, you must get him back or forget about us, just forget about all of this and go away."

Goldenberg slumped down and tried once more for Lunin's approval, "Tell them the truth, Doctor, that we can't go on if he's gone. It's just a waste without him, tell them, please, sir."

Doctor Lunin said nothing, which I suppose was an answer in itself.

The important response was from Uncle Alexander, who mumbled one of his choice obtuse verdicts, "It's done."

What he meant was that he had made his decision and that, given the character of the man, the decision was inarguable, written in stone and pitiless.

Katya understood none of this, however, and jumped toward my uncles with an argument. "You said you were going to help me! You can't leave it like this! You've got to get them!" Uncle Dmitry tried to soothe her but Katya pushed him aside and continued her complaint, and the next moments were confused shouting. I suppose it sounded ridiculous to everyone else to hear Katya telling Uncle Alexander that he should fight back. I heard her words as serious and desperate and felt wretched. Katya would shout, "Some bloody brave men! He's my family, and I'm holding on to him, and I came here because you must do something! You must! Is he just another old Jew to you? You're just like them!" And when Uncle Dmitry would say, "Katya, don't, we'll talk later," Katya would only shout louder, "You said you'd help! You must do something! Shoot them! Get him back! You must!"

Uncle Alexander might have helped if he'd clarified his judgment. That wasn't his way, and he sat silently at the table while Katya wasted her voice and then, as she cursed him as "Stalin's bloody great hero" one last time, he ended the briefing by walking out of the barracks, head down, sucking on his pipe, off to pace the airfield and brood.

Uncle Konstantine ordered, "Lights out thirty minutes, early call," and then turned to flirt with Doctor Mometov. The cosmonauts broke up into groups to smoke and eat while Katya continued to berate Uncle Dmitry, though eventually even she weakened and let Uncle Dmitry escort her to her quarters at the back of the barracks, where the Kazakh women bunked. I wanted to follow them to see if she would talk to me, yet I didn't do anything but sulk. What's funny to me now is that I was so fixed on my doubts and desires that I missed the point of the decisions made around me as badly as Katya had. I sat stupidly asking myself what had happened. And why was the Grand Constructor abducted? And what were my uncles doing about it? And what did they want from me?

I didn't have the confidence to ask anyone, and I waited at my bunk. It would have been so easy—if I'd just asked any one of them he would have told me what my uncles were going to do was what the Air Force expected, "Attack, attack, ram the enemy, attack." But no, I was cozier with my self-pity. Much later however, with the barracks quieted down so that the wind was like a woodwind instrument over the camp, Goldenberg came over to introduce himself to me and to help me think better about events. He'd not gone back to the oasis with the other rocketeers, and he'd been bumping around out of place among the cosmonauts until he'd come to me. "You're the one who fought them, yes?" he asked. I admitted to this hesitantly, and he said that he'd learned that I'd been beaten for defending Mrs. Prishkin, that I'd alerted them to the abduction, and that I was the one who knew who the Chekhist general was who was behind this. He was trying to be kind. He thanked me for what I'd done and sat down on the adjoining bunk. "I was wondering, Lieutenant, can you tell me what's going to happen tomorrow? What are your colonels going to do?"

I glanced around at the cosmonauts playing chess, drinking and joking and wide awake despite Uncle Konstantine's order, and then looked back to Goldenberg. I realized he thought I was one of the elite and not supercargo like him. I said, "I wish I knew."

"But, sir," he whispered, "are you going to get him back? Is it true? Can you do that?" Goldenberg's narrow face dimmed, and I remember how sadly he spoke when he added, "I'm a Jew, too, you know, and so's Doctor Lunin. Most of the boys on the program are, you know. You have to understand, we're good socialists, but I know how it is. If you're a Jew, the Organs don't let you forget. Lieutenant, it's not like they say, is it? That you don't care about the Grand Constructor because he's a Jew."

What Goldenberg said was more true than not (and you should know this about the so-called socialist paradise of the CPSU) in that Russia remained the same land of pogroms that it had long been under the tsars, and in that State Security was as grotesquely anti-Semitic as the Nazis had ever been; and yet what made me feel especially rotten was to think just then of all the anti-Semitic remarks and jokes I'd laughed at and passed all through school about boys just like Goldenberg—the intellectuals, the earnest, long-nosed Jews, the cosmopolitan Zionists. I'm trying to be very accurate here. I felt guilty for the fear I saw in Goldenberg. I tried to deny what he said: "No, no," I started, "nothing, no, there's nothing of that."

In my urge to console Goldenberg, I saw what my uncles were going to do about the Grand Constructor, and, as I saw the future, my self-pity vanished for a moment. I'd spent three days camped in the desert with my bold uncles and their squadron striding around me like predators, with military preparations moving in one obvious direction, and I'd seen nothing until I saw myself through Goldenberg's eyes. I realized that I'd been Iagoda's stooge not because anyone else thought I was but because I thought I was; and now I realized all I had to do was to stop thinking like a victim and to start thinking again like a conqueror and I could right myself. I found my voice to boast to Goldenberg like a genuine hero. "Colonel Oryolin's in command," I said, reiterating Stumpelkin's philosophy, "and anything's possible." To bolster Goldenberg the more, I added my own assumption. "If we want the moon, we better get the Grand Constructor back. And we do want the moon, so I think what's going to happen is we're going to go get him."

Goldenberg asked, "But how, sir? I mean, the Organs have him, don't they? Can you fight them? Can you do that?"

All I had for him were Uncle Alexander's words, "It's done, isn't it? It's done."

Did I believe this? Did I believe that when you think a thing done, as Uncle Alexander had thought the rescue done, that it becomes true? It didn't seem to matter to Goldenberg, who gazed at me as if I were a golden hero. He was a gentle man, the one of us who loved the unlovable Grand Constructor unconditionally, and he gripped my hand when he asked me the crucial unsolved question: "Why did they take him, sir?"

The correct answer was to bait a trap for Uncle Alexander, but I didn't know this and didn't even guess at it; rather I avoided the question in the way Uncle Alexander might have done. "Don't bother explaining them. Our job is to get in line and to do what we're told."

I wonder now if I believed what I told Goldenberg. The truth was I probably didn't believe it—I was talking puffed-up trash, and I had no information of what was going to happen next. But there was a part of me that could pretend to be this fearless, tight-lipped, hard-minded hero like my uncles, and, strange to admit, the bragging fool in me did know what he was talking about. Does a boy become a hero because of what he does or because of what he pretends to do? Because of the truth or because of make-believe? What is a hero? A truth or a lie? I'm far older than I should be not to have answers to such questions. And I know that Russia is over a millennium more ancient than I and yet still can't answer any better than I. I suppose the simplest way to state my puzzle is to say that my Russia believes in heroes, but are heroes believable?

It didn't matter what I believed, for the next morning began the treachery, murder, and heroism of the next two weeks. I got up early with the Kazakh women in hopes to find a way to get into the back of the barracks to speak with Katya. I dressed quickly, visited the outhouse, idled around the kitchen annex that was built underneath the rear of the barracks, but could find no way to get past those squat grandmothers. Perhaps I didn't try too hard, since I didn't know what to say to her; all I could have done was sob and ask empty questions. Not too long after, my anxiety was settled when I heard Uncle Konstantine banging a pot on the stove inside and calling the squadron awake with the orders of the day. Eight of us, including me and Stumpelkin, Isaacii Goldenberg, and the Kazakh boy, Abdrahman Godzihkty, were ordered to get our breakfast and to assemble with our kits within the half hour.

No one talked much. The Air Force in us knew not to ask where we were going until we got there, and anyway I think by then the word had been passed that we were bound for Dzhezkazgan District. You see how useless debating what was going to happen had been. My uncles were always going to do what they were going to do; Uncle Alexander was always going to take revenge for the abduction of the Grand Constructor; and who could have been surprised to learn that it mattered not in the least that State Security knew we were coming or that my uncles were plunging us into a baited trap. We were going because we were going. This is how the heroes I've seen truly were—they went right at the center of the line with main weight and they didn't wait and they went regardless of and in spite of and without any thought to reason—and if you don't understand this now, much of what I have to say will be impossible to you. Heroes are hardheaded battering rams; they go and go; they are what my father's motto makes of them: heroes keep going.

Witness that at first silver light on a dark blue Monday, November

11, we eight would-be heroes happily kept going right behind Uncle Konstantine, boarding the Il-14 and lifting off for Dzhezkazgan District 350 kilometers northeast. I confess that I was probably gladdest of all to go in order to get free of Katya's cold moods. Then, too, the boy-man in me had a naïve ambition that I could win Katya back by rescuing her grandfather from some fantastic wall of flames. I can remember searching from the port to see if she was there to watch our lift-off, and when she didn't appear I told myself that she didn't need to, because she could hear the engines roar off. The truth of it was that while my head was light with victory tomorrow, my heart was heavy with failure yesterday; and I was far from a prince of the steppe when I told the tiny blur the barracks soon became, "I love you."

Planet Stalin

We eight boys weren't the strike force, we were the reconnaissance team, and for ten days we roamed the wintry plateau of Dzhezkazgan District in search of the Grand Constructor. I know now that we were also decoys. My uncles well understood that Iagoda's game was to lure them from the relative refuge of the Cosmodrome and into the pit (and it was actually a pit) he'd prepared around the Grand Constructor, who after all had been abducted in such a crude, noisy fashion that it could only mean Iagoda wanted us to follow the trail. My uncles aimed to play the game to the end, first by making noise with overeager boys and then by striking as swiftly as falcons just when Iagoda thought he was winning. As it happened, our time in Dzhezkazgan didn't work out well for anyone, but then I have learned since then that when you pick up a weapon in anger you're soon going to have to look into the face of a tragedy.

Our reconnaissance base was a hardscrabble sheep farm that was named the Fifth Anniversary of Sputnik Collective, located on the western shoulder of a thin river about twenty kilometers south of the rail junction at New Dzhezkazgan. Glavtop and Grin flopped the Il-14 down on a muddy road that no one but they could have used as a landing strip. Our first sight was a wilderness of naked muddy scarps and little wind-twisted trees, and I can remember being impressed by how dramatically the landscape had changed from the salt-pocked desert of the yellow steppe to this high purplish plateau that the natives called the dead steppe.

We were greeted by a gang of cheering, hatless shepherds who were retired Air Force officers now come to running the collective farm. The director was a hairless, scar-faced older man named Tolya Ten, who had once been Uncle Konstantine's flight instructor at Orenburg. Tolya Ten was also a roaring drunkard and gambler, and he was quick to wager that the Il-14 couldn't get off again from the mud. Uncle Konstantine took all our pocket cash to raise a pot to match Tolya Ten's, and the two of them stood arm in arm in the mud howling and laughing as Glavtop and Grin turned the plane and powered up. The Il-14 cleared the road well before the fence line, and as we cheered, Tolya Ten back-flopped in the mud, crying out his pet vulgarity, "As I live and frig!" Tolya Ten was a strange clown, a man who seemed to laugh all the time. The biggest, blackest joke was that there were almost no sheep left at the collective, because the breeding stock had been wiped out by some sort of epidemic the spring before. What we found were two dozen Russian settlers and their families wasting away the months drinking home-brewed vodka and eating up the rest of the livestock and cabbage stores while they waited to be restocked from the state farms in Armenia. For no known reason the new herd wasn't due until January—the very month ingress would be most difficult—and until then the only diversion for the men was watching the gray skies fill with blizzards and beating their wives. (I don't know what the children did through the winter, since when the snows came they couldn't get to school; and the two weeks I was there they just stared at us like hungry dogs.)

I doubt my uncles had told Tolya Ten much about our mission before we arrived. It was soon obvious the shepherds didn't care for politics or intrigue, though not because they were afraid of state authority. The trick of the shepherds was that they were all not only former falcons but also paroled zeks, ex-convicts, who had been ex-

iled to Kazakhstan after they were released from the slave camps. You
must know much about how vast the slave camps had been under
Stalin both before and after the war, but back then I knew very little
about the truth, and spending time with old zeks was a hasty education. They didn't seem bitter about their fate; they just seemed
drunk all the time, men who loved to laugh hard, weep harder, and
tell wild tales of the old days and the teeming dead. We young falcons were a gift to them—a captive audience—and they took the
opportunity to spellbind us with war stories. Each night in the
squalid bunkhouse, Tolya Ten and his pals would paint a hideous
picture of the old days in the district when the slave camps had been
scattered about like dead groves. Tolya Ten's own story was a calam-
ity that had started with a fistfight over a dice game in 1944 that had
brought him a ten-year sentence in a camp and a five-year internal
exile in the district. Since then he'd married and raised a giant family
that had been cut in half one summer by diphtheria. He told us he'd
become the collective farm's director three years before, when he'd
won the job in a dice game with his predecessor. "As I live and frig!"
he'd cry out as he punctuated his odyssey with harder and blacker
laughter.

It was Tolya Ten who invented "Planet Stalin" in honor of our
visit. Maybe it was one of the other old falcons, but I can clearly see
Tolya Ten sitting there over another overcooked mutton and cabbage stew, sloshing his juice and bellowing, "You bet it's Planet
Stalin out here, haw-haw. You've flown millions of kilometers to
Planet Stalin, and nobody leaves Planet Stalin, nobody's sober
enough to get off!" At the time I thought Planet Stalin a lunatic
notion that mocked the importance of our work—more of the rocket
ships and Martians that children made of space travel—but now I've
changed my opinion and agree that Planet Stalin was accurate for the
so-called dead steppe. They were all dead men, you see, and their
wives and children were as condemned as they were. Out there on a
frozen plateau of desolate soil and monstrous storms, they had all
been buried for years by the time we came their way; and we must
have looked to them like spacemen from another planet named
earth, landed here with pretentious talk and ludicrous hopes of a
tomorrow that would never come to Planet Stalin. I wonder now
why they didn't deny us, unless that's what that black laughter was,
the jeering of the entombed.

We pursued our reconnaissance mission with the sober zeal of youth. Uncle Konstantine told us to go out and "mix with the masses," and we took him literally. We made a masquerade ball of it, dressing as shepherds or layabouts and using the farm's small autobus to ride into New Dzhezkazgan each morning as if we were looking for work. We stood with the natives at the various hiring stations and told anyone who asked that we were shepherds who needed new jobs. Our daily hope was that perhaps we'd run across Kuznetsov in the market squares. At the same time, Uncle Konstantine told us to ask no questions, since that would give us away as intruders. We were to roam through the public areas and get comfortable with the terrain and the schedule of the shifts at the copper mines. The copper pits in the craggy hills to the west dominated the dead steppe's fortunes and made New Dzhezkazgan little more than a sloppily built shock-labor town at a bend in the river. The smaller Old Dzhezkazgan, a few kilometers north, was the headquarters of the copper bosses and the crossroads for the pits and the smelters. Everything in both towns stank of sulfur from the smelting process, and the bleak winter sunlight was often cut to nothing by the black smear of smoke thrown by the coal-burning power plants at the mines.

I've told you we didn't actually sign on to day jobs; we just stood on line and pretended we were new to the region and looking for easy posts. This got a derisive roar from the other vagabonds, who assumed we were Army deserters and Miserbiev was too well fed to be anything but a general's son. In that district, you either went into the mines or you ate rodents and barley through the winter and found what work you could in the spring.

We accomplished nothing significant in the next ten days waiting for Uncle Alexander to arrive—not one word about the Grand Constructor, not even an unconfirmed sighting of Kuznetsov, nothing but sore backsides from riding the autobus in and out like commuters and sore feet from walking the towns all day like beggars. I realize now that we weren't supposed to make progress. We were there only to attract the attention of any local Chekhists who might be watching for us. Those empty ten days were like a long fuse burning toward a catastrophe. I suppose we did make something of our time. We did draw up an accurate map of the region. We also learned who the local bosses were, how many police were stationed in both New Dzhezkazgan and Old Dzhezkazgan, where the airfield was and what its traffic was, how long it took to drive the muddy roads from the sheep ranch to the rail junction to the airfield. We also reconnoitered Old Dzhezkazgan's sports club—called the Stalin Sports Club—and made sure that two of us were watching its entrance at all times in the hope we might spy Kuznetsov. We didn't spot him, but we did become comfortable with the ebb and flow of the club, and this later proved critical. The granite-faced sports club was next door to the district's Party headquarters, which was also State Security headquarters on the dead steppe.

I see now that I also gained something in those ten days. I stopped worrying about myself and returned again to my fantasy life as an all-conquering falcon. I didn't forget about my shame; I just ignored it like a low-grade fever. I couldn't forget about Katya's troubles, but I could convince myself that she was safe with Uncle Dmitry and that when I had the chance I could make up to her. I felt healthy, vigorous, and dutiful, and, if my thoughts were narrow and my conduct immature, at least I was in good company with the cosmonauts. I was young, and it was fun to dress in ragged jerkins and felt boots and buy "juice" for ancient vagabonds in order to get them talking about local conditions without actually asking direct questions. It was special fun to follow the Kazakh boy Abdrahman Godzihkty into the native quarters and buy drinks for the whores, who sat with us complaining about the whoremongers, smugglers, and police.

We blossomed in the romance of our mission, carrying on as if we truly were explorers on an alien Planet Stalin. Uncle Konstantine was the ideal master of boys. He knew to approve of every sort of scheme we proposed and not to burden us with strict rules that wouldn't have mattered anyway. He knew we were decoys, and he knew that high spirits and tireless gimmicks suited the game. "You look too pink today, my darlings, much too pink!" he'd instruct us in the mornings about our complexions. "Walk slower, slump lower!" he'd instruct us about our posture. "You're out of work! Cry over yourselves! Convince them you need help!" he'd add, then he'd limp around the bunkhouse, showing us how to beg for half of a cigarette, how to drink three-on-a-bottle (the local talent), how to search the mud for coins. His best charade was quarreling with Little Laika over a bowl of scraps.

Abdrahman Godzihkty was the one of us who wouldn't mock the

local people for their poverty and depravity. "My people hate the khans," Abdrahman confided to us, meaning the Russian settlers, who by then had reduced the Kazakhs to less than four out of ten in Kazakhstan. "Our camels outlive us; our goats outlive us. The khans have stolen everything and killed the steppe." This was the boy, remember, who fifty years later would rise to be prime minister of the Kazakh Republic. Even at sixteen, small and always hungry, he was most outspoken and adversarial, and his natural intellect soon drew him close to softhearted Isaacii Goldenberg. Goldenberg had volunteered to come along out of his devotion to the Grand Constructor, making him odd man out, so it was easy to pair him with Abdrahman. And since Goldenberg had decided that I was a hero to be followed, he and Abdrahman tagged along behind me and Stumpelkin, making us the oddest quartet in the district.

We were also the luckiest four, because that first weekend we ran into trouble that only luck and Abdrahman's quick eyes saved us from. It happened Saturday afternoon on the market square in Old Dzhezkazgan; and the incident was most significant because it was when I first saw the local police chief at work, a tough-minded sadist named Major Lazursky, the very man who would almost destroy my uncles the next weekend.

The market square was a naked, half-frozen lot that was filled with merchants' stalls and trash heaps. The market was surrounded by the best buildings in Old Dzhezkazgan, including the state stores, the Ministry of Nonferrous Mining, Party headquarters, and the Stalin Sports Club. In the morning the market was an open-air bazaar of trade goods; however, once the state stores ran out of food or closed early on the weekend, the square teemed with shoppers. That Saturday afternoon Stumpelkin and I were on duty keeping watch on the sports club. It was a frigid, windy, dark day, and the only good of the cold was that the mud was frozen enough to walk on. Stumpelkin and I were dressed in rags that had been deloused but still made us itch. We were taking turns scratching each other's backs while huddling out of the wind behind a stall, when there was a disaster right in front of us.

The trouble started as an argument over blood. A butcher jumped out at an old Kazakh woman who was scooping up the animal blood on the icy patches beneath his stand. He yelled and tried to shove her away with his foot, but she just folded into a tighter ball on the ground and continued her scavenging. I thought the argument was done, but then the butcher reached into his stall for a club and smashed the woman's head. The grandmother collapsed face forward. I doubt the butcher had meant to kill her, and he backed away in shock, looking around for help, as if he could explain his crime. A crowd started to gather around the corpse. There was a call for a policeman. The butcher panicked and tried to roll the body away with his feet, making things worse, because her head left a bloody streak on the ice.

I must have been staring in disbelief—the scene was no more than ten meters from our position—because something happened that I missed, and the next I realized Abdrahman was pulling at my sleeve. "We must get away now, khan," he told me. "Hurry away, we can't stay here, we must run before the police come."

Abdrahman had realized that the crowd was fast becoming a mob aiming to kill the butcher in revenge. The butcher grabbed the back of his head, and then I saw an ice ball smash his eye, and then he went down pleading for mercy. Everything was so fast it was like a gale that came from nowhere. We four were trapped more by the speed of the violence than by the terrain. Within a minute, the mob had stoned the butcher to death and had surged forward to overturn the stall and plunder the meat, tearing sheep carcasses apart by hand and fighting over the bones. I can remember standing back to back with Stumpelkin as the mob swept around us, more women and children than men, all picking at the ground and wailing in a frenzy that soon overturned and ransacked the two adjoining stalls. It was like being penned in with starving animals pushing their snouts at a trough. I say this not to derogate but to show what life had become in the workers' paradise of the empire—that after all the fancy talk about Marxist-Leninism and the radiant future, what truly drove the folk was the search for food, and whoever controlled the food supply in the empire controlled everyone. Do you understand that when you're hungry you will say and do anything to eat, and when you're fed you will say and do anything to keep eating? Have you ever been hungry enough to lie? to steal? to kill? If not, then there is little I can say that can help you understand that what I felt that day wasn't disgust for the mob or even pity for the mob, but rather a fear that I was being dragged into it, that I could feel as those people even though I was rich and well fed and blessed. I felt their ravenousness and it paralyzed me. I wonder now if all my pride of place isn't just a mask over the man who could have gone to his knees and fought for meat.

The police chief, Major Lazursky, knew that to control the food was to control the mob. I first saw him as he led a dozen or so well-armed policemen into the heart of the riot. My most vivid memory of Lazursky is my last of him, when I saw him dying broken-backed and paralyzed on the tarmac at the airstrip, but that terrible day I recall a dark, nimble little man with a narrow mustache and sharp nose, carrying a walking stick that he used like a whip. He was fear-less in the face of the mob and didn't back away even when some fool threw a rock to strike his greatcoat. I watched him react, taking his time to turn from side to side to measure the threat, and then looked to his men and raised his stick. As suddenly as that, there was a single volley of rifle fire into the back of the mob: no threats, no challenges, no orders, Lazursky just signaled and his men shot down half a dozen women and children. The people fled in slow motion, leaving Lazursky and his men standing over several fallen bodies, and at the center of the carnage, the corpses of the butcher and old woman. Lazursky turned around and strolled back across the lot toward Party headquarters.

I saw Lazursky's withdrawal while on my belly, since we four had long since thrown ourselves down on the ice. I don't know how long we lay there, perhaps three minutes, long enough for the scene to change again as the crowd returned to care for the wounded. I sup-pose we were in shock. I don't now recall getting up, though I must have in order to lead us out of there. We took refuge in the eaves of a state store across the square. I got my breath enough to think and asked Abdrahman, "Is that all there's going to be? Are they coming back? Are they going to arrest anybody?" I couldn't accept that we could have been so close to slaughter and yet be able to walk away untouched. Abdrahman had his own version of events. Pointing to Party headquarters he said, "No arrests, khan, no jails on the steppe. Russian justice." He waved at the market square where the crowd, no longer a mob, was returning as if all was well, as if nothing had happened at all. "My people know Russian justice," Abdrahman ex-plained. "They know it's the way. They know they were stupid. My people are stupid people, more stupid than your people, khan."

It didn't seem to matter that the policemen had been Kazakh and only Lazursky was a Russian, and I didn't bother arguing. Isaacii Goldenberg couldn't recover so easily. He wept uncontrollably, and we had to help him walk to the rendezvous point for the autobus. He kept crying, "It didn't mean anything. What did it mean? It didn't, did it? It was so fast, they were dead, and no one said anything. I saw them die like nothing! They were children and old women, and they killed them like nothing."

Stumpelkin and I comforted him as best we could on the ride back to the farm. Later that night, in the bunkhouse, Uncle Konstantine and Tolya Ten took pity on Goldenberg and, rather than mock him, tried to get him to laugh by telling him serial fairy tales that always ended with the same verse, *"Any day without cruelty is like a day in heaven."*

That night Tolya Ten told us about Major Lazursky, and I suppose we should have anticipated how tough an adversary he would become. "He's a rare one, ain't he? Even out here he's a rare one. Just out from Leningrad District, not a talky man, on his way up, a comer." Tolya Ten related how Lazursky had tried to clean up the gambling dens after he'd first arrived, but he had learned to stand back and take his share from the top of the pile as every other boss did. Tolya Ten joked, "On Planet Stalin, you do as Stalinists do or we do you, haw-haw!" and then he roared out a strange curse that made the other shepherds raise their glasses. "Long life on Planet Stalin!"

After ten days we were exhausted with our search and with our conviction that we could locate the Grand Constructor as if he were a foundling. We all welcomed the rest we got on Thursday, November 21, when a wild snowstorm struck the steppe and blocked the roads with wet drifts. The wind was like a tidal rip, blowing off the chimney pipe from the bunkhouse and piling up so much wet snow on the roof that we had to shore up the central beams. Throughout the day we huddled around the stove working on our collective map of the district and the twin towns. We did have several guesses as to where they might be imprisoning the Grand Constructor, and I mention the most logical as at Party headquarters in Old Dzhezkazgan, or at the big police barracks in New Dzhezkazgan, or—Uncle Konstantine's choice—at the lime pit at the slaughterhouse.

I can see now that my uncles had sent us to the dead steppe not to find anyone but rather to wait for that storm to find us. My uncles knew that Iagoda expected us to mount a rescue. My uncles knew that Iagoda would counterattack with Special Action Troops that would have to be airlifted into the district. My uncles knew that the only thing that gave them an advantage was bad weather. And so my uncles had busied us with idle investigations until a big storm rolled in from Siberia, promising three days of blowing wet snow and icy rain. Only the Air Force would try to operate in such conditions; only bedazzled falcons like Glavtop and Grin would try to land in such a blizzard. Perhaps you can appreciate what a thrill it was to hear the unmistakable low roar of two props skim over the bunkhouse at twilight. We raced outside to light the oil beacons we'd arranged and then gathered to watch the Il-14 dart out of blackness, flop on runners, bounce twice in the crosswind, and skid several dozen meters to the back wall of the feed barn, trailing fence wire from the rear skid. Uncle Konstantine led the charge to pull open the cabin door, and out came the rest of the squadron as well as some surprises. The fifth figure out was Katya in a heavy parka. I assumed nothing had changed her mood toward me, and I didn't want to risk another rejection, so I stayed back from her as if we were strangers.

What was clearly changed was that Uncle Alexander was no longer the reticent, brooding figure of two weeks before, but rather arrived in full battle dress with more violent momentum than the wind. He had brought with him a dozen Kazakh gunmen chosen by Mullah Orzabai from the caravan guard to serve as a strike force. There were also several crates of assault rifles and small arms in the cargo hold to support what Uncle Alexander intended to be a murder raid.

However at first Uncle Dmitry seemed to be in charge of the mission, just as, at first, the operation seemed to be a ransom negotiation, not an attack. Uncle Dmitry helped Katya off the plane and then ordered us to get down five black strongboxes that turned out to be gold ingots raised by the mullah from Star City's traders. In preparation for the exchange, Uncle Dmitry had also brought along the two pharmacists from Star City—Doctor Mometov and Illina Ivanov—both as medics for us and to treat the Grand Constructor once we got him out.

There was a briefing called for after supper, yet well beforehand it didn't take more than a half hour of gossip for Fedyuninsky and

Cherryntevsky to bring us up to date. They said that what Uncle Dmitry had arranged so far was the beginnings of a diplomatic settlement. For the past two weeks, Uncle Dmitry had been in Moscow with Fedyuninsky, Cherryntevsky, Artzybashev, and Kandidim, calling on their friends in the Air Force, Army, and Party to find out what they were up against in Iagoda and looking for a way to negotiate the crisis. In consequence Uncle Dmitry had raised the ransom and made contact via an intermediary in the Kazakhstan Central Committee with those who were said to be behind the abduction: the entire Executive Committee of Dzhezkazgan District. We were up against hired thugs working for the local bosses who were in turn working for Iagoda, and we were told that we could buy back the Grand Constructor as if he were a prize ewe. As Fedyuninsky phrased the challenge: "Crime makes a market. And we've doubled whatever Iagoda can pay. The local bosses are mulling it over."

If this bloodless negotiation seems to you antithetical to Uncle Alexander, it was, and it was actually only another aspect of my uncles' plan, yet another decoy to make Iagoda think he was winning. Yet at the time most of us were persuaded that my uncles did intend to settle the trouble with gold. In fact no one was more convinced that all could be solved diplomatically and peacefully than Katya.

Katya was as changed as Uncle Alexander from the last I'd seen her—no longer an avenger calling for killing but rather a conciliator returned to her high-minded opinions of human nature and calling for compromise. As supper was served in the bunkhouse, she approached me with explanations and new demands. I was wary of her, and when she took me aside to give us privacy, I was even more nervous for the stares of the cosmonauts. I kept one eye on my friends and the other on Katya's lips, and it was some time before I understood what she was saying. "I know I scared you before, Peter," she told me. "I know I did. And I'm not going to go on about it, though I want you to know that I've much to make up for. I scared myself. I was so angry and so scared, and I wanted to get back at them for making me feel so scared. It was like falling down. I couldn't stop myself. It felt as if there was no one and nothing to grab on to. Do you understand?"

I claimed I understood her, though I didn't. I wish I'd been mature enough for her. She was telling me what hopelessness felt like, and it would have been so easy for me just to sympathize. Instead I sat by dumbly, worrying only that the others would call me "lover boy" and would tease me for our intimacy. I remember thinking that at least my friends couldn't eavesdrop on us because of the clatter of pans and shouting over food at the tables.

"I talked a lot of foolishness," Katya continued. "I wanted to fight back at everyone, and I guess that meant that I wanted to quit, just to quit and run away from you and everyone and hide. I made it worse the way I acted. I was blaming you for something you couldn't stop. I know you tried to help me, and I'm grateful. I promise after this I'll try to trust you and everyone more. I'll try to trust them more." By "them" she meant my uncles, and she looked in their direction and smiled as Uncle Dmitry winked at her. Katya sighed and asked me, "Do you believe me, Peter?"

I said I did, though I didn't.

She also asked, "I hurt you the way I acted, didn't I?"

I didn't answer. My feelings must have showed, because Katya rewarded me by taking off a glove and brushing my face with her hand. Her touch made me forget about the others in the room and what they might say, and I fell in love with her again. I think now that I was right to be in love with her touch and not her talk. She always said so much that I have forgotten many of her remarks, but what I do remember precisely is the smooth, warm feel of her hand. I would have happily lost myself in just holding her hand, yet what she wanted was to preach her passion for politics to me again. I listened as closely as I could to please her.

"Listen to what's happened," she charged. "There's not all bad news." She said that over the last two weeks Uncle Dmitry had opened communication with everyone who might be able to help—not only with the chief rocketeers at Star City but also, in Moscow, with General Krylov of the Rocket Forces and Academy of Science President Keldysh of the State Space Commission. Uncle Dmitry had learned that the rocketeers didn't care about the Grand Constructor at all—they regarded him a potent rival for funds—and that the state commissioners didn't care about the Grand Constructor as long as Doctor Lunin was able to go forward with the superbooster. Uncle Dmitry had then petitioned the Air Force high command for relief, had appealed to Marshal of Aviation Vershinin himself, and had been told that, given the crisis in Czechoslovakia, it was not the right time for bad relations with the Lubyanka lords—in other words, wait and see. My uncles waited for nothing, and so Uncle Dmitry had directed Fedyuninsky to use bribery and favor-calling to penetrate the Lubyanka itself to find out what Iagoda had up against us. Soon Uncle Dmitry had put together a picture of the crisis and a way to solve it.

"We've found their chink," Katya announced, "and it turns out to be *gold*. Why didn't that ever occur to me? Why didn't I see all these years that no one grubs more for gold than a socialist superman? They're for sale, Peter, all of them, for sale! Dmitry Mikhailovich says that I shouldn't be so shocked, but I am. For sale, anyone or anything, from the Vorkuta mines to the Kremlin suites, it's all for sale under the table."

Much of what Katya told me was repeated in the briefing later that night, again led by Zhora Fedyuninsky, but not attended by Uncle Alexander. The revelations were simple, and I've told you most of them. General Iagoda was chief of the notorious Fifth Directorate and a favorite of several principal bosses at the Kremlin. Fedyuninsky characterized Iagoda as "a bloodless bastard from the Leningrad apparatus," also as "an orthodox hangman." And yet, Fedyuninsky said, Iagoda was not omnipotent. It was Fedyuninsky's best intelligence that Iagoda had ordered the abduction on his own authority and that Iagoda was acting without tacit approval of the other Lubyanka lords. What this all meant, Fedyuninsky construed, was that we were not up against State Security regulars but rather hirelings. The Grand Constructor had been taken by a small team of retired Chekhists who were under contract to the Fifth Directorate. Our local adversaries were a network of old wolves who lived and thrived in Dzhezkazgan District under the protection of the local bosses. Fedyuninsky concluded his part of the briefing with flair as he spun to reintroduce the strongboxes. "This is a copper field," Fedyuninsky said, "and in a copper field there's nothing that can move men's souls more than gold. We've brought more of it than the bosses around here could filch from their smelters in a year." A Kazakh gunman opened a strongbox to let us glimpse the ingots, and I realized that it was true, that gold did shine and make you want to pick it up like a small animal. "Now," Fedyuninsky added, "we're going to move their souls from Iagoda's side to ours."

Uncle Dmitry thanked Fedyuninsky and then addressed us in such a relaxed, sanguine fashion that he convinced us all that he did intend to ransom off the Grand Constructor. "You've done well," he told the eight of us of our wasted two weeks on the dead steppe, "however, now it's time we settled this quickly." He said that the next day he intended to go into Old Dzhezkazgan and make contact with the chairman of the district's Executive Committee at Party headquarters. "I'll sit down and talk with him and we'll settle this," Uncle Dmitry explained. "His name is Egan Odersyats, and he's an old, old soldier, or so we're told, from the Twenty-seventh Guards Rifles, from Volgograd District. We've made sure that our friends in Moscow have alerted Comrade Chairman Odersyats that we're calling on him with significant proposals. What we've heard back is that he's most ready to hear our proposals and wants to help any way he can. Of course, he's also ready to sell us whatever we can pay for. What you see there is about twice the regular rate for missing Grand Constructors."

To the squadron, especially to me and my friends, this was a joyless anticlimax. After the briefing, I can remember carping with the others that we'd spent two weeks trying to be heroes and now all we were going to do was eat more mutton stew and go home. It's strange to me now to think how little understanding we had of my uncles, how we could worship them and yet not see that they never didn't attack, that their lives were what they were because they didn't trust any result to a battle but the destruction of the enemy.

I don't recall talking much with Katya after the briefing—with the crowding in of the Kazakhs and all the others Katya had to stay at Tolya Ten's house with the two pharmacists—but I do recall that she approached me again after breakfast the next morning, Friday the twenty-second. She said she wanted to walk with me outside. It was another gloomy black day, though not as cold, a momentary break in the serial storms that were whipping around the steppe. The snow had changed to a light rain that was washing down the snowbanks. We strolled by the frozen reservoir, and, not knowing what she wanted, I tried to make conversation about idle things that had once pleased her, such as pointing out a flock of black kites that were skimming the ridge line.

Katya would have little of my bird talk and soon cut me off to ask me about Iagoda. "Tell me what he's like. Tell me what he said about me. And tell me what you told Colonel Oryolin. I know some of it, but tell me from the beginning. And tell me everything about this woman, Romodanovsky. Don't leave out a thing. I want to know how many teeth she has."

Remember, Katya had been left out of my confessions to my uncles and had learned what she had from Uncle Dmitry. Katya's curiosity was aggressive. Her new mood made her look less rundown and put some false color in her face. Overall though, she was too thin, much too fragile for a woman in her first months of pregnancy. Her mind was ceaseless, however, and when I mentioned what I knew of Madame Romodanovsky, she became as hot-bloodedly intuitive as I'd ever seen her. To give her credit, Katya's diligence was appropriate, since she was on the trail of a secret so dangerous it would eventually destroy us.

"She was his wife?" Katya would repeat about Uncle Alexander and Madame Romodanovsky. "My god, what a thing. He was married? My god. What's she look like, what's she like? What did she say? No, no, tell me exactly what she said to you. You met her at Saint Sophia? Where else? At the Bolshoi? Where else? There was a child, a daughter? My god, my god, polio? How do you know? When? While Oryolin was in the camps? Oryolin was in the camps? They were in the camps? When? Are you sure? You must remember!"

Katya was fascinated that my uncles had been zeks. "My god, they did that to them," she said of their imprisonment. "My god, I never knew. Angelicka never told me. You see how sad it all is; I'm her best friend and she wouldn't tell me that Dmitry Mikhailovich was in the camps. My god, Stalin was insane—to put them in the camps—my god, they were all insane, weren't they—they made the camps true communism, didn't they? Everyone suffers the same, my god."

Once she had hold of Madame Romodanovsky's story, Katya wouldn't relent, pushing me further and further. "But who is she?" Katya would demand. "Why should she have a bodyguard? What's she want in all this? Don't you see, Peter, that she's behind this? What sort of woman can have the Fifth Directorate for a bodyguard? And what rubbish about a feud—what sort of feud? You're saying that because she hates Oryolin she wants him dead? Is that what Iagoda said? Are you sure? You've got to tell me more about her! Tell me all of it again!"

I did complain to Katya that I had wanted to tell her everything two weeks before.

Katya dismissed my complaint with the same high-handed argument as before. "I was sick with fear, I thought you were one of them. I told you, I didn't trust you or anyone then. Now I feel different about it; I see that I have to try to trust more. Let's not make too much of it."

I wanted to make a lot of her lack of trust—what I see now as her general shortage of faith in me and those who loved her. Katya's mind was so superior to others' that she spent most of her time entirely concerned with her own thoughts. I wanted to warn her that trust and faith weren't something to jettison one day and retrieve the next. I wanted to make her see that our only safety was to stand fast together as the Air Force taught, that what she thought so brilliantly wasn't as important as the steady way we all worked together. I said none of this. I didn't even think to say something as simple as I love you.

The secret that Katya was after demanded most of her attention. "If it's a feud like Iagoda says," she would argue with herself, "what kind of feud brings you and me into it? What have you got to do with them? And what do I have to do with it? And what use is all this anti-Semitism? If the feud's between her and Oryolin, why involve all of us?" Katya kept repeating, "What kind of feud? It doesn't make sense!" and "Who is she that she can do this!" and "There has to be an explanation!"

I had no answer then, and though I have one now, I still can't say it's a satisfactory explanation for the feud. Madame Romodanovsky and Alexander Oryolin hated each other in the way other folk love each other, I understand that much, but why did they have to destroy each other, why did they feel they could wreck whoever stood in their ways? What are we to make of folk who do not care how much damage they cause? Who think that their lives are more worthwhile than ours? The truth might have been that Madame Romodanovsky and Alexander Oryolin were the same sort of despots, that neither of them bothered with reasons for the damage they did, that they were just well-matched dark souls who trampled the innocent and the helpless as thoughtlessly as a beast charges through a field. It could also have been just fate that they came together and fell apart, just as it was all our fates to be born in Russia in a day where the world was turned upside down and those who hated and killed without reasons were far more powerful than those who loved and helped with all the best reasons.

Katya must have seen something of the darkness of the feud. She told me how Uncle Alexander had deteriorated in the two weeks since he'd learned his wife had returned. The militancy and determination I'd spied in his face, I realize now, was more likely a bloodlust that blocked out all senses. What I'd seen were the first stages of his madness of war-making and murder for murder's sake, and I will show you how depraved Uncle Alexander's madness became on the dead steppe. "Dmitry Mikhailovich's very worried," Katya told me about Uncle Dmitry's concern for Uncle Alexander, and she went on to portray the problem with insight as well as intellectual bluster. "Dmitry Mikhailovich is trying to help everyone, and he can't help Oryolin, and he knows it, and yet he keeps trying. I forced him to tell me something of what's wrong. He said your brave Oryolin's gone back to his heavy drinking. I've heard them argue about it. Your brave Oryolin is a very sick man, a very cruel, very dangerous man, the worst I've ever seen. There's this look of his that makes me think he's the enemy. Listen to me, Peter. Oryolin doesn't care who lives or dies. He's a killer, do you understand me, he'd kill anyone, you, me, even Dmitry Mikhailovich, he'd kill any of us, and he wouldn't even think about it. If we were in his way, he'd kill us. I'm sure some of the problem Dmitry Mikhailovich has is that Oryolin wants to shoot his way in."

At this remark Katya frowned. "I know, shooting is what I wanted at first, but I was feeling crazy. I've told you, I was frightened. I see now that we can get Grandfather back by buying him back. Dmitry Mikhailovich knows what he's doing. He's smart and cautious, and we can and will get Grandfather back tomorrow, and that will be the end of it."

I was bothered by how sure Katya sounded of her opinions, as if my uncles were chessmen she could put where she wanted. Katya was condescending about men like my uncles and also about men like me, and I wonder now if she ever understood how much violence there was in us in those days, how very, very dangerous we were all the time—that it wasn't just that Uncle Alexander was a killer, as she said, but that we were all of us soldiers trained to follow men like Uncle Alexander to the finish. Like most intellectuals I've known, she thought she could control the evil in men with talk. From what I've seen in my life, I'm confident that the only way to stop a hard man with a gun is to send at him another hard man with a gun. It's dismal to admit, and I wish Katya had been right, yet I know she was wrong. We were all of us killers, and once the shooting started there was nothing to be done but survive it and live on with the regrets.

I can also fault Katya for all that she didn't speak of that morning. There was nothing about Daniel, left with Mrs. Zhukovsky like extra baggage, and there was nothing about our future or the baby she must have realized she was carrying. There was also no effort to show concern for the Grand Constructor. She called him "Grandfather," but otherwise treated his welfare as indifferently as Uncle Alexander had with Doctor Lunin.

Late Friday morning, November 22, my uncles' plan for the Grand Constructor advanced with a start when Uncle Dmitry organized his embassy to meet with the Dzhezkazgan District Party committee. He told us that he had altered his plans a little, that he would be traveling into town that afternoon, spending the night with friends of Tolya Ten's in Old Dzhezkazgan, and then making contact with the district chairman, Egan Odersyats, on Saturday morning. It was all a ruse, but at the time it looked to us to be a most risky operation. Uncle Dmitry asked for volunteers to help him handle the strongboxes and security. Everyone stepped forward, yet Uncle Dmitry chose only Fedyuninsky as his assistant, Abdrahman Godzihkty as a translator, and two Kazakh gunmen to handle the gold strongboxes. Katya was going along as a principal negotiator, Isaacii Goldenberg as an aide, and the two pharmacists as medical support. I see now that if sending Little Laika and a dozen children along would have made the expedition appear more peaceful, then my uncles would have added lambs, too. Uncle Dmitry chose the collective's big troika instead of the autobus, ostensibly because the roads were difficult and the sleigh could go overland, but more likely because horses with bells hauling gold would make even the most suspicious wolf lick his lips.

I held my place and didn't break discipline save right at the end, when the troika was set for departure. I knew that everyone was watching, but I found courage and walked up beside Katya and pulled at her coat. She let me touch her hand, and I whispered, "I love you. Please, I didn't want you to go without me telling you I love you."

I'm glad I did this, even with the cosmonauts staring, and it didn't upset me when Katya patted my hand as if I were a child.

"Yes," was all she said, "we'll talk about it tomorrow," and then the troika tore off with bells ringing.

Uncle Alexander didn't come out to see Uncle Dmitry off, and that alone should have warned me that all was not what it appeared. I saw nothing but my anxiety for Katya's safety—which would have tripled if I'd known the truth—and I fell in with the general opinion that the big bad wolves of Dzhezkazgan District were greedy oafs and that we had wasted our time being so cautious about our reconnaissance.

We continued wasting the day with routine housekeeping and later with target shooting. You would think that one of us would have looked at two dozen well-oiled automatic rifles with folding stocks and another half dozen Skorpion machine pistols and asked why we were such heavily armed negotiators, or looked to the dozen Kazakh gunmen who could shoot the fingers off a hand at fifty meters and asked why Uncle Alexander had brought them along, but I can't recall any such remark. We were lightheaded with such good weapons and endless ammunition. In the Friday afternoon drizzle, we blasted away at fenceposts, scrub trees, and several snowmen we made from the slush. We were so fatheaded, I think we would have tried to shoot out the black clouds that rolled in from the north. Soon enough I was greatly enjoying myself. I hadn't handled a weapon since Orenburg, yet my reflexes, eyesight, and training in those days made shooting as easy as looking. Despite all the misery I'd seen, everything was still a boy's challenge for me: that sheepless sheep farm, those sarcastic shepherds and their sad-eyed wives and children, the craven mob in town and the pitiful miners at the derelict pits, all of it a fantastic landscape of suffering and death, and there I was chopping up the firing range and admiring my prowess. I was becoming as perverse as everyone else on Planet Stalin. I can remember how, when I spotted Uncle Alexander coming out to watch us shoot, I tried even harder to splinter a post, as if I could win a sharpshooter medal as well as his approval.

The day's games went past sundown. The shepherds set up a phonograph in the bunkhouse to play German recordings, and we sat around singing along without a word of worry about our envoys. Later I took my tea glass outside and sat under a shelter from the wind. My friends joined me, and we took advantage of a break in the rain by building a campfire with dry wood from the shed. All my best friends were there, Stumpelkin, Miserbiev, and Adama-Bibliov, and I think we were convinced we'd be going home soon and this would be our last night on the dreary dead steppe. After two weeks we needed baths, clean clothes, sleep, and something beside mutton, and we complained as soldiers do about trivial things, such as the gagging smell of wet sheep wool. Other cosmonauts drifted out to us and there was more song singing. Stumpelkin provided some Siberian lore when he looked at the black sky, sniffed like a sheepdog, and pronounced, "Big storm tomorrow. I can smell it."

What had delayed my uncles' plan the extra day—from Friday night to Saturday night—was that they were waiting for a low-pressure range to deliver one more freezing rainstorm out of the north to cover our attack and retreat. Uncle Konstantine gave away the plan that night, though none of us was perceptive enough to understand him. He came out to the campfire with Tolya Ten and other shepherds, all of them very drunk, and after some typical vulgar song singing, he told us that there was nothing like a wonderful woman to make a man feel young, and wasn't Doctor Mometov a wonderful woman, and wasn't he a fool to let her out of his sight? Someone asked why he hadn't gone along with her into town, and Uncle Konstantine roared out a broken proverb: "When you're surrounded by wolves, darlings, howl like a wolf and don't ever sleep with the lambs." In other words, we had sent our lambs to decoy a wolf. Now it was time to close the trap and to close it with the same wolfishness of our enemies.

The waiting, teasing, and decoying ended Saturday morning before first light. I was already awake when Uncle Alexander and Misha Cherryntevsky walked into the bunkhouse and stood by the stove. They were both in full battle dress. I hopped in my bare feet toward them to ask why. This got me close enough to see that Uncle Alexander's face was awful—dark-skinned, dark-eyed, dry and hard like stone, now and again glowing red from the coals in the stove. I was frightened of him; he seemed sinister, and there was something wrong about his posture, as if he were crouched to spring. I know I'm making him sound barbarous, but I'm trying to describe what it felt like to be near him that day, and why I recoiled to bump against Cherryntevsky.

I asked him, "What is it?"

Cherryntevsky said, "We're going to go now. The colonel says go now."

I asked, "Is there trouble?"

Cherryntevsky checked his watch, and, because I'd not gotten a new one since they'd stolen mine at the Lubyanka, I peered over his shoulder. At 0400, Saturday, November 23, 1968, I watched as Alexander Oryolin went to war with his wife, his past, and also with his own fate. In his obtuse way Uncle Alexander told Cherryntevsky, "It's done, finish it." He meant the waiting was done and Uncle Dmitry's embassy had accomplished all that was asked of it. He also meant that now came the ruthlessness in him to finish what he wanted. I don't know if it will bother you, but I do know it has long upset me to realize how very many heroes have hard hearts, and that when men like Alexander Oryolin say, "Finish it," they become executioners.

Cherryntevsky shouted the squadron and Kazakhs alert, ordering everyone into full winter gear. "Greatcoats, strip off the tabs, get the boots right, load up bandoliers, cover those gun barrels, by the numbers, it's today!"

No one complained. The cosmonauts knew as quickly as I did that the next step wasn't going to be negotiations. Uncle Alexander didn't even have to address the others; he just loaded extra clips for his Skorpion and walked out of the barracks. By dawn—and there wasn't much sun that day—we were on the road in the autobus and the farm's two canvas-backed lorries, making slow headway in an ice shower that required us to get out every half kilometer and haul the bus or the lorries out of the mud and slush by hand. Counting the shepherds who came along with Tolya Ten as scouts, we numbered nearly three dozen heavily armed, silent, wet, obedient men. We reached the outskirts of Old Dzhezkazgan just as the morning shift came out of the buses from the mines, and it was easy to mix into the crowd of miners and drift into the town.

Uncle Alexander's orders were simple: stay in fire teams, do nothing until we were told what to do, and keep shut regardless. I stayed tip to tail with Stumpelkin, and through the afternoon we wandered the streets and alleyways, passing the other teams silently, snacking when we could on dates and bread for a long night ahead. If you'd spotted me walking with Stumpelkin around the market square, you would have seen an inconsequential vagabond in a plain great-coat carrying a shepherd's sack that concealed my assault rifle and ammo—nothing more than a discolored and restless young man down on his luck with worse to come. I felt the usual contradictions that you do before combat, confident and anxious, strong and weary, trusting and doubtful, overbearing and frivolous. I held on to my training and tried not to think too hard. I understood by then that all my assumptions about the mission were useless. I also realized that Katya had been placed in much danger and that her predicament was probably for a purpose. I can't say that I fretted about this at length, since I was too involved in the small details of walking the streets anonymously. I remember that day so graphically, as if I am reliving it, because of a wonder of manhood that Uncle Lev taught me—that what a boy does first makes him the man he is at last. My first love was Katya, and I'm stronger for it. I first killed men that day for nothing, and I'm weaker for it.

Uncle Alexander's plan was so bald it didn't require rehearsal. We were told that Uncle Dmitry and the others were being held in the Party headquarters building on the market square in Old Dzhezkazgan. We were not told if they were prisoners or not, and no one asked. We didn't question Uncle Alexander at any point; we just did what we were told and concentrated on our individual parts of the operation. What I know now is that the overall plan was based on a rough timing. Cherryntevsky was to lead six of us, including me and Stumpelkin, into the Stalin Sports Club so we could work our way to the back of the adjoining Party headquarters. Uncle Alexander and the Kazakh gunmen were to invade Party headquarters from the front. Simultaneously Artzybashev and Kandidim, who were already in the sports club gambling with Tolya Ten and the shepherds, were to set fire to the sports club with incendiaries. Uncle Konstantine was to stand by with the autobus to get us all out and back to the collective, where Glavtop and Grin were waiting with the Il-14.

The centerpiece of the plan was the diversion. Every Saturday night the sports club was frenzied with miners gathered for the wrestling matches in the yard out back, where fat, naked, greased-up men bit and gouged each other like wild pigs. We were going to make our assault while every eye was on the arena, especially the eyes of the Executive Committee, who were the sponsors of the matches.

You might notice that Uncle Alexander's plan wasn't much concerned with casualties. The truth was that it wasn't a rescue at all, it was vengeance, and, as I'll explain, the truth came to me slowly and left me disillusioned.

At 2130 hours, the night black with a damp wind but no rain as of yet, Cherryntevsky took a position at the bus stop on the market square and signaled us by holding up his arms. We were all close at hand, sheltering where we could under the eaves, and the six of us— Stumpelkin, me, Miserbiev, Adama-Bibliov, Schtange, and Tevye-look—maneuvered through the vehicle traffic to Cherryntevsky and then started across the road for the sports club. It was swing time between shifts, the square turbulent with buses and lorries either arriving from or going to the mines, the sports club raucous with drunks and whores spilling up the steps and into the building to get to ringside. Our first step was to find and join Artzybashev and Kandidim inside, who were supposed to be playing dice games with Tolya Ten and his cronies. The size of the crowd forced us together, and we pushed in like a phalanx. I didn't intend to take the lead, it just happened that I was first through the antehall and into the public bar. The only sport the Stalin Sports Club cared about was gambling, and the bar was arranged like a poor man's casino with rough tables along the walls for dice and cards. The place stank of men, beer, and cooking grease from the kitchens below, and there was such a din of laughter and cheers that if you didn't know these men were cutthroats you'd think this was a festival.

I was impatient. Stumpelkin kept telling me to ease up and, "Wait on orders, Peter. Wait now. You know we're to wait on the colonels' command." I couldn't control myself, I wanted to be at the front because I wanted to be first into Party headquarters. I'd figured by then that if I didn't get to Katya first, there might not be anyone else to protect her. Uncle Alexander's orders hadn't mentioned anyone's safety; and if Katya was in there she was left to her own chances, and I'd elected myself as her main chance. I admit I was making selfish decisions that to another might look heroic. Yet I didn't feel like a hero; I felt frightened and even wrongheaded, since I was breaking ranks. I pushed through the bar and found the back exit to wooden stairs that opened on the arena in the rear yard. There must have been seven or eight hundred men gathered around a crude, elevated ring that was lit by light stands from the sports club and Party headquarters. Except for the wind, the outside celebration was as cheerful as the inside and the wagering was more frantic. In the ring, two giant naked figures were rolling over each other like muddy boulders while the miners pelted them with slush balls and roared for blood. It was all a phenomenon of cruelty; and it wasn't limited to the ring, because I saw fistfights among the crowd at the foot of the steps. I moved into the back of the crowd in the way I might have waded into a pack of wild dogs. I was so scared I was aggressive; I couldn't stop myself from trying anything to get to my goal. Only fear can explain how reckless I was—I was too terrified to think about what I was doing. I saw an opening from the yard. Party headquarters next door was three stories high and brick-built, with bars on the ground-floor windows. We'd been told the best way in was to get atop the attached shed and through the second floor's unbarred windows. Importantly, I saw that there was a small balcony out over the alley-way, a sort of open-air royal box that had been constructed to allow the local bosses to watch the wrestling matches. The district's gambling and prostitution were controlled by the Party, so the bosses had much reason to keep a close watch on their operations. That night there were several squat old men in heavy coats standing on the balcony smoking cigarettes and watching the match. I studied them long enough to see that what they were really watching were the gambling receipts, which were brought up to them as soon as they were collected. The cash was always in their sight, for various toadies would carry the money in boxes across the yard and up an iron staircase to the balcony, as if making deposits in a vault. I was sure of the arrangement as soon as I saw it, but I waited awhile to see how it was done—several old men seemed to be the designated carriers—and to note the two armed policemen at the base of the iron stairs.

I must have been crazed with fear. What else explains what I wanted to do? I wanted Katya safe, that was all I thought, nothing more complicated, nothing more reasoned. I grabbed around for Stumpelkin, who had followed me outside, and I pointed up. "It's better to try now while they're all out there," I said. "Let's try it. We get up there and we're inside. You see them—we'll go up with one of the collectors."

Genka told me, "No, no, what are you doing? We're to wait for the signal. You know that. What's wrong with you?"

I exaggerated my hope. "It's Katya, she's up there. I'm sure she's up there. You've got to help me." I didn't know any of this and, as I listened to myself, I became more and more aggressively panicky. "I'm going now. You can wait," I told him. Stumpelkin grabbed for me but I dodged him and headed toward the alleyway.

It was fate that delivered up Kuznetsov to me. I didn't recognize him beforehand, and I didn't think about who he might be when I chose him. I just followed one of the old men with a money box into the alleyway and to the iron stairs. Yes, he walked lopsided and dragged his left foot like a man with a bad hip, and yes, his teeth were either missing or made of steel and he had "dung-colored eyes," exactly as described by the pharmacists, but I didn't think about it, no matter how it looked later. It was fate that drove me, and it was fate that gave me Kuznetsov's arm. He must have thought I was a thief, because he cried "You shit!" and covered up the box. The crowd noise buried his voice. I shut him up by leveling my knife into his ribs and yanking him onto the blade. It punctured him like a needle, and he wheezed.

I told him, "We're together, say it, we're together."

He wheezed again and said, "No," and tried to break free. He was a very strong old man, his arms were like iron, and I had to stick the knife in hard until he stopped struggling and conceded, "All right, you little shit."

I lost my courage then, not when he resisted but when he surrendered, and I was left realizing the flimsiness of my plan. Also: if you hold a knife on a man, you have to be ready to kill him, and I wasn't. Kuznetsov was tough and angry. His strength of will weakened me. I looked at the face of the police guards and figured they wouldn't let me pass. And even when they did, distracted by the match, I saw I couldn't get Kuznetsov up the stairs. He was too massive, the steps were too slippery, and what was I going to do on the balcony? We struggled up a few steps anyway until I just stopped. I glanced over the whole field lit blue-white by floodlights, the wrestlers, the miners and drunks, the brick rear wall of the sports club, the miners hanging on the wooden fence that lined the alleyway from the street, and what I felt was defeat. The moment I thought I was beaten I was, and all I could think then was that unless I ran I was going to die. I'm being exact here. I'd quit and given up my life just when fate reached in and pushed me toward a victory. I was grabbing for the rifle in my bag, or perhaps I was just getting set to fling the bag and jump free, at just the moment an explosion tore out windows in the sports club.

I heard the first explosion. I heard Kuznetsov drop the money box with a bang. I didn't hear much else, and I didn't look at anything but where I pointed the rifle. My panic gave me extraordinary energy, and all at once I had dragged Kuznetsov up the balcony, and drawn down on the Party bosses.

Those savage old men were generations beyond me, the sort who'd fought each war and revolution of the century, and they knew long before I did that they were dead men by the fact of my rifle in their chests and by the chaos in the yard below. What had happened was Uncle Alexander's assault. Artzybashev, Kandidim, and Tolya Ten's crew had set off incendiaries in the sports club's bar that cracked windows and poured black smoke from the doorway. Meanwhile, Uncle Alexander and his Kazakh gunmen were assaulting the front of Party headquarters, and Uncle Konstantine was plowing the autobus up the alleyway and directly into the crowd as it tried to flee. There was the dull crack of gunfire beneath screaming, and then a second and third explosion spewed glass onto the crowd; then a fourth ripped out a support beam and the rear wall of the sports club started to collapse; then a fifth sent flames through the roof. We weren't making a rescue operation, we were making gross mayhem and butchery; and the truth was that Alexander Oryolin was leading a murder raid. He had sent us in and then he'd ordered the sports club set afire and then he'd started shooting. I wonder now if there can be said to have been a plan beyond the revenge, and, though we did win our way, how can I call that massacre a victory?

I wasn't thinking much inside the chaos. The same fear that had gotten me to the balcony fixed me in place with the old men. I did fire one burst at the window just above the balcony, because I saw a young man's face, and I reacted as I'd been trained. My memory can fool me here. I think I shot the man through the throat. If it wasn't me who shot him, it could have been. I remember the gunsmoke burning my nose and feeling the heat in the trigger and that my ears rang like a threat alert warble. I shot without thinking, I shot without reason. He was just a boy like me, and he looked out to see what was happening, and then he was gone, and I was shaking, and my ears hurt.

The next I remember is that Uncle Konstantine was on the balcony with me and yelling at the old men to get inside. "You know why we're here, boys. Don't make a fuss!" Little Laika darted around my feet. Cherryntevsky boosted me forward and told me to keep my rifle at the biggest old man's head. Stumpelkin was there, too, and he clubbed another man, and then we were all inside from the balcony to a long, carpeted room, like a lounge room set with a table of food, and my memory is that somehow Uncle Dmitry was yelling at Uncle Konstantine: "What! Where's Sasha! What!" Uncle Dmitry had gathered Katya, Goldenberg, and the pharmacists behind him and was struggling to keep them back from the line of fire on the bosses.

I shook my head to clear my ears. I'd lost my right-side hearing and everything sounded dull.

Katya and Goldenberg were also yelling at Uncle Konstantine. What I could understand of their complaint was that they weren't prisoners, and why had we done this? Like the rest of us, excepting my uncles, they knew nothing of the fact that they had been used as decoys, and that the gold ransom was only meant as a way to get the district bosses together that night at Party headquarters. It seemed that we'd crashed into the Executive Committee's emergency session just as they were trying to decide how to cut up the ransom. The bosses' greed had done what a battalion probably couldn't have done—made them targets for our coup de main. There was more shouting, everyone at once; and then the floodlights outside went out, and the lamplights in Party headquarters went out, and Uncle Konstantine cried, "Down!" Instantly a huge explosion cracked the windows. The sports club was an inferno. Smoking cinders shot into the committee room.

Uncle Konstantine was first up again. He went over to lean against a giant portrait of Stalin on the front wall and to poke at it with a burning chip. He was in a grandiose mood, laughing as he burned out Stalin's face, and he kept making Little Laika bark at his remarks about "the greatest pipe smoker of all time."

The room was bright and hot from the flames next door. Every now and again we had to stamp on the carpet or shake out the drapes as they smoldered. Uncle Konstantine ordered us to get the district bosses—there were six of them—up against the Stalin portrait. The biggest old man wouldn't move; and he turned out to be Egan Odersyats, the district chairman and big boss. He kept telling us,

"You're dead, you're all dead," but no one responded to him. He must have once been a very strong man, with massive shoulders, long arms, huge hands, but he'd settled to stoutness at perhaps seventy, and he was even pink-faced, grandfatherly, gouty, in a very good fur coat and black riding boots. He repeated himself, "Shit, you're dead shit; you're all dead shits."

Uncle Dmitry had recovered himself and answered Odersyats, "Now, we're men of the world, Comrade Chairman. We'll get through this without that sort of talk." He kicked a cinder off the carpet and asked Uncle Konstantine, "Where's Sasha?"

The shouting started again, everyone at everyone else—pleas, threats, denunciations—and I told you that it wasn't clear to anyone that this had all been purposeful, since it appeared a disaster. Katya cried some of the loudest at my uncles: "Why did you do this! You're no different from them!"

We'd gotten several lanterns lit and had cleaned away the broken glass by the time Uncle Alexander came in from the hall door. He had his Skorpion pistol out, he reeked of nitrates and smoke, and there was ash on his boots and face. Two of the Kazakh gunmen came in with him and there was blood on them. The shooting had stopped, and the building was secure, all the policemen either surrendered, run away, or dead. Fedyuninsky had been gathering up the gold bars into one of the strongboxes, and he walked over to whisper to Uncle Alexander, who called for the Kazakhs again, and they came in to remove the strongboxes. The Kazakhs moved as smoothly as desert animals, and it was clear watching them that they had no limits.

Uncle Alexander spoke to Uncle Dmitry, "Which one?"

Uncle Dmitry indicated Odersyats and said, "He's stalling us, of course. He was satisfied with the price and was just being a good host and lifting a glass before settling up."

Uncle Alexander addressed Odersyats. "Tell me what we came for. Tell me where."

Odersyats tried his theme once more, "You're dead!"

There was a new voice, "He won't tell you," and I turned to realize it was Major Lazursky, the dark little police chief with the little mustache. I either hadn't recognized him until then or, more likely, just didn't concentrate on anything but my duty to hold down on Odersyats. Without his greatcoat Lazursky looked even smaller than Uncle Dmitry, but he was as tough-minded as my uncles. "You can see he won't tell you," he said. "He thinks he's an immortal."

Uncle Alexander ignored Lazursky and repeated to Odersyats, "Tell me where."

"Say nothing," Lazursky told Odersyats.

"Hey now," Uncle Konstantine told the chief, "wait your turn." He looked down at Lazursky and stepped on his foot.

It was then it first came to me that we were going to kill them all if we didn't get what we wanted; perhaps I also realized we were going to kill them in any event. I wasn't clairvoyant about this, for all I was sensing was what I'd seen that morning in Uncle Alexander's predatory posture and that blackness in his face.

Odersyats must have seen something like it, too, for he weakened suddenly and argued, "There's no call for this. We've cooperated. The old man is alive and healthy, I can tell you. It's difficult, it's taken time, you can have what you want. We'll take you to him. You can have him. There have been mistakes here. I can see that."

Uncle Alexander said, "Tell me who made the mistakes."

Odersyats looked past me to the old cripple, Kuznetsov, who had been forgotten in the pack of bosses. Kuznetsov knew he was finished and collapsed and crawled toward Uncle Alexander. "Mercy, shit, shit," he begged. "I was ordered, it was orders, shit, shit, we didn't hurt him; he's very old, and we just did what we were told."

I saw Uncle Alexander tilt his head, that's all, and then a Kazakh grabbed Kuznetsov by the hair like a dead thing and dragged him out the door. I expected a shot. There was only a small cry, and then the sound of a man trying to get his breath with his throat cut, and then silence from the hall. I didn't have any thoughts until Katya started cursing my uncles. As I listened to her, I felt confused by what she said, possibly because there was half truth in it.

"You devils," she screamed at my uncles. "You're just like them, you devils, you crazy, sick devils! All of you, Stalin's devils, you're as sick as he was! And he's dead, and you can't stop killing and killing!"

Goldenberg held on to Katya. He was moaning against her shoulder, mostly about his fears. "Please, no, no, they've killed him, too."

Odersyats now understood that he was negotiating for his life. "We can settle this," he cried to my uncles. "We were ordered!" The other bosses kept gasping and crying out that Odersyats must make a deal with us. Some of them were arguing in Kazakh, which Abdrahman translated for Uncle Dmitry. Odersyats made a show of listening to his committee and then stepped closer to Uncle Alexander. "What do you want? Just tell me. The old man? You can have him. The gold? You can have it. Is that what you want?"

My uncles had worked for two weeks to get to this point where Uncle Alexander could make any demand and be answered, and he went after the critical details about Iagoda. "Tell me who ordered you," he said.

Odersyats growled out, "Moscow, the Organs, this Iagoda bastard. We were ordered and we were paid."

Uncle Alexander demanded, "Tell me when you alerted Moscow."

Odersyats admitted he'd betrayed us—"It was orders!"—and then told us how. "This afternoon, but it was orders! I wanted to make a deal. I tried to. But he found out about it." Odersyats betrayed Lazursky, too, by pointing at him. "I tried to help you. He ordered me to call Iagoda! He said if I didn't I was out. What could I do?"

I finally understood what my uncles had arranged and why all the ruses. They'd known that Iagoda expected us to move on Dzhezkazgan, that's why it had been so easy to get in. They'd also known that Odersyats was under orders to call Iagoda for Special Action Troops as soon as he made contact with us, to bottle us up and destroy my uncles outside the protection of the Air Force. Yet they'd further known that Odersyats wouldn't betray us until he had the gold in his hands. The protracted, slow-paced, almost casual negotiation over the last week had all been to convince Odersyats he could have the gold and give us up, and the way Uncle Dmitry's embassy had approached him had convinced him there was no hurry to call for help.

Odersyats was now trying to blame Lazursky for the treachery of the call to Moscow. Odersyats looked again at Uncle Alexander's black face. "I can help you. You've got time to get away. We didn't call until late. They can't get here until morning. I can help you!"

Lazursky shouted, "Shut yourself!" and might have had a weapon in his hand, I couldn't see clearly, before Uncle Konstantine knocked him down. I am focusing on Lazursky now, as I didn't at the time, because he turned out to be an intractable foe, and what mistakes my uncles made were in not watching for Lazursky's tricks. Uncle Konstantine picked Lazursky up with one hand and pushed him face first against the Stalin portrait. "Shut your mouth, little fellow," Uncle Konstantine remarked.

Odersyats gave almost everything up. "You can go there, where we've got him, to Number Two." He pointed to the west. "He's at Number Two, a pit called Number Two, an old pit they use as a special prison! It wasn't me, it was him"—he pointed at Lazursky— "and Iagoda and them! It's a Chekhist operation. It's Iagoda's operation. It's his! What can we do about it? At the Three-hundred Level!"

Odersyats was talking about a copper pit that had been turned into a special transfer prison for the Fifth Directorate. You must understand that State Security supervised a vast tyranny of prisons, slave camps, and dungeons. On any given day, State Security was capable of making anyone, no matter how prestigious, disappear into the camps, out of reach of even Party bosses. The most successful way of all to make someone vanish, even more useful than killing him—where there was after all a corpse that could suddenly bob into sight—was to throw the victim into dungeons that didn't exist, the so-called special prisons. Why we'd not been able to figure out where they had imprisoned the Grand Constructor was that he was stowed in a special prison that was three hundred meters underground in a very old, played-out copper mine, Number 2, located in the hills to the west—a pit that was maintained by the Executive Committee of the district as a profit-making enterprise. Odersyats was one of Iagoda's well-paid wardens; Lazursky was one of Iagoda's well-motivated captains of guards.

My uncles had at last learned what we needed. Uncle Alexander gave orders around the room, chiefly to do with Odersyats and Lazursky, who were bound up by the Kazakhs and taken out of the room the front way. The other old bosses were forced to lie down beneath the Stalin portrait. Some of them were crying. Fedyuninsky knelt down to talk to them, and I overheard him tell one weepy-faced little man, "Try to think of your family now." Uncle Konstantine grabbed handfuls of food and told us to get plenty for the others. I stuffed my shepherd's bag with cheeses and bread and was going to eat some myself when Uncle Dmitry came over and told me to take Katya out. "I want her in the bus with you and the rest," he told me. "She's upset, and I don't want her near Sasha."

I didn't understand him, but I think now he was telling me that

Uncle Alexander was not to be challenged. Katya wouldn't go, and I needed Goldenberg and Abdrahman's assistance to get her moving out onto the balcony. "You're murderers," she kept accusing everyone; and to me she said, "Get away, you're just like them. Don't you see what they're doing?" Abdrahman carried my weapon and also Stumpelkin's, and Stumpelkin and I were obliged to lift Katya down the iron stairs and push her into the autobus. All this took very little time, much less than it takes to describe. The rain had started as icy droplets by then, making the sports club a smoking lump of flames, with the roof falling in on the upper story. The yard was spotted by glowing debris and many dark clumps that were probably bodies.

Stumpelkin and I were in the alleyway outside the autobus door when I heard the pops of the executions. I knew that those hollow *tphutt* sounds were a machine pistol, and I guess I knew as quickly that Uncle Alexander had murdered the old bosses. I confess now that it sickened me. Those old men had known what he was going to do, and they'd begged him for their lives. Odersyats had given us what we wanted. Uncle Alexander had shot the old regime anyway.

What I could do about my upset was to hold on to my duty. As I have many times since then, I ignored everything but the task at hand. I kept Katya and Goldenberg on the autobus, as if they were my prisoners, and I waited for the rest of the squadron to join us. They blew out the roof of Party headquarters and used incendiaries to ignite the top story, and then cosmonauts came running from every direction reeking of smoke and gunfire and shouting for speed. Uncle Konstantine was last on, herding the two pharmacists in front of him like ewes. He rolled the autobus into the street about the time the sports club walls started to collapse. The big statue of Stalin out front stood alone like a scorched champion.

We were a makeshift caravan out of the town and into the hills. Uncle Alexander led in a police van along with several Kazakhs and the prisoners Odersyats and Lazursky. The other Kazakhs followed in one of the lorries (Tolya Ten and his fellows, after collecting a large sum of cash from the Party's gambling coffers, had returned to the farm in the other lorry). Last came the squadron in the autobus. Uncle Alexander turned on the police van's red lights and used the siren. We rolled through the town like officials, even if there was no traffic and no one to be seen on the roads. Uncle Konstantine struggled to keep up on the washed-out turns, bashing the autobus into several gullies that required us to get off and push, and that was the level part of the trip. Then we were in the naked hills of the pits, with the temperature dropping and the rain dripping an oily sleet that ruined traction, and we had to get out to push at least once every kilometer. Still the bad weather was our best ally by delaying any flight of the Special Action Troops from getting in from Moscow. Uncle Konstantine shouted at the storm as he drove; he encouraged us to cheer like lunatics each time we went out to boost the rear wheels. The cosmonauts were in verbose moods, commenting on everything as if the trip were a jaunt. I suspect now they were concealing the same fear I felt that either we won the night or we were finished. We'd massacred dozens, and only getting back to the Cosmodrome could give us shelter. I was shaking all the time from my fear, not the ice. I refused to think about what Katya had said about us. She sat with Goldenberg and the pharmacists, and when I tried to get her eye she looked past me, as if I were nothing to her. The truth was, I think, that she was drained by the horror, that she knew she could no longer help herself or anyone.

We fell farther and farther behind Uncle Alexander and the Kazakhs. When we reached what turned out to be Number 2, there were two Kazakhs with lights waiting for us with Uncle Alexander's orders. The autobus stopped on an incline, Uncle Konstantine popped out to confer with the Kazakhs, and when he came back he called for volunteers and then chose the four most junior, Miserbiev, Adama-Bibliov, Stumpelkin, and me. "The works are up there," Uncle Konstantine told us of the blackness to the left. "And you lot are to get up that slag and watch the road for lights out from town." He handed over a flare pistol to Miserbiev, adding, "And shoot this off, nothing else—you see lights, you make lights, then you run for us!" Uncle Konstantine did show some pity however, making Artzybashev and Kandidim give us their excellent oilskins so that we could rig a lean-to.

We jumped from the bus and watched it move in jolts up the turnoff. Miserbiev was in good spirits. "You boys don't know works like this," he told us of the mountain above us. "You stay near me— this slag is treacherous." Miserbiev was a blowhard, but we listened to him this time because he was from the Donetsk region, one of the first of his family since the Revolution not to die in the coal pits. He sensed our obedience to his big mouth, and he lectured us at length about the dangers of mine works. We were standing at the foot of a three-peaked mountain with treeless slopes that were scarred by rocky mud slides and the always threatening slag avalanches. Above us there were the backlit profiles of three big works, including the smokestacks of the power plants, the lights on the shafthouses, the lights on the rail spur. These three mines were wedged up against each other. Number 2 was the lowest on the hillside—a long-abandoned works marked off by a strong new fence and darkened except for where we could see the autobus's headlights. The main road bypassed our position by a hundred meters; while the rail spur, winding off the hill, crossed the road just below us.

It's important to note here that the nearest threat we could presume was from the smaller works across the road and lower on the hillside. It was lit by guard towers and ringed by barbed wire–topped fences, because, as Miserbiev told us, it was a convict works, a slave labor camp. "You can see the zeks. Those're all zeks," Miserbiev said, pointing to the gangs of men by the shaft building, walking so slowly it was hard to see them move. "It's a convict works," Miserbiev explained. "They work them in the oldest drifts. And since they don't pay them, it's worth it, the silver they get out of the rubbish alone is worth it. The zeks like it because it's easy to loaf below. They don't harass them much in the galleries. Only the black lung can get at you down there."

Adama-Bibliov complained about Miserbiev's ghoulishness, "Stow it, Trifya, and keep alert," but there wasn't much else to do but talk and get wet. Soon Miserbiev was explaining how silicosis was what killed miners and that very few were ever killed in the pits; they died much later.

I half listened while watching the vehicle lights on the main road for any hint they were police coming out from town. It was midshift, so there was light lorry traffic from the hills, and soon after a train of empty ore cars churned up the incline. In the distance the lights of the town were a yellow stain. I took the glasses from Stumpelkin and tried to pick out the flames from the sports club and Party headquarters, but that wasn't possible in the low visibility. I also kept checking to the north for any landing lights, since whatever was coming from Moscow would come from that direction. There was nothing but blackness, and in truth wouldn't be anything but blackness, for the threat to us that night was underground.

Miserbiev weighed us down with dire estimates about State Security's infamous Special Action Troops. "I figure the bad boys can get here in under twelve hours. Depending on when they got the alert, I figure before dawn tomorrow. We're underwater here, but they have an all-weather field at Karaganda, and they could come over by train, which would add maybe four hours to my estimate."

We were annoyed with him and countered. Stumpelkin said, "Not before daylight is all that matters." Adama-Bibliov said, "Stow it and eat something. You're running on because you're hungry." I handed Miserbiev bread and told him, "You don't even know they're coming, just that Odersyats said they were." We were jittery like this for at least a half hour, with only the haphazard protection of the oilskins pinned on the slag and braced by two rifles, and I suppose Miserbiev did keep us from worrying by talking about the worst aloud.

Fate delivered the worst anyway, but not anything as we expected, when Abdrahman and two Kazakhs came running down to find our patrol. They didn't locate us right away, since we were on the lee side; but when they did, the news was alarming and the order was for Miserbiev to get up to the shafthouse, Abdrahman crying out bluntly, "Khans, come, khans, they need the fat khan!"

We gave the flare gun to the Kazakhs and got back up the hill behind Abdrahman. What had happened was that Lazursky had sprung a trap, though at the time all we knew was that Uncle Alexander and Uncle Konstantine, Katya, the pharmacists, and Goldenberg were stuck at the 300 Level in a blacked-out pit. What we learned was that the police guard had surrendered much too readily when ordered to lay down their arms by Lazursky. Upward of a dozen men, some heavily armed, had just laid down in defeat and allowed themselves to be marched out of a strong defensive position and stuffed in a shed. The same loose sequence had served below as well, when Lazursky had gone down the two-decker elevator with Uncle Alexander and the Kazakh gunmen and ordered the prison guard to surrender and go back up quietly. The word had then been passed for the pharmacists to care for an overwhelming number of casualties among the prisoners. I don't know how many round trips the elevator made; however, the pharmacists sent up more than twenty men and women, most of them unable to walk. The special prison was a charnel house; and since I never learned what happened to those inmates, I have to rely on what Doctor Mometov said later, that there was nothing her medicine could do for them, they were all mind-broken from the drugs. I would learn someday myself what was meant by State Security's drugs. That night I only cared for Katya's safety, and the news was that she and Goldenberg, impatient with how long it was taking to bring up the Grand Constructor and worried for his health, had gone down in one of the trips to transfer up the guards and inmates. Abdrahman said all had been going well, if slowly, until the power had shut off: no elevator, no lights, no telephone communication below, no way to get our people up, no explanation for what was wrong. That was when Uncle Dmitry, in command at the shafthouse, had sent for Miserbiev—"the fat khan"—as the one most likely to have a technical opinion of the crisis. We arrived at the shafthouse as Uncle Dmitry was shouting orders to drive the autobus up to the main door in order to illuminate the workspace with its headlights. The shafthouse was a wood-built three-story structure; the first level was made over into a barracks for the guards, with kitchens, an armory, officers' quarters, and a radio room. Uncle Dmitry had already directed the Kazakhs to strip out the armory and lock down the police guard, but, without power for lights, security was fragile. We crashed past several cosmonauts in the dark, and Miserbiev had to call out his own name to announce we'd arrived. The place reeked of creosote, cooking oil, foul clothes, and what must have been the stink of the unwashed inmates, who were huddled together by the stove. We had to follow the sound of Little Laika to locate the black hole of the pit—because she feared elevators, Laikushka had been left up top and now harried everyone's thinking with her barking and whining.

We reported to Uncle Dmitry, who showed his distress by making hard demands. "You know about this?" he said to Miserbiev about the works. "Then you find me a way down or fix it, just get us down. Do you think it's the generator?" Schtange and Tevyelook were already in the headgear checking the winch; they called down to Uncle Dmitry that they needed more time. Uncle Dmitry appealed to Miserbiev, "Trifya, help us here."

I followed Miserbiev as he raced around the shafthouse looking for what he said would be auxiliary airshafts. Outside again, we went over the timbers to a mud- and ice-packed declivity, where Miserbiev located a trash heap piled over the skipshaft. Miserbiev kicked at the mess. "It's sealed, look!"

I asked, "Can't we get down?"

Miserbiev did know the solution, but he didn't know where it was. He announced, "There must be an auxiliary shaft. They build them with one just in case of disaster. And since the skipshaft is sealed there must be another one somewhere. If not, why'd they seal this one?" He turned back toward the looming shafthouse and asked himself, "This is wrong; what don't I see? One way down doesn't make sense. How would they get out, climb?" Miserbiev was a bold fellow, overweight like a clown, wiser than he acted, and he knew he could solve this if he had time. We jogged back inside just as they were barricading the windows and stringing lamplights off the battery in the autobus. Miserbiev reported to Uncle Dmitry, "It's sealed back there, sir. But I'm going to say there has to be an escape route. Get them to tell you where."

Uncle Dmitry called for Odersyats and the officer of the guard to be brought out of the armory. Odersyats didn't look the immortal bear anymore—his hands were bound behind, and he was breathing heavily, as if his heart was working too hard. "You've got to tell me how to get down there," Uncle Dmitry said.

"It's Lazursky," Odersyats said, lowering his head to take a cigarette offered by Fedyuninsky. He was no longer holding back anything and sounded weary as he muttered, "I tried to tell you. Lazursky's done it. He always meant to do it. I think he planned it. I can't help you now. I told you, Lazursky's Iagoda's man; this is his operation. He knew you were coming. He's been waiting for you."

What Odersyats said turned out to be true: just as my uncles had used us as decoys, so Iagoda and Lazursky had used Odersyats, Kuznetsov, and the Executive Committee to decoy us.

Fedyuninsky also gave a cigarette to the officer of the guard and then placed a roll of money in his tunic pocket. "You can be the new police chief," Fedyuninsky told him. "The district needs a new chief."

The officer of the guard was a rugged Kazakh with a mustache that covered his mouth. He smiled to show his broken teeth and said, "Major Lazursky did it from below. He cut the power from below. It's an emergency procedure. He arranged to do it. It was orders. He told me to step aside, and he'd take care of you himself. He's a rough one for a Russian."

"How do we get down there!" Uncle Dmitry demanded. Laikushka barked, and Uncle Dmitry yelled, "Shut up!"

The Kazakh officer smiled. "You can jump."

Miserbiev applied his genius to solve the dilemma. "That's it, isn't it? If he cut the power from below, then there must be a power cable from another works, because there's no power plant up here. The power's from another works! My guess is that they've got a cable in from the convict works down there. That way they can pay for this place on the books of the convict works. And if there's a cable in, that means there's an auxiliary shaft out the same way. There must be an escape route to the convict works. Am I right? Yes, I'm right. There's a shaft out to the convict works." Miserbiev made a fist and hit his own forehead. "Make him tell me, sir."

Uncle Dmitry hesitated in order to think about Miserbiev's presentation, which was accurate but argumentative. It wasn't Uncle Dmitry's nature to make a decision without talking and debating, and he probably wanted to open the question to all of us. He crossed his arms and glanced at the black hole of the shaft.

Odersyats made his last mistake by trying to make a deal at the wrong time. "You're beaten," he told Uncle Dmitry. "Lazursky's men will be here soon, first Lazursky's, then Moscow's. They expected you to try this, and they planned to trap you down there. You're beaten, so just clear out with what you've got. If you save me I can help you clear out. Save me and save yourselves."

Uncle Dmitry didn't hesitate this time, firing one shot that flashed a white flame out and set fire to Odersyats's overcoat as it heaved the old man back onto his bound arms. The corpse was on fire until Uncle Dmitry kicked it over. The squadron said nothing, watching and waiting. The nearby Kazakhs checked their weapons with equal patience. I don't recall having a reaction, there were too many murders already, and I suppose now the only thing to make of the way Uncle Dmitry had shot without a word is that even the most reasonable and compassionate of the three of them was, when it came to it, as bloody as an axman. Uncle Dmitry turned his machine pistol toward the Kazakh officer.

"At the Three-hundred Level," the officer conceded. "Southeast, there's an exit. Like he says, an escape route. You can follow the conduit to the gallery. It's behind the elevator shaft." Fedyuninsky released the officer's hands and gave him paper and pen to draw out his facts. "Here and here," the officer said, indicating the escape route with a hole in the paper. "It's a single shaft out of an old stope. It's not marked, but there's a hatchway."

Uncle Dmitry asked, "What about the power?"

"It can't be done," the officer said. "Lazursky cut it from below. He knows the way out. Lazursky is going out this way."

Uncle Dmitry asked, "How long before your reinforcements arrive?"

The officer answered, "They should have been here." The Kazakh shifted his feet and looked west. "You must've frigged 'em badly in town."

You can see what a simple trap it was, the sort that the victim closes on himself: we had gone down to the 300 Level; Lazursky had cut the power; and now he was walking out to supervise the assault on the shafthouse that would deliver my uncles to Iagoda, perhaps even before the Special Action Troops arrived. Major Lazursky was ambitious, ingenious, and about to win everything.

I didn't wait to hear how desperate things were, because the hopelessness of the crisis helped me make my decision to go down the pit. After all, if we were beaten, then I could try anything, and what I worked up was so rash I had to pull Stumpelkin aside to check on the facts. "They can't come up, but I can go down, can't I?" Stumpelkin agreed. We stripped off our coats, cut up our leather jerkins into strips with which to wrap our hands and knees, then rushed up to Uncle Dmitry to volunteer together. "It's the fastest way," Stumpelkin presented to Uncle Dmitry. "Straight down on the elevator cable, sir. Just like training. And we can lead them out the escape shaft."

Trifya Miserbiev not only said we were crazy—"That cable will cut your hands off if it gets through that leather"—he also said it might work: "They can get to the zek works down there. There won't be much security. And they'll be out, maybe."

My impression was that Uncle Dmitry wanted to shake us off and send someone senior down, but it was then that Lazursky's trap on us started to close. Word came of a flare signal from the main road, and then a Kazakh came up from the slag pile to report that there was a police van parked at the railbed and there were two policemen halting lorry and bus traffic up the hillside. It looked as if some of Lazursky's men had rallied, though not to attack us, rather to bottle us up until the Special Action Troops could arrive. Perhaps the flare signal came after Uncle Dmitry agreed to our proposal; it's difficult to recall the sequence. The result was that Uncle Dmitry chose us over the others who tried to take our place once they'd seen my scheme.

"You two are enough!" Uncle Dmitry told Stumpelkin and me. "I don't care what it takes; get them out. We'll hold here until you're clear." Uncle Dmitry also said he was sending Misha Cher-ryntevsky and the last shepherd (the lorry driver) back over the hills the long way to get to the collective to alert Glavtop and Grin at the Il-14 that the new rendezvous would be at the Dzhezkazgan airstrip at dawn. "Tell Sasha not to wait for us," Uncle Dmitry said to me. "And if we miss the rendezvous, we'll get out overland. We'll walk out."

Uncle Dmitry issued us several battery torches and gave me another flare gun. "Tell Sasha to fire when you're clear. We'll wait here as long as it takes."

As Stumpelkin and I were climbing up on the crossbeams, Uncle Dmitry gave me advice that I thought was odd. "Stay with Sasha," he said. "Do what he says and stay right with him and don't do anything unless he says, and if he gives you an order you do it." I took his advice as a warning not to break ranks again, as I had at Party headquarters—that was a stupid episode and yet was probably what my mind was worth that night, as panicky as cocksure—and I responded, "Yes, sir, I understand, sir," before I let go. What Uncle Dmitry was actually telling me, I think now, was that Uncle Alexander was a dangerous creature when he was on the attack, and that I should neither expect nor ask for reasons. I wasn't thinking much at all as I found my strength and swung out on the cable for a moment, mighty pleased with my daring and with the gaze of the squadron. I felt like a man who could not fail, which is a ruinous attitude, and I didn't even flinch at letting up my grip and plunging alone in free-fall as the cable sliced into my leather handholds. I slid down in jolts of ten meters, spinning into the frigid updraft and the hot odor of creosote with pockets of gases and bad air, and then, because I felt the cable shredding the leather, I started dropping faster and faster, a race between the length of the cable and the insulation on my knees and palms. The descent couldn't have taken more than three minutes. I was probably lucky to get down with just the heels on my boots worn off and a bad burn on my right thigh that I can still find today. I didn't care about the burn at the time, only with landing atop the steel cage of the double-decker elevator.

Stumpelkin landed behind me. We lit our battery torches and dropped down to the wooden planks. We were surprised by another bounce on the steel cage and found that Abdrahman Godzihkty had imitated our leather handholds and sneaked past Uncle Dmitry to follow us down, both because he thought it was his place to stay with me and Stumpelkin as he had for two weeks and also because he, too, had been warned—told by the mullah not to return to Star City unless he came back with the Grand Constructor.

I didn't comment, I just pulled Abdrahman down to us, checked the drawing Fedyuninsky had made, pointed my torch, and called once tentatively for my uncles, "Air Force!"

Uncle Konstantine called back, "Stay down, black out!" At the same instant there was a white flash with the dull echo of a shot, and then three more from the right. Stumpelkin and I went on our bellics to firing positions. I called back to Abdrahman to stay where he was. Because I was exposed on the wooden deck, I started to crawl to Uncle Konstantine's shouts. "Good, good," Uncle Konstantine coaxed me. "Keep down—it's Lazursky. He's got one of the rifles and half a clip left." Stumpelkin, Abdrahman, and I were separated in the dark, and I reached Uncle Konstantine's position having lost sense of them behind me. I wanted to turn back to locate them, yet Uncle Konstantine yanked me to him and asked, "Laikushka's good?" I told him that Stumpelkin and Abdrahman were cut off back there. Uncle Konstantine kissed me and ordered me to crawl on to the left and not to use my light until I was inside a big door. I knew there was trouble with how quiet Stumpelkin and Abdrahman had become; however, I obeyed Uncle Konstantine in starts, moving in a blackness so complete that I felt senseless, as if I were easing up a wall rather than along a floor. I reached out and felt a corpse, perhaps two corpses, and this panicked me to use the torch. I just flashed it once, but at this two hands grabbed my rifle and dragged me by the strap on my face forward over floorboards and gravel, and then hurtled me over my head and onto my back into a long low chamber. I felt a knife at my throat, and then I didn't.

What had happened was that Uncle Alexander had decided not to kill me. "Give me your torch," he said, "and report." I gave him all the extra torches in my shepherd's sack. He lit one and checked out the doorway into the triple compartment of the main shaft, and then flashed back into us and along the ceiling before announcing to the others behind us, "It's Nevsky. Get back to work. And use this." He tossed a torch to Doctor Mometov and said to me, "Tell me what's cut the power?"

I started talking and only gradually glanced around to see where I was. We were inside an old stope, carved out of rock and secured by pillars and plank work, that had been turned into one of the wards of the special prison, the floor covered with straw and the wall lined by low wooden cots. What I saw was a dungeon's dungeon, more a holding cell for the living dead than even a prison. Lazursky's trap had caught my uncles in the worst position. The Grand Constructor hadn't been jailed so much as drugged to insensibility and left in this hole like a comatose patient. The delay getting him to the surface had been because Doctor Mometov wanted to get his pulse up with one of her drugs. The prisoners who they'd sent up had been much younger men, yet I'd seen that what was left of them was trash. There were still five prisoners in the room, laid out on the cots like corpses, and I suppose that's what they were. I didn't then know about the torture drugs, and I had no way of knowing that what I saw in those skeletal faces was what a ghost looks like looking back. I breathed the stink of old flesh and kept talking to Uncle Alexander, who sat back on his heels and focused on the doorway.

What had happened, I learned later from Goldenberg, was that Lazursky had produced a pistol he'd known to find in the cell, perhaps even one he'd hidden in the Grand Constructor's bedding; and when my uncles had been out supervising the sending up of the drugged prisoners, Lazursky had grabbed Goldenberg, Katya, and Illina as a shield to make the Kazakh gunman guarding him lower his rifle, had murdered the Kazakh anyway for his rifle, and had then gone out into the corridor to open fire on my uncles and several ambulatory prisoners. The lights and power had gone out before my uncles could return fire. They had worked back to the cell in the dark, leaving behind several dying zeks, two of whom I'd crawled across in the dark.

What I'd found was a room of the dead, dying, tortured, and

trapped. Doctor Mometov was using what antibiotic and morphine injections she had on the prisoners and also doctoring the pharmacist Illina Ivanov, whom Lazursky had bashed on his way out. The dead Kazakh gunman was on the floor. Katya and Goldenberg were over with the Grand Constructor's prone form, staring at me as I talked.

I finished my report to Uncle Alexander and gave over the flare gun. He didn't comment on what I'd done to get down, only demanding again, "What's cut the power?" I told him that the officer of the guard said it had been Lazursky, and that Odersyats had said that Lazursky had arranged all this beforehand and was acting according to a plan.

Uncle Alexander asked about the drawing I'd given him. "You say we can get out here?"

I tried to sound confident. "Yes, sir, the next works down the hill, the zek works. Trifya says there must be an auxiliary shaft, an escape route, that we can find by following the power cable."

Uncle Alexander turned his head to Doctor Mometov and told her about the Grand Constructor, "We're moving him now."

The reason for the delay down here had been that Doctor Mometov was adamant about her patient. "He needs critical handling and emergency care," she argued back. "His pulse, I can't answer for it. And if you're asking me can he be moved, I say not unless you're prepared to kill him."

Katya came out of the shock she must have been in. "Go on," she told Uncle Alexander. "We'll stay here with Grandfather and them."

"No, you go with them, Mrs. Prishkin," Goldenberg told her as he slumped beside the old man's body. "This was my fault, I let him grab me, and they're going to die too." Isaacii was talking about how Lazursky had used him, Katya, and Illina as a shield to draw down on the dead Kazakh gunman's rifle—all a fiasco that was no one's fault except perhaps my uncles' for committing us to a dead end.

Uncle Alexander showed me that the way to command is to command; he ignored all their complaints and ordered Doctor Mometov, "Get him ready, make litters, do it." Uncle Alexander took the drawing and told me, "We're going to find Kostya and the shaft."

We moved out but didn't get far, for we came across Uncle Konstantine carrying Stumpelkin in his arms. Inside the chamber, Stumpelkin tried to sit up and then claimed, "It's like a kick in my back somewhere," before he collapsed in shock. Doctor Mometov stripped his coat back and told us there was an entry hole at his hip, and she couldn't find the exit wound.

I panicked about Abdrahman: "He's still out there; let me bring him in."

This helped nothing, since my fear spread to Katya and Goldenberg, who complained to my uncles, "We can't go. You can't make us. We'll stay here. We can't leave all these people. You can come back for us." Goldenberg started to cry and maybe Katya did too, though perhaps it was Illina—I couldn't be sure, and I might have been crying myself, the air was foul, and there was that sweet rot of death like a taste of poison.

There are times when the bloody-mindedness in heroes is the only thing that stops a defeat. My uncles took control by just taking control, no tricks about it, just standing up and ordering us. "We're going, darlings, all of us," Uncle Konstantine told Katya. Uncle Alexander ordered Doctor Mometov, "Up, up!" and when she hesitated, wanting to stay with the tortured and wounded, he yanked at the Grand Constructor's cot. "If he's done," Uncle Alexander declared, "we're not." Doctor Mometov saw as I did that my uncles were going to leave regardless, and she submitted, directing Goldenberg and Katya to help her make field litters for our two wounded out of planks and the straw mattress.

Within minutes, without reconnaissance, pause, or discussion, we'd gathered our invalids, the Grand Constructor and Stumpelkin, and started into the triple compartment toward the lift to find the escape route.

I felt my failure for abandoning Abdrahman and asked Uncle Konstantine to call out for him. I don't know what happened up front—I was back carrying the Grand Constructor's litter with Doctor Mometov—but I think I heard a muffled, "Khans, here, khans!" and then Abdrahman was jumping into Uncle Konstantine's arms like a child and calling, "I found it!"

Abdrahman had figured that Lazursky had ambushed us because we were between him and the escape route, and that once we were out of the way, Lazursky would flee. So Abdrahman had played possum and watched Lazursky go to the correct stope, or, as Uncle Konstantine roared when we lit up the escape route, "The fox's flown the coop!"

The escape route wasn't promising, a single low compartment into blackness. I doubt if we would have found it on our own just because it looked caved in and flooded, but it appeared the same pathway as on the drawing. There was an insulated cable strung along its plank work. My uncles made the choice and told us to close up, and then Uncle Alexander and Uncle Konstantine took up Stumpelkin's litter and plunged in first.

I was waiting my turn when Katya bumped over to peer into the compartment. I wanted to act as stouthearted as my uncles, and so I told her, "About a half kilometer, I estimate, mostly downhill, and we're following Lazursky, so we know it's clear."

Katya upset me when she responded, "We're not getting out, are we? You know it, don't you? We're going to die in there, aren't we?"

I could hear that her exhaustion had disabled her and she'd quit, she didn't want to get out; yet I didn't have enough strength for both her, myself, and carrying the litter, so I said something foolish such as, "They can get us out, you'll see."

Her reply was broken-voiced, "I'm so scared, Peter, oh, shit, oh. Why does this have to happen?"

It was time to go. I obeyed my duty rather than my heart and plunged into the gallery. Today, when all I have to offer her is love, I don't have any more of an answer for her question—"Why does this have to happen?"—than to say it wasn't your fault, Katya, none of it; it was done to you; you were not to blame.

The route became narrow and hazardous, just enough for a modest-sized man to go through widthwise and someone Uncle Konstantine's size to squeeze sideways. There was one stretch where a dip in the line had filled the compartment with ice-caked water to my knee level, and we had to crash through and drag the litter across the ice chunks. We kept on in torch-lit darkness, bashing our heads on the timbers, breathing that creosote-soaked air. I would have quit if that had been a choice and don't know how the others kept on, since it was too much for me. I was in something like a trance as we cleared the route in stages, out of the narrowest confines and through a stope where we had to crawl under an overhang no more than a meter high, and then found a triple compartment of the convict works. It wasn't the same as getting free, but at least it was lit by overhead lamps and our footfalls were dry and firm. There was a railbed that showed the way to the exit shafts. I could hear the distant roaring and sucking sound of air pumps and told myself that we were half clear, we'd half made it; and I turned to encourage Katya, "We're halfway out, see?"

Katya had been crying as she and Goldenberg struggled to keep up behind me. I heard Katya tell Goldenberg, "I can't anymore," before she fell back into Illina. Goldenberg called out, and Doctor Mometov told me to put our load down—stopping us well behind my uncles—and then she went to help Katya. "I can't, I can't," Katya was ranting, "I can't, I can't!"

We were crumpled on the gallery floor, on our hands and knees in fresh and ancient mule dung (mules hauled the ore), and Goldenberg was crying again, and what I could think to do was to call for Uncle Alexander. Uncle Konstantine, many meters ahead, called back to me to get everyone up and keep the pace. I couldn't even rouse myself. I called out again for Uncle Alexander, "Please, Colonel Oryolin, it's Katya. She's down, sir!"

I was doing what Uncle Dmitry had warned me not to—I was not obeying orders exactly—and I soon suffered my mistake, for when Uncle Alexander came back to us he was pitiless. I revealed my weakness: "Katya's collapsed, sir. Let me carry her, and Goldenberg and Abdrahman can handle my end of the litter."

"You have a post," he said.

"Katya can't go anymore," I protested.

"Get the litter up, Lieutenant," he said.

I'd like to report that he didn't mean I should leave her; I'd like to say that even Alexander Oryolin wouldn't abandon the wounded; I'd like to make more of him than there was. The truth was that Uncle Alexander was what I confronted on the floor of the gallery— a black-eyed, black-faced, blackhearted shock commander—and he would have sacrificed any of us and carried out the Grand Constructor's corpse if that's all that was left to him to win. He might have shot Katya himself if he thought she was holding me back, and I think now that if I had hesitated to obey much longer he would have shot me too. It didn't happen. I thank fate for it and for delivering up suddenly those five wretched convicts who walked out of the crosscut at Uncle Konstantine's point position and saved us. They didn't mean to help us—the five were too slavish and reduced to think about compassion or charity—they just bent their heads to Uncle Konstantine's coaxing and bullying and served us like human mules. "Here now, boys," Uncle Konstantine told them with the same tone he used for Little Laika, "here now, you come with us; we're getting out of this hole, yes, yes, you're with us." They were gnarled, toothless, filth-caked little men, but I'm sure their arrival saved Katya's life and probably Goldenberg's and Illina's, too, who were shivering too much to have gone on. Only Doctor Mometov was solid enough to supervise the convicts. I can't describe how inhuman it was down there; nothing could have endured there long and not turned into what those zeks had become, subterranean animals like their blind mules, brainless creatures, gaunt, diseased, scarred, two-legged pack animals.

A pair of zeks took up the Grand Constructor and then another pair took Stumpelkin, and the fifth supported Goldenberg and lifted Illina onto his back. This freed me to help Katya. I pulled her onto my back too, a difficult load in those low spaces, but she'd stopped making any sounds and, though she could walk, I was concerned she might fall again on the railbed. We were spread out some twenty meters like a beggars' parade shuffling down the centerline of the triple compartment; and as we came upon new crosscuts, other convicts appeared and fell in behind, none of the zeks addressing us or their mates, just following the momentum. It was as if my uncles were shepherds to the zeks, and Uncle Konstantine did cajole the newcomers like lambs. "Easy now, boys," he'd say. "We're going on with our business, you go on with yours, lads. Make way, now, boys." At some point the line stopped; I was far enough back not to know right away what was happening ahead. I settled down by several skips and waited for Doctor Mometov to come over and check on Katya, who had become glassy-eyed and speechless. What had happened was that my uncles had scouted ahead to the elevator shaft and there was gunplay, for when they came back to me I could smell fresh gunsmoke on their greatcoats, though I'd heard no shooting, nothing but the distant air pumps and the screeching skips down other cuts.

"This is the last push," Uncle Konstantine told Doctor Mometov. "You with us?"

Doctor Mometov checked her patients and wiped Stumpelkin's

face. "Whatever we do, we must hurry. I need a surgery for the young man. I have to seal the exit wound before he bleeds to death."

Uncle Alexander squatted next to me. "No one stops," he told us, and he went down the line, to Uncle Konstantine, Abdrahman, Goldenberg, Illina, Doctor Mometov, not bothering to notice our five slaves, repeating, "No one stops. No matter what you see or hear." He spoke to me, "No one stops."

I asked, "Is Lazursky ahead of us, sir?"

Uncle Alexander replied, "You follow me. That's what you do. And you do what I tell you when I tell you." He reloaded his Skorpion pistol in front of me, and he did it so deliberately that I realized at the time that he was asking himself if I was going to break. I knew not to speak up, just to obey, and even when Uncle Alexander lifted Katya's head a little to see if she was conscious, I said nothing.

He went to the lead, and we followed. The elevator shaft was at the end of a two-story-high chamber that was used as a switching yard for the skips and a stockpen for the mules. There were two elevators side by side, one going up and one down on the same cycle. Each elevator was a triple-deck cage that didn't stop moving, just jerked by, and you had to leap on an open deck as fast as you could as it moved up or down. We reached the mouths of the shafts without interference, no supervisors, no guards, no zeks, and gathered at the two black pits waiting for a transport up.

Uncle Konstantine told me, "You're first, Petya, get the women up," and then indicated the zeks with the litters, "and we'll send this lot after you."

I obeyed and didn't think to ask what I should do up top. We had to wait some time, listening to the cranking cable and banging chains, for the approach of a triple-decker was like a sea monster rising from the ocean floor; and then I could see the top of a cage and lowered Katya down as the top cleared and the first deck came up. We were quick to get on, Uncle Alexander boosting Goldenberg, the zek with Illina leaping on ably. I looked back and waited for my uncles to speak, but they said nothing.

This next incident weighs on me to this day. Neither of my uncles bothered to prepare me for the guard in the shafthouse. I was left to my own, and my fear increased in the ride up, passing level after level without anyone senior to rely on. I believe now that I killed out of fear, not anger or cunning, or perhaps I killed for no reason at all, a pathetic reflex, a predator's instinct. What happened was that, as the deck cleared the platform surface at the shafthouse, I had to leap off before the others. As I landed, my weapon tangled behind me, and, as I turned, I was faced by one greasy-faced guard in a greatcoat and two zeks watching him watching me. The three were just standing there, thick-tongued, slow-witted, the guard holding a glass of tea at his lips, not one of them moving. So why did I shoot them? I don't know; it was as if I weren't in control of myself. I could claim that I was so certain I was going to come upon Lazursky that I didn't think, but that wouldn't be all the truth. I crouched and unslung my rifle and released the safety and shot, *pop, pop, pop,* three shots in their chests at close range. I saw their eyes as they felt the pain. I saw each not believe he was dead as he collapsed backward. There hadn't been a word between us, not a sound but the rifle and the grinding of the winch, and there were three dead men already starting to rot and shadows darting in the periphery of my vision that must have been other zeks hiding from this monster who killed without talk or cries. I'd become no different from the killers my uncles were and maybe worse, in that I wasn't in command of myself, I shot without sense, I shot as I'd been trained by the Air Force to shoot—no plans, no doubts, no thoughts at all, just shoot. I'm confessing my crimes now not because I hope for forgiveness, but because I need to show myself how little point there is to murder. Murder is the stupidest of crimes; it means nothing and comes to nothing; for what solution is there to casting men into an abyss? I shot three men, they were dead, and, as Goldenberg had said, "it didn't mean anything," it didn't change anything. I still had to keep going, though the killings must have hurt me somehow, made me duller witted, since after that I moved without much reasoning at all.

By then, my uncles had come up with the zeks and the two litters. They scrambled to get Katya, Illina, Goldenberg, and Doctor Mometov down from the top deck. Uncle Alexander saw what I'd done—he checked the guard's face—and then gave me another clip, which I understood meant he approved of me.

Those shadows I'd spotted were in fact other zeks in the shafthouse. As we organized ourselves for the next leg, they emerged to watch us like carrion animals waiting on death. We had turned their world upside down—armed men up from the circles of hell—so that the longer they watched the more frantic they became, some of them heaving rocks at us to see if we were genuine. Uncle Konstantine barked at them to get away, and when that didn't stop the rocks, Uncle Alexander fired a warning shot at a light stanchion. We moved out in a tight line with Uncle Alexander's same order: "Don't stop."

I recall coming out of the barnlike sliding door of the shafthouse, and yet much of the escape until we got to the airfield is lost to me. I know what must have happened, but I can't remember feeling much of it, and I have to guess at particulars. I suppose now my memory loss is because those three murders left me in shock; I could neither think nor remember to think. I was only able to concentrate on my duty to haul Katya and tend to Goldenberg, and I followed Uncle Alexander's footsteps carefully. I know my uncles shot whatever moved around us as we staggered across the yard. However, the gunfire neither scared the zeks off nor alarmed the guards. I also know we got up to the lot of vehicles by the power plant, where Uncle Alexander chose a vehicle—a small Volga sedan—and told me I was to drive out. What I didn't know at the time was that Uncle Konstantine and Doctor Mometov had broken off from us in order to carry Stumpelkin to the works infirmary. Nor did I realize then that I'd carried Katya in such a way that her head had struck something. When we got to the sedan, I saw her bleeding and thought she'd been shot or hit by a stone.

It must have been Uncle Alexander who fired the flare gun to alert Uncle Dmitry up on the mountain that we'd gotten out. I'd turned from him by then, helping up Goldenberg, who'd broken his toe and damaged his ankle, and Uncle Alexander grabbed me and jammed me against the sedan. "You must follow me!" he shouted, and then he ripped up the hood and started the engine. I couldn't have managed any of this; I had lost all dexterity; I was a brute obeying dumbly. He shoved me toward the door and ordered, "Follow me!" and waved at a canvas-backed lorry beside the sedan. "I'm taking that lorry," he told me. "Lieutenant, do you hear me!" he demanded.

I answered, "Sir."

"Get the rifles and put them in the lorry cab!" he told Abdrahman. He gave me his best advice, "No one stops! Don't stop!"

There never was an alarm in the works. The only difference our murderous progress seemed to make was that many zeks trailed behind us like dogs, staring at us, doing nothing to protect themselves.

The guards in the towers never reacted, even after the flare, and were either asleep or wanted no fight with our weapons. I pushed Katya into the front seat and got in to find that the engine was already hot and the petrol gauge was broken. Meanwhile, two convicts manhandled the Grand Constructor into the backseat. Goldenberg crawled in and covered the old man's body. There was banging on the back door—the zek who had been hauling Illina, protecting her like an infant. He laid her in the backseat gently, and I yelled for him to get in with us, but he was afraid and retreated off, bobbing his head and weeping.

I found the gear box and played with it a little—I'd only driven an automobile once before—and then got us moving in first gear just as Uncle Alexander's big, canvas-backed lorry churned up the rise and turned in front of me, its taillights flashing red to guide me. As the lorry slowed, I saw the other four zeks leap onto its cargo bed—the only four zeks who tried to escape that night. Uncle Alexander drove point like a pathfinder, bashing aside a water lorry at the mine gates. That parked water truck was the only resistance we met on the drive to the Dzhezkazgan airfield, back over the same route we'd plowed with the bus, this time downhill. The drive was soundless to me, since I couldn't hear properly, both my ears damaged by the gunfire. I stank of nitrates, oil, dung, and my thigh was burned from the cable, yet in all I was sound and lucky. Katya was down on the seat beside me, bleeding from the head, and as I drove I pressed my palm on her skull as if I could keep her alive with pressure. She wasn't breathing evenly—it was a bad concussion that I feared was a gunshot—and when she spoke it was a gasping, rattling noise that sounded like "can't, can't, can't."

The district airfield was rudimentary, with an operations shack and a single iced-up strip located about eighteen kilometers and a forty-minute drive from the works. Uncle Alexander found the strip in the rain as if he'd been there before, though I knew he'd just had our map to guide him. He navigated us across a mushy snowfield and then we were on the strip, heading for the flight line. There were four An-2s—a twenty-year-old, small, underpowered, metal biplane that was best for light cargo hauling—parked beside the doorless hangar, and Uncle Alexander's big lorry circled the flight line quickly and then stopped, its headlights illuminating the lead An-2.

Presently Uncle Alexander was at my door, ordering me, "Get her loaded. Just our people, not the zeks, and move it."

I opened my door and looked around for Uncle Konstantine. It was the first I'd realized he was missing, and I asked, "Where's Colonel Strogolshikov—where's Genka and the doctor?"

Uncle Alexander pulled me from the sedan and raised his voice to be clear above the rain. "Dump the cargo and preflight her. Light as you can, she's got to clear the hills to the east, and there's a five-hundred-meter peak around here somewhere. She'll ice up in this. I'll get you what I can from the ops. And you'll need to top her fuel, she'll need her range."

I protested, "What about the squadron and the rendezvous at dawn?"

Uncle Alexander ignored me. "Get the zeks off-loading any cargo, strip her! I'm to the ops to get you what I can!" He patted Abdrahman and told him, "You're with me, bring the rifle!" I watched him trot toward the ops shack, a one-man assault force with a Kazakh gun-bearer, and then I did my duty to marshal the convicts, who were standing like apes beside the lorry. I soon found the work kept me from fretting. I had two convicts clean out the An-2, dumping crates of pamphlets and mailbags, while I took the other two to roll over the fuel wagon, which was like directing a runaway train, so that we almost clipped the An-2's wing. We had to pump the fuel by hand, and it took longer than it should have, but it gave us time to help the two zeks in the plane pull out the storage shelves and anything else that could be detached. I had Katya, Illina, and the Grand Constructor shifted from the sedan into the forward bulkhead of the plane. Goldenberg limped in on his own with blankets he'd found in the next plane over, and we tucked the Grand Constructor tight, not truly knowing if he was alive or dead, since he was breathing imperceptibly. Once we'd bedded down the wounded as best we could, I let the zeks huddle inside the hatchway.

The four convicts didn't talk to me or each other, they just gaped like orphans and made it clear they wanted passage. I knew Uncle Alexander wouldn't permit them with us, but saw no use in arousing them beforehand by forcing them out of the hold. I circled the An-2 to check the rudder, elevator, ailerons, flaps, and props and then rechecked under the engine cowl for birdlife sheltering from the storm. I'd done all I could—she was a stocky, solid aircraft that could probably have flown through a mountain—and rather than exhaust myself with another reconnoiter, I popped the canopy hatchway from the outside and climbed up into the flight deck to study the flight controls. Everything looked crude and simple. I figured Uncle Alexander could fly anything with wings.

What I didn't understand was that I was to be the pilot. After nearly thirty minutes away, Uncle Alexander appeared at the hatchway like a drowned fisherman: he'd lost his cap; his hair and face were caked with rain and sweat; his breath was puffy and his voice guttural. I raised the hatchway and let Abdrahman slide up into the second seat while Uncle Alexander leaned in under the canopy. "Here's what we could find," he said, dropping his shepherd's bag and sorting out a thermos of tea, a map case, and a bag of hard-boiled eggs. Abdrahman was wearing two greatcoats over his own and pulled them off to get at extra heavy woolens and a jerkin underneath. They'd pilfered all this from the ops shack. I assumed the sentries were dead. I learned later from Abdrahman that what had taken so long was that Uncle Alexander had interrogated the two police guards with a knife, with Abdrahman translating, before he'd murdered them—all to learn that they knew nothing about any inbound flight from Moscow or anywhere and that they'd had no call from Lazursky or anyone that night. This was likely a lie that condemned them, given that they'd been seated at the powered-up receiver waiting for a call during a rainstorm despite the fact this was not an all-weather field. "This rain might be snow to the west," Uncle Alexander continued, leaning in over the map. "I make a left-to-right head wind. You won't be able to get above the storm. You haven't got the ceiling in this. But you can get over the rain, and it should break to the south. You'll pick up Star City's beacon inside two hours."

I heard what he'd said—I was the pilot—and didn't comment as he continued to instruct me with the An-2 specifications, the climbing and cruising speed, the range and fuel consumption. "She rides like a plowhorse," he said, tapping the stick, "so fight the rudders, fight them. She won't break before you do." He settled back, his head and shoulder still inside the cabin and his torso out in the rain. "Start and go," he commanded.

I knew not to question his decision to make me the pilot, yet I had to ask, "What about you, sir?"

He tossed a pack of cigarettes to Abdrahman and told me, "Here's your copilot; he's earned it." He looked back to the cabin and added, "Get those zeks out. Go!" before he stepped off and walked to his lorry.

I obeyed. A thousand-horsepower engine needed at least fifteen minutes to warm up. After I ignited her, I ordered Abdrahman to get into the dry clothes while I helped the invalids. Goldenberg took the tea and bread and started feeding Illina, but Katya just lay there, open-eyed by then, but feverish, her lips cracked. I got her boots and socks off and dried her feet with a blanket, and then pulled her parka free and wrapped her in one of the stolen greatcoats. In the shadows she looked most damaged to me, a slim woman with pasty skin and blood-matted hair, and I couldn't tell if the bleeding had ceased.

The four convicts were still huddled at the hatchway. I knew I either had to lie to them or use the rifle on them. "You're on the next plane out!" I lied. They pleaded and resisted, scared little dead men who could have broken me in half but were so wasted by years of slavery that they just watched Goldenberg eat the bread and waited in hopes that I would feed them. I gave them the bag of hard-boiled eggs and told them to get out and join my colonel in the lorry. They knew I was lying, but they slipped away in defeat, and I sealed the door straightaway.

Goldenberg asked me, "What will happen to them?" meaning the convicts. I think he knew the answer, because he started whimpering again. I told him his job was to hold on to the litter as we climbed, and then to get some water into Katya. Illina was alert enough to help, and she moved over to embrace Katya, understanding as I didn't that the worst danger here was shock from exposure.

I didn't like making so many critical decisions, and I felt that every choice I made was half-wrong. I got back to the flight deck and poked out to give thumbs-up to Uncle Alexander at the cabin of his lorry. He blinked his lights then shot ahead to lead me out the taxiway and to mark the end point of the runway.

My duty came down to my driving a lumbering craft that I'd never flown, and I could only depend on my training: I released the brakes to taxi out after Uncle Alexander's lead and found she did handle heavily, like driving a team of plowhorses, and then I brought the nose into the wind, rechecked the tachometer for carburetor ice, throttled down to check the fuel pump and tank, released the brakes, and tried not to think about it, just to watch my ground speed and react. I throttled up and found the bumps and ice slicks survivable, and all was in order as my speed climbed to fifty, then sixty, then seventy-five kilometers per hour. I don't know why I looked around, since my job was straight ahead. I did though, a driver checking his field of vision, and I saw a second pair of headlights on the snow field ahead, running to intercept me.

I decided to abort, guessing the headlights were the squadron in the autobus. I throttled down hard, putting flaps down, working the rudder pedals to steer into the skid, fighting the jolts as I skidded and left the strip for the frozen mud banks. We spun portside about one hundred degrees before she settled. I idled and feathered the engine, popped the canopy. Do you understand? I thought the second set of headlights was the squadron, that's why I disobeyed Uncle Alexander's order to take off. I was wrong regardless how it worked out. What I learned that night more than anything else on Planet Stalin was that once you throw in with men like my uncles, you throw in with them, you don't decide you know better or, worst of all, are better. At twenty-two, you are only as good or bad as your leaders. Make sure you feel right when you choose them, and then keep going wherever they send you and go till heaven or hell turns you back. I didn't keep going, I aborted; and my disobedience led to a dreadful turn that still confounds me, though I suppose what happened was the common sort of confusion in a battle. The second set of headlights wasn't the squadron's autobus but rather another Volga sedan in Uncle Konstantine's hands. He had stolen it to follow us with Doctor Mometov and Stumpelkin. Yet Uncle Alexander, who saw me abort at the approach of the sedan, regarded the Volga as a threat, and he came banging across the runway to shield me and ram the sedan. Because Uncle Konstantine veered as he neared my position, the big lorry only caught the sedan's rear and then bull-dozed it sideways to pin it between its bumper and the snowbank. Uncle Alexander was quick out with his pistol to kill any survivors. Uncle Alexander aimed to crush them, and it was happenstance that he'd missed a broadside on the first pass, and it was happenstance again that when Uncle Konstantine came out of the sedan waving his pistol also, the two of them like pack leaders squaring off to fight over me and mine, that one or both recognized the fiasco and dropped their guard, Uncle Konstantine beginning a roar, "Balls, Sasha, balls!"

The scene was even stranger, for the indomitable Major Lazursky had been trussed up and stowed in the crushed boot of the sedan. Uncle Konstantine had captured Lazursky at the convict works infirmary, where Lazursky had gone after emerging from the shafthouse no more than a few minutes before us. Uncle Konstantine had just walked in on Lazursky at the telephone—as obliging and feeble as that, the enemy undone not by cunning or force but by the simplest of coincidences, as if all there was of our besting Lazursky was a last-moment accident.

The accident was stranger still. After my uncles had untangled their vehicles, and Uncle Konstantine had driven the sedan over to the An-2 to help the transfer of the unconscious, now bandaged Stumpelkin into the aircraft, it was time to deal with Lazursky; but when Uncle Konstantine pried open the trunk to fetch him out, he found that the impact had broken Lazursky's back. Lazursky lay on his side, bound and helpless, screaming, "Help me, God, God, help, I can't move! I can't feel my legs! And it hurts, my god, it hurts!"

All this was in the rain, under steaming headlights, with those gasping wails, and I suppose Uncle Alexander's expedience was predictable. When Doctor Mometov tried to examine Lazursky, Uncle Alexander blocked her path. When Uncle Konstantine told Doctor Mometov to give Lazursky morphine, Uncle Alexander cut them both off and laid his knife blade along Lazursky's shattered spine to check if he was faking. "Tell me!" Uncle Alexander demanded. Lazursky was screaming too hard to hear the order, and if he had it was unlikely he would have given up any information about the ambush he'd planned, either the disposition of the police forces encircling the squadron or the arrival of any troops from Moscow. Uncle Alexander quit his effort short of torture and pulled back from the boot of the car, telling Doctor Mometov, "You have patients enough. This one's done."

Doctor Mometov protested, "Colonel, I won't leave any citizen like this."

"Kostya," Uncle Alexander ordered, "get her up," meaning Uncle Konstantine was to take charge both of Doctor Mometov and the

An-2. With a savagery that stunned me, Uncle Alexander reached inside the boot and pulled Lazursky out by the legs and let him fall onto the runway, so that he was face-up into the rain. Mercy would have been to shoot him, yet that wasn't for Uncle Alexander, who walked away while Lazursky cleared his mind long enough to ejaculate the blackest of curses: "You're damned like me!" and then he repeated, "Damned!" again and again until his mouth filled with rainwater and he gagged to silence.

I was standing at the hatchway of the aircraft, and as Uncle Alexander passed me he ordered, "Take charge of the zeks."

For my disobedience I was stripped of my command, yet admit now I was relieved to fall back into line. I confess there was an undeniable sense of security in bowing and bending to a man as tyrannical as Uncle Alexander. To challenge him wasn't credible and would have felt crazed. He was the most violent human being I'd ever witnessed and, in the sad way of young men, I was entranced by his cruelty. I'd struggled all night to show my courage by trying to protect Katya, by volunteering and risking my life, yet in the end I'd only been a subordinate to the strength of our attack, Alexander Oryolin's blood-lust.

I corralled the four convicts back into the big lorry bed and climbed into the cabin to wait for Uncle Alexander. He stood alone in the rain until Uncle Konstantine had warmed up the An-2 engine again, and then he tramped to the lorry, climbed in, and started us out to repeat the takeoff procedure. Uncle Konstantine taxied the aircraft, powered up, and lifted off, vanishing into the curtain of rain.

Uncle Alexander and I didn't talk the remainder of our time together that night, and I don't care to relate in detail the final hours of our hazard, since it was uneventful. Within two hours—dawn somewhere up above the storm clouds—Glavtop and Grin came in over the field at zero altitude, and, as soon as Uncle Alexander lit up the strip with the lorry, they skated the Il-14 to a firm landing. Not much more than a quarter hour after that, Uncle Dmitry and the squadron with the Kazakh gunmen turned up in the autobus with a most anticlimactic tale of the resolution of the standoff at Number 2. After the flare, Uncle Dmitry had waited long enough to be sure we were clear, and then he had escorted the tough Kazakh police officer to the police at the roadblock, where the Kazakh had told them that Lazursky was finished, that he was probably the new chief, that this wasn't theirs to get shot over. Uncle Dmitry had talked his way out after all by breaking the will of the opposition and also by dangling a vision of the Dzhezkazgan District without the old bosses.

There wasn't much talk as the squadron and Kazakhs boarded the Il-14 (which we had to strip to bones to accommodate twenty-two of us plus the gold bars: twice the safe load). Everyone was exhausted by a night in which they'd expected the worst and yet had ended with an icy drizzle and one KIA, the Kazakh gunman Lazursky had shot down in the mineshaft. The police ambush at the works had disintegrated, the Special Action flight from Moscow either hadn't been able to get in through the storm or had never been dispatched in the first place, we never knew which; and so by the time we quit the district, there was no opposition left standing. In retrospect the only human adversaries we'd faced were Major Lazursky and a few greedy old men with bad hips and worse hearts. The trap that General Iagoda had set for us from Moscow had failed at the point of attack because my uncles had crashed the walls and burned the fortresses and slaughtered the bosses. The truth in the empire in those days was that if you killed wantonly long enough, and especially if you killed bosses such as Lazursky and Odersyats like flies, then you could have your way in any direction and have the last word, too.

I was glad for the silence on the flight out and hunched up in a half-fetal position against the bulkhead, quietly grieving with the sort of shock that remains after combat. I was so worn down by the danger that I didn't care for the facts of what we'd done; or for the fact that Uncle Alexander had turned the four zeks who'd helped us away from the overloaded Il-14, abandoning them to their fates; or for the boasts of the squadron (who dealt with their shock in several ways, from silence to incessant chatting); or even for my grinding shame for starting all this as Iagoda's stooge. The only thing I cared about was that I was still moving and that somewhere ahead of us I was sure Katya was in safe hands.

What I do care about now is to speak of Lazursky, whom I saw only twice and yet remember better than many men I've loved: remember for his dark, sinister little face and strong voice and for how I watched him die. There are thoughts you have that you bury for decades that can come back to you of a sudden. I realize now that I have long carried within me such thoughts of Lazursky. I can recall now how, after the An-2 had gone but before the Il-14 or the squadron arrived, I sat in the hangar looking out into the rainy darkness toward where we'd abandoned Lazursky. I couldn't hear him, couldn't see him, but I believed I could, and the image of Lazursky lying out there in the ice frightened me. I think I could see myself out there, paralyzed and alone with a mouthful of sleet, and I cringed at the picture of my own death. But there was more to my fear than fear of death. I was also frightened of Uncle Alexander. I couldn't explain to myself how he could have done that to Lazursky regardless of the provocation, how the man I worshipped as a hero of heroes could act like a monster.

I remember that while I sat nearby Uncle Alexander, who was fixed cross-legged on a crate smoking his pipe and studying the storm, a tired, soaked man showing little of his power at that moment, I wanted to ask a dark question of him. I did nothing about it. I can ask it now, since it's for me to answer as well. "What did Lazursky mean that we're damned like him," is what I wanted to ask. "Are we, sir, damned like him?"

You can see how disillusioned I was about my uncles. Lazursky wasn't correct that night, yet such a curse follows men like a shadow. It sat hard with me that there was some justice in damning my uncles for their ruthlessness. The paradox still confounds me that so many of the heroes in our history are also infamous murderers. What is it in folk that makes us turn again and again to the awful strength in men like my uncles? What explains why Russia, then and now, elevates and venerates and even sanctifies bloody fools like Lazursky, like Iagoda, like Uncle Alexander, and like me? How does telling the truth of us make us into heroes?

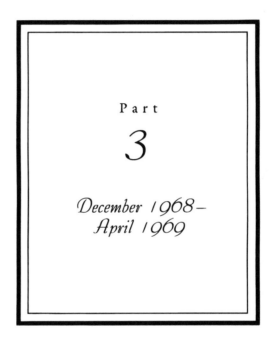

Part

3

December 1968–
April 1969

$\textcircled{1}$

My Mother

The Dzhezkazgan raid advanced my uncles' reputations ever more
notoriously. It was as if the very lawlessness of their dare to attack
what they wanted made them all that more legitimate as heroes of
the empire. I can't explain this paradox any better now than to say
that in those days, if you won a victory, it didn't signify what you'd
done, it only mattered that you'd triumphed, and soon enough all
the fools, liars, thieves, and bullies in the empire were eager to acknowledge your prowess and call you an ally. Within a week of our
return the Army and Air Force bosses offered their roundabout approval of my uncles by publishing their photographs in the military
newspaper, *Red Star,* using their official cosmonaut portraits with a
collective caption that resurrected their nom de guerre, the Martian
Troika, and made a pun out of it, saying that perhaps soon they'd be
the Lunar Troika. Do you see the size of the endorsement? Not only
was it all right that my uncles had shot up and burned out a town for
their own purposes, but also this strange achievement qualified them
once again to go from war heroes to space heroes and lead to the
moon.

None of this spontaneous appreciation surprised the Cosmonaut
Corps, since to us my uncles were high-performance audacity, the
Air Force's most outlandish stars, heroes of legends written and un-
written. Can you see them now as we did then? All their lives my

uncles had beaten monstrous odds and cheated anonymous death to survive the barbarities of fifty years of the Red Terror. It was not that much of an exaggeration to say that Lenin had hanged their fathers and Stalin had shot their brothers and the Party had crushed their children. We saw my uncles as the luckiest few of our very few heroes, the remnant of millions of sacrificed boys, and we didn't ask if they were good or bad, grand or ignoble, we only asked that they keep going for us and with us. Then as now Russia believed in heroes; then as now heroes were the Motherland's only passion. That's why my uncles could walk on the fires of Dzhezkazgan and not even the biggest bosses would move against them as long as they won. The Party, the Army and Air Force, the multitude of the folk, all understood that the empire had to have heroes like my uncles— valorous, undisciplined, selfish, and selfless champions. My uncles were what we could see and touch of greatness. We didn't have the wealth of the West; we didn't have the might of NATO; we didn't have the luck of the Americans. What we had was three colossal heroes proved in battle and sanctioned by fate.

In plain talk it was the Dzhezkazgan raid that elected my uncles to get what they wanted, the moon landing. Not sense, not science, not political favoritism, none of that moved the decision. Plain heroism won out. Everyone knew that moon-driving called for heroes, so the rhetorical questions were put at Starry Town: Why waste time trying to make new heroes out of men like Beregovoi and Shatalov when three were at hand? Hadn't the State Space Commission set us backward and made a mess by granting *Soyuz 2/3* to lesser men? Wasn't it time to turn to our best and trust their furious souls?

All this high talk of my uncles didn't take me from the low facts of my own return to Starry Town. I didn't see Katya again for over a month, not until Christmas week. Her worst wound was a bad concussion. She didn't respond well either to first aid at the Tsar Cannon airstrip or to the care she received back at Starry Town, and so, wasted and invalided, she and Daniel were taken by Mrs. Zhukovsky to convalesce at Katya's mother's in Petersburg. Our other casualties mended variously. The Grand Constructor was alert within days of his return to Tsar Cannon, but his health was mortally damaged. He never recovered from the effect of the drugs—his speech slurred and often inaudible—and he required a wheelchair and much medical attention from then until his death. He was no longer healthy enough to go on as the absolute boss of Tsar Cannon, and yet he was too much of a Bolshevik fanatic to relinquish any of his power short of death, and so he agreed to the compromise that he would retain his post while allowing Doctor Lunin to assume the acting directorship. The young nurse Illina Ivanov healed at Star City's hospital and soon joined Doctor Mometov out at the Tsar Cannon infirmary with responsibilities to care for the Grand Constructor. Isaacii Goldenberg repaired quickest of all and limped himself back to duty, no longer just the Grand Constructor's devoted acolyte but also the newly promoted acting deputy director of the project—as the rocketeers jested, Nikhon Univer's old brain in a young man's body. And my dear friend Genka Stumpelkin was too Siberian to die on us. After he had emergency surgery at Star City, I helped take him back to Starry Town's medical center on November 25.

Uncle Alexander didn't return to Starry Town. He set up camp at the Tsar Cannon works. Uncle Konstantine stayed on at the Cosmodrome to help supervise the heavy construction at the airfield and also to romance Doctor Mometov, whom he persuaded to come out to him at Tsar Cannon. He would soon marry, his sixth and final wife. Only Uncle Dmitry came home to Starry Town, though despite the *Red Star* promotion and the general hoorahing of the Corps he didn't come home in a triumphant temper. To my uncles, Iagoda was their enemy until he was dead, and the Dzhezkazgan raid had only foxed Iagoda, not defeated him. Dzhezkazgan was a victory that left my uncles fatalistic, and they were never lighthearted again, becoming instead most stern and pious about duty. The squadron also put aside most of its high spirits, and I never saw any of them irresponsible again.

My situation wasn't bright-faced. I returned to the candidate barracks to find that I was again stuck between the warring worlds of the Corps and State Security. The other candidates had heard exaggerated versions of Dzhezkazgan, and they'd also heard that I'd done something reckless against State Security. They certainly could guess that my return had something to do with the fact that Lieutenant-Colonel Maximov, deputy commander of the Corps, and Chekhist rat, was thrown out of Starry Town like a rat. Rather than making me a hero to the candidates, however, these developments just made them doubt me more. Was I a stooge or one of my uncles' darlings? Either way, for a candidate I was too flagrantly AWOL too often, and without bothering with an interview Khitrovo again reduced me to the bottom of the class, stripped me of all privileges, docked me two months' pay, and this time penned me up at night by moving my bunk beside the watch officer's desk. I heard that Khitrovo wanted to have me on charges, and that he threatened to resign if he wasn't satisfied about my future discipline. I also heard the word had been passed to all Starry Town that my candidacy was guaranteed by my uncles and my safety was guaranteed by the Corps.

I became something like a ward of the squadron, and my friends Trifya Miserbiev and Yurka Adama-Bibliov were assigned to accompany me everywhere outside of the barracks, including to class. I was told to go nowhere unless my companions were along, and I was told that if I tried to put one foot outside of Starry Town without authorization I would wear a ball and chain the remainder of my candidacy. Uncle Dmitry delivered this threat in person at the end of November, "No more surprises, Petya, and no more questions! You behave yourself and you tell me everything—who calls you, who writes you—and if you satisfy me that you're the best you can be, then I'll pass on any letters you might write to Katya. Agreed?"

My obedience was heartfelt, "Yes, sir, I do have letters for her, and thank you, sir."

I understood that these arrangements were to protect me from Iagoda's reach, since it wasn't impossible he might try to abduct me in retaliation for Dzhezkazgan. What I didn't understand was why I should continue to be the battleground, why I was part of the so-called feud between Uncle Alexander and Madame Romodanovsky. Yet when I asked Uncle Dmitry to answer what I regarded a straight-forward question—"What am I to them, sir, why do they care about me?"—I was returned another version of Uncle Dmitry's "No more surprises, and no more questions!": "You do what you're told," he said, "and we'll sort this out."

What my uncles claimed they were going to sort out, but were actually keeping from me, was that I was at the heart of the feud. I didn't then think to solve the mystery, I just waited on their orders, but you might be able to look at the facts and see as I did not. Why did Uncle Alexander and Madame Romodanovsky hate each other? Why did they include me in their feud? The truth was that it was a blood feud to do with my dead father and with Uncle Alexander's dead daughter Sophia and with me. The truth was that Madame

Romodanovsky had been my father's mistress before she was Uncle Alexander's wife. The truth was that Madame Romodanovsky was my mother.

Yes, Uncle Alexander's daughter was my half sister—Sophia and Peter: we had the same mother and different fathers—and to Uncle Alexander's mind, once he'd learned that my mother was back in Russia, my life was as forfeit as his unless she was stopped, for my mother regarded me almost as much a threat to her power as she regarded Uncle Alexander a threat to her life. I was one of two children she had abandoned who lived. He was one of two lovers she had abandoned who lived. She wanted us destroyed because she feared us, because she hated what she feared, because she was certain we wanted revenge on her, and also because she wanted us destroyed—no reason, no sense, just because she wanted it.

Now you can appreciate how shocked my mother must have been when I walked in on her at Saint Sophia and pulled her out of Ivan the Terrible's pew. Now you can understand why she pounded on me to tell her that Uncle Alexander had sent me to intercept her. Now you can sense her conviction that unless she struck at us we were going to strike at her. It was impossible for her to accept that Saint Sophia was an accident, a coincidence, just fate. She must have regarded Saint Sophia as a dark stab at her heart, the judgment of heaven on her soul.

I know the whole truth of my mother takes explaining, and I must get on to tell how I learned of her identity. For now I can say that my father Apollon Nevsky was a strong, ambitious, lucky man with a lifelong weakness for strong, ambitious, and dangerous women, which is what he found exactly in the young Daemonia Romodanovsky. When he accepted my mother as his mistress early in the war, he must have known that she was an agent who'd been sent to him by State Security, he must have realized that her role was to spy on him and, if necessary, to inform on him. Father was already too prominent for his flying in Spain not to perceive that Stalin was a jealous god, and that those who most threatened Stalin's might were the celebrated heroes of the people. But then I can also imagine the bawdy game a man as cocky as my father might have made of my mother, the informer, in his bed. They were said to have been most compatible, and they were inseparable for three years, 1942 to 1945, sharing the privations of combat from Stalingrad to the Byelorussian front. Yet then Mother became pregnant again (with me, her second or third pregnancy according to what Uncle Dmitry said, but the first one to survive the first several months). Soon after, my father, who had assumed acting command of the Fourth Air Army at war's end, left my mother behind at his corps headquarters in Ukraine while he went on to Germany to oversee the forward basing of our air regiments. My mother was left in the temporary care of my uncles, especially Uncle Alexander, who, as my father's wingman, took special responsibility to find transport for her back to Moscow (and I have often puzzled if he was in love with her at this point, his commander's woman and by far the most alluring creature in his young life at twenty-four). I don't turn from the truth here: my father abandoned my mother as soon as the war was done and just as he gained prospect not only to rise to the highest Air Force ranks but also to return to his wife now liberated from Leningrad—abandoned her as he might have tossed aside a junior staff officer. My uncles soon moved on to postwar Vienna with the regiment, and my mother was obliged to return to Moscow, where she gave birth to me in April 1946, and where she found herself discarded by her Chekhist handlers as the forgotten bitch of a hero's forgotten bastard. Alone, penurious, her parents dead and her brothers and sisters scattered by the war, jobless in a desolated Moscow filling with the war's returning victors, my mother faced no future but perhaps being passed from old boss to new boss as a whore of the state.

My mother, Eudaemonia Petrovna Romodanovsky, was a beautiful, resolute woman, born in 1918, the youngest daughter of a Moscow silver merchant—Peter Alexandrovich Romodanovsky—who had long prospered buying and selling religious paraphernalia and who, after the civil war and the massacre of the priests, had thrown in with the Bolsheviks and befriended Stalin over some inconsequential trade matter that allowed him an opportunity to show his loyalty first to Stalin and second to the Party. My grandfather had prospered under Stalin's five-year plans and endless purges until he died of influenza on a trip to France in 1938. There was reason to believe that my grandfather at his death was a Chekhist agent masquerading as a senior trade official. He certainly placed as many of his children as he could into the prestigious State Security schools. My mother was well educated in Moscow and abroad in Paris as well, and she did not hesitate, at nineteen, to accept her posting as a Chekhist seducer to entrap any enemies of the state left after the purges. My mother's radiance and intelligence made her a natural treasure, and I suspect she was a natural choice to become the mistress of the leading air ace of the Spanish War, who soon became the leading air ace of the winter of 1941.

My mother's crisis in the spring of 1946, left with me and little else, must have looked to her as a seminal moment—either she won her job back at the Lubyanka or she sank into deprivation. My mother decided to fight with what weapons she'd learned to use, chiefly her extraordinary skills to deceive and hate, betray and abandon. My mother decided to do to others what had been done to her.

I admit I don't know all this for sure—none of the principals were frank with me, and I have what I do from what Great-Uncle Lev told Katya and she told me, and also from what Uncle Dmitry told his wife, Angelicka, who then passed it on to Anna who told me many years after my uncles were gone—but I can guess much of the chronology and piece out the rest from what I've learned from the stories of State Security. I think my mother must have gone to her bosses at the Lubyanka and proposed that she was ill used in Moscow as just another consort for old men when instead she was schooled to go abroad to lure and corrupt any of the mighty war heroes that State Security might want brought under control. Then again perhaps the Lubyanka lords recruited my mother as part of a new legion of treachery incarnate to be dispatched throughout a newly won empire. In any event the plot to spy on and undermine all war heroes wasn't a political or philosophical decision on anyone's part—it was simply the Bolshevik Party under Stalin, a bawdy house of lust and assassination, a pit where my mother could thrive as long as she denounced on command.

You might shake your head and conclude that my mother gave herself to be one of Great-Uncle Lev's "whores of Babylon," and I don't disagree, though I sometimes do try to see how my mother might have seen. What righteous choices were there in a Russia where the bosses had sold their souls to Stalin and his gang of fratricides, and where the people had stood by and let their souls be stolen by the worst among them? Yes, my mother could have quit her ambition, raised me as best she could, sacrificed her health and mind like the rest of her generation. Perhaps that was what a better woman would have done. My mother was not a better woman or even a

good woman: she was a child of the bright lies of the burning Bolshevik Revolution; she was a corrupted, cornered, vindictive human
being facing stark temptation. Her temptation was not singular in
1946, in a Europe that had disgraced itself for a decade with war and
in a Russia that had disgraced itself for centuries with slavery and
infanticide, and when she chose of her own to sell her soul to
Stalinist devils she wasn't the first or even of the first ten thousand to
walk that path. My mother gave herself to power, she became a slave
to power, she chose power as her profession, and what she gained for
her bargain was authority to roam Europe and destroy men like ants,
and what she lost for her bargain was love. The first love she lost was
me when she gave me up to my father's wife, Marya, at Leningrad,
who took me in resignedly since she'd lost her two daughters to the
famines. The second love she lost was Alexander Oryolin, whom she
married to assure he couldn't escape her as my father had. The third
love she lost was my sister, Sophia, whom she abandoned when she
left Uncle Alexander for grander assignments in Western Europe.
And the fourth, fifth, and sixth loves she lost were my father and
uncles Konstantine and Dmitry, when she gave evidence against
them as well as her husband during State Security's purges of the Air
Force in 1949, 1950, 1951, 1952, 1953. Yet none of this history is
to argue that my mother should be forgiven for her crimes. My
mother sent my father to the camps where he was murdered, sent my
uncles to the camps where they were broken, sent so many unnamed
potentates and worthless despots to their cold ends that by the time I
met her at Saint Sophia she was not much more than a denizen of
the worst that men can do to each other. Yes, I admit she was a
whore of Babylon; and yes, she was a cold-blooded Chekhist agent
who practiced nothing but treachery. She was wrong, most wrong.
There can be no justification for such a life, and if my presentation of
her story sounds as if I am holding back from condemning her
completely, it's because I am still struggling to accept the truth.
Daemonia Romodanovsky was a private terror, and I am ashamed
that she was my mother, and I confess my shame. It's the shame I
first felt the Saturday night they locked me in the basement cell at the
Lubyanka. It's the shame of a bastard of the Lubyanka. It's the
shame that I was born to a woman who betrayed because she wanted
to betray, who condemned and murdered because she wanted to
condemn and murder, who was evil because she wanted to be evil.

The truth was that my mother chose to become a black, rotten soul who, once she'd won the chance, did the devil's work with a passion rivaled only by that of the Four Horsemen of the Apocalypse, and who I can imagine, with what irony I possess, finally went on to hell because she wanted to seduce, betray, and abandon the devil, too. Then again the hardhearted in me wants to ask: Wasn't my mother one of the supreme achievements of the Bolsheviks, wasn't she the tempter's seductress, the maligner's denouncer, the forsaker's deserter, wasn't she the perfect communism of perfect depredation?

Now you can see how very much I, at twenty-two, had to learn about Madame Romodanovsky and my uncles. My education began again in the last days of December, nearly six weeks after returning from Dzhezkazgan. The Corps had gone on two weeks of New Year's leave, and I was the last candidate left in the barracks. Colonel Khitrovo hadn't said I had to stay on over the holiday, but then he hadn't said I was released from my punishment restrictions either, and anyway I remained grounded by Uncle Dmitry's order. My chaperons, Trifya Miserbiev and Yurka Adama-Bibliov, checked on my whereabouts day and night, and the only unusual place they'd let me go after hours was to the medical center to visit Stumpelkin. The rest of the squadron was scattering to their own homes or off to the Cosmodrome. Uncle Dmitry remained at Starry Town, yet he hadn't called on me for weeks; according to Miserbiev, he was momentarily to depart for the Tsar Cannon works.

This all left me as ignorant as ever of my plight, and it's worth asking why my uncles were so pigheaded they wouldn't tell me the truth of the threat. I don't have an answer other than to guess that it was Uncle Alexander's refusal to confront his own history that kept him from helping me with mine. The darkest part of him, the blackness in his character, was a tyrant who would rather attack some fantastic enemy than pass a moment in reflection about his doubts. It might not have occurred to him that there was someone like me who deserved his mercy, if he had any left to give. Whatever the explanation of Uncle Alexander's silence to me, Uncle Dmitry went along with it, though I wonder now if he avoided me those weeks at Starry Town because he felt remorse for denying me.

My self-denial about Katya was what burdened me. I had written her several imploring letters and had sent them via Uncle Dmitry. She'd written back nothing, leaving me hostage not only to State

Security and my promise to Uncle Dmitry to remain in check but also to my heartsickness. It might seem a slim motive now, but at the time my longing for Katya and for making love to Katya and for just plain sex with her—she was an articulate lover—was what drove me more than the moon talk into the trouble of those four bad weeks of January 1969.

My frustrations about Katya boiled over on Saturday morning, December 28. With everyone away, the only recreation I had was to linger in the duty room, where it was warmest and where I could listen to the shortwave radio with the cook, Lukacs. Lukacs was a Pole who understood German, and his custom after finishing his chores was to tune in to the morning news broadcast from East Germany. The most important news item to me was still the American triumph of *Apollo 8,* which had just returned from its five-day mission on a fly-by of the moon. I was most blue; the more I listened to news about *Apollo 8* the more miserable I felt about being stuck in the barracks, where I only wanted to listen for news about *Apollo 8.* I knew that the squadron down at the Cosmodrome had been able to track the Americans and to argue about the particulars of the mission and about why it was that we were so slow to launch our own lunar fly-by. I was stuck with a cook who could only talk about pastry and only cared to talk about how little he was paid for his pastry. You can anticipate how easy it was for me to convince myself that I had to break out. When Miserbiev and Adama-Bibliov came in out of the weather—it snowed steadily that day—for coffee and some of Lukacs's famous pastry, I was barefaced about my intention.

"I'm leaving here," I declared in a pout. "I must get out of here. Don't try to stop me."

Miserbiev took up two puffy rolls and changed the subject. "The Americans splashed down last night, did you hear?" He blinked at the radio, which was once again playing symphony music. "We were over at ops for the debrief. They came down last night about twenty hundred hours our time. They double-skipped the capsule like we knew they would, for a ballistic reentry, just like we did with *Zond 6*—like a flat rock on a lake—and the word is that the crew came out good, without any injuries, very neat. They were down in the Pacific within a few miles of the recovery ship. It was a godlike mission, like you'd draw it down, godlike."

Miserbiev's jargon was meant to intrigue me and coax me out of my funk. All week Miserbiev and Adama-Bibliov had been dropping by to brief me on *Apollo 8*—from the Saturn V's "godlike" launch to the "godlike" translunar and transearth burns—and they knew how hungry I was for details. Our opinion was that the Americans were not only rich like gods but also lucky like gods. Yet everything Miserbiev said only made me feel worse about being the commonest serf in the universe. "I've got to leave for a while," I repeated. "You'd do the same as me."

Miserbiev and Adama-Bibliov were sympathetic, and they'd arrived that morning with special news they knew would cheer me greatly; yet they were going to tease me awhile beforehand. Miserbiev licked his lips of butter and tried first with a tidbit of gossip from the Cosmodrome. "There aren't any more whispers about a *Zond 7*, if you want to know. And they're not asking for pilots at all. The lunar window's slammed shut, like we thought. It's a disgrace, isn't it?"

He was talking about the aborted plan to follow November's unmanned *Zond 6* shot on a Proton rocket with a manned lunar fly-by on a Proton rocket in the December lunar window. Miserbiev knew my opinion about the failure and shared it. The State Space Commission had let the rocket chiefs back out of the shot over some minor foul-up with the booster. Who can care now about all the what-ifs of those days? Still it infuriated us to think about what if we had been permitted to send a manned *Zond 7* to a lunar fly-by before *Apollo 8*? What if that had been a Russian broadcast back to earth? What if Uncle Dmitry had been allowed to ride to glory? Instead all we had was another unexplained abort and another dumb humiliation, while the Americans grabbed gold rings off the moon.

My pout deepened as I declared, "I won't hear it anymore. I need to get to Leningrad. I have to see Katya. It's wrong to keep me here; no one else would do this."

Miserbiev tried once more, "We weren't ever ready, you know, and now with *Apollo 8* back, the whole Zond program is useless, just like Colonel Oryolin said it would be. He told them, and they didn't listen. He was right, one thousand percent right."

I whined, "At least let me telephone her. No one would know. What would it hurt?"

Adama-Bibliov decided to spring the special news on me, stretching his long legs and grinning as he spoke, "You should hear us out, Peter. There's good news about our colonels."

"What good news?" I asked.

Miserbiev continued teasing, "The big bosses are trembling in their beds! The Americans are jumping over the moon! The masses are clamoring for a savior, a savior for all Russia!" He spoke more nonsense, however the kernel of what he said was that, since the state space commissioners had canceled the Zond program, they were desperate for a propaganda victory, for any victory at all. "The big bosses have to make good. They have to deliver the goods, and now with this"—he gestured up toward the moon where *Apollo 8* used to be—"the State Commission has come on its knees to Starry Town, begging us for a victory, for a savior, for three saviors!"

Adama-Bibliov explained, "The word we've heard is that the State Commission has asked our colonels to take charge of the next mission, for the rendezvous, link-up, and spacewalk."

"Begging them!" Miserbiev repeated. "Anything they want, begging them!"

I demanded, "When!"

Adama-Bibliov said, "Colonel Zhukovsky is to drive the lead ship, Colonel Strogolshikov is to drive the follow-on—*Soyuz 4/5*. And there's more and better, because the word is that Glavtop and Grin are chosen to crew with Colonel Strogolshikov, to transfer between the ships, a dual spacewalk!"

"When!" I demanded again.

Adama-Bibliov declared, "January, as soon as possible. The word is that the orders are coming through here tonight, and we're off to the Cosmodrome when they do. Maybe as soon as tomorrow."

"Is it confirmed?" I asked.

Miserbiev said that Artzybashev had called a gambling associate at the Academy of Sciences to confirm the rumors, and that according to a friend of a friend of President Keldysh, the silver-maned dandy who liked to cozy up to the Corps, it was firm that Uncle Dmitry was to command the lead *Soyuz 4*, and Uncle Konstantine was to command the chase *Soyuz 5* with Glavtop and Grin as crew.

"Also," said Adama-Bibliov, adding a crucial piece of information, "we hear that Colonel Oryolin has been given ground control command, to run the mission his own way from the first. There won't be any more flip-flops, no more backwardness, as Colonel Oryolin says. They're finally sending the right men. We've got two R-7s, two Soyuzes, a twinned launch date, *Soyuz 4/5* within a month!"

We laughed and pounded our boots on the floor, and Lukacs brought out more rolls and butter and rich new coffee. "Ooray for Old Number Seven!" we toasted the boosters. "Ooray for the Soyuz!" we cheered the ships. "Fly-by is for tourists!" we taunted *Apollo 8*'s success. "Ooray for the State Commission!"

My mood soon plunged back down again, and I felt more left out and forgotten than ever. I warned them with more whining, "I can't just stay here. How can I? With all this news, and you'll be at the Cosmodrome, and what about me?"

I let them put me off with more gossip and their chitchat about how unfairly I was being treated after what I'd done to make up for being an idiot with State Security. I even acted thankful when they promised to ask Uncle Dmitry if I could come along to the Cosmodrome. It was all a ruse, since I'd already made my decision to bolt.

I didn't wait to think about it again; I grabbed my kit bag and was on the flight line before midday in order to bribe a ride to Leningrad. The snowstorm kept the heavy transport stuff grounded, so the only thing I could do was harry the flight mechanics until they told me there was a messenger flight departing at 1400. I took it as a good omen that the aircraft was an old An-2 like the one we'd stolen at Dzhezkazgan, and I made the flight easy by daydreaming of Katya's white body. By late afternoon I was on the ground in Leningrad, and by midevening I was stepping off a commuter bus into a whirl of snow on the Nevsky Prospect about a half kilometer from my home. I figured it was best I waited to call on Katya in the morning, and besides I was eager to see Great-Uncle Lev.

The entryway to my apartment building was locked. I had to use the back way I'd used as a boy, over the wall and down between the buildings to the primeval Siberian pine tree in the courtyard, and then up to the second level of big branches to the windows off the communal kitchen. I knocked on the kitchen window, and it was my good luck that Great-Uncle Lev's true love, Golda Rinsakov, a tiny and very tough seventy-six-year-old widow who'd won two medals as a firefighter in the war, was in the kitchen making tea. Eventually she opened the sash and challenged me, "You want what?"

"It's me, Golda Pavelovna, Peter."

Golda was so nearsighted she couldn't make out my face in the snow, and she asked, "Petrushka?" and peered out hard, not wanting to admit she couldn't see me. "You're in the tree? Why are you in the tree? Come in here, instantly!"

Golda had moved in with Lev two years after I'd departed for the academy, the widower and the widow living side by side in a communal apartment of eight (there'd been eleven when I lived there), and she had become like a long-distance stepparent to me as I'd gone through my adolescence, faithfully writing me letters and generally treating me as if I were one of her numerous grandchildren (she'd buried two husbands). I was always comfortable with her as a friend, and we went down the hall arm-in-arm to surprise Great-Uncle Lev in his room. We found he'd fallen asleep while reading in the damask chair. He looked wonderful, exactly the same as he had looked to me lifelong, a small, sturdy, dark-skinned, big-eared, and giant-handed serf with a long nose as bumpy as a pine cone, a beard so thick it was like undergrowth, and a sweet tooth I'd prepared for, bringing along two apple pastries from Lukacs. When she saw the food Golda raced to make me a quick supper, returning with a heaping plate of eggs and cooked mushrooms for me and a tea tray to help Great-Uncle Lev wake up. By then he'd put his teeth in, pulled on his heavy dressing gown, cleaned his eyeglasses, and found his ironic voice.

"Now you come home like a conqueror," he began. "Here, look into the light. Yes, what I thought I'd see, your cheeks are swollen with arrogance and you've grown more teeth, at least four extra teeth."

Golda contributed, "He's lost weight. Petrushka, you're thin. They must feed you worse than that school. How can they? I thought this was a rich bunch you were with?"

We chatted and hugged like this for some time before Great-Uncle Lev, in his cagey way, introduced the critical topic of Katya. "Your friend Ekaterina has called on us several times this past month," he said, nodding to Golda, "and we've enjoyed talking with her about you. And we want you to know, she's lovely, very lovely."

I demanded, "Katya was here? How is she, she's been here in this room, is she better? I've written her and she won't write back. Is she all right?"

"She told us how you've been," Great-Uncle Lev said and then lowering his voice added, "and she told us how very, very foolish you've been, about the gunplay in the south that you mentioned far too briefly in your letter"—I had written Lev an abridged version of Dzhezkazgan in a flimsy try at humility and manliness—"and about many sad things I hoped I'd never hear again."

I didn't know what he meant about "sad things" he didn't want to hear again—remember he'd kept the truth of my birth from me—however I defended myself, "I told you, it was something we had to do."

He underscored, "A long life is what you have to do."

I tried, "We were attacked, I was attacked, Katya was attacked. And I wrote you, I didn't go myself, I was with my uncles, with my colonels, you know, Father's men, Oryolin, Strogolshikov, and Zhukovsky, I wrote you that much."

He underscored, "God gave me two cheeks."

Golda tried to make peace, "We sometimes only have worry on our plates, Petrushka."

Great-Uncle Lev glanced away from me. I can guess that he was pained that he'd not told me of my mother all those years, and that the version of the Lubyanka arrest and the Dzhezkazgan raid he'd heard from Katya had frightened him that my mother was not only returned but also openly menacing. He must have felt miserable for his dilemma—to tell me the truth and perhaps lose me to disgust or to continue the lie and lose me to my mother's malevolence—and so he showed his upset by flapping at me about "gunplay," as if he were a pacifist.

I can see now how he, just like my uncles, twisted himself to avoid my mother, as if there was something about Daemonia Romodanovsky that made it easier to deceive and deny than to confront her. My mother made you want to lie to others about her. She was the liar who conjured lies; she was the betrayer who made you betray yourself.

Great-Uncle Lev offered a strange kind of compromise about my mother by speaking of Katya's motherhood. "Your friend, Ekaterina, asked us many questions about our family," he said, lowering his voice again, "because she is very concerned about our family, about who we are and who you are, because, you see, or do you?"

I knew he was going to surprise me, yet still I wasn't prepared for what he had to say.

He knew it was a surprise too, because he spoke gently, *"For your child,* Petrushka, for yours, the two of you," and then he spoke more ironically, "for this child of a married woman whose husband is a runaway lout and a young officer who falls in love as quickly as his father, and now there's a new child in the family!"

Golda grabbed my hand and kissed my fingers. "God bless, do bless, a son, I'm certain, it's a son. She's full of sons. She's brought her Daniel, and what a treasure he is. And how he needs a brother. How he needs a papa!"

I must have asked him to repeat himself many times, and I must have gone over the facts a hundred times in my brain, but the lovely aspect of having a child is that you don't have to do anything but enjoy the news. Katya was three months pregnant, and I could expect a child by summer. I staggered around the little room I'd grown up in and asked myself how I could be anyone's father. I doubt if I slept three hours that night. I had every mood: awe, bravery, terror, guilt, anger. I interrogated myself in circles: Why hadn't she told me? What was I supposed to do? Would she marry me? Was I right to ask her to? Had the baby been hurt by her concussion? Was she all right? Must she marry me?

I remember Sunday with joy. Golda woke me with a heavy breakfast that she forced me to eat before going to Katya. "Tell her you love her, say it first and last," Golda instructed me. "Ask about the child *after* you tell her you love her." Great-Uncle Lev's advice was simpler: "Be calm." At that hour it was still black outside, the city like a crystal palace, with snow heaped to the second levels on the main thoroughfares. I bypassed the overcrowded trolleys because I could travel much faster on foot. Katya's mother's apartment was on the prestigious Theater Place across from the Kirov Theater, about a kilometer from my home. Along the way I couldn't find any flower vendors who had stock, no matter the price I offered, and I felt empty-handed when I stopped running and stood at Katya's mother's large, polished door on the second landing of a very beautiful apartment house.

I didn't even get to surprise Katya, because she unceremoniously opened the door just as I rang the bell. "Come in, Peter," she said. "They called from Starry Town; I knew you'd be coming this morning."

Katya was wrapped in a housecoat, and she wouldn't look into my eyes as I moved past her into the baronial foyer. I glanced into the vast, chilly, unlit, Romanov-age apartment, and then I turned to stare at her midsection. I was disappointed that I couldn't see any change at her waist, and I didn't know enough about pregnancy to take account of the new fullness to her face and her flushed complexion. The most obvious change was that she'd cut her fine hair very short to complement the fuzzy growth where they'd shaved her head around the wound.

Katya didn't wait to show her bad temper; she sat on a chair beneath an oil portrait of a ballerina and then she accused me of stupidity. "I knew you were coming, and I don't want you here, it's futile," she said. "And you're causing more trouble by coming here. Angelicka called me last night to say that Dmitry Mikhailovich knew immediately what you'd done and was very annoyed and was blaming me for your coming here, which is unfair. I didn't make you run away. You did it on your own."

I asked, "Are they coming for me?" Katya said that Uncle Dmitry was sending "two boys" to fetch me, which I knew meant Miserbiev and Adama-Bibliov. "I'm not going back unless you tell me to go," I said.

Katya returned, "I don't care what you do, I'm not your guardian," and then she brushed past me into the vast front parlor, where in the first dim light from the outside she looked so wan she might have been transparent. Katya stood against a drape as if to hide herself from me and then thought better of her position and came out into the center of the room, speaking with a less angry, more scolding tone. "Angelicka says that Dmitry Mikhailovich feels sorry for you, if you want to know. He's the one who's treating you like a child. If you want to stay in Leningrad, then stay, you don't need my consent."

"I've got a New Year leave and I'm staying to be with you," I declared, and then remembering Golda's counsel, "I'm staying because I love you and want to be with you."

"The two boys they're sending are coming here today," she said.

"I can handle them," I said. "Just tell me you want me to stay and I'll stay, and they can't make me go until I want to." I was half sure I could deliver on my boast, that I could convince my uncles to leave me be as long as I accepted Miserbiev and Adama-Bibliov as chaperons, but I was not at all sure I could overcome Katya's refusal. I tried once more, "I love you, Katya, and I know about the baby, Uncle Lev told me. I love you and want to marry you. We need each other now. The baby needs us."

I didn't understand how profound an argument I was making intuitively, and I was surprised to see Katya's tears. "What's important," she said in a frail voice, "is that you do what you want. Do you hear me? This isn't a game for me like you make of it. This is my life, and Daniel's life, and my baby's life." She held her arms as if to cradle her waist. Then she looked at me with her watery eyes and spoke out her fear. "Peter, what are we going to do? We're not all going to make it, are we, not all of us? And I can't fight them like I wanted to fight them. What I did last month was crazy, I was crazy to go with you, it was like going mad it was so crazy. You killed dozens of men, maybe hundreds, and you and your friends are crazy! I almost died down there. That mine was terrible, God!—and what do I care about your ridiculous Oryolin. My grandfather can go to hell for what I care! I must have been mad! I'm thirty-five years old, I'm broke and I've lost what job I had, and my husband's deserted me, and my Daniel doesn't understand why his mother's so crazy. I have to think about Daniel and the baby. I have to stay here." Katya sagged sideways and asked, "Don't you understand? How can I marry you?"

What I understood was that Katya had reversed herself once more and returned to her original opinion of my uncles as "Stalin's damned little heroes," her grandfather the Grand Constructor as a fanatical stranger, and the Cosmonaut Corps as meaningless puppets. However, rather than point up her contradictions, I responded with all the hope I could marshal, "We're going to be happy together, Katya, and I'm not leaving you."

Katya approached as if she was falling into me, and then she was in my arms, shaking and weeping and grasping my shoulders. I realized that my prideful Katya, who said she needed no one, now was admitting she needed me. I also realized that I liked being needed and that being needed made my decisions clearer and easier. "I'm staying," I said. "And Trifya and Yurka, when they get here, they can stay, too. We'll have a week together, and then you'll see that I'm right that we should get married."

"Marriage is impossible," Katya whispered. I didn't argue further because I didn't want to take advantage of my first victory over her willfulness. I did want to take advantage of her tenderness, and we went back to her bed for an hour of lovemaking and the sort of repetitive promises and hopes that lovers manage as if in a dream. Her body was still bruised from Dzhezkazgan, and I stroked her back where there was a scar from some unknown scrape. We recovered ourselves and dressed in time to greet Daniel when he woke up for breakfast. And, a little later on, I was mostly prepared for my introduction to Katya's imposing mother, Mrs. Univer, an elegant, bright-eyed woman, about sixty, very slender and fair but not as tall as Katya.

Mrs. Univer was no less demanding than her daughter and showed her precise intelligence by asking forceful questions such as, "You know Katya's Boris, don't you, you know he's deserted her?" and "You're the father of the new child, aren't you? And you're merely a candidate-cosmonaut, aren't you? What kind of security is that for a woman with two children?" and of course the distinct, "You say you intend to marry my daughter, well, that's not going to happen today, is it? We can forswear that topic for now, can't we? I don't have to worry about another peacock of an officer this morning, do I?"

I fumbled all my answers, yet this seemed to assure Mrs. Univer that I was sincerely in love with Katya and therefore acceptable as a son-in-law for a daughter who was, after all, still married, recuperating from a head wound, abandoned by her husband, penniless with a son to raise, and now pregnant. I suppose Mrs. Univer concluded that only love could overcome such troubles, and while we dined on cold fish and omelets in the sunroom, overlooking Theater Place and the ice-caked statue of Glinka, I tried to get used to having two sharp-witted women on either side of me like a crossfire.

At some point in our conversations there was an odd turn that clouded the otherwise hopeful morning, and I must mention it because it was a clue to later events. I asked Mrs. Univer, trying to please her, "Your apartment is enormous and grand. Is it all yours, just you, the furniture, too?"

Mrs. Univer smiled. "It's been in our family for a century."

I waited for an explanation, since it couldn't have been her property, it was clearly part of the privilege of being a Univer, at one time one of Leningrad's first families, and the benefit of her being a senior instructor at the Kirov Theater across the plaza, and yet Mrs. Univer continued to talk of the apartment as if she owned it and the furnishings as if she'd inherited them from progenitors. The truth was that Mrs. Univer was living in a fantasy. Later that afternoon Katya told me that her mother often talked as if she were living in the past, when her own family had indeed lived in luxury. "Since my father died, Mother falls back to pretending now and then. Don't say anything about it, please, it's harmless, and she knows she's doing it. We were a very large family here once, when I was growing up, and Mother knows she keeps the apartment because of Grandfather. Once, a long time ago, my mother's family had an apartment like this on the other side of the Prospect. Mother sometimes likes to forget what's happened since, I suppose."

I said, "I suppose I understand—she's pretending it's before the Revolution."

Katya responded, "You know about growing up with pretense, with a mystery." She didn't begin to explain this remark until five days later, though it's clear to me now that she was referring to her curiosity of my origins.

I remained ignorant for the moment and celebrated that week of radiant, cold, wind-biting weather and the constant companionship of my true love. As I'd boasted to her, I was able to control Miserbiev and Adama-Bibliov when they arrived, all the more easily because it turned out that Uncle Dmitry had anticipated my temper and ordered them only to remain with me like watchdogs, not to drag me back to Starry Town. It was after all New Year's week, and it wasn't difficult to find amusement in Leningrad. Each night we bunked at Mrs. Univer's—there were two unused bedrooms in what were once the servants' quarters—while each day we explored the city with Katya and Daniel and often Great-Uncle Lev as our tour guide. Miserbiev proved an excellent companion for Daniel, and Adama-Bibliov was the best antidote to Miserbiev's constant chatter at the museums. I was grateful to them that they didn't fuss about being assigned to me rather than going to the Cosmodrome with the rest of the squadron to help prepare for *Soyuz 4/5*. I was grateful to Katya for being so good a sport about having three falcons trail her like lost boys, and soon she and I found a rhythm that suited us. I would say I loved her at every opportunity. She would boss me, Daniel, Trifya Miserbiev, and Yurka Adama-Bibliov. Now and again, when she said she was feeling "small," she would ask me to hold her in my arms and not talk. My reward for my obedience was that each evening, after we'd gorged ourselves on Mrs. Univer's generous meals of roast pork, cold sturgeon, kasha, cabbage cutlets in sour milk, cheese dumplings, boiled potatoes covered with hot cracknels, and after we'd had enough of the esoteric debates between Miserbiev and Mrs. Univer over drama, dance, cinema, and all the rest the know-it-all Trifya could opine of, after all such family entertainment and comfort, Katya and I would slip off to kiss Daniel good-night and then patter into her snug room that looked out on the snowy central courtyard and talk and make love and dream and begin again while the first quarter moon set each morning in Taurus.

I could have gone on with that week forever, my New Year's days with my newfound love, yet Katya felt compelled to move our passion out of the dreamworld I made of it, or off the star she'd once said we lived on together, and into a place where she could control our future. This sounds unfair, but she was a proud, domineering, contrary, often vexatious woman who borrowed trouble and who believed she could dominate fate with her intellect. She said she wanted to solve what she called the mystery of my life, and solve it regardless of how dangerous the solution might be to us. I suppose she also wanted peace of mind about the father of her child and the man who claimed he was never going to leave her. Whether she did it for herself, for me, or for the baby, or just because she wanted to, Katya kept on pursuing the many clues about my birth until she uncovered the secrets of my mother, and then, with the persistence of a soldier, she kept on until what she'd discovered came down on her as murderously as an avalanche.

The way Katya went after my origins was to trick it out of Great-Uncle Lev, who often accompanied us as we wandered Leningrad that week. The first instance I witnessed her methods was Thursday afternoon, when we were all walking back from ice-skating at the Tauride Gardens. "Why don't you tell me again," Katya began to Great-Uncle Lev, "how you used to bring little Peter here?" Great-Uncle Lev was pleased to reminisce about how he'd raised me, and he began a long tale about making skates for me for Christmas week every year. Katya interrupted him, asking a strange question, "Did you bring him here with his mother, Marya, before she left him?"

Great-Uncle Lev evaded the question, "It was a sad time."

Katya told Daniel to run ahead with Miserbiev and Adama-Bibliov and get in line for chocolate at the confectionery's. She took my arm close and told Great-Uncle Lev, "I want to know about those days. I want you to tell me about Peter's mother, Marya." Katya knew she was probing sensitive matters and yet didn't hesitate. "I want to know why she left him with you."

Great-Uncle Lev tried more evasion, "Marya and Petrushka lived in a small room on the Vyborg Side. It was rough as usual that winter, 1949. And I was still working then, so I couldn't get over to visit them as often as I should have."

Katya cut in, "She just called on you. She just turned up on your doorstep with a three-year-old. She just said, 'Here, I'm going away to bury my husband, and I might not come back, so love him for me, goodbye'?"

Great-Uncle Lev tried one last time to avoid the topic: "It was a bad winter, you don't know. There wasn't fuel. We ate rodents, bugs. There wasn't any heavy clothing for Petrushka. We had to wrap him in old silk pieces for warmth. And Marya was sick with grief over Apollon. She'd just had the news that he was dead. She wasn't herself and had to go immediately—" Great-Uncle Lev looked away, and for the first time I knew he was lying to me about those days—I could feel that he was holding back on something crucial.

Katya sensed the same falsehood and bore down on him. "I don't understand it. How does a woman who's buried two daughters in five years just give over her last child and go away for a funeral? I don't believe it. There must be more to what she was feeling." Katya pulled on my hand to make me pay mind to her argument. "When I was in that mine with Peter last month, I learned something important about life. I learned that death is easy to accept. It's a finish, and you get used to it quickly. But what's hard is that death takes you away from love. Death is simple. It's leaving those you love and who love you that you fight against. It's leaving love that you won't do."

"A good lesson," Great-Uncle Lev said.

"Not just a lesson," Katya said, "it's also why I don't believe that

Marya could leave Peter with you out of grief for Apollon. You're not remembering everything for me."

"Those were sad days," said Great-Uncle Lev, and then he said he was tired and needed to rest his feet, so he hurried ahead to sit with Daniel at the confectionery's.

I asked Katya not to press Great-Uncle Lev anymore about my mother and father. I thought what she was after was more of her speculation about how my father died, and I didn't want to think about that on such a happy day. I told Katya, "He only knows what they told him, that my father went down in a training accident, and that my mother got word of his death and went out to Siberia to bury him. She didn't come back. That's all he knows; it's all anyone knows."

"You've asked your great Oryolin about what happened to your father?"

I snapped, "I don't want to talk about it."

Katya said, "Fine, neither do I. It's not your father I'm asking about, it's Marya and why she did what she did, what her state of mind must have been when she left you."

We walked on silently awhile, and I pretended to be concerned with herring gulls roosting by the quay. Katya couldn't be content, and she told me, before we rejoined the others, "Your kind and wise old Uncle Lev, he's lying to us, Peter, he's lying about Marya somehow."

I pretended I didn't hear this, but I wonder now if I was being so reticent because I sensed that Katya was on to something profound. The story of my orphaning was a tidy story that Great-Uncle Lev had told me so often over the years that I believed it the way a child believes a fairy tale. My father Apollon died in a test plane accident. My mother Marya received a telegram of his death and dropped me at Great-Uncle Lev's room on her way to the train station. We never heard from Marya again. And yet, on that Thursday afternoon, with just a few comments, Katya had turned the story inside out and made me doubt all of the details.

The truth of it, I can surmise now, was that Marya was probably informed by State Security that her husband was under arrest for treason and that she was to report to his trial to give evidence. She must have known when she put me with Great-Uncle Lev and Great-

Aunt Elizaveta that she'd never see me again. I have no distinct memory of Marya, just as I have none of my father, but I admire Marya for taking me in as her own child for three years, especially since her two children, my half sisters, had died horribly in the famines. She must have felt cursed by God for her fate. I also honor her for standing by my father to the end, though she must have realized that he had been denounced by his wartime mistress, my real mother, Daemonia.

Katya wouldn't or couldn't quit her probing of Great-Uncle Lev. On Friday evening, the night before Miserbiev, Adama-Bibliov, and I were due to return to Starry Town, we enjoyed a fancy farewell supper at Mrs. Univer's apartment. Great-Uncle Lev and Golda Rinsakov were also there, bringing Golda's prize dish of calf's tongue in white sauce with raisins and lemon juice. Mrs. Univer toasted the future and said how lucky she was to have a big family again at her table, adding that she had beautiful young dancers for Miserbiev and Adama-Bibliov to meet. Miserbiev blushed and started a speech about marriage's effect upon what he called "space psychology." Daniel saved us from Miserbiev's monologue by asking Adama-Bibliov to tell the story again about how Peter the Great founded rocketry in Russia. We were happy and noisy like a family, feeling safe, consoled, easy-hearted, well fed, timeless. And when we took coffee in the front parlor, I thought Katya and I were going to slip off for a few embraces in the bedroom, but no, Katya moved past me and asked Great-Uncle Lev to help her put Daniel to bed.

The two of them were in the back bedroom for an hour, through the cakes and sweets and stories, and when they returned Great-Uncle Lev looked sad and very old, and Katya looked grave and heated. Katya explained her flushed complexion, "I'm on my feet too much sometimes."

Great-Uncle Lev didn't explain his sudden gray mood, though he did bid me goodbye oddly, "You're good and lucky like your father, Petrushka. Never forget that you're good and lucky."

I believe this talk of goodness was Great-Uncle Lev's roundabout way of telling me that I could survive any blow including the truth about my mother. I also believe that it was that night that Katya broke through Great-Uncle Lev's evasions and both figured out the mystery and forced him to admit to the truth. She was an intuitive thinker who could make a grand whole out of just a few pieces of a puzzle. She had been brooding about Madame Romodanovsky for some time, packing and unpacking what I'd told her of my meetings both at Saint Sophia and that night in the limousine after the Lubyanka. Katya had put all this singular information together with what she was able to trick out of Great-Uncle Lev about my father and his wife, Marya, and then she must have demanded that Great-Uncle Lev stop lying. She had made a leap to a conclusion and then she'd pounded Lev with the facts until he'd confirmed her intuition.

Still the truth of me must have darkened her—hence her grave, burning look—and then, in one of those demonstrations of the unpredictable potency of truth-telling, it emboldened her to go much farther than interrogations. It's my conjecture that Katya first hatched her plan to trap Madame Romodanovsky in the lies as soon as she determined I was her son. I can't prove this, but I can guess that as soon as Katya saw the truth she planned premeditatively to confront my mother with me, herself, and our baby in order to force my mother to relent or recoil or retreat, or whatever Katya thought would be sufficient surrender. It was a most wrongheaded decision, but I can sometimes see as Katya must have that the only way to make us safe from my mother was not to hide from her under a bushel but to go right to her and demand our freedom.

Katya began her plan right that night. She took me to bed straightaway and, after some wordless lovemaking that alerted me she was feeling assertive, even predatory, she pulled me beside her and gave me my orders. I was to obey my uncles and remain at Starry Town until she came to visit me. I was not to make any mischief for her about her divorce, which she said would require negotiation, and which she said she would obtain as soon as Colonel Prishkin repaid her the debts she'd paid off for him over the last four years. I was also not to complain anymore about her former lover Ara Ovchennikov, the Moscow University professor who was imprisoned at Lefortovo Prison awaiting transportation to a prison camp and who needed her friendship and support. I was also not to harry her about marriage, because she would marry whom she wanted to marry when she wanted to marry. Once all this had been presented to me as fixed— and I've left out the arguments we'd had that week that led up to her orders about Prishkin and Ovchennikov—Katya said that she believed I loved her, that she believed she loved me, and that she believed our baby deserved his or her father close at hand. "I'm not going to tell you how right now," she told me, "but I will do what I can to end my old life and get on with a new life. And I need you to have faith in me and do what I say."

I agreed—receiving several firm kisses for my pledge—and then I tried to win more from her. "I'll do it because I love you," I said. "And I'd love you the better if you promise you'll come back to Starry Town."

"I promise," Katya said. "I swear I'll see you soon. First I have to contact Boris about the divorce. But I do have to go down if just to close the apartment and pack mine and Daniel's things. Perhaps I'll see you as early as next weekend."

I pleaded, "Will you promise that marriage isn't impossible?"

"Maybe anything, Peter," she trailed off, "although marriage is a long way from being possible."

Katya's promise was a ruse, part of her plan to confront my mother. What she needed the week for was to get a message to my mother. Katya proceeded most audaciously, as I learned later, by telephoning her husband, Prishkin, at Starry Town's medical center and telling him not only about the divorce and his debts but also that he was to contact his handlers, the Chekhists he'd informed on us to, and tell them he had a letter for General Iagoda. Katya had then written a long letter to my mother, care of Prishkin, in which she had included everything she knew about me and had demanded my mother meet with us the following weekend in Moscow. I never saw the letter, but I can imagine it was direct and received all of Katya's sharp gift for rhetoric. Katya meant to do more than win us freedom from persecution: she wanted to hurt my mother as she'd been hurt by her; she wanted the sort of vindication that might not be credible in this life.

I don't have to imagine the results of Katya's challenge, because within two days Katya received an anonymous call from Moscow telling her to attend the Bolshoi that Friday evening, a performance of the ballet *Spartacus*. Katya accepted the counterchallenge and immediately moved to put into place the other parts of her plan, including the critical detail of contacting Uncle Dmitry at the Cosmodrome, when it was too late for him to stop her but just in time for him to attend the confrontation.

At Starry Town I knew nothing of Katya's extravagant recklessness and glided through my week awaiting news from her. I was hopeful I could overcome her reluctance and win her as soon as I had her in reach, or, if not then, then as soon as the baby was born. I think now that the fact of the baby was growing in me as it grew in Katya, so that every day I felt less the naïve boy and more the man of the world. I also felt anxious my hopes could fall apart, and at mid-week, when I received a note from Mrs. Zhukovsky, I jumped at the possibility in it. "I need a driver Saturday," Mrs. Zhukovsky wrote, asking me to fetch a car from the motor pool in her name at 1830 hours and to pick her up at her building. "Full-dress, don't be late," the note read.

I was sure this somehow meant Katya was coming to Starry Town Friday night and perhaps we were going to fetch her at the train station. My fantasy quickly fashioned Friday night as a rendezvous and elopement, and for the next day I schemed not only where we should go for our wedding night but also the practical matter of how I was going to lie my way out of the barracks for the weekend. My biggest worry was how I was going to escape the watch of my chaperons Miserbiev and Adama-Bibliov, who I knew would be checking on me before curfew, and who I knew would alert my uncles as soon as they'd discovered I'd sneaked off again. In the end I decided not to think about consequences, waiting until the last possible moment, at 1800 hours, and then charging the duty officer with my request to leave barracks for the evening. He refused, since I was still on restrictions from November, and so I played my only card, which was to show him Mrs. Zhukovsky's note with a hundred rubles attached. He took the money and told me that anything for the wife of Colonel Zhukovsky was fine with him, "All power to *Soyuz 4/5.*"

The power that evening was Katya's willpower. I remember it as a gingery, frigid night under a gibbous moon, no snow until much later in the evening, and when I hopped out of the car, feeling I'd eluded all of my keepers, I was holding out a lap blanket and wasn't prepared for the three of them—Katya as well as Mrs. Zhukovsky and her daughter Anna—to come carefully toward me down the frozen pathway. At the sight of Katya on Anna's arm I leaped to attention and controlled my glee.

"We're off to the Bolshoi, Peter," Katya told me. She seemed composed and serene to me, her white skin glowing in the reflected light off the snowbanks, her eyes focused as if her intelligence were devoted to me alone. "You're taking the three of us to the ballet," she added and then, though her lips moved another beat, she let her thoughts wander and said nothing more about why she'd arrived without telling me, or how long she was staying, or who was waiting for us at the Bolshoi.

I didn't fuss because I was caught up in the glamour of the three of them wrapped in good furs and dressed in fine gowns for the bel étage at the Bolshoi Theater, and they smelled deliciously of scented soap as they swept past me like swans. Anna was carrying a bouquet of some sort of white flowers, probably hothouse gardenias, and was most animated about the evening, cooing, "We're to see *Spartacus,* Peter Apollonovich, oh, isn't it wonderful!" and then purring about the performers, "Maximova's dancing Phrygia! And Vassilev's tonight's Spartacus! Maximova and Vassilev both, tonight, oh, isn't it wonderful!" I tried to ask Anna more about the dancers, since I liked her black-eyed enthusiasm, but Katya told me to keep my eyes forward and to drive carefully. Katya was not especially loving toward me, having only kissed my cheek as she got into the backseat of the car with the other two, and I accepted her coolness as perhaps discretion in front of Anna. My fantasies were racing ahead with the car, already changing from my notion of elopement to the prospect of going to the theater with three beauties and then returning to Katya's bed. I noted Katya's contradictory, volatile mood—she kept telling me to drive fast, then slow, then fast again—and yet I told myself this was all meant as a surprise, and hadn't she come to Starry Town as she'd said, and what was I worrying about?

The exceptionally tolerant Mrs. Zhukovsky, who was going along with her best friend's plan despite what must have been deep doubts about Katya's thinking, did try to fill up the silence in the car by offering tidbits from the Cosmodrome. She said Uncle Dmitry had called to tell her the Soyuz missions were behind schedule and yet, "It's what Mitya always says. We're behind schedule, we're falling behind, we're late, slow, tardy. 'I'm late, I'm late!' "

Katya hinted at her plan by saying, "He'd better be almost on time this time."

I didn't understand that Katya meant she had waited until noontime that day and then had telephoned for Uncle Dmitry at the Cosmodrome and challenged him to attend the Bolshoi that night with us, adding that we were keeping a rendezvous with my mother,

Madame Romodanovsky. This last-moment call had given Uncle Dmitry enough time to reach Moscow for the ballet but not enough time to reach Starry Town before we departed. In my ignorance I supposed that Katya was referring to the Soyuzes and asked, "Is the mission really on schedule, Mrs. Zhukovsky?"

Mrs. Zhukovsky laughed and replied, "Mitya wouldn't feel useful if it was entirely on schedule, would he?"

I liked how she said this—I liked everything about the extremely elegant Angelicka Zhukovsky—and I wanted Katya to love and admire me the way Angelicka did Uncle Dmitry. Then again there was a part of me that felt less than useful attending the theater with three beauties rather than weathering the preparations with the squadron at the Cosmodrome. I didn't mention my self-pity until after we'd parked the car among the buses and joined the theatergoers trekking cheerily up the rise to the shining theater. "I've missed you," I said to Katya as I helped her traverse an ice patch. "I don't have much to do but miss you. No one else wants me for anything but you."

Katya diverted me, "You're good for me, aren't you, darling?" The truth was that what I was good for that night was a phalanx to be used against my mother.

The Bolshoi's lobby was a waterfall of theatergoers from the sixth level cascading down the scarlet carpet to the blue-suited concessionaires, and all of the scene was lit up like a launchpad and buzzing with talk about the famous ballerina Maximova and dancer Vassilev. It was my first time inside the building and I was dazzled, bending my head back to peer all the way to the plaster figures on the ceiling. Anna Zhukovsky had attended the Bolshoi before, but never dressed as a grownup, and it was especially fun to enter the lobby with her on parade in her pale blue dress gown and fine blue shoes. I did try to flatter her though my remark came out most confused, for, when Anna asked me what I thought of the Bolshoi, I said the building wasn't Air Force—with its marble archways, grotesque chandeliers, giant friezes—but that she was most definitely Air Force. "I'm Air Force?" she asked, glancing down at her clothes for what might be wrong, and asking again, "I'm Air Force?"

My compliment had failed, so I retreated to Katya's side of the trio, and I laugh at myself for how awkward I was talking with gorgeous dark-eyed Anna the twelve-year-old that night, an episode that she and I would tease each other about the rest of our lives together, for a critical detail I haven't mentioned before is that Anna and I married many years later, in 1987. I mention this now just to jolt myself that the two women I loved deeply in my life were the same sort of contraries whom I couldn't ever solve. "You treated me like a child!" was always Anna's complaint, and "You were a child!" was always my complaint, a sweet standoff that still lightens my heart.

We had seats on the bel étage in box No. 26, usually reserved for Starry Town (Anna was my source for this and many of the details of the events leading up to this episode), and I noted the four empty chairs and wanted to ask who might be joining us. I said little, entertaining myself by studying the dark-red-upholstered canyon of the audience and counting general officers' stars, but then Katya kept glancing back at the door so often that I leaned to ask what was going on.

"Never you mind," Katya scolded, and I suppose from that moment I was aware that something was out of the ordinary here—that Katya was hatching something. I know I didn't guess the truth that Uncle Dmitry was expected, and I think the most I suspected was that Miserbiev and Adama-Bibliov had been invited too, so I relaxed to enjoy what I could of the evening. Soon after the music started, the curtain came up, the dancers paraded and twirled, and though I don't recall a sound of the music, and still have no notion as to what *Spartacus* was about, other than about some gladiators in Rome, I can't say it was humdrum, and I do recall enjoying some of the springing and leaping.

The first intermission provided me another good clue as to what Katya was about, when Katya and Angelicka sent me out to walk the staircases with Anna and Anna told me more than she was supposed to know. "I'm so happy!" Anna announced to me. "When Mama told me that Papa would be late, I thought we'd have to wait for him and miss the curtain. But now, oh, isn't it wonderful? Isn't Vassilev wonderful?"

I asked, "You say your father is coming from the Cosmodrome tonight? Why?"

Anna turned us up the main stairs and answered, "Aunt Katya asked him, and he promised he would. It was Aunt Katya who said I could come along too. This is her theater party."

I guessed a little more of the truth. "Has Katya been with you more than just today?"

"Since Wednesday," Anna said. "She came down to pack up her apartment. She's moving to Leningrad, you know, and I've been helping her pack. Tonight's my reward."

I was heartsick at all this, not because Katya was said to be moving to Leningrad (we'd discussed her closing down her apartment), but because she was clearly intriguing in some way and especially because she had been at Starry Town ninety-six hours without contacting me. I hurried Anna back to the box and found Katya and Angelicka bent in close conference. I know it sounds immature of me now, but I felt like their child and I was indignant. I might have muttered unintelligibly before I asked the important question, "Why is Colonel Zhukovsky coming tonight? What are we doing here?"

Katya shook me off. "Sit down, Peter," she ordered, "and don't ask more." I knew from looking at her that there was something very troubling ahead, for her pale cheeks were flushed a sad pink and her back was so straight she looked pinned to her chair. "You promised me you would do what I say, didn't you?" she added.

I tried, "Katya, please," and then lost my point and sagged back down beside her as if I were Anna's age. I ask myself now what was I to have done? I knew this was all wrong, but I wasn't strong enough to overcome Katya's willpower. Later, I was hardly alert in my funk, watching the dancers writhe on the stage and feeling no less tormented myself, when the door of the box opened and a black-leather-jacketed Chekhist bodyguard popped in to hover over Katya's shoulder and press a note into her hand. The note was my mother beckoning Katya, of course, but I didn't know that and started to react when Katya told the bodyguard, "Yes, we'll be along soon."

I couldn't stop my protective reaction and followed the bodyguard outside, demanding, "What do you want? Are you one of Iagoda's?"

The bodyguard walked on. I was ready to take him down, but then two pairs of hands grabbed me back against the wall, and before I could push them off I heard Miserbiev's voice, "None of that, you're with us until Colonel Zhukovsky gets here." It was both Miserbiev and Adama-Bibliov, whom I'd thought I'd slipped away from and who were not now fooling around, since they were armed with revolvers in their greatcoats. They were under orders from Uncle Dmitry, who'd called through to them from the Cosmodrome as he'd lifted off homeward bound that afternoon, and they were to stand guard outside the Starry Town box throughout the performance.

The intricacy of Katya's plan was upon me—the letter to my mother, the theater party, Uncle Dmitry and my chaperons, and now this note delivered by one of Iagoda's goons—Katya had arranged all of this as scrupulously as a shock commander prepares a front. She wasn't going to stop now. Everything had come together except for the vital matter of Uncle Dmitry, who was late arriving (it was never clear if Katya expected all three of my uncles or just Uncle Dmitry to help her with my mother), yet Katya knew not to wait.

How stupid I was, how bullheaded Katya was, how our lives might have been if she hadn't attacked into my mother's power. I can't recall if I went back into the box, or if Katya came out, but I remember that before I had a chance to quiz Miserbiev and Adama-Bibliov, Katya was swirling past me down the curved corridor. "You must do what I say," she told me. "You promised. Now do what I say and come with me."

Hanging back I asked, "Where are we going?"

Katya was off, not waiting for me, and it was Mrs. Zhukovsky who settled the debate by coming out and telling us, "Stay with her, Lieutenants. She's not to be left alone." Mrs. Zhukovsky knew the risks and let her fear show. "You go, and I'll try to find what's happened to Mitya."

"Right you are," Miserbiev agreed, who at least had more of the plan than I did, since he knew Uncle Dmitry was expected and was late. We three, me, Miserbiev, and Adama-Bibliov, raced on after Katya, who'd gotten ahead of us to the staircase. We had to go down a level before we continued on to the other side of the corridor to the entrance of the most famous box at the Bolshoi, the old Romanov apartment box and also Stalin's favorite, No. 2. The bodyguard who'd delivered the note was standing by idly, and Katya waved to him to open up. He obeyed and the thick paneled door swung back to reveal the depth of a small, luxurious apartment that was attached to the box like an annex.

"Now, Peter," Katya said to me in that bossy tone she used when she would not compromise, "this is something we have to do, and you must believe me that I know what's right for us. We have to go in there. We have to. You must help me do this." She reached out for

my left hand. "You two wait for Colonel Zhukovsky," Katya told
Miserbiev and Adama-Bibliov, who, though nervous about this,
obeyed.

"What?" I must have demanded, though I can't recall challenging Katya, and though I gave her my hand and let her pull me
forward. I can ask now, did I know what was happening, and did
Katya know what she was doing? The answer to both is no. No.
Katya's plan was a catastrophe from the start. You don't correspond
with murder; you don't bargain with murder; you don't challenge
murder; you don't walk into the grasp of a whore of Babylon and
walk out again whole.

The apartment was laden with Romanov and French furnishings,
and the inner parlor was lit by golden sconces. We could hear the
orchestra music, for the stage was no more than twenty meters from
behind the heavy gold drapes and drawn doors at the front wall. My
mother, whom I thought of as Madame Romodanovsky, was seated
in an armchair by the old gas-lit fireplace. She was alone, smoking
casually with her scepterlike holder, and, as we came in, I saw she had
been reading a foreign magazine while she waited for us. She was
dressed in a black gown with a fur collar, but she didn't look so
intimidating to me as she had in the limousine or at Saint Sophia,
and perhaps my mother's power was diminished by Katya's energy. I
think my mother looked older to me, not so captivating, her dyed
hair a little lifeless, her complexion painted on, her red lips too thin,
and those almond-shaped and burning black eyes of hers, while still
threatening, seemed drained of their full power. I wonder now if the
slight dimming I sensed in my mother's aura might be the only proof
I shall ever have that my mother in some way understood the truth
of her crimes once she was confronted with one of the most helpless
of her victims.

Katya took charge with her devout intelligence, as if this was a
moral debate and she could chastise my mother to defeat. "You
know who I am, and you know why I'm here," Katya started. "And
I know everything about you. Everything from the war until now.
And I've come here to tell you that you're done with, you and your
kind are done with. *You are done.* I know it, and you know it, and
soon everyone will know you're done. The end won't come tomorrow, and maybe not ten or twenty years from tomorrow, but it will
come in my son's lifetime, in my new baby's lifetime, and you know

it as well as I do. You are done, my little mother." Katya was using a peasant phrase as an insult, and she repeated it with a harsh whisper, "My little mother." Then she continued, "I'm speaking so there won't be any misunderstanding, since I know you have a way of breaking the backs of words like zeks. You're a Chekhist bitch, neither less nor more, and what you are would make me hate you if I could afford to think like that. But I can't, because I've got children to care for. I don't think much about you at all, and what little I do think, my little mother, is that I'm looking forward to a world where you're a forgotten nightmare."

While Katya talked, my mother lifted her face first to me, then to Katya, then back to me, and what I saw was that queer transformation I told you I saw at Saint Sophia, when her face aged suddenly and changed from a hot radiance to a dry blankness and beyond that to a cold blackness, like a gem losing its beauty as a shadow drops across it and then darkness falls. As Katya finished, my mother turned her burning, black-eyed gaze once more at me, and Katya, seeing this, began again: "He doesn't know yet," she said, "and now I'm going to tell him and help him understand." Katya took my hand again and pulled me close to her side. "You're mine, Peter," she told me. Then, addressing my mother as she touched her waist, Katya continued, "He's mine, and his child's mine."

My mother reacted with an exhale of disgust and then, as she drew breath in, her slender frame seemed to fill up with strength, as if she were coming alive or, if she'd been a beast, as if she were rising on her haunches and expanding her chest and warning us off.

Katya understood my mother's defensive posture and snapped, "You're afraid, aren't you? You are done, and you know it, and the proof is us, isn't it? We're supposed to be your children, but we don't want you. We think you're old and tired and lost, and that makes you afraid of us, doesn't it?"

My mother didn't respond so Katya pressed her advantage. "You don't want me to tell him, do you? He frightens you, your child frightens you, my child frightens you—children frighten you! You're afraid of your own children!" Katya pulled me closer still and spoke passionately to me. "She won't tell you, no one has, so I'm going to do it, and I want you to know it's because I love you that I have to tell you the truth. She's your mother, Peter. She was your father's mistress during the war. She's your mother, your mother. Look at her face, Peter, it's your face. She's your mother."

Katya spoke the truth, and yet I didn't or couldn't understand what she said, not the first or second time she said it, though I did hear her words and did look at Mother's face. Katya kept repeating the declaration, "This is your mother, Peter, your mother, she's your mother," and in between she added hard facts such as that Great-Uncle Lev had lied to me, that my uncles had lied to me, that everyone had lied to me, and that she'd brought me here to stop the lying. "She's your mother," Katya said again and again like a chant, "your mother," and then: "She had your father killed. She had Oryolin, Strogolshikov, and Zhukovsky imprisoned. She had us attacked. She was responsible for what happened to my grandfather. She's behind it all, Peter, your mother. She's another Chekhist monster, your little mother."

I still couldn't react, and at some point Katya turned to my mother and said, "Why not tell him now? He's your son, look at him. Doesn't he mean anything to you? What are you waiting for? He won't go away. He's here. Tell him the truth."

And then to me Katya said, "Ask her the truth, Peter. She's your mother. Ask her. Your father abandoned her, and she abandoned you, your mother, your real mother."

I couldn't obey, and I couldn't break away, and I stood locked down and speechless. My memory is that there was very little time between when Katya told me and when the others came in, though it might have been many minutes, even a long time, because I remember hearing the orchestra finish and a booming ovation and then pounding sounds outside that were probably the audience leaving the building.

What I didn't hear was the apartment door opening behind us and both General Iagoda and Uncle Dmitry walking up across from me. "Good evening, Lieutenant Nevsky," Iagoda said to me with strained formality. He was polite enough, if his eyes looked unusually weary behind his eyeglass lenses, and he hadn't removed his overcoat, since my guess is that he'd just rushed in from his car to safeguard my mother, though I can't explain why he should have been as late as my uncles, nor why my mother should have wanted to see us without Iagoda's vulturelike watchfulness. "Good evening, Mrs.

Prishkin," Iagoda spoke to Katya. "I hope I haven't come in too soon and your conference has been helpful."

Uncle Dmitry interjected, "We'll do without the pleasantries, General."

Iagoda bowed and stood behind my mother's chair like her courtier. "Yes, Colonel, I agree," he said, and then fell silent at the bad blood in the room.

Uncle Dmitry, who was in his parade-dress uniform but was unkempt after a half day of flying, addressed Katya. "I'm sorry I'm late, but then, you wanted it this way, didn't you? And now you've had it this way."

Katya said, "I've told Peter the truth."

"I expected you would," Uncle Dmitry replied, though he sounded most fretful when he continued, "and I'm glad you have. It was time it came out, and now that it has we can get on. There's little for us here, Katya, believe me, and we can talk more fully back at Starry Town."

"You're too late for everything," Katya said. "I've already told her what I think of her, and she just sits there like the dried-up little mother she is."

Uncle Dmitry sighed, since he knew that Katya was daring the devil in my mother and that if there was a chance left he had to get us away before my mother counterattacked. "We must go, Katya. The ballet's done, and Angelicka and Anna should be seen home."

Still my mother had not spoken, still my mother continued to smoke and gaze at me, at Katya, at Uncle Dmitry, then again at me, as if she were measuring her thoughts, as if she were waiting for her moment to strike. And yet still Katya kept talking as if she could overthrow my mother with fine words, and yet still Katya hadn't understood, as Uncle Dmitry did, that we were no longer in a world that heeded pious talk but rather in my mother's world of seduction and treachery. Katya had thought she could orchestrate a vindication by telling me the truth in front of my mother, as if all that State Security had corrupted in fifty years of terror could be saved by some sort of virtuous magic of the word, but Katya was wrong, wrong, wrong, as many a prideful intellectual had been wrong before her when faced with adamant evil; and, as Katya kept talking, haranguing, bullying, and bluffing, it became more and more apparent that Katya was losing what she thought she was saving, and that my mother's silence was in fact what evil always does when challenged: it goes to ground and lets you spend yourself looking for meaning in the battle when there is none, just malignant creatures like Iagoda, just rotten souls like my mother's, and if you want to stop folk like them, don't talk about it and don't argue with them, rather take your own soul in hand and strike them down hard.

"I'll go when you've told him the truth," Katya accused Uncle Dmitry. "You're his great dear godfather, his 'uncle,' his great hero of the Martian Troika, and what have you done for him but forget about him? And when he came walking back to you, because he wanted to be just like you, what did you do but lie to him!"

Uncle Dmitry pleaded, "Please, we'll talk about this later."

Katya went at my mother. "Why don't you tell him what you felt when he walked into your arms in Novgorod. And you blamed Oryolin! It's God who sent him! You got another chance, and what did you do but try to kill me and his baby!" Katya pounded her point, talking very smart and loose with her genius in a rage. "And why? Why? I'll tell you. Your kind is as sick as ever! You tried to kill me and my baby because I'm a Jew, because my grandfather is a Jew! He's the most famous engineer in the state, but he's my grandfather, and that makes me as much a Jew as he is, and you wanted us dead just because we're Jews. It doesn't make any more sense than that. I've asked myself over and over why you're doing this to us, and what I think is that it's because we're Jews! You had my grandfather abducted and tortured and nearly killed not because of what he's done but because we're Jews. Because your son, whom you threw away like a rag, is in love with a Jew! It's your incredible sickness, isn't it, all of you Chekhist monsters?" Katya pointed at my mother like a prosecutor at the bar of history. "Your grandchild will be a Jew like me, and you're so sick at this fact, so sick at everything good in the world like your son, all you can do is give the same old sick Stalinist order, 'Kill the Jews!' "

At last Katya had penetrated my mother's fortress temperament— for my mother wasn't that much different than an old-fashioned anti-Semite who used race bigotry as readily as she did other prejudices to confuse and corrupt her victims. What my mother and Iagoda had done with the Grand Constructor had been not much different from the old tsarist trick of using a Jew for a scapegoat because no one was likely to object when another Jew vanished. My mother emerged from her silence with a heavy gesture toward Iagoda, telling him, "Shut her up, will you. I've heard enough. And get her out of here."

"You try!" Katya yelled back.

Uncle Dmitry didn't just try, he embraced Katya and whispered to her, "Please, please," and then they were both moving away from me like a doctor and invalid.

My memory could be deceiving me here. It might be that before Uncle Dmitry took hold of Katya, Uncle Alexander and Uncle Konstantine had entered along with Mrs. Zhukovsky, Miserbiev and Adama-Bibliov, and two of Iagoda's bodyguards. This sequence would explain why I seem to recall Katya being led out by both Uncle Dmitry and Angelicka Zhukovsky, and why I think there was a screaming argument before Katya withdrew or was taken out. I would like to be more exact, yet at the time I was still so weak-willed in the face of Katya and my mother that I can now only approximate many of the events. I think I recall Katya cursing everyone, my mother, my uncles, State Security, and the Corps, and me too, and I think I remember Katya, overheated in her fury, twisted into a hurt posture, flailing at us as if we were her enemy, telling my uncles, "You're no better than they are! You're the same monsters!" and telling me, "You can't get away from them! They won't let you go!"

All this is unclear, and it might be that I only think it happened this way because otherwise I would never have an explanation for why Katya abandoned me that night, left me behind just as my mother had, quit me with more of her absolute curses that my uncles were "Stalin's damned little heroes," and that I was another one of Stalin's "damned little bastards!"

At least I'm sure that after Katya had gone with Uncle Dmitry and Mrs. Zhukovsky, I remember Uncle Konstantine scooping up a flimsy white chair and sitting himself across from my mother and speaking tauntingly to her, "You're older, Monya. We're all older."

I'm also sure I remember how Uncle Alexander walked into the apartment like an executioner in parade dress, his face that same horrible blackness that I'd seen at Dzhezkazgan, and how he took a position just behind me in a paternal posture, but then again also like my ally, as if he were backing me up rather than commanding me.

There might have been aimless, menacing words between Iagoda and my uncles, for Iagoda was most uncomfortable face to face with men he knew were likely armed (Miserbiev and Adama-Bibliov certainly were armed and stood with an easy field of fire on the two bodyguards), but the first lengthy remark I can recall was that of Uncle Konstantine, who made it clear to me that he thought lying to me had been wrong. "You know who Monya is now, don't you, darling? We should have told you, and we didn't." He addressed Uncle Alexander. "Sasha, we should have told him. You should have, and I'm saying you were stupid not to." He glanced to me. "We were stupid, Petrushka, and for me and Laikuskha, we apologize."

I nodded at Uncle Konstantine, and Uncle Alexander told me, "It's enough you know now."

My mother's black eyes were on her husband, and as soon as he'd spoken she loosed her tongue. "What does he know?" my mother said. I saw her hands shake, but her voice was supreme. "How you sent him against me like a prank at Novgorod? How you're doing all this to me as you've always done it to me because you hate me for standing up to your sort and for leaving you? I'll tell him, Sasha, if you want me to, I'll tell him what you want me to tell him. Lieutenant Nevsky," she addressed me coolly, looking into my eyes with what I had to accept were my same eyes, "that woman who was here, she told you you're my son. You are. Now I've told you. And Sasha, he sent you to me last summer, didn't he? And you lied to me about it, didn't you? What else? How else have you lied to me? You know I gave evidence against your father, don't you? And you've been told I gave evidence against these two also, against the three of them. If you want to believe any of this, then believe it. They must have also told you that your sister died because of me. You can believe that, too. It isn't true, she died of polio, but they like to blame me for their own failures, so blame me, you can blame me, too."

I heard all this, the logical parts as well as the large irrational patches, but all that I understood was that my mother was beyond me, incomprehensible to me—as if she were speaking in French not Russian, as if she were an alien remarking on this poor little human race.

Uncle Alexander understood her for his own purposes and knew not to waste words on her. "Enough and enough," he said, "you leave them alone"—he meant me and Katya—"and we'll leave you alone, and that finishes it."

My mother argued back with a raspy, nagging voice I'd not heard before, the voice not of an empress but rather a middle-aged woman, even a crabby babushka. "You did this to me," she told Uncle Alexander. "You sent him at me like a prank, and you sent her at me, and you know you did. To me, why are you doing this to me? You're doing this."

It was stunning to hear this mature woman—my mother—proclaiming such obvious nonsense. She was arguing that Uncle Alexander had sent me to intercept her at Saint Sophia, that Uncle Alexander had sent Katya here tonight, that Uncle Alexander was trying to get at her somehow. I couldn't explain then, and can't now, how a woman who'd so frightened me moments before had changed into such a shrewish fool, other than to say that folk aren't all the same way, that even monoliths like my mother have seams of triteness and absurdity in them that come out at odd times to reveal the brat or coward or abandoned child in their hearts.

Uncle Konstantine wasn't bothered by the contrast and used his farce cleverly. "Now, darlings, now that we've rid ourselves of twenty years of sweet talk, let's get on with it." He also used his cigarette smoke to make those O's of his like a clown. "I'm speaking for Sasha, and you there, Comrade Four-Eyes," he addressed Iagoda, "you can speak for Monya." Uncle Konstantine leaned forward to draw up his boot and to make everyone pay close attention to his voice. "It's a simple trade-off," he said with a grunt. "You don't come at us anymore, and we don't come at you anymore." Uncle Konstantine had the voice of a jester, jovial, relaxed, self-mocking, and he'd removed his cap so that his bald pate reflected all the reds in the room as if he were lit up pink, but what he had to say was militant. "We want to decide this tonight, Comrade Four-Eyes, because we've got work to do back at the Cosmodrome and up there, too." He rolled his eyes up to the ceiling, meaning the orbital rendezvous mission. "You can see that we're good for what we say. That scrap down south showed you that, didn't it, Comrade Four-Eyes, and also settled our past differences, didn't it? So now let's let this little parley settle our present differences. All clear? You have your way. We have our way. No more grumbling."

Iagoda straightened like a general officer reaffirming his potency and responded, "A fair offer, Colonel," and then, placing his hand on my mother's shoulder, he added, "and we agree."

"We have a cease-fire," Uncle Konstantine judged. "Good for you, Sasha?" Uncle Alexander didn't react, so Uncle Konstantine prodded him, "Anything you want to say?"

"Yes." Uncle Alexander squared his big shoulders and put his prowlike jaw out even farther. "You leave them alone," he told my mother, again meaning me and Katya. "This is between us, Daemonia, between you and me. It started with us and it's to end with us." He addressed Iagoda, "You shoot again, General, you shoot through me. You don't shoot at my people. You shoot through me."

"No more shooting anywhere," Uncle Konstantine contended. "Tell him, Comrade Four-Eyes. It's cease-fire for us, isn't it?"

"Yes, yes," Iagoda lied to us.

I knew he was lying, and my uncles knew he was lying, but it was one of the strange rules of Russia in those days that tyrants like Iagoda and Uncle Alexander didn't go at each other without a provocation. There was also the strong likelihood that Iagoda was intimidated by Dzhezkazgan and by the fame attaching to my uncles looking toward *Soyuz 4/5*. Iagoda was making a deal with men who were too well regarded for him to attack, and my uncles were making a deal with a man who was too well placed for them to attack, and this was a cease-fire and standoff, not a peace.

My mother didn't care for such cock-of-the-walk grappling, and, as soon as Iagoda and Uncle Alexander had agreed, she lifted like a black bird of prey and exited the apartment in a rush of bodyguards, leaving Iagoda to finish for her. By leaving so suddenly and silently, my mother had maintained her pretense as the victim here. Yes, incredibly, I'm convinced that my mother believed that she was the victim in the feud between her and Uncle Alexander, and that her queer statement to Uncle Alexander, "Why are you doing this to me?" was a glimpse into her dark mind. My mother thought she was under attack, thought that Uncle Alexander and I and perhaps the Corps and all Russia were persecuting her. All these decades later I can only account for her inside-out-upside-down thinking by suggesting that evil is self-ignorant, the very opposite of wisdom, a know-nothing-of-yourself worldview. What had started as a feud between the betrayer Daemonia and the betrayed Alexander had become in my mother's mind a plot against her, and her proof of the plot was me at Saint Sophia, was Katya at the Bolshoi, was the frightful fact that I was my father's son come to worship her enemies and to haunt her.

Fate had delivered us all together, and after the Bolshoi our last parley was done, like a clan that had met one last time to make certain we hated each other and that the end was inevitable. Like feuding field marshals, Uncle Alexander and Iagoda had met under a truce flag, had shown each other they were equally bloody-minded, had bowed out ceremonially, Uncle Alexander warning my mother to go no further, Iagoda lying to us that he would cease his rot. The ceremony continued to the last, for on the way out of the apartment Uncle Alexander and Iagoda brushed very close, and Iagoda said, "Excuse me, Colonel, I'll bid you good-night here," and Uncle Alexander, not bothering with civility, mumbled a redundant warning, "You come at my people again, I'm coming for you, General, for you."

It felt liberating to get out of the Bolshoi, and it felt wonderful to walk abreast with my uncles and Miserbiev and Adama-Bibliov. There was a staff car waiting for us, since Uncle Dmitry had taken Angelicka, Anna, and Katya on home already, and we three (Miserbiev and Adama-Bibliov had their own car) sat mostly in silence as we headed back to Starry Town, though I recall that Uncle Konstantine chatted about the upcoming Soyuz missions: They were flying back to the Cosmodrome immediately; all was well; Little Laika was in love with a Kazakh stray; Doctor Tatyana Mometov was a superb cook and by the way, said Uncle Konstantine, he and she were getting married soon, just before the launch. Through this chatter Uncle Alexander stayed stern, smoking his pipe, watching the road, not speaking to me.

Not until we neared Starry Town did Uncle Konstantine address the events of the evening. "No time to worry ourselves," he said. "Too much work ahead. On the run. All's well. No more of that business with Comrade Four-Eyes, Petya. That Blue Tab boy will stay at his desk. But there's this thought," he warned with another broken proverb, "Make friends with the wolf but sleep with your ax at hand."

I thought this good advice and felt better about Katya's future. I was most confused about much of what I'd learned, but I could hold on to the idea that something had been accomplished if Katya was now to be left out of the feud and could stay safe at her mother's in Leningrad. From what I figured at the time, Katya had only ever been a ploy for Iagoda, a turn of the screw, and once Uncle Alexander had challenged Iagoda face to face, it was unlikely that Katya would be bothered again. The feud, I told myself, was between Iagoda and my uncles.

No, I do remember now that Uncle Alexander did speak to me in the car, and he spoke generally of the feud and even made something of a confession about him and my mother. It's surprising that I forgot until now, but then how else would I know what I do about them unless he'd told me? Right near the end of the car trip he started speaking abruptly to me, as if he'd been rehearsing his thoughts and they poured out in a single stream. "Lieutenant, I was your father's wingman, and he was the best commander I've known. He and Daemonia were together until you were born. He left her behind with us, and we took care of her the best we could. I didn't take up with your mother until later. We had a little girl. Your father wanted a son, and you're his son, and that's enough for any man. You're with us now."

I don't remember that I remarked about what he said, and it wasn't possible to question him, but I can say now that I later learned from Anna, who overheard Angelicka and Uncle Dmitry talking, that Uncle Alexander had left out some suggestive details about him and my mother. It might have been that he and my mother had become lovers before I was born, and that perhaps one of the reasons my father abandoned my mother was jealousy of his herculean young wingman and protégé Alexander Oryolin. None of the three of them did very well with the triangle, and, if what Anna overheard was true, then it makes some sense that my mother should accuse Uncle Alexander of persecuting her, and that Uncle Alexander might revile my mother while at the same time feeling some responsibility for her fall, and that my father, whom no one ever represented to me as less than a holy champion, might have been a very ordinary failure at love, and that Uncle Alexander, who was very unlucky at love, might have had great difficulty in dealing with me, since he might have come very close to being my father instead of cuckolding my father.

At twenty-two I was respectful of Uncle Alexander's confession and said nothing but, "Yes, sir, I understand, sir."

I got out of the staff car at the crossroads near the candidate barracks, when my uncles told me they'd see me soon—"All's well, darling," Uncle Konstantine said with a double thumbs-up for the imminent Soyuz mission—and then they turned toward the field to be airborne for the Cosmodrome within the hour. They had devoted a half day of their preflight time to come to Moscow to protect and help me. I should have felt better for their attention, but didn't. What I felt was another flicker of my shame of having done something wrong. What I wanted was to go with my uncles, to run away from what I'd learned that night, and I recall sitting on my bunk later brooding about my predicament. I had no more genuine feeling for Madame Romodanovsky then than I do now, and, after some naïve self-pity, I was able to push aside any deeper thoughts about my mother and think about Katya. I could see that, for some time to come, she and I would have to remain apart. I also had reason to hope that, once I'd become a cosmonaut, once my uncles had triumphed, once all the trouble of the past months had been forgotten in the celebration of all Russia for the moon landing, then I could win Katya as sure as the moon. I overlooked Katya's parting curses, "You'll never get away from them. They won't let you go!" and held on to her soft promises and my own dreams.

Soyuz 4/5

I didn't have long to dream, for my uncles were not going to leave me alone at Starry Town to get into more trouble or to give in to my heart again and dash for Leningrad. The next morning, Saturday, January 11, Lieutenant-Colonel Khitrovo called the candidates to assembly and announced that the launch dates for *Soyuz 4/5* had been moved up a week to the next Tuesday and Wednesday, January 14–15, and that it had been approved that we were to participate in the mission.

We candidates were delighted by the news, especially because Khi-trovo then told us that our task was to deploy with the cosmonauts to the string of ground tracking stations across Europe and Asia where we would supervise the communication network with the two spacecraft. Khitrovo had us break into two-man teams and draw from a cap for our travel orders, and soon my mate, Doctor Gogol, and I chose the plum post, the Caribe station off Cuba. I had a moment to consider eating papayas and sending a letter postmarked Havana to Katya, but then Khitrovo stepped in to say I hadn't earned such luck and to hand Doctor Gogol and me a grim assign-ment, the Magadan Air Defense station on the north Pacific coast, code-named (by the color-coded regions) Gold No. 3. Khitrovo gave the same assignment to my friends Volgamints and Lympyet and said, "You lot deserve worse but there isn't any."

We laughed this off in our glee for the adventure of it, and there were jokes about going to count the trees, and that it was shorter to Magadan going west than east, but we four took the teasing easily as we packed our heaviest clothes, found a ride on a transport bound for Omsk, and were airborne by noontime on a sixteen-hour-long series of short hops into a Pacific dawn. En route I did brood about my mother in a sort of aftershock of the Bolshoi meeting. I think I was more curious about her than upset by her, and I touched my nose and mouth to try to verify what Katya had said about Madame Romodanovsky and me having the same face. I did wonder what she'd been doing the past twenty years, and I did speculate what was going to happen now: Was I supposed to see her again? Did I have any obligation to her? You can see from my fleeting notions that I wasn't a deep thinker about all this, and that I was willing to go along with whatever Katya said about my mother and to obey my uncles as to how I should conduct myself. Vaguely I understood that my mother was most dangerous and that the feud was not a game, it was deadly and final. Yet these observations didn't burden me, and I think now I know why. I was ashamed for what I'd learned, that such a woman should be my mother, that I should be a bastard of the Lubyanka, and perhaps the only way I could accept such at the time was to skirt it as a baffling tale I'd heard and not as my own story. I fixed a few of the details in my mind like constellations in my brain's firmament, and I was satisfied to navigate by my certainty that Katya loved me, that my uncles cared about me, that I could make right whatever I'd done wrong so far, and that whatever happened I must keep going until I got my heart's desires, or most of them. One significant thing more: en route I prayed for the first time since I'd lived with Great-Uncle Lev. It was a short prayer to my father, and I asked him to look after me and make sure I didn't make any more mistakes. It can seem odd now that a boy who was a tabula rasa of religion should address a prayer to a man he'd never known, yet at the time it made me feel better and also gave me the resolve to begin a long letter to Great-Uncle Lev to ask for the facts about me he'd avoided all my life.

My prayer was the wisest choice I'd made in months, for I was going to need all assistance the next week as I discovered just exactly how degenerate Russia had become under the rule of rot of men like Iagoda. On Sunday, January 12, we four landed in a runner-fixed light transport at Magadan's icebound airfield during a routine late-morning blow of perilous cross gusts, and we staggered across the tarmac to the ops shack to wait for the Air Defense car that was supposed to meet us. After hours of heatless waiting and failure to get through by telephone to Air Defense headquarters in Magadan, we purchased our way onto the lorry that had brought out the air-field relief (the field was only open four hours a day), and after a bouncing frigid ride we reached the train depot on Magadan's de-serted main thoroughfare overlooking the ice-caked Pacific shore and a deserted-looking dockyard. In relief for finding a building with some heat we ate two meals each of good potato pancakes, sweet onion soup, handfuls of sour cream, and three liters of bad coffee that sent us all to the latrine. Threatened with a night in the depot before we could rouse Air Defense headquarters to provide us proper transportation, we decided to go it alone and bribe our way onto the baggage car of an ore train heading up into the hills and, according to the stationmaster, past the drop-off for Gold No. 3. Because we arrived in a blow and left at dusk, I saw little of Magadan, and what I saw was snow-heaped paths and squalid wood-built barracks fitted against the sudden ridges and hills that rose as if straight out of the sea; the only folk I saw were like two-legged insects whose daily chore was to crawl along a coal-stained ice sheet in search of food, warmth, and enough vodka to get to spring. Magadan was an old timber and ship-building town that Stalin's five-year plans had trans-formed into a gold-mining depot and then a zek way station to the infamous slave camps up, the Kolyma River valley. By the time I saw it in the winter of 1969, the town had disintegrated to no more than a warren of former zeks who lived on in permanent internal exile, making the town an arctic Dzhezkazgan-by-the-sea populated by drunken outcasts and several packs of wild dogs. We four felt as if we'd escaped a timeless disaster when we boarded the ore train and churned north toward Gold No. 3. We left the black hump of the depot behind and moved slowly up a river valley among pristine taiga hills, the quarter moon lighting slender larches and swaying Siberian pines on the ridges and sturdy stone pines in the small clearings. The evening was radiant, an intimidating fifty-five degrees centigrade below zero, and the only sound was the muffled clacking of the train that soothed me like a friend's voice and made me talk to myself as I lay out with my feet to the baggage handler's wood stove. I didn't say anything noteworthy to myself, just the babbling of a boy intoxicated to be on the move again, to be doing something manly, to be away from all that confusing, painful business in Moscow and off into the fabled wilderness of farthest Siberia with a defined mission ahead of me. "Magadan! The Pacific!" I announced to myself, and you can hear how unironic I was in those days, how very childlike, thinking more of bird-watching than Soyuz-watching, "Reindeer herds! And five-meter-high brown bears! And three-meter-long black wolves and wild weasels, and the capercaillie and the eagle owl!"

The weather deteriorated with heavy clouds pouring in from the east, and it was starlessly black when the ore train halted a moment around 2100 hours to drop us off on a low wooden platform. Gold No. 3 was said by the trainmen to be a kilometer up the big hillside. We'd prepared ourselves as best we could with snowshoes bought at exorbitant rates in Magadan, but still it was hard-slogging with electric torches across a gulch and then up a sharp hillside path that had been constructed with log steps at the steepest sections. We didn't know we were on the correct path until we spied a green electric light through the tree line above us that had to be the Air Defense compound. What made us certain was that the Air Defensemen had cut back a circle of larches, firs, and underbrush to make the compound a bald roost that commanded the lower hills. The station itself was built like a short lighthouse topped by the communications-and-radar array, but nothing about it was well built, part concrete and part cut timber, and only that green electric lamplight marked the half-buried entrance for us.

We were winded by the climb and at first wondered if the station was abandoned. Volgamints pounded hard enough to shake loose small icicles from the overhang, and then we all called out in unison until the crew eventually opened up. We were most discouraged after two days of traveling to find a foul-smelling hovel and a sleepy-eyed detail of four middle-aged Air Defense drunkards and a twenty-one-year-old commander named Lieutenant Vladimirovich. We were wrong to dismiss Vladimirovich, but at first his runtish size, sloppy deportment, indifference to the morale of his command, and especially his soft-pitched voice were most off-putting. It turned out he was the hearty son of a lumber boss from down the valley, generous like all Siberians and extremely bold, one of the bravest men I've ever known. It's my belief that he gave his life for me and the others, and I wish I could now say that I'd been more generous to him. But that morning what I made of him was a scruffy boy in greasy woolens who came out to us yawning and grinning and whose notion of ceremony was to call, "Welcome, cosmonauts, welcome to Fool's Gold, welcome most honored cosmonauts!"

We were half a day early, according to Vladimirovich, who'd been told to expect four cosmonauts Monday morning not Sunday evening, and he begged our pardon for the mistake and blamed himself for not getting confirmation. "Fool's Gold" was what he called Gold No. 3, because the shallower north and east slopes of the hill had once held an old gold-mining camp working the placer deposits in the ravines. Volgamints made a joke about washing out the snow in our boots for gold, and Vladimirovich joked back we were welcome to whatever gold we could find except his gold teeth. He grinned at us to show two beauties, a jest that delighted Volgamints and Lympyet and made Doctor Gogol laugh hard. Vladimirovich offered us the freedom of his command, though he again apologized for how poorly prepared he was for our visit, nearly all his electronics either failed or unreliable. Fool's Gold was no longer the first or even second line of air defense. While the station had once served ably as a watchtower against American bombers, it had been largely obsolesced by ballistic-missile technology, and so what good the station served was as a listening post for orbiting spacecraft. Yet the space program hadn't invested much in updating the facility, and the result was a moss-covered two-story-high hovel with the radar-and-communications array propped atop it like a tired dunce's cap. The tiny living quarters were insulated with animal hides; the radar room was usually kept sealed to preserve the equipment; the radio room was a closet with a twenty-year-old transmitter that hadn't been reliable for a year; the generator room had a big hole in the wall and the generator had to be shut down at night to conserve fuel; the telephone was so vulnerable to ice on the lines that they only trusted it in the summer; the only working light was the green lamp at the entrance, the water was from a well down the hillside, and the cooking facilities were a wood stove and a brick-built open fire attached to the living quarters like a shed.

I list all this deficiency to show you that outside Starry Town and Star City the space program was an illusion. After our initial disappointment passed, the station didn't look impossible to us and our hunger made it an agreeable refuge. Vladimirovich did know how to provide a midnight supper, and we were treated to a most honored feast of grilled reindeer steaks, roasted rabbit meat, and a vegetable-thick rabbit stew along with good kasha, decent beet soup, and canned tomatoes and more gobs of sour cream, washed by lethal vodka cut slightly in the Siberian way. I liked the thick rabbit stew and ate ravenously. One of the Air Defensemen could bake bread when he had the flour and had made us dense loaves of black bread in the wood stove. We ate until we groaned and by the time we retired everyone was cheery with drink and pleased to be well fed and warm while that lethal night wind outside tried to tear out the hill. I bedded down across from sour Volgamints—who of course had been the worst complainer en route—and even he was willing to admit as we went to sleep, "Fool's Gold, well, ha, who's the fool? But the food's not bad, ha!"

The next day, Monday, January 13, we were invaded before dawn by real cosmonauts, my friends and watchdogs Miserbiev and Adama-Bibliov, along with the squadron's best engineers Schtange and Tevyelook, who awoke us all by pounding on the door and shouting, "Hello, the camp! Hello, Peter Nevsky!"

Vladimirovich hadn't been wrong after all to expect cosmonauts on Monday morning, it was just that he hadn't been told to expect us candidates on Sunday—a distinction that was wasted on Vladimirovich, who was in awe of anyone from the legendary Starry Town.

The new arrivals had traveled nine thousand kilometers from the Cosmodrome on a hurry-up transport with great news that all was on schedule at T minus approximately thirty-six hours for Uncle Dmitry's *Soyuz 4.*

My narrow-minded thought was that Miserbiev and Adama-Bibliov had come to guard me, and I was resentful that I still wasn't trusted despite all that had happened. In fact the four cosmonauts were not there for me but as part of the general deployment of the squadron around the globe to supervise crucial posts in the communications network. Moreover my uncles knew that Fool's Gold was a very weak link in the network—the last station before radio contact was lost over the Pacific until the Caribe station in the Caribbean—and so they had dispatched four of the ten of the squadron available along with a half ton of communications equipment and parts that had been flown into Magadan on a big Antonov (Air Defense headquarters had met the cosmonauts at the field properly) and transferred by lorry to a flatcar and then plopped down at the wooden platform on the rail line. All that was left was for the thirteen of us to haul a half ton up the hillside using pulleys and hand-built sleds and to do it double-time.

That afternoon another half ton of equipment arrived by ore train at the platform, and we were at work again in gusts that kicked snow sideways in waves, and it wasn't even storming yet. By then we'd all had time to puzzle over my uncles' intentions. Our opinion was that my uncles had not only known Fool's Gold was inoperative, they'd also known that just sending parts into Siberia wouldn't fix it, and so they'd arranged for Khitrovo to send four reliable candidates (Khitrovo had lied when he said he'd sent us for punishment), and then they'd dispatched four of their own squadron, including their two best electrical engineers, Schtange and Tevyelook, and enough paraphernalia to remake the station. The final consideration was that the eight of us carried enough cash to buy or bribe whatever additional supplies we needed from the military stores and black market in Magadan, and Tevyelook and Schtange quickly worked up a shopping list to send into Magadan on the Monday afternoon southbound train.

Monday was perpetual labor, and by Tuesday morning's northbound train drop-off, after working and sleeping in six-hour shifts, we'd repaired, cleaned, checked, and rebuilt the communications array, the radar room, the radio room, and large parts of the genera-tor. We'd even rigged new wires and mounted big lights outside and bright overhead lamps inside. Schtange had also ordered a gas-lit bread-baking oven from the black marketeers in Magadan and was waiting for a free moment to install it in the kitchen annex. Despite our frantic pace we ate like taiga lords on reindeer steaks, and we celebrated the end of Monday's labor by sharing fresh-baked bread, a kettle of onion soup, and more and more of the cut vodka as we sang Siberian hunting songs and speculated about *Soyuz 4/5*. I enjoyed the work as well as the companionship of men who could labor shoulder to shoulder passionately, but what I most treasured was how I was able on my breaks to get up on the catwalk around the array to listen for the caws and hoos and guttural screams of the birdlife whenever the wind eased. My finest moment Monday was when I heard an eagle owl very close by at feeding time.

As we worked we reorganized the station from each according to his gifts to each according to his needs, a phenomenon that doesn't come by mandate but out of necessity and desire. For example Vladi-mirovich, grateful for our competence and unfazed by our bossiness, gave over his command to us and devoted himself to hunting for the table with his two handsome .22 rifles and single-shot birdguns. Tuesday morning he and Lev Lympyet, who was thrilled by the hunting, brought in a fat hare, a hazelhen grouse, and a giant caper-caillie. Doctor Gogol took charge of the Air Defensemen, who were all suffering from intestinal ailments, and gave them hand-mixed bromides that improved their moods if not their health. Miserbiev and scrupulous Adama-Bibliov appointed themselves co–executive officers of the station and posted a duty schedule that divided the maintenance chores into shifts. Schtange and Tevyelook, who did all of the skilled work on the electronics, passed their time tinkering in the communications room, and if I haven't said much of Vasya and Tima until now it's because they were the most unprepossessing of the squadron, men who asked little and said less and yet were always dependable, as you shall soon see. My job at the station became a jack-of-all-trades, passing from place to place to lend a hand and chat with everyone at work, and I can suppose now that the reason I so quickly assumed command once we fell into trouble was that I didn't have anything more significant to do.

By Tuesday noontime, 1130 hours our time at Magadan and

0330 hours Cosmodrome time, we had satisfied each of Schtange's and Tevyelook's demands, and we all crowded around as we turned on the generator, lit up the radio room, and reached out to join the worldwide network prepared for the *Soyuz 4* launch at T minus approximately nine hours.

"Dawn, this is Gold Three, over to you," Tevyelook called through via satellite uplink to the mission control center at the Cosmodrome code-named Dawn. "Dawn, this is Gold Three, over to you."

At first only broken chatter came back, and then after adjustments that did little but make us sweat, the transmission cleared up. The message was no-nonsense, "Roger, Gold Three, this is Dawn, very well, welcome to the net, now get off the air, over to you and out."

I recognized Fedyuninsky's voice and snobbery, but my candidate friends were annoyed by the curtness after all the work we'd done to get on the air. Arkady Volgamints went so far as to curse my uncles, "What big bastards, you'd think they owned the airwaves!" and later to me he also spoke against Schtange and Tevyelook, "Those brains in there, they treat me like a babushka, they treat me as if I ain't never put a receiver together one-handed at fifteen thousand meters! Frig 'em." I didn't bother to defend either my uncles or Schtange and Tevyelook, who weren't the pleasantest personalities, because Volgamints wasn't wrong. My uncles and their squadron were cocky about their work, and to outsiders it was hard to tolerate all the attendant bullying. This was my uncles' moment to qualify for the moon landing, so they didn't have any need to be diplomatic if they succeeded and no amount of generosity would have mattered if they failed. The pressure was probably greater still, because the mission as planned by the State Commission was most risky. In addition, my uncles aimed to perform all the tasks with minimum fuss and maximum speed and then get down so perfectly that the Corps would recover all its reputation lost in the failures of the first three Soyuzes.

I want to be exact about the size of my uncles' ambitions, since what was ahead of us might look unchallenging now but was unprecedented back then: *Soyuz 4*, code-named Amur and commanded by Uncle Dmitry, was scheduled for lift-off into low earth orbit on Tuesday morning Cosmodrome time, January 14. *Soyuz 5*, code-named Baikal and commanded by Uncle Konstantine and crewed by Glavtop and Grin, was set for lift-off to a parallel low earth orbit on

Wednesday morning, January 15. The mission called for the two tandem spacecraft to rendezvous by radar and manual flying, to link together with drogue docking mechanisms at the prows, and then to transfer the crew of Glavtop and Grin from *Soyuz 5* to *Soyuz 4* with a spacewalk. Uncle Dmitry was then to land his ship and new crew immediately and Uncle Konstantine was to follow after another day of sightseeing. We were launching two spacecraft and four men within a day, tracking and supporting all systems and crew, overseeing the never-before-attempted transfer of two men in orbit, and then bringing everything down within three days. The only thing my uncles weren't attempting was landing in Red Square tip to tail, and there was no reason to doubt they wouldn't have done this if it would have persuaded the Kremlin bosses more to the Corps. If and when my uncles achieved *Soyuz 4/5*, then all the systems were in place and man-rated for the moon-driving; because if we could do all this in earth orbit we could do it in lunar orbit, and all that remained for the moon was the raising of Tsar Cannon.

Uncle Alexander came on the radio at T minus five hours in order to certify his chain of command and the worldwide communications network. Uncle Alexander was called the mission control commander, though what this actually meant was that he was boss of the total mission and could not be overruled by the rocket chiefs from first to last. When he came to Gold 3, Uncle Alexander told us that we'd share the communications link each ninety minutes with two other stations in eastern Siberia. He also told us that, since we were easternmost, we must maintain communication as long as possible as the spacecraft moved out over the Pacific headed for South America, circling the earth clockwise every ninety minutes. Uncle Alexander underlined our critical job, "Establish your duty roster. Lieutenant Schtange, Lieutenant Tevyelook, one of you on call at all times. As for the rest of you, I want one man on the up-link and one at the ready in three-hour shifts. You don't interrupt, you pass through the link to me, understood? You must remain up and operative. Understood?"

We understood: we were passive go-betweens and not active agents, and we must remain on the net regardless, and therein was the challenge. The ever dangerous weather conditions were a constant threat, and almost as if the storm gods were eavesdropping and had decided to play us a trick, we had watched Tuesday morning as the thick cloud cover moved across the hills again. Unlike the previous two days, when the dark had passed us by about midday, the wind changed, backing to northerly, which Vladimirovich said was a sign that heavy snow was imminent. By late afternoon our time, at approximately T minus four hours, the wind was most definitely northerly, like a warning wail promising trouble ahead. Even before the snow came we were already scrambling to keep the array's housing free of ice and to keep the generator running on heavy fuel that we had to fetch from the buried cache behind the station and warm up before we could pour it like tar.

Those storm gods were busy pranksters, because there was also bad weather closing on the Cosmodrome, and at T minus one hour we overheard on the network that there were crosswinds and light snow striking the launchpad and a low center closing from Siberia. Meanwhile we were also able to listen in on the open line in order to enjoy Uncle Dmitry's witty style as he prepared to launch. The rocketeers had sealed Uncle Dmitry in the spacecraft sometime before, and while he waited he was able to chat with whomever he wished via radiophone, including his wife, Angelicka, and daughters, Anna and Marya. He was shrewd to call through to many of the big bosses, so that the ever obstreperous Secretary Ustinov was obliged to wish my uncles well.

The final hour passed in a wink, and our transmission remained clear to lift-off at 1249 hours Cosmodrome time (2049 our time). We were all crowded in outside the radio room listening on the speaker Schtange had rigged for us, and what we could hear over and over was Uncle Alexander's measured monotone marking the countdown to launch and then calling the post–lift-off time incrementally, "T plus thirty seconds and nominal . . . T plus sixty seconds and nominal."

Uncle Dmitry didn't respond until he was in orbit. I found it most frustrating to hear and not see the launch and prowled restlessly as far as I could into the station without losing the transmission to the wind noise. I remember talking to myself like a child reciting his lessons and trying to imagine what the launch must have felt like. There would be first-stage cutoff, with g-forces easing, followed by cutoff of the strap-on boosters and then separation of the strap-ons confirmed. Then there would be a rip-sounding bump at the bow of the orbital module that was the separation of the nose cone and escape tower. Then there would be a slight pop and the spacecraft shroud would be gone and confirmed. Uncle Dmitry would be breathing easier now as the g-forces lifted. Then would come the second-stage cutoff and separation, all confirmed, and Uncle Dmitry would feel the weightless drift. Then third-stage ignition would jar some of the loose bolts and make a whooshing sound through the cabin that Uncle Dmitry might hear through his headset but would certainly feel like a pilot feels all power thrusts. Cutoff would follow presently and then Uncle Dmitry would be able to peer through the portal to see the black wall of the earth terminator where night crept west toward Kazakhstan and the Urals.

My heart was racing as I heard Uncle Alexander announce, "Amur, this is Dawn, orbit confirmed," and then in the mumbly monotone of his that meant he was firm in command he read the orbit, 225 by 173 kilometers.

The first words to be heard from the spacecraft were Uncle Dmitry at his pedantic best, "Dawn, this is Amur," he started, "Amur has wings, Dawn, Amur has wings." And then we heard a radio-crackling version of some especially apt and sentimental Pushkin lines recited slowly and lovingly, "In alien lands devoutly clinging / To age-old rites of Russian earth. / I let a captive bird go winging / To greet the radiant spring's rebirth."

We at Fool's Gold toasted the earth, the moon, and the heavens with sloshing cups of coffee and tea. Then we roared our approval for the Cosmonaut Corps and also wept, me included, at Uncle Dmitry's brave sentiment, though I suppose I should note that all Russians always weep at Pushkin. Uncle Dmitry continued his sentimental journey apace, for the second transmission from the spacecraft was a live television broadcast. We couldn't receive it, only overhear, yet it was obvious from the first that the broadcast had little to do with flying. I learned later that Uncle Dmitry smiled politely into the camera and then moved the lens to show the two empty couches to his left, the control panel, then the hatchway to the orbital module. Moscow never announced launches beforehand and certainly didn't announce mission goals, but a fool could have guessed that Uncle Dmitry wasn't in orbit for another attempt at a rendezvous with a robot ship. That television broadcast was like a boast that my uncles were aiming very high and that everyone should stay in touch with the imminent news from space. Even Volgamints was impressed with my uncles' showmanship and told me that they were turning the mission into a "frigging space circus."

Rather than remain at the radio, I got my greatcoat and went up top to the catwalk. There was still no snowfall though I could smell it coming like a damp piny perfume. I braced myself against the gusts and stared into the black sky as if I could spy Uncle Dmitry as he passed overhead. I was also thinking that perhaps my gaze, even down here below the storm, could hold him aloft. I knew it was superstitious of me, but all that night I was either on the catwalk staring as if I could keep Uncle Dmitry safe or at the radio room listening in as if I could talk Uncle Dmitry through any errors. There wasn't anything more I could have done, there really wasn't more that had to be done; however, my imagination made me feel better and eased me through my first duty tour at the communications room, when, about midnight our time during Uncle Dmitry's fifth orbit, Uncle Alexander gave Uncle Dmitry permission for a circularizing burn of the spacecraft engine. "Amur, ten seconds, five seconds, initiate," Uncle Alexander called. Uncle Dmitry then very neatly slipped *Soyuz 4* into a more circular orbit, approximately 237 by 207 kilometers, that was more appropriate for the rendezvous the next day. Even a maneuver as simple as this excited me so much that I couldn't sit and I had to stand and turn around in that closet-size room like a cooped falcon. I continued like this throughout my duty tour and right up until Uncle Dmitry called once more to say he was shutting down for four hours of sleep. We were the last station to track him as Uncle Dmitry passed quietly once more east on to the Pacific, and once we'd lost his track on the radar screen Miserbiev took pity on me and made me eat some rabbit stew and bread to calm me down (he had a kilo of reindeer steak) and then insisted that if I couldn't sleep I should at least lie in my bedroll while I listened to the network chatter. Trifya was most kind, and he helped me the more when he spoke of the mission so far as a dream, since that's what it did feel like to me, a fantastic dream. "Easy now," he told me. "You know the Soyuz drives like a dream and that Colonel Oryolin was always right, and we've let them waste years robot-testing a dream. The Soyuz drives like a dream, she's the Corps' dream."

Our part of the dream turned perilous at midday on the fifteenth when the long-expected storm struck hard and quickly pressed in on us. We were ready when it hit, and scrambled to our prearranged posts to keep the snow from building up on the flat roof, the exposed catwalk, the very vulnerable array, and particularly to keep the fuel cache from being buried in drifts. Yet as the snow increased and the wind pounded almost straight down, it was like working at the bottom of a frozen lake. We knew we were fighting and losing and that in time the storm would wear us down. Still our duty was to maintain generator power and to keep the array operational. The Siberians showed us how to tie on lifelines to stretch out to the fuel cache and how to use pickaxes on the ice, which was like chipping concrete.

Those storm gods were grisly, because at the same time we were struggling with our blizzard, another snowstorm hit the Cosmodrome nine thousand kilometers to the east. My uncles had dared fate by risking the natural consequence of a double launch in deep winter. The storm at the Cosmodrome wasn't as severe as ours, but then it didn't have to be bad to threaten the launchpad. We listened in on the network as Uncle Alexander overcalled all cautionary words and ordered Doctor Mishuk to roll out the R-7 from the Rocketage and raise it for launch. The rocketeers had worked through the night to clean and ready the launch gantry, and at dawn they had to redouble their labor to raise and fuel the booster in the wind. The chief concern was that the fuel lines might ice up and fail, and so they delayed the kerosene fueling until the last. The conditions on the pad worsened to the point that Uncle Konstantine and his crew of Glavtop and Grin had to bypass the jammed high-level servicing platform and climb a forty-meter ladder to their craft. What I most remember about the crisis at the Cosmodrome was not the threat but rather Uncle Alexander's message over the network throughout the countdown: "Finish it," he'd say again and again. "Finish it." Whenever the rocketeers argued for a hold, such as when one of the two communications antennas snapped like straw, whenever the meteorologists would call in with news that the storm was breaking up or the front was stalling, whenever any dissenting voice sounded on the network, Uncle Alexander would order all of us with a mumbly, "Finish it." "Finish it." "Finish it."

At T minus sixty minutes to *Soyuz 5*'s launch, Uncle Dmitry broke in to the network to divert everyone with another television broadcast as he passed over Asia. It was a guileful maneuver by Uncle

Dmitry, because while the state audience didn't know of the storm at the launchpad those of us who did couldn't both worry and listen to his artful performance. He not only gave a speech about the beauties of the earth's blues and greens, and spoke of the white cloud banks as gossamer companions, but he also gave an interview by answering questions from schoolchildren that were relayed to him by Fedyuninsky at the Cosmodrome. "There's no upside down or backwards," he told the audience. "Wherever I am is the right side up and forward." And as anxious as we all were about the storm on the launchpad, we all laughed at the answer to a child who asked, "Where's the W.C.?" because Uncle Dmitry replied sincerely, "It's in the next model."

Uncle Konstantine's *Soyuz 5* launch was not routine not only because of the blizzard but also because it had to go within twenty-four hours of Uncle Dmitry's launch, and this meant all the routine sort of problems of a countdown had to be fixed instantly or ignored. Uncle Alexander overrode several warning alarms in the heat exchanger on a strap-on, in various vernier engines, and in the electrical control system on the RD-108. Doctor Mishuk, deputy chief of the R-7, was said to have collapsed four times from exhaustion yet wouldn't let them carry him from the pad. Because of the way the wind gusts were buffeting the booster, the rocketeers waited as long as possible to fold the service platform back from the gantry, and even then the booster, held up only by its own weight, swayed so badly that Uncle Konstantine, not a man to panic at disaster, cried out to Uncle Alexander on the open line, "Burn us or lose us, Sasha!" I'm certain that the reason Uncle Alexander decided to override the last thirty-five minutes of built-in hold time on the countdown and fire a little early, at 1214 hours Cosmodrome time, was that the booster was trying to tear free of its electrical connections. They fired so early they didn't have time to clear off the empty fuel cars before Uncle Alexander skipped the count ahead from T minus forty-seven minutes to T minus eight minutes when he ordered and confirmed onboard power. I have been hard on Alexander Oryolin as a tyrant, but that day only such a man could have risked those conditions and fired ahead of schedule.

I ask myself now, did I doubt my uncles that day? With the weather and clock against them and all the rocket chiefs and meteorologists contradicting their conviction and the fate of the space pro-

gram in their hands, did I doubt their command? Yes, I did, the
truth was that I doubted them all the while I cheered them. I
thought they were taking uncalled-for risks and carrying on as if they
were losing a battle rather than winning the moon. I ask myself now
what was it that they were truly fighting against? Not the weather
and the clock, no, for I knew that they could beat the weather, and I
also knew that Mishuk's booster was a hardy plowhorse and that
Uncle Dmitry and Uncle Konstantine could drive whatever flew, so
that once in orbit the mission was secure. What made me doubt
them was not just that they were taking perilous risks but also my
suspicion, which I was only half aware of, that my uncles were going
harder than sense because of Iagoda and my mother. Alexander Oryolin's war against Iagoda, Alexander Oryolin's feud with my mother,
the darkness in all their souls that they wouldn't or couldn't solve,
these were what drove my uncles to force their will on men and
machines, and my uncles made *Soyuz 4/5* into a contest meant not
only to win the moon assignment but also to blunt Iagoda. I think
fear drove those spacecraft as much as pride. My uncles had to have
been apprehensive that by taking on Iagoda they had weakened and
possibly wrecked their plans for moon-driving. Iagoda was not a
commonplace enemy—he had cunning to corrupt men's souls, just
as he had turned Doctor Lunin against the Grand Constructor—and
even if my uncles weren't afraid of Iagoda in a way that I can understand, they had to have acknowledged the fear in the conflict. I felt
the fear at Fool's Gold, and the anxiety that kept me awake and
working, or up on the catwalk trying to hold the spacecraft up with
my eyes, was more my fear of Iagoda than of failure. To me, Iagoda
was out there in the dark with my incomprehensible mother at his
side, and they were coming to get me when I was at my most vulnerable, with my eyes on the sky and my back to the wilderness.

I'm trying to tell you how I felt the wolf coming for me before I
knew how or when; and if you've ever been stalked you know how
you can't explain the prickly feel of your skin and the weight in your
heart, but that you know anyway you've been marked.

The wolf wasn't coming that day, for Uncle Konstantine's *Soyuz 5*
lifted so perfectly on course that Uncle Dmitry in *Soyuz 4* in his
sixteenth orbit reported that he saw *Soyuz 5* come up to him. Uncle
Dmitry even called Uncle Konstantine "my wingman," and the two
of them bantered like MiG drivers on a sortie. After six revolutions of

flying in tandem, my uncles altered their orbits to 253 kilometers apogee, 211 kilometers perigee, and then Uncle Alexander ordered the crews to sleep. Before they shut down their communications, Uncle Konstantine fussed that he was fresh and wanted to get on with the rendezvous and link-up, some "hot driving" he called it, but Uncle Konstantine was silenced by Uncle Alexander. "You're standing down, and you're napping because I say you're napping."

It was the next day that the wolf showed himself to me at Fool's Gold while I was least looking. The two spacecraft began their rest period about dawn our time, Thursday, January 16, and Uncle Alexander told all ground stations that we had eight hours before the scheduled link-up and rendezvous so that we should get our rest and check all equipment. We at Fool's Gold relaxed as best we could by sleeping or loafing. I was still too excited to rest, however, and because the storm had broken during the night and the morning was frigid but relatively calm I decided to ask Vladimirovich if I could go along with him on his morning hunt. He said he was delighted for my company and offered me his birdgun, which I refused. What I had in mind was some bird-watching, particularly to spy the nests of the black-billed capercaillie, and I asked if we could try the thick Siberian pine copses by the river where I expected the best results. Vladimirovich gave me his best skis, and we made good time a few kilometers down the west trail to the rolling fields in the glen, where we ran across a mysterious hunting party. There were four men in heavy, greasy parkas and animal-hide leggings. They said they were rail workers from the construction camp down the valley out for some fresh meat after the blow and before another one. They were authentically hungry, with bad skin color and red-shot eyes, and the biggest of them, who was cross-eyed and filthy-faced, asked us if we'd seen any big game, perhaps a reindeer, and then he spoke very menacing words, "What about them cosmonauts, hey? You seen them? We heard there's frigging cosmonauts up the way?"

I started to answer, "Well," but Vladimirovich interrupted me to ask, "What's that about cosmonauts, comrades?"

The cross-eyed hunter said he'd heard there were cosmonauts up the trail. "Everybody knows there's frigging cosmonauts come up from Magadan," he claimed. "Everybody knows they're going to land a frigging spaceship up here!"

Vladimirovich grunted and countered, "What's that about a spaceship, comrades?"

The hunters laughed at Vladimirovich's ignorance and said they were moving on, though they didn't go right away, instead obviously coveting our boots and coats and especially my wristwatch, a good new one I'd bought in Leningrad at the New Year. Finally they lowered their eyes and left us, sliding quickly off the main trail and back toward the rail line.

I didn't understand what had happened. Once we had gotten clear of them, continuing lower toward the river, Vladimirovich stopped at the edge of a frozen marsh and asked me, "What did you notice about those fellows?" I said, "They looked rugged," and shrugged.

Vladimirovich didn't correct me right away, yet after he'd unslung his .22 and crouched down to get a sense of the field, he said, "You see those two rifles they had? Mausers."

I crouched down beside him and tried to figure what he meant about Mausers. Vladimirovich lay down on the snow in the firing position, a tiny, dark-faced boy soldier in a prehistoric world, as motionless as a rock for several minutes, and then, even though I didn't see anything, he fired once and grinned. At twenty meters there was blood in the snow where he'd shot dead an Arctic hare coming out of buried brush. When Vladimirovich had fetched the hare he spoke again, "Mausers, Lieutenant Nevsky, they were packing two Mausers, and they looked well-oiled. You wouldn't want to eat what a Mauser can bag." He tapped his .22 rifle. "This is all you need around here. Whatever's big enough for a Mauser is either hibernating or wears boots like us."

"Then what are they?" I asked. "They said they were from the railroad camp."

"Bandits," Vladimirovich said. "They're bandits, and they ain't from any railroad camp."

I understood what he was saying but asked anyway, "What are they after?"

"What are bandits after?" Vladimirovich replied, and then he looked around once more. "We best get back to the station and chew about what we saw."

We did much more than "chew," we argued loudly and anxiously. Vladimirovich reported what we'd witnessed and then said there were many bandits upriver in the hills who were usually too timid to approach a camp, but that in this instance he thought they'd been stirred by the rumor of rich cosmonauts and a spaceship in the area. Vladimirovich also said that he and I had escaped trouble probably because the bandits had only been a scouting party for a larger band and hadn't wanted to give away their intentions by attacking us. Vladimirovich said it was his opinion that we should take those four seriously. "I've not known them to come so close in before," he added. "They must be crazy with the word of you and the spaceship." The debate that followed was troubling. We were divided by our fears. Volgamints said it didn't matter what the bandits wanted, we couldn't fight them off with rabbit and bird guns, a few knives, and a radio (Air Defense camps were not routinely issued firearms) and that the sensible course was to abandon the station and get back into Magadan by the afternoon train. "They're going to cut our throats while we're on the radio! They're going to shoot us through our frigging radarscopes!"

Lev Lympyet was less concerned, saying that he'd been stationed down near Vladivostok before joining the Corps and had seen many scavengers like that, and that to call them bandits was an exaggeration. "They don't attack military camps," he said, "but if you're alone they'll jump you if they're in a pack. Mostly they pick over rubbish, really, they're just poor bastards who are usually starving to death and don't know enough to come in. I've seen what happens to them. You find mummies in the spring, faces picked to the bone by the birds, another poor bastard who died calling himself a bandit."

The four Air Defense crewmen shivered and disagreed with Lympyet, preferring to run for safety because they said they were too old to fight and weren't paid for it anyway.

At this point Doctor Gogol spoke up with some wise comfort, "What are we afraid of? We're thirteen men in a military compound, and what are they but four starved beggars?"

The four cosmonauts didn't need to speak because to them our position was clear. We were going to do our duty and stay on the network until my uncles were returned to earth. Vladimirovich understood that he'd upset his men excessively and spoke out about our prospects, "We're secure here, and if we have to we'll radio in for backup, and for now we'll stay up here on the hill, and we've got plenty of stores, and besides the weather's going to get worse again, no man's going to last long out there when it comes to a blow."

We broke up the debate. If trouble was coming we knew we had to stay alert, and there was nothing more to say until trouble came on. Volgamints tried to repair his misbehavior by howling like a sickly wolf and mocking his own fears: "Werewolves," he said, "who's afraid of skinny little werewolves?"

There wasn't time to make more of our scare—and what choice did we have but to keep going?—because it was time for my uncles either to win or lose with the boldest space mission ever attempted, a manned transfer in earth orbit, and I'm going to outline the procedure in detail because I want you to appreciate the unknown challenges my uncles overcame with their pigheaded courage. The ground station network was up and all ears when Uncle Dmitry in *Soyuz 4* began the hard task of closing on Uncle Konstantine's *Soyuz 5* by radar guidance and eventually by feel. This wasn't a ground-controlled mission, my uncles were driving their own ships, and by sunset our time Uncle Dmitry had maneuvered to a 253-by-201-kilometer orbit and within ten kilometers of *Soyuz 5* in the lead position. Uncle Konstantine pitched his craft on the x axis and steadied on the plane to prepare his bow for the close of Uncle Dmitry's bow. Uncle Dmitry guided closer and closer by radar, the two vehicles like iron butterflies sailing together on a breeze while they tried to kiss tip to tip. It took ninety minutes to close to ten meters, and then another fifty minutes to ease forward to contact.

"Steady, on my count," Uncle Dmitry called out, and we could hear his concern, since this was by feel, there'd been no way to rehearse on the ground the docking assembly or drogue docking collar. Uncle Dmitry started, "Ten, nine, eight, seven, six . . ."

"Contact!" Uncle Konstantine yelled, and of course he was vulgar about the operation, calling to Uncle Alexander, "Dawn, this is Baikal, I've been frigged!"

Uncle Alexander ordered, "Get on with it." And then he asked, "Confirm?"

"We have inboard com," Uncle Dmitry said, meaning they were now linked by communications and power lines as the earth's first space station—with a crew of four. "Dawn, confirm," he added, "Amur meets Baikal, confirm."

It so happened that just as they kissed and coupled they were above us at Fool's Gold and heading out over the Pacific toward South America. However, the day's work was only half done, for Uncle Alexander, before he lost good radio signal while the space-craft crossed over the Pacific, canceled the rest break and ordered Glavtop and Grin to get into their spacesuits and prepare for their spacewalk on the next pass over Asia.

What I know of the next forty minutes is from the transcript of the mission, since we at Fool's Gold didn't pick up communications again until the spacecraft were acquired by the Caribe station. In *Soyuz 5* Glavtop and Grin floated forward through the hatch into the spherical orbital module where their spacesuits were stowed. Uncle Konstantine, who was the only spacewalker in the Corps, harried their preparations with small talk such as, "In my day there was none of this dressing and undressing, I just took a big breath and popped out." The spacesuits required patient assembly and checks, and the telemetry and safety halyards had to be certified repeatedly, since no cosmonaut had dressed in free-fall before (in *Voskhod 2* in 1965, Uncle Konstantine wore his suit at launch). Glavtop reported on the weightless phenomenon that while he worked, whatever object he didn't hold on to tended to orbit around him like a satellite. Throughout the dressing Uncle Alexander harassed them, "Baikal, I want them out, out, I want it done!" and yet when Uncle Konstantine went forward to help, Uncle Alexander ordered him back to his command seat to monitor the life support system and to remain in communication with the Cosmodrome.

Sixty minutes after link-up, Glavtop and Grin were dressed and ready to open the exterior hatch. The two spacecraft were then over North Africa approaching the Mediterranean, and so we had reac-quired them on the network and could listen in to the final prepara-tions. Uncle Alexander ordered Uncle Konstantine to seal the interior hatch and added, "Baikal, you don't go out of the ship, you stay at your post," which was a blunt way of saying that if Glavtop and Grin failed outside they were not as important as the return of the spacecraft.

Valya Glavtop was first out. He reported every move to Uncle Alexander, who was watching on a television camera mounted exter-nally on the orbital module. This wasn't a public broadcast however, for there was nothing certain about the outcome. "Dawn, my head's out, do you have me?" Glavtop asked Uncle Alexander. "I've got my leg out," he said as he struggled to clear the life support system that was strapped on his left thigh rather than on his back. "I'm out!" he announced.

Uncle Alexander broke in, "Valya, the tether, test the tether now, and move it!"

Glavtop obeyed by pulling hard on the tether and then spinning himself out along the superstructure, but even then Uncle Alexander wasn't satisfied with the progress and demanded more speed. "Move along, Valya, move along," Uncle Alexander said. "Keep pressure on the tether, move it, use the handholds, move it!"

When Kolya Grin got out, he ignored Uncle Alexander long enough to name a new color he called "earth blue," which he then applied to everything below, "It's earth blue, the browns are blue, the whites are blue, the blues are blue-blue."

Glavtop also misbehaved long enough to spin himself on his x axis and report on a phenomenon of spacewalk: "I know I'm doing the rolling," he said, "but it's as if I'm stationary and the earth's moving."

Uncle Konstantine broke in to contribute his own peculiar perspective of spacewalking, "The stars don't twinkle, don't forget to mention, they just shine and shine."

Uncle Alexander would have none of their play, rejecting their requests to dawdle on the handholds and ordering Glavtop and Grin, "I want you inside now, close down, now."

The spacewalk and transfer ended without incident at thirty-seven minutes when Uncle Dmitry, dressed in a spacesuit, opened the exterior hatch on *Soyuz 4*'s spherical module and welcomed his new crew. Uncle Alexander didn't slacken the pace however, and two hours later, at fifty-five and a half hours into the mission, after Glavtop and Grin had undressed and assumed their new couches in *Soyuz 4*, Uncle Alexander ordered the two spacecraft to separate and take up parallel orbits, and then, when the maneuver was satisfactory and all systems were nominal, he ordered the crews to cease their excited banter and rest.

We knew that the mission wasn't successful until all were down safely, yet we also knew that my uncles had driven the Cosmodrome to the brink of a trailblazing achievement. We could now construct the sort of spacecraft that was required for the moon landing—a command ship and lunar lander coupled like a mother and her issue—and we could transfer cosmonauts from one module to the other. My uncles had satisfied the Grand Constructor's bargain that if we were ready with the driving he would be ready with the superbooster, and all that should have been ahead for my uncles was the assembly of men and machines on the launchpad for the moon.

Instead there was the wolf ahead. The first attack came matter-of-factly after dark on the evening of January 16. Volgamints and Adama-Bibliov went up on the catwalk to check on the radar array and spotted a body on the snow near the half-buried outhouse. It was one of the Air Defense crew, and he'd been shot in the back near the kidneys. We got him inside quickly, and he was conscious, if in shock, and commented, "It doesn't hurt." Doctor Gogol couldn't stop the internal bleeding, and the man died while talking of his parents about dawn on Friday, the seventeenth. By then we'd done what we could to make the station a fortress, sealing the windows and doors with planks and getting in extra fuel barrels so we wouldn't have to expose ourselves in daylight at the fuel cache. We had also worn ourselves down debating whether we should retreat to the rail line and hail the morning ore train or use the field phone to call Air Defense headquarters at Magadan for support. The argument went back and forth, and nothing was decided, because we still believed that the bandits we'd seen were scavengers who didn't have the firepower or nerve to assault the station, but who would wait for us down the trail to pick us off if we ran for it.

Doctor Gogol declared, "We're secure here."

"We're on the net and we're staying on the net," Miserbiev added unnecessarily, since the cosmonauts were clearly not leaving. Uncle Dmitry was scheduled to burn retros and land *Soyuz 4* in ten hours, and Uncle Konstantine was due down tomorrow evening, so the station had to remain operative for at least another thirty-six hours. Adama-Bibliov told the Air Defensemen, "We're not saying what you have to do, but this is our post."

Vladimirovich was angry about his dead man and complained, "They killed Vasily without a chance, it's not right," and yet he said he wasn't going to quit his station just because of a pack of back-shooting cowards. "We're staying until we're relieved."

We eventually called Magadan on the field phone. I recall now that we had to wait until dawn because Vladimirovich said they didn't man the field phone at Magadan overnight. We got no answer, either because the storm had taken the wire down at our end or because the Air Defensemen in Magadan just didn't bother coming into the office every day.

"They're old men, pensioners," Vladimirovich remarked, "and they only pay them four times a year."

We'd done all we could to prepare for the worst, and yet it didn't seem enough, and Volgamints insisted we vote on our choices. "I'm ranking here," he said, "and I say we quit. We've got a couple of popguns and they've got at least two heavy rifles. I vote we go."

There was no support for Volgamints's position, but he kept complaining, "Then let's use the radio and the up-link! We can call the Cosmodrome and they can call Magadan and get the police up here!"

The four cosmonauts were firm in their rejection. "We stay on net and we stay off the air," Adama-Bibliov said. Miserbiev added perhaps too proudly, "We don't cry wolf, Major, and we don't call nine thousand kilometers because of a handful of beggars."

Volgamints cursed, "Frigging brains and your frigging net."

I admit now that our stubbornness was wrongheaded, though at the time I felt we were doing right by maintaining our strictest duty as a ground control station. The argument faded, and in the end we compromised that we'd stay on net and radio silent until the Soyuzes were safe on earth. However, for our own safety we'd send Vladimirovich and a party to intercept the afternoon southbound train and alert the police at Magadan that we needed support—though we decided not to flag down the train at the usual platform on the fore trail, but rather use the railroad camp platform several kilometers down the valley.

We did take some comfort from the natural defense of the weather, for the backside of the storm fell on us that morning, not nearly as violently as the day before but blowing steadily, spewing the fresh snowfall like waves of ice crystals. Vladimirovich said it was going to blow harder still, and so he chose only the best skiers of long-legged Adama-Bibliov (a winter Olympic medalist), rugged Lev Lympyet, and me as the odd man out. We took both .22s and left the two birdguns (I remember now there was both a single-shot and a side-by-side) with Volgamints and Miserbiev to guard the main door. To avoid any possible detection we went out through the generator room, through the generator containment, down along the rotted-out gold camp barracks' foundations to the tree line, moving in pairs, each partner covering the other. Though the visibility was under fifty meters we would have made the trek easily but for some bad luck. About six kilometers out, Lympyet went through ground ice and tore up his ankle. We had nothing for his pain, and since we were less than midway to our destination with two hours of light left we decided we should turn back to Fool's Gold. Vladimirovich showed us how to cut birch limbs to fashion a makeshift sled for Lympyet. Vladimirovich then made a brave offer to push on alone to the rail platform line, saying he could make the round trip before dark and probably catch up with us before Adama-Bibliov and I got Lympyet back to the station.

Adama-Bibliov thought Vladimirovich was taking on too much, and he added, "We should stay together. If we get separated and the storm gets worse, we're done."

I overcalled Adama-Bibliov's caution with the same assertiveness I had first used at Dzhezkazgan, surprising myself by sounding a mimic of Uncle Alexander's flat tone of command. "You're right, you're going," I told Vladimirovich. "Go and come back quickly and don't miss us in the dark." I added with my own more sympathetic voice, "And soft landing, Lieutenant."

Vladimirovich plunged into the blowing snow, and Adama-Bibliov and I struggled with the litter back up our own tracks as the light faded. Adama-Bibliov was a strong, expert companion, and we cleared the last ravine past dark and spied a glow above us that we instantly realized was Fool's Gold station on fire. We watched as the flames snapped sideways in the wind, and if our first reaction was to rush in we checked that and settled Lympyet down to make a plan. Lympyet said, "Leave me here and go in slowly, they'll need your rifle if it's the bandits."

I asserted myself again, "We'll go in after dark; now let's make you a shelter." Within the hour at full dark, Adama-Bibliov and I went in on our bellies over the generator containment area and toward the kitchen annex. By then the flames had died after eating through the timber and hides on the north wall and collapsing the back part of the roof, so that there was a hole in the wall between the concrete abutments. I called for Miserbiev, "Trifya! Hello! It's Peter and Yurka!"

Volgamints answered me from the hole in the wall, "The bastards are out there! Do you see them? Five or six of them!"

We raced into the smoke and found everyone barricaded at the front of the station in the living quarters and the communications and radio rooms. The generator was still running, so we still had power to the communications and radar room and were still on net, with Schtange and Tevyelook at their posts. Miserbiev said that an undetermined number of bandits had charged the camp at twilight, shooting wildly and yelling like crazy men to cover their main effort to pour kerosene and set fire to the roof. Volgamints said that he was sure he had hit one of them out back before the bandits had retreated into the tree line to let the fire rage. Fortunately, after burning out the hole in the wall, the roof had collapsed, burying the fire with snow.

I took command of the station as easily as I had of the scouting party by posing questions and giving practical orders. "Any casualties?" I asked. "Have you kept trying the field phone?" "How much fuel have we got inside?" "How many shells left for the shotguns?" The answers were predictable, and I gathered everyone outside the communications room to give our assignments. I wasn't so much ordering as I was taking the lead; however, the effect was that I was in command, and yet no one challenged me, not even cynical Volgamints. I told them that Vladimirovich had gone on to meet the southbound train, that we could expect him to return before very long, and that we could also expect relief from Magadan on the morning northbound train. I told them that we were secure inside as long as we didn't panic and that what was important was to keep the generator running and the station operational on the net. When no one contradicted me, I pressed on with remarks about our immediate duty to get Lympyet in from the storm, to get the generator refueled, and to get more barrels in from the cache. Soon I was speaking as if the bandits were no more significant a problem than a put-out fire. I appointed Adama-Bibliov, Doctor Gogol, and Volgamints to bring Lympyet in from the shelter, and I told Miserbiev to get dinner ready and to make it heavy and plentiful. Finally, with everyone off on the double, I asked Schtange and Tevyelook for a report on Uncle Dmitry's *Soyuz 4.*

"Amur is down on target, parachutes were good, retro was

good," Schtange reported on Uncle Dmitry's successful reentry and recovery. "He was down at seventeen fifty-three hours our time, about forty kilometers outside of Karaganda. All onboard were healthy and secure. Major Cherryntevsky reached them five minutes later." Cherryntevsky was in command of the search-and-recovery operation in north Kazakhstan, and to be on top of the command module within five minutes of landing was excellent even for a mother hen like him.

I asked after Uncle Konstantine, who wasn't scheduled to reenter for twenty-four hours, and was told by Tevyelook that Uncle Konstantine was so happy to be free of Uncle Dmitry's hectoring and Uncle Alexander's bossiness that he was singing desert ballads and love songs to his wife Doctor Mometov. "Good," I said, and then I gave Schtange and Tevyelook their assignment. "You two are going to have to go on all the remaining tours, because we'll need everyone else for security and the generator." I added, "We can do this easily."

I believed what I told them, but now I can see that much of my conduct was problematic. I was too much in charge, I took too much of the planning on myself, I didn't let the others make choices for themselves, and the result was that I wore down faster than the rest and found myself frightened of things that didn't exist or at least were farfetched. Sometime that night I started to believe that the bandits were in fact State Security goons who had been sent by Iagoda to capture or kill me, that what was really happening was a general attack on my uncles, and that this station was only the first of the coordinated campaign to wreck *Soyuz 4/5.* This was all nonsense, of course; those bandits were just bandits, sent by no one and after nothing but our cash, watches, and clothes—I repeat so that you won't make the same mistake I did and think that Iagoda was all-powerful and all-seeing: the bandits that attacked us were not Chekhist agents but drifters who were so desperate they threw their lives away for nothing—and yet I weakened myself with vain fears.

Once Lympyet was brought in safely—no sign of the bandits in the tree line—I ordered the hole in the wall sealed up with empty fuel barrels and floorboards, ordered the stove built up high to keep the instruments from freezing from the breach, ordered everyone to eat to their fill of the reindeer steaks, kasha, and bread. Serving out the food right away was smart and was the best order I gave all night. Soon after supper the wind shifted northerly again and strengthened, so that the cold stabbed into the station and threw drifting snow into the corridor like white ash. We were all upset that Vladimirovich didn't return. We argued among ourselves that he was all right, that he'd probably signaled the train and started back only to get lost in the storm, and so he was sheltering until daylight. Another version was that Vladimirovich had gone into Magadan himself to make sure there was relief for us on the morning train. Yet another version said that Vladimirovich had returned and, seeing the station was under siege, had gone down to the railroad camp to get help tonight. Our speculations were empty but they passed the time, and at first light on Saturday, January 18, we had fourteen hours to last out before we could shut down.

I slept sitting up in the corridor just down from the burned-out north wall. I had strangely comforting dreams of my father despite my distress. A phenomenon of desperation, I have discovered, is that when you are most at the bottom and should be feeling most hopeless you dream of finer things. What I dreamed was of a large, handsome general officer, all bright white like the snow in sunlight and carrying a box of fruit like a treasure. The fruit was for me, and I was allowed to approach this great white general who I knew was my father but looked both like my father's photos and like Uncle Alexander. I cried I was so happy to be getting a gift, and I was sure I would never be hungry again. The dream didn't make any sense, yet when Miserbiev and Volgamints woke me for my turn on the dawn watch I felt restored and resolved. I broke the ice-caked blanket from my face, took my bearings, and asked for the time. Miserbiev said it was 0530 and asked, "Not a sound all night out there. You figure they might be run off?"

Volgamints overheard us talking and remarked, "Shit, they're just waiting for the light. They'll wade in here and cut our throats as soon as they can see 'em. And for what? For the gold in our teeth, for the price of our boots. Shit." Dear grumpy Arkady Volgamints always had more and more cheerily depressing thoughts, and his rambling that morning seized upon an especially grim notion: "I don't mind dying, but you know I've always minded being turned into bones. It's seeing myself as just more bones that makes me feel I want to go on living, miserable as life is. What are we really but more bones for more walls. I'd like to think that the hard time I've had in this life should get me more than turning into bones."

I didn't pay close mind to his bones talk, too busy cinching up my greatcoat and leggings and trying to drink powerfully hot soup, but, after we'd awakened the rest of the station and certified all was well and gone out to position ourselves on either side of the shored-up hole in the wall, Miserbiev asked Volgamints, "What was that about bones, Volgamints, has the cold dried up your brainpan?"

Volgamints told us something that hadn't ever occurred to me. "This whole hill's built on bones, that's how crazy I am." Volgamints kicked out a cinderblock to make old chunks of concrete tumble from the wall. "See that there, in the masonry, those chips that look like pebbles, that's human bone."

Miserbiev was fascinated and stirred around the concrete with his fingers, saying, "It might be bone, but how do you know it's human?"

"Shit, boy," Volgamints said with a vile grin, waving out into the wind and the north slope of the hill, "this whole hill's built on bones. This was a slave camp, and they didn't bury them that deep, the ground's too hard in winter and too wet in summer. I can smell the bones, can't you? The whole place is bones. Bones, bones, it's like they grew bones up here, bones for the gold, bones for the bones, and bones for the mortar, too, ha!"

I was so stunned I didn't have anything to say. I'd known that Fool's Gold was built on the remains of a camp working a gold placer deposit, and I'd realized that this actually meant that there had been a slave labor camp here filled with zeks in the 1930s and 1940s, when the Kolyma River was like the valley of the shadow of death, but to my mind that was all generations ago. Now Volgamints made me see that those murdered tens of thousands had remains that couldn't be hidden. Stranger still than my astonishment at the bones was that the facts of it all made me feel stronger. I asked myself what could be worse than this, what else could go wrong, and having no answer I decided that it was time to put on an imitation of the shock commander's mask that I'd seen Uncle Alexander wear. The dawn came on very dimly and thickly through a dark gray cloud cover. Though it wasn't snowing, the wind was flinging the fallen snow sideways from the tree line into our faces and making us nearly blind if we stared straight out. Momentarily it was full light, and I heard myself using Uncle Alexander's stern, mumbly voice. "They'll come now," I announced to Miserbiev and Volgamints. "Pass the word; they'll come at us here."

"How do you know?" Miserbiev asked.

Volgamints said, "Shut yourself and tell the boys. Nevsky's right, shit, he's right."

"Here's what's going to happen," I told Volgamints, as if I were prescient, though that's what it felt like to see the whole battle in my mind as if it had already happened. "They're going to rush us and try to get inside with their rifles, since they can't see to shoot us at range." I got up from my position and took the side-by-side shotgun, giving over the single-shot to Volgamints. "Arkady," I added, "I'm going out left to give us flanking fire, you go out right. Lie down in the snow and let them pass you, then come on in shooting."

I took up my half-buried position in the soft snow and waited calmly. I think now that the explanation for my self-confidence, in profound contrast to the panic I'd felt the night before when I'd imagined Iagoda coming for me, was that peculiar dream I'd had of my father, which might have made me less afraid of death. In any event the battle was also like a dream to me, and perhaps the strangest of all facts that morning was that I went through the fighting and killing as if I'd done it all before, as if this were yet another in a lifetime of wars, as if I were both my father and myself at the same time, like father like son, a legacy of savagery for the Motherland, and if I seem forlorn about this, I suppose I am. We did fight savagely, for within moments of taking up my position, the bandits rushed the north wall from the tree line, firing their rifles and pistols blindly. There were at least a dozen of them, but they weakened their superior numbers by attacking in a pack and trying to overwhelm us in the first rush. My plan of flanking fire worked well. Volgamints and I gained sudden advantage as we came at the pack's back and blasted into their center. Then they were inside the wall where Miserbiev, Adama-Bibliov, Doctor Gogol, and the two Air Defensemen blocked them by using a post like a phalanx into their ranks. The battle was hand to hand and crazed. We had to close on them to overcome their pistols, which they used badly anyway, shooting into their own backsides when we counterattacked. I fired both barrels into them several times, and Arkady picked off their cross-eyed leader. When we were out of shells we used the shotguns like clubs. One of the bandits penetrated to the communications room, stabbed Schtange through the leg, and started to tear at the transmitter before Tevyelook brained him. Two of the bandits, trying to escape the trap we had them in, climbed atop the roof, and I went up with Adama-Bibliov to keep them from the array. I had shot many with buckshot, yet I helped kill those two with my hands and boots. Adama-Bibliov and I hacked at them with rods and then stomped on them until they stopped moving and threw them off. It wasn't courage, it was battle, and it kept on until I lost a sense of the field and could neither see nor hear. We wrestled and stabbed and kicked until there was no more screaming in the station and then we stopped. What must have happened was that the bandits, more beaten up than defeated—only the three confirmed dead—had broken off their attack and fled back through the north wall to the tree line. I don't recall all of it, and I depended on Doctor Gogol to tell me how bad things were for us. He said he wanted to treat two wounded bandits left behind in the station, and I told Volgamints to toss them out, and I said it again with Uncle Alexander's cruelest tone, "Get them out, now!" We interrogated one buckshot bandit, a gnarled little creature with his nut-brown face shredded by blows, and when he wouldn't talk we kicked at him until he cursed us. "Frig yourselves!" was all he said before he passed out, and I ordered him tossed out, too.

After the first attack we all knew that no rescue was coming for us. Either we fled the station or we were going to be overwhelmed and killed in the second attack. We also knew that we were staying on out of fury as much as our strict obedience to duty to maintain the station. The day dimmed as we waited for the second assault that didn't come. By last light Volgamints and I were propped back to back at the north wall, both beaten down, dizzy and exhausted by the waiting to die, since all we had was a captured pistol with several rounds. The others were also in poor shape: in the communications room Tevyelook was at his post, and in the radar room Schtange, despite his thigh wound, was propped up at the panel, while Doctor Gogol was moving among us with water and antibiotics, Adama-Bibliov and the Air Defensemen were loading more fuel out in the generator room, and Miserbiev and Lympyet were feeding wood into the stove. As hopeless as our circumstances were it made sense to me that Arkady Volgamints started singing. We might very well have all sung along for what use we were, since nothing we did kept us secure from another attack. Instead it was Siberia and the wretched January weather that came back on the station again midafternoon to heave a heavy snow up onto the north wall and west door, drifting snow as high as the array and sealing us up like hares in a burrow.

The only progress more important to us than the storm's was *Soyuz 5*'s, for, at 1840 hours our time, Uncle Konstantine pitched his spacecraft, burned his main engine for two and half minutes, jettisoned the orbital module and propulsion module, and then fiddled with the six thrusters on the command module as he rode his ship like a flying rock to ten kilometers altitude, where the parachute system activated, popping the drogue out at nine kilometers and the main chute at eight kilometers. The heat shield separated and *Soyuz 5* dangled toward a gentle landing—with one more blast of the solid-fuel landing rocket at one meter—and then plopped in a snow field near Karaganda at 1900 hours exactly.

At Fool's Gold we never heard the landing, because a half hour before the reentry procedure our communications and radar array failed in the wind, rendering us useless to the network. I ordered the generator shut down to save fuel. I gave the proper order, "Stand down," and it was like the air rushing out of our lungs. *Soyuz 4/5* was history, and we were released from our duty. We celebrated by lighting a lamp, pouring vodka and tea, eating from a collective pot stuffed with all the kasha, stew, onions, beets, potatoes, and meat we could fit in. It tasted as good as any meal I'd ever had. It also gave us heart for the howling night ahead and our thin hope that perhaps relief would yet come up from Magadan in the morning. I slept sitting up on a stool against the front door, and if I dreamed, it must have been of more food or maybe just a month's sleep. Doctor Gogol woke me at full light on Sunday, January 19, and said there were several men outside, hailing the camp. Volgamints warned me, "No deals with the bastards." Adama-Bibliov and I, who were the two fittest, dressed correctly in our greatcoats, cleaned our faces with snow, and went out to parley with what we thought were the bandits asking for terms.

What we found instead were reindeer herders, eight of them,

squat, savvy strong-backed Siberians, who were out early searching for strays after the five-day blow. They'd seen our stove smoke from the rail line and trekked up on the fore trail in hopes to take tea with the rumored cosmonauts and our spaceship, or so their thinking had been on the way up. Adama-Bibliov and I stared at them as if we didn't believe what they'd said, and they repeated themselves, "Comrade cosmonauts, we're poor herders, comrade cosmonauts!" We continued dumbfounded, staring for a long moment at our deliverers and then up to the sun as it broke through the crystalline tree line like a blaze in the sweet blue sky.

"Comrade cosmonauts, our dogs have found bodies, comrades!" the herders called and then pointed back to the fore trail. "Comrades, come and see!"

Soon all the cosmonauts were out in the clean white snowfield and, after pounding on the herders like maniacs, we followed them to see what they had discovered off the fore trail. There were four bodies scattered around a collapsed lean-to beneath the bows of a spruce, all of them greasy-coated bandits, and then farther down the fore trail, there were five more dead bandits. When we looked closer we found that they were all shot in the head. We reasoned that it could only have been done by Vladimirovich. After some arguing we figured he'd come back to the station sometime on Friday night and killed the four of them as they sheltered at a lean-to, reducing the first attack force by a third. And for some unknown reason he'd stayed out here and waited for us to fend off the first attack and then he'd killed five more bandits as they'd fled down the fore trail after breaking off. Vladimirovich had picked off nine men with a .22 in a blizzard; he'd brought down more than half the enemy with one shot each to the head as if they were game springing from buried brush. The explanation for why there hadn't been a second attack all day Saturday was not just the weather but also that the bandits were frightened off by an invisible partisan. But why hadn't Vladimirovich come in Friday night or Saturday after the attack? Where was he? We searched around the bodies and then spread out with the herders and their hunting dogs and swept along the steep south slope, but we found nothing. Our best guess was that Vladimirovich had been wounded when he'd shot the first four and had waited bleeding and immobile out here for his chance to kill more. We reconstructed his firing angles as best we could, but still the snow was so fresh and heavy that he could have been under meters of drift.

We broke off the search at midday in order to get our wounded ready for departure. With the help of the herders we hauled out Lympyet, Schtange, the Air Defenseman's corpse, and the fifteen bandits' corpses (the two I killed, the two we threw out who died of their wounds, the one we kicked to death, the cross-eyed leader Volgamints shot, the nine Vladimirovich shot), and flagged down the southbound train at the platform late afternoon. The trainmen told us they'd heard from their mates that Vladimirovich had signaled the afternoon train two days before, and that the trainmen had passed on word to the police at Magadan that there was trouble at Fool's Gold, but no one knew why the police hadn't come up for us. Perhaps it was the storm, the trainmen said, or perhaps the police didn't get paid enough to go out into the wilderness to battle marauders. We didn't stay at Magadan long enough to find out why we'd been left to die. We'd outlasted stupidity, so what was to be gained by trying to outlast lies? Bold, brave little Vladimirovich had saved our lives and then vanished into the wind to become a corpse for the birds and rodents to pick clean in the thaw, more bones in a wilderness of bones on the Kolyma.

My thoughts that day were most mundane, all to break camp and get back to Magadan and get out of Siberia. I wanted a flight for Moscow as soon as possible to find proper care for our wounded and for the infections we'd all picked up from exhaustion. Our concern about the weather deteriorating again meant that as soon as we reached Air Defense headquarters at Magadan we demanded to use their telephone so we could call Fedyuninsky at the Cosmodrome to have him assign us a good Il-14 out of the Sakhalin fields that could be diverted north to us. I can't remember thinking much more than about the weather reports, and my remark about Vladimirovich's bones was an afterthought. Volgamints wanted to make a fuss about how the Magadan police and Air Defense headquarters had ignored our pleas, but I told him to shut up, that it wasn't ours to worry about them not doing their duty as long as we'd done ours. There was brief excitement over the fifteen bandit corpses we'd brought in; however, even that faded when the local police chief, who wouldn't come himself, sent word that if we wanted the bounty on bandits we'd have to prove we killed them. Miserbiev's ironic comment at this outrage was, "If they were wolves we'd get the bounty in gold on the head." It might be news to you that we could find such corruption and dereliction and just walk away from it; however, at the time it seemed sensible to us to leave town quietly. What my uncles had taught us was that you took care of your own and kept going; there was nothing to do about the rot of the empire but to leave it behind. Magadan District was no worse than Dzhezkazgan District, and neither were any different than all the other towns that were burdened with millions of zeks and children of zeks who'd been abandoned by Lenin and Stalin and their Motherland to die alone like Vladimirovich.

By full light Monday, following a bad night at that drafty hovel of Air Defense headquarters fretting about how no one at Magadan seemed to care about Vladimirovich's body (the headquarters captain, a rotten little pensioner, said he'd write Vladimirovich's father a letter once they'd confirmed the death), we left all that folly behind and got airborne for Moscow. Fedyuninsky had used my uncles' prestige and sent us an Il-14 outfitted with litters for Lympyet and Schtange. I had a cushioned seat over the wing and was able to relax enough to sleep ten hours of the hopping flight. When I awoke I tried to finish my letter to Great-Uncle Lev and to start one to Katya, and yet after a few sentences in each I quit and started weeping. I thought it was fatigue, but I think my desolate mood was also because for eight days I'd done everything I could to do my duty, and yet what I had come to was sorrow. I balled myself into my seat, covering up with a blanket to hide my face from the others. I kept saying to myself, But we won, but we won, but we won, and yet I didn't believe it. I wonder now if the reason I didn't believe it was because I saw that by doing my duty I had become just another damned little hero who was getting used to the killing.

③

Assassination

Two days later the Corps celebrated the victory of *Soyuz 4/5* in front of an all-union television audience at Moscow. It was a bright, seasonal Wednesday, January 22, and the television cameras showed my uncles dressed in their parade-dress uniforms with all their medals beaming in the sunlight disembarking their special Party airliner at Vnukovo airport south of Moscow, then showed them parading down a red runner to a reception line made up of the highest Party and military bosses, then showed Chairman Brezhnev himself kissing them on the cheek, Prime Minister Kosygin giving them each bouquets of red flowers, and President Podgorny declaring in honor of my uncles' triumph that this was "Soviet Friendship in Space" week. Meanwhile the general staff primped and applauded, the Army band thundered brassy victory music, and thousands of airport workers and bussed-in schoolchildren cheered and sang songs and heaved flowers. We of the Cosmonaut Corps stood at attention on the airport tarmac, saluting our three greatest heroes.

You might know that this day was soon scarred by an assassination attempt on Chairman Brezhnev by two gunmen in Army uniforms who opened fire on the motorcade when it passed into the Kremlin yard. You might also know that State Security later claimed that it captured the gunmen and that, after a lengthy investigation, it was determined that the two assassins were mentally ill Army officers who had recently returned from Czechoslovakia, where they had been deceived by Western propaganda into thinking the empire was corrupt. If you check closely you might also find a footnote of that day that says that the assassins' gunfire missed Chairman Brezhnev's car and struck several cosmonauts riding in the open car just behind in the motorcade; however, no one was seriously wounded and all soon recovered easily and returned to duty.

I'm writing to tell you the truth of that day was that those assassins didn't aim for Brezhnev—he wasn't even in the motorcade when it reached the Kremlin yard—but rather they fired on my uncles and especially on Uncle Alexander. My mother finally used all her power over Iagoda and ordered him to launch an operation to gun down my uncles. My mother so hated and feared Uncle Alexander that she didn't even recognize a limit like the Kremlin when it came time to give him what he'd boastfully demanded, "Shoot through me!" I look at what she did that day and still struggle with the size of her crimes. Could it have been as simple as that as she was condemned, so she condemned? I wonder if somewhere in the wretchedness I saw at Dzhezkazgan and Magadan might not have been an explanation for my mother's evil. She wasn't born a betrayer, she had to learn how to damn as she was damned; and she learned from the most damned men in all Russia, she learned from the damned lie of the Bolshevik Revolution.

It's eerie and most sad how it can feel just last week that I was at Vnukovo airport, in the crowd at the landing gate, cheering my uncles as they were kissed by Brezhnev and flattered by Podgorny. I had recovered from my grieving fit with two sound nights of sleep at the barracks and with two noisy days of telling and retelling my adventures at Fool's Gold to all who'd listen, and I was again an arrogant little cosmonaut candidate. My version of Fool's Gold was most of what was heard at the barracks, because the disabled Lev Lympyet and ill Volgamints (who had caught the flu) were in hospital, and Doctor Gogol was not a boaster like me. Soon the gossip at Starry Town was that I'd commanded a last-ditch defense against a horde of Chinese invaders, and I didn't discourage Lieutenant-Colonel Khitrovo from thinking that I'd amounted to more than a truant. My head was so big that I rehearsed what I was going to say to my uncles when I saw them ("It was our job, sirs," was my favorite possibility), and I was ready to show my humility by crediting Schtange and Tevyelook with the true heroism of remaining at the station during the battle. In sum I was the happiest gamecock of the Corps, and I cheered and cheered when my uncles passed by arm-in-arm with the Air Force's Marshal of Aviation Vershinin and Corps Commander General Kamenin.

After the reception line broke up, the Corps was permitted to move in a mass over to the microphones to watch the award ceremony as it was televised. Genka Stumpelkin, who was just out of hospital, took my arm for support and, as we moved, mentioned what might have been the first warning sign of the plot against my uncles. "Did you see how the Chekhists backed off, Peter?" he asked, pointing to the uniformed State Security generals in the reception line who had indeed shied back from shaking hands with my uncles. "Peter, can you see General Iagoda? I doubt he's here. I'll bet he can't show his face, that bastard."

I told Stumpelkin to forget about Iagoda, he wasn't present and wasn't likely to cause any more trouble. "It's all over for him," I said, using Katya's argument at the Bolshoi, though I winced at this notion because I didn't believe it. I hadn't talked with Stumpelkin about the Bolshoi and wasn't sure I wanted to because of my lingering shame. He knew about it, of course, all the squadron did and probably also most of Starry Town, thanks to Miserbiev and Adama-Bibliov and the grapevine. "We've won, Genka," I said. "We've won and they've lost."

"Quivering Chekhist bastards," Stumpelkin emphasized. Getting shot in the back had made Stumpelkin temperamental and even cranky. He'd lost weight, and his dark good looks were fragile in the strong breeze. I'd missed him for the past two months, and I'd most missed his levelheadedness at Fool's Gold. I held him close by the arm now as if to keep from losing him in the crowd. We wedged forward to get as close as possible to the microphones, though before we could get a clear view, Marshal of Aviation Vershinin, a blocky, deeply jowly old grandfather, had already pinned gold stars on uncles Dmitry and Konstantine, and General Kamenin, flapping his somewhat smaller jowls, had pinned gold stars on Glavtop and Grin. Then it was Uncle Alexander's turn, and Secretary Ustinov himself pinned Uncle Alexander—a very gratifying moment, the boss of the space program congratulating the rebellious king of Starry Town as if they were old allies. Uncle Alexander saluted with his square shoulders like a launch platform and his chest a galaxy of decorations. Secretary Ustinov hadn't been able to add another gold star (Uncle Alexander already wore the limit of three), so the Party had given him his second Order of Lenin and, almost as if in apology, Ustinov had to tell Uncle Alexander that he was due a large salary raise. Hearing this the squadron smirked at each other, since Uncle Alexander lived like a pauper and no one had ever seen him handle money. The ceremony concluded with Chairman Brezhnev kissing my uncles and then losing his head and kissing the entire

State Space Commission including wizened little Blagonravov. Brezhnev was acting softheaded—and was probably more than a little drunk in celebration for having a victory-in-space to boast about on television after the ongoing fiasco of Czechoslovakia.

The television cameras turned to the Army band's performance while off camera Marshal Vershinin addressed the Corps as if it were his family of sons and nephews gathered around his hearth. Stumpelkin and I had to push closer still to hear him over the music. Vershinin surprised everyone by immediately promoting my uncles to general officers, so that the squadron now saluted Majors-General Oryolin, Strogolshikov, and Zhukovsky. I envied them extremely, and I imagined what I would look like up there if it were ever my day to be decorated and promoted. I specially admired Uncle Dmitry for taking time to duck aside and greet Angelicka and his daughters in the VIP area. I knew then he was the sort of man I wanted to become, a good father and loving husband as well as a hero. I also wanted to be like Uncle Alexander, though without his wrath and loneliness. The truth was that I wanted to be like both of them and perhaps also like Uncle Konstantine, too, and the contradiction here didn't interfere with my fantasy of becoming a happy, well-married, paternal, beloved, ferocious, hilarious, well-decorated, and wise major-general of the Corps.

Marshal Vershinin ended the ceremony by leading one more cheer, "Ooray!" and then escorted my uncles to the front of the airport to their open car in the motorcade. Stumpelkin and I detoured around the crush of the crowd and found Miserbiev and Adama-Bibliov at the parking area. We four had joined to persuade Artzybashev to call a debt and provide us a car of our own for the day. While we could have ridden in one of the Corps' autobuses, we wanted to get ahead of the motorcade for a good view of the procession as it reached Red Square. Stumpelkin and I hadn't been invited to the state reception in the Great Kremlin Palace, since I was still a lowly candidate (no longer on restrictions) and Stumpelkin was supposed to be in hospital, so that on the drive in we debated our tactics to crash the reception. Stumpelkin's opinion was, "They won't ask us for I.D. It's too big a day. We can just walk in with the others; we've got the right uniforms."

Miserbiev teased, "You think you can just stroll into Saint George's Hall? You don't know those thieves who run that place.

They'll want a hundred rubles each and your watch." Miserbiev, who'd been gorging since our return from Fool's Gold, was chewing so rapidly on buttered rolls that he became unintelligible, "Leave it—— I know ——"

We rocketed up M2 to reach the Garden Ring Road ahead of the roadblocks. Tens of thousands were already gathered along the route, because they had let out the government offices and schools to attend the motorcade, and the crowd had been swelled by the pensioners and loafers come out to enjoy the largest Cosmonaut Corps procession since Gagarin's seven years before. All Moscow looked to be singing, dancing, and particularly drinking three-on-a-bottle, and the crowds were soon so rowdy waiting for the motorcade that we had to quit our car near the river and dash across the Moskoveretsky Bridge on foot. Two policemen challenged us on the bridge, which I thought strange at the time, since we were clearly falcons and three of us wore the cosmonaut badge, and we ignored them as if they were pickpockets. I didn't make more of the policemen, nor did I make anything of the fact that there were squads of State Security regulars—the Blue Tabs—deployed throughout Red Square from the river to the Hotel Moskva. The Blue Tabs weren't armed but they were obviously on duty and in communication by radio with a central dispatcher. Now and again, as if practicing for trouble, the Blue Tabs linked arms by fours and eights and marched into the back of the crowd in order to cause sudden shifts. The most intimidating force was the Blue Tab guard mounted atop sorrel stallions, a squadron of horsemen stationed at each exit off the square. I ask now, since there never was an answer, was there supposed to have been a coup that day? Did other Lubyanka lords know that Iagoda was going to have my uncles shot, and so the Lubyanka lords decided to prepare for the worst and ready their troops to support a takeover of Red Square? Did they mean to go further and take over the Great Kremlin Palace too? How close did Russia come to a Chekhist coup against Brezhnev that day? I still can't figure all of what I saw, and the most I can guess is that the Blue Tab regulars and cavalry were probably working for Iagoda, too, and were standing by should the assassination go wrong.

It was about 1300 hours when the motorcade crossed the bridge and started up into Red Square. We four had made our way up to the other side of Saint Basil's, near the old execution block, and we could look back to see the crowds part like a grass field as the motorcade pushed through. The lead car was for the bodyguards; behind that came Brezhnev's car with Kirilenko and the now-ascendant Secretary Ustinov and Blagonravov; the third car contained my uncles with Glavtop and Grin; and behind them the general staff's cars followed in order of title, with Marshal Vershinin's car fourth or fifth in line. The Corps' buses were still on the bridge as my uncles' car reached the middle of Red Square and halted for the crush of the cheering crowd.

Despite the cold my uncles were in a topless limousine, one of the older kind, a gigantic black Zil, with jump seats and running boards. It was draped with red-and-yellow flower chains, its interior heaped with white blossoms. Uncle Konstantine was standing, and he had Laikushka at his chest and was waving her paws to the cheers. The schoolchildren responded wonderfully, crying, "Laikushka, we love you!" Many beauties crooned for Glavtop and Grin, and several girls ran up to kiss them. My uncles ordered their car on a little farther and then paused not far from Lenin's tomb, so that when they stood the photographers could frame them waving in front of the tomb itself. I could see how calculating my uncles were to encourage the tumult—Uncle Konstantine hoisting Laikushka over his head like a trophy, even Uncle Alexander raising his right arm to acknowledge the roars—and I could also see it was all a cunning performance. This was politics, Starry Town–style, for all Russia believed in heroes, all Russia was mad for heroes, and the Corps gave Russia what it wanted most—spacemen, rocketeers, cosmonauts, and those heroes of heroes, the Martian Troika, on parade. My uncles cooperated because they understood that as they gathered the passion of the people like flowers they could use it like thrust to drive the moon. This was such a triumphant day that no big boss could ever forget that the Corps was not only loved but also worshipped as the grandest socialist achievement, and that to deny the Corps anything was to deny the people's dreams everything. I felt the mass passion for the Corps, too, and it made me feel at the center of history, with the quarter moon in the luminous blue sky above, ours to take as all Russia cheered, "Hoorah! Hoorah!"

Miserbiev broke my mood with his idea to get into the Great Kremlin Palace. "Follow me," he said. "We have to get ahead of the motorcade, run." He meant that while the motorcade was going counterclockwise around the Kremlin via Karl Marx Prospect, we'd go directly to the Borovitskaya Gate and bluff our way into the Kremlin yard ahead of the wake of the procession.

I want to report now what I saw at the Borovitskaya Gate, because I want to show how carefully Iagoda had prepared the attack: Across Karl Marx Prospect there were two columns of Blue Tabs in single file with weapons raised at attention; on my side of the crossroad there were two columns of the Kremlin garrison's puppet troops also with weapons raised. The tower gate was open wide, and just outside the tower there was a squadron of Blue Tab mounted troops flanking the approach, while just inside the tower there was an armored personnel carrier decked with red carnations. I saw no officers in charge of the mounted troops or the puppet troops, just noncoms, and I saw no Chekhist goons in black leather.

I watched as the motorcade, which by then had circled the citadel, came slowly down the road while the crowd pushed out from the Alexander Gardens. At the turn into the tower gate, the lead security car veered off so that my uncles' limousine was first in line. Brezhnev's car had quit the procession in Red Square and entered the Kremlin at the Spassky Gate. I underline this detail, because the official explanation later claimed that the attackers fired on the lead limousine in the false belief it was Brezhnev's. This was all a lie, since an open car filled with Air Force officers was nothing like Brezhnev's closed-top limousine.

Miserbiev was still game for his plan to crash the gate, and he approached a puppet noncom at the foot of the gate and tried, "We're from Starry Town, comrade, we're going in now."

"Stand back," the noncom ordered us. "Give way."

We were ten meters outside the huge portals of the gate. I glanced inside and saw a mass of milling figures—cooks, servants, gardeners, all types of uniforms, also VIP Party men in sable caps and many small children raised on their fathers' shoulders, all come out to glimpse the famous cosmonauts. Then my uncles' car was even with us and halted when two blond teenage girls in national costumes climbed up on the runner in order to kiss Glavtop and Grin. Miserbiev, Adama-Bibliov, Stumpelkin, and I all cheered, "Keep kissing!" and that's when Uncle Konstantine spotted us and shouted, "Darlings, come aboard!" and indicated we should climb onto the running boards. "Give way, toy soldier!" Miserbiev told the noncom, and we four stepped out and started walking behind the limousine. Stumpelkin and I hopped onto the left running board, next to Uncle Dmitry, just as the car rolled forward again and through the gate. I remember how Little Laika was jumping from side to side, yapping at the horses, and how it felt as if the Great Kremlin Palace were looming overhead like a monster. I also remember how Uncle Alexander turned his head to us and, just when a normal man would have smiled tightly, he nodded forbiddingly. Stumpelkin nodded back in imitation, and I did too, and as I did I looked instinctively to my right side to gaze at the open vista of the Kremlin grounds and the merry, windswept blue sky beyond the Annunciation Tower.

That's all I can recall up to the instant of the shots. And then there were two muffled reports from a large-caliber automatic— *tphut, tphut*—and then there was a pause, and then one of the shooters emptied the rest of his clip, six more quick shots, *tphut-tphut-tphut-tphut-tphut-tphut*. I didn't know what was happening, but I felt the spray of glass shards and blood hit my face, and when I looked to where the noise came from I smelled the gunsmoke and spotted the last blue flame cough out of an automatic pistol. There were two shooters standing at the car's right front fender, and the shots had come so rapidly and wildly that they'd blown out the windshield. I don't recall hearing anyone's voice, though I clearly remember the screams. The limousine braked, and I was thrown forward and down, so that I had to keep my balance by grabbing the door handle. As I came up I was staring through the gunsmoke cloud directly at the shooters, two Army officers in black-tabbed tanker uniforms, each with a pistol, though the only one of them to have fired was the smaller of the two, a stocky blue-faced fellow. The larger, bug-eyed shooter stood frozen with his weapon hanging unfired in his hand.

The screaming became louder, and I looked to see that it was Little Laika, wailing like a dying human with holes so large in her intestines that her blood was spewing in an arc. Uncle Konstantine was hugging her to try to seal the holes. Her screams were awful to hear, a desperate, pleading screech. I looked for sympathy to Uncle Dmitry and didn't understand why he was so calm and glassy-eyed. At the far side of the couch Uncle Alexander seemed to be wiping his mouth and reaching out for Little Laika, while Glavtop had turned away from Little Laika as if to shield the girls from the blood spray. I could see that one of the beautiful girls had her mouth open crookedly and her neck was scarred across a dark line.

All this came to me as if in slow motion, and yet it must have been less than a second between when I regained my balance on the car door and when I attacked the shooters. I leaped forward and used my forearm on the big, bug-eyed tanker, and he crumpled down so that all I had to do was kick up once with my knee to catch his head. His neck snapped back like a hinge, and he fell against an edge on the car's undercarriage. Later they claimed he gashed his head on the car and that the puncture wound caused brain damage, though I doubted this then and am sure now it was a lie. State Security probably used the torture drugs on him until he had no brain left and then tossed him into one of their dungeons. I learned later that his name was Junior Lieutenant M. N. Gorky, twenty-one, who was said to be a distant nephew of the famous Soviet writer. The rest of his life was a horrible injustice, and it was said that he died seventeen years later, forgotten by his family and friends, alone, at thirty-eight, and I'm sorry for what I did to him, since he didn't shoot; he was a dupe of Iagoda and my mother and the Lubyanka lords.

The genuine assassin was the blue-faced shooter who had emptied his pistol into my uncles. Miserbiev and Adama-Bibliov dived over the limousine hood and ran after him, almost tackling him at the first rush but losing their grip as they struck the wall of bystanders. The blue-faced shooter was up like a gymnast and was too quick even for Adama-Bibliov's strides, and he soon vanished into the palace. State Security claimed later his name was Yeropkin and that they arrested him two days later, after he'd been denounced by his brother officers in the Kiev District. State Security also claimed that he'd confessed he'd meant to shoot Brezhnev, and that he'd confused the limousines, and that he was just back from Prague and mentally ill. All these were obvious lies, though I don't doubt there was a real Yeropkin whom they arrested and condemned to an asylum, but he wasn't the blue-faced shooter.

Everything happened at once, the shooting, the screaming, my attacking, the blue-faced shooter's fleeing; and while I was still bending over the felled shooter, Stumpelkin shouted at me to drive the car out of the yard, "Get the wheel, Peter, the wheel, get us out of here!"

It wasn't until then that looking back I realized my uncles were shot. Uncle Konstantine was struck in the hip, Uncle Dmitry was hit in the ribs, and Uncle Alexander was wounded the worst, two bullets between his lungs and stomach, so that he was sitting still in shock as he sucked air for a rattling breath.

The limousine driver's face was shot off, and I had to yank him over the side of the door and climb into his blood in order to get the car in reverse gear and back up. In my haste I backed up against the personnel carrier, and it rained flowers on the rear couch. I tried to get us started again, but we were blocked by Marshal Vershinin's car and it was impossible, so I shut off the engine. We were surrounded by general officers, and there were many hands reaching to help my uncles. I specially remember Corps Commander General Kamenin crying, "No, no! Please God, no, not like this, not them!" and also how Marshal Vershinin took off his hat and cradled Uncle Dmitry against his breast. "For God's sake," Marshal Vershinin kept repeating, "for God's sake, for God's sake—"

What I could do was stare at Uncle Alexander sitting stiffly and squarely against the leather couch. Kolya Grin had ripped opened Uncle Alexander's tunic coat and shirt and jammed a linen into the hole in his belly to stem the bleeding, but it wasn't working. Uncle Alexander's breathing was more labored, and his eyes weren't fixed, as if they wanted to roll upward. I remember thinking, He's going to die, that's what death looks like. And I remember wanting to tell Uncle Alexander something important about death but I couldn't think what, and I suppose it was fear of death more than good training that made me stand up on the front seat and call out for help, "Medics! Medics!" After Little Laika's screams died, Uncle Konstantine caught my trouser leg and spoke flimsily but clearly to me, "Here now, Petya, here now, no hurry now, here now, let's have some peace."

Off to the side of the car Valya Glavtop wept over one of the teenagers, who died within the hour, seventeen-year-old Tula Volkhov, as innocent as imaginable, murdered for nothing by my mother.

Shock explains some of why I have so few memories from the Kremlin yard until the following week, and I wonder now if the shootings coming so close on my exhaustion after Fool's Gold didn't crash me into black and blank despair. It was as if my world had dimmed when I saw my uncles shot down. I'm sure I saw the ambulances, the medics, the transfer to the polyclinic where they took all three of my uncles into surgery; I'm sure the squadron met several times in the next days at Black House to hear medical reports—Uncle Alexander was wounded very badly and faced many operations—and to review repeatedly the sequence of events that led to the shootings (Zhora Fedyuninsky led our discussion, and I owe my assumptions about the assassins to his genius); I'm sure, too, that I was with the squadron at the funeral for Tula Volkhov, whom we buried with military honors at her parents' home. And yet I can't picture any of those days as wholly as my usual memories, as if I were physically present but mentally AWOL. I know I wrote all the events down in several letters to Katya, and if I had those letters now I could verify the details to myself, but I don't, and so even the writing of the letters is sketchy to me. It might be that over the years I've seen so many struck down, I've waited on so many surgeries, I've buried so many friends, I've lived so long with the heartbreak of irreparable loss, it sometimes feels as if I'm always knotted up inside, afraid and dumbstruck, at the hospital or bedside or graveside and helpless before fate. Perhaps, too, I didn't want to think clearly about what had happened because I'd realized as soon as I heard the shots that it was my mother who had ordered my uncles shot down, that I was the son of a woman who would murder heroes and innocence and the hope of all Russia. No one spoke to me about it, but then no one had to say anything for me to know as I stood by listening to the discussions about the assassination that I had been an impotent dupe in the conspiracy against my uncles. If I wasn't to blame for the ruin, then I was undeniably part of the blame, and I speculate now that, as shame-scarred as I was, I might have collapsed from self-disgust if not for the miraculous antidote of grief.

What I next am clear about, and what was next critical to the ongoing catastrophes that now came at Starry Town like death blows, was my visiting Uncle Dmitry at the Starry Town medical center. It was a blizzardy day, and my diary has it marked Sunday, February 9. I had been told to go to see Uncle Dmitry; in fact I was told by Lieutenant-Colonel Khitrovo, who, since the shooting, had become markedly sympathetic toward me. My heroics at Fool's Gold had boosted me in his eyes, and I was again at the top of the class by scores and performance, but the real reason he was kind toward me was that I had knocked down one of the assassins at the car. Khitrovo was like many at Starry Town, who had learned something of the whole story and didn't choose to get involved more than to show their prejudices; and Khitrovo's prejudice was that my uncles were now immortals so that anyone whom they favored he favored. There was a wild rumor at the barracks that I was Uncle Alexander's bastard son, which is a good example of how some people wanted to deal with the tragedy—that it was a family affair, that they should stay out of it and wait to see how it turned.

At the medical center the nurses guided me to the second floor, and I found Uncle Dmitry seated in a wheelchair by the window in an otherwise empty ward room. He was in a new blue dressing gown and seemed very composed as he smoked slowly and watched the snowfall. I announced myself with a salute and offered the well wishes of the candidates' barracks and tried a brisk, "Sir! It's great to see you, sir! And that's a handsome new robe, sir."

"Yes," he said, patting his dressing gown, "Anna made it for me, isn't it fine to have a daughter who can make such a thing, isn't it fine?" He sounded most gentle. He touched the chair by the window. "Sit yourself, Petya. I've called you because we have to come to some understandings; this is personal, sit by me." I obeyed quickly, and as he saw my forlorn look he started again, "We've had some excitement, there's no denying it." He tried a paternal smile and continued, "And you had some excitement at Magadan, I've been told, Trifya and Yurka told me, you had too much excitement out there."

My fantasy version of my report of Fool's Gold faded in my mind and I said, "It was bandits, sir, and we were very lucky to get away."

"Yes, you were," he agreed. "They've let Vasya and Tima out of here now, and I don't want any more of you checking in. What were you lot thinking to hold on to a post like that? Did you think it was more important to us than you are?"

In response I mentioned some details of Schtange's and Tevyelook's woundings, and I brought him up to date on my friend Lev Lympyet's broken ankle and my friend Volgamints's bad cough, and how Doctor Gogol was the real hero for nursing us through the ordeal. All this talk was stalling on my part, for I could feel that Uncle Dmitry was about to be very grave. I think I used the word *setback* when I talked about Lympyet's ankle not healing correctly.

Uncle Dmitry interrupted me, "Yes, we've all had a setback, haven't we?" and then he smoothed the mound of dressing on his left side under his robe and said, "It's right to speak aloud what's happened, and what's happened is that we had some good luck, and then we had some bad luck, and there's no need to go on about the bad luck. Everyone's still with us, and we have much more than we did before. We have a man-rated Soyuz, and we're all ready to go again, aren't we? All except for Laikushka, all of us are ready to go except her. Almost all."

We had buried Little Laika beside the Black House in a grave so small that it hurt me to look at the little mound and think of how she'd died—but I knew that wasn't why Uncle Dmitry was sounding so grim, and I was afraid it was the rumor that Uncle Alexander wasn't recovering and that the last operation might have left him critical. Still I didn't know how to ask such a thing and said, "Little Laika, sir, and that poor girl, Tula Volkhov."

Uncle Dmitry slumped a moment. I learned much later that the death of Tula Volkhov had struck him very hard because he'd pictured his own daughters lying there; and it had hurt him to think of his dying and leaving Anna and Marya vulnerable to a world that could gun down a seventeen-year-old beauty. Then Uncle Dmitry came out of his cloud, sucked his cigarette, and said, "All bad luck, Petya, all bad luck behind us, and we're due for some soft landings ahead. There's not time for us to sing sad songs of the dead." And with that he raised his bony head to the light so that the reflection off the snow made his face glow bright white. Having steadied his mood he said, "Now that's done, and we know better luck's ahead, we can talk about some of the good things to come, such as you and Katya."

I was prepared for him to mention Katya and replied, "Yes, sir, I've been writing her every day. I'd call her, except that you said it was best I didn't. I do wish she'd write me back."

"She's well, and she's healthy. Angelicka talks with her almost every day, and Katya's very busy. I haven't said so before, Petya, so I want you to know that I think the news about the baby, about your child, I think it's great and grand news. A child is the best news. I think marrying Angelicka and having Anna and Marya was the best news of my life, and I want Katya and the baby to be the best news of your life."

I wanted him to be my father so I could share with him all my doubts. "Yes, sir, thank you, and I'm hoping we can be married soon—if her divorce is done, and if I'm invited into the Corps, and if we can find a place for us and Daniel and the baby, and if Katya says she'll marry me—because you see, sir, since she hasn't said she will marry me, not definitely, and the way she left at the theater that night, well, I keep writing her and asking her, and she hasn't replied, not once."

Uncle Dmitry wasn't listening. He was preparing to tell me what he knew I didn't want to hear. "Here is what's so hard to understand, Petya. I'm asking you to delay your future. For a while. I'm asking you to put off your plans about marriage."

"Yes, sir," I said without meaning it.

He said, "You have a right to know why I'm asking you. I can't and won't order you, so you should ask."

I knew why, and my throat felt lead lined when I swallowed and declared, "It's because of my mother, sir, my mother and General Iagoda and my mother's feud with General Oryolin."

Uncle Dmitry leaned to the side of the chair and began his version of the story of my birth and the feud, and while it was similar to the three discrete versions Iagoda and Katya and Uncle Alexander had told me, it was also helpful to hear Uncle Dmitry shape the details for his own purposes. He said my father was an extraordinary officer, who, if he'd lived, would now be standing side by side with Marshal Vershinin at the head of the Air Force. He also said that my father was a man who had a very high opinion of his own abilities as a lover of women, and that he had taken up with a beautiful young woman named Daemonia Romodanovsky during the war, even though he'd known she was a Chekhist agent. Uncle Dmitry said that State Security had spied on everyone as successful as my father and that my father had boasted that he was so important he deserved the most beautiful informer in Russia. "The queer thing is that they loved each other," Uncle Dmitry said. "I'm certain they did, no two people who act like they did—happy to be around each other, always laughing at good news and fixing each other's meals or worrying when either was away—no couple acts like that unless they're in love. Perhaps it wasn't a mature love, maybe they were careless and troublesome, but it was the war. It was like that for all of us. None of us thought we'd live. None of us at all." Uncle Dmitry said that near the close of the war my father had been promoted to take charge of all the Fourth Air Army's fighter commands for the final campaign on Berlin and then, at war's end, had been elevated to command of the Fourth Air Army. This had meant my father had to leave his air regiment behind in Byelorussia, and so he had appointed Uncle Alexander to take charge. He had also asked Uncle Alexander to look after my mother, who was then pregnant with me and whom he didn't want to take with him to his new headquarters. "He left her with Sasha, with us, he left her behind," Uncle Dmitry said. "It was something that we did then. None of us didn't do it, none of us didn't have a girl that we left, none of us didn't do things we were ashamed of afterward." Uncle Dmitry reminded me that my father had tried to provide for my mother. "It might seem strange to say now, Petya, but then we felt that your mother needed looking after, and leaving her with us was a way of helping her. You see, she and Sasha had grown close by then. You might say they were the two people closest to your father, they had your father in common, and they were drawn together, you understand."

If my mother and Uncle Alexander were lovers while she was still with my father, or if she and Uncle Alexander became lovers in the period between my father's leaving and my birth, nevertheless my mother didn't stay long with Uncle Alexander. Uncle Dmitry wasn't forthcoming about what happened afterward, between 1945 and my birth in 1946. I've already told you what I know of this period (which I learned from Anna many years later): that my mother went back to Moscow, submitted herself to the Lubyanka lords to become a whore of the empire, and then abandoned me to my father's family in Leningrad—just sent me to my father's wife, Marya, as if I were a suit of clothes my father had left behind.

Uncle Dmitry skipped ahead to my mother's return to Uncle Alexander in the winter of 1947. They married, and my mother took up a privileged position as a hero's wife, except that she was now spying and informing on every officer she met, especially the decorated heroes like my uncles. Soon my mother was pregnant again, which caused a falling-out between her and Uncle Alexander— "Your mother didn't think she was someone who should have children," Uncle Dmitry said, "and she wanted to end the pregnancy but didn't, and I suppose she blamed Sasha for her situation"—that led to her leaving him as soon as she'd had the child, Sophia. My mother took Sophia with her, yet, when Sophia fell ill with polio in 1949, my mother put her in a sanitarium in Moscow, where she died alone, before her second birthday. By then the Stalinists had launched new purges against the Party and military. My mother had denounced and testified against my father and my uncles, and they were all condemned to the slave camps.

"I don't know what happened to your father, Petya," Uncle Dmitry said, "but he was probably shot in early 'forty-nine with the first executions of senior staff, when they shot four thousand officers in a month. I don't know where, but it was probably in transit. They sent our cadre to hell that year. But they didn't keep records you can rely on, so all we have are rumors, and dead men don't carry tales."

Uncle Dmitry didn't pause to describe his own imprisonment; he just said that he and uncles Konstantine and Alexander had spent five years in several camps, mostly together with other Air Force veterans, and that they'd been released to internal exile in 1954 and pardoned in 1955 to become test pilots in the Kazakhstan ranges.

Uncle Dmitry did want to address what he made of my father's and Uncle Alexander's love for my mother. "They were two very fortunate men—your father was only thirty-four when he left your mother, and Sasha was only twenty-four when he tried to take her in the first time," Uncle Dmitry explained. "And your mother was a very, very proud and difficult woman. And beautiful, you can see that, she was always very beautiful and a great pleasure for the eyes; the priests would have once said she was a sin of the eyes. It wasn't right what they arranged, trading her off between them like that, trading you off too, but they did it, and at the time they thought it was what she wanted, too, and what they thought had to be done. Your mother said she liked it. She even teased about getting a younger hero for an older one. But I knew even then she was angry, and when she left us the first time to have you we didn't feel right about what had happened. And when she came back, after leaving you with your father's family, we knew she was still angry. It wasn't all one thing. I can remember thinking that it was probably best that she'd left her baby—you—with your father's people. She wasn't a woman who cared for motherhood. She's a passionate woman, she was once, and she was treated badly, and I suppose she's had her revenge."

Uncle Dmitry finished sadly as if the memory of my mother made him feel his regrets for his own life. "What happened later doesn't change what was between your father and mother when you were conceived. They made you with love, Petya, you should always remember that. What happened later, now we all have to live with it."

Uncle Dmitry had talked for a half hour, perhaps more, and I didn't interrupt once and waited for him to ask me if I understood him or had any questions. Instead he stopped talking suddenly and stared at me. "You're a good young man, Peter Apollonovich, and your father would have been proud to know you."

I wasn't mature enough to accept this compliment as profound and burst out instead with my darkest question, "But, sir, you haven't told me why my mother had my father arrested. Why did she have you arrested? Why has she done this to you now? Because she was angry with you, is that the reason?"

Uncle Dmitry nodded. "I don't know. She was angry, but I don't know."

I complained in a shaky voice, "There must be a reason."

"I don't know," Uncle Dmitry complained back, "though I once thought I did, I once thought she struck back when she felt attacked, and if we didn't threaten her she'd leave us alone. But I was wrong, and what I know now is that she will strike at us again and again until she's finished us. If that's a reason, that it's her nature to act like this, then that's the only reason I have, that your mother's been the same as long as I've known of her, more than twenty-five years now she's been a woman who's true to herself."

I declared my confusion, "You mean that my mother abandons and destroys people because she wants to? That's not a reason!"

"No, it's not a reason," Uncle Dmitry agreed, and then he changed his manner and spoke to me as a commander. "There is a reason why I've told you all this about your mother, however, and you must hear what I'm asking you. You must not leave Starry Town. There can be no exceptions, no trips with your friends, no running off to see Katya. You must not try to see Katya, Petya, you'll only give them an excuse to hurt her, and you'll accomplish nothing in any event. We can protect ourselves here, but not away from here. We're badly off now. I'm telling you how it is and must be. We're in a bad way. Sasha needs time to heal as best he can, and Kostya and I need time to get back to duty, maybe within a month. But for now it's as if we were under siege, exactly like that. And you must listen to me. Your mother and General Iagoda are a constant threat. She's a threat to all of us, including to you. This isn't bandits. Iagoda is powerful, and all the more so since they've done this to us and we couldn't stop it. For now, they're too powerful to take on. Understood, Petya?" he asked.

My "Yes, sir," was hushed.

Uncle Dmitry didn't sympathize with me, for he had harder goals, and he spoke as sanguinely as he could, "Our luck's not with us just now. Iagoda has the high ground for the moment, and the Chekhists are in control now, and what we have to do is bide away the winter and wait for our time again. It will come, maybe in the spring, but not now; now we need time to heal."

Uncle Dmitry's try at optimism about our dilemma made it possible for me to hear and understand the deep level of defeat in his voice, and this rocked me more than anything he'd said. "What's happened, sir?" I demanded. "Is it Katya?"

"No, no, she's well, I told you."

"But sir, why are we pulling back now? You said we have more than before. We're hurt but we're all still here, you said so. So what's gone wrong, can you tell me?"

"Your mother's had her revenge," Uncle Dmitry said, "and it's a complete revenge, and we have to live with it."

Then Uncle Dmitry showed me the truth behind the rumors about Uncle Alexander's condition. He tried to stand but it made him dizzy, so he sat back in his chair and had me push him across the corridor to Uncle Alexander's room. Uncle Konstantine, who seemed robust in his gray hospital gown, had been seated by the bed reading a book aloud when we came in, and he stood quickly on his good leg and tried a toothy smile, asking Uncle Dmitry, "Have you told him?"

I looked at Uncle Alexander and felt the horror before I understood it, for though he was napping quietly in his bed he was laid out like a dead man, unshaven, yellowy, his hair gone white, tubes down his nose and throat. The worst of it was that from the way he was arranged I could guess at the truth that he was paraplegic.

Uncle Dmitry told me anyway, "He's lost the use of his bowels and such. His colon's wrecked and his intestines are all wrong, and his spine was cut so that nothing works below. They've operated again and again, and we should have lost all of him in the last one."

Uncle Konstantine slumped to the side and used his walking crutch to move to the wall, and just when he might have bent a proverb to spread hope about the room—something duly jovial such as "There are three ways to do it, the right way, the wrong way, and the Russian way!"—he said nothing and settled back heavily against the wall with such a broken heart that I could hear a soundless groan.

"We should've lost him," Uncle Dmitry repeated about Uncle Alexander, "but he wouldn't go, or he doesn't know how to go, or he wanted to go but he came back for us, something like that." Uncle Dmitry touched the bedstead and stated the worst. "Sasha's permanently crippled, Petya, and he won't fly again, or walk again, or"—he waved at his waist—"be a man again, not that way."

I felt as if I should touch Uncle Alexander's legs to prove it wasn't true, but it was, and through the blizzard that afternoon I sat with my uncles and tried to accept that Alexander Oryolin was half dead. We might have been there for an hour waiting for him to wake up, with the hospital sounds around us and a solicitous nurse or two who kept looking in on our needs. Eventually Uncle Alexander did wake up; however, it took him much too long, and as he came out of his sleep his breath made such sorry sucking sounds that I worried he was going to gag for air. Then he opened his eyes and looked at me, and I told him how good it was to see him. I was lying—he looked worse alert than he had asleep and he smelled of medication and bandages and the sweet-sour odor of dying flesh—and he knew I was lying and didn't care to respond. I felt worse again when Uncle Alexander started to urinate and we could hear the urine trickling down the tube into a bag. Soon I found myself sitting with the three men I worshipped like gods and yet feeling that I was alone in the room. It was even worse than this, it was as if they were dead, it was as if they were long forgotten and only I were able to recall how they'd once been the greatest of the great; the king, the prime minister, and the jester, the Martian Troika. I can still feel my disorientation at sitting there among them and sensing that they were already gone and that they wanted me to remember them but didn't know how to say to me, "Remember us for what we were, Peter Apollonovich, not for how we fell to earth."

When the nurses brought supper, small trays of oatmeal that Uncle Konstantine wouldn't have noticed a week before but now ate meekly, I made excuses and left the medical center in a daze, struggling through the drifts back to barracks and letting my tears freeze in the wind. I wrote Katya that night that I was for the first time ever scared in a way that I couldn't make go away. I also told her what Uncle Dmitry had said of my mother and that no matter what happened I would never leave her and the baby, but that for now Uncle Dmitry had asked me to remain at Starry Town and not risk provoking more trouble for her. I told Katya that she had been right about my mother being done, but that it was too soon to know how we could stand up to my mother's and Iagoda's evildoing. I also told Katya that I loved her more than ever before, and that if I couldn't marry her now, then someday soon all this would go away, and she and I and Daniel and the baby would escape to our private star.

You might think that my attachment to Katya was forced, that I made too much of our love, given that we'd been together perhaps three or four months in our lives and that what we had in common was failure and an unborn child; but I remind you how fiercely a boy can love his first love, and that if I put too much on Katya then I'm glad now that I did, she was my salvation for all the years afterward when I was alone. Also writing such a heartfelt letter while sitting in the orderly room at the barracks, midwinter at Starry Town in a Russia paralyzed by fear as profoundly as Uncle Alexander was crippled by gunshot, was all I had to hold on to of my dreams of a new world to conquer, and I clutched for Katya in my imagination and wept for what was lost.

"Fools Shoot, God Reloads!"

February was the darkest month in the history of the Cosmonaut Corps. The hard fact of Uncle Alexander's crippling injuries leveled the squadron and then knocked down all Starry Town. The Corps' morale was so low it was as if it had been robbed of children and savings as well as health, and that everyone was old and abandoned without rest or hope, for the greatest among us was grounded by his all-ascendant enemy, and our ambitions for the moon were gone with Alexander Oryolin's strength.

What made this defeat even worse was that Iagoda grew stronger and stronger. Midmonth there was a raft of harsh editorials in *Pravda* and *Red Star* and *Izvestia,* all to the point that Russia had been safer and stronger under Stalin and the might of State Security than under today's vacillating bosses and their compromises with foreigners and weaklings. The editorials called for a new crusade of law and order that would not tolerate any more protests, dissent, wrecking, or hooliganism. The editorials topped their menace with a call for an all-union celebration of Stalin's ninetieth birthday the following December, a spectacle that would have been unthinkable in the hazy climate before Czechoslovakia but now seemed logical as a symbol of absolute state power. February saw the rebirth of the potency of the Lubyanka lords, and though their tyranny had been coming for over a year, and certainly since the Czechoslovakian invasion, the shootings at the Kremlin made it clear to us that State Security had regained its suzerainty.

I recall all this stated ironically by Zhora Fedyuninsky, the squadron's chief in the absence of my uncles, when one night at Black House he summarized the current politics: "The fools want Stalin back. It's the Stalin cult, they want him back. We're still burying his 'errors,' and they're digging him up. We're going to bow and scrape to his mummy. They're going to put a mummy on television and move his mouth while they tell us to fall down and love him for being our leader despite his death." We didn't laugh; instead we lowered our heads and mumbled and drank and complained that what did politics matter, Alexander Oryolin was down.

You might ask why I go on about all this treachery and tyranny now, when it's long since fixed that the Stalinists and their offspring were stupid monsters and that the only thing they accomplished was to torture Russia with fire and knout for several generations and then vanish into their own lies as if they'd never existed, but I answer back that unless you take into account that it was Russia's fate to suffer those rotten souls like a bear tied down and tortured in pieces, you can't understand why my chronicle from the white nights of June 1968 until the dark nights of February 1969 is a miserable record of reversals and losses. All Russia is fate, true; however, fate doesn't come clearly, it comes mysteriously. It was the Corps' mysterious fate to lose and lose, it was State Security's mysterious fate to win and win. What you've watched happen from summer until winter was in fact the strangulation of the Corps and the ascension of State Security. I know I haven't deliberated over the mountains of facts of the reaction, yet look at what I have mentioned—the invasion of Czechoslovakia, the persecution of Katya's university friends, the flagrant abduction of a state scientist into a secret dungeon, the total depravity of Dzhezkazgan District and Magadan District, an attack on heroes in the Kremlin yard—and realize that, despite all this rot, there was no law to make the criminals answer; and the reason I haven't wasted words carping about crimes is that there was no court to go to and say, for example, that my uncles were shot by a hired assassin. What I have been able to show you in particular is some of the rise of General Robespierre Iagoda and his Fifth Directorate. Simultaneously all of State Security was reaching for the crown of the empire with a slow-motion coup d'état. The truth of it was that by February the Corps' bright hope for the moon was as imprisoned as if it were in the Lubyanka's dungeon, and there was no one who could stand up and take back our own, and only the mystery of fate could save us.

In March there was fate aplenty. I was at Black House the wet night of March 8 when there was the first break in our state of siege. I recall it as another gloomy Saturday in a string of them since the shootings. The Corps' mood had fallen so far that the past week the grapevine at Starry Town actually had welcomed the news of the new American orbital mission, *Apollo 9,* since even if our moon-driving was now out of the question then at least we could participate like a good audience for NASA. That evening the whole of the squadron, absent my uncles but now including not only me but also my friends Volgamints, Lympyet, and Doctor Gogol, who had earned their invitations at Fool's Gold, had drifted through a raging sleet storm out to Black House in order to drink and complain and also to hear a briefing on *Apollo 9*'s mission by Fedyuninsky and his studious protégés, Tima Schtange and Vasya Tevyelook. We settled down in the living loft and heard that what the Americans were doing was imitating the success of *Soyuz 4/5.* Five days before, the Americans had used their big Saturn V booster to launch an Apollo command capsule with a three-man crew along with a lunar lander housed in the booster—the premier spaceflight of the lander. The mission's aim was to practice the rendezvous and link-up of the two spacecraft, to certify the spacesuits and spacewalking abilities of the crew, to transfer the crew from the command capsule to the lander via the internal hatchway (the Americans didn't plan to spacewalk between craft as we did), and then to separate from the lander and bring down the crew as if they were returning from the moon. In all we were told that the Americans were rehearsing the same steps my uncles had made two months before in order to prepare their systems for an LOR moon-landing mission perhaps as early as summer.

The American mission did not meet our approval, and after a half hour of numbers and tangential anecdotes Tevyelook summarized *Apollo 9* condescendingly as he pointed to his charts. "Their spacesuits are overbuilt but adequate for short bursts. The rendezvous and docking maneuver today was barely adequate and sluggish, very messy toward the lock-on and, for all the backups they've got, not worth the trouble. They've spent dearly for what they've got up there, and they haven't achieved any more than we have. Much the same sort of problem actually—ground control won't let them fly their own ships, they look over their shoulders and overcall their commanders' instincts, and the missions are burdened with busywork and chatter."

Schtange smiled at his friend's fussiness and remarked, "In any event the result, comrades, is that the Americans are now as ready as we are for an LOR. They can do it as soon as the next shot, if they want, though for now they're saying that *Apollo 10* won't be the landing but a rehearsal in lunar orbit."

What Schtange said was dazzling—that the Americans were now so skilled, confident, and wealthy that they could schedule an LOR rehearsal in lunar orbit with all systems and yet not actually have to land—and perhaps just because of the grandeur of the American feats the squadron responded to the news with jeers and the wild claims, "We've got them where we want, right behind us!" and "We're ahead!"

"No, we're not," Schtange countered.

"Yes, we are!" we declared, pigheadedly ignoring that we lacked a booster, a spacecraft, and an assignment.

Schtange and Tevyelook restated their conclusions, since they'd devoted five days to eavesdropping electronically on the American mission and had acquired many details that no one cared to hear. They kept talking regardless of our catcalling, two fastidious engineers who were worse about their obsession for chess and numbers ever since Fool's Gold had elevated them into unselfconscious heroes. Fedyuninsky stepped in to arbitrate and, when we wouldn't quiet down, he taunted us, "The Americans are ahead of us. And they're more ready than we are. And they're so close to the moon they can touch it anytime they want. They've got Saturn V. They've got a man-rated moon lander. They've got a garage full of capsules and money."

We protested, "We've got Tsar Cannon."

Fedyuninsky insisted on being as realistic as he was provocative. "Where is it?" he challenged. "Have we launched Tsar Cannon? Is it man-rated? When do we see it? What good is a booster that hasn't launched a lander that doesn't exist with a spacecraft they won't give us for a crew we haven't got?"

This was so negative an accounting that we threw food and hooted him down with more of our nonsense. The Black House was only a step above a hovel, and we were crowded like poultry among the rude benches, burlap walls, and the roasting tile oven. We had slabs of salted fish, many cooking pots spilling over with kasha and onions and several racks of lamb brought up from the open fire they kept in the stockpen below, and our big mouths took comfort not only in boasting but also in imitation of Trifya Miserbiev's ceaseless gluttony. The plank floor had become a smelly heap of food scraps, and with Little Laika gone there was nothing to be done but heave the bones and bits out the cracks in the windowpanes. I admit that in spite of the bitter conditions—the sleet was raking the roof and the wind made the chimney sound like moaning—I was enjoying myself and felt blessed to be present. It had been my idea to get my friends Volgamints, Gogol, and the still invalided Lympyet invited (Fedyuninsky had said, "No need to ask, Lieutenant, they are most welcome"), and I was mighty pleased at how they admired the squadron. I was more mightily pleased with my dear Orenburg brothers—fat Miserbiev and skinny Adama-Bibliov, earnest Stumpelkin and felonious Artzybashev and Kandidim, the maternal Cherryntevsky and haughty Fedyuninsky, and of course the beautiful Glavtop and Grin—all of them selfish, vulgar, reckless rascals, yes, but they were the sort of rascals I'd come to understand were the backbone of the Corps just because they were endlessly loyal to my uncles' dream of the moon. It made no sense for us to brag of our tattered chances to drive the moon or to deny NASA's impending victory. And yet together we happily ridiculed the Americans for their overbearing wealth and overbuilt spacecraft, and together we just as merrily ignored our poverty and want. If braggadocio could have launched a superbooster, we could have parked Black House in lunar orbit that night.

We knew our high spirits were a sham. Without my uncles we were helpless to go anywhere but to bed; and my uncles weren't even up to the walk to Black House anymore, perhaps not ever again, so the moon for them was a lost ambition. Also the reports from the medical center were solemn: Uncle Alexander was said to be weaker still while recovering from his third major operation to resection his bowels; Uncle Dmitry was said to be coughing blood and was confined to bedrest; Uncle Konstantine, who had been mending, had broken his foot in a rage at the weakness in his bad leg and was said to be hobbling the halls of the clinic talking to the ghost of Little Laika. Given such unrelieved bad news, we swam in our noisy self-deceit, and by the volume of juice being consumed no one was planning to go home gently. Great-Uncle Lev might have said that we laughed not to cry and we drank to drink. My memory is that I was trying to join in by sipping at the vodka and was feeling flushed and dizzy when the moment came for fate to turn our way.

It was a miraculous fate, and it arrived very late in the evening with a pounding and helloing from the stockpen below: "Darlings!" came the unmistakable bellow of Uncle Konstantine; "Darlings! Here's the dead risen! Here's the main chance! Come down and hear all about it! Darlings, God reloads! Haw haw! We've got the main chance! God reloads! Fools shoot, God reloads!"

We rushed out of the living loft and swung down to the stockpen floor to greet Uncle Konstantine and Uncle Dmitry both surprisingly out of the hospital and arrived in their own staff car (as generals they now had a car and driver). Uncle Konstantine was on crutches for his smashed left foot, and Uncle Dmitry stepped cautiously like an invalid, yet they looked grand to us in their beautiful general's greatcoats, rich fur caps, and white silk scarfs. Also surprising was that they were arm-in-arm with a colonel in bomber command who was still in his flight gear. Uncle Dmitry recommended, "Put up with Kostya, I'll explain when he calms down."

"God reloads!" Uncle Konstantine kept broadcasting, "Haw! Haw! Fools shoot and shoot and what happens but God reloads, and now it's our chance, now it's our main chance. God reloads!"

What Uncle Konstantine was ranting about was the miracle of fate that had suddenly set China against the empire in a major border dispute west of Vladivostok, with the very real possibility of a major nuclear war within the month unless one side or both backed down from mobilization and what was then called brinksmanship. From out of nowhere fate had delivered an unpredictable turn of events that had panicked the Kremlin and, as Uncle Konstantine explained in headlines and I shall explain in detail, now reinforced us. "Mao's mobilized!" Uncle Konstantine boomed. "The Chinese have mobilized! Millions on the march! Across the Ussuri! Vladivostok is defenseless! The Kremlin is wetting its pants. The Chekhists are hiding under the covers! God reloads!" Uncle Konstantine swung himself back and forth before the open fire on his crutches, bellowing, "Don't you understand, darlings, God reloads us! We're back on top! We're armed again! God's reloading our bombers tonight! They have to bargain with us! Fools shoot and God reloads!" and then finally, "Give me a bottle, what's the delay!"

The juice finally cooled Uncle Konstantine's performance long enough for us to help him and Uncle Dmitry up the stairs to the living loft. Uncle Dmitry with his greatcoat removed still looked frail from a chest wound that never truly healed, but he sounded even-voiced again and most in control of his emotions. He started by asking for some tea and then introducing his companion, Col. Oleg Furnin of bomber command, a tall, round-backed, balding senior falcon who, I would learn later, was an Orenburg man who had once served under my father in the Fourth Air Army and who was also a lifelong friend of my uncles since their cadet days and who had even spent two years with them in a slave camp in north Kazakhstan in the early 1950s. Uncle Dmitry spoke affectionately while he introduced Furnin and then presented the pertinent facts, "Colonel Furnin's just landed. He's come straight to us with confirmation of the rumors we've been hearing out of headquarters the past week. It's confirmed that the Chinese have mobilized along the whole of the

Ussuri River. And that all week they've been probing us. And we've been probing back. Tell them, Oleg."

Colonel Furnin was weary from his flight from Vladivostok and gulped from a mug as he talked. "As I was telling Mitya and Kostya—the generals—I've seen them, this isn't secondhand. I flew over their recon battalions; they aren't worrying about air cover. There are tens of thousands on the move out there. It started a week ago with a brawl over an island in the river. From what I hear there's no one on the island. So you can guess that this is a planned provocation and that the Chinese have been ready for their mobilization since Czechoslovakia. They know we're skin and bones along the border." Furnin spoke like a man used to making cynical remarks about command decisions, "We're reinforcing at division level so far, though by now they've probably discovered that we haven't got a full corps within a week's march of the river. The Navy panicked first and ordered the fleet to make steam and get out of port. That will take time, and I hear the submarine fleet can't put to sea for at least a month. Our dauntless bastards have discovered that if Mao crosses the Ussuri in corps strength there's not a chance of stopping him from taking Vladivostok and most of the border as far north as Sakhalin, which is why I'm here, comrades, and what I'm telling you— we've been ordered to load the bombs from the stores, the tactical weapons for now. At least I got my boys back here to load the good stuff. The tacticals they're loading at Vladivostok are garbage that I wouldn't allow in my planes even with a radiation check. Tonight, comrades, out there tonight, they're loading tacticals, and for all I know someone's loading strategics too, though what they can use that crap on, God knows. By tomorrow our dauntless bastards will be telling me that now we have to be ready to stop those poor yellow hordes the only way we can, stop them and Vladivostok and a chunk of the Pacific coast. I'll have to order my boys to dive-bomb with tacticals."

We were open-mouthed at Furnin's tale of imminent apocalypse. Uncle Dmitry took up Colonel Furnin's tale by restating the facts that the fighting had started March 2 on an uninhabited island in the middle of the Ussuri River when both sides had fired on each other's patrols. The potshotting had quickly escalated, and a week later both sides were reinforcing with regiments and alerting whole divisions.

Uncle Dmitry said that it looked as if Mao Tse-tung was deliberately challenging the Kremlin bosses to stop his land grab for a sizable portion of the border, including the Vladivostok corridor and our major port on the Pacific.

"The Chinese are speaking in aphorisms," Uncle Dmitry said, "and that means they're serious. The latest from them is 'Our enemies quiver like ginkgo leaves.' "

We didn't laugh out loud. It was more true than not that the Kremlin bosses had long been intimidated by Mao Tse-tung and his forty-million-man army. And it was easy to assume our bosses were now frightened of the Chinese with our Army overwrought and overextended in order to support the expedition in Czechoslovakia. There was no likelihood of mounting a major ground defense in the east at least until after the spring thaw. This left the safety of the empire to the omnipresent Air Force, and the big bosses, convinced they were going to lose the Pacific coast in a massacre, had called on the Air Force to open our nuclear-weapons lockers and deploy our air wings against the Chinese threat. Of course there weren't sufficient stores at Sakhalin and Vladivostok, since no one had planned for an air-launched border war. Colonel Furnin had brought his Tu-142 air wing to Chkalvo to fetch ordnance from the stores buried beneath the airfield, and all that night flight crews were stacking small atomic bombs called tacticals in the bays.

After Uncle Dmitry had defined the strategic crisis, he then argued the new state of affairs not only from the Air Force point of view but also from the Cosmonaut Corps' vantage. "They need us now. They have to need us now." (He meant the big bosses whom Furnin called "dauntless bastards.") "We're what they've got to hold on to a third of Siberia. We're what they have to keep their jobs. And it didn't take Marshal Vershinin long to answer the call with a simple proposition that if we protect Siberia then we can pick our price. We're the Air Force, and the Air Force attacks. And now that they see what life would be like without Siberia, they didn't call on the Organs, they called on us."

Uncle Konstantine argued our position more vulgarly, "What've the Chekhists got to stop four hundred and five heavy divisions? Denunciations? Backshooting? Newspaper articles!" Uncle Konstantine roared between bites of lamb and gulps of juice, "What're they going to do, arrest a billion Chinese? Reeducate forty million soldiers? Make Father Mao fall down the stairs?" He thundered at the ceiling as if he were addressing God or Laikushka, "God reloads, I tell you, God reloads, and it's our turn to get back at those Chekhist backshooters!"

Arkady Volgamints interrupted to question Furnin about bomber command. Arkady was respectful of the colonel's status, but he pressed him with technical questions, such as the number of air wings available, the commanding officers, the size of the nuclear locker opened, and Furnin answered with thorough explanations of the crisis. We fighter pilots sat by appreciating their rigor and waiting for them to come to a conclusion. Finally Volgamints thanked Furnin, sucked on a cigarette, and told us: "It's bad, like the colonel says; it's very bad out there. They've loaded tactical, the kiloton range, and God help us, that stuff is garbage, like the colonel says. It might just drop itself it's such junk. And if it's good news we lose Lake Baikal, then drink to it."

It wasn't good news to lose Lake Baikal, but the threat of losing Lake Baikal and Siberia was, since as Uncle Dmitry explained, the threat of war provided a bizarre solution to our troubles with the Lubyanka lords. At the climax of State Security's grinding coup d'état, just when the Lubyanka lords seemed to be in control of the Kremlin, the Party, and the military, the Chekhists had lost their hold and their mastery for the simple reason that, while they could terrorize the empire's leadership, they couldn't stop China's army. Only the Air Force could save the Kremlin now, and our big bosses knew they must satisfy the Air Force in all directions in all things. Uncle Dmitry declared that now was our chance, our "main chance," to regain some of what we'd lost. Just as Czechoslovakia had offered my uncles an opportunity to grab at Tsar Cannon for themselves, now the Chinese mobilization offered them a chance to grab at the moon too, and they were aiming to transform the defeat of the shootings into a victory in space.

"Prepare yourselves, do what you can to get ready," Uncle Dmitry told us. "Soon, very soon, we'll be moving again, and when we do we've got to move fast for what we want before the window closes on us." Uncle Dmitry wasn't able to match Uncle Alexander's fiery talk on the eve of battle, so instead he invoked the fallen icon himself, "Sasha told me to tell you, here's our time, this is our time, now, our time for our job. Sasha also said to tell you that the Americans are good, very good"—he waved at the charts of *Apollo 9* on the wall—"very, very, very good." Uncle Dmitry imitated an Oryolin grimace and made his voice sound like a recording of the original. "And so we're going to beat the best. We're going to do our job and drive the moon. We're going to 'Finish it.' "

We cheered passionately for the first time since the shootings, calling out " 'Finish it!' 'Finish it!' 'Finish it!' " as well as the drunken "Keep pouring!" We celebrated like idiots who'd dance on the graves of the empire as long as we won our way to the moon, singing bawdy songs about the Chekhists and rowdy songs about the Chinese and also leaping up onto the beams and out the windows onto the slippery porch roof to howl at the skies, "Bombs away!" and the inane, "Ka-boom!" My uncles and Colonel Furnin remained for much of the foolishness, and by the time we carried them down to their car, and promised them we'd be good, and promised Uncle Konstantine he could stay with us the next time when he was off his crutches, we had exaggerated the plain advice to ready ourselves for action ahead into plans worthy of full mobilization.

"We're the high ground," Uncle Dmitry told us in parting. "And the high ground is what we can sell dearly. What we want is everything they've got and then twice that again."

Uncle Dmitry just repeated his broken proverb drunkenly, "God reloads, God reloads—Fools shoot and God reloads!"

I am sure you can hear the forced note in all this inspirational tomfoolery, and my confession here is that after my uncles had left us that night I felt more despair, not less. I wasn't alone in this odd despair. My memory is that after they'd gone, even as we continued our celebration at Black House, there was an understanding among us that my uncles hadn't told us anything new, but instead were doing what they had always done in the face of disaster—speaking tough and demanding big and making us feel like privileged conquerors. There was no reason to believe that my uncles' present demand of the moon would come to more than had the one they'd made after Czechoslovakia, and, given that my uncles were now invalided, there was good cause to believe that "Finish it" meant we were finished, too. No one spoke this aloud, but it was there to hear in our boasts and taunts and particularly in the way no one had been bold enough to ask after Uncle Alexander's failing health. My confession in sum is that immediately after my uncles had told us we were going to get back our own, we didn't believe them anymore, and worse, there was a sense that whatever was ahead, it would come to more disaster. Perhaps I shouldn't put this onto the others and should blame myself, confess myself, that alongside my hopes for the next months was my sense that my mother had struck my uncles and the Corps a death blow and that I was watching my beloved heroes pass painfully into their fate.

Still, there turned out to be call to have faith in my uncles' great expectations. Over the next month all Russia reloaded with threats and bluff and more sinister ordnance, and no faction did better than the Air Force and the Corps. I didn't look much beyond my duty and didn't care much beyond Uncle Dmitry's opinion that the Air Force was going to sell the high ground dearly, so I missed or ignored much of what happened out east on the Ussuri River, or down south at the Party's spring plenum on the Black Sea, or just forty kilometers away in the renovated, soundless corridors of the Lubyanka. I do know that Father Mao didn't launch his hordes, and we didn't launch our bombers, yet other than this bald fact I can't now say and can't even find the history books to explain what was done to back down or appease the Chinese, or what happened to soothe the Kremlin bosses, or what trade-offs were necessary to unseat the Lubyanka lords from their high perch and restore the Air Force to the high ground.

I do know that Starry Town came to life again as if the thaw had arrived just for us. Whatever reloading God did that spring he distinctly smiled upon the Air Force. An entire new fighter division was formed at Chkalvo, nearly doubling the size of the airbase and increasing the Air Force's power over Moscow proportionately (and also in the sky over the Lubyanka), so the price the Air Force asked for the Ussuri River had to have been staggeringly expensive. Army engineers and construction battalions descended on the base to begin a massive earth-moving scheme to rebuild the flight line so the Cosmonaut Corps would have its own hangar, an extravagance that meant the falcons in the Corps could fly on demand. At the end of March each of the Corps' fighter pilots was assigned his own new 21. My uncles' squadron received the best of the best: fourteen new MiG-21 Pfs delivered direct from the shakedown range, each with two replacement engines that were not the standard R-13 but were the twice-as-powerful Tumansky R-25s. And for Starry Town there was the most lavish price of all: a mission control center to be built just down the road, on the other side of the lake. Soon enough the engineers broke ground for a gigantic brick-built facility that would someday direct all orbital and interplanetary missions, so there would be no more depending on the whims of the rocketeers at Star City.

Through March and into April it became apparent to the squadron that much of what Uncle Dmitry had said was coming our way. Soon the question of the moon-driving rose up like the moon itself. It was still not possible to believe that we could get back what all we'd lost in January in the Kremlin yard, but it was possible to believe we could return to the Cosmodrome. Remember, the Corps in general and the squadron in particular had been shut up at the fortress of Starry Town since the shootings, under siege from State Security and without boosters or ships or missions, and just the freedom to go back to Star City looked to us to be a prize. My uncles were after the dearest prize of all, however, and a hot rumor swept Starry Town in early April that there had been a tempestuous meeting of the Corps' most senior cosmonauts and staff at the medical center, at Uncle Alexander's bedside, in which my uncles had demanded of Corps Commander General Kamenin to demand of Marshal of Aviation Vershinin and the Air Force to demand of the State Space Commission and the big bosses the king's ransom of the moon. The word was that Uncle Dmitry had put his case as diplomatically as possible for a demand—though with a measure of Uncle Alexander's rhetoric, "Tsar Cannon for us or nothing for us. That's what we've earned. That's what we're owed. That's what we want"—and that Uncle Konstantine had sealed the demand with his by then well-known opinion, "God reloads!" It was also said that Uncle Alexander had lain silently by, unable to speak for himself for the medications.

I wrote Katya with all the rumors and often mentioned my worries about my uncles and their plans of moon-driving. Since Katya never wrote me back, I was free to speculate about the Corps' future as if I were a potentate and insider. "I know you don't think there was ever much to the hope for the moon landing," I wrote her. "I know you think it was always propaganda, but surely you can see that we were very close to it and that it's awful to watch while the Americans take the moon while we have nothing to show." I rambled on some until I came to my borrowed-from-Oryolin explanation for why the moon landing was important to me. "I believe this is my job. I don't make much more of it than as my job, and getting to the moon can't hurt anything, can it? And what has your grandfather worked for his whole life and why should it be wrong he wants his Tsar Cannon to drive the moon? And what have my uncles worked for since they got out of the camps? And how can it be a bad thing that they want to go where no man has ever been? I feel lucky to be here. And even if the Americans beat us to the moon, I think we should keep trying to get there. And if it takes ten or twenty more years we will." This was such big talk that it makes me sigh now at what a big head I had at twenty-two, what a long way I had to fall. I crossed out "my uncles" and started to put in their formal titles of generals, but then left it alone, since by then I'd decided that, if I couldn't let down my guard to Katya, then there was something wrong with the way I loved her. I did love her deeply, and though I didn't know how to win her to my side other than to keep writing letters, I did have as many schemes for Katya as my uncles had for the moon, and I laid out my latest appeal to her with not a little strategy: "I learned today from Colonel Khitrovo that I'm graduating into the Corps on June 1, at the top of my class. I've asked Uncle Lev to come down to attend the ceremony. Could you join him? He doesn't travel easily and would appreciate your company. I don't know if he's left Leningrad since the war, and you might be able to persuade him. Perhaps by then I'll be able to come and get him. I could bring you and Daniel back with us. I'm not trying to trick you. I know you hate Starry Town. But it's different now . . ." I reiterated how rich and powerful we were, and I even mentioned that I'd had a raise in salary. "Please try to come down for my graduation. I love you in Leningrad or anywhere, but please, this is my life. I want you to share it with me. I want to be with you for the baby."

I still have a draft of this letter—I sent her a longer version—and as I read it over I can see that while I was prescient about the Corps' future I was witless about Katya's future. What did I know about marriage? What could I know of how it was for Katya to give birth alone, divorced, penniless, with the father of her first child a coward and the father of her second child a wet-eared fool? What did I know about Katya more than I loved her? She'd shown me my mother was a hate-mongering assassin, and I'd had nothing to say in reply. She'd left me to my duty and gone to make a separate life for herself, and I wouldn't stop pestering her to come back to a place she denounced as a fraud. She'd risked her life several times in standing up to killers, and what did I offer her but more of the same ugliness. I suppose what I can make of this letter now is how stupid love made me, a boy deaf to reason and too thick-witted to see the truth that Katya could not come back to me, that Katya was gone to me. And I suppose, too, now that seven decades have gone, I'm not a day wiser either about Katya or about love.

I've told you that I don't think anyone in the squadron or in the Corps believed my uncles could exact the moonshot out of the Air Force and the bosses. I've confessed that when I looked down at Uncle Alexander in his sickbed I'd seen that he was not ever going to lead us again. I've argued at length why it was beyond reason that the Corps could reorganize itself and return to the Cosmodrome and man-rate Tsar Cannon in time to beat the Americans to the landing. All this was convincing, and all of it stepped aside when my uncles attacked again. My diary says that the critical date was Friday afternoon, April 18—the day my uncles played their hand at a parley called at Black House, and the strength of the hand was Alexander Oryolin risen from his own death.

I was out at the new flight line with Genka Stumpelkin, waiting for an opening in the weather, when I first heard of the parley. It was raining steadily, and Stumpelkin and I were at the door of a half-built hangar propped atop a ferry cart in our flight gear and helmets, shielding ourselves with the hem of a tarp and watching the wind wreck the tarpaulins they'd draped over some exposed diagnostic equipment. The new flight line at that point was half built—a tangle of sand piles, brickyards, earth-moving equipment, loose lumber, naked beams piled like sticks, and all of it sinking in the mud—and in order to escape the worst of the pandemonium Fedyuninsky had directed the squadron's new 21-Pfs to be moved out here to a temporary bivouac at the edge of the construction. Fedyuninsky had also said I could use one of the squadron's three surplus aircraft (that is, one of my uncles' 21s), and so of course I'd been camped either at Black House waiting for a ship or at the flight line waiting for clearance every free moment since, getting as many hours as possible in the northern range. I was living at mach speed, either in class or in my dreams or in the air, and in just such a cheery, cocky mood I'd decided that life was good even if I worried too much. I was chattering with Stumpelkin about some new daredevil maneuver I wanted us to try when I spotted Miserbiev and Adama-Bibliov veering toward us on my BMW, which had been renovated anew to become the squadron's favorite toy. I figured they were going to try to take our place with the two prepped 21s once the weather lifted, so I called out, "We're next, go away!"

They shook me off and, pushing back the hoods of their rain capes, they called over the bike's roar, "You're scrubbed! All flights canceled!"

We waved them away, and Stumpelkin called back, "We've been waiting all morning. It's our turn!"

They jerked the bike to our feet, and Miserbiev insisted, "Big briefing! The generals! You're scrubbed! Major Fedyuninsky says so! A hurry-up at Black House!" Adama-Bibliov pointed up and shouted, "You can't fly in this anyway; you're scrubbed!"

"What is it?" I asked.

"Big!" Miserbiev answered with the proper tone to make us hurry. The sky obediently cracked like a big egg, and the rain became a downpour that dropped visibility so fast the tower had to pop on the runway lights, as if lighting our way to Black House. Stumpelkin and I tossed our helmets to the flight crew, pulled our greatcoats over our bare heads, and somehow found footholds and handholds on the BMW so that the four of us churned off into a gray wall of rain for a ridiculous kilometer of slipping and blind driving. We found our way by guess and by accident until we went through the cut in the fence, over the bank and down, to sink like a team of horses into the muddy field behind Black House, where our clowning ended, because Black House was surrounded by a security cordon of gigantic paratroopers. My first thought was that there was trouble, perhaps another attack on my uncles, but I was wrong. There were many vehicles parked in the field off the road, both staff cars and light armored lorries, and the paratroopers wore the insignia of the Steppe Eagle regiment of the famous 103rd Airborne Division. Several paratroopers in battle dress approached us in the mud and ordered, "Stop it there, comrades, let's have identification." To indicate how unexpected this all was to us, I note that not one of us, big-ears that we were, had heard any word beforehand about paratroopers, and we had not one clue as to why an element of the 103rd should be up from their base at Tula. We were openly flabbergasted and obeyed their challenge meekly. They passed us through the cordon to a formidable Black House, not only for the vehicles and guards outside but also, inside in the stockpen, for a gathering of the Air Force general staff. Our surprise was total when, after wrestling my BMW out of the mud and getting it into the stockpen, we four recoiled from the amount of gold epaulets in the arena. Uncle Dmitry was the host of the affair, and he was standing with the supremely powerful Marshal of Aviation Vershinin and his aides-de-camp slightly off center stage because of a cascading leak. Marshal Vershinin did glance at us struggling with the motorcycle as if we were crazed children, but he soon flapped his jowls like ermine folds and turned back to Uncle Dmitry and his aides. The not-much-less-jowly Corps Commander General Kamenin, who was chatting with Major Fedyuninsky and Colonels Beregovoi and Shatalov, also stared at our entry, but not so disapprovingly, and then nodded to us as if he understood our embarrassment. By the rear post, where we wanted to park the motorcycle, there was an especially large light colonel of the Steppe Eagles who stared silently at the BMW and then stepped aside. I'd soon learn that this Goliath was Lieutenant-Colonel A. K. Strogolshikov from Rostov-on-Don, Uncle Konstantine's eldest brother's son or, as Uncle Konstantine said, "my favorite nephew."

Yet the most telling surprise was little Isaacii Goldenberg, who was seated quietly by himself in a soaked slicker, squeezing and fussing with a large portfolio case. I didn't spot him right away, but then, to conceal my disrespectful condition, I retreated from the center and found him like a long-lost brother. I was too excited to wait, and I grabbed him up in a hug and whispered the critical question, "Why are you here?"

His answer told the tale, "Peter Apollonovich, we're ready."

We couldn't talk normally for the VIPs nearby, but we could whisper to each other in bursts of communication, and what I learned was that Misha Cherryntevsky had flown Goldenberg up from Tsar Cannon that morning and that Goldenberg was here to give a briefing on the superbooster. "We've got two built," Goldenberg whispered. "We're starting long count tonight. For a June test."

I whispered back a question, "How is the Grand Constructor?"

"He's not good," Goldenberg replied. "He doesn't complain.

We're ready, so is he." The truth, I'd learn later, was that the Grand Constructor was very sickly and could only visit the Tsar Cannon vehical assembly barn in a wheelchair every few days. Goldenberg no longer fretted as sentimentally about his mentor as he had, and he seemed willing to accept the fact that an old man with broken health was not in fact the same as a superbooster, and that one could rise while the other faded. The Goldenberg I met that day was a much more confident, mature man than I'd last seen off to the Star City hospital in November. His promotion to deputy director of the program, his frantic winter of work, his complicated and compassionate soul, all this had put weight on him and his manner, and, if he'd been a falcon, I would have called him cocksure.

The cocksure originals of the squadron as well as a fair number of the Corps' senior cosmonauts (mostly of Beregovoi's and Shatalov's cliques) were arriving in stages as Goldenberg and I whispered together. The Corps had been called out to this briefing as suddenly as Stumpelkin and I had, and each of them arrived in a rush of curiosity at the security and the VIPs. The full assembly couldn't have taken more than a quarter hour from when I first entered and when the briefing began; however, in the meantime, I managed to park my motorcycle, question Goldenberg, and also signal Stumpelkin, Miserbiev, and Adama-Bibliov by sign and whisper that we were here about Tsar Cannon.

While the arena filled to standing-room-only, Uncle Dmitry beckoned me over to introduce me to Marshal Vershinin. "Apollon Nevsky's son," Uncle Dmitry said. "He was at the attack. You remember, sir."

Marshal Vershinin, who was so ancient that he'd pounded my father's chest to congratulate him for raking Prussia and Berlin to rubble, now pounded my chest and said, "Good, good, good for you." Vershinin had a growl for a voice, after decades of tobacco and absolute power, and he'd learned to use his voice as a way of putting off real conversation. Something brightened in his jowly, pitted face when he pounded me, and after a pause he asked, "You're Nevsky's boy?" He glanced at Uncle Dmitry, and I don't know if he was registering more than some distant memory of my father, though at the time I flinched that he might be thinking what he knew of my mother. Whatever was in Vershinin's mind didn't come out, because he grumbled, "Good, I knew your father. Good. He was one of my best. Good," and then pounded me again so that I backed away with a salute.

The last VIP to arrive was President Keldysh of the Academy of Sciences who, tossing off his rain gear and brushing his long white hair with his fingers, held himself back like a prince among serfs, but then thought better of it and pushed in among the crowd to offer foreign cigarettes to Vershinin, Kamenin, and others. What was significant about Keldysh's presence was that, as a principal member of the State Space Commission, he had come to the briefing as a representative of the other space bosses, which suggested that Secretary Ustinov and Chairman Blagonravov were unsure how to balance themselves between the demands of the Corps and the Kremlin.

Fedyuninsky played master of ceremonies and called out, "Comrades!" ceremonially, then looked up to the living loft. We watched the door open, and Uncle Konstantine, free of his crutches, carried down Uncle Alexander like a broken caricature of himself. I was prepared, I suppose, but I was still startled to see what damage had already been done. Uncle Alexander had lost so much weight his general's tunic covered him like a blanket, and with his gray skin, brittle hair, slack jawline, yellowy fingers, there was almost nothing left of the hero but bits of his mumbly voice and all of that terrible black gaze. Uncle Konstantine placed Uncle Alexander on a chair at the foot of the stairs and held him in place like a doll. The VIPs approached and bowed their respects. Marshal Vershinin showed his upset by reaching to touch Uncle Alexander's cuff as if he couldn't believe this was the same man. Fedyuninsky put a second chair down so that Marshal Vershinin could sit beside Uncle Alexander, and the two of them looked like a grandfather and a frail child facing each other.

Uncle Dmitry had changed too, though not as physically as temperamentally, and there was little of his tact when he began the briefing soon after. "Comrades, we've asked you here to give us a free hand. We're asking for a free hand." He addressed Vershinin directly. "We're prepared to move now, sir, and you know we are. Now we can show you how. This is Deputy Director I. M. Goldenberg of the Tsar Cannon works."

Goldenberg was fully prepared and handled his briefing not only with the photos and charts he'd brought in his portfolio case but also by anticipating problems—posing challenges to his own talk and then answering himself succinctly. He summarized, "We have two boosters in the palace, what we called the palace, which is the vehicle assembly barn. And we have three more in stages on the blocks. We've scheduled a test launch with a fourth-stage mock-up in forty days." Goldenberg repeated his hard fact. *"Forty days."*

Keldysh interrupted as if he were in command. "You're saying a Tsar Cannon test launch by June first? You can't mean it. How?"

Goldenberg found his strongest tone. "Yes, sir, in *forty days*. And we also expect to mount a man-rated booster in *sixty days.*"

Keldysh complained, "You can't—think this through. The Americans can't do it that soon. You're not thinking this through."

"Sir," Goldenberg replied, "I'm not reporting what we can do. I'm reporting what we're doing. *Forty days* primary test, and the long count starts tonight. *Sixty days* for man-rating, and the long count starts mid-May. It's on my charts, sir, and there's no mistake. It's thought through, sir. I am telling you what is already in motion."

Marshal Vershinin wasn't so easily answered. He announced his dissatisfaction by crossing his arms and pushing his face down into his jowls. It was a crowded room, cosmonauts bumping each other both to see the action and to avoid the worst leaks, and still we waited on Vershinin's favor as the rain pounded, the roof leaked, the door banged in the wind, a heavy Antonov swept overhead like an avalanche. Finally Vershinin used the weight of his office and grumbled, "What do you want, Comrade Deputy Director?"

"Comrade Marshal, sir," Goldenberg started, checking Uncle Dmitry's nod before he declared, "we need two heavy construction battalions with equipment. We need immediate release of ten million liters of kerosene. We need two work trains. We need a transport squadron to airlift supplies from the Smolensk plants. We need another one hundred volunteers from the Cosmodrome—men I'd have to hand-pick from the R-7 teams—and we need all this immediately."

Vershinin motioned as if he'd expected no less. "What else, Comrade Deputy Director?"

Goldenberg reported, "We need thirty million rubles credit in our account, and we need two Soyuz spacecraft with spare equipment from the Rocketage."

Vershinin asked, "What's thirty million for?"

"For the lander, sir," Goldenberg replied. "We need a lunar lander." Goldenberg flipped his portfolio case open again and brought out a drawing of a moon lander. It was a simple one-man craft with two modes (descent stage and ascent stage) and four landing legs, not unlike the ugliest spider ever created.

"That will fly?" Vershinin asked.

Goldenberg looked at the photograph. "It should."

"Speak the truth," Vershinin demanded.

Goldenberg blinked and didn't mean to joke when he said, "We could test one for five million rubles more credit."

Corps Commander General Kamenin tried to help the proceedings. "We probably could get by with less than thirty million, sir."

Vershinin asked President Keldysh, "Would your lot pay for this?"

Keldysh answered, "If we had it, yes, I suppose, Marshal, if we had it. But we don't have it, and we don't know where to get such a sum. We gave Tsar Cannon all we can last September. There's no new source."

Vershinin barked at Keldysh, "Answer me clearly; would you pay for this if you had it?"

Keldysh quivered at Vershinin's temper, and I saw in the way Keldysh didn't respond that the Air Force frightened even Kremlin pets like the boss of the Academy of Sciences. Keldysh, trying to conceal his anxiety, stepped toward Uncle Alexander and asked as if he were conferring with a colleague, "Can you do this, General Oryolin? There are limits, aren't there? I mean, it's better that we get there in an orderly fashion, not hastily in untested craft. The Americans aren't there yet. Perhaps we can have more time to prepare. I've heard out what we have. I'm asking you, as a friend, do you think we're ready for a lunar lander?"

Uncle Alexander ignored Keldysh and kept his black eyes on Marshal Vershinin.

Vershinin certainly understood he was in absolute control of the day, since he had the resources, the money, and the power to grant Goldenberg all he asked, regardless of what the State Space Commission offered. "Good, good," Vershinin said to Goldenberg. "That's everything you want from me?"

Uncle Konstantine returned, "Haw!" and then stepped over to knock the arm of his giant nephew as if he were a fir tree growing among us. "We want the Steppe Eagles at the Tsar Cannon works," Uncle Konstantine added, "and we want them with battalion air defense from division."

Lt.-Col. Alexey Strogolshikov wasn't a talker like his uncle. He saluted Vershinin and said, "We're volunteering, sir, for security duty."

Marshal Vershinin spat in the mud as if he were feeling young, indomitable, and all wise, though the truth was he was a very old and tired soldier who, I would learn later, knew that day that he was on his last legs as an autocrat and wouldn't last out the year as Air Force boss. The moon landing was his last campaign. If there's a good explanation for what he did that day, it was that he was the Air Force incarnate and believed only in attack, attack, ram. "I suppose you know what my staff makes of spacemen," Vershinin grumbled to my uncles while his chief of staff and aides-de-camp stood noncommittally in front of him. "I suppose you can see they think I'm nuts to be listening to you spacemen."

I thought we were rejected and that Vershinin was going to stand and growl and leave. Instead Vershinin held out his hand to our boss, General Kamenin. "What've you made of this, Kolya?"

Kamenin rotated his head like a turret and blew out his cheeks in exasperation, making a fog of smoke in the damp. "It's theirs to do," Kamenin told Vershinin. "I'm just an old housekeeper. If it was mine to go I'd be right with them. But I'm just an old housekeeper." As an aside Colonel Beregovoi, who was a dutiful officer despite his failure with *Soyuz 2/3* and who would one day succeed Kamenin as the second Corps commander, bent over to whisper to Kamenin, and Kamenin, nodding at the information, added to Vershinin, "I was going to say, sir, that the Corps is yours to command, and that if you are asking for the Corps' belief, I am confident that the Corps stands with Generals Oryolin, Zhukovsky, and Strogolshikov on this matter. For myself, I yearn for the day we stand on the seas of the moon."

Kamenin was so eloquent that Marshal Vershinin spat again and growled at my uncles, "They're all for you and I'm not surprised. You tell me why I should go along with it. The moon? Who needs the moon? What can I do with the moon? How many divisions does the moon have? Can I go there? Is there any money there to pay me back for what you want? Why should I give you what you ask?"

Just when I thought Uncle Dmitry was going to reply graciously, he coughed and closed his eyes in weariness and nodded to Uncle Konstantine, as if passing the burden. Uncle Konstantine made a disgusted face and spat back at Vershinin, "Bah! You didn't ask us at the Volga. You didn't ask us at the Oder. You didn't ask at Nikita, nor at Prague. And now you ask us why? Now you ask us? Bah!"

Uncle Konstantine's disrespect was heroic. In the pause after the outburst, Uncle Alexander said something that was lost in the clatter of men moving around. Uncle Alexander started to repeat himself when his voice failed, and it was only the third time he spoke that he was loud enough for all to hear his response to Marshal Vershinin. "It's your job. The moon's our job. Do yours, we'll do ours. Finish it."

Alexander Oryolin was a dying man, more ghost than human as he struggled to hold himself up against the back of the chair, and every man in the stockpen could see that he might not last the sixty days he asked for his moon landing. Yet no one moved to refuse him when he asked for the moon. Though his conduct was mostly a mystery to me at the time, I think I know why now. The man who asked for the moon in the stockpen was doomed by fate, so that to refuse Uncle Alexander that afternoon would have been the same as refusing a fate none of us could know.

"Finish it yourself, Sasha," Vershinin ordered.

I know I heard Marshal Vershinin say this. I've described the day and moment carefully to prove it happened. I know I saw three dozen others in earshot who heard the same and I can name them: the squadron, Marshal Vershinin, his chief of staff, Polotoi, and aides-de-camp, Volstad and Danovinn, also Lt.-Col. (later Lieutenant-General of Airborne) Alexey Strogolshikov and his staff majors and captains; also, from the Corps, General Kamenin, and future Corps commanders Beregovoi and Shatalov and eight Corps staff officers; also there was Goldenberg. Of these three dozen men, three of us are still living as of this writing, Isaacii Goldenberg, Genka Stumpelkin, and me. I'm telling you the truth of it when I write that the full authority of the Air Force signed on for my uncles' campaign. My uncles were neither mutineers nor wreckers, nor were any of the thousands who worked on Tsar Cannon. What happened the next forty, sixty, ninety days was provisioned and paid for by the Air Force general staff with the compliance of the State Space Commission. I repeat that I saw and heard it, this isn't secondhand tale-telling or speculation, this is my eyewitness. On the stormy afternoon of April 18, 1969, my uncles were granted the power to test-launch a Tsar Cannon with a mock-up Soyuz within forty days and then to launch and man-rate a Tsar Cannon on a voyage to the moon within sixty days.

I remember the moment Vershinin said, "Finish it," and I remember the celebration afterward. I remember walking on Black House's roof with my Orenburg brothers as we hailed the black sky and imitated bird calls. I remember how we wouldn't sleep that night or that weekend as we sang, drank, danced, and boasted our luck. I remember most dearly what it felt like to stand atop the universe, up there astride Black House, face to face with a shivering forest and the boundless heavens, where I thought it was my fate to soar like a falcon. And I remember how fate doesn't stop just because you think you have what you want and that, within a week of that vertiginous day, I tumbled from Black House's peak to one of the worst dungeons in the empire, where I lost my love to my mother's damned soul.

Part

4

April – July 1969

1

Surface of the Sun

I fault myself and my stupid pride for falling into Iagoda's final trap. Three months of solid security at Starry Town had made me casual about any threat from my mother, and I told myself that I was foolish to have thought the attack at Fool's Gold had been Chekhists, and that I had to take courage and stop seeing bogeymen in every treetop. My uncles had withstood the assassination and risen again, so it seemed right for me to absorb the worst of the news of the winter and not let it hold me back now that spring had brought the hope of a moonshot. In all I was swellheaded, brash, game, spirited, and most ready to get going again after feeling like a child of bad luck and loss for too long, and I suppose I was about as ripe for a trick as I could have been. And a most simple trick was all it took to get me out of Starry Town, where Iagoda couldn't reach me, and to get me out in such a way that no one would know I was gone until it was too late.

My fall started the Tuesday of May Day week, when I slipped away early from a class exercise at the Devil's Windmill (Khitrovo no longer bothered to monitor my comings and goings) and headed for the field for an hour in a 21 with any of the squadron I could find available at Black House. Halfway to the wood path I realized I'd left my new flight boots at the barracks and, in just such a casual way, I discovered on my bunk the first real letter I'd ever had from Katya. I pounced on it like a starved cat and had to settle down before I could comprehend what she said. Once I had focused, I had to read it over and over in shock, because she'd written she was "fond" of me and always would be, but that she had others to think of, and that it was time for me to accept that our lives were "profoundly apart."

Katya's letter was Iagoda's trick meant to draw me out of Starry Town. And yet it was a genuine letter. She'd written it spontaneously and meant it ardently, and if she wasn't candid in the letter she only kept from me what she knew would have hurt worse than her fare-well. For the fact was that Katya had taken up again with her univer-sity lover, the professor Ara Ovchennikov, who had been released from Lefortovo Prison in Moscow several weeks before. And the complete facts, which even Katya didn't know, were that Iagoda had released Ovchennikov in such a way that he'd known he would go to Katya in Leningrad and that eventually Katya would write and tell me. As it happened Katya didn't tell me the details of Ovchennikov, who was then living with her at her mother's, but she did mention in her letter that she was well and that her "friends" were standing by her through her last months of pregnancy. The sentence that hurt the most was: "I'm going to try to make a new beginning again for myself and my children, and I know someday you will see this is for the best for all of us."

As I read Katya's argument I remember feeling my heart ache as if my chest were made of wood and then feeling my senses succumb to a rage so black that soon I couldn't see or hear properly. I think now that my rage was also part of Iagoda's trick, since he'd anticipated that I was my mother's son and wouldn't accept any abandonment without fighting back. How well Iagoda knew my mother, how well he knew me, for as I sat there alone and abandoned I lost my reason and found that blackness that I'd seen in Uncle Alexander. As I tried to think what to do my mind wouldn't obey me. I didn't care about my duty or about my life or about anything but getting Katya and my child back. I especially didn't care about my promise to Uncle Dmitry to stay secure at Starry Town. I think now that this might have been the first time I experienced directly my mother's passion for vengeance, which I acknowledge is as much a part of my nature as my sense of forgiveness. I was forgiving nothing that day. My mother in me made me stupid, violent, ruthless, very stupid, so that

all I thought was, My Katya! My child! My life! and that all I wanted
was to grab back what was mine. I had no other motive than revenge
and no other plan than to go to Leningrad and confront Katya. In
my stupid mind I could see the trip, I could see how I would face
her, I could hear what I would say, and before I thought more I was
dressing for my stupid scheme in my woolens, flight suit, flight
boots, double gloves, and then my best rain cape. I took up all my
reserved cash, nearly a thousand rubles, and filled my kit bag with
rolls from the kitchen, fruit from the locker, a canteen of warm tea.
My preparations for the trip were desperately controlled, and I
would have attacked anyone who blocked me, and when the cook
Lukacs asked me if I wanted his fresh rolls instead of the old ones, I
passed him as if he were stone and marched out for the new flight
line. I wasn't flying. I was stealing my BMW, which was at the hangar in the crew chief's cubicle for a routine tune-up. I walked right to
the crew chief and lied to him that Major Fedyuninsky wanted four
21s prepped for a night flight. The crew chief complained so much
that I had to invoke Fedyuninsky's name repeatedly and agree to sign
for the work; yet I would have broken any rule to get rid of him and
his men because I needed to get my motorcycle out of the hangar
without them seeing me. When I got the BMW out of the back of
the hangar and over to the motor pool I bribed the airman with one
hundred rubles for two petrol cans and another one hundred for his
silence. He did ask me where I was headed, and I lied, "Moscow, a
girl," and laughed as if it were a lark. I lied again to the sentry at the
checkpoint that I was running a dispatch into Moscow, and though
he didn't like it, since I didn't have papers, I bribed him a hundred
rubles and said I was also off to see my fiancée in town. By midafternoon I was on the Leningrad road, cruising hard between two
Army lorries as if I were part of their escort. This ruse carried me past
the checkpoints until dark. It was a twenty-two-hour trip on frost-
scarred roads, and I doubt I rested more than four hours, and even
then I just sat by the motorcycle staring at the empty roadway and
wilderness of woods. The single comfort I permitted myself was listening to the early morning ground feeders, like the waxwings and
dippers, but I didn't let my pleasure last and even cursed the buds in
the birch trees as if they were my enemies. I burned my hand on the
tailpipe during a refueling stop near Volochek and yet hardly felt the
pain. I was through the Volhkov vales at first light and remember

actually glimpsing Saint Sophia's dome on the other side of Lake Illmen as I worked overland to the Pskov road to bypass a large checkpoint.

Past dawn, as I entered Leningrad District, there were gunsmoke clouds ahead with a driving rain that slicked the road. Forty kilometers from the city I was pushed off the road by an autobus and lost a gear. Soon after that I ran short of petrol and bought some from two soldiers snoozing in a military car parked at a campsite. By then I was suffering from the beating I was getting riding hard over the torn roads, but nothing, not exhaustion, hunger, desertion, betrayal, lies, theft, none of it mattered to me, for it was my rage more than the motorcycle that carried me to my fate. I couldn't have understood this then, but now I know that my rage was like a monster that was taking control of me. And it wasn't just a rage of hurt feelings or heartache anymore, it had grown to become a rage of vengeance, and it was still growing to become a rage of damnation—the rage to damn Katya for betraying my love for her, the rage to damn myself for failure to hold on to her, the rage to damn everyone for abandoning me—and, yes, it was also a rage to condemn and to murder, for I was my mother's son. Perhaps the most understanding I shall ever have of the feud between my mother and Uncle Alexander is that the love they probably felt for each other at one time had turned into the same sort of monstrous self-condemning madness that drove me to Leningrad.

At Leningrad I circled Theater Place counterclockwise past the Kirov and back to glide by Katya's mother's apartment building and to park near Glinka's statue. The closer I got the stronger I could feel my self-righteousness, and I stripped off my helmet, poncho, and gloves like a man ready to do battle. I didn't look for any evidence of a State Security trap and didn't even imagine it; nor did I think of going home to Great-Uncle Lev for his help beforehand, since I knew he'd probably take Katya's side or, worse, no side at all, and I wouldn't hear of conciliation, I wouldn't hear anything but my inner voice, Mine! Mine! I leaped off my bike and walked in long steps across the road and up the stairwell to pound on the door like a battering ram. I waited a long pause, knocked again, and then Mrs. Univer opened the door. She was polite and tried, "Come in, Peter, we're sitting down to breakfast." I didn't reply; I just dumped my coat and crossed the foyer to the dining room.

Katya was at the table in her dressing robe, and beside her was sleepy Daniel in his nightshirt. In the guest chair was Katya's lover, Dr. Professor Ara Ovchennikov, a lanky, red-bearded, large-headed man, about forty, with a pleasant face that was much too thin. I never saw him again, but I can suppose he was one of those foolishly noble men, once called dissidents, who in those days used big words about big ideas to try to shield himself from the fact that he was helpless in the face of tyranny. Yet I don't blame him, not now and not then, since I was a greater fool to stare at him as if he were sitting in my chair.

Katya's mother came in behind me and said something suitable to break the silence. All I could do was stare at Ovchennikov, and then at Katya, and then back to Ovchennikov.

Katya started talking softly, and what I heard was, "Peter? Why are you here? Has something happened?" Katya was vastly pregnant in her eighth month, puffy-faced and weary-eyed, and she half stood as she asked again, "Peter, why are you here, what are you doing?"

I'd lost my angry words and what I managed to say was, "I thought I should. I wanted to. I wanted to see you." Perhaps I said more to her, but I don't remember the words, and in any event I didn't finish my thought before there was a cracking thud in the outer hall and then heavy footfalls as eight Chekhists came through the door like paper and charged into the apartment to close Iagoda's trap on me and my love.

Katya's scream was horror and, after a lifetime of missing her, I can still hear it. "No, not here, not now!" she begged. "No, not here, no, no, not now!" Daniel screamed too and lunged for his mother while Ara Ovchennikov sat stunned at the invasion. The Chekhists filled the foyer entry and didn't speak. The leader pointed at me. The bravest of us was Mrs. Univer, who turned to shelter her family from what she must have known was death; and she tried in a strong voice, "Please, what do you want?"

The Chekhist leader again pointed at me, and I reacted in a panic, because as soon as I'd seen the Chekhists my stupid rage had left me to be replaced by my terror at what I'd done to bring Iagoda down on me and Katya. My panic made me fight wildly as I took a step back for momentum and then charged them, head-butting the leader and tackling his partner. My aim was to get them away from Katya and her family, and I cried out much foolishness to the Chekhists such as, "Leave them alone, I'm what you want!" It was no use, for they dragged me down and beat me with blackjacks and booted me until I couldn't move. The biggest one brained Ara Ovchennikov and killed him, I suppose, though I never learned his fate; and since they carried him away, perhaps he survived that blow. They also arrested Katya and her mother and abandoned Daniel—just closed the door on a child screaming in an empty apartment. Ask yourself what sort of men arrest a pregnant woman and her mother and then close a child in an empty apartment and you will know what I mean when I call Iagoda's Fifth Directorate the rot of the rot. Katya's screams for mercy were dreadful, and I recall them acutely now that I'm telling you, and they hurt me all again, "No, no, no, not here, not now, please, what have we done, please!"

I suppose they beat me some more in the car and then later at the Big House, yet I can't be sure. I know they stripped off my flight suit and boots and put me in a holding room with crushed little men like myself, some of whom told me where I was when I came alert and realized that I was helpless. I was at least a week at the Big House before they transferred me downriver into the hands of State Security's Special Hospital. I have little to say of my time there—Leningrad's ramshackle prison looked like an abandoned warehouse with all the windows broken out and the foundation crumbling to mud—for it was all the same sort of deprivation. I was an anonymous prisoner in with thieves, killers, misfits, who were either too stupid or too cruel to talk much to me or anyone else. I was abused impersonally along with many others in the holding cell and another larger common cell, and they never fed us without kicking someone down first. The brutality was halfhearted and just hurt me, and I didn't get sick until later. It wasn't until they transferred me to the Special Hospital that I had someone to talk to. Then I was in the hands of State Security, I wore a numbered tunic, the beatings stopped, and the torture began.

It was called the Leningrad Special Psychiatric Hospital, a wood-built complex with a central administration building and annexes like wings on the river out toward Lake Ladoga. You would better understand it as a madhouse. I was put in the ward called the Third Department, a narrow, long room on the upper floor of the north wing, with straw on the floor, bedsprings on wooden frames lining the walls, barred windows on three sides, and another window high above the latrine. All the wards in the Special Hospital looked alike and reeked of the same mix of disinfectant, urine, filthy men, and that sour rot of death. I was there two months and saw at least three men die each week just on my ward, and so the smell of death was usually strong enough to penetrate the perpetual cloud of tobacco smoke spread by the warders and inmates.

I'm sure of the death rate, because the man I knew best while I was in the Third Department was an inmate named Markovich, who was in charge of clearing out the corpses and cleaning up afterward, and he made me his assistant. I owe my life to Markovich's generosity toward me. He was another in the line of men, like the nameless zeks at Dzhezkazgan and Vladimirovich at Fool's Gold, who gave up their lives in such a way that I could keep going. Then again Markovich wasn't a decent man and was probably criminally insane by the time I met him. Markovich told me he'd once been a sailor at the Kronstadt fortress, where he'd killed his superior officer in a fistfight, and he'd been either in jail, in the camps, or at the Special Hospital, since 1941. He also told me that he'd had to kill seventy-nine other men in his twenty-eight years in prison, and that he expected to die when one of his victims' relatives caught up with him. He was hairless and toothless, he said, because of starvation over the years and the drugs they'd used on him. Yet he also bragged that he wasn't ever sick, because he always found a way to get vitamins no matter how little food he received. His body showed the decades of abuse, for he walked stiff and hunched forward like a chimpanzee and his left ear was swollen like a red knob, from pneumonia Markovich said, but also probably from beatings by the warders with their switches. Markovich had been beaten for so long and so routinely that he didn't talk about it. It had just become part of his nature to ignore cruelty and carry on with his day as if we were on a cruise. I repeat that he was generous to take me on as his assistant; however, he didn't do this out of kindness, he said he could "taste profit" in me. He called me his "new baby," and he cared for me just enough to keep me alive during the injections. "My beautiful new baby needs a diaper," he'd say to me after the injections had wrecked my bowels again. "Sleep, my new baby, we'll work you later," he'd say when he knew I couldn't get up because of the burning in my legs. "A little work for my baby will take your mind off it," he'd say when I was too hurt to sleep. My job for Markovich was washing corpses and scrubbing the bed frames with the corrosive disinfectant, and though it sounds repulsive it wasn't. Corpses aren't frightening. What's more, the Special Hospital had many rules about disposal of the dead, and it encouraged me that, if I died, I wouldn't be thrown away like trash.

The injections they gave me were the torture drugs I've mentioned before, some of the same drugs they gave those poor folk we found and left at Dzhezkazgan. Dzhezkazgan had been a transfer prison, where they drugged inmates to insensibility; whereas State Security used the special psychiatric hospitals as torture chambers to break their victims. Markovich told me that every inmate in the Third Department was diagnosed as dangerous and suicidal, and he also told me that the doctors claimed their injections were to cure us. Why debate such lies here? There were real maniacs on the ward but, like Markovich, they were often the most considerate among us; and I particularly recall a riverboat pilot who had scuttled a loaded ferry and now spent his time writing letters for the illiterate. Markovich also told me that only the most "special" prisoners like me received "the course," which was the doctors' euphemism for the injections. Markovich called the drugs the witch's brew. The warders came for me every other day in the morning, sometimes in the afternoon. They carried me down to the doctors' quarters in the administration building. They put me in various small rooms, like miniature clinics, with examination tables and surgical tools, where two warders held me down on my chest while a white-coated doctor injected me in the rump. The injection itself felt like a dull pressure until the air got to it, and then the spot swelled and burned. The burning spread like coals under my skin that became redder and hotter until the coals felt as if they were crumbling and slipping down my legs, or back up to my shoulders. It was as if I were roasting from the inside out, and, even after the burning sensation eased, the spot where they'd stuck the needle, on my buttocks or back thighs, would turn black and remain painful to the touch, so that I couldn't sit down or sleep on my back.

I've told you what it felt like, but the sickest and strangest part of the experience was what the drugs did to my mind. Whenever the burning cooled, usually at night, my dreams became fantasies which I've forgotten, all except the most unusual of them. It was that I was alone on the surface of the sun. I knew plenty of astronomy and could recognize the gases jetting up waves of molten walls at 580 degrees Kelvin. I could admire the phosphosphere as if it were the dry steppe. I could look up into the chromosphere as if checking the flying weather. It was a very vivid and queerly comforting dream, and it never felt like a nightmare. I think part of my comfort was that whenever I went to the surface of the sun, I was out of reach of the Third Department and the doctors. The surface of the sun could feel like a good refuge to me, and I think now that my dream was probably a fantasy version of what Katya had once told about our love. "Love is a star," she'd told me, "a great red giant burning quick and wild. You go there with someone you love, and it's your private sun forever. You know you can't live on it. You know that it can't last and it will burn out and cool and empty someday. But it's yours, ours. Isn't it like that for you, Petrushka, my companion, my dear, dear lover."

I didn't have Katya to be with, I had hairless, toothless, rubbery, and bent Markovich, and when they carried me back from another injection tied on a stick like a captured creature, Markovich would help me find a way to lie on my hip that didn't hurt and then he'd make me talk to him. "Talk about the cosmonauts," he'd prod me after an injection. "Talk about these generals, your uncles." "Talk about your mother, Eudaemonia Romodanovsky." "Talk about Katya. Tell me how beautiful she is. Talk about love, my baby."

I can't reproduce dialogue, since I don't think our exchanges were rational. He would pick a topic that pleased him and question me, and I would babble. He knew most everything about me by then, having emptied me of information as a man might devour books in order to amuse himself and also, I believe, in order to keep his own sanity by thinking about a world beyond his prison. He favored my more Oriental tales, and he would ask me about the places I'd visited, such as the Urals or Kazakhstan. He was specifically interested in exotic foods such as koumiss, and he giggled at details about both sweets and Katya's body.

I knew even then that Markovich was mad. Who knows what a real doctor would have made of his character? Then again it didn't bother me that he picked on me when I wanted to be alone or that he made me talk when I wanted to cry for the pain of my damaged bowels. He'd cup his hands over mine and imitate my howls as I strained at the cramps, "Owww, ohhhh!" Then without any complaint he'd clean me after my diarrhea or after I'd vomited in my sleep. How best can I illustrate such hellishness? A screaming, tortured, dying boy locked in mock philosophical debate with a thieving, grinning, deathless madman, both of us surrounded by a ward full of abandoned human husks in a Special Hospital run by torturers.

"All Russia is fate?" Markovich would challenge me. "Not so, not so, all Russia is eating. All about food, I'm saying. Talk to me about koumiss."

"Landing on the moon?" he'd say about my tales of my uncles, and then he'd taunt me with a stupid pun, "Who's a lunatic, baby? Me? Landing on the moon? I'm not that crazy, I'm saying. I'm not a lunatic, I'm a Bolshevik. Why do they want to fly to the moon? Have they run out of cheese, ha ha! Talk to me about cheese."

I've already noted that Markovich wasn't a decent man. I know he stole food from me. I know he sold my services as a corpse-washer and bed-frame scrubber to the warders in exchange for cigarettes and his infatuation with vitamins. I realize that Markovich had probably used boys like me before as his private slaves and had then tossed them aside when conditions pinched or another came along. Nonetheless Markovich saved me and my sanity when no one else could have, and, if he used me, then I also used him. I suppose for all his crimes he deserved to be condemned, but not by me. Isn't he also proof that in every heart there is some goodness no matter how degraded? Isn't Markovich evidence that God's grace is for the least deserving of us just as it is for the most admirable, and that it's not for us to say beforehand who is saved and who is damned?

I'm skipping the repetitive facts of the six weeks of my torture by the so-called course or witch's brew. I've told you that I screamed constantly and that the injections left me very sick, coughing blood and urinating blood and passing blood, and that's enough detail. What was significant about the torture was that it had no rational point. To make the pain stop I would have done anything they asked—I would have lied, cheated, betrayed, condemned, and denounced anyone—and yet I didn't, because my torturers didn't ask me to, nor did they accuse me of any crime, interrogate me for any information, talk to me at all. What I've recounted is all that happened: the warders dragged me down to the clinic; the doctors stuck me; the warders carried me back to the Third Department; and no one said a word unless it was me screaming. In the dumb routine of the horror, I felt myself changing into a creature who breathed, sweated, defecated, screamed, and wept, not truly a man, just a creature that wanted nothing but another breath to scream again. And then after six weeks of this meaningless punishment they took me to my mother, and she made me see that I had become not just a creature of pain but also a hopeless child abandoned on the surface of the sun.

My memory, which is unreliable here, is that they came for me on a white night, midmonth certainly, and since I recall speaking of the new strawberry moon to Markovich, that would make it June 14. My memory gives me a picture that I was up late scrubbing a bed frame while the rest of the ward was asleep, and that Markovich and I were catching the breeze by the big barred window overlooking the river. The white-night sky was that sheer powder blue that mixes faint starlight with the quiet reflection from the sun just below the horizon, and it was that time between midnight and 0100 when, despite the light, the birds are at rest, so the forest is hushed like a netherworld. There was no sound on the ward except the muted sobbing of one of the madmen, when Kok, the chief warder of the Third Department, appeared suddenly and came down the length of the room right at me. He said, "You again, our favorite," as he thumped my ear just a flick with his baton. Kok was a wide-faced, fair-complected Lithuanian who, according to Markovich, was a former inmate and a half-Jew (Markovich was also a half-Jew, he said, and he claimed that's why Kok hated him). "It's always you they want," Kok added. "And they only send for you when I'm trying to sleep," and then he thumped my ear harder. I lowered my head to avoid another blow and put up my hands to him to tie to the stick.

Markovich protested, "It's late for witch's brew, ain't it? What do you want my baby for now?"

Kok swung at my ear again and missed, so he pointed the baton at Markovich's nose. "He's off from here," Kok said. "Orders came. He's off to the Center."

Markovich didn't like this and demanded, "What's he done they want him there? You got it wrong."

Kok got me up roughly, and I became very frightened when I saw Markovich standing defiantly and demanding to know why I was being taken to the Center. It was too late, Markovich complained, we were busy, there must be a mistake. Kok swung at Markovich to end the argument. I didn't know what the Center was but soon learned, after I'd been manacled and transported in a van up and across the river to the Petrograd side, that it was just a zek's euphemism for Leningrad's State Security headquarters, an old imperial court building that was built flush against a quay on the Neva. The reason I soon became afraid of the Center was that Markovich had told me that as long as I stayed at the Third Department I was safe, since they never executed prisoners at the Special Hospital, only at the Big House. "Nine grams waiting at the Big House," he'd told me. "You do what they want to stay here." Markovich hadn't distinguished between the ramshackle prison of the Big House and the stone fortress of State Security headquarters, because they seemed the same execution block to him. Markovich had told me very specifically about what "nine-grams-waiting" would feel like, since he'd been waiting for his own execution half his life. "Like a blow, baby," he'd told me. "But you'll see white not red. And you'll bite your tongue off. And it won't hurt long enough. And you'll see your skull bone fly off before you fall into a hole. Bang!" His tale had terrified me more than the torture, though I can't now tell you why, nor can I say why State Security murdered prisoners in such a ghastly way, firing a bullet into a man's brain when his back was turned.

At the Center's courtyard drive, all I could think was my fear of nine-grams-waiting and that I didn't want to bite off my tongue. By then I was so certain they were going to shoot me that I'd stopped crying and was walking silently again with some conjured boy's notion that a falcon should die without tears. The Blue Tabs took me down two levels of stone stairs to a low, broad corridor that ran under the length of the building's river wing. The corridor was lit by a few dangling bulbs and filled with odd trash, such as bags of hardened concrete, broken furniture, piles of broken bricks, and there was standing water in every rut from whenever the Neva flooded. I recall that corridor as clearly as my own closet. At one end of the corridor there were the stone stairs down from the courtyard drive; at the other end there was an antechamber that opened onto the river quay. The Neva was so close I could smell the rank damp along with the wafting poisons of a sewer drain, and I wanted to faint from the stink, but I couldn't. I wanted to ask them why they were shooting me, but I didn't. Markovich had told me you'd hear a double click as they cocked the pistol hammer, and so I paused between every step to listen. I counted twenty-seven paces before they stopped me, each step like my last, each step expecting the blow that wouldn't hurt long, each step trying not to weep or plead for mercy. I can still sicken myself about this. What I hated the most was that I didn't want to die in a sewer, alone, without a brain—I hated dying in pieces like garbage without a brain or a skull or my tongue, and maybe it was that dread of dismemberment that kept me moving. Then it was over; and they were unhooking my hands and ankles and boosting me into a shallow cell that had been cut in the corridor's wall, without light except what seeped through the ventilation hole, without room to stand up or stretch out so that I had to lie on my side (my sores kept me off my backside), with only a chamber pot and foul water on the floor from river seepage. There were dozens of similar cells down there, but I heard no sounds from them and didn't hear any other footsteps the days I waited. The corridor was like a garbage chute into the river. Even though they hadn't shot me at first, I convinced myself that soon they'd kill me and throw me away like waste. I'd float to sea on the ebb tide.

My fear of nine-grams-waiting started again that evening (I can't be sure only one day passed, but it's my best guess), when two Blue Tabs pulled me out of the cell and manacled me again, hands and ankles, and then pushed me toward the long end of the corridor. It was the same slow walk over brick shards and rat bones (there were cats everywhere in Chekhist dungeons). I counted another sixty-five steps to the riverside, where the standing water was icy and like sludge. I was too weary to beg and obeyed as they shoved me into the antechamber and opened the outer portal to the quay. I glanced at one of the Blue Tabs' watches. It was 1830 exactly. If I have the date correct, Sunday, June 15, the time is strangely significant, for, as I shall explain, down at the Cosmodrome it was 2030 hours, desert twilight in mid-June on the yellow steppe at Tsar Cannon.

Outside the Leningrad evening was like a mural painting—the choppy blue river and the mellow golden sunlight of another sweet white night. I was staggered at first by the brightness and overcome, too, by the good air and cool breeze. The Blue Tabs had to boost me by my arms. We worked down the steps of the concrete embankment to the greasy waterline where diesel fuel floated like black grass. I tried to relax but my fear rose up once more. I begged them to tell me if they were going to throw me in. They shared cigarettes and ignored me. I stood between them for some time, looking out on the busy harbor. There were freighters loading at the Navy Yard, ferries crisscrossing the main channel, smaller craft tied up at other official quays. It was such a beautiful white night, a scene of such pleasant normalcy, that I was disoriented. I can remember listening to schoolchildren singing a folk song on a ferry that passed perhaps a hundred meters offshore.

What we were waiting for wasn't my nine grams, but rather Iagoda and my mother. A small white river cutter approached from the Big Neva and churned the channel until it backed its engines and drifted to a neat touch at the landing. Several green-suited Border Guardsmen jumped to hold the cutter in check, and two more took me from the Blue Tabs. I didn't resist, for by then I'd spotted General Iagoda under the awning on the aftdeck of the cutter, standing bareheaded and cheery and beckoning to me as he puffed on his cigarette holder and called, "Lieutenant, good, good, come aboard," as hale as a yachtsman.

I ask you now what could have been more lunatic—and I mean to mock—than stepping out of a dungeon to go aboard a trim white cutter in the blue Neva on a fair, breezy evening, and then to sit in manacles under an awning with General Iagoda and my mother? My mother came on deck after we'd shoved off from the quay, and she looked self-possessed and haughty in creamy bright clothes and a very white wool shawl. She sat in a canvas-backed chair across from where they'd flopped me on the deck. Iagoda took a seat beside her, and they both gazed out onto the sun's long rays reflecting off the waves, neither of them taking notice of me. It was as if I were their privileged guest for a day cruise—without shoes or hat or coat and shivering in the sea breeze, my face pocked with scabs, my gums bleeding so that I leaked blood onto my lips, my fingernails broken off and infected—and they were letting me enjoy their discreet hospitality before bothering me with conversation.

Eventually my mother did notice me, and when she did she emphasized her disappointment. My memory is particularly untrustworthy in this part of my story, and I can only recall that evening in the Gulf of Finland like a child's nightmare, filled with giants, witches and ghouls and a long falling into a hole. My recollection is that my mother began by scolding Iagoda for how poorly I looked. "What've they done to him? Why didn't you tell me they were doing this? What have they used on him? Look at what's been done. Did you decide on this? I said to make progress with him. Is this progress to you? I said I didn't want this, I very clearly said I didn't want this. You and your people, I know what you'll say, it couldn't be helped, or mistakes have been made, but I didn't want this. This is shocking, look—shocking." They were discussing me the way they might have discussed a sickly domestic animal—not quite a dog—and there was some give-and-take about which of my injuries were attributable to my defiance and which were caused by other zeks or my jailers. Iagoda was defensive throughout and conceded, "Yes, yes, I see what you mean. They've made a mess of it. I take responsibility," and other apologies and concessions to my mother's opinions.

I've mentioned that my mother was dressed in layers of beautiful cream-colored clothes, with some sort of wool shawl over her head and shoulders, with jewelry and cosmetics, but I must emphasize that to me—lying on my side and gazing up at her—she seemed much more beautiful and very much more alluring than she had at the Bolshoi. Her rich black Eurasian eyes, which had seemed faded when she was facing Katya and then Uncle Alexander, glowed once again with her furious passion. I was confused by how much younger and more awesome she looked to me in the golden light of the white night. Her tone was vigorously disapproving again, and there was none of the shrewishness she'd used with Uncle Alexander. "I didn't want this," she told Iagoda. "No, no, you've done it wrong. If I didn't know what he looked like before I wouldn't have recognized him. He was a handsome young man. He had a profile to him. And now look at what's been done. You weren't to do this, God, not this—" At this point she reverted to her rapid French-speaking to voice a much longer version of her complaint.

Iagoda answered in Russian, trying to defend himself. "I understand, yes. It hasn't worked well enough, yes." Iagoda explained, "It's called 'the course,' " and he puffed on his cigarette as if he were most intimidated by my mother's temper, and then continued with many empty details about the drugs. As he talked he shimmered like a deity in my eyes, so potent with his chivalrous manners, his scholarly eyeglasses, his fine-boned Nordic features and neat lips and bright even teeth, that he might have been the most completely perverted version of the New Man of Bolshevism I would ever meet—a sleek, articulate, sympathetic gangster. Iagoda told my mother, "The doctors said he was a routine case of schizophrenia. It was an inconsistent diagnosis, I knew that, but it was what they usually say, and it was the best advice I had to rely on. They said he was suffering from 'sluggish schizophrenia' and that he was a typical delusional case. I asked for their help in cleaning him up. I didn't know they were going to do this. I'm as shocked as you about this. If I'd known, I wouldn't have permitted it."

There was much more French between them, and I listened in a woozy state of curiosity. This mention of "sluggish schizophrenia" was the first I'd heard that those doctors had opinions of me, and I turned over their idea of me as mind-sick in my very damaged mind. I know now it was all so much naked cruelty to torture a man for being a man, but back then I was reduced to accepting a world where cruelty was healing and doctors were monstrosities. I do puzzle now if Iagoda believed what he was saying. Did the infamous chief of the Fifth Directorate believe the lie that the Special Hospital was actually a house of healing? How self-deluded was Iagoda? I don't know. I've waited and watched for seven decades, and still no one has given me a good answer to the simple question: Did men like Iagoda know the lies they told from the truth?

On the cutter I was lost in a firmament of lies and didn't respond for some time. Then again, neither Iagoda nor my mother addressed me, and I suppose my mind *was* sluggish. Meanwhile they pattered on in Russian and French about my "shocking" condition, but I've shown enough to make a good and simple case—now, sixty-eight years later—that my mother and her lover Iagoda were insane. Only insanity could explain their aberrant conduct that evening, plucking me from a dungeon, bickering over me as if I were a mistake, and yet not offering one hand to help me. What I'm arguing is that my mother had gone mad after decades of promiscuous and homicidal corruption. She could no longer carry on rationally, so that her talk, her conduct, her devotions, were as mad as Markovich's and the whole of the Third Department. My mother had gone mad by making herself a slave to power in the debauched and degraded and upside-down-inside-out world of the Lubyanka lords, as if she were a daughter of Hell, as if she were the first and last paramour of the Judas incarnate that was the Bolshevik Revolution.

And yet, saying she was insane doesn't satisfy me now that I've

written it. Great-Uncle Lev would have called my mother a whore of
Babylon and walked away. Uncle Dmitry told me she was true to
herself and that he pitied her; and I suppose that was a way of saying
she was naturally evildoing, though it might also have been his way
of telling me that he felt guilty for what had happened to her in the
war. Uncle Alexander told me not to bother explaining my mother
or any enemy, rather to fight back and to keep fighting in the Air
Force way until I got what I wanted and won out; but then his
opinion about his wife was always presented fragmentarily, and he
was not to be trusted about his heart. Uncle Konstantine, who didn't
waste words on foes, explained my mother to me that night after the
Bolshoi as a wolf in wolf's clothing, and this might be the most
concise and clever picture of all, a wolf in wolf's clothing in a wilderness of wolves howling like wolves. Yet, now that I'm brooding
about my memory of my mother, I confess she seems left unsolved
by the sum total of her crimes, her history, her rotten soul. The truth
might be that the facts of her demonstrate what a fraudulent human
being she had become by the time I met her. She was hardly alone in
her transformation into a human hoax—she was merely representative of the human hoax of the whole state after fifty years of blunders,
theft, butchery, cowardice, and lies upon lies. It was all lies, as Katya
told me so bluntly once: everything I learned as a young man, everything that got me into that cutter, was based upon the lie of the
Revolution. There was no peace, no bread, no land; there was no
defeat of backwardness; there was no toil, no struggle, no ideology,
no collectivism, no socialism yearning toward true communism, no
defeat of the Kulaks, no crushing of the wreckers; there was no Lenin
the Father; there was no Stalin, Leader of the Genius Toilers of the
Whole World; there was no truth from one border of the empire to
the other. It was all lies—"Lenin" was Ulyanov, a barren, loveless
fantasist and soulless tyrant not that far in temperament from the
nasty Grand Constructor; "Stalin" was Dzhugashvili, a base, homicidal maniac not that far in cunning and talents from Markovich—
and the very first lie told by those few envious, pompous, under-
handed, cowardly middle-aged men who called themselves Bolsheviks was the falsehood that they could build a paradise on earth
without a God Almighty in Heaven.

I have held myself back all these pages from venting my deepest
prejudice against my mother and Iagoda and the whole pack of such

wolves, and so, now that I'm here to face down my mother's madness, I write candidly my confession that I believe in God the Father Almighty Maker of Heaven and Earth and in His Only Son, Jesus Christ; and so I am not declaring anything unusual when I say that my faith in God is what gives my life purpose and meaning to me and that what my mother lacked more than a heart was a faith. My mother, by the time I met her, believed in nothing. She had turned from God as the Bolsheviks once turned from God. In so doing, of her own and their own free will, she and they had made themselves into small, fearful, stupid animals, not men and women; she and they had condemned themselves to a life without love or hope or faith; she and they had abandoned themselves in the shadow of evil where only God's grace can redeem the evildoer. If you ask me now, at the end of my tether, what was the worst sin of the twentieth century, I will say flatly that it was in listening to all the men and women who said that they could make a better world without the mystery of the grace of God, who said in their unearned arrogance with guns in their hands that they knew best who should prosper or fail, wed or love or eat or die. It's my belief that all such profound decisions can only be made by responding to God's grace in the mystery of life, and that there is no freedom possible without the grace of God, and anyone who tells you so even now is a liar who wants to make you a serf, and so show him or her the truth and then the door.

My mother was one such liar, a counterfeit human being, a beautiful, loveless, hopeless, faithless, heartless, spineless, mindless animal, a damned fool, and I suppose I reject her now as the first liar in my life. But back then my dilemma was much more acute for the choice I had between accepting my mother's lies and losing my truth and freedom, or denying my mother's lies and losing everything I loved. You can see the crisis starkly now as I couldn't or wouldn't then, though I do believe I felt it in my heart inarticulately, and that my way of resolving the choice was a confused refusal to quit, a stubborn belief in my father's motto to keep going, a hardheaded hold on the Air Force's crude rule to fight and ram.

Certainly none of this God talk would have made sense to what was left of my mind on the deck of the cutter. I thought I was dying, I was holding on to my life weakly, and yet I found a way to deny my mother. I have no good memories of what I said, but it must have been something hysterical such as "Why are you doing this to me?"

or "Please, Katya's pregnant, she didn't do anything!" or simply "Please, help me, I don't want to die!"

I don't think they responded, but my mother did change her focus from complaints about my condition to her lingering suspicions about me and my uncles, and most especially about our meeting in Saint Sophia. I can recall my mother asking Iagoda, "How did they know, do you think, that we'd be there? How could they have known? How could they have gotten him there so exactly? Last year, you know, at Novgorod, when they sent him to me. Why haven't you found out for me? I asked you to, and you said you would. And don't tell me it was an accident again. I won't believe it and you don't either; there aren't accidents like that. To have him there to meet me, and I hadn't been back more than a week? I've waited, and you've wasted all this time, and nothing—nothing but this. Why was he there? How did Oryolin do that?"

Iagoda had no answer other than to repeat his excuses and say he hadn't had reliable information for some time coming out of "the other camp," by which he probably meant Starry Town. Iagoda did not mention what he'd told me at the Lubyanka, that he knew my presence at Saint Sophia was an accident of fate and that I was a "go-between chosen by fate to preserve the peace." What's strange about this was that, despite all the evidence, my mother refused to accept it was an accident of fate—the river barge accident—that had delivered me to Novgorod, and until the end my mother demanded to know how my uncles had conspired against her, how I'd been so clever as to be present to touch her hand when I helped her from the pew in Saint Sophia. I can only guess that my mother kept at her crazy inquiry because she'd been very frightened of me that day and ever since, that is, not of me but of the turn of fate that had set me at Ivan the Terrible's pew.

You might ask now, why did they torment me that evening, what did they want from me? Did they want me to obey them, denounce my uncles, renounce the Corps? But then why didn't they mention any of this? Why did they just look me over and not talk to me? Was the reason as trite as my mother's wanting to see what had been done to me and my sluggish schizophrenia? Was the reason as bizarre as my mother's fretting about Saint Sophia? Again I don't know the answers, so I must guess that they themselves didn't know the reason, that they might not have had a reason. It might just have been a whim of my mother's to come up to Leningrad—where Iagoda was very powerful as the former boss of the city's State Security—and it might just have been a momentary curiosity on her part to take me out for a cruise, as if I really were her heir. Why my mother remains such a mystery to me might be that all the while I have been searching for her deepest motives, she had none—other than the time-worn sort of anger, lust, pride, envy, and mental sloth.

I'm struggling to get on to the worst part of my time with them—when they showed their depravity nakedly—and I'll write it down quickly so I can get past it.

My mother sounded exasperated when she took a new cigarette from Iagoda, glanced at me, and remarked, "I don't like what you've made of this. I don't like what's happening. You've promised me a lot, and you've shown little of it. Can you at least clean this up so I can stop thinking about it?"

Iagoda looked at me and said, "Yes, yes."

My mother continued, "And the rest of them, you'll clean that up, too. Oryolin most of all, Oryolin finally this time."

Iagoda nodded at me. "Yes, yes. But I thought we were going to try to make something of him, you understand, to save him."

"Save what?" my mother asked. "After this mess you've made, save what? Do what you must and don't bother me with it anymore. And make sure you don't come to me with more of your 'mistakes-were-made' explanations. I don't want to hear it anymore."

Iagoda stood as if his joints hurt, and from my position he seemed on the great heights of a cliff as he responded to my mother, "Mistakes are always made, Daemonia. It is the nature of mistakes."

My mother's last spiteful verdict before she rose and left us was, "I don't want to know, just clean it up quickly."

The worst words I've ever heard were so simple for her to say. "I don't want to know," she said. "Just clean it up quickly," she said. My mother might have condemned a multitude as easily as one with those same words: "Just clean it up quickly." Clean up me and my lovely Katya and our unborn baby and my valiant uncles and any and all she thought rubbish she didn't want to know about anymore. The books say that Lenin and Stalin, who took special care to seduce and betray and condemn their enemies in person, were often frustrated by the delays that rose up in the wars, purges, and other orgies of cruelty in the name of perfect tyranny, and I have long imagined both of them at various times telling their toadies, "I don't want to know, just clean it up quickly."

Before Iagoda swept me into the rubbish bin I did make one small rebellion, and yet because my memory is so poor here I can't be certain that what I said and did wasn't just in my mind. What I think happened or imagined happened was that, as I lay there, I had a vision of my uncles on the yellow steppe. This vision convinced me that my uncles were winning. I think I stopped crying and begging long enough to yell at my mother and Iagoda something incoherent such as, "They've done it! You're beaten!"

What I must have been speaking of was my wild hope that, since it was more than forty days since the April 18 parley at Black House, that meant that out on the yellow steppe my uncles had launched the first Tsar Cannon test. "She drives, she drives the moon!" I shouted. "We drive the moon!" Then again I can't recall my mother responding to my shouting before she left me, so perhaps this defiance was in my mind's eye. "It's the moon!" I screamed. "We're going to the moon! We've won!"

Iagoda didn't respond either. He followed my mother below and left me on the deck with the Border Guardsmen. I can't remember anything after that until the Blue Tabs lifted me off the cutter and carried me back to my cell like a sack. I'm sure I didn't see the cutter depart, and so I can't provide any last image of my mother. After that evening, I never saw her again; that was the end for us.

I was dead both to them and to myself. When those Blue Tabs dropped me back in the shallow cell, I lay down to die in the seepage. My heart was broken, my mind was shredded, my body was ruined, I felt abandoned by everyone on earth and most especially thrown away by the person who was truly my mother, and so I must have told myself that it was all right to sleep awhile, that it couldn't make it worse if I just closed my eyes and didn't wake up. What death feels like is a mystery to me. I do know what dying feels like, and it's so stifling, blinding, and gagging that it makes the falling-down sensation that then comes on seem a relief. I felt I was falling down and down; I felt as if I were wasting to a husk while my cell became a gigantic pit. Then I stopped feeling anything at all, as if I were adrift in starless zero-gravity, and my thoughts turned to fantasies of free-fall and flight, and I felt I'd escaped my fear of death. But I was afraid, and my fantasies didn't prove to be a refuge, for sometime in the dark of that brief white night they came to get me out of my cell. What's maddening here is that I might have dreamed what I can remember, and the dream is more powerful than the facts. When you lie down to die as I did, when you decide it's permitted to quit if just for a while, you lose the ability to know what's real and what's a dream. I can remember the door opening. I can remember getting up from the floor and going into the corridor. I can remember the Blue Tabs directing me to walk toward the Neva. I can remember hearing my manacles scraping the stones and bricks. I can remember thinking that this was the end, that I'd hear the double-click and then the shot, and then my skull bone would be flying out in front of my eyes. After a dozen or so paces, I can remember the Blue Tabs opening a cell door just behind me and ordering me to get "it" out. I remember clearly how they said, "Get it out," repeatedly. I can remember what it felt like to step into the muddy sludge of the cell and then to knock my sandal against rags that I knew were human. I can remember the cold terror I felt when I got down next to the human rags I knew were my Katya.

Here's what I know for certain about that white night, whether or not it was a fantasy. I know that I didn't get to say goodbye. I have lived out my life knowing that she died like that, alone and abandoned, in rags, with scabs and a rasping breath, and that I was no comfort, and that I won't ever find a way to tell her I miss her.

I also know how I can remember a dream of that night: wrapping my arms around her and taking her with me down the corridor and then down the quay steps, but not to the Neva, rather to a hydrogen and helium land. Together we strode a quiescent prominence like a violet, pink, and white plateau where the darting X-rays tickled our feet. Hand in hand we moved north for a while, strolling past the wonder of it all, until a solar flare lifted us up as if on a falcon's wings and then, when the flare snapped back, we were as one diving into the furnace of our fate. You see what my memory has done with my grief. My Katya and our baby were condemned to death by my mother, were sent into an abyss and murdered so that there was no record, were cleaned up quickly so that my mother didn't have to know any more, and yet my memory only wants to picture how I was the hero who rescued them to escape hell on earth for the surface of the sun.

②

Driving the Moon

The moon race didn't wait for me or love or memory or anything but driving there. I'd doomed myself to defeat in a dungeon and a madhouse, but out there on the yellow steppe my uncles aimed to win for the plain reason that it was their job to win. The truth was that, for my uncles, all Russia and every fool in it could be damned, they were still bound for a new planet and their own hard fates.

It was the same leap at the moon and fate for the American astronauts. In March NASA's rocketeers might have imitated my uncles' *Soyuz 4/5* with their extravagant *Apollo 9*, yet in May, with their trailblazing *Apollo 10* LOR mission, they surged ahead to the brink of a moon landing. On May 18, a perfect Saturn V boosted a three-man command capsule and lunar lander into earth orbit, and then, after the transposition and docking that fashioned the moonship, the astronauts fired the main engine on an excellent translunar trajectory. Three days later *Apollo 10* achieved lunar orbit, and twelve revolutions after that two astronauts (Stafford and Cernan) entered the lunar lander code-named Snoopy and descended to within fifteen kilometers of the moon's surface at the Sea of Tranquillity, in order to inspect several potential landing sites. There was a freak incident during ascent, when the lunar lander went into a flat spin for eight seconds, but the American luck held as Stafford composed himself and regained control to redock with the command capsule. On May 26, the crew splashed down neatly in the South Pacific within eight kilometers of the recovery ship USS *Princeton;* this heroic and risky and most lucky dress rehearsal accomplished, the American moon landing was waiting on *Apollo 11* and a July launch.

While the Americans were harvesting the bounty of their work, wealth, and fortune, the Tsar Cannoneers were falling behind in the long countdown for the Tsar Cannon test-launch premiere. Burdened by shortages, sandstorms, late deliveries, a breakdown of the two work locomotives—delaying the transfer of the booster from the palace (vehicle assembly barn) to the launchpad—and many minor errors, losses, and setbacks such as a flu bug, heart ailments, and other stress-caused ailments among critical personnel, the forty-day countdown proposed by Goldenberg in April stretched to forty-four days, then forty-nine, and eventually, with a major delay for not only the kerosene cars promised by Marshal Vershinin but also the hydrazine and nitric acid propellant needed for the upper stage, to sixty days. Finally in mid-June, at T minus four days, with the superbooster in place at the launchpad and the gantry raised for final preparation, the Tsar Cannoneers approved a short count of fifty hours of working time and forty hours of built-in holds. At T minus sixteen hours, Isaacii Goldenberg intervened during another sandstorm and took over supervision of the fueling of all stages simultaneously. At T minus forty-five minutes, the gantry was peeled back to reveal a behemoth rocket ship, ninety meters high, seventeen meters across at its fins, like a great desert onion dome amid billowing clouds of LOX.

Obviously I wasn't present. I did later see the films of the launch, and my eyewitness account depends upon Goldenberg, who, along with Doctor Lunin, ran the launch, so I can report accurately that, at T minus fifteen minutes, it was Goldenberg's voice on the loudspeaker at test control announcing, "Status board clear, switching to internal vehicle power."

I must mention that I think I sensed the countdown, though I won't press my claim. Perhaps it was chance and perhaps it was a second sight that as I was boarding that cutter in the Neva on Sunday, June 15—1830 Leningrad time, 2030 Cosmodrome time—the Tsar Cannoneers were directing the last minutes of the countdown. While I was crying before my mother and Iagoda, while I was ranting "She drives!" and "We've won!" or thought I was, Tsar Cannon truly was driving and my uncles truly were winning. At T minus five minutes, the Tsar Cannoneers pressurized the fuel tanks; at T minus three minutes, they initiated full internal power and engaged automatic sequence. Only a catastrophe could have stopped the shot then, and Goldenberg on the loudspeaker counted down from twenty seconds. At T minus seventeen seconds, the booster's brain locked on its target coordinates; at ten seconds, water was dumped on the pad to cool it for the blast; at nine seconds, there was automatic ignition sequence followed by the profound earth-rumbling of six thousand metric tons of thrust fighting to be free of gravity. All at once superheated steam cloaked the pad, the restraint points released, the internal gyroscopes steadied the vehicle, and, at T plus four seconds, the largest booster on earth began to rise with thunderclaps, shock waves, and a burning orange tail that picked the ship up and flung it into the pink twilight.

I can see the flaming thrust and hear the rumbling cracks and smell the surging kerosene cloud as if I were there at the test control bunker. I can also hear how the dying Grand Constructor, wasted not only by his abduction and the drugs but also by a stroke he'd suffered over the winter, would have harassed Goldenberg and Lunin with a muted but aggravating fanaticism, "Get it right, do it!" I can also watch the monitors as the eight strap-ons cut off and separated at two minutes and twenty seconds, as the core-stage engines continued twenty more seconds, as the Proton third stage burned another two minutes forty seconds and cut off. At T plus five minutes thirty seconds, the drone payload (a robot Soyuz) was inserted into orbit at 178 by 366 kilometers. I can still feel the whole perfect operation as if I were everywhere in it at once. And what do I now feel about the fact that while I lay mad in a cell in a dungeon my Cosmonaut Corps was one shot from the moon? I feel empty about it.

My uncles felt empty about my ruin, too, according to what I've been told by Stumpelkin, who was my informant for much of what happened next. My uncles knew where I was and what had been done to me and Katya and her family. They also knew who'd done it, how it was done, and why it was done, that is, that it was done for the feud and nothing more—and this meant that I was trapped and Katya was murdered for the nothingness of my mother's vengeance. All the evildoing by Iagoda and my mother was for nothing in the end. My uncles knew this and knew they must not turn back to it, as Uncle Alexander had threatened madly at the Bolshoi, and they also knew they must not and would not try to save me. I was lost to my uncles just as I was lost to myself, and my uncles accepted the sentence just as I accepted it. Uncle Alexander, who was dying in bits from the bowels up, had rejected me silently, for I had disobeyed, I had broken ranks with the Air Force and Corps, I had thrown away my life. I was as dead to Uncle Alexander as I was to my mother, and no matter how the squadron appealed he ignored the arguments and refused to hear out its rescue plans.

If you're surprised by this, recall that I've told you the truth, that Alexander Oryolin could be as hard-hearted and damnable as my mother. What Uncle Alexander held to was his duty, what he called his job, and his job wasn't to save me or to stab Iagoda or to make good on a feud; his job was to drive Tsar Cannon to the moon landing and in the meantime to guard the Tsar Cannoneers from the threat of Iagoda's reach. Expansion of the Tsar Cannon airstrip had started the fall before with work battalions, earth-moving equipment, tank farms, revetments, and hangars, and all that was in place even before the massive construction project that expanded the small-gauge rail line that connected to Star City and raised the vehicle assembly barn on the steppe. After April, with Marshal Vershinin's authority, Tsar Cannon works had become a five-hundred-square-kilometer theater of operations with the introduction of the thousand-man Steppe Eagle regiment, three work battalions to augment the heavy construction, a SAM-equipped air defense battalion from the 103rd Air Assault Division, and the deployment of not only a helicopter regiment and a transport aviation squadron but also my uncles' squadron's fourteen 21-Pf air interceptors along with ground and repair crews.

My uncles were expecting the worst, and they prepared for it as morbidly as they'd once dug in their air regiment from Stalingrad to Berlin. If General Iagoda aimed to finish the assassination before the moonshot, he would have to come through a ground and air defense that was comparable in quality though not in quantity to Starry Town's security with Chkalvo Airbase. By June my uncles ruled more sophisticated firepower than any command in Kazakhstan except State Security's Border Guards at Tashkent.

Regardless of Uncle Alexander's prejudice, my friends would not stop pleading for me. Stumpelkin told me about the first confrontation at Black House the day after I disappeared in late April. "He sat tight, and we asked him again, because we weren't sure he'd heard us," Stumpelkin said of Uncle Alexander, who'd been moved from the medical center out to Black House along with nurses and a bodyguard of paratroopers. "But he'd heard us and didn't want to answer. General Zhukovsky was there, and he said, 'We'll see,' but I knew he wasn't going to do anything. It was clear by the way General Strogolshikov walked out on us that they wouldn't listen. And we knew the Corps wouldn't listen if they wouldn't. You were off the roster, Peter; they'd just removed you like a deserter."

(I once asked Genka—this was many years later—"Did you think I'd deserted?" and he answered, "No, but I thought you'd done something very selfish that was close to desertion.")

Again in mid-May, about the time the squadron transferred from Starry Town to the Tsar Cannon airstrip, my friends appealed to my uncles that they were ready to volunteer to go for me, and again they were rebuffed. Through May and into June the squadron set up their flight plans, flew daily patrols, worked at the palace on the spacecraft and the critical moon lander, and waited for victory, and all the while they debated among themselves what Iagoda might have to send against Tsar Cannon if he were to be so desperate as to try at a desert fortress. My name always came up in these debates, Stumpelkin said, and along with the defense plans for the airfield my friends proposed plans to rescue me. However, each time the discussions went as far as to spell out methods and to list volunteers, my uncles rejected my friends, no counters, no recons, no patrols, no expeditions. The standing order at Tsar Cannon works was "Finish it" and that meant the moon landing and not a feud over an absent-without-leave boy like me.

Stumpelkin said that the break in the gloom came after the successful Tsar Cannon test launch, when the squadron actually tried to rebel from my uncles' rule. Stumpelkin said it started spontaneously at a morning preflight briefing on a dirty Saturday morning in the desert—June 21, T minus twenty-three days on the long count for the moonshot. With a gusty yellow wind bending the radio towers and filling the air with engine-beating sand, the squadron decided to delay the dawn exercise and eat more breakfast, and it was then that they found themselves gathered in a rump war council that was essentially a mutiny. I don't judge them for it, other than to agree that they were wrong to defy my uncles and to come for me, and to admit that if I'd been there I would have spoken against them.

Stumpelkin remembered the scene years later with a mix of regret and self-righteousness: "We knew they weren't going to help you whether or not we made the test shot," he said of my uncles. "They'd been spending their time over at the palace with Lunin and that lot, and we were on our own at the field. Zhora [Fedyuninsky] called the meeting, after breakfast, and we were of a mind to have it out, at least Yurka [Adama-Bibliov] and I were, and Trifya [Miserbiev] was even crankier about it. Your Kazakh pal was there, that boy Abdrahman, and he spoke up too. And so did Isaacii [Goldenberg], you know. Isaacii made long speeches about you, he must have told you. It got noisy. We were disgusted you'd been left to die. We made sure everyone heard us sound off."

Stumpelkin said that Fedyuninsky had chaired the meeting and had used his procurator style to outline the crime, the culprits, the solution, eventually summarizing, "He's been at the Special Hospital since May fifth, and he's back now after four days at the Center— that's Chekhist H.Q., the Detention and Interrogation Center. We got word last night that yesterday they transferred him back to the Special Hospital and he's on the ward again, the Third Department. No special guards, just the warders, and no special treatment since they brought him back. We think they've stopped the drugs."

Artzybashev had purchased or extorted most of Fedyuninsky's intelligence from sources in Leningrad, so he was able to expand upon the latest information. "They didn't shoot him like they were supposed to. We don't know why," Artzybashev said. "It's what they do at the Center—after they work on them, they shoot them. Where they put him there, you're not supposed to come back. I don't know why they didn't shoot him. No one knows. He should be dead."

Stumpelkin told me that my friend Arkady Volgamints had teased, "Maybe they screwed it," and had made everyone laugh and grumble. (The squadron didn't know about my boat ride with my mother and Iagoda, which was the true reason I'd been kept four days at the Center before being transferred back to the Special Hospital.)

Goldenberg had then made one of his speeches, and because he was now a crowning Tsar Cannoneer, the genius protégé who'd taken the Grand Constructor's place to launch the test booster, what he'd said had authority for the squadron. Goldenberg told me years later that he was so annoyed with the wandering argument that he'd dared sarcasm to stir up the proceedings. "What Peter Nevsky did was ridiculous," Goldenberg had started, "and none of us would have done such a thing, would have gone to our girl because she was in trouble. I'm sure not one of you would have tried to help Mrs.

Prishkin. A man like that deserves what comes and should suffer for being so ridiculous as to get caught by the Chekhists and tortured for six weeks."

When Fedyuninsky had responded, "We get the point," Goldenberg had quipped, "Then go get Peter Nevsky, too. He saved my life and the Grand Constructor's life once; now let's go save his life, or what's left of it."

Stumpelkin said that Fedyuninsky had sighed and tried to finish his briefing, "What we know for now is that Peter's back on the ward. He's probably out of his mind. But he's not dead yet."

It was Misha Cherryntevsky who had then asked, "What's left of him?" And it was Doctor Gogol who had contributed facts: "The drugs they're using are crude and short-lived. The more serious threat is to his mind. He'll have flashbacks forever. It's something like epilepsy. The mind doesn't recover for a long time, if ever, and there are missing pieces, as if your brain's packed with sawdust."

Stumpelkin said that he had not felt more upset than when he faced the fact that my mind was being damaged irreparably, and that this revelation had pulled the squadron's mood down hard.

Fedyuninsky had returned the meeting to the rescue plans they'd worked out, the maps, charts, diagrams, timetables, and the typical paperwork of an operation. They had reviewed similar material before, when they'd petitioned my uncles, and there was nothing new to discuss. The discussion had remained businesslike, with the whole squadron contributing along with my friends Arkady Volgamints, Doctor Gogol, and Lev Lympyet, who were now cosmonauts and who had been invited to the Cosmodrome to participate in my rescue. No matter how long they talked however, the question hadn't been how to get me out, but rather who could command the mutiny that could do it. Stumpelkin said that the sun had come up so fast on the steppe that, by the time Fedyuninsky had finished going over the timetables for a rescue raid, the barracks windows were rectangular ovens. Fedyuninsky had pushed his charts aside and concluded, "We can get into the Third Department. We can buy the ward. We can get out. There might be a problem, if Iagoda expects us, there might be a problem, but I doubt it. I think they've thrown him back into the Special Hospital because they don't care what happens to him. I think Peter Nevsky's there for us to retrieve like a lost watch."

Because he was still an outsider, Volgamints had said aloud what everyone was probably thinking anyway, "I'd say there might be a problem if we get shot down like ducks and clapped in there with Peter, wouldn't you, boys? Just a little problem that the Chekhist bastards are waiting for us to knock on the door."

Cherryntevsky had snapped, "We don't need smart lips."

Goldenberg told me later that at this point he'd deliberately baited the squadron. "No, let him talk. I'm not sure they're waiting for us, but did that stop you before? Is this the same bunch of hot falcons I saw last fall who dropped into the Dzhezkazgan like avenging angels? It must have been some other flight of avenging angels."

Tempers worn down by the heat and the subject, there had followed much carping and challenging, and the squadron had drifted in doubt. If my uncles had been present, here was the moment when Uncle Dmitry would have thanked Fedyuninsky and the rest for their contributions and would then have led the squadron to a collective recommendation for action, and then Uncle Konstantine would have joked, and then Uncle Alexander would have sat forward and commanded. But without my uncles the squadron was headless, and Stumpelkin told me that after a while the cosmonauts had become too disagreeable to argue and had just flopped despondently about the barracks. It had become hotter, duller, closer, and the molten wind had cut through the cracks in the walls, and still no one had wanted to leave the barracks for relief, because, according to both Stumpelkin and Goldenberg, they'd realized that when this meeting ended I was dead to them: Glavtop had pulled on his flight boots, Grin had napped, Schtange and Tevyelook had unfolded their chessboard, Miserbiev had eaten cold porridge, Adama-Bibliov had finished sewing on a button, my friends Volgamints, Gogol, and Lympyet had tried to cool themselves with hot tea, Artzybashev had dictated a list of money figures to Kandidim, and all of them had watched for one of their number—perhaps the senior Fedyuninsky or Cherryntevsky—to take control of the failing mutiny and declare of my rescue, "Finish it."

Stumpelkin told me years later—I think it was eight years later, while we were training for our first spaceflight mission—that he doubted anything more would have happened that morning without the sudden intervention by my uncles, that is, by a surrogate for my invalided uncles: "The sun was like a torch when we heard the chopper outside," Stumpelkin told me. "We knew it was the paratroopers moving around—they'd been racing around the airfield on full-battle-dress drills for weeks, and over the last week they'd been running night exercises over the airfield. What was odd was that this Mil came roaring overhead and held there, beating us in the downdraft and rattling the walls. Someone opened the door to go out and wave them off—it was like inside a drum in there—but when the door opened there was dust like an avalanche into the room that made it hard to see, and we yelled at him to close up. And then, it was just like this, the door was shut, and we realized that Strogolshikov had come in with one of his company commanders and several noncoms and the regimental intelligence officer. Strogolshikov, you know how black-faced he was in those days, a big, big black-faced bully, remember?" (Stumpelkin told me this version in 1977, before Alexey Strogolshikov became commanding general of the 103rd, a decade before his wretched humiliation and court-martial in Afghanistan as the Butcher of Kabul, two decades before he was installed as the commanding general of the Russian Airborne Corps.)

Stumpelkin laughed at this part of his remembrance. "He looked like he'd been painted by dust, and only when he blinked and opened his mouth could you see he was alive—you remember, Strogolshikov was an ugly bull, and when we asked him what he was doing all he said was, 'We're ready.' Then he pointed out to where an Antonov was taxiing at the ready. You know what happened next." Stumpelkin laughed harder. " 'We're ready,' he said. And I guess he was, since we were airborne within twenty minutes and down at the assembly point ten hours later—a by-the-numbers exfiltration, in and out and no waiting, all the briefing and debriefing while in flight, and back at Tsar Cannon within twenty-four hours of his 'Ready.' But you know."

I know very little of what happened next other than the fact that I was rescued in a small-scale airborne helicopter assault on the Special Hospital using the same tactics that the Steppe Eagles had been practicing during those night exercises at Tsar Cannon—which of course was demonstration that my uncles had decided to meet the squadron's demands rather than to continue to erode morale. Then again it might also have been a demonstration that my uncles had decided to keep their troops sharp-minded with a military problem, for, as you shall see, Alexey Strogolshikov was sent more to end me than to save me.

What I do know of the rescue is that, by the time Alexey Strogolshikov was "ready," I was more comfortable than I had been since my arrest because I'd decided to stop fighting and quit. I'd been put back with Markovich. There'd been no more injections, at Iagoda's order I suppose, but perhaps, too, because no one expected me to live much longer. I couldn't eat at all. Markovich forced me to take water, and he bathed the infected scabs on my thighs and hips. I still couldn't lie on my back or sides, or sit, so I spent my time lying on my face. If everything went well I slept heavily and blankly, and there were no more dreams about the sun, I'm sure of that. After whatever happened to me or to my mind at the Center, I felt very content to think or dream of nothing. My body ached, and I could feel my gums rotting and my joints hardening, but my dreams were gentle, woolly, unthreatening. What I didn't know then, and do now, is that when your dreams turn strangely sweet despite your deprivation it means you're probably done, just as in the slave camps the zeks often reported tender dreams in the worst circumstances.

My dreams must have been like that the Saturday evening they came for me—June 21, a smooth, partly cloudy white night in Leningrad—because I can recall being in a hazy mood after awakening from a long sleep. I found a sitting position that didn't hurt and yet allowed me to rest at Markovich's feet, in order to listen to him sing lullabies. Markovich had a whispery voice, and I don't know why he sang most every night, but then, I don't understand most of what I found in the Third Department. It was as if men can only be bashed down so far, and then they reach a bottom and that's where they last out for much longer than expected.

The moon set over the Neva early that night, into Virgo according to my charts now, and I seem to recall leaning against Markovich's knee watching the quarter moon fade into the skyline on the far side of the Neva. I was very keen on where the moon was, I'm sure, and maybe my attention was some sort of passive strength, since the moon represented my uncles and the Corps to me. This memory might be confused in my mind with other nights, but it seems correct now that Markovich was being especially kindly to me, stroking my ear to make it hurt less and singing lullabies again and again. We were fastened together like a father and son, a hairless nut-brown man and a pale shrunken child, and our devotion might have lasted minutes or hours until it was broken by the attack. I can distinctly remember how Markovich pulled away from me to stare out the window. I can picture the half dark in the long gray chamber, the slumbering lump of dying men, the broad choppy Neva, the serene blue glimmer of that eerie twilight time of a white night—and then Markovich was pawing at the screened window and whispering, "Here, now, baby, here now, isn't this them? Isn't this yours? Ain't I right about you, isn't this them?"

What Markovich heard and saw were four dragonlike heavy Mils fitted with pontoons skimming over the river in from the direction of the old steelworks and heading directly for the boggy ground behind the annex of the Third Department. The front of the Special Hospital's grounds was dry and piny and ringed by barbed wire, but the backside dipped into mud and silt flats that appeared and disappeared with the river's irregular flood tides. There was a capsized hulk of a barge in the flats that held grebes and other shore nesters, and the lead Mil aimed for a landing zone between the capsized barge and the soggy flats. I didn't see much of the initial operation, but I do know the airborne drill. I can suppose that the four Mils would have worked in teams of two, with the lead Mil touching down to unload strike teams of paratroopers designated for the annex while the second Mil hovered offshore to provide covering fire, and then the two Mils would have exchanged places. The second pair of Mils would have gone over the hospital and matched the arrangement on the street side. The grinding noise of the engines must have terrified the few warders still awake, and there was no one in the Special Hospital with the know-how or will to resist an airborne strike force. Alexey Strogolshikov was a shock commander who knew you take a target by brute force from all sides at once, and the Air Force in him told him not to wait or creep but rather to go directly at the main gate with main force and maximum firepower. The only part of the strike that suggested any finesse was that it came in the blue light of midnight, but then the Mils made enough noise to shake awake the river gods. I don't know if Alexey Strogolshikov actually expected State Security to counterattack—there was no reason to believe State Security cared at all about me or anyone at the Special Hospital, and the field intelligence Artzybashev would have bought would have told the Steppe Eagles that the Special Hospital was nothing other than a worthless human trash heap on the outskirts of the city—but then Alexey Strogolshikov's expectations wouldn't have signified, since he was trained to come for the worst case and to find it.

The worst in this case was contained in Alexey Strogolshikov's orders from my uncles, and I have to tell you what you might not understand: The paratroopers weren't sent to extract me and carry me back to Tsar Cannon—they were sent to find what was left of me and, since I was brainless, to shoot me like a mortally wounded animal. It was the way of the world in those days that a falcon must not be left in the enemy's hands, and, if he was, then he was no longer a falcon, he was a forfeited casualty. Even this explanation probably doesn't help you comprehend how the empire had been built on a rigorous cruelty that was usually logical and always final, but I am telling you as best I can that the viciousness I have shown you in the Chekhists was matched in all ways by the brutality in the Air Force. Rather than get nine grams from Iagoda, my uncles had sent Alexey Strogolshikov to give me nine grams from them.

I missed the assault because I was clinging to Markovich's legs and whimpering at the roar of the Mils. Down below, the strike teams tore down the barbed wire, catapulted into the annex through ground-floor windows, bashed off locks, crushed anyone in their way, and came on shouting, "Out, all of you, out!" In the Third Department the inmates fled toward Markovich at the end of the ward, and soon the warders did, too, particularly the little sadist warder Kok, who tried to hide among us. When the troopers finally cracked into the ward, someone boldly kicked at Kok and cried, "Him, get him!" and Kok scrambled out like a cat, begging for mercy until one of the troopers brained him flat.

The Steppe Eagles were mammoth, stone-faced, cold-blooded men who were much too quick for our nerves, and they used their bayonets and rifle butts to corral us into a heap. Then they ordered us to count off by fours, but because few were sensible enough to count anymore this failed as a way to separate us. At some point a noncom called out my name, "Nevsky! Report! Lieutenant P. A. Nevsky, report front and center!"

I didn't respond, since I was too slow-witted to do anything without a long delay; and yet—and here's a deep mystery to me—by the time I was able to respond, Markovich stopped me by holding his finger to his lips and whispering, "Sshh," and I obeyed him.

Given my silence, the search had to fail, because neither the warders, the inmates, the doctors, nor the administrators knew my name, I was just a number on the ward to them, and only Markovich could have identified me. The Steppe Eagles, baffled by the sobbing chaos, swept us all up and pushed us out of the ward and down the stairwell out to the swampy grounds' riverside. The paratroopers were emptying the whole annex of the Third Department in order to locate me, calling repeatedly, "Nevsky! Lieutenant Nevsky, sound out!" Soon there must have been three hundred inmates and several dozen warders spread out in clumps along the wet shoreline, surrounded by paratroopers who kept calling out for me and looking back at the big Mil hovering just offshore that was their command post. The troopers began to interrogate the warders savagely in the Airborne way of beatings and slashings, and still there was no order to search, and still I remained huddled with Markovich in the mud. I wasn't coherent enough at the time to help myself, yet Markovich was clearly in control of himself, and I have long felt frustrated that I don't know why he did what he did. He'd said I was his treasure, his baby, and he must have known I was his way out of the Third Department— why else had he coddled me those weeks—so why didn't he let me answer?

The search for me continued, and though I didn't see or hear them, my friends Stumpelkin, Miserbiev, and Adama-Bibliov were there, along with Volgamints, Gogol, and Lympyet, all of them volunteers from the squadron under the command of Misha Cherryntevsky (the whole squadron was not permitted to accompany the Steppe Eagles), and they were scattered around the grounds checking from inmate to inmate for me. Stumpelkin told me later that the depravity of the inmates had shaken him, and that he'd hoped I was dead rather than one of those wailing madmen.

Stumpelkin said, too, that he was only ten meters from me at the crisis when suddenly, for no rational reason, Markovich had bounded up like a rubbery monkey and cried out, "I'm here! I'm Nevsky! Catch me! I'm Nevsky, the little man in the moon!" Markovich bounded away screeching, "Here! Here!" and when a trooper blocked him, Markovich scrambled back toward me, crying out insanely, "Nevsky! It's me, here, here, catch me, babies!" Markovich was in midair flight when he dropped into the mud.

I lunged atop him like a child to a parent, though I knew he was dead. His mouth and eyes open, his fingers like claws, he was clearly gone, and whatever killed him—stroke, burst heart, exhaustion, perhaps even a bullet, though I don't recall a wound or blood—I would never know. It was as if he were playing tag with the Steppe Eagles and then he was dead. I can recall very little more than knowing I was dead with him. Stumpelkin told me that I had clutched the corpse and wailed hysterically, and it was then that Doctor Gogol had recognized me. Gogol had rushed over to make certain it was me under the grime and scabs, and he had waved over Stumpelkin and Miserbiev and ordered them to fetch Major Cherryntevsky. "We were afraid they'd spot what we were doing," Stumpelkin told me. "You were out of your head. We knew what they'd do."

The Steppe Eagles were already shooting warders, doctors, and madmen as they finished interrogating them. I haven't illustrated this detail until now because it's mad too, but I suppose the truth doesn't have to have an explanation. The Steppe Eagles were shooting men in the head at the direction of the noncoms. Many begged for mercy, but no one fought back, and though I guess I understand why they shot the warders and doctors, I don't know how they judged which inmates should die.

Doctor Gogol didn't wait for Cherryntevsky; he just grabbed me up and with Stumpelkin's help carried me over the shallows to the Mil straightaway. My friends wouldn't let the troopers see me. They kept me under blankets in the Mil, and according to Stumpelkin, when one of the noncoms came over to question them, Volgamints threatened to shoot him. Stumpelkin also said that, by the time they found me, the grounds were pandemonium—squads of troopers crisscrossing between madmen, corpses lined up like wood, warders gagging and vomiting as they were led to execution, and over it all Alexey Strogolshikov on the field phone, calling his Mils to lift off. Stumpelkin told me that Alexey Strogolshikov couldn't have known that I was found, that he must have regarded his mission a failure, that he'd probably decided to pull out because he was under orders that, if he couldn't find me, he was to level the Third Department.

Stumpelkin told me, "They left a smoking wreck. Amazing to see. As soon as we lifted off, they fired the incendiaries, and the whole building where you'd been fell apart and caught fire. It was amazing—right on the river, warehouses all around, and boom! Just like Dzhezkazgan."

My friends carried me from the Special Hospital, past the eyes of the Steppe Eagles and back to the airbase, where our Antonov lifted us back to Tsar Cannon works; however, I carried nothing from the Third Department, not even the dreams that had sustained me as I lay dying, and I have no memory between Markovich's death and when I awakened in the hazy heat of the yellow steppe a week later. I lay insensate for five days and nights, and when I started to come up out of the stupor, when Doctor Gogol and Doctor Mometov (who was now Uncle Konstantine's sixth wife) eased back on the tranquilizers and antibiotics, I was moved from the humidity of the barracks to a cool, dry underground chamber. I must have thought I was in a tomb, for my dreams returned, and this time they were chilly, shadowy, black, and hollow. Now and then I would wake and feel the chill air and reach for Markovich and find a cold concrete wall and darkness.

It turned out I wasn't in a tomb. I was in the big bomb shelter bunker that had been built for the squadron just off from the old barracks. It wasn't until the eighth day after my rescue, Sunday, June 29, that I woke up enough to take control of my surroundings and take stock of my body. It was very important to me that my bowels worked again and that I could urinate without pain. My feet were gruesome with swollen, blackened heels and several toes without nails, but I could stand without shaking, and just holding still, half naked and erect, was an advance. Yet there was no improvement in my ability to think. I lay passively on my stomach (my sores were still too bad to sit on) until Doctor Gogol and my friends came to check on me. They were excited to see me acting alert and tried to tell me everything at once about what I'd missed since May—the move from Starry Town, the building of the defenses, the test launch of Tsar Cannon, my rescue—but after a while Doctor Gogol realized I wasn't responding correctly and quieted everyone down; he also gave me more drugs that soon helped me go back to sleep. I obeyed him without question, and didn't talk much to anyone, going along with whatever was asked. What I recall about my state was that it was as if I had awakened in my body and yet my mind was still lost, and for long afterward I remained aware of but numb to my surroundings.

For those days of convalescence in the shelter, I remained on my bunk as if all that had happened was that I had exchanged the Third Department for the yellow steppe. The others were good to me, sharing quips and jokes with me, but they soon learned to treat me as a vacant-eyed invalid who wasn't going back to duty anytime soon. And once Doctors Gogol and Mometov had determined I wasn't going to lapse back into any infections or fits—I was told I dry-heaved for eight hours after they tried morphine on me—even the doctors left me be. My new rhythm was to doze through the heat of the day and then to lie awake in the evening listening in on the cosmonauts. Meanwhile the squadron came and went, speaking cheery encouragement to me, chatting among themselves about air patrols and the construction projects. The squadron was flying so many practice alerts, in addition to maintaining a round-the-clock air patrol, that it felt to me as if I were a fly on the wall of a continual air raid drill. Whenever I looked most animated, my friends patted my head and teased me with remarks such as, "Who's the loafer down here! Wouldn't I like such a big sleep!" or "Keep snoring!" or similar nonsense. My bunker soon became a popular refuge, since it was well ventilated, mostly quiet, good for napping between combat air patrols, and also because it was convenient to the new-built air control tower. By then the cosmonauts had rejected the torrid barracks above and were competing for bunk space below, and I was sharing my little chamber, at various times depending on their schedules, with all members of the squadron as well as with several officers from the Steppe Eagles' attached air defense battalion.

One of the Steppe Eagles was the extraordinary air control officer Lieutenant S. T. Zvorrov, who was mocked behind his back as "Fats" because he was skeletally thin. I first met him there in the bunker beneath the desert and knew him for nearly fifty more years, until his death more than a decade back now of cancer. Most things about Zvorrov invited mockery, for as long as I knew him he ate only yellow rice and peppers, chain-smoked hand-rolled cigarettes hypnotically, and had a very annoying way of speaking with an affectless monotone that usually made him sound disdainful. In truth, Zvorrov was a contemptuous, impatient, autocratic fellow who took getting used to, and that was just when he was a young officer still establishing his reputation. When I first met Zvorrov, he was already well acclaimed for having been master air controller of the 103rd airlift that had captured Prague in one night, and, by taking on the assignment as master controller of the defense of Tsar Cannon works, he was reaching for legendary status.

Perhaps I should say that Zvorrov first met me, because on the tenth morning after my rescue, Tuesday, July 1, I was stumbling around in trousers and a cotton blouse looking for a pair of boots that could fit over my swollen heels, when Zvorrov came down the hatchway from the surface and peered in at me. Dressed in starched tropical whites with highly polished buttons and boots, he looked to be on parade except that he was smoking a cigarette with one hand and swatting flies with the other. He started dully to me, "You look like crap."

I responded just as dully, "Sir."

"Very smelly crap," he added. Zvorrov's face was fleshless and nearly lipless, and when he talked the only part of him that seemed to move was his cigarette hand. "You're Nevsky, right," he asked. "And you're the one they brought back in a bag?"

I returned, "Yes, sir." I wanted to sound firmer but couldn't manage it and instead just waited and watched passively. My eyes must have wandered, because Zvorrov turned to look where I looked at the sun's rays blazing down from the hatchway. Sunlight still held a very unhealthy attraction for the most damaged part of my mind, and I suppose I was always in danger of slipping back into my hallucination about escaping the earth for the surface of the sun.

Zvorrov didn't care about my health. "Reporting to duty, are you?" he asked with that ruined smoky voice of his, like an arrogant parrot. "I need a servant, not an assistant, a servant. None of your sort know crap about taking orders and shutting up. They'll probably give me you if I ask. You want a job?"

"I don't know," I said, without meaning anything.

"You don't need to know crap," Zvorrov said. "I know what I want, and I'll tell you, and then you fetch me a glass of tea or more cigarettes or whatever I ask. I want a servant, not an assistant."

My next questions were a muddled way of asking about my circumstances, but they were also my way of making sure what I thought was happening was the case. "You're Steppe Eagles, sir?" I asked. "You're one of them who brought me here? You're one of Colonel Strogolshikov's command? You know General Oryolin, sir?"

Zvorrov answered, "All crap. You're a servant, and you should remember that I don't attack anything anywhere. I'm the master of the game, I'm the cow that slaughters the butchers, I am the best at it, Nevsky, the best." He'd had enough of conversation and yanked at me to follow him up the stairs to the hatchway and then out onto the roasting landscape of a windswept world. The light and sounds of aircraft paralyzed me for several moments, and I sought some relief in the shadow of the air control tower. The tower was really a wooden shack on a platform raised twenty meters high on latticed wooden beams. Zvorrov pointed to the wooden ladder up to the shack. "You're my servant if you can get up there," he challenged me. "Think you can do that? I'll need tea, lots of it, and you get the water boiled over there at the barracks, and you carry it up to me up there. That's the job."

I was too stupid to understand and kept staring at the shack, asking, "Tea, sir?"

Zvorrov said, "Let's see if you can climb it."

I did understand this was a test that I wanted to pass. Barefoot and silently I started up the ladder, taking too long between steps, sweating much too heavily even in that heat, picking up nasty splinters in my palms and soles, but eventually I reached the platform and pushed myself flat out on my stomach, feeling accomplished. Skeletal Zvorrov joined me so easily he didn't even have to throw away his cigarette as he climbed. He told me, "You'll have to do that a hundred and fifty times a day. Do it with a pot of tea and whatever else I want. Day and night, got it? And you'll need boots; have you got boots?"

I couldn't breathe well enough to say more than "No, sir."

Zvorrov shrugged off my answer and pointed down to the barracks. "Fetch me tea. Now."

I remember little from those drowsy first days after I awakened, but I certainly recall my great satisfaction as I climbed down from the air control tower and looked around at the clouds of dust of thousands of men and women working out there on the steppe and knew that now I was part of the whole again—an entire Air Force construction brigade with heavy equipment, the Kazakh village drafted as day laborers, a reinforced Airborne regiment, a squadron from transport aviation, a regiment of Mils, a squadron of interceptors, the teams of rocketeers at the palace and launchpad in the distant rolling ocean of hot yellow salt flats, and now breathless, bootless, wordless me. My willpower was minimal; my body was still shot through with boils; I was half mad with thoughts and fantasies I couldn't fend off; and yet I felt thankful to have a job that I could do as Zvorrov's factotum.

Did I have any thoughts for Katya? I must have thought of her, I must have also thought about Markovich, I must have lain there for hours on my bunk or up in the tower at Zvorrov's bidding while I reviewed all the recent disasters, and yet I can't remember any of my worry, as if my mind has protected me from those days by erasing the worst of the darkness. I add here that it wouldn't be for some months that I learned that Great-Uncle Lev and Golda Rinsakov had been bypassed by the violence, left to petition the Cosmonaut Corps for news about me until Major Tronko took pity and wrote them at year's end with an official version of lies that nonetheless communicated that I was alive.

I went through those days without hope or meaning. I wasn't dead, yet it was as if I had died to what I was, for what those drugs had done worst was to make me numb to my own heart. None of the normal passions any longer affected me. Not only was I empty of love, hatred, joy, revulsion, and the shame that had followed me like a shadow since the Lubyanka, but also I'd lost the sense of self-preservation that makes for anxiety and fear. I was purposeless, too. I could remain in a trancelike position indefinitely; I could stare at the horizon and see nothing; I could talk and not understand what I'd said; I could wander the edge of the airfield without a direction. I suppose now an even better way of describing this numbing phenomenon of the drugs was that, when I awoke from my stupor, I was a man reborn without my soul. My weakened body and damaged brain were on the yellow steppe, but my soul was still with Markovich or with Katya and Great-Uncle Lev, or just missing in action.

Two days after Zvorrov gave me a job, my uncles sent for me along with the rest of the squadron, and that was when I finally faced what had been done to me, with my broken heart and absent soul, and also saw for the first time what all the sacrifice had brought about. It was July 3, T minus eleven days on the long count for the moonshot. My memory is that Stumpelkin came for me in the bunker around suppertime (I had to be reminded to eat) and told me that the squadron had been ordered to report to my uncles at the palace for a briefing, and that Major Fedyuninsky had said I was to be included along with Volgamints, Doctor Gogol, and Lympyet. I dressed in a loose tunic, making sure I didn't miss any buttons and that the sandals I had to wear were both on—it was also hard for me to get shaving and washing details right—and I followed Stumpelkin like a child up to the mess at the barracks. Everyone greeted me generously, and, in the fading heat of the late afternoon, I stood by happily (I couldn't sit) while the squadron ate potato pancakes and barbecued lamb with bowls of cucumbers and debated what my uncles might want of us at the briefing.

The general opinion was that it was time to choose the crew for the moonship. Artzybashev was busy making wagers on who would be named. Since to a man everyone expected Glavtop and Grin to crew, along with either Uncle Konstantine or Uncle Dmitry as commander, there wasn't any play until the odds were extreme. The squadron laughed hard and drank too much and made Misha Cherryntevsky get out his guitar and invent a new stanza about how brave we all were, how truly vainglorious. The cosmonauts were their usual noisy, impetuous selves—and Volgamints's vulgarity, Doctor Gogol's irony, and Lympyet's calmness fit in neatly with the others' strong personalities—yet to me their talk seemed incomprehensible and somehow useless. I tried to act alert, but when someone like Miserbiev or Doctor Gogol noticed that I wasn't eating more than a handful of food, like a sickly rabbit nibbling at cabbage, I retreated to crouch against the wall and wait for Stumpelkin to tell me what to do.

Eventually Major Fedyuninsky telephoned to the new motor pool for an autobus, and the squadron took their last drinks, lit their cigarettes, and strolled outside in the easiest of moods. Stumpelkin and Doctor Gogol took my hands and led me into the shade of the building, where I started a coughing fit and spat some blood with my phlegm. Doctor Gogol thought I should rest, and he asked Fedyuninsky if I could be excused from the briefing. In reply Fedyuninsky stared at my pale, blank face and said sharply, "You're coming along, on your own or on a stretcher, right?" To get me through the fit Abdrahman Godzihkty, who was always about the barracks like a head boy, ran up with goat milk for me. When he saw the blood on my tunic, he protested to Doctor Gogol that I looked worse than ever, and Gogol agreed. I recall Abdrahman was very kind and told me, "You are as brave as any of them, khan. You must be brave enough to rest yourself." Doctor Gogol told me candidly, "You're not fit, Peter. I think your lungs could collapse on you. Without rest they will."

I told them I was fine and to leave me be, but the truth was that I was worse, and the further truth was that I didn't care about my health. Do you understand how much I'd surrendered at the hands of State Security? I know I haven't gone on about what the pain and the terror of the pain did to me over the weeks at the Third Department, and yet the result was I'd quit my life and didn't care to fight to hold on to my worthless body any more than I cared to hold on to my empty desires of conquest and heroism.

On the slow bumpy drive out to the palace, Genka Stumpelkin, seeing my vacant eyes, tried to interest me in the squadron's affairs and also in his concern for my uncles. "They're not the same, I hear," he said of my uncles. "I've just seen them from a distance, but Major Fedyuninsky, he says that General Zhukovsky is so changed we won't recognize him. And General Oryolin—they say he just writes out his orders, he doesn't say anything to anybody. General Strogolshikov's the only one who'll talk. The big news with him is that he's grown a beard, though nobody knows why. They say they're so sad it's like they're in mourning."

I didn't respond, because I could hardly understand what he was saying, but, now that I think about what Stumpelkin told me, I think I can explain my uncles' transformation—I will show it to you soon—as that of men who were in the presence of their own fates. They could see that their fate was damnation. I know, it must sound to you as if I am letting that curse hurled at us by the devil Lazursky color my old-age doubts and regrets about my life, but, if that's true, then it's also true that even damned men like Lazursky have powers to see into the future, and the future he might have seen as he lay there dying in the sleet was that, no matter what would come, his killers were as damned as he. You see, as much as I have presented my uncles as ruthless and limitless, they must have come to see after the assassination that there was no way out for them—that, if they didn't reach the moon, they would have sacrificed everything for a damned failure, that, if they did reach the moon, they would have sacrificed everything for a damned success. Either way my uncles must have understood that damnation was their inevitable fate, just as it was Russia's inevitable fate in those days. Everyone was cursed by the rot, everyone was damned by the rot—most definitely the valorous, the good, the innocent, the old and young and unborn, the victorious fools everywhere, most especially our heroes of heroes who could drive the moon but couldn't walk the steppe free of damned Chekhists like Lazursky and Iagoda and my mother.

We reached the oasis at desert twilight, and in another few minutes of bad driving I got my first close look at the gigantic vehicle assembly barn, or Tsar Cannon palace. Genka was still trying to cheer me up; he pulled me out of the autobus and spoke like a big brother, "Look at the size of it, Peter. Isn't it stupendous? Isn't it worth it all? Come on now, I want to show you the ship. Follow me closely now, watch your step for the cables."

I looked up, and I probably did want to reply, but what happened instead was another coughing fit and more blood spitting. The palace was spectacular. There has never been another such building in Asia, raised like a titanic tent built with ascending staircase levels of tin, canvas, pressed wood, thin steel beams, and whatever else they could buy, barter for, or pilfer. The palace was so giant—one hundred and eighty meters at the peak, a half a kilometer stem to stern— that it threw a long blue shadow on the purplish-yellow desert floor as the sunset directly west of the massive main entrance doors colored the whole building a strange pink and white. The grounds outside the palace were a chaos of heavy lorries and day laborers coming and going among a jumble of discarded building materials such as sand piles, pyramids of bricks, and scattered woodpiles, and, as we passed inside through actual canvas flaps, it was clear that the inside grounds were a similar wild commotion of laborers and rocketeers rushing about among stacks of floor planks, naked cables, overhead ducts, discarded railbed, swinging catwalks, overhead cranes, and unrecognizable discarded machinery. The interior of the palace was so vast that there was room for the two work locomotives that were to haul the booster to the launchpad. The Tsar Cannoneers hadn't bothered with arranging avenues through the refuse and equipment, or with lighting what avenues did exist, so we were soon lost in dark blinds and had to question stray laborers to find our way to the clean room. "You want the clean room?" they asked us. "Follow the runners. Stay on the runners," they warned us, waving us across an expanse of desert floor, since they'd not bothered to lay planks everywhere, and we had to pick our way over a black runner that was the only protection from exposed cables.

The centerpiece of the palace was what could be seen of the vertically raised Tsar Cannon. The main fuselage was generally hidden by the encircling platforms; all that showed to us below were the gray fins of the strap-ons and about twenty meters high of the main stage. The whole ninety-meter-tall booster stood beneath a hammerhead crane at the apex, and amidships the booster was wrapped by about twenty stories of catwalks and other lesser cranes. What it most resembled was a whale hanging from the scales of a god of fishermen, and oddly there was a distinct fishy odor mixed in with the diesel oil and acetylene-torch smells—perhaps because of all the dried fish the rocketeers ate while they worked. There were dozens of Tsar Cannoneers in dingy white coats and threadbare overalls gathered around an exposed panel over the vernier engines, and we came very close to them as we slid around the steam clouds from one of the locomotives. The engineers were arguing vehemently about something in the exposed panel, but I have no idea what. What I know now from reconstructing the events of those last days was that, since July 3 was T minus eleven days, the locomotives were making steam because they were scheduled to begin the rollout of the booster that night for the two-day trip to the launchpad. The Tsar Cannoneers were probably arguing over some emergency detail that they believed in their frantic, fussy ways could destroy the mission. There wasn't anything magical about their task; it was just a mountain of detail turned into a tower of machinery and materials—tons upon tons of fuel lines, heat exchangers, gas generators, swivel-mounted vernier engines, combustion chambers, fuel tanks and LOX pipelines, tank apertures, turbo pumps, injection jets, regulators, ventilation ducts—and all these hammered-together systems connected to hammered-together instruments, and none of the parts any less important than any other part, for if one failed, the whole failed, and hence the arguing of engineers.

Our destination was the clean room where the Tsar Cannoneers had prepared the spacecraft for the booster payload. This restricted area—sealed, air-cooled, harshly lit by banks of fluorescent lights—showed the most expense in the palace. The construction bays for the spacecraft were empty now, with the Soyuz (designated *Luna 15*) and lunar lander (designated *Laikushka*) mounted on the booster's third stage, so the rocketeers had ripped out the bank of cables and moved aside the two overhead cranes in order to make room on the linoleum floor for a round table.

My uncles were hunched over the table listening to a briefing by Goldenberg and Doctor Lunin, with occasional contributions by Doctor Mishuk. What was most striking about the conference was that the Grand Constructor sat in a wheelchair beside Goldenberg saying nothing and perhaps hearing nothing; his eyes were shut, and he looked either asleep or medicated, wrapped tightly in a blanket with his black forage cap pulled down to his ears. The Grand Constructor's condition was at least expectable for a tired old man, while the look of my uncles was so shocking that many of the cosmonauts lowered their heads and whispered together as if we were visiting a hospital ward and not a briefing. Uncle Dmitry, always gaunt-faced, sat in a sullen, pinched silence, his lips bluish, his complexion deeply lined, apparently unaware that his cigarette had burned to his fingertips, and inconsiderate of his oily tunic coat—one of the most fastidious of men, almost as prim about his grooming as Fedyuninsky, now reduced to sleeping in his uniform. Uncle Alexander was so much worse than when I'd seen him in April that it was as if his torso were shrinking to bones inside his uniform. His face was bloated by painkillers, his skin was so waxen it seemed painted on, and his paralyzed legs had twisted inward so that they couldn't even get his boots on anymore; and he was wearing sheepskin slippers. Uncle Konstantine looked vigorous enough, with a patchy white beard that emphasized his sun-browned bald head, but upon closer examination his temperament was out of character and had become antagonistic and impatient. "Get it done," Uncle Konstantine would order, or "Now, it must be now." And, as Goldenberg continued his report, Uncle Konstantine interrupted him, "You need more men, get them!"

I remind you that I was not only sickly, I was also absent of any normal sentiment. I could find no pity for anyone else's tragedy. My last interview with my uncles that evening was feeble, spare, broken, without love, loyalty, tenderness, and, though it was the last time I would ever see them, what I can remember now is that I didn't feel anything as I talked with them, as if I were doing my duty on auto-pilot, as if I were no more than an obedient serf.

Uncle Konstantine began his remarks by cutting off Golden-berg's, Lunin's, and Mishuk's remarks and waving at the squadron like children to come forward. "Let's do this," he said. "You rest yourselves. Let's do this." The squadron pushed into the center of the clean room and acted in the routine relaxed manner—leaning against rails and partitions, blowing cigarette smoke and joking that all the cool air on the steppe had been locked up in the clean room. The squadron's mood was cocky, for the cosmonauts expected noth-ing other than the usual succinct laying out of options and then firm decisions by Uncle Alexander. However, it was obvious that this was a briefing unlike any other before, because Uncle Konstantine, not Uncle Dmitry, was going to do all the talking: "Two weeks back, you wanted a fight. You went to Leningrad and found a fight. Not much of a fight, but you had your day, darlings, and that's the meat of it." The cosmonauts were relieved that the near mutiny was not going to be held against them, despite the facts generally known that Alexey Strogolshikov had been dispatched at my uncles' orders and that one of the orders had been to leave me dead rather than bring back the brainless specimen I seemed. "That's the meat of it," Uncle Konstantine repeated. "You wanted to bring out the ax, and the ax is out, and though you know it wasn't going to scare off the wolf, you wanted the ax out. That's the meat of it."

Uncle Konstantine was speaking in his customary proverbial style, and, without Uncle Dmitry's help to interpret, the briefing was go-ing well off course. Fedyuninsky spoke up to try to restore the train of thought. "Sir, if you mean the wolf is coming on at us, if you mean it's to be Iagoda, we understand, sir, that we might be attacked here. We're at our most extreme readiness."

Uncle Konstantine ignored Fedyuninsky's coherence. "It's enough that the ax is out. You can't hide the ax. You shouldn't hide the ax."

Fedyuninsky again appealed for clarity, "It's Iagoda, sir. He's go-ing to attack us? With what, sir? We don't have any good intelligence of what he's throwing against us."

Uncle Konstantine avoided plain sense. "Eleven days from now we're attacking," Uncle Konstantine declared about the moonshot. "Our ax is out, and we're attacking."

"What about our friends in Moscow?" Fedyuninsky asked of the Kremlin bosses and Air Force high command, who had made concessions to my uncles back in April.

Uncle Konstantine responded with more imprecision. "About two weeks from now, we'll have friends everywhere, or we won't." At least it was clear by this that Uncle Konstantine meant that, if we landed on the moon, it didn't signify what wolf came our way. The cosmonauts nodded at Uncle Konstantine's proof.

Fedyuninsky was still concerned with operational details and asked, "Will the Steppe Eagles stay, sir? If we're attacked, will they stay and hold the field? Will Moscow reinforce us if we're hard-pressed?" Fedyuninsky sounded frustrated and tried again. "What we want to know, sir, is are we going to be attacked by State Security? And if we're attacked, are we going to be left to fight on alone?"

Uncle Konstantine didn't answer. The truth was that the Airborne regiment would stay unless they were withdrawn by the Air Force, and the Air Force would reinforce us unless it didn't, and the rest of the Corps would keep out of our fight unless it didn't, and in all, there had been no promises made by Marshal Vershinin in the event of a battle, and none had been asked. What Uncle Konstantine had told the squadron in his peculiarly metaphorical way was that we were on our own and should not look for help from outside. Uncle Konstantine had said all he wanted about any possible battle with Iagoda. He waved at Goldenberg to add another bizarre detail about the preparations for moon-driving.

Goldenberg started, "You should know—General Strogolshikov wants me to tell you—that we've been advised, by the State Space Commission and Chairman Blagonravov's office, that Marshal Vershinin has denied our request, previously agreed upon but now withdrawn, for funds to build the moon lander at this point in time." Goldenberg indicated the empty bay where they'd built the moon lander. "*Laikushka*," he said, using the pet name for the lander. "You should know that we can't afford to build her."

Fedyuninsky returned, "You're telling us that you can't afford to build the lander that you've already built and mounted on the booster, is that it? This is some sort of double-talk to give the Air

Force a way to deny that we had permission in the event of a catastrophe?"

All Goldenberg did in reply was to acknowledge his invalid mentor with a shrug and remind us, "He is the Grand Constructor." Years later, Goldenberg told me that what had happened was that the Grand Constructor, in what turned out to be his last official act, had signed correspondence that denied that the lander had been built with Air Force funds, thereby providing all parties—the Air Force, the Corps, the Star City rocketeers, the Tsar Cannoneers, and especially the State Space Commission—a way to blame any failure on only one man, Academician Nikhon Univer, and yet to claim any success as their own. At the close of his long, cold, merciless life, the Grand Constructor committed one selfless act of giving away his triumph while accepting all the condemnations of the age. Goldenberg later philosophized to me about his boss, "We all knew his faults. We all knew Russia's faults, didn't we, Peter? And didn't we love him and Russia the same, knowing they couldn't change, knowing we couldn't change? Wasn't it like that for you, Peter? Knowing it could have been done right but staying on anyway and to the end?" Such a generous summary speaks better of Goldenberg's heart than it does of the Grand Constructor, who lived a selfish zealot and who died speechless and alone but for his one true friend, Isaacii Goldenberg—and yet I wonder, if I were given the choice between solitary conquest of the stars and the love of men, would I choose other than had the Grand Constructor?

Goldenberg closed his presentation to the squadron by handing over a copy of the Grand Constructor's letter to the State Space Commission. Fedyuninsky read it and tossed it back on the table, adding, "We're not here to talk about a catastrophe." Uncle Konstantine snorted at this in his old familiar way, and the squadron welcomed the comfort of old-fashioned bravado by laughing a little and teasing back, "The wolf can't read anyway!"

I felt none of this troubled exchange, of course; I stood to the side and watched my uncles like a servant watching his masters. Only Uncle Konstantine showed emotion at all; so it was easy for me to match the blankness of Uncle Dmitry and the lifelessness of Uncle Alexander. I think there was more conversation about the likelihood of battle; and there was mention of a joint command by Fedyuninsky and Alexey Strogolshikov; and I think members of the squadron spoke up with boasts about how well prepared the airbase was to fend off all assaults. From what I can remember, there was no special reason to bother my uncles with operational details about our CAPs, our 21s, our depot stores. Uncle Konstantine cut off the technicalities by asking each of the squadron to stand and receive a salute from him and a few words of encouragement, the usual proverbial remarks about wolves or swords, such as "When the sheath's broken, you can't hide the sword!" He worked through each, from Fedyuninsky down to the newest members, Volgamints, Gogol, and Lympyet, and, as each man returned the salute, a kind of storm cloud came over the squadron's faces. They realized this was a farewell.

Everyone was addressed but me, and my memory is that Uncle Konstantine was gentle with me. "Here's what it is, Petya. Come here. Come closer. You were brought back. They wanted to bring you back. Your comrades wanted you back. And we let them. Do you understand me?"

I tried hard to snap my salute. "Yes, sir, I do, sir."

Uncle Konstantine wanted more from me. "Iagoda took you, didn't he? Do you remember it to tell it?"

I felt nothing when I answered, "Yes, sir, some of it, sir. And it was my mother, sir, Madame Romodanovsky, she ordered it. And General Iagoda, he did what she ordered. I can remember much of it, sir. They took me on a boat in the Neva. They told me they were going to clean me up. They said they were going to clean us all up, sir."

My uncles didn't react, but the cosmonauts made a sound behind me that I can remember as an exhale, for, even though they'd known the facts about me and my mother and father, I think it must have been much to hear, on the eve of battle, that all this trouble had been caused by the direction of an insane Lubyanka lord and his insane mistress.

Uncle Konstantine coaxed me. "They worked on you?"

My mind slipped. I probably sounded very weak when I got stuck on an irrational answer. "They said they were going to clean us up, sir. Clean us up like they were going to clean the deck of the boat, sir. They said they were going to clean up Katya. Like she was dirt, going to clean her up."

Uncle Dmitry came to life at Katya's name and moved his hand to his mouth to ask, "What about Katya?"

I answered with too much confusion to be convincing. "They've cleaned her up, sir, I think. I think that's what they told me, what General Iagoda and my mother told me. They might have shown me her body. I'm not certain, sir. I was out of my head, and I thought I was on the surface of the sun."

Uncle Dmitry could see I wasn't making sense and asked Fedyuninsky and Artzybashev, "Is she dead?"

"We don't know," Fedyuninsky answered. Artzybashev contributed his best intelligence, "She disappeared is what we know, and she might be dead. It's the usual muck-up until we spend a lot of money to find out."

"Find out what you can and tell him," Uncle Dmitry ordered Artzybashev, who wasn't able to obey that order because he was dead himself in two weeks' time. And even if he had lived, Artzybashev wouldn't have been able to buy the truth, for the truth was that once Katya disappeared into the Big House, or the Center, or wherever they put her, she wasn't coming back, there wasn't anyone or any way to get her back. I know this now, but at the time, if I'd been sane, I might have grasped at the ambivalence in his opinion. Nothing showed my soullessness more starkly than the fact that I stood there blank-faced before my uncles while they speculated about Katya's murder.

The question was dropped, and Katya was dismissed along with me. "Very well, Lieutenant," Uncle Konstantine said. "You have your post. I'm told you're assistant to Zvorrov."

I answered, "Yes, sir, Lieutenant Zvorrov, sir."

"Very well," said Uncle Konstantine. He looked away to the squadron to speak of final things. At the finish, you see, my uncles were only heroes of heroes, and by this I mean not only brave and bold but also savage, unrelenting, and unforgiving of anyone. If I could have thought clearly at the time, this bloody-mindedness of theirs might have confounded me the more; however, what I've learned all these years since then helps me understand that you don't measure heroes as good or bad folk; you don't need to measure them at all. Heroes carry on regardless of praise or blame. Heroes are what they do, not what you make of them, not even what they might make of themselves. At best heroes are folk who meet their fate gracefully; at worst heroes are vain fools who chase the very fate that's coming for them. I didn't see the truth that day, standing before my uncles like a ghost of myself, but now I see the truth, and it doesn't make me love them any less. It makes me miss them all over again. Damned or not, beaten or not, my uncles didn't pull back to make amends at the brink; they kept going into the mystery of their fate.

Uncle Konstantine laid his huge hands palm down on the table. "The last of this is the choice of the crew."

It was time for judgment and command. The squadron gathered as one and watched as Uncle Alexander wrote out a note and passed it over, first to Uncle Dmitry, who passed it on one more place to Uncle Konstantine, who read it and repeated, "The crew, the crew." And then he let the note fall to the floor like trash and added, "Get your sleep. It's the last you'll have of it. Sheath's broken, dismissed."

The squadron obeyed. There were no careful words from Uncle Dmitry, no bent proverbs from Uncle Konstantine—just the morbid "Sheath's broken, can't hide the sword"—and, hardest to accept, no overheated charges from the demagogic Oryolin. Uncle Alexander had made the crew assignment, and his command was that it would be the Martian Troika alone driving the moon.

War of the Worlds

Iagoda's forces launched an air assault at first light, Wednesday, July 9, 1969. If you're a student of those days, mark it in your copybooks as one of those small black days that mar the twentieth century, for that morning the might of the Lubyanka lords stabbed at my uncles' backs while the Kremlin bosses closed their eyes and the Army closed its ears and all Russia turned away from the Corps and fell back into the rot. The truth is that my uncles, aiming to conquer a new world, were betrayed by the old world, and the further truth is that, though it has been sixty-eight years since that day, I have yet to find any man or woman who can tell me why my uncles were abandoned for noth-

ing, for an insane feud between my mother and Alexander Oryolin—
for nothing, and yet back then that nothingness was our fate.

Our fate turned grim at 0417, when three bogeys, a Yak-28D
recon with two MiG-17PF escorts, appeared on Zvorrov's radar
screen. I saw the three echoes pop up from my roost, leaning against
a stool in the corner of the air control tower over the Tsar Cannon
airfield. I remember that I was cold and had pulled a blanket over my
shoulders while waiting for Zvorrov's next command to fetch him
hot tea or tobacco or fruit from the barracks below. I had been
wakeful all night, yet felt content to climb up to my duty to wait on
Zvorrov. Zvorrov himself not only always seemed awake but also
always seemed in constant motion back and forth in front of his
several radarscopes and radio links, rolling fat cigarettes, listening to
chatter on his headset, drinking scalding tea like water, eating whole
apples in three bites, muttering to himself or to his command in that
hypnotic voice of his; for after days of chain-smoking and talking,
Zvorrov's voice had become a dry croak that sounded like a strange
insect buzzing against the background noise of the rattling field generator hum below us.

"Stay hot, stay hot," I can remember Zvorrov croaking into his
headset at the sight of the three bogeys. "Give me a moment. A
moment. There now." He talked faster, calling Tevyelook and
Schtange, who were on sentry flight more than one hundred kilometers to the south at ten thousand meters, up where there was a
cloudless purplish black sky as the stars winked out with the approaching dawn and—weather forecast clear and hot—the high sky
of dogfighting. It was then that the bogey Yak-28 recon with escort
made a break toward us on a photographic run. Zvorrov called his
radar pickets for identification and confirmation and then, after
checking there wasn't anything more behind the three bogeys, he
ordered Tevyelook and Schtange to a new altitude and heading. "No
intercept," Zvorrov croaked. "Come to one-nine-five at my
count. . . ." and then he read off a list of numbers so fast he didn't
bother to take his cigarette from his mouth.

I can picture how quietly the battle started as the amber radar
display blinked bright at echo points and identification numbers
flashed to locate Schtange and Tevyelook and our Antonov air picket
as they responded to Zvorrov's orders. I knew most of what was
happening even without a headset—it was all right out of a field

exercise in air defense—and, whenever I lost the flow of the CAPs, I could check the transparent map overlay that showed the locations of SAM sites, Mil depots, and AAA guns in order to see how close in the bogeys were to our counterfire. (The screens were supposed to have audio signals, a clear beep, but Zvorrov was one of those hot types who turned off and ripped out all standard aids.) At this point the bogey contact was still nothing new. We'd had five days of similar sorties by reconnaissance aircraft that had come probing our perimeter at dawn and dusk. Though Zvorrov had sent our sentry flight to answer the probes, no shots had been fired yet, just a run in at us at high altitude and sudden break-off and run out as our sentries closed. The Tsar Cannon airfield's defense was being photographed, mapped, and sounded meticulously, all standard preparation for an air and ground assault. After five days it was easy to assume that the enemy had gained a working knowledge of the vital details of the airfield, such as Zvorrov's tower, the 21s' revetments, the fuel depots, perhaps the underground arsenal.

I do not mean to make our defenses sound easy. The Tsar Cannon airfield's considerable strength was its isolation. We were more than six hundred kilometers from the Border Guard bases at Chimkent and the Air Defense airfield at Tashkent and therefore well out of range of a forced march. To reach us Iagoda's forces would have to come by lorry overland or by armored train up from the south, and both routes would expose them to airstrike or the shock tactics of airborne assault by the Steppe Eagles. What was apparent to all strategists was that the most effective assault on Tsar Cannon would be the most difficult—an airborne drop of Special Action Troops in coordination with an overland armored column, all supported by air-to-ground fighter-bombers. To initiate such a complex operation successfully, it would be necessary first to destroy the Tsar Cannon airfield. The battle for Tsar Cannon was to be won or lost not in the air or out on the yellow steppe but at the airfield, where the squadron's 21s were stored and armed, where the only Antonov air picket was serviced, where the Airborne's Mils were fueled and repaired, and where the brain of the whole rested in the head of the unpredictable master air controller Zvorrov.

The puzzle by July 9 was why Iagoda's forces hadn't yet launched airstrikes against the airfield. I didn't bother myself with debating these matters then—I wasn't capable to do more than scurry around for Zvorrov and sometimes look in on his work like a child watching his big brother—but it interests me now to wonder why Iagoda had hesitated. The two possibilities are either that he was more cautious than he'd evidenced before—this was the same man who'd sent assassins into the Kremlin yard during an all-union celebration—or more likely that he'd had difficulty raising an order of battle from the available State Security combat forces. Iagoda's closely held Fifth Directorate itself was chiefly goons and torturers, not soldiers. He would have had to appeal to the Lubyanka lords for use of the Border Guards, the Special Action Troops, various Interior Ministry troops (mostly prison-guard trash), and State Security's own closely held air power available from the Air Defense forces. Some of this order was first-rate—and the Special Action Troops were most formidable—but the bulk of it was inferior, and the aircraft were outclassed by our equipment. Iagoda must have found, in his haste to obey my mother's order to "clean it up quickly," that he didn't have the time or ability, during the lingering Czechoslovakia crisis and the still dangerous Chinese crisis, to mobilize an overwhelming, first-rate strike force and get it to assembly points such as Chimkent and Tashkent. The truth about the delay, I can now suppose, must have been that Iagoda had wasted weeks assembling a hodgepodge of air and ground troops and even then must have been forced to wait until the last possible hour to pull together a coordinated offensive operation. From the tardy and slipshod way his forces finally came on, he must have known that, at T minus five days on the long count, he had to begin the battering down of our defenses regardless of his preparedness or lose any chance of stopping my uncles.

I have said that the battle that morning began quietly. It is more accurate to say that it began with Zvorrov's intuitive genius that the three bogeys on the first-light run hadn't come for reconnaissance, but rather as a decoy for an airstrike behind them. It was just eight minutes after first contact that Zvorrov, a one-man radar-netting station supported by three EW/GCI picket units, four mobile SAM sites, a heavy 21 squadron, a transport regiment, an armored Mil squadron, two light Mil squadrons, and six light spotter planes all plugged into his headset, that this vast network of air defense in one man's brain, began reacting even before there was anything out there to see or counter. It was as if Zvorrov knew what was going to happen before it happened, a second sight that was as much a result of training as talent. Then again Zvorrov was facing strike tactics that he'd helped perfect in the preparation for Czechoslovakia and a NATO counterattack (an airborne assault and/or an armored stab must be prepped by shock bombardment). He knew there were no variations permitted. He also knew that somewhere out there, at either the Border Guard base at Chimkent or at the Air Defense airbase at Tashkent, there was an air traffic controller like himself, who was following line by line the same textbook that said take the high ground by flattening the airfield in order to destroy any credible air defense.

"On your toes, now," was how Zvorrov croaked his alert into his mouthpiece. The three bogey echoes were changing course. Zvorrov called out numbers and then tapped his ear and said, "Starters up, ready, ready. On my count," as he called the squadron to attention. It was exactly 0425, and, by the book, the squadron was already scrambled in their cockpits and awaiting orders to launch. Zvorrov glanced at the winking radar screens and rolled another cigarette, a habit of his that I knew by then meant he was about to make a decision and immediately call for a glass of hot tea. I moved away from the screen to get the tea before he demanded it, feeling competent that, just as Zvorrov ordered the squadron, "Launching now, strike away," and just as six orange flames burst out on the dark field a kilometer from us, and just as Zvorrov held out his hand to me and ordered, "Pour a glass, boy!" I was ready with a glass of hot tea and a lump of sugar.

I was a servant, and while the half-mad part of me was missing in action, the half-sane part of me was alert to Zvorrov's needs. When Zvorrov didn't need me I was useless and stood aside like a pot, watching for Zvorrov's orders and feeling neither fear nor peace of mind, just a dull-eyed sobriety. I was little more than another one of Zvorrov's machines waiting on his whim, and this might explain why I remember the battle as passively as a camera.

What I recall next is that Zvorrov made and smoked two more cigarettes while he waited for the squadron's strike flight of Glavtop and Grin, Artzybashev and Kandidim, and Miserbiev and Adama-Bibliov to get to their altitude and station. In the meantime, Zvorrov called his ground command to check on the alert, ordered his SAM sites locked and loaded, dispatched scout Mils away in four directions, pulled his Antonov airborne radar picket back into the interior, and dispatched a Steppe Eagle recon company south on heavy Mils. This took another eighteen minutes to confirm. At 0443 hours, the eastern horizon was a bold red-and-orange streak, the airfield was still colorless gray, and only the distant blue-white lights at the launchpad marked the desert as populated. Zvorrov made his third cigarette and stared down at his main radar screen. I thought he was going to demand another glass of tea and approached with one in hand, but I was wrong; he was just standing there staring. I looked where he looked and saw an amber blur at the south edge of the radar screen, a phenomenon that was distinctive of a dawn sandstorm in the desert sending dust as high as a thousand meters.

Zvorrov saw something much worse and called, "Board clear, reserve away," to launch four more 21s, the reserve flight of Fedyuninsky and Cherryntevsky, Stumpelkin and (in my seat) Volgamints, and then he called the Steppe Eagles' recon company and directed it to veer off from the axis of the sandstorm. Zvorrov stepped away from the screen, muttered to himself, checked his watch, and then started a whispery staccato of numbers that I couldn't follow. I was sicker in the mornings, the residue of the drugs weakening me when I might ordinarily have been dreaming, so I could only concentrate in bursts, and I missed the detail of the next minutes until full dawn light illuminated the air control tower and the airfield. What must have happened is that Zvorrov confirmed that his sentry flight, strike flight, and reserve flight were all at their stations, and then he must have committed himself, for the next I knew the air raid klaxon sounded on the field and several heavy Mils, launching from the Airborne bivouac to the south, flung themselves over us in a roar. Zvorrov was croaking orders at everyone in his command, "Multiple bogeys, inbound, threat axis bearing one-two-five, two elements, high lead and trailing medium. Sentry flight, close and engage. Strike leader, close on . . ." and so on, telling them what he'd already figured out, that the enemy had used the recons to decoy us and the sandstorm to conceal an airstrike coming in behind it. Zvorrov gave out numbers upon numbers. Sometimes I knew what he was saying, sometimes I could hear the crackle from the headset as the command talked back to him, sometimes I could only guess at Zvorrov's logic as he vectored the squadron to intercept the threat, as he ordered strike flight leaders Glavtop and Grin, the two purest 21 drivers in the Air Force, to close on the bogey strike flight. This was an air battle some seventy to one hundred kilometers from the field. The only sign around me that there was any strike imminent was the air raid klaxon and an occasional lorry racing across the field; otherwise everything was buttoned down and secured and only Zvorrov's brain could be said to be on the front line. As I watched him dodge, wince, smoke, and twist, I was watching a peculiar version of the contest, and, though at the time I could hardly follow his struggle, I have reconstructed enough of the details from others, such as Stumpelkin and Miserbiev, to present an outline of the next twenty minutes.

On Zvorrov's screen multiple echoes emerged out of the sandstorm's blurred tail, and then there were more echoes approaching from another axis parallel to the sandstorm's, two bogey strike flights coming on toward the field. Zvorrov had launched all his aircraft in correct expectation of the dual-axis raid, and his first order was to direct an intercept before the two bogey elements could join up. The lead bogey element was MiG-17 fighter aircraft—gun-mounted, slow-footed, and day-only interceptors; the trailing bogey element was Yak-28 fighter-bombers—a fast, long-range ground-strike aircraft that loaded contact bombs and heat-seekers and carried no gun. Zvorrov sent the sentry flight of Schtange and Tevyelook into the 17s, two against twelve, in order to break them up, and to slow them from rendezvousing with the bombers. Zvorrov continued croaking out his staccato numbers as the two friendlies darted into the many bogeys. Our 21s were so superior, with both heat-seekers and a gun, that Schtange's and Tevyelook's first pass was like smashing fireflies. Several amber echoes blinked out at once, and all of the 17s scattered lower to run for their lives. Schtange and Tevyelook were climbing back up to make another pass when Zvorrov ordered, "Break off, sentry flight, now." When Schtange and Tevyelook tried to resist, though critical on fuel, Zvorrov repeated, "Break, now," and then more numbers.

The trailing bogey element of Yaks, stripped of fighter cover, were defenseless prey. Zvorrov called strike flight leaders Glavtop and Grin with a heading, altitude, and airspeed to bring a half dozen 21s into two dozen bogeys high and hot. Less than a minute later, Zvorrov croaked, "Strike leader, engage," and a crackle from the headset indicated that the ambush was right on target. Zvorrov switched his attention to his ground command and called his most outlying SAM site, fifty kilometers downrange, along the main air corridor from

Tashkent, to tell the weapons officer to maintain blackout and wait. "Stay down, salvo on my call."

Within moments two first-class Yak squadrons were either falling out of the sky or scattering in all directions as the strike flight salvoed its heat-seekers and went to guns. The only hope for the Yaks to continue their attack was to get down on the deck and try to run in at shrub level. Zvorrov was prepared for the leakers. When a few echoes disappeared of a sudden, Zvorrov called reserve flight leader Fedyuninsky to stay high in order to keep the leakers at shrub level. Zvorrov's trap was baited and set, and, while he croaked more numbers and watched the clock, the Yaks came closer and closer until they were in easy range of the SAMs. Zvorrov called his SAM site, "Illuminate. Fire at range. Shoot, shoot, shoot," and the radar screen showed scratchlike echoes that intersected with several of the bogeys and vanished. Of two Yak squadrons, there were only six still coming on; and then there were two, and Zvorrov ordered Fedyuninsky's reserve flight, "Close and engage." After another few moments of silence and more crackles, four 21 echoes on afterburners closed on two fleeing Yak echoes; and then there were no bogeys on the screen or in the air.

The end of the battle was as quiet as the beginning. Zvorrov made another cigarette and held out his hand for tea and fruit, complaining, "I want fresh," when I handed him a warm peach. In less than twenty minutes, upwards of sixty men had been knocked down, and what Zvorrov wanted was a colder peach. There were a few more details to conclude, and Zvorrov ordered all the flights back to altitude to hover on station before turning home. He also ordered the SAM site shut down and moved, and sent light Mils around the sandstorm to patrol behind the path of the storm and search for any enemy sappers that might have come in on a helicopter, but overall the battle was won and Zvorrov was triumphant. His victory didn't change his mood. He continued to smoke and demand and croak, never looking up from his screens even when a big Mil shot by the air tower so close the beams shook like paper and dust filled the shack, never even acknowledging the calls from Schtange and Tevyelook, who were first down on the field to refuel and rearm. The all clear sounded, lorries crossed the field at normal speed, air crews unbuttoned the storage depots and prepped rearmament, the Kazakh laborers who hadn't evacuated were poking out of the bunkers like blind men, it was full dawn and white hot on the yellow field, and yet still all that Zvorrov cared about was a colder peach.

After all these years, I should have found a way to explain to myself how it was that we could kill each other so routinely. I wonder if there might be something to Zvorrov's appetite for tea and fruit while he ordered men to die. Perhaps it was that the battle for Tsar Cannon was joined as if it were an exercise. We all conducted ourselves as carefully as we might have eaten peaches. You don't think about eating while you're doing it, and perhaps it can be said that you don't think about killing while you're at it. I mean this to be a hard comparison; for now, at the end of my life, I regret the brutal way I've carried on, eating and killing thoughtlessly. I want to tell you that it is better to think about it; it's always better to hear and see and turn and think before you bite.

Back then the battle carried on like a feast. The first airstrike on Wednesday morning was followed by a smaller raid that evening, when what must have been remnants of the dawn debacle tested our readiness at dusk and fled like rabbits as soon as Glavtop and Grin closed within ten kilometers. At midday Thursday, the Steppe Eagles found and engaged an enemy long-range scout force that, according to prisoners, had lost contact with the main body of an enemy armor column advancing slowly overland from the northeast, from the railhead at Dzhezkazgan. There was a second body of enemy armor coming from the southwest on the Turkestan road, and Zvorrov fretted that his scouts couldn't fix the battle axis. Also Thursday evening, Zvorrov received word that an armored train of Border Guards had started north from Tashkent. There were many rumors from Star City that Kazakhs and other non-Russians were evacuating the river quarter in fear of reprisals, and also that the families of rocketeers and other Russian officialdom were about to flee north on a special train. By dark Thursday, Zvorrov's spotter planes reported that the main rail line from Uzbekistan was backed up with stalled rolling stock, evidence that State Security had delayed the freight and passenger trains for two border republics in order to rush through its armored train. On Zvorrov's map it was clear that Iagoda's strategy was gradually beginning to close a pincer on Tsar Cannon—three armor units from the northeast, southwest, and southeast—in expectation that the airstrikes would eventually prevail.

There was a second major airstrike Friday dawn—more Yaks and

17s and a new element of the fast but poorly armed Su-11 interceptors—and Zvorrov lost one of his SAM sites when it lit up to salvo too early and, exposed to counterfire, was slammed by trailing defense suppression. That morning several Yaks did penetrate our defenses by coming in at shrub level through the breached corridor to hit the airfield with contact bombs that damaged underground fuel lines and the doors of two buried revetments. The day got worse when there was news of a food riot in Star City that had started a refugee column out to us for our stores. When Steppe Eagles flew down to try to turn the refugees back, they were shown leaflets that had been dropped that said State Security was coming to restore order throughout the district. The refugees said they all knew this meant there would be a massacre and mass deportation. On Friday afternoon, Zvorrov sent teams of Steppe Eagles hopping up and down the rail line from the south to blow out half-kilometer sections. The armored train was coming on with its own repair unit, however, and a scout flight estimated that, despite the Steppe Eagles' efforts, it would only take another forty-eight hours before the train was in position to dismount its armor column to come at us from the south.

It was well understood that the enemy armor could not and would not accelerate until the airfield was destroyed. Accordingly, Friday evening before sundown, a massive and well-coordinated enemy strike showed echoes on the radar screens like the torches of a mob. It was about 1930 hours when the air raid sounded. I was alone in the bunker fetching more fruit for Zvorrov. My friends had been sleeping beside their 21s, so I'd spent the last three days by myself, except for waiting on Zvorrov or now and again enjoying a visit from Abdrahman, who brought me goat's milk when he could. I think I might have been singing to myself when the klaxon sounded. No, I remember now that Doctor Gogol was with me in order to check the infection on my thigh. The reason I was singing was because the injection he wanted to give me frightened me. The air raid was a relief to me, and I told Gogol I had to get to my post. "Peter," I remember him telling me, "your fever's up, and I don't like what I'm hearing in your chest. There's fluid in your lungs. I can't say it's not pneumonia. You're not fit for duty. I'm telling you to rest. Will you listen to me? You could get badly sick again. I'm not sure you understand what I'm saying." I understood, but I responded unconvincingly, something like, "Zvorrov needs me," and tucked up my clothes and slipped on my sandals and got up to the surface. I found the field covered in foul-smelling smoke, because the wind had shifted from the still-burning underground stores. I lost focus, starting for a stroll out away from the smoke, until I heard Zvorrov shouting down to me, "Tea! Quick! Where's my tea!" By the time I could obey Zvorrov and carry his tea up to the air control tower, Glavtop's and Grin's strike flight was airborne and the sentry flight was vectored to attack the lead bogey element. Artzybashev and Kandidim were sentry flight, and they followed Zvorrov's order to go high for the 17s, which turned out to be a disaster. The 17s that night were PFUs, that is, missile-mounted, and they salvoed at maximum range then rushed at the sentry flight, sixteen against two, so that Artzybashev and Kandidim had too many targets to fight off and blew up midair, the squadron's first two casualties.

Zvorrov saw his sentry flight vanish, and it must have been then he concluded that the enemy had changed tactics—swarming to kill—and that we were going to be hit hard. He took off his steel helmet, made another cigarette, called for tea, and then, while sipping and smoking, went back to work calling his command; yet I am almost certain that there was less energy in his croaking—there was resignation that this was the way the battle had to turn. I wasn't any more concerned that night than before, so I think I stared out on the field as if it were just another evening. I saw several Kazakh laborers changing a tire on a flatbed lorry in front of the barracks, four burly little men in black cotton clothes sweating and grunting to get their vehicle and themselves to safety. I gazed up dreamily ten kilometers distant to the top of the profile of Tsar Cannon that showed over the lip of the man-made bowl like a fat needle. The air was cool and clear enough by then—the wind must have shifted, because I don't recall any more problems with the smoke—for me to make out a railcar rolling from the palace out to the launch area. I watched it slide from right to left as if it were a toy train. Out there on the launchpad was a man-made kerosene bomb of a superbooster, and it all looked so serene to me that I wanted to reach out and play with it.

The battle continued without me, and from what I have reconstructed from talks with Stumpelkin, and from my memory of talks with Zvorrov before his death ten years ago, I can report some of the highlights of that night's devastating strike. After the bogey 17s had killed Artzybashev and Kandidim, two different squadrons of Su-11s came on from the southeast like spears of luminous white echoes on the screen, penetrating our defense at three thousand and four thousand meters. From the southwest, another spear of white echoes approached, Yak-28s carrying antirunway bombs, so that Zvorrov was faced with three bogey air-to-ground elements coming on three different battle axes at once. He only had one six-aircraft strike flight and one four-aircraft reserve flight. He had to commit the strike flight to the very dangerous Yaks and back them up with the reserve flight (those antirunway bombs would crater the field and make it unlikely the 21s could get down safely), and that left only one SAM site to stop the Su-11s. Within minutes, Zvorrov didn't have that much, because the outlying SAM battery in the Su-11 corridor failed to respond to his call and winked out, struck by bogey free-floating defense-suppression sorties firing missiles that homed in on radar signals. Zvorrov tried to compensate by risking his second battery, ordering it to light up and salvo, "Shoot, shoot, shoot," but he knew this was too little and too late. The Su-11s kept on. Zvorrov was taking another critical loss, too, because as he launched a Mil recon to see what had happened to his lead SAM site, the third and last SAM battery called in to say it had to shut down and run because there were reports of enemy sappers on the ground.

Glavtop's and Grin's strike flight hit the Yaks high and hot as usual. Fedyuninsky's reserve flight met and broke up the leakers as usual. Yet there was nothing left to stop the threat of the two Su-11 elements from the southeast, and, as Zvorrov croaked, he communicated the inevitable in matter-of-fact terms: "Multiple bogeys, inbound on the deck," he warned the Steppe Eagles on the airfield in order to get them to clear out their Mils; "Multiple bogeys," he addressed Fedyuninsky's reserve flight that was now trying to get back to defend the field; "I am salvoing to your northeast, breakthroughs, breakthroughs," he added to warn Fedyuninsky to stay away from the field, because the Steppe Eagles would be firing their handheld SAMs. "Breakthroughs," he repeated in a harsh croak, "at shrub level, bearing one-six-seven, breakthroughs."

There was booming to the south and hollow cracks that reverberated toward the east, probably the 21s, or perhaps it was ground explosions of expended ordnance. I could see white streaks like scars on the orange-and-purple sky, then lots of drifting dots, and, since by then the pops of gunfire were incessant, those puffs must have been the Steppe Eagles' air defense battalion's radar-guided guns peppering the air corridors, and those spiraling white trails were probably from the shoulder-fired SAMs. I remained numb and dopey at my post, indifferent to the fact that the airfield was naked to a strike of radar-homing missiles and contact bombs.

What happened next was miraculous to me. Zvorrov, having identified the threat, started calling out warnings to his command such as, "ETA three minutes. Twelve breakthroughs at shrubs," and then updated, "Sixteen leakers, shoot, eighteen leakers, shoot," and finally, losing count of all the echoes closing on the field, told his command, "Multiple inbound warheads, multiple warheads, inbound, inbound," as the Su-11s popped up and fired all their ordnance at us. At this point Zvorrov was a dead man—those inbound warheads were homing on the air control tower while the other leakers were coming on to bomb the naked field—and I don't believe Zvorrov would have left his station if not for Alexey Strogolshikov's intervention. I was watching the tiny puffs in the air when a heavy Mil swooped past the tower and slammed to the blacktop below, Steppe Eagles pouring out and a huge officer hailing Zvorrov to come down. I didn't understand what the troopers wanted and shrank back into the corner. The next I knew Alexey Strogolshikov was in the tower, barking, "Get out, both of you, get out, get out, now, shut down!" Zvorrov ignored his commander and kept muttering orders into his headset, such as, "One minute, stragglers coming your way," to Fedyuninsky, and more numbers to Glavtop and Grin. Just when it seemed Alexey Strogolshikov was going to have to brain him, Zvorrov broke off his croaking and kicked at his panel. I think it was then that Zvorrov initiated the big trick of barrage-jamming that scattered the homers and saved our lives.

I get confused about the last moments before the blasts. The best I can say is that Alexey Strogolshikov threw me down to another trooper, who manhandled me across the tarmac. He wanted me in the bunker, and I resisted, probably because I didn't want to leave Zvorrov. The missiles started arriving like falling splinters. I don't know how it was that I neither got into the bunker nor on the Mil. The pounding explosions made the ground jump up and shake with white dust, and soon I was wandering the field alone. I can picture the sky bluish to the east, and the roar of a Yak engine overhead, but that must be out of order, because the homers hit first. There was a wall of sparks behind me, which must have been a bomb hit on an ammunition dump. I could see these fat arrows coming in at ten meters and could hear the rocket engines clicking like plates breaking. Three swept over me and struck the barracks, and then I was on my face and rolling over and over as if I were on fire. I have another memory of the field becoming as red as the sunset, except that it was near dark by then, so I must have been dreaming again of the surface of the sun. I suppose my memory of my burning feet was because the flight line was ablaze.

Long afterward the klaxon stopped screaming. I remember walking away from the field coughing and retching, because of the hot smoke from the fires at the fuel stores and the Antonov flight line, where two big transports were ablaze and disintegrating like melting skeletons. The airfield burned all night in the strong northerly wind, a throbbing white glow under a boundless display of July stars. The next I'm sure of I was at the tents of the Steppe Eagle field hospital, and Doctor Gogol was leaning over me and checking my temperature. Maybe all this isn't accurate, but somehow I got from wandering the shattered airfield after the strike to the quiet recess of the field hospital in the last hours before dawn.

What's wrong with my sequence is that I'd lost track of two days. It wasn't Saturday morning when I woke up, as Doctor Gogol checked on me, but rather Monday morning. What I can reconstruct now is that I must have collapsed Friday night and gone in and out of fits in such a way that I didn't realize that I'd been raving, shaking, sweating, and coughing for forty hours. What made me collapse was the walking pneumonia Gogol had detected Friday; what woke me was that the last of the fever broke. I was on a ground cloth, surrounded by wounded and dying, and Doctor Gogol was speaking softly, "Welcome back, Peter. Welcome back." I asked him where we were, but I didn't think to ask him what day it was. After he told me, "You're being well cared for. You're one of my successes. Rest now, and I'll see you at breakfast," he left me. I dozed for another few hours before I got up for a drink of water. The black night was softening to the east, and I was able to find my way past the laid-out invalids to the water lorry. The wounded made no noise, and it seemed to me as if they were all asleep while wide-eyed; indeed, the only disturbance was when a light Mil slammed down to deliver wounded and roared off again into the general drone of faraway helicopters. I was extremely thirsty and hungry, and when I mixed in with the walking wounded Steppe Eagles, I asked them if there was a field kitchen. The troopers were kind to me and shared their rations—bread, rice with some sauce—and it was one of them who remarked to another, "I hope this frigging thing's done today, my feet quit on me Saturday." I realized then that something was wrong with my sense of time. After a few questions, I discovered it was about 0200 hours Monday morning. This knowledge made me weep. The Steppe Eagles reassured me, but it was no use, I was a rag of tears, and I collapsed on my sore bottom and sobbed. I don't understand why losing track of two days affected me this way. I wasn't upset; I wasn't scared; I wasn't even sad. The strangest part of my gap in time was that it was a little while longer before I finally realized that, since it was Monday morning, July 14, it was the day of the moonshot—in fact, while I was weeping, it was approximately T minus three hours.

My crying fit drained me to silence. Sitting there sore-bottomed and as empty as a cup, I came alert enough to smell my stink from soiling myself. I went to wash and fell into line at the water lorry behind a young man about my age in a torn flight suit with his hands bandaged like mittens. I didn't talk to him at first, but after I'd gotten some water and cleaned off my legs, and after I'd found a fresh pair of trousers in a heap of discarded clothing, I got back on line for more water and the young fellow pointed to my torn tunic coat. He asked me, "You're one of them?" and indicated my falcon's wings and cosmonaut badge. I told him my name and rank and asked his. He said he was Cadet T. V. Vunder of Stavropol Academy, the Air Defense training academy. I realized he was a captured enemy pilot out of a Su-11 that had disintegrated under him Friday night, which meant that Iagoda had drafted students to fly against master 21 drivers. Vunder had a narrow face that made his bruised jaw look gigantic, and he was still in shock for the pain of his burns, so he was timid about himself and thanked me repeatedly for talking with him. (About twenty-five years later I saw this same T. V. Vunder on a television business news show, in which he was praised for owning some sort of innovative transport company in the south. I presume he lived well after his ordeal in the desert.) Vunder wanted to smoke, and I helped him light a cigarette. All the while he kept asking me,

"How is this?" He couldn't think to make more of his question, just "How? How?" as he puffed and looked around at the field hospital. I mention Vunder out of all the outlandish things that happened during the battle, because it still amazes me that there's still no answer for what he asked, "How is this?" At the time what his question did for me was make me think about where I was and what was happening. Perhaps you know that in a catastrophe like a battle the brain doesn't work well—you do what you're told, what you're trained to do; you don't speculate, contemplate, or in any way think for yourself; and time seems to crumple all around you. Considering that I'd gone into the battle with half of a brain, I was probably lucky to have any sense of proportion. As Vunder kept asking, "How is this? How? How?" I stood bent like a gorse bush and let the night wind hold me up while I thought about his question. I could see the lights of the gantry tower to the left and the palace to the far right, and behind me was the burning tank farm. As I kept studying and reviewing the landscape, I was able to force myself to think logically if crudely: it was Monday morning, it was July 14, it was before sunup, therefore, Tsar Cannon is launching, I told myself. I wanted to get excited about my discovery and looked again at the blue lights of the palace. Today was the day, I told myself; the lights were still on; and the Steppe Eagles hadn't pulled out or surrendered or quit; we were winning; we'd held out; we'd held the airfield. Despite my argument, I still couldn't feel what I was saying. The sane part of me was too weak to respond to the facts, and the mindsick part of me— what I now think of as mad—was faraway. It was many years before I was able to think over all this confusion between what I did and what I felt, and it was decades before I was able to come to an explanation for my condition. During the battle I was not only lost and alone, not only without my soul and heart, not only lost in time, I was also lost between the real world of the Motherland where men murdered each other pitilessly, and the make-believe world of my youth where I was a hero bound to conquer the moon. Do you understand the conflict? I was lost between what my life was and what I'd dreamed it to be, and I couldn't accept the truth. The real world contained my uncles and their drive for the moon landing, yes; and yet it also contained Iagoda and my mother and their rot; and I didn't want to live in such a paradoxical place any longer. I wanted to flee to my childhood world of adventures in outer space. I suppose a simpler way of saying this is that I didn't want to be the boy who had grown up to a manhood of disasters and abandonment. I was standing at a field hospital for a war between two ruthless factions; however, in my mind, the battle was more like a war between worlds wholly alien to each other—their cruel, starving, hopeless Russia and my starry-eyed, muscular, utopian Russia. "How is this?" Cadet Vunder asked me. I answer him seven decades later that how "this" happened is that we were fighting to win the wrong world, the world of heart-break, when what we both wanted was the world up there in heaven, a new planet of a new day. I also want to say now, before I get on, that perhaps why we fought so hard to drive the moon was not to lord over our foes, not to breach the cosmos, not even for what I have said of the single-minded march toward the planets, but rather because to touch the face of the moon was also to realize our finest dreams.

This yearning might explain why I wandered away from the field hospital and toward the distant gantry tower. I wanted to go see the moonshot. Somehow I was next on a lorry that was headed along the railbed back toward the airfield. The lorry was loaded with rock-eteers and other volunteers going over to the field to help with re-pairs on the cratered runway. They were mostly middle-aged, gray-headed, overweight, frail-looking fellows, but they were very cheery about their task. Without my asking, they passed on to me news from Tsar Cannon. They told me all operations outside of the launch control had been suspended because of a fire in the palace on Satur-day—set by a saboteur or a drunkard—that had eaten away much of the clean room and damaged one of the two half-built superboos-ters. They also told me that Doctor Lunin had fallen sick after fight-ing the fire, and that the launch control was now in the hands of Isaacii Goldenberg. They said Tsar Cannon's countdown was on in-definite hold—more trouble with the bug-ridden vernier engines—but they were quick to assure me that the problems could be solved with luck and time. If I had been more sensible, it would have been wonderful to hear the pleasure they found in their jobs. Though their palace was heavily damaged by fire, though State Security was closing in on the works, though the moonship's fate was unknown, the Tsar Cannoneers insisted that all was well with the launch se-quence and that the next few hours would decide the matter. Mean-while they were going to stay busy at the airfield. I did ask after my uncles, and a coiled little man in a heavy sheepskin coat, a rocketeer by his educated manner, told me he'd seen them at the launch control with Goldenberg. "General Oryolin's not going to make it," he said. "He isn't," he repeated. Others in the lorry agreed, though another man said that he'd seen General Oryolin enter the spacecraft within the hour. They took delight in explaining to me how they'd built a spacesuit that could accommodate Uncle Alexander's broken bowels, and added that a man as disabled as Oryolin, if he could stand the g-forces at launch, would do better in zero-g than he did on earth. Then we were at the smoking airfield, where the work battalion's heavy equipment and the Kazakh laborers were hastily filling bomb craters on the runway. We were handed shovels and pickaxes and told to pull apart a mound of concrete thrown up like a mud pile. I started digging; however, my companions were distracted by the bizarre sights of a battlefield, and they kept breaking off work in order to stare at the small gas fires, the ruins of cracked Antonovs and Mils nearby, and out to the south for advancing enemy vehicles. There was only the wind and a smoky moonless sky, for it was the night of the new moon, and the moon had set by then. The Tsar Cannoneers remained talkative—much detail about the booster's fueling—and, though they were frightened whenever a Mil flew over, they were good company, and I was lucky to have fallen in with them.

It was a half hour before it came to me that I could just walk across the field and check on the squadron at the bunker. One moment I was digging with older men, the next I said to the rocketeers, "I'm going over to see my friends," and they said, "You take care, Lieutenant, take care," and the next I was finding my way in the dark for the old barracks. The compound was ruins; the air control tower was scrap; the starlight was just enough for me to locate the fused lump of the field generator. I searched around in the ashes for the entrance to the bunker and found a hole where the hatchway had been. I called down something knot-headed such as, "Anyone down there?"

Zhora Fedyuninsky flashed a torch up into my face. "Well, Peter Nevsky's ghost again," he teased me. "Hungry are you? Ghost has to eat, too; come on down, Lieutenant. We're brewing water and introducing it to tea." It was the last time I would ever see Fedyuninsky alive, and it is dear to me how he greeted me at the base of the stairs as if we'd just left each other: "Good, yes," he said. "It seems we're very light on the duty roster just now. So good, you're just the man. How're your feet there?" He looked handsome in his flight suit, and the only signs of his last five days of combat were his bright red eyes and a singed red left ear. He offered me a cigarette, then took it back and said, "Right, you don't smoke. Good. Come in. Plenty of room down here on a dreary night, good company. It's good to see you, good, good. How are you feeling?"

I tried not to wobble on my sandals, and I grunted in my most manly voice. Inside the bunker Genka Stumpelkin was stirring tea in a pot on a gas oven and tried not to sound unmilitary when he greeted me warmly. "Peter, oh, Peter, they said you'd run away. The troopers said you'd run off Friday. We figured you were lost on the steppe, and we didn't know what—"

My best explanation was, "I've been sleeping, I think. I've been with Doctor Gogol, at the hospital, and asleep almost since Friday, I guess."

Arkady Volgamints was seated on a bunk eating sausage, and he teased me while chewing. "Sleep's a popular decision around here," he said, waving the sausage at the blanketed hump of Trifya Miserbiev asleep and snoring in the upper bunk. Glavtop and Grin were asleep in bedrolls on opposite top bunks. "Grab a blanket," Volgamints told me. "Sleep's what we've got plenty of, sleep and for some reason a crate of this excellent sausage." I told him there was hot food out at the field hospital. Volgamints rubbed his red curls and smirked. "Order me up some perch stuffed with pepper and bay leaves," he teased, "and white bread and horseradish. And sailor's macaroni. And strawberries, yes, big ones from Tashkent. Instead, wait, a bottle will do."

Stumpelkin set me down on a locker. I bounced up for my sore backside, and he peered into my face in the lamplight, asking, "How're your shakes? And that cough you've had?" I didn't want to talk about my illness and asked after the others. Stumpelkin replied, "You say you were with Doctor Gogol? We've not seen him or Lev [Lympyet] since Saturday. This is good news to have you here, oh, good news, how about tea? It's sort of tea."

I thanked him and looked around for my friend Adama-Bibliov, and, when I didn't find him in the other bunks, I didn't ask Stumpelkin the obvious. I just took the tea glass and lay on my belly across a bunk, sipping and waiting. I was looking at all that remained of the squadron: six gone—Artzybashev and Kandidim blown up, Cherryntevsky down and badly wounded, Schtange and Tevyelook down and captured by enemy forces, Yurka Adama-Bibliov wounded badly landing a crippled 21 and not expected to live—and five survivors plus Volgamints, and out in the desert, somewhere with the troopers, Doctor Gogol and Lev Lympyet. Why no one told me the facts was because of the Air Force superstition that it's bad luck to talk about the missing in action, in fact it's bad luck to say anything meaningful other than graphic duty-talk while you're waiting to fly a combat patrol.

The general wordlessness continued, and the only sound in the bunker was the hiss of the gas stove. I was drifting to sleep, feeling painless, but then Fedyuninsky squatted beside me. In my half trance, I heard him ask me if I could fly. "You have to tell me straight, Lieutenant," he said, "since we're one short on the roster—at least you could say we have a Twenty-one we can't man. You're my choice if you say you can go."

No one else spoke up; they just watched my reactions, which were more a lack of reactions. Then Genka Stumpelkin objected, "He's not going, you can't ask him to. Look at him, he can't even sit, and his feet are awful."

Fedyuninsky showed his exhaustion by replying, "This is my decision. We have six nominal aircraft, and we must launch what we have. If he says he can go, he can go. What is it then, Lieutenant Nevsky?"

I faked a firm, "Yes, sir."

"Questions?" Fedyuninsky asked the others. "Good. It'll be first light in thirty minutes, and we'll get up as soon as we can see the runway for the rubble. Let's try not to get on anyone's nerves."

Volgamints mocked, "Oh, my, yes, shit. Let's frigging finish it, oh, my," in a wild parody of Uncle Alexander. When Stumpelkin protested his blasphemy, Volgamints laughed at all of us and added, "I'm too hungry for this anyway, and I can't eat any more sausage. It's given me an elephant's bellyache."

"I told you to quit it about food!" Miserbiev cried as he shoved himself around. I saw his trousers were cut open and both legs were in splints from the thighs to the ankles, for he'd fractured his knees in a runway mishap. I stared at the splints, and Miserbiev saw me staring and called over, "It was ugly, Peter. I taxied into a pothole." Miserbiev shrugged and then again challenged Volgamints, "But not as ugly as your lip!" Nothing came of their spat but some huffing over hastily lit cigarettes. I mention the incident at all to show that, even in such presumably heroic circumstances as the last ditch of the last battle of the last war, men are going to remain vain, prattling fools living for the moment and ready to cross each other over trifles, while at the same time they are also ready to sacrifice all they have for flags and esprit de corps and sometimes something you can't even name.

Zhora Fedyuninsky busied himself at the table writing down the duty roster in the squadron's flight log. It was a measure of his backbone that he was struggling to be worthy of a post no one else wanted—the shock commander who must order us to the finish. "Genka," Fedyuninsky started, "you and Peter on reserve flight launch, and stay on the field until you're called, there's no need to get up until you're needed. We're not going to have that sort of time." He nodded to Volgamints. "We'll take the strike, Major, with them in reserve." Waving at Glavtop and Grin in their bunks, he said, "Wake our sentry flight. We best get up."

I took too long pulling on Miserbiev's baggy flight suit, and so Miserbiev lowered himself to a stool to help me button and buckle. He was tender when he helped me into the g-suit and flight boots. It was time to go; and Stumpelkin took me by the arm while Volgamints carried Miserbiev over his shoulder and up the steps. The air crews had sent a cart for us, and we rocked over the rubble to the flight line. Miserbiev rode beside me to prep me on his aircraft's peculiarities. "She probably handles heavy since the pothole," was his clearest advice. Our six 21s with starting carts and minimal crews were scattered along the field for cover, and the cart dropped me off last so Miserbiev could stay and jabber at me. The air crews had fueled us as close as possible to dawn to avoid risking the incoming fire, which was sporadic but dangerous long-range mortar stuff from enemy sappers on the run from Steppe Eagle patrols in the desert. Tactical ground battle, as I know it, isn't valiant warriors on an honorable field but rather wild shots in darkness, rattling noise, men and body parts tossed up like gravel, the stench of burning fuel, and also queer events such as a double-splinted chubby little fellow like Miserbiev sitting on a cart and jabbering away. "Your J-band is spotty, don't trust it,'' he told me as the airman helped me into the cockpit. "Follow Genka's lead. Get behind him and do what he says. You stay on his tail feathers!''

As reserve flight, Stumpelkin and I weren't to launch, just sit at the launch point and wait for alert. All I had to do was start and roll a half kilometer. Yet as I settled in the seat with difficulty for the sores on my backside, and as the crewman slapped my helmet and watched closely, I couldn't figure what to do and just sat limp. The crewman called up his chief, and the old man checked my avionics settings for the field and time and then, when it was time to go, he started the engine for me by reaching over my shoulder for the contact. Miserbiev watched the struggle and called up, "Peter, get out of there if you can't drive her,'' but I must have ignored him, for the next I realized I was shaking and coughing as I rolled the 21 with the canopy up from the arming area to the taxiway. I was last in line and watched the strike flight take off in twenty-second intervals: a hollow roar and then a rush of air and the wail of the afterburners as the orange glow of each 21 lifted off and broke left or right in case of shoulder-fired SAMs from sappers. Then the strike flight was gone, and there was just the vibration of my Tumansky engine and, to my right, the flat lemon glow of Stumpelkin's exhaust and, in my ears, the crackle of the radio. There was no one out there to be heard, just empty air except for the squadron's band. After that my numbness actually helped me. I felt no fear at the mortar rounds that landed down the line nor the flashes of small-arms fire way upfield. My mind was empty. I might even have dozed as first light filled my cockpit with dirty colors and the dawn breeze threw dust into the cockpit. What next I remember was Stumpelkin squawking, "Peter, button up, Peter! On my count, Peter! Roll! Peter, answer me back. Peter, call back!'' I neither felt nor thought, I just obeyed, calling back, "Roger, rolling,'' and finding that my training didn't need my mind. I lowered the canopy, released the brakes, rolled to the launch point, and then powered up to bolt forward and bump and bang over loose stones. Lift-off was clean into that soft sensation of floating at the head of a rocket until Stumpelkin ordered me to break on his tail when my threat alert warbled warning of SAMs. Again what helped me was that I didn't have to think. I just obeyed and moved both hands and both feet to push over with full power. I was like a broken body that was reborn a brainless gyrfalcon. As long as I obeyed

Stumpelkin's lead, I found no difficulty climbing to our patrol station. We throttled down to conserve fuel and circled above wisps of smoke as the sun caught me in the eyes and lulled me back to my dreams.

I don't know how long we waited, it might have only been moments, but then a new call came over the squadron band. "Warning! Multiple bogeys, ready, ready, come to . . ." and I knew the croaking was Zvorrov, who had survived all the airstrikes by driving around in a convoy of lorries loaded with a mobile EW/GCI net. Then again, I understood little of Zvorrov's orders and had to jink to avoid Stumpelkin as he broke down to a new altitude and heading and called me to follow him.

I can't provide a blow by blow of the last strike. I can say that Zvorrov's foreshortened pickets meant that, by the time he called us, it was too late to do more than get in the way of a bogey juggernaut. What Stumpelkin, Volgamints, and Zvorrov later told me (and this was over the years, so even they could have confused certain details) was that Fedyuninsky and Volgamints took on a lead element of 17s and cut into them easily until Fedyuninsky blew his engine somehow and caught a 17's tail in a dogfighting freak that sent his ship down like a dead thing and killed him. Volgamints was soon overwhelmed but survived ejection with a broken sternum. Soon after, the 17s joined up with the main element of Yaks—the enemy replaying the same tactics of Friday—and within minutes the battle was down to Glavtop and Grin chasing the strike in and Stumpelkin and me over the field waiting for the strike to come on. Glavtop and Grin took on everything at once and, when their bays and ammo boxes were empty, they flew down into the gamut anyway and didn't come up. How they survived ejection at those speeds and altitude was a dogfighting miracle.

The battle was lost when Glavtop and Grin went down. Zvorrov made his decision to commit Genka and me anyway and ordered a new heading. My J-band radar was so bad that I didn't know we'd met the enemy—at least eighteen aircraft—until I saw Stumpelkin lock on a target and salvo, though I didn't see the hit. Our 21s could outturn, outclimb, and outrun anything out there, and initially it was like swimming through twigs. The only thing that could stop Stumpelkin was the odds and the fact that I couldn't fight. Also, I abandoned him and tried to run away.

I've told Stumpelkin the story of my failure so often over the years that it's odd I still find it hard to write down the truth that I let them shoot down my best friend. What happened first was that we rolled out of a pass and came back to chase bogeys so close in to the field that I could see swirling SAM contrails come up and the black puffs of the bomb hits down below. The Yaks were cratering the field at will, and it was futile to continue, but Genka lined up two bogeys pulling out of a bombing run and used his guns. The trailing Yak broke down and blew up. I saw Genka fire again, and then I saw a black dart pass over me. Genka called, "Peter, what's on me? What's on me? Get it off!" and then a heat-seeker tore a hole in his fuselage. I was less than two kilometers back at five o'clock, so I saw it all as if in slow motion, the missile, the detonation, the popping of the canopy and his ejection, and then Stumpelkin was gone and, in a phenomenon of dogfighting, I was alone in the sky, no bogeys, no friendlies, nothing on my failed radar or crackling radio.

My reaction was to run away. Without anyone to give me orders, the sane part of me looked around at all the danger and told me to run away. I dropped my ordnance and auxiliary tank, worked the pedals and throttle, lit up my afterburners, and pushed into the vertical. My worn aircraft soon started bleeding hydraulics, and, as the indicators flashed, I shut them down and turned off the warblers warning low fuel. I turned up the cabin heater to maximum and increased the oxygen flow in my mask to keep me awake. I was climbing at eighty degrees into a hot blue sky with no one or nothing to go back for. I didn't kick over even when the drag warned me I was losing control. I kept on until my engine failed in the rare air of twenty kilometers high and I began to wallow ballistically. I knew I had to pop the canopy and get out, and within moments my reflexes or perhaps my deep sense of obedience made me save my own life; yet I remember very clearly the love of freedom I felt in the vertical, and how I didn't want to get out, I wanted to keep going through the blue and into the stars. My flight still feels to me like a dream. I can't promise I saw the phenomenon I think I saw when I finally swirled over the top and blew myself out of the cockpit. Genka Stumpelkin claimed that it was unlikely, but at the time I was certain that across the cloudless canopy of heaven I saw Tsar Cannon enter space.

(4)

The True Story of the
Russian Moon Landing

What I know to be true of the moon landing I have from Isaacii Goldenberg. He served as the mission control boss, and little over those six days of the voyage happened without his knowledge and approval. Isaacii is dead now, just this past winter from pneumonia and old age; and because it has taken me seven years to compile just this much of my draft, I find that, now that I've come to the part of my story that needs him most, all I have of him are my memories and the notes I took from our many conversations of the events. He did leave me his log of the mission, before the signals started to break up and fail, and I have studied the transmissions so closely that it can feel as if I were there at mission control, sometimes as if I were in the command module with my uncles as they drove the moon.

Tsar Cannon burst restraint points at T-00:00:07, and the moonship began its job in a crude rage of orange fire, twisting to get free of gravity while the gimbal motion of the core engines fought to keep the thrust aligned with the center of the mass. Simultaneously the launch tower burst with a flood of water to cool the pad, so that eighty-eight meters of LOX-frothing rocket ship seemed to float both inside a superheated steam cloud and atop an upside-down volcano. The contest between Tsar Cannon and gravity was fair equal for one second, three seconds, ten seconds, and then the black-smoking fury of the core and strap-on R-300 engines overwhelmed the earth's invisible chains and the booster lifted free of the tower in a thunderclapping roar and began to accelerate into the pure vertical.

Inside the command module, my uncles had little to do but wrestle with four g's and listen to the angry engines. I never rode a booster as big as Tsar Cannon, but I am sure they could hear the crackling sounds right through their couches. I know the g-load felt like being flattened by an ocean wave that wouldn't quit. They shook like aspic while they tried to remember to breathe. My uncles would have been most alert to any sudden pitch that would mean the very failure they had risked in their haste. They had ordered Goldenberg to override the systematic hold for the flawed vernier engines and to jump the countdown ahead through two hours of checks in order to make the shot at 0441, July 14, twenty minutes after sunrise.

At T plus two minutes twenty seconds, the strap-on engines cut off and were jettisoned by explosive bolt. Goldenberg announced, "First stage away, confirmed. Core engines nominal, confirmed." Goldenberg said he knew my uncles couldn't answer him, but he couldn't not do his duty, and besides, he said, there was no one else senior to talk. Goldenberg became boss of the mission by default, since the Grand Constructor had become an artifact in a wheelchair and since the Saturday before, Doctor Lunin, while fighting the flash fire in the clean room, had collapsed with a stroke that paralyzed him for the last eleven years of his life. This left Goldenberg and the tireless Doctor Mishuk of the R-7 as the ranking senior rocketeers for the mission, and, while they shared the job like brothers, there was a burden on Goldenberg's talent and intuition, as I shall explain.

At T plus two minutes forty-nine seconds of the mission, the main engines cut off, the core second stage was jettisoned, and the third stage (a rebuilt Proton) began the longest, most dangerous burn, six minutes and twenty seconds to push the spacecraft past escape velocity and into orbit. The whole machine began to bounce and shudder with the feared pogo effect of the superbooster launches (the American Saturn V suffered the pogo as well), and there were tearing sounds amidships. During the burn, the nose shroud parted correctly, exposing the spacecraft to space, and while the tearing sounds continued my uncles shook in silence and patience. There were no emergency procedures, indeed to save weight there was only one spacesuit among the three of them. Goldenberg said that the tearing sounds were likely the Proton's fuel tanks emptying unevenly and that, as far as he could later determine, the damage caused by the vibrations was not major. The burn cut off, and the spacecraft rode the third stage into earth orbit at twenty-four thousand kilometers per hour.

From his monitor, Goldenberg deployed the spacecraft's high-gain antenna radome like a toadstool tower atop the orbital module.

From then on there was a two-way link between ground control and the spacecraft. "Earth orbit, confirmed," Goldenberg announced to my uncles. He told them they had achieved a low orbit of 247 by 182 kilometers at 51.6 degrees inclination. When he asked for confirmation, my uncles remained silent; and Goldenberg had to insist that they respond if just to verify the high-gain antenna was nominal.

Uncle Dmitry was command pilot in the port-side couch, and he answered curtly, *"Luna* here, orbit confirmed," and then continued with acronyms and numbers, but according to Goldenberg he sounded subdued. Uncle Dmitry did add, "Rough, rough, rough," and it was Goldenberg's assumption that Uncle Dmitry's upset was because of the Proton's sloppy burn. Goldenberg and Doctor Mishuk determined that the spacecraft, designated *Luna 15,* had been late getting into orbit because of power shorts in the modified Proton. Goldenberg passed on to Uncle Dmitry that the deviation in the orbit was a problem but wouldn't delay the schedule.

Uncle Alexander was flight engineer in the starboard-side couch. Through his porthole he would have already been able to see the Kamchatka peninsula beneath broken cloud cover on a torrid mid-summer day in most-eastern Siberia. I can't know how much he suffered in the launch, but I know that he'd gone into space without feeling below his chest and without eating solid food for several weeks. Whatever pain he felt must have been offset by the gentleness of zero-gravity. Uncle Alexander was wearing the special orange flight suit that the engineers had built for his broken bowels, and he had been fixed to his couch like a corpse with a brain and hands. Goldenberg told me that Uncle Alexander's voice remained strong throughout the mission and that his opinion commanded all debates. "I'd like to think that getting up gave him strength and some peace," Goldenberg told me. "Or maybe it was because he was the one of them who left no one behind. Or maybe it was because he was even stranger than we ever knew—I don't know." In any event, Uncle Alexander overcalled Goldenberg's remarks and declared, "All nominal. We want three orbits. Give us a good TLI."

More than two hours later, behind schedule but not as late as it could have been, due to some inspired recalculation by the engineers, the Proton third stage relit and burned for six more minutes, pushing the spacecraft to earth escape velocity at approximately forty thousand kilometers per hour. This was the critical translunar injection or TLI—they were leaving earth's orbit like a slung shot—and *Luna 15* shook badly again as it aimed for a long elliptical trajectory for the moon. Cut-off was on time. Goldenberg called, "Confirmed," and read out the numbers while waiting for the engineers to determine how effective the TLI had been. To this point the moonship had been ground-controlled, a robot ship, and Goldenberg was pleased to report that the best of the news was that the time of the TLI burn had been nominal. Soon he had to pass on the bad news that, according to his numbers, *Luna 15*'s pericynthion, or closest pass to the moon, was calculated at a very wide two thousand kilometers, and that they would have to make at least three midcourse corrections to bring the pericynthion down to an acceptable 120 kilometers. Goldenberg urged the first midcourse correction, "We'll start with a ten-second burn."

Uncle Alexander rejected the request, "Get on with the link-up," and then he ordered Uncle Dmitry to initiate the transposition.

My uncles were in their usual pigheaded rush, waving off caution and taking the driving away from the Tsar Cannoneers as soon as possible. What had to be done was some fancy flying in order to reassemble the moonship like a freight train, placing the caboose before the locomotive—a complex maneuver called transposition that included separation from the third stage, extraction of the lander from the bow of the trailing Proton, and then the docking of the two craft into one. More than twenty-five hundred kilometers from earth, outbound to the moon, Uncle Dmitry took control of his ship and fired the bolts that decoupled *Luna 15* from the spent Proton. Firing the reaction control thrusters, Uncle Dmitry rolled, pitched, and yawed like a cork in water to bring the command ship head-on to the bow of the Proton core, where the moon lander was stored as if in a garage. Uncle Dmitry closed on the garage with his rendezvous radar, and he eased the last meters by sighting through the belly-mounted periscope. This was the maneuver that Uncle Dmitry had practiced in *Soyuz 4/5*. He made a neat fit as his probe-docking apparatus slipped into the lander's drogue-docking apparatus and the capture latches closed with a pop. Everything had gone so well that Goldenberg insisted on slowing down for checks, and he made my uncles wait seventy minutes before confirming the dock and letting Uncle Dmitry back the lander out of the Proton garage while rolling and pitching to test the hitch.

Four hours into the mission, *Luna 15* was a whole mooncraft that looked as if the iron butterfly of the command ship had been captured by a little black spider of a moon lander, designated *Laikushka*. Goldenberg asked for a ten-second burn for the first midcourse correction, or MCC1, and this time Uncle Alexander approved. By remote command Goldenberg fired the command ship's main engine, expending fuel as dearly as if it were blood. After cutoff the engineers rushed to calculate the new pericynthion. The result was again wide, though it did lower the gap to eleven hundred kilometers. Goldenberg showed his concern when he called my uncles with the results. "This won't do, sirs. We've got to cut down the flight path. We'll have an MCC2 as soon as we can work it up." In return Uncle Konstantine spoke for the first time in order to tease, "A miss is what we want, darling, no bull's-eye." Goldenberg told me he and Doctor Mishuk noted Uncle Konstantine's quip. They were encouraged that my uncles were jesting, because perhaps this meant they were feeling better about their ship and the way they had to share the flight with the Tsar Cannoneers (for, unlike the Apollos, *Luna 15* had no onboard guidance and navigation system and my uncles were dependent on Goldenberg's monitors and calculations). Goldenberg took back control of all the ship's systems and told my uncles to rest, and this time they obliged. For my uncles, the bright full earth was behind, the dark new moon was ahead, their spacecraft was a sound if ugly ship in a mysterious sea. I think I know why, after the tragedy of the countdown and the troubles of the Proton burns and TLI, they were able to find some humor again and relax. It was because of what they could see from the porthole. I have driven the moon in my time, and I know that as soon as you have done your job to the limit, as soon as you have your thoughts to yourself, you look back at where you've come from and feel reverence at the beauty of the phenomenon that I have learned to call earth blue—a planet like a freak of a color in the black of the cosmos, a globe that can look like a glistening blue gem nestled into those feathery clouds hugging the white poles. With ETA eighty-five hours to lunar orbit insertion, my uncles did as I have done and said their fare-thee-wells to the comfort of earth blue and their hellos to the aura of the rising moon.

Back on earth the race to the moon took flight when, approximately sixty hours later, a majestic American Saturn V burst restraint points and lifted *Apollo 11* through the pogo effect to a low earth orbit of 192 by 190 kilometers over the South Atlantic. Three orbits later, the spacecraft rode the TLI burn for six minutes to approximately forty thousand kilometers per hour outbound to the moon. The transposition and docking were handled expertly, and the moonship was assembled and certified ahead of schedule. Soon they fired the command ship's main engine and scooted into a flight path with a pericynthion of 333 kilometers, which would have to be corrected midcourse. The three astronauts were lighthearted with excitement, and Colonel E. E. Aldrin gave a whimsical weather report as he looked back to earth, "It looks like L.A. doesn't have a smog problem today." The astronauts weren't unaware that there was a rival spacecraft ahead of them. Then again, there had been no announcement from Moscow, and the assumption was that *Luna 15* was a robot craft launched to steal headlines and possibly to attempt the not unspectacular feat of landing a robot soil sampler that could return some lunar rocks in a small capsule. If you're surprised that there should have been so much confusion about what was the greatest footrace of the twentieth century, then perhaps you still don't understand how the Cold War had made all public discourse a clatter of lies and half-truths. The raising of the two moonships was as if prideful mankind had again erected a Tower of Babel only to tumble to mayhem. I promise you that you can look at the records of those days for yourself and find no remark at all from the Russian side, and from the American side only the assertion that *Luna 15* was no more than an unmanned stunt meant to take advantage of fate should *Apollo 11* fail to make a moon landing.

Fate took advantage of my uncles, for their first emergency was one of those freaks of flying that kills. It came about seventy-five hours into the mission, when events were already beginning to unravel, for the poor flight path had put them behind schedule and short of a solution. Three midcourse corrections had not lowered the pericynthion adequately, and the fourth try was scheduled in eight hours. The result of all this error was that, rather than a tidy eighty-five hours to lunar orbital insertion, or LOI, the ETA had been recalculated to ninety-six hours. In order to make sure the ETA didn't get any worse, Uncle Dmitry was much on the line to Goldenberg whenever Goldenberg's ground stations could give them a clear signal. (Transmission was not continuous, because we maintained only one ground station in the Western Hemisphere; all operations had to be timed to when the face of Asia looked at the moonship.) Goldenberg's memory was that, right before the accident, he was talking with Uncle Dmitry about the BBC report on the moon race. "The BBC called them an enigma, or mystery in an enigma, or an enigma in a shroud, or something like that," Goldenberg told me. "And General Zhukovsky thought it was funny and wanted to cheer everyone up with it. We were talking back and forth freely, and then I heard him suck in air and say, 'Alert, we have impact.' "

The first impact sounded like a thump forward on the orbital module's wall. Following Uncle Dmitry's alert call, there were two more thumps and a scraping sound, as if a giant hand had clawed the ship stem to stern. The worst sound was a sharp bang that came amidships, and instantly afterward the radio communications started breaking up at random.

Uncle Dmitry repeated his emergency call several times; when he was sure he'd made himself clear, he added, "I show venting of the main approach and orientation fuel tank."

Goldenberg glanced over his monitors, saw nothing as of yet, and asked, "What is the nature of the alert?"

Uncle Dmitry reported, "We've lost pressure in the main thruster tank. Repeat, I am showing bleeding in the main thruster fuel tank." Uncle Alexander came on the line: "Isaacii, we have impact in fuel tanks aft. All secure forward. There is possible high-gain antenna damage. We need you to correct pitch, or give us the rudder and we'll correct."

Goldenberg was still not reading the damage that my uncles could see on their monitors and demanded, "*Luna*, impact with what? You've hit something? What've you hit?"

Uncle Dmitry took control of his own ship to steady the pitch. Meanwhile the radio transmission continued to show mixed weakness, and from then on the two-way link was a constant threat to fail. Uncle Dmitry called Goldenberg with his assessment that the emergency alert was because *Luna 15* had collided with space debris. Uncle Dmitry said that large stonelike objects were whirling around the craft, some of them pockmarked ovals, some of them pristine obelisks. "We've flown into a swarm of junk," Uncle Dmitry called. "When you do your numbers you'll find that we are at an equigravisphere point. We talked about this once a long time ago. We dismissed it as improbable."

Goldenberg answered, "It is improbable and impossible!"

Uncle Dmitry reminded Goldenberg, "If it happened then it must be possible."

Such a collision *was* both improbable and as close to impossible as imaginable, and yet my uncles had indeed flown into one of the equigravisphere points of the earth and the moon and had indeed struck debris that over the eons had collected in permanent orbit, like a Sargasso Sea of space waste. No one had ever regarded such a collision a credible danger and, in all the planning for the moon missions, there had not been one calculation of the probability. The impact was a freak of flying that the lucky Americans in *Apollo 11,* sixty hours behind my uncles, would also experience and survive without damage: Collins reported he felt a thump just before he spotted an L-shaped rock swim past the porthole.

Onboard *Luna 15,* the impact caused wounds that weren't mortal, though they were very threatening. Uncle Dmitry took time to study all his systems and reported a dire number to Goldenberg, "We're down to forty-seven percent for thrusters." Before Goldenberg could call back with his opinion that this was not acceptable, Uncle Alexander declared, "We're nominal for LOI."

Goldenberg took this exchange as evidence that, from the moment of the preliminary damage control, my uncles were reckoning to the limit of the envelope. I think Goldenberg had this right, and that, by facing the likelihood of failure as soon as they could, my uncles made their subsequent discussions easier. For example, Uncle Dmitry proposed a plan to evaluate the collision damage by sending Uncle Konstantine outside to walk over the ship. Uncle Alexander rejected the idea. Goldenberg said there was much argument over this point, Uncle Dmitry saying that they must locate the anomaly in the high gain or the solar-panel array, Uncle Alexander maintaining that the spacesuit must be preserved for the moon landing. I can guess now that perhaps this disagreement was also early evidence of a change in my uncles' mood. As early as the collision damage control, Uncle Alexander was prepared to trade a round-trip for a moon landing. Whatever was true, Uncle Dmitry prevailed with a compromise decision to give Uncle Konstantine an EVA once they were in lunar orbit.

By the time Goldenberg's machines were able to read the anomalies on the spacecraft, Uncle Dmitry was ready with a firm opinion to keep going despite warnings. "We can fly around the thruster fuel drop-off," Uncle Dmitry told Goldenberg. "The high-gain signal isn't critical. You give us a good MCC4, and we're nominal."

Goldenberg told me that he pressed Uncle Dmitry about internal damage and got him to admit that there was an obvious problem with the condensers that was making the command cabin cooler and damper. Goldenberg said this news frightened him and made him feel as cold as death, because it probably meant that *Luna 15* was losing irreplaceable stores. "It was too much to hear," Goldenberg told me. "We had launched without a margin for any such failure. Here we were three hundred and eighty-four thousand kilometers from earth without adequate backups, without an onboard guidance system, without a certifiable radio signal, and they were telling me the life-support system was breaking down. I knew what it meant, and they did, too. I figured it wasn't my job to tell them the ship was dying; it was my job to help them fly through the troubles. But after that, after the accident—what was holding her together was them. You know what I told Mishuk? What you told me once, Peter, the first time we met. I told Mishuk, 'General Oryolin's in charge, anything's possible.' "

The next emergency followed the first predictably. After a fourth midcourse-correction burn that wasted fuel but brought the crucial pericynthion down to a barely acceptable 160 kilometers, *Luna 15* was ready for the critical LOI burn to slow it down enough so that it could slip into lunar orbit. The six-minute burn was scheduled on the far side of the moon, where it would begin and end while my uncles were out of communication with Goldenberg. "I was worried about that LOI burn even from before the accident," Goldenberg told me. "And since before they went over the hill we weren't getting good reads from the engine, it told me that even if the firing went perfectly we might get a bad burn out of it, too long or too short." Goldenberg's concerns were well taken. After the ship had gone behind the moon, or over the hill, into the twenty-five-minute radio shadow or loss of signal, it emerged with a weak and patchy radio transmission and much too late for the burn to have been nominal. It took Goldenberg several calls to get through. When he did, Uncle Dmitry reported that during the burn there had been more shaking aft. It took Goldenberg and Doctor Mishuk eight more hours to confirm the bad news that the LOI burn had been too long and had inserted *Luna 15* into too elliptical a lunar orbit—the apocynthion too high, the pericynthion too low. This meant that, until the orbit was corrected, my uncles couldn't launch or recover the moon lander. "She should have been two-hundred-and-three by one-hundred-and-ten kilometers," Goldenberg told me. "She was three-hundred by fifty-five kilometers. It was messy, messy, with an inclination one hundred and ten degrees. She should have been reliable. She was all over the sky."

The worst of it was the slow-motion bleeding of the stores. The bad LOI burn had used too much nitric acid oxidizer for the hydrazine fuel. Goldenberg said that the collision had damaged the primary turbine pump for the main engine. Without that pump flowing evenly, Goldenberg said, he couldn't drive the ship reliably from earth. "I called them with my damage assessment," Goldenberg told me. "My numbers were convincing and awful. They didn't listen. They didn't want to listen."

Uncle Dmitry told Goldenberg, "We're in orbit, and we're staying in orbit. What we want now is some rest. Then what we want is numbers for a circularizing burn."

Goldenberg replied, "Affirmative," and lost contact altogether for several minutes. From then on radio contact was haphazard, and without good signals Goldenberg couldn't monitor the already dubious machines. "I put the best case on it," Goldenberg told me. "They were there, and they didn't need me to stay there. What I had to do was improve their orbit."

Four hours and two full lunar revolutions later, Goldenberg had a change of heart and decided it wasn't his job to be a handmaid to a catastrophe, it was his job to get his ship and crew home. After several attempts, he got through to list what he knew of *Luna 15*'s failures and to suggest a cautious plan to extract my uncles from lunar orbit. "I told them they were redline in oxidizer," Goldenberg told me. "I told them they were redline in the condensers and that there was a transient in the electrical system that flashed a warning light on my board but not theirs. I told them their high gain was critical, and I was assuming there'd been damage to a solar panel. I told them that maybe the impact had torn one of the panels loose, since that would explain the power dips, or maybe one of the panels had never fully deployed. I told them a lot more—though it wasn't possible to know how much of my speech got through with that bad radio—and I made sure they understood that I couldn't read what fuel was left to any accuracy, but that whatever was left was sufficient for a good TEI burn if we went immediately, and by that I meant within one orbit. I wanted them home. I told them with numbers that couldn't be argued. I did my best to tell them the worst. Then I waited."

There was a long delay before my uncles' reply, with much breaking up, and when a call did get through it was Uncle Alexander. "Negative abort, repeat, negative abort, repeat, negative abort. Come back."

Goldenberg obeyed. "Roger, *Luna,* negative abort at this time."

Uncle Dmitry asked again for a circularizing burn to correct the bad orbit. "How long to work up numbers on the burn?" Uncle Dmitry asked. "If you don't trust the signal, we'll fire it manually."

Goldenberg told them he wouldn't have numbers until he and Doctor Mishuk worked up a model. Eventually Doctor Mishuk delivered an opinion that designing a new circularizing burn to take into account the questionable firing mechanisms would require at least twenty-four hours of plotting and planning. Goldenberg passed this on to my uncles and was firm that they could not fire the circularizing burn manually. "It cannot be done, sirs."

Uncle Dmitry came back with a fresh cheerfulness that Goldenberg took as intimation that my uncles had decided to fight on as if they were still the shock falcon commanders of their youth, when there was never a possibility of retreat or surrender. "We're parked," Uncle Dmitry called, "and we're putting Kostya over the side to see what ripped us, and how."

Goldenberg listened in as Uncle Konstantine, forward in the orbital module, pulled on his spacesuit and prepared for EVA. Uncle Alexander urged haste in order to conserve the oxygen pack for the lunar landing. Uncle Konstantine was a brave man, but not even valor can describe all of what it must have taken for him to mount the orbital module with only a single lifeline, knowing no one could come out for him if he got hung up. Uncle Konstantine moved over the ship laboriously, handhold to knob, breathing heavily like a mountain climber. He hitched and curled out the lifeline to float off a few meters to inspect the moon lander. On the intercom he reported Goldenberg's worst suppositions: the high-gain antenna was bent sideways; one of two solar panels dangled like scrap; there was a dark smear of fuel on the command ship's skin.

Uncle Dmitry called Goldenberg to pass on the details and a preliminary diagnosis, "Our opinion is that the impact clipped a solar panel and sent shards into the main engine. Maybe into the turbine feed. We have a spook in our guts."

Goldenberg appealed to them to abort, and this time he was ominous. "The electrical system, the high gain, the main engine, the life support, my board, your board, all of this—it's either critical or will be. I can't drive what I can't read, and you must abort, now, sirs. You must abort."

Uncle Alexander countered, "No abort."

Uncle Konstantine contributed on the intercom, "My *Lai-kushka*'s in good shape and ready to fly—no abort."

Uncle Dmitry called Goldenberg with a compromise, "We'll hold on the decision, Isaacii. For now, I'm shutting down all systems except minimal life support. We're waiting on you to give us the circularizing burn."

As many as seven decades later, Goldenberg could still get teary and agitated when he described this part of the ordeal. "I should have forced it," he told me. "They wouldn't listen to me how bad it was. I was right, I was right in every detail! No matter what Mishuk worked up, I knew we couldn't fire the burn accurately, because the signal was bad, and the engine just wouldn't respond. I knew they were stalling me to the point where I couldn't get them home, and I let them! My checks were right. That circularizing burn wouldn't ever have worked. It didn't have a chance. They were asking for a miracle!"

For more than fifty dark hours and twenty-nine orbits, my uncles waited for Goldenberg's and Mishuk's models and systems checks to deliver that miracle. Meanwhile, *Apollo 11* closed the distance on schedule; seventy-five hours into the mission, it swung over the far side of the moon for the LOI burn. When the spacecraft emerged twenty-three minutes later, it was in an excellent lunar orbit, with an apocynthion of 312 kilometers and a pericynthion of 113 kilometers and an inclination eighty-five degrees west. Command module pilot

Collins reported on the LOI: "It was like, it was like perfect." Mission commander Armstrong was whimsical about the surface of the moon below: "It looks very much like the pictures, but like the difference between watching a real football game and one on TV—it's no substitute for actually being there."

My uncles were there, too, crisscrossing the same pitted, colorless wasteland in a crippled ship. I can't know what they said among themselves. I can guess that they slept as much as possible. They had reduced light, heat, and condensers to save the stores, and those two days must have been increasingly colder, damper, more and more foul in bad air. The only consolation they would have had was that there might be a solution to the orbit and a way to launch the lander.

"I knew they wouldn't come back, and I couldn't bring them back without their help," Goldenberg told me about those two days of calculations and failures to work out a credible circularizing burn. "It was either give them what they wanted or let them die like that, freezing and gasping until they passed out. They knew we had to do something for them. They knew they were extorting that burn from us. They knew everything and handled me like a child."

At 137 hours into the mission, Goldenberg and Mishuk gave up on all their models and designed a twenty-second circularizing burn that Goldenberg told my uncles was no more than a wild guess. He read the numbers to Uncle Dmitry and argued that the burn had to be programmed into the main engine; it could not be fired manually. My uncles were reluctant to trust the robot control again but finally relented and went over the hill to the far side, where the burn cut in and off. When the ship emerged, it took several minutes to reestablish contact and not much more time for Goldenberg and Doctor Mishuk to determine that the new orbit wasn't any better than before, with an apocynthion of 221 kilometers and a pericynthion of 95 kilometers and with an inclination 126 degrees.

Luna 15 was a dying bird. Goldenberg's team couldn't put her back together again, and it was at this desperate point that, according to Goldenberg, Uncle Alexander took complete charge with a plan that showed the genius of a shock commander to find a way to attack. First, he ordered Uncle Konstantine back outside with tools and wire to tie up the high-gain antenna; then he ordered Goldenberg to prepare a model for what he called a bumper burn.

Goldenberg explained to me, "General Oryolin wanted to use the lander engine to bump the ship into a good orbit. They didn't trust the main engine anymore; the turbine pump made it useless for any discreet calculation. But he knew we could count on the lander's engine. No more spook in the system, you see. Mishuk and I liked the idea right away. Yes, it was high risk; but yes, too, it was an inspired risk."

Uncle Konstantine suited up and went outside again with a repair kit, including surgical tape and electrical wire in order to tie up the high gain the way you might repair a broken umbrella. This took time, expending much oxygen and wearing Uncle Konstantine down. I have worked in suits most superior to his, so I am sure that his heart rate must have skyrocketed. After all this struggle, he was only able to achieve a marginal improvement in signal, though even this was enough to encourage my uncles. Uncle Alexander called Goldenberg, "Get the model worked up. We want the burn at the first available long window. We want an orbit of one-ten by ninety, and get the inclination corrected."

Goldenberg, Doctor Mishuk, and their team of Tsar Cannoneers responded like men thrown a lifeline. "When I heard him," Goldenberg told me, "I knew we had a way to do it. It was something we could do—I mean we didn't have to keep sitting there moaning about everything, we could try to save what we could. General Oryolin was like that, wasn't he?—a man who made you feel you could do the job. If he said it, you believed it, even if you were sure it was crazy. There wasn't much more to worry over except disappointing him. We went to our models on the bumper burn, and we worked almost happily—we did our job because General Oryolin had given us the strength to do our job."

Goldenberg and the Tsar Cannoneers did their job in safety at the command bunker. I've forgotten to mention that, despite the loss of the squadron, the Steppe Eagles had held the airfield and the oasis. Iagoda's forces had bombed the field to rubble but had broken off all air and ground attacks as soon as Tsar Cannon had launched, withdrawing the armored train and two armor columns and abandoning Star City to the Kazakh refugees. Within a day, train service had been restored from the north and the Air Force had sent in support and supplies. The ceasefire was as if a windstorm had passed over the Cosmodrome. The yellow steppe returned to the timeless heat of midsummer. I have no final explanation for why Iagoda had backed off after the launch—I know enough not to ask for reasons for anything done in Russia in those days—but I can suppose that Iagoda might have been checked by the other Lubyanka lords because, after all, my mother's feud was done, Alexander Oryolin was gone, Iagoda had cleaned up the Cosmonaut Corps of my uncles. Then again, the Lubyanka lords were such cunning wolves that I also have to suppose that they might have checked Iagoda because, once my uncles had launched, there was a possibility that Oryolin, Strogolshikov, and Zhukovsky could return as the first men on the moon.

While my uncles waited for the bumper burn, Houston control awoke *Apollo 11*'s astronauts for the day of the moon landing, Sunday, July 20, 1969. After a neat circularizing burn, the moonship's orbit was excellent, at 99.6 kilometers by 121.7 kilometers, driving at 5,800 kilometers per hour in an equatorial orbit. Records show that Houston control joked with the astronauts about how well they had slept and how their mission dominated the day's headlines. I note that at no point in the conversations was my uncles' spacecraft mentioned. Ninety-three and a half hours into *Apollo 11,* there were eight more hours to the landing sequence. The records show that Collins talked about the systems checks in his command module *Columbia,* Aldrin talked about systems checks in his already powered-up lunar lander module *Eagle,* while Armstrong kept his eyes on the potential landing sites below in the Sea of Tranquillity, a huge plain of sterile dust in the northeast quadrant. The Americans were giddy for their good luck so far. Houston control told the astronauts a Chinese fairy tale about a beautiful girl named Chango, who had been exiled to the moon and lived there in the shade of a cinnamon tree, alone except for a large rabbit. "Okay," Aldrin replied, "we'll keep a close eye for the bunny girl."

On *Luna 15,* fifteen minutes to the bumper burn, Goldenberg locked down his last numbers and read them again to Uncle Konstantine in his *Laikushka.* The burn, already programmed into the engine system, was only to last for twenty-two seconds. Uncle Konstantine had transferred to the lander an hour before to certify all systems, and also because the air was better in the lander and he'd need his strength for the landing. Also, Uncle Alexander wanted Uncle Konstantine's observation of what the bumper burn did to

Luna 15. Uncle Dmitry congratulated Goldenberg and Doctor Mishuk for their model. "You've done it, I'm impressed. You've done everything we've asked. You should know we're grateful." Uncle Dmitry was so pleased he even recited from Pushkin for them, a verse that Goldenberg recalled began, "Why does the wind revolve inanely?" or something similar.

Goldenberg told me that he kept shut in spite of my uncles' exhilaration. "There wasn't much to say after the housekeeping," Goldenberg told me. "We knew they were going for the DOI no matter what the burn did. We knew that this was the first step down to the surface for them. They weren't thinking about coming back."

Luna 15 went over the hill; *Laikushka*'s engine fired the burn; Goldenberg reacquired the signal and did the numbers. Presently he called my uncles to tell them the results were poor but not failure. Apocynthion was down to a manageable 110 kilometers, though pericynthion was dangerously low, at 16 kilometers, meaning the ship was zooming right over the big mountains of the moon. The inclination was still bad at 127 degrees; the revolution was down to 114 minutes.

Uncle Alexander called Goldenberg with his verdict. He wanted the calculations for the lander undocking as soon as possible—that is, the separation of *Luna* and *Laikushka*—and he wanted the lander's descent orbit insertion and powered descent immediately afterward. He wanted all this worked up within two revolutions. Uncle Alexander ordered Goldenberg, "Get it done."

Goldenberg told me, "He sounded angry when he said it in that way of his, you know, like a terrible boss. I believe he knew it was wrong to force the DOI, but we didn't challenge him. We'd gone along too far to raise more obstacles. The bumper burn had worked half well. He didn't care if it had worked at all. You see, by then my checks showed there was sufficient fuel to boost them into the TEI, but there was insufficient to slow them down on the way home. Maybe there was enough, my reads were all messy. Still, it didn't come to arguing TEI or not. General Oryolin didn't care about my numbers. He'd decided for all of us that this was a one-way mission."

I remember thinking, when Goldenberg first told me of this turn, that a dying man shouldn't have been the man to make this decision.

Alexander Oryolin was doomed, and perhaps he was also damned, and it's my experience that such men are not trustworthy decision makers. But then I want to be fair-minded about Uncle Alexander's position. I know what it means to obey regardless of your feelings or desires, and perhaps when it came to it Uncle Alexander chose to go for the landing because he thought it was his job. "It's the job," I can hear him say, his shoulders squared, his chin out, chewing on his pipe stem, those black eyes faraway, repeating in his mumbly voice, "It's the job."

Meanwhile *Apollo 11* reproduced like an amoeba to fix the command module *Columbia,* crewed by Collins, in a high orbit and the lunar module *Eagle,* crewed by Armstrong and Aldrin, in a low orbit. In the one hundred and third hour of the mission, on the far side of the moon, the programmed ignition fired a thirty-second DOI burn in order to send the lander *Eagle* into a still lower orbit with a pericynthion of sixteen kilometers. Houston control reacquired *Columbia*'s signal first. All was well aboard the command ship. Houston control reacquired *Eagle*'s signal and discovered there was an anomaly in the transmission. At first the signal was strong, but then as Houston was calling the lander, "If you read, you're a go for powered descent," the telemetry died. What had happened was that the high-gain antenna on *Eagle* was out of line to transmit and receive from the earth, and, without that two-way link, the lander was helpless. The rocketeers compensated as quickly as possible, calling Collins in *Columbia* to act as a go-between, so that he could tell Aldrin in *Eagle,* "They recommend you yaw right ten degrees and try the high gain again." The astronauts used thrusters to reorient the lander, and the high-gain signal was reestablished, yet there would be more difficulty with it ahead. I note these troubles not to take from the American triumph but rather to help you marvel at the size of the achievement. After all the expensive, painstaking preparation, the American moon landing came down to the courage and luck of the astronauts driving the vehicles, and at the end their success included some breakneck decisions.

Eagle was cleared for automatic powered descent within twelve minutes. Fifteen kilometers from the surface, Armstrong manually fired the lander engine. Here again Houston control lost the signal from the lander, and again Collins on *Columbia* had to serve as the go-between, telling Armstrong to switch to *Eagle*'s omnidirectional antenna to maintain communication in case of an emergency. The signal to earth remained weak, and Aldrin reoriented the lander's high-gain antenna once more. This time the signal got through perfectly to Houston, but you can hear how the astronauts' and rocketeer's voices sounded their strain and caution as they chatted among themselves, "See if they got me now . . ." "Yeah, you should have him now." "*Eagle,* we've got you now."

The next problem tumbled atop the first as the lander swooped lower on its final landing approach. At this point the landing radar and the rendezvous radar on the lander read two different altitudes from the surface, and accordingly the primary guidance computer onboard *Eagle,* unable to solve the discrepancy, gave an alarm signal, 1201 or 1202. In abort simulations, the crew had prepared for this possibility by deciding to ignore the alarm and bail out or reboot the computer—in other words, the astronauts were trained to be good pilots who trusted themselves and not their robots. As the lander settled forward into an upright position, however, the high-gain signal again started breaking up. This time the lander was too far committed to the landing approach to reorient. If the high-gain transmission had failed at this moment, Houston control would have been blind and Armstrong would have been deprived of the elaborate backup checks on his ship.

The astronauts' luck held. The lander again flew through its signal troubles to the point of no return, called High Gate. Houston control gave its final approval to Armstrong: "*Eagle.* Houston. You're go for a landing."

From then on down, the lander was in the hands of fate and its pilots, and if you have ever thought that the moon landing was straightforward and inevitable you have not listened to the recording of the descent: "Roger," the copilot Aldrin replied to Houston control, "understand, go for landing. Three thousand feet. Program alarm!"

Houston control responded, "Copy."

Aldrin warned again of the computer alarm, "Twelve-o-one."

Armstrong confirmed, "Twelve-o-one."

"Roger," Houston control responded. "Twelve-o-one alarm. We're go. Hang tight. We're go."

"Hang tight" tells the tale better than facts. I translate it now as the American way of saying, "Keep going," or "Finish it," or "It's the job," since during the final approach, the rocketeers and astronauts ignored the robot controls that had got them there and chose to "hang tight." At 125 meters, Armstrong loaded a new program that he hoped would stop overloading while *Eagle* continued to settle on its programmed landing sequence toward the Sea of Tranquillity. At thirty-five meters, Armstrong was permitted to take over from the robots, and from the moment he took the controls Armstrong drove his ship not by the numbers but by the feel of a high-performance pilot. Here was the time for dare, here was the moment only a man could have solved, here was the proof that the Americans won the moon not just by money and luck but also by the grace of God. Armstrong flew the lander lower to look over the terrain, and in a glance he decided to reject the first spot because there were too many ruts and boulders, too much soft dust. Armstrong moved on, hovering forward at twenty-five meters, and he rejected a second spot in a broad, pitted crater. From his portal view the dust stretched out endlessly, the boulders threw sharp shadows, the craters opened into crevasses. Armstrong knew he was taking too long to find a landing zone, knew he was expending too much fuel, knew time was the enemy.

Houston control called the threat to Armstrong, "Sixty seconds," when the monitors on earth said there was less than a minute's worth of fuel in the lander.

Copilot Aldrin responded with numbers and added what he could see on the surface, "Lights on. Forward. Forward. Good. Forty feet, down two and one half. Picking up some faint dust . . . Faint shadow."

Houston control called the frightening fact, "Thirty seconds," which meant, because the monitors were useless below thirty seconds, there was no more margin; the engine was redline and at the edge of failure; and either Armstrong landed or he aborted or he rode *Eagle* to a catastrophe. Armstrong decided to find his fate on the surface of the moon, and Aldrin proclaimed the victory as it happened, "Engines stop."

Houston control responded, "We copy you down, *Eagle*."

Armstrong confirmed the victory, "Houston. Tranquillity Base here. The *Eagle* has landed."

Nineteen hours after the American landing, my uncles were prepared to go for their own moon landing. The long wait had been necessary because of *Luna 15*'s difficult orbit and because of the need to wait for a transmission window between the Cosmodrome and the moon, and it wasn't until approximately 187 hours into the mission that the Tsar Cannoneers were in position to lock on to the high-gain antenna on the lander in order to fly her down. By this time all extra fuel and stores had been expended onboard the command ship, and Goldenberg and Doctor Mishuk had been obliged to design a landing sequence that used the remainder of fuel and stores aboard *Laikushka*.

"It was orders," Goldenberg told me. "They'd worn us down. We were like shroud-makers. There wasn't any way but to give them a chance to make the landing. They didn't have twelve hours of air left, and by the next good window they'd be dead."

Luna 15 went over the hill once more. Uncle Dmitry used his thrusters to pop the command ship apart from Uncle Konstantine in the lander. Separation instantly turned disastrous, for the spook in the electrical system caused a thruster to stick open, and the command ship yawed badly on the z axis, in a flat spin. Uncle Dmitry shut down the thruster system and used his unreliable main engine to stabilize the ship, which altered his orbit dramatically. At acquisition of signal, Goldenberg read the command ship in an unstable orbit, but much worse was the fact that the flat spin had collapsed the jerry-rigged high-gain antenna. After a sputter and screech, the direct radio link died. This was the opposite of the problem that had faced the astronauts, for now the command ship was deaf and dumb and the lander was the go-between. Uncle Konstantine and Uncle Dmitry opened communication and discussed the facts of the separation, and then Uncle Konstantine called Goldenberg with orders from Uncle Alexander, "Sasha says he wants me to start down in five minutes. Give me a DOI and a powered descent all together, I'm so low I can pick the flowers now."

Goldenberg shot back, "I can't do that, sir. We have to check your new orbit before we can trust the landing sequence!"

Uncle Konstantine repeated, "Five minutes and get me close; I'll set her down."

Goldenberg told me that he was still unable to accept that my uncles were going to die. He called Uncle Konstantine with a plea,

"You can't go down without checks, sir. You have to tell General Zhukovsky that his orbit is deteriorating, and he has to boost to a higher orbit."

Uncle Konstantine returned, "The orders are to get me down, and wouldn't you know they'd leave you and me with all the work while they sit there snoozing. Let's get me down, and then we can lend a hand over there."

Goldenberg called back an obedient, "Yes, sir." Decades later Goldenberg reflected to me, "In other words he told me to shut up and get on with my work. I felt bad right away, since he was the one who was going down, and yet I was the one crying about it. I shouldn't have lost my head. What could he do about *Luna*'s orbit? It was too late for them; it was too late for him. Do you know what it was like to pretend I could help him? If he got down, if he got back up, what was there to rendezvous with? *Luna* was drifting down, she was unrecoverable. Generals Zhukovsky and Oryolin had sacrificed their ship in the undocking. It was a disaster. I had three doomed cosmonauts up there, and only one of them was still talking to me, and he wanted me to fly him down to his own death—a disaster."

Goldenberg's disaster got worse, because what he next had to do was approve Uncle Konstantine's descent, though he knew that the programmed sequence in the lander was inappropriate to present conditions. Uncle Konstantine called Goldenberg, "Sasha and Mitya say I have their best wishes. I'm all green lights, darling, we're driving home. Give me a countdown by the minute to ignition."

Goldenberg responded, "Five minutes and counting, sir." And then he added, "You're redline on oxygen, redline on nitric."

Uncle Konstantine didn't dispute the figures, reading them back while he waited. The lander *Laikushka* had a cramped flight cabin that had been fortified to withstand space exposure and arranged to make her as easy to fly as a Mil. Uncle Konstantine would have spent his last minutes in a half-crouched position, and he would have buttoned up his spacesuit again after breathing internal air for the last half day. The lander looked like a mechanical spider that could divide in half, the descent stage of four legs to be left on the moon, the bell-shaped ascent stage to be flown back up into lunar orbit. Return wasn't any longer an issue, however, for in the overlong struggle in orbit, Uncle Konstantine had exhausted his reserve stores except for water. Goldenberg told me he assumed that Uncle Konstantine must have drunk liberally those last minutes, because his voice strength-ened. He called Goldenberg, "How's my signal? Five by five? Good. Time?"

"Three minutes, sir," Goldenberg called and counted down to ignition. He told me no one wept in the control room. "We were exhausted. We told ourselves that he was going to try to land on the moon and that was what we'd built the ship for."

Uncle Konstantine's last remark before ignition was everything I loved about him—brassy, crude, stubborn, funny: "Holy Mother-frigging Russia's great, darling, but the moon—just look at her—she rises!"

Twelve kilometers from the surface, the engine fired automati-cally, the lander pitched upright, the radioaltimeter measured the horizontal and vertical planes, and *Laikushka* started the powered descent toward the chosen target area in the Sea of Fertility. The original landing sequence called for the main engine to burn 850 seconds to a preset cutoff, and then the lander was to settle in free-fall to six hundred meters, and then, with a combination of the vernier engines and a boost from the main engine, the lander was to settle down to fifty to twenty meters, where Uncle Konstantine was to take control and land manually.

Goldenberg told me that what went wrong was unclear, though he supposed it must have been caused by a bad landing sequence. What happened was that the main engine refused to cut off at 850 seconds and the lander overflew the target area. At the emergency, Goldenberg overheard Uncle Konstantine talking to Uncle Dmitry. "No cutoff," Uncle Konstantine said. Then, "Negative, I'm on a ride." Then, "I'm north, way north. Twenty-two hundred meters. Goodbye Sea of Fertility. On a ride!"

Goldenberg called a warning, "Your fuel is redline. Shut down, abort," because he wanted Uncle Konstantine to punch out of the sequence and escape in the ascent stage. "Abort, abort!" he re-peated.

The lander overshot the target area and swooped onward to the northeast. "Sea of Marsh," Uncle Konstantine called and then, "Cut off, she's cut off!"

Goldenberg explained to me that the main engine must have ex-hausted its fuel and shut down, leaving the lander in free-fall. Uncle Konstantine wasn't powerless, because he had the tiny vernier engines for lift, and he could stabilize with his orientation thrusters. He must have gained some control of his flight, for his next call was confident.

"Two hundred meters," he reported, "and I'm going down. A little hard. Landing sequence. Initiate."

Goldenberg said that Uncle Konstantine must have stabilized his ship and fired all his vernier engines to slow the fall. What happened last is impossible to say, perhaps total engine failure, perhaps a tumbling spin. All I have is Goldenberg's remark that Uncle Konstantine's last call was buried in static and sounded like, "Alert."

Goldenberg recorded *Laikushka*'s impact in the Sea of Crisis at the base of a minor mountain range, seventeen degrees north, forty-nine degrees east. The lander's small cabin crumpled like paper and slid like a flat rock across a crater rim to come to rest at the lip of a shallow crevasse. There was no fire. Uncle Konstantine died on impact. I know this to be true, because I was able to locate the crash site in order to dig out the cabin and the spacesuit and to bring what we could of him back to give to Uncle Konstantine's widow, Doctor Mometov, who buried his remains on the banks of the Don on the fortieth anniversary of his death.

After Uncle Konstantine's crash, Goldenberg lost all sign of the command ship. *Luna 15* went over the hill one last time and was not seen again. My uncles either crashed on the far side of the moon or blasted out of lunar orbit. Since there can be no final version, I am free to imagine their last flight, and I have made my choice of their end. *Luna 15* would have continued through lunar darkness and then once more over the west limb of the moon into the earthlessness of the far side. I can picture Uncle Dmitry in his couch, arms crossed on his chest; and I can see Uncle Alexander turned sideways to his portal, his withered legs tucked underneath to hold him up. The cabin would have been dark, icing along the walls, very rank and close, and they couldn't have known how much longer they would have before blackout. It would have been best to get the finish done soon, for the job on the moon was done and their duty was answered.

I imagine Uncle Alexander touching his engineer's panel and ordering, "Trim her on my count."

I can hear Uncle Dmitry chatting as he prepared to change orbit, and I can suppose he talked about Angelicka, Anna, Marya, and how he missed them. Certainly I would have said something about how much I loved my family, even if the only person to hear was Alexander Oryolin, a man who loved no one at the end.

Then again, it isn't fair to say that Uncle Alexander was loveless at his death. He had lived so long as a larger-than-life hero, always driving himself for greater gain and victory, that perhaps the finality of his last flight gave him peace enough to relax and to love. It's important to me to say that he wasn't alone at the end, that he'd listened to his devoted Kostya's last transmission, that he died beside his dear friend Mitya. He surely loved them. I don't know. I loved him. When I think back, of all the men I have known, Alexander Alexandrovich Oryolin is the one I most wanted to be like and yet the one I have long worried I might have become—brave yet tyrannical, passionate yet unforgiving, ambitious yet despairing.

I am sure that before ignition Uncle Dmitry would have said, "Soft landing, Sasha."

I am sure Uncle Alexander would have mumbled back, "Finish it."

My version of their end is that, at approximately T plus 189 hours, *Luna 15*'s main engine would have fired one last time. Goldenberg told me there would have been fuel for a two-minute burst, not nearly enough for a transearth injection, but sufficient if timed correctly to get out of lunar orbit. All Goldenberg knew for certain was that *Luna 15* was in orbit and then she wasn't. In my time in command of Tranquillity Base, I directed several searches on the far side for impact zones. The moon is a solemn landscape that burns the soul and freezes the heart, and there are millions of holes left unexamined, yet I don't believe that was their end. I believe my uncles got free at last and boosted themselves into the long fall that would make their spacecraft a man-made satellite in eternal orbit of the sun that gave birth to us all.

⑤

My End

I'm ancient now, ninety-one years is more than old, and when you're the same as me you'll know how one of the thrills most available is to see the world again with twenty-two-year-old eyes. Now I have and I'm happy for it. I have also told the true story of the Russian moon landing, and I'm much happier for it. If this were to be my memoir of those days, Air Force rules say that I should continue with the rest of the tale of my service, but I don't want to. The Cosmonaut Corps has a history, and you can find the volumes in the library; and somewhere you will find that I was the sixth commander of the Corps.

My life was Starry Town from the first day I arrived to the last day I departed. I know that I wasn't worse than my predecessor, just as I know I wasn't better than my successor. I confess that as commander of the Corps I was stern, short-tempered, long-winded, judgmental, and orthodox, and when I wanted to be I was ruthless. I was sometimes called a hero, and sometimes I was, yet none of the ribbons have ever looked as good to me as they once did on the breasts of my uncles, the Martian Troika, who taught me how to be heroic and, more importantly, taught me how to carry on without heroes like them as my shock commanders.

I should speak some of my time in the Corps after my uncles were gone. The Cosmonaut Corps took those of us left back like orphans and buried our dead decently: the high-minded Zhora Fedyuninsky, the lionhearted Misha Cherryntevsky, the dice master Artzybashev and his bookkeeper Kandidim, and the last to go, my friend Yurka Adama-Bibliov, who died of his wounds eight months after the battle. There was no blame for what we'd done, and there was no discipline. The Corps stood by us, and the Air Force stood by the Corps, and we stood together as falcons. I returned from the medical center as a member of the Corps, a senior lieutenant, and took up my post as best I could, given my poor mental health. Eventually I recovered all of my sensibilities and the maddening numbness of the drugs faded, and I was able to look around me and feel what had happened. By then more than three years had passed since Katya's death, and I fell heartsick as my memories overwhelmed me with nightmares. My friends Genka Stumpelkin, Trifya Miserbiev, Arkady Volgamints, and Doctor Gogol helped me get through my crisis by standing by me and making the simple argument that doing my duty was the best way to remember my loved ones. Still, the shock of what had happened burdened my life for years, and even now I have to believe that the energy I have found to tell my story has come as much from my grief as from my pride.

When Great-Uncle Lev died in the early 1970s, my whole family was gone, I was truly alone and abandoned, and yet I was still moving, so there was nothing to do but to keep going. I think that one of the tricks I used to carry on was that, because I didn't wholly believe what had happened to me, it was possible for me not to think about it except when I felt weak and alone, so I made sure I was always in good shape and always with my friends.

My duty saved me. I did my job, and years later it was my job to go into orbit on the Soyuz-Ts and the Salyut and Mir stations; and by the mid-1980s, when I made full colonel, I had compiled over two hundred days in orbit and was, with Genka Stumpelkin, at the top of the list for a trip to the moon. Moon-driving wasn't ever straightforward, and our voyage had to wait out the hand of all Russia's fate that swept aside the Kremlin bosses and the Lubyanka lords and also the empire. By the time I was able to reach the moon, at the first of the century, it was my last mission into space. Genka and I did help to raise Tranquillity Base, and we did make a show of exploring the terrain, and I've mentioned that we found Uncle Konstantine's crash site and recovered his remains. I wanted to go back to the moon again, we all did, but it wasn't possible for us then, and so the seniors of us—including Stumpelkin, Miserbiev, Volgamints, Gogol, and me—stayed on at Starry Town to train our successors. For many years there wasn't much money or prospect at Starry Town, and yet we persevered in our efforts to work with and often for the Americans and the others, and it certainly helped our progress that by the turn of the century Glavtop and Grin were co-chiefs of the Russian Air Force. When I retired from the Air Force, the

Cosmonaut Corps was two thousand strong with cadets from six continents, and by today the Corps has grown into what I'd like to think of as a merchant marine school to service Tranquillity Base, the orbitals, and the probes and generally to do the rugged and thankless work of maintaining the frontiers of interplanetary flight. I realize that the Corps hasn't become the legion of champions and conquerors I first envisioned when I arrived in 1968, but then a boy has big eyes and there are ages ahead for my dream to come true.

I did marry and have a family of my own, and I hope you'll be pleased that I married Uncle Dmitry's elder daughter, Anna. Our marriage didn't happen for many years, and I wasn't Anna's first husband, but when we did meet again—on the Black Sea—we fell together like the dearest old friends. I have loved her dearly ever since, and this last year without her here wouldn't have been possible without my sustaining memories of her and without the joy I can see of her in our children and grandchildren. Anna's daughter Natalie grew up as mine, and our sons Mitya (named for Anna's father) and Apollon (named for mine) were our strength after we lost Natalie in India. Anna and I never had much savings, and when I retired we stayed on at Starry Town as scruffy pensioners, but then Mitya turned a small land investment into a modest fortune and Apollon transformed the wealth into a great and worthwhile enterprise. It might be the most curious-turned corner of my life that Apollon Nevsky's son and Dmitry Zhukovsky's son-in-law should turn out to be the father of two Siberian railroad magnates and the grandfather of nine men and women who have nothing to do with the Air Force and the great-grandfather of, so far, twenty-three boys and girls, none of whom say they have interest in moon-driving or space travel—though there is dear little Sasha, who has shown promise since I bribed him with my old cosmonaut badge.

I am also my mother's son. I would prefer that I could write firmly of her end, but I can't. After the moon landing she withdrew back into her own lies and the protection of the Lubyanka lords. I can assume she went back abroad to Paris sometime in the 1970s. I can also assume that she outlasted the fall of her Lubyanka lords in the 1990s and found a way to live out her life in splendor and to die surrounded by friends and lovers. I can't assume much more, and, though I once wasted much time hoping she paid for her crimes, I can now write that I no longer hate her and, now that I've written down what happened back then, don't think much of her at all. She was my mother, and I should have loved her, and I didn't and don't, and this in itself is as sad a sentence as a man can pronounce on his mother. I know I am not the first man to have a mother who tried to destroy him, and I know I am not the last to say that only the grace of God can finally answer the fate of evildoers such as Eudaemonia Romodanovsky.

Does it surprise you that there was no more meaning to my mother's feud with Alexander Oryolin than the violence I've told? It probably does, and there's no better way to make clear how rotten Russia was then, than to say that all such tragedies could happen as senselessly as I've described. I've told you the truth as it happened, and if it seems incomplete it is because there were no rational explanations in the Russia of the bosses. If you asked why this man or woman was killed, or why this one disappeared as if he or she never existed, you found the same annihilating silence we fought on the yellow steppe. Brutality and depravity have no reasons, murder comes and then it goes, and no one remembers for very long, since there's always another vicious servant like Iagoda, there's always another infamous mistress like my mother. What was the Russia of the bosses but a sly assassin like Iagoda and a beautiful betrayer like my mother, and what did the bosses do in those days but waste Russia's heroes and abandon Russia's children and destroy hope for everyone? And all for what? At the end of my tether I am right and past due to say what I believe about those days. I saw generations of cruelty for nothing; I saw betrayal and abandonment and murder for nothing; and worst of all, I saw myself join in with the crimes for nothing. For the whole of the twentieth century my Motherland shamed all of us who wanted to love her, and what little was accomplished was buried beneath the suffering that was done to my Motherland's own children.

At the very end I must tell you the whole truth. I've deceived you that I don't know about my mother's fate. I do know some of it, because of a newspaper clipping Isaacii Goldenberg sent me once, while he was traveling abroad as a consultant on the equatorial spaceport project. He never mentioned the clipping again, and it was easy for me to put it away and pretend that I hadn't seen it until now,

when it's time to confess. My mother died in a hotel fire in Paris in
the Year Seven. The item wasn't from a daily newspaper, but rather
from an arts periodical, so I didn't gain all the details. It said that a
well-known patroness of the opera, "Madame E. P. Romodanovsky," had perished in her sleep during a fire in a prominent residential hotel. The item said that friends of the deceased had established a
memorial fund in her name for the Paris Opera (which had burned
badly that year) and that contributions could be made to the Opera
Reconstruction Fund. There was no mention of a family. I know
"Romodanovsky" is not an uncommon name, and I know that I
could have checked the facts thirty years ago and confirmed all this
finally, but I didn't. I confess it now. I believe it was my mother, and
I believe she died alone in her sleep of smoke inhalation, and I believe there was someone kind at her graveside to grieve for her.

What is left of all of those days now is grief, and there is too much
of it for me if I let myself think about it. I have missed Katya ever
since, and if there were a magical way to trade my few hundred steps
on the moon for a single step with her I would do it right now. I
want to go to her and say I'm sorry and please forgive me and I love
you. Then again, it comes to me that I did say those things back then
and saying so didn't stop me from carrying on with my bloody-
minded pursuit of heroism and the moon. What did my ambition get
me but all this grief for my lost Katya? I have spoken so judgmentally
of others it is time for me to judge myself, and my verdict is that I
obeyed my duty to my Motherland so well that I failed my duty to
the soul I loved the most; and yet this, too, was my fate, and the
truth of it burns me like the sun.

What I want to do now is to think of my two uncles still up there
in orbit around the sun. They are free-falling there forever, you understand, an eternity in their own tomb, the only two human beings
who have never gone back to dust. I adored them so that, despite all
the troubles I've told you of them, I can still feel the thrill of meeting
them and walking behind them and watching them soar. Perhaps I
can do more now than simply mourn them. After all, there is a part
of my mind that is still the twenty-two-year-old boy who came to
conquer new worlds, and perhaps I can use this power to star-drive
again. I confess that even now, given the choice between the sweet,
rich, warm earth with my father, Great-Uncle Lev, Katya, Anna,

Natalie, the squadron, Little Laika, Goldenberg, and all whom I've loved—Uncle Konstantine too—and the relentless hurly-burly of the heavens with them, I would choose the stars with Uncle Dmitry and Uncle Alexander. In my confession is my next step: I will lay aside my storytelling and close my twenty-two-year-old eyes and launch my soul to keep going until I find them.

ABOUT THE AUTHOR

John Calvin Batchelor was born in Bryn Mawr, Pennsylvania, in 1948. He lives with his family in New York City. This is his seventh book.